Sugar Rush
By
Sarah Anne Craik

To Amy and Rosa. The friends who encouraged me to write xxx

Prologue

I can't believe I did it! Mummy said that this Lego set would be too tough for me because the box had twelve plus on it. The box was wrong. I'm nine and I built the whole thing all by myself.

It's a boat. A big boat too. It even has toy sharks to go with it.

I should show her. She'll be proud! Maybe she'll give me one of those chocolate cookies!

"Sofiaaaaa!"

I hear my name but it's not a voice that I like.

No! He can't be here. Mummy and Daddy said they weren't going out today. I don't need a babysitter.

Why do they always ask Brian? Someone else could look after me. Someone other than a cousin who hates me.

"Sofia, where are you?"

His voice is louder...closer. The feeling I always get in my tummy when he's around, makes me want to cry.

I can't cry. That always makes him mad.

Footsteps make the floorboards in the hallway creak and I jump up from my bedroom floor.

The boat falls from my hands as they shake. A few pieces fall off but the rug under my feet stops any noise.

Glancing around, I try to find a place to hide.

"You in here brat?"

He's outside my room now. Why does his voice always sound so mean?

I don't want him here. Maybe he doesn't know where I am?

Holding my breath, I count the seconds and hope that he keeps on walking.

He doesn't.

As soon as the door begins to open, I run.

Pulling my closet open, I get in and shut it behind me. Pushing the hanging clothes out of the way, I hide behind them and pray they protect me.

I know they won't.

Pressing my back against the wall, I try to become invisible. I wish I could disappear. I wish Mummy and Daddy wouldn't leave. I wish I could tell them about him.

Through the wooden slats on the closet door, I can see part of him. His black boots. He always wears them. They hurt when he kicks me.

"Sofia, you really need to get smarter. I guess that's impossible for you though huh?"   He laughs, just like always. He likes to makes fun of me.

I cover my mouth with my hand to stop myself from gasping. My cheeks heat and my eyes sting.

Squeezing them shut, I slide to the floor and wrap my arms around myself. He knows where I am.

I keep my eyes closed.

As soon as I hear the closet door opening and clothes being pushed aside, I can tell he has a smile on his face. I don't even have to look at him to know.

"There you are. You shouldn't hide from me. It's inconvenient" He sighs. I don't know what that last word means but I know he's annoyed.

Annoyed is never a good thing. It makes him worse.

I don't want to be afraid of him but I can't help it. Maybe I'd be less scared if I knew why he did this to me.

He always tells me it's because he can.

"Leave me alone" I whisper. I want my words to be a yell but I can't make my voice any louder.

"You know that I can't do that idiot"

That's when I open my eyes.

I see his evil smile, his black clothes and even blacker hair.

Mummy and Daddy say that he's a 'responsible young man'. I don't know what that big word means either.

It can't mean this.

"Move" he snaps and reaches for me before I can blink. He's only five years older than me but that's enough to make him stronger.

I scream and the same thing happens that it always does.

Kick. Slap.

Today I'm going to have to lie to my Mummy and Daddy again. I'll have to tell them that I fell. Silly me. Always falling over.

Tonight I'll cry because of the pain in my sides from his boot.

Tomorrow it could happen once more.

And there's nothing I can do about it.

Sofia

University. It's everything I ever wanted. The one thing that meant I could have freedom from my past and gain a future.

After years of working shitty jobs to save up the money and securing the best high school grades, I had gotten two different acceptance letters.

One for a university in my home town in Ohio and one in Chicago. It was an easy choice for me. The University of Illinois not only gave me a better chance at success but it also meant I could escape the town I lived in. I wanted that for many reasons.

So I left my crying Mom and proud Dad behind.

Four more years of hard work and study got me the degree that I dreamed of.

Web Design and Development.

I had been given a little toy robot that allowed me to programme its movements, for my twelfth birthday. I've been obsessed with programming and code ever since.

With everything going so well for me, I should have know it wouldn't last.

My life was looking up until I reached a dead end. That's exactly where I am right now.

The part where I'm supposed to get a job with my degree and support myself, hasn't quite worked out yet.

I know not many people get a job right away. Although I'm pretty sure most people definitely get employed within a whole year of graduating.

Not me. Not one interview. Not one chance.

Maybe it's the degree I went with? Maybe Web Design was a bad choice to make. Although surely in the twentieth century web tech is important.

There's nothing else that I can see myself doing. I still want to learn more. To work with experienced people who have knowledge I don't.

I have to know how it all works. It was all I did at home and all I still do.

I'm trying to keep positive. However, I'm beginning to worry that university was just one big scam to get me into debt and crush all of my hopes and dreams.

They gave me a piece of paper and a status. None of which can save me from being stuck in a studio apartment with no heat twelve months after graduation. As well as the fact that I'm thousands of miles from home and those loans I took out to get me by are now spent.

Sometimes I wonder if I'd have been better off staying at home. If I'd stayed in Ohio I would have had my family to support me. No, that would have been a bad choice. I'm glad I left.

I know I can do this without support. I have dreams and I'm still trying to achieve them.

I got here myself. Sure I had to start University a little later than most people because my parents couldn't afford to help me save but I did it. I worked those shitty jobs a little longer than most people need to. I was twenty when I got to Illinois.

I was able to get this apartment near campus. Which was a smart idea at the time. All of it was smart at the time. Even the loans that paid my rent.

Now I've got nothing left. Well, two dollars sixty to be exact.

This situation is a lot worse than I'm acting like it is.

The easy solution is to go back home.

Admit to my parents that I've failed and accept defeat. Except I can't bring myself to do that. I'm too proud. Oh and every time I think of going back there my stomach ties in knots. I can't go home. Not when he's there.

Stop thinking of him. Stop thinking of home!

I'm trying to distract myself the same way I always do. Staring at my laptop screen filled with lines of html and css coding. I'm telling myself the better I make my websites, the more chance I have of a job offer.

Someone has to give me a job. I don't care if it's not related to my degree at this point, as long as it can buy me food.

My laptop is five years old now and is just about the only electrical device working in this damn place.

3:05 am is the time displayed in the top right corner of my screen. I should be in bed, having nightmares about waking up in the morning and still being in this real life disaster.

My eyes are burning because I've been staring at this screen for over three hours. Previously to opening up my current prototype, I was actually being productive.

Two more job applications sent off. Usually that would make me feel a small sense of achievement but with the drought of replies in my inbox, I just don't feel happy about it.

3.06 am. Damn two whole minutes of my life that I'll never get back. Yet surely that means I'm two whole minutes closer to the part of my life where those inspirational people go "it gets better". I can guarantee I'll never be saying those words myself.

I wonder what percentage of jobs in Chicago I've already applied for. Definitely near the fifty percent mark at this point. Surely!

Would I rather be a waitress than a qualified web designer? Sometimes I think the answer is yes. If it's easier.

Considering I want to stab my eyes out every time I can't find the misplaced comma within my html document. Serving food sounds relaxing.

Could I settle with that though? Knowing I'm capable of more? Knowing that I don't know everything there is to know?

3.10 am. Wow, now we're making some progress. I just covered four minutes this time. I'm insane, talking to myself in my head as if someone is going to answer back.

Actually I wish someone would.

***

5.36 am. I may have fallen asleep on top of my keyboard. I can confirm from the moisture on the R, T and Y that clearly I was drooling.

Sitting back up in my seat makes my head spins. At the same time my stomach growls, begging for food.

Of course I'm hungry. I haven't eaten for at least a day and I can't afford to buy anything. I'm sure I have some microwaveable noodles in the kitchen cupboard.

Ping!

My eyes focus back on my laptop screen and I realise the reason I woke up was because of a notification. This ping is a second reminder.

My eyes squint through tiredness and I see the email icon bouncing joyfully. I wish I had that much energy.

This happy alert would usually have me jabbing the left click button in excitement. I used to believe it could be a job interview. It's clear now I've lost hope as I lazily tap to open the email.

Shocking. It's junk.

"Thank you. This is exactly what I wanted" I sigh and roll my head a little to relieve the stiffness in my body. My back aches. My head pounds.

On the plus side, I do enjoy getting junk mail. I like to scrutinise all of the fake websites and learn exactly what not to do when building one. It's kind of a way for me to improve my skills. So maybe it's not all bad.

Inspecting the email closely, I see it's an advert of sorts. The opening line says 'MAKE MONEY QUICKLY'. Which is always a lie. It no doubt should be called 'GET KIDNAPPED QUICKLY'.

Still, let's see how good they have faked their website.

Under the subject line is a link that has me curious.

www.sugar.com/rush

Sugar? Are they selling candy? No, it's probably some weird porn thing. Definitely porn!

Clicking it anyway, I immediately regret it.

Cringing away in shock, a very bright and colourful layout is displayed. Wow, I'm gonna need sunglasses for this.

In huge neon pink writing the words 'SUGAR RUSH' cover the screen. The background contrasts with an even brighter green which I hate. That's all that's on the page apart from a little button underneath that says 'enter your wildest dreams'. Hmmm, that's a bold statement.

The web designer in me has to notice that not only should that button be bigger but there's nothing on here that tells me what I'm clicking on. Not really.

Maybe that's the point...

Click.

My eyes squint in preparation for another blindingly colourful page. Only this one is much more mellow. The same green from the background of the welcome screen greets me but the text and images are actually reasonably coloured and spaced.

The first line of text reads:

'Which SUGAR Daddy is right for you? Haven't picked yet? Why not?'

Sugar Daddies. What a concept. I'm not surprised really. Most of these emails are in some way morally messed up.

I'm kind of disappointed really. I was hoping the 'make money quickly' part would be true. Even though I know it never could be.

Do people actually do this stuff? I can't imagine myself spending time with someone for money.

I mean, it must feel horrible. Totally degrading and not worth it.

Why the hell do I care?

My eyes fly over the photos of older gentlemen. Some are quite handsome but I'm guessing a lot of these people are fake. I'm also unsure if this is even legal.

I don't know why I'm scrolling down. Or why I'm reading the details of these men instead of criticising the bad font choice but here I am.

Maybe it's because I've never given this lifestyle much thought and now I have far too many questions. Maybe it's because the concept doesn't sit right with me. Or maybe I'm just bored.

Do these women just go to meet random men? Men that could hurt them?

No, I'm not going to go there. Not every guy is evil. I need to remember that.

Are these men respectable? Do they treat these women well?

I decide that I don't want to know either way. Because if I let myself think about it then I'll end up making a whole fantasy. One where a Sugar Daddy saves me from my hell. Which is the most ridiculous thing I've ever heard.

I do it all the time. Imagining a lottery win or landing a well paid job.

It only makes me sad when I snap back to reality and my life is still the same.

6:00am. Time to try and sleep anyway.

No one is going to save me from the situation I'm in. No knight in shining armour and certainly not a fake sugar daddy.

I'll do it myself. I'll save myself from this horrible nightmare.

There's no other option.

Sofia

A few days have passed since I discovered the sugar daddy website. During that time I've wondered about it far too much. It's completely irrelevant to my life but just like always, if I don't understand something, it makes me really want to.

I googled the words 'Sugar Rush' last night but stopped myself from scrolling down the search results. Sure, I could find the page through my junk mail again but I want to know if its accessible through a good old search engine.

Anyway, it's completely pointless. I don't want to focus on this. Instead I should be more interested in getting my life together.

My friend Annabelle had called last night to ask when we could catch up again. I met her at university and sometimes she was the only person who kept me going. She graduated with a Journalism degree, which meant we obviously never had any classes together. We met because she tripped in front of me in the hall and the water she'd been drinking went all over me. I'm glad it happened.

She doesn't know how much I'm struggling and I don't intend to tell her. So instead of saying that I couldn't afford to catch up with her, I said I was busy.

Busy...what a joke.

The only thing that keeps me busy is counting down the days until my rent is due. Rent that I can't pay.

I don't think i'll be able to keep my lack of money a secret for long. My Mom will no doubt be visiting soon. She tries to do so a couple times a year. Sometimes Dad comes too. It makes me feel bad that I haven't travelled home within the five years since I left. I'm also running out of excuses as to why I can't.

Dropping down onto my bed, I stare at the paint chipped ceiling. I can't keep living this way.

Ping!

My phone lights up beside me, the cracked screen showing a notification. I'm not even sure how this phone still works.

It's another email. Junk again. This time the subject reads:

'DID YOU FORGET SOMETHING?'

Creepy.

Opening it up, I'm blinded by pink and green just like a few days ago. Oh no. I should have known this would happen. Of course I'm going to get more emails from the 'Sugar Rush' website. This is why you don't click on junk.

I wouldn't be surprised if I get bombarded with all different sugar daddy companies now, real and fake.

Fuck!

Swiping my thumb upwards the screen reveals more tag lines to pull me in.

'SIGN UP NOW!'

No absolutely not. No.

A little voice in my head pipes up, asking the question: *why not?*

Why not? Because its stupid and irresponsible. Plus, I have much better things to do.

Do I though?

Maybe I could just take a look. Do some research. That can't hurt anyone. Except me.

No, I won't waste my time on this.

Getting up, I decide to try and distract myself. This time without building a website.

Maybe I should go for a walk. Fresh air will do me some good and it's free.

It's June and for Illinois that means its humid as hell. However, all of the years spend outside during summer in Dayton prepared me for it.

Switching jeans for shorts and a hoodie for a cami, I stand in front of the mirror on the wall beside my bed. I try not to look at myself these days because all I see is a pale sad face, tired blue eyes and the evidence of lack of food.

Pulling my hair up into a bun, I grimace at the brunette pieces that stick out. It's too long now but this will have to do.

***

For a good few hours I wonder around the city, taking my time. I have nothing to get back to. People watching has never been my thing but today it's interesting.

Sitting on a park bench, I glance around at families and business men. Women running and couples walking hand in hand.

Is that something that I want? A partner? I'm not too sure. I had my fair share of flings in university like everyone else but I never got close to anyone.

Is it worth it? I'm not sure it is. Not if most people end up hurt. Emotionally or otherwise. What a sad thought.

Using one of my last two dollar, I grab a hot dog and keep on walking.

What the hell am I going to do? My parents can't afford to send me money, I know that for a fact and I simply won't ask them anyway.

With that depressing thought, I make my way back home. A home I may not have in the near future.

As soon as I get back, I'm throwing myself onto my bed again. This time face first so that when I scream the sound is muffled.

It feels good to let out the agony and frustration inside of me.

My fists punch the duvet in anger before my body goes lax.

Naturally, once I've pulled myself together, I check my phone. Of course I left the 'Sugar Rush' email open. Of course!

Well, you know what? I don't care how pointless it is, I'm going to feed my curiosity.

This time when I open the website, I don't scan over the sugar daddies quickly. This time I pay attention and analyse.

My eyes glance over the profiles. Photo after photo of older men. Some with grey hair, some who clearly dye their hair to keep the grey away. A lot of these men are in suits, standing beside some fancy vehicle. I guess that's how they prove they're rich.

How is anyone supposed to choose a Sugar Daddy this way? Do the women choose or are they chosen?

Scrolling quickly, I stop suddenly and let my finger choose a Daddy for me to investigate.

My thumb hovers over a Howard Green. His photo shows him on a yacht, wearing black shorts and a polo shirt. I can't make out much of his features because he's wearing sunglasses but I can see he's one of the men who has opted to let his hair go grey. Brave. He's forty five and is apparently fifty kilometres away from me.

Next up! Darren...no second name which is a bit strange. Although I've seen a few profiles like this. I don't think these men want anyone to know that they're sugar daddies. Probably because they're married or something.

So Darren...he's less grey than the last guy. Probably because he's a little younger at forty. Lovely blue suit though. One of his pictures is of a horse stable but I'm not sure if he actually rides or just owns the place to cash in.

The only information I'm really getting from these profiles is age and how far away they are from me.

A love heart sits under every guys photo, which I'm sure is for sugar babies to match with them. The words 'more info' is next to every love heart. I've been trying not to tap any of those links because I don't want to admit how interesting I'm finding this.

But I guess I'll just have to be disappointed in myself.

Hitting the button under Darren's photo, I wait in anticipation, until a log in screen pops up.

Ah shit! I need to sign up if I want to see his whole profile.

Well that's not going to happen. I've already went too far.

'LOG IN OR SIGN UP TO BECOME A SUGARY SWEET AND GET THAT RUSH NOW!'

A 'sugary sweet'?

They really changed the term sugar baby to 'sugary sweet'...ugh.

Which reminds me, I should be looking at the terms and conditions of this website. Are there rules?

Finding the page I'm looking for, I curse out loud as I'm met with the same sign up page.

This is the point where I should go back to applying for jobs. The part where my curiosity needs to stop.

My fingers drum soundlessly on my duvet by my side.

Option one: get up and do something productive. Face my reality and cry some more.

Option two: sign up and spend the rest of the day snooping on men who may or may not be real people.

The second option means I can pretend my life is normal.

Oh fuck it!

Hitting the sign up button, I feel a sense of excitement that I can't explain. As if I'm doing something I shouldn't be.

All of the standard information boxes pop up. Name, age, email address. Oh and a little icon that suggests I download the app. An app! I'm starting to think this website is very much real. I'll know for sure if they ask for my bank details. If they do then it's a scam.

Scrolling further, I see that there are a lot of boxes and questions to answer. Great. This is a detailed profile.

Name: Sofia Westwood
Age: 25
Location: Chicago, Illinois
Occupation (if applicable) : Web Designer

Okay so maybe I'm not actually employed but no one needs to know that.

Interests: Gaining a better future, coding, graphic design, movies and eating too much chocolate.

It's all true. Especially the chocolate part. There's nothing better than movie marathons and lots of chocolate. Maybe it would be nice to have someone to snuggle up to but I'm certainly not writing that. Just in case someone actually reads it.

It's takes me half an hour to complete the profile. Everything from loves and hates, body type to what food I like. They even require a photo. Which I really don't want to have to add but it's mandatory.

So I try my best to find a half decent picture in my camera roll. I settle on one from a few months ago when I had stupidly gone out for drinks with Annabelle. I should not have spent that money.

Regardless, the pictures we took are nice enough that I can use one for my profile. I'm in a little black dress, my hair is curled and my makeup is light.

That'll do.

With a sigh on relief, I click 'submit' and am overjoyed to see an acceptance page. I'm also informed that I will be alerted to 'daddies' who view my profile or like it.

Fantastic.

Except I don't care about that.

I'm here to scrutinise them for fun and now I can see all of their information and the website rules.

I've suddenly gotten an urge to laugh maniacally but I'll refrain.

So here we go.

My scrolling continues for a good hour. It's almost embarrassing how engrossed I am but this is extremely interesting to me. The truth is, I'm just plain nosey.

I click on lots of profiles and read their interests. A lot of them say they want a women to make them look good and some admit they have wives but would still like some 'fun'.

Yuck!

A man named Barry states that he wants someone who he can look after. Someone who needs him. He also mentions that he doesn't want a women over twenty. He's fifty-two...

Double ew!

Goodbye Barry you creep.

Who's next?

Scroll. Scroll.

My finger stops dead as something catches my eye. Something that I haven't seen yet.

A man under forty.

All I notice is the number thirty-four in the age box and my eyes focus in on the anomaly.

I read his name first.

Elijah Everett.

Then I see his photo and I stare.

And stare some more.

He's gorgeous! Soft brunette hair with a hint of red, lovely tamed beard. Light green eyes. The photo of him is waist up so I can see he's wearing a dark blue suit. It shows off strong looking shoulders. He looks confident in the photo but not arrogant. Like he knows he's more than capable of getting things done! There's a slight smile on his face that makes his eyes crinkle at the sides and it's so very charming. I wonder if he's kind? This isn't a man that has a six pack under the suit. His cheeks are a little more filled out than most of the sickly slim men on here. It's extremely refreshing and attractive. Sexy even. I wonder what it would be like to lie down on his chest and just kinda be there?

Woah Sofia! That escalated quickly.

Blinking in confusion, my gaze darts to his information.

Mr Everett is only five kilometres from me. He's 5,8" and is the CEO of 'Everett and Son Industries'.

Very nice.

Let's see what he's looking for.

He says:

"I don't have much time to date due to the nature of my job, so this seemed like the easiest option. I'd like a women who I can take to dinner, bring to corporate events and keep me company on lonely nights. Snacks and music provided"

It takes me a few seconds to realise I'm smiling.

Ew! I have to stop whatever the hell it is I'm doing.

However, my mind is already wondering about those snacks.

Shaking my head at my own stupidity, I squash down any intrusive thoughts. I'm not on this website because I actually want a sugar daddy. I'm here just to look. I'm interested about it all.

Hunger hurts my stomach again and I wish for a few seconds that I could be that person. The women who meets men for dinner and gets paid. Hell, I'll just take the meal right now.

Where would Elijah Everett take me to dinner?

Nowhere! I'm pretty sure I'm not the type of women he's looking for. In fact, I'm positive.

Pressing the more info button again, this time so it disappears and I can leave his profile behind, I'm met with a different notification.

'YOU LIKED ELIJAH EVERETT'S PROFILE. WILL IT BE A MATCH?'

What?!
No! No I didn't! Oh no!
I hit the love heart by mistake!
Oh shit!
Throwing my phone away in horror, I cover my face with my hands.
If he's a real person he's going to see that and he's probably going to laugh at me.
Maybe I can unlike it?
Scrambling for my phone again, I try to unlike the heart.
Nothing happens.
I'm not sure why I'm surprised. The world is against me right now. So why would a little bit more embarrassment hurt?
Well, I guess that's what I get for being too curious. Curiosity killed the cat and now it's going to kill me.

Elijah

The ticking of the clock on the wall is amplifying my pounding heartache and the buzz of twenty people conversing doesn't help either.

I'm supposed to be the one leading this meeting but no one has stopped to consult me for a while. Quite honestly, I don't care.

Usually my brain would be switched on. I'd be engaged and actually doing my job but right now I'd love nothing more than to get in my car and drive far away. From all of this responsibility.

The only thing stopping me is guilt.

This was my father's company.

Everett and Son Industries.

He worked hard to build it up so big that every other corporate company in Chicago and most of the US desired to be like his.

Which had its downfalls of course.

It meant he had zero time for his wife or son.

The only time he paid attention to me was when he wanted to groom me to take over his legacy one day. So it could live on for years to come.

I guess he didn't expect that day to come so quickly.

He definitely didn't expect to wrap his car around a tree, killing himself and my Mom in one sweep. Gone.

The irony of it is, they were on their way to have a vacation. One he kept putting off.

Getting a phone call at nineteen to say your parents are dead is not exactly something that I'd ever imagined could be in the realm of possibility.

Yet that's why I'm here in this boardroom. That's why I'm now CEO and somehow this multi-billion dollar company is mine.

Not because I want it but because I know that if I gave it up, he'd start rolling in his grave.

My relationship with my parents wasn't great but I always wanted their approval and pride. I'll be trying to make them proud until I die.

"Mr Everett, I think this deal could make more money than this company has ever seen" Jack chimes, making me pay attention. He has a triumphant smile on his wrinkled face, his eyes alight with success.

He's in his fifties and has been employed here long before I took over. He has helped me more than I could ever thank him for.

I nod and try to return his smile but he no doubt knows that I'm lacking enthusiasm. I always am. Yet he can't say anything because I'm his boss. Which doesn't seem right. Maybe my father should have given this company to him. They worked closely after all.

I know that I'm good at what I do but that doesn't mean I want to do it.

This deal involves swapping data and technologies with a similar company in Japan. We both have something the other doesn't.

"Great work Jack" I tell him and wonder how much more money we really need.

I certainly don't need anymore.

I'm extremely grateful that I was born into money and I know how privileged I am.

Yet there's no mistaking how much money changes people. I fucking hate it.

Since this company has been around for decades, that meant that everyone knew I was the son of a rich guy. Even as a kid.

Every 'friend' I thought I had or girl who said they were interested in me, really only saw dollar signs attached to me. Any affection towards me was well thought out and fake.

I always wondered why so many kids at school wanted to have sleepovers on the weekends.

Although I suppose I don't blame them.

Add in the fact that I find it hard to stay interested in anyone or anything for a long period of time and I'm basically destined to live a lonely life.

It's sad really.

I've tried to date the normal way. I've even introduced myself with a fake name so my date couldn't google me.

They always find out who I am or know me before hand. Not that it would make much difference, I can't connect with any living thing on this planet. I'm just not good at it.

My eyes flick to the clock that is still hurting my head and I see that's it's just gone five pm. This meeting is over.

Scratching my beard, that I really need to trim, I clear my throat.

"Thank you everyone for coming today. I'll update you within the next week with any correspondence from Japan. Have a good weekend"

I use the lightest tone I can to disguise my disinterest and am met with a chorus of 'thank you' and 'goodbyes'.

Men and women, rise from their seats and move towards the door.

Jack hovers beside me until I nod at him once more. He probably has something to say but I'd rather not hear it.

Once the room is empty and I'm alone, I get up and walk to the floor to ceiling windows. From forty stories up, I get a good view of the world below.

Everyone is getting ready for a good Friday night. The ant sized people below move in crowds, on their way to bars and restaurants.

This weekend should be relatively empty for me. Apart from any left over work. Which is rare.

Not so long ago I'd have went online and found a women to take out.

Except that chapter of my life ended swiftly, with an incident I'd rather never think about again.

What a stupid idea it was anyway.

Becoming a sugar daddy at twenty-nine is something else I didn't expect to happen. I thought it would help me defeat the loneliness I feel, while knowing that I can't get hurt.

It made me feel safe, knowing that these women wanted me for my money meant there would be no surprises.

They'd get paid and I'd feel more human.

Nevertheless, four years of that was enough.

I never want to go on that website aga-

Ping!

Pulling my phone out of my suit jacket in annoyance, I glare at the screen. I'd love to have a day when no one contacts me.

'SOFIA WESTWOOD HAS LIKED YOUR PROFILE. REPLY NOW!'

It takes me a good few moments to realise what I'm seeing. I haven't gotten a notification like this in about a year. I thought I deleted my account. No more sugar daddy bullshit.

Swiping my screen, I mean to delete it but instead my phone opens up the app that I clearly failed to delete.

I've still had this app installed on my phone for this long and I didn't notice? I really need to pay more attention.

A 'sugary sweets' profile appears and I have to roll my eyes at the name. I always thought it was weird.

Sofia Westwood huh?

Sorry Sofia, I'm out of business.

My eyes glance over the information in front of me, a frown tugging at my forehead as I read her interests.

She wants to gain a better future. That's inspiring and an unusual thing to write on a sugary sweet profile. She also mentions coding and her occupation states Web Designer.

Impressive.

I've never understood any of that stuff. She seems ambitious, which is refreshing.

I'm used to seeing women write about the car they'd like or the restaurant they want to eat at. After all that's what the website encourages from them.

Maybe she didn't read the suggestions on 'how to get a daddy'.

Well good for her if that's true. Those guidelines are dumb.

She also mentions movies and eating too much chocolate. That line takes away my frown and has me pausing.

I have a certain adoration for a good snack and she loves chocolate. It's kind of amusing that we both mentioned these things in our bios.

Without much thought, I scroll further down to her photo.

Then I stand there like an idiot staring at it.

She's...lovely.

I mean every women on here is attractive. Yet she is a different kind of attractive.

Loose curled brunette hair, blue eyes and a black dress that hugs her petite figure. There's no seductive pose or serious expression. She's smiling.

No. I'm not doing this.

Shoving my phone back in my pocket, I stare back out to the world below.

I'm not a sugar daddy anymore. Plus, it never really made me happy anyway. All I did was meet woman after woman. I took them to dinner, sometimes only once. On occasion I'd have a sugar baby for a few months before it was clear we didn't even like each other's company.

It's was a vicious cycle.

I'd feel lonely so I'd find a woman. Then I'd realise that I'm no good at having anyone around or that trying to talk to someone who I have nothing in common with is hellish.

Sometimes it would just be a one night stand but I don't have to be a sugar daddy to do that.

I need a new hobby.

***

My apartment sits at the top of one of the many skyscrapers in Illinois. I chose it because the view isn't restricted by other buildings. I've moved around a lot since my parents died. Fifteen years of never being able to settle.

Lying on my black leather couch, I watch the sun go down.

Usually I'd be in my office with my face in a computer screen but I'm feeling particularly unsettled. It may be tiredness or it may be my constant thoughts about the notification I received earlier.

I've been wondering about Sofia.

A women I've never met, who I know nothing about. For all I know her bio could be bullshit and her name might be fake.

Why am I wondering?

If I'd gotten the same notification with another women's profile attached, I know I wouldn't be thinking this way.

Something is bothering me but I can't quite put my finger on it.

Pulling myself off the couch, I make my way to the kitchen. Grabbing a glass from the cabinet, I place it on the marble counter and pour myself some whiskey.

I don't like to drink much but it might stop the niggling in my head.

There's an urge that's growing more with every passing minute.

I want to like her profile so we match because I'm curious if she's as endearing by direct message as she is in her bio.

It's not a good idea.

So why do I want to know what her favourite movie is? Or her favourite chocolate?

Maybe she could teach me about that coding stuff?

Closing my eyes, I sigh loudly, letting out the annoyance at myself.

I already know that I'm going to follow my urge. Which is not something I ever have to stop myself from doing. I'm level headed and direct.

I usually have control over myself.

Except right now.

"Fucking hell!" I snap and it echoes slightly around the empty apartment.

Ignoring how it makes me feel, I march back to the couch and snatch my phone off the coffee table.

I pause, remembering what happened the last time I had a 'sugary sweet'.

Nothing good. Everything bad.

I keep telling myself that it wasn't my fault but it still feels like it was.

Lucy.

We only met once for dinner. We had sex. She was nice.

She certainly didn't deserve what happened. I wish I could have stopped it.

If I keep thinking about it, I'll go insane.

Unfortunately, I can't change the past. I just need to focus on the future.

What happened to Lucy won't happen again. I know that for a fact. So I have to bite the bullet and try to let myself live.

Before Lucy, I had almost given up the sugar daddy lifestyle anyway because it made me feel just as shit as trying to date for real did.

Now though, I'm hoping that maybe I can find out why Sofia's profile has me so interested. So confused.

Before I can change my mind, I find the long forgotten app, open her profile and jab the little love heart.

My screen burst into a tiny fireworks display as the words 'IT'S A MATCH' appear.

I should leave it at that but I still want to know something.

Tapping the direct message button, I feel a shot of excitement zap me. I'm a fucking idiot.

Anyway, here goes nothing.

Elijah: What's your favourite movie of all time?

Sofia

    I spend the rest of the day and into the night, praying that Elijah Everett doesn't see the notification.
    I have visions of this rich handsome man, scoffing at my profile. Laughing at it and shaking his head. It's not something that should bother me because my intention was merely to research a lifestyle I don't understand.
    Yet here I am, nervous. Worried that a man, a complete stranger might think I'm lame.
    I've been burying myself in my portfolio of websites.
    Tweaking things that don't need tweaked. Watching videos on Java Script that I've already seen twenty times. All because my brain is focused on this one thing.
    Something that shouldn't even matter to me.
    Is it because he's good looking? Or because I know he's probably stuck up and will look down on me?
    I'm not sure what my issue is but somehow I'm becoming angry at profile of a man who doesn't know I exist.
    The light is fading through the windows of my apartment, the sound of a busy street below echoing up.
    It's Friday night. The beginning of another weekend in which Annabelle will ask me to go for drinks or to a club.
    I'm surprised she hasn't called since the other day. She doesn't give up easy when she wants something.

Yet I'll have to lie. Maybe I can say I'm unwell this time.

Just as I'm thinking of a good illness to fake, my laptop alerts me that my inbox has refreshed and I'm met with a bunch of new emails.

My stomach drops immediately as I see the words 'SUGAR RUSH'.

Oh no.

Is it him? Or maybe some other man in his fifties has liked my profile. Which is something I hadn't considered. All of the sugar daddies can see me now. They can interact with my profile.

Shit!

Opening my inbox, I have to take a moment to process the chaos I'm met with.

Five different emails.

Three from the Sugar Rush website. Three?

Jesus Christ!

The fourth is from a place called 'Brew House'!

I've no idea what that is and I have much more pressing matters.

Focusing back on the first email, I open it up and sigh.

I was right.

Apparently a man named Jacob has liked my profile. The email invites me to view his and like him back.

No thanks Jacob.

Delete.

I'm assuming the other two emails will be similar, so I click onto the second one without much thought.

That's when my heart stops.

'ELIJAH EVERETT HAS LIKED YOUR PROFILE. YOU HAVE MATCHED'

This has me jumping out of my seat with an emotion that I can't quite place.

The feeling only gets more intense when the third email informs me that I have a message from him.

WHAT THE FUCK?!

What have I done?!

Am I a sugar baby now? Totally unintentionally.

Pushing aside my shock, I go to the fourth email with the intention of deleting it. It's probably nothing.

'You have been invited to an interview at Brew House'

Oh! Shit!

Oh my god. Yes!

FINALLY!

An interview. On this coming Monday.

It's a coffee shop. Obviously I've applied for so many jobs that I've forgotten about this one. It's not web design but it could mean money to keep me going!

"YES!" I yell, jumping around like an idiot. Too much enthusiasm has me stubbing my toe and yelling in a completely different tone.

"FUCK OUCH!"

Falling back into my desk chair, rubbing my toe to soothe the ache, I click on the last email.

My soaring joy plummets to the ground.

My rent is due by the end of the month. I mean I knew this information but the email really drives it home. I've got two weeks to find four hundred dollars.

Even if I somehow get this job, it won't be quick enough.

I don't want to think about that right now. So I go back to the interview email and make sure that I accept the invitation. I won't miss out on this.

Logically the next thing I should do is research the company. So that I'm prepared for any questions that they might ask. But I have all weekend and there's something that I want to do more.

Moving back to the first email, I grin a little too widely as I see that Elijah Everett and I are now classed as a match.

Who'd have thought it and how frigging strange?

What is he thinking? What am I thinking?

The next email informs me that to see his message, I have to download the app. Of course.

There's no hesitation from me, I'm in the App Store in seconds, logging on to see what he has said.

I feel kind of giddy, like a teenage girl who's crush has just text her.

Except he's not my crush. Just a random man who I'm curious about. There's that word again, curious.

I'm nervous to read the message, unsure of what he could possibly say. Yet when I finally bring myself to look, it's not what I expected.

It shows he paid attention to what I wrote.

Elijah: What is your favourite movie of all time?

My favourite movie...

That's something that I'll have to think about for a long time. I've seen more than the average person but choosing a favourite is never something I've done.

I could name a few that I hate. Any of the Saw movies for a start. Gore isn't my thing.

The Invisible Man, because of the abusive asshole in it.

But love?

What do I love?

Anything Disney but as a twenty five year old women I don't think that's something I should admit.

Maybe I should be honest. Just tell him the truth.

Sofia: I don't have one. There's no way I could ever possibly choose.

I type the words and my thumb hover over the send button. I could just delete the app, delete my account and never reply.

Yet I know that I won't do that .

As soon as I tap the button, my heart thuds because of my decision. I've never done anything like this before. I haven't even been on a normal dating website, let alone one of this kind.

My pulse quickens as a little chat bubble appears.

This indicates he's typing.

Oh wow, was he waiting for my reply?

I watch and wait in anticipation for his answer.

Elijah: Can I tell you mine and see if you approve?

Well this is serious. What if he says Saw.

Sofia: Be careful what you choose. I might judge you.

The chat bubble pops up again. I wonder if it'll be an action film. Or horror?

Getting up from my chair, I sit in the middle of my bed with my legs crossed.

I guess this is happening. I'm chatting to a sugar daddy about movies.

Elijah: I'm trying to figure out what would impress you. Would you rather I tell you the truth?

Sofia: Honesty is always best.

Elijah: Okay, then it's the Lion King.

The Lion King. No way. That can't be true. He has to be messing with me. Although, I hope he's not.

He messages once more.

Elijah: I've scared you off already haven't I?

Sofia: No, I'm just contemplating whether or not you're joking.

Elijah: Would you prefer it to be a joke?

Sofia: No...I love Disney. Even though I maybe shouldn't.

Elijah: Why not?

Sofia: I'm supposed to be adult.

Elijah: So am I but I don't give a fuck :)

This is so strange. He's the CEO of a corporate company. He wears suits and is no doubt very serious. But look at that little smiley face.

Sofia: Then I guess I won't give a fuck either.

Elijah: That's the spirit. What's your favourite Disney film then?

Sofia: Lilo and Stitch.

Elijah: Yes! Good choice. I'll remember that.

Sofia: You will? Why?

Elijah: I might need it for later.

Cute. Really cute. So cute my face feels hot.

Get a grip!

Sofia: You shouldn't have said that. I'm going to make up a quiz for you.

Elijah: If I get all the answers right, can I ask you more questions?

Sofia: You could just ask me now. I'm a very busy women you know.

Elijah: Of course! So sorry, I'll get right to it. First of all, I want to know what you'd like from this website. What are you looking for?

Smooth. Right to the point. I like it but I'm also terrified because now I have to choose to lie or tell the truth.

I'll use a similar line that he did earlier.

Sofia: Would you rather I was honest? I could make up a fantastically impressive answer for you.
He's quick to reply.
Elijah: Honestly is always best.
Copy cat!
Sofia: Okay you asked for it. The answer is, I don't know. I didn't sign up to be a sugar baby. I did it because I wanted to know what all of this was about. I was being nosey and I haven't got a clue what I'm doing. Sorry to disappoint.
This time the chat bubble appears for a lot longer.
It's probably only a minute but it feels like a lifetime.
Maybe he feels like I've messed with him.
I don't realise I'm holding my breath until I let it go when he replies.
Elijah: I'm not disappointed at all. I don't blame you for wanting to know. It took me a while to understand it all myself. Tell me, are you looking for a sugar daddy now or is this part of your research? Either way, I'd like to help you.
The obvious answer is no. I don't want a sugar daddy.
Yet for some reason I don't want to say no. I don't want to stop talking to him yet. Does that mean I do in fact want one? Could I take money from someone?
No.
Sofia: I'm also not sure. Sorry.
Elijah: Don't apologise. I have to know, did you like my profile as part of your investigation? I'm not sure if my heart can take the answer. :O
I can tell he's kidding. His feelings won't really be hurt but shit, he's perceptive.
Sofia: Small confession. It was an accident...

Elijah

An accident. Well I'd be lying if I said that doesn't hurt my feelings a little but I also want to laugh out loud.

Miss Sofia Westwood's intentions weren't to find a sugar daddy. No wonder her profile was so different.

I like it.

A lot.

In fact, I'm even more intrigued than I was before. She's went to all the trouble to sign up, liked my profile by accident and is now engaging in conversation with me. That's dedication if I've ever seen it. If she genuinely had wanted to find a sugar daddy, would her bio be the same? My immediate thought is yes.

If this wasn't her intention, does that mean she's just being polite? I don't want to make her uncomfortable. I also don't want to stop talking to her. I wanna know more. Maybe I could really help her out with her curiosity and questions.

Elijah: You mean to tell me you're just humouring me? My feelings Sofia...

Sofia: Another confession. I liked your profile by accident because I was looking at it for so long. You're not the same as the others.

The others? What does that mean?

Elijah: I'm not?

Sofia: For a start you're younger. You have all your hair and it look like you take care of your beard.

Ha! She's not wrong about the age thing. I've noticed myself that I'm from a whole different generation to most sugar daddies.

Elijah: A man who doesn't take care of his beard is worth nothing.

Sofia: I like that.

Elijah: Do you? I have to make sure of something. I don't want you to feel like you have to speak with me because I liked you back. If you're uncomfortable please let me know.

I send the message and wait with baited breath. Why would it matter if she wasn't interested? Her profile made me curious but that's all. So why am I worried about her reply?

Seconds tick by making me nervous.

Sofia: I'm not uncomfortable at all. I chose to answer you remember? Why did you like me back?

How do I answer this? Truthfully? I've never had to message a women this way. Never wanted to. It's usually a simple match and then a date. Then again, she isn't here for that and I want to answer her.

Elijah: I loved your bio. It was refreshing and different. And well if I can be blunt, you looked beautiful in your photo.

There I said it. Complimenting a women is never hard for me. Apart from now. Have I ever felt worry when telling a women she's beautiful? No, not once.

Sofia: Thank you, you're rather handsome yourself.

Huh. I'm extremely glad she thinks so.

Elijah: Is it the beard?

Sofia: Yup, all the beard. Nothing else.

Elijah: I thought so. By the way, I was being serious earlier. If you want to know more about this lifestyle. I'm more than happy to help you.

I may not have been in this game for a while but that's okay, nothing has changed.

Sofia: I'd like that. For educational purposes only of course.

Elijah: Of course. What do you want to know?

Sofia: What is it you require from a sugar baby?

Elijah: Me personally? Or in general?

Sofia: You

Interesting. And oddly flattering that she wants to know about me.

Maybe I'm her test subject.

Elijah: Mostly someone to take out, someone who is okay with coming to corporate events as my date.

I pretty much repeat my bio because telling her I'm lonely and not good at being with someone is less palatable.

Sofia: So it's all for show? Or is there some form of intimacy? A friendship even?

I've never had a friendship with any of my sugar babies or anyone for that matter. As for intimacy, not really.

Unless it's sex but I'm not sure that's what she means. I don't know what else to say.

Elijah: I've been fond of some of my sugar babies but I wouldn't say a friendship formed. They are more acquaintances.

Sofia: Do you require sex?

Well, that was blunt but very relevant.

Elijah: No it's not required but sometimes happens.

Sofia: And other sugar daddies? Is it the same?

Elijah: No. Everyone has their own reasons. I'm sorry if I sound cold. That's not my intention Sofia. Unfortunately it's just how my life has turned out. I'm not cruel or disrespectful to any women. I've just never felt the desire to be any more than polite. They seem to feel the same way. It's more or less a business transaction at times. Having someone to take to dinner every now and then is better than sitting alone.

Shit. I didn't mean to type that part but I don't want her to think I'm a monster. I haven't gotten close to any women, sugar baby or not. Hell, I haven't gotten close to any other human. That's just what happens when you're born rich and your future is written for you I guess. God, I sound pathetic!

Sofia: I understand. You don't have to say sorry. I'm not here to judge your life choices. Tell me about something else.

We talk for the rest of the night. She asks me more about myself than the lifestyle. I tell her about my job and she seems genuinely interested. Which is unusual. No one really ever cares about my job unless they're doing business with me. She asks what I like about it and how I cope leading so many people.

I tell her that luckily it came naturally to me. Which is true. I leave out the part about how I got the company.

She quizzes me on what music I like and it turns out we have similar taste. I list the artists I'm fond of as does she.

There's quite a few matches on our lists including Metallica and Fall Out Boy.

I take my turn asking her questions too, which I enjoy much more. She's definitely more interesting than I am.

I ask her about web design and she gushes over the topic. She writes about it as if it's her one true love and I read with rapt interest. She even asks if I hate the design of the sugar rush website.

I do.

I'm disappointed when she stops telling me about it. I could have read her opinions and annoyances for hours more. This is an unusual experience but it's also undeniably fantastic.

Sofia: Do you find the name 'sugary sweet' as creepy as I do?

Elijah: It's the worst choice the website made.

Sofia: I'm so happy you agree :)

Elijah: I have another burning question.

Sofia: Ask away.

Elijah: You mentioned you like eating too much chocolate. What kind of chocolate?

Sofia: All the chocolate.

Elijah: Perfect answer.

Sofia: Do you consider chocolate a snack?

She's paid attention to my bio as much as I have hers.

Elijah: Anything can be a snack if you try hard enough ;)

Eventually it's clear that we're both too tired to keep our eyes open. A glance at the time on my screen and I see it's just passed three am.

When a message from her is sent half written, I assume it's because she's fallen asleep.

For all that time, sending her messages, I felt something that I haven't for a long time. Or maybe ever. Happiness, excitement. Calm. All of those things.

Elijah: Goodnight Sofia-

Before I send it, I pause. Wondering if I should ask her the one thing I've been contemplating for a while. I don't know if it's a good idea though. It might scare her off.

Typing it out anyway, I read it back to myself.

Elijah: Can I take you out? I'll give you the full experience. I hope you sleep well.

Am I doing this to help her queries? Or do I simply want to take her out?

Both.

It's both.

Send!

Sofia

I'm woken up by the sun beaming through the window, my eyes squinting from the brightness.

As soon as my brain fog lifts, memories from last night surface.

Oh shit!

Sitting up in bed - still wearing the jeans and t-shirt from yesterday - I search my bed for my phone.

Did I really spend all that time talking to a sugar daddy? Flirting with one? Honestly I'm not sure what I'm trying to do with my life at this point.

Elijah Everett.

My face heats at the thought of him name.

How can I be blushing over a man I've never met?

Yet he's so sweet and direct and...

Pull it together Sofia!

Finally finding my phone, I shove it in front of my face.

The first thing I notice is that I've slept until eleven am. The second thing I notice is a missed call from my Mom at nine-thirty this morning. Shit! I'll have to call her back.

Before I can, my eyes land on an array of messages from the sugar rush app.

Swiping away likes from three different men and a couple messages from others, I find the message I'd hoped for.

One from Elijah.

I fell asleep in the middle of our conversation so now I should probably apologise.

Assuming he will have just said goodnight, I open his message without much thought.

Then I have to read it over multiple times to let it sink in.

He wants to take me out.

Wow.

Me, really? Why?

Could I do that? Do I want to go that far?

Yes I suppose I do. There's so much more I want to ask him. Not just about his lifestyle choice either. About him.

Maybe I should analyse why? Why am I so interested in a stranger so quick?

Part of it could be that I want to pretend my life is okay. Although it seems more likely that while talking to him last night, I didn't feel guarded.

Which is strange because when it comes to men, I'm always guarded.

Would I feel that way if I met him in real life? Or would I feel the slight twinge of nerves that always prickles in the back of my mind when I'm around a man. It's not overwhelming but it's always there. Present.

Maybe that's why any of the flings in University never turned into a relationship.

What would my Mom say?

She'd say no. That meeting a strange man is bad.

I'm not dumb. I know that's true. I'm aware of how stupid it is.

She'd be disappointed and I may very well end up disappointed in myself.

I should be focusing on the interview. On my future.

Not some new hobby of quizzing a sugar daddy.

I'll say no...

For sure.

So I type out the the message.

Sofia: I really appreciate the offer but I don't think that's a good idea.

Yet I can't bring myself to send it. I'm not sure what I want to do. I know what the smart answer is, the safe answer.

Frustration creeps in with the inability to decide.

Dropping my phone onto the bed, I leave it behind as I walk to the bathroom. A shower will make me feel better. Even if the water only stays hot for about five minutes.

Removing my clothes, I let them fall to the floor. Without waiting for the water to get warm, I jump in and let the cold shock me.

That's what I need. A shock back to reality.

I stand there for as long as I possibly can, through the water getting hot until it goes cold once more. My finger tips wrinkle from being under the spray too long and my thoughts wander.

What's the worst that could happen if I say yes? That's probably not the best question to ask myself.

It could only be one time. Just to see.

See what?

If he's real? If he looks as good face to face? If the continuous desire to know more about him will go away...

Letting the water hit me directly in the face, I let out a defeated sigh.

I know my answer.

With a towel wrapped around me and hair that is still damn, I delete my original message and change it.

Sofia: I suppose you could take me out. If I can fit you into my busy schedule :)

It's ridiculous how quickly I feel better. How happy I am now.

The chat bubble appears immediately and my stomach flutters.

Butterflies? Oh come on.

Elijah: I feel so very privileged. When can you fit me in? I have most of this weekend free if that's any good for you.

This weekend. As in today or tomorrow. Already? Well duh Sofia, he doesn't have much free time to play with.

Sofia: It turns out I am also free all weekend.

Elijah: Perfect! How does tonight sound? We could go to dinner. That's a pretty standard thing for a sugar daddy and sugar baby to do. It'll help with your experience.

Okay, tonight is good. I can totally do this. No big deal right? Just meeting a rich stranger. This is what I wanted. Deeeep breaths.

Sofia: Tonight is great.

Elijah: Seven pm? I could pick you up.

Sofia: Seven is perfect but I'd rather make my own way if you don't mind.

Safety first. Don't get into a strange mans car.

Elijah: Of course I don't mind. Do you want to pick the restaurant or shall I?

Sofia: You can. Just let me know where and I'll be there :)

Elijah: You got it. I'll message you soon. I'm looking forward to this.

Sofia: Me too.

With the conversation ending and my heart in my throat, I let out an excited squeal. Well partly terrified too.
Oh my god.
Oh my goddddd!
What is it about this man? I'm worried that it has nothing to do with him being a sugar daddy. If that's true then I'm in trouble.

***

I'm a panicked mess as I throw all of my clothes out of my wardrobe and onto the floor. I don't have a huge collection to pick from but it's still a task to sift through it all.
Why the hell do I have zero nice clothes? I'm by no means a glamour model but I do try to take pride in my appearance...sometimes. My favourite thing to wear these days is a sweat pant-hoodie combo.
I certainly can't meet Mr Elijah Everett wearing that. He will no doubt be dressed from head to toe in designer clothes.
Come on! There has to be something!
My frustration is almost driving me to breaking point when my hand grasps a pale pink strapless dress, complete with sweetheart neckline and skater style skirt. I can confirm I've worn it once since I purchased it. Because I haven't been anywhere recently that would require a fancy dress. Actually it probably isn't fancy by other peoples standards but it is to me.
It's perfect for tonight.
Couple it with the only black heels I have, straighten my brunette crazed locks and maybe I'll look presentable.
At least I already showered today so that's one thing out of the way.

***

A few hours later I receive a message from Elijah with the details of the restaurant. It's called 'Maple and Ash' and according to Google maps, it's only a twenty minute walk from my apartment. Thank god.

It also has a whole five stars.

I'm not sure why I expected anything less. The man I'm going to meet is obviously a millionaire. Or a billionaire? Who knows but he's classy and probably wouldn't eat anywhere that's less than five stars.

I gotta admit it makes me a little nervous. Elijah doesn't know how much I'm struggling. He probably assumes I don't have much money but he doesn't know to what extent. Technically he thinks I'm an employed Web Designer.

Shit.

What if sees me and immediately decides he's made a mistake?

Well that doesn't matter anyway because it's not a real 'sugar' date. It's just to kill my curiosity.

On the plus side, at least I'll have a real meal tonight.

***

At six pm I tug on my dress and realise it's less fitting than I remember. That's probably because I've been on a new diet of air. Luckily my ankles haven't shrunk any and my heels fit perfectly.

I spray so much perfume over my body that I begin to choke on it. Lord Sofia, you don't want to smell like a hookers handbag!

Oh a purse!

I better find that too! Even though I'm not sure what I'm going to put in it. My phone, keys and empty wallet?

I should have a black one, it can just be for show I guess.

Shaking my head to escape the cloud of perfume, I step in front of my mirror.

Staring at myself, I see the lack of colour in my cheeks and zero light in my eyes. I try to ignore it as I straighten my hair and apply a little lip gloss. There's no point in adding lots of makeup because it's just not who I am.

As I stand there fully dressed an onslaught of emotions hit me. This is probably the most risky thing I've ever done in my life.

One particular feeling takes hold, one from my childhood that has me frozen. What if I get hurt?

I grit my teeth and push it away.

This is the present and my past can't hurt me.

Stepping away from my own reflection, I find my purse, throw in what I need and exit my apartment building.

It's six thirty now, so I should be ten minutes early when I get there.

The cool breeze calms my nerves as I walk, the sky clear and light.

Maybe I should have put a jacket on for when I have to walk back home. It won't be as warm then but it's too late now.

Taking my time, I enjoy the walk. It helps me clear my head and makes my decision seem less crazy.

This is going to be fun and it's about time I had some of that.

Twenty minutes later I make it to 'Maple and Ash' and from the modern white brick exterior, I know I'm going to feel extremely out of place in there.

I take a deep breath before entering the foyer to collect my thoughts. It's probably best to meet him in here.

I wonder if he's the early type too.

My eyes scan the area just in case, taking in lovely velvet seating for those who are waiting for a table. The decor is dark and sophisticated. It feels expensive.

Maybe I should have waited outsi-

My eyes land on a lovely gentleman waiting at the bar a few feet away. He leans on it, no drink to be seen.

Lord have mercy.

Elijah Everett.

He's glancing around too but it doesn't take long for him to stop.

When his eyes meet mine all of my nerves disappear and my body relaxes. What is this witchcraft?

I think I'm drooling...am I drooling? It has nothing to do with the fancy expensive decor. The chandelier is pretty and all but that's not why my jaw is on the floor.

Elijah is dressed in a gorgeous blue suit. His hair is nicely styled, his beard groomed perfectly. Oh and the little smile on his face suggests confidence. He's a very handsome man. His photo didn't prepare me for this and I'm going struggle to form any sentences.

Especially now that he's walking towards me.

"Sofia?" He questions, his eyes slide down my body and back up so slowly that I can literally feel it burning me.

Does he like what he sees? I sure hope so.

God, I love how he says my name.

Breath!

"Yes, that's me" I reply and he steps forward, leaning into me subtly. He's taller than me by a few inches...just right.

"May I?" He asks and I realise he's asking if he can kiss my cheek. Wow, what a gentleman.

"Of course" I reply, a blush creeping onto my face.

The cute smile he gives me before closing the distance causes butterflies to go crazy in my stomach. His lips press onto my cheek while his hand rests gently on my arm.

Let's just say my body reacts.

A lovely cologne fills my senses and I have to refrain from trying to smell him further.

"You look beautiful" he whispers in my ear and I can feel my blush amplifying. I probably look like a bright red tomato.

"Thank you" is my high pitched reply. I literally sound like a mouse.

He's going to think I'm a idiot!

Lord, he's so dreamy though. Maybe I should be his sugar baby.

No! Focus!

As he steps aside to let me go ahead, my heart beat picks up and it's all to do with him.

His hand meets my lower back, guiding me gently inside the dinning area. He asks a waiter about his reservation but I can barely focus on the words.

As we're led to our table, I try to distract myself from the way he's heating me up.

This is ridiculous!

I try to take in the decor some more as a distraction.

Perfectly white and pristine table cloths underneath identically placed plates and cutlery. The lighting is low, the atmosphere almost seductive. That's the only way I can describe it. The tables are a nice distance from one another which seems like it would provide just the right amount of privacy.

That's not something that I have to worry about as we stop at a table situated away from all the others. It's a little bit more fancy too and spacious with plush black chairs replacing the wooden ones that the other tables have.

I'm speechless as his hand leaves my back so that he can pull my chair out for me. I've never seen such grandeur.

All I can do is mumble a quick thank you as I sit and my eyes follow his confident walk around to his own chair.

There's something about this man that suggests even though he's all polite and perfectly dressed on the outside, there's someone a little more rough underneath.

Maybe it's the way he gazes back at me with light green eyes that hold so much curiosity for a normal women like me. I imagine my gaze looks the same. I feel hungry for food and information. And other things...

When he begins to speak I'm pretty sure a gun shot could go off and I'd be unaware.

"Are you okay?" he asks, his expression completely genuine. I've forgotten how to speak.

Use your words Sofia! He's just a person!

"Yes, sorry this is just all new to me" I reply, my voice so low I'm surprised he heard.

"Don't apologise. Is there anything I can do to make you more comfortable? I promise you don't need to feel nervous. I'm here at your service remember. Anything you want to know..." he trails off as my brain processes his kind words and soft tone.

I'm not nervous Elijah. I'm...something else.

I have the answer to a question I asked myself earlier. The calm I felt when messaging him does extend to real life. It baffles me.

What is it about him? I'm usually unsettled around men.

"I am comfortable. Thank you for this" I reply, my voice more even now.

"No, thank you. I'm glad you agreed to come out with me. I really enjoyed our conversation last night" he says, his eyes flicking to the menu. It's as if had to break eye contact with me, his throat clearing as he reads.

Hmm. What was that?

"So did I" I tell him and follow his lead.

My eyes widen immediately when I see the price tags on all of the food. So much so that I consider getting up and leaving. This is crazy.

This is what I wanted.

Are women comfortable with this? With someone paying all of this money for a meal for them?

"You look a little white" I hear and find Elijah smirking at me.

"This is expensive" I state the obvious like a fool. Why am I shocked?

"Yes. I know I'm not your sugar daddy but I will be paying for this meal. The full experience remember?" He winks and it kills my worry. I don't think I'll feel good about him paying for it but it's not as if I can.

"I remember. Although I'm unsure of what you get out of this" I wonder out loud.

He places his hands on the table, clasping them together.

"I get to spend the evening with a gorgeous women who I am just as intrigued by as she is me. I liked your profile Sofia. It was like a breath of fresh air and now I want to know more about you"

There goes my blush again. What could he possibly want to know about me?

We stare at one another for what feels like forever until a waitress appears next our table, hovering awkwardly.

I'm kind of glad. If I'd stared any longer I'd have melted into a puddle on the floor.

"Sir, Madam, what can I get you?"

Considering the lack of time spent actually looking at the menu, I ask what she recommends.

Apparently the most expensive steak they offer is the best and I reluctantly agree to it. While Elijah opts for a burger, which doesn't sound all that sophisticated but I bet it it. Maybe it's laced with gold!

Once we order drinks too – a white wine for me and a red for him – I feel a little bit less out of place. No one has looked at me funny yet.

"So this is what a normal dinner or meeting would be like with a sugar baby?" I ask as the waitress leaves.

"Yes, apart from the fact that I haven't sent you a payment to be here" he replies in a wary tone, that suggests he doesn't want to scare me off. Huh?

"What? You have to pay a women to be here? Even the first time you meet?" I'm pretty sure my eyes are almost popping from my head.

"Mmmhhmm. Does that surprise you?" He questions, his gaze filled with amusement. I think he's enjoying my shock.

"Well yes, what if you don't like each other?"

"It doesn't matter either way. The sugar daddy still has to pay. Although every website has different conditions. The first meeting payment is exclusive to 'Sugar Rush' apparently. I think it's fair though. A lady should get a payment if she's went out of her way to meet a man" he explains before tilting his head. "Did you read the information page?" His tone is almost teasing.

"No, I didn't get that far" I state, giving him a slight glare.

"What stopped you?" He leans his elbow on the table, his chin resting in his hand.

My mouth goes dry. My body heating again.

Does he know how I'm reacting?

"Some fancy rich guy liked my profile" I tease back.

"That's unfortunate" He grins, showing perfect white teeth.

Ugh. He has a gorgeous smile.

"What does it say?" I ask.

"A lot. Too much for anyone to remember but in short, it gives both sugar babies and sugar daddies some tips and guidelines. What to do and what not to" he explains.

"What's something that shouldn't be done?" I wonder.

"One thing is that a sugar daddy must not have more than one sugar baby at a time" he tells me.

"That seems reasonable"

"I agree"

"You do? Wouldn't it be easier to have more than one. You could have them on a sort of rotation" I joke and he raises his eyebrows.

"I've never thought of that. Maybe you're right" he replies and I scrunch my nose in disgust. In reality, that's not a pleasant thought. "No, actually that would mean I wouldn't be able to give all my attention to one woman" he continues.

When he says this, his gaze bores into mine as if he's trying to tell me something. Something that I can't work out.

This time I'm saved from the intensity by our food.

As soon as I see it, my stomach growls and I pray he hasn't heard. I'm going to have to try to eat slowly so that I don't give away how much I need this.

Cutting into the steak, I place it in my mouth and have to fight not to let a moan out. My eyes close as the flavour explodes in my mouth. I've never had a meal like this is my whole life.

When I open my eyes again, Elijah is sipping his wine. His focus on me.

What is he thinking? Does he know I'm starving?

If he does, he doesn't mention it.

So I change my route of inquiry and ask more about his work as we eat. I liked reading about it when we messaged last night. There isn't much that I understand about the business world but I enjoy hearing about it from him. Maybe it's the lovely way he enunciates words, or the fact that he knows what he's doing. It's…dare I say…sexy.

He tells me about a recent deal with Japan that he's in the middle of but then pauses abruptly.

"I'm sorry you probably don't want to hear all of this"

"I do. It's interesting"

"Really? Not many people would say that" he tells me, a slight sadness in his voice.

"I like to learn about new things"

"Yes, I'm starting to realise that" he smirks.

"I have an idea. I'm going to ask you some quick fire questions so that I can get all of the more personal questions out of the way. That's if you don't mind" I suggest.

"I don't mind at all. I'm excited for this" he smiles, looking eager.

"Okay, how long have you been a sugar daddy?"

"About five years"

"How many sugar babies have you had?"

"Twelve"

Wow. Anyway…

"What makes you decide to end it?"

"There's always a point when I realise that neither I nor the sugar baby is happy with the arrangement. When we no longer can stand each other's company"

Oh. That's a shame.

"You've had twelve sugar babies in five years. Is there breaks in between?"

"A lot of breaks. Some of them I only saw once or twice"

This continues for some time. I pick his brain and ask about his type, his favourite sugar baby and if he has to pay more for sex. His answers make me stop.

"I don't think I have a certain type of women I prefer. That's always been a strange concept to me. I've found different types of women attractive. Sexually speaking. It hasn't ever been emotionally speaking"

When he stops talking, he blinks and shakes his head as if he's confused. Maybe he hadn't meant to say that. "As for a favourite sugar baby. I don't have one either. Also no, sex doesn't cost more as that would suggest prostitution and that is not what this is. I hope you don't think that"

The way he looks at me is like he's almost pleading. "I don't want you to think bad of me"

Oh. Wow.

"I don't" I assure him. "Like I said in our messages, I'm not here to judge you"

Once again he looks confused before he covers it up with a smile.

"I think it's my turn to ask you some things" he replies, looking mischievous.

Our empty plates are removed at that moment and dessert menus are put in their place. My stomach is aching in a different kind of way at this point.

"First question is do we share dessert?" He asks and my mouth falls open.

"Yes. Absolutely we do. There is no other way to have dessert"

"What would you like?" He questions, quirking his eyebrow in question.

"Is my answer going to change how you see me?"

"Oh it's make or break"

Taking my time I scrutinise then menu. There's a lot of things with fruit which personally I don't think should be on a dessert. There's chocolate eclairs and tarts. Cheesecake. Except the only thing that makes sense to me is just simple.

"Chocolate fudge cake with ice cream" I announce and wait for his opinion.

He doesn't give anyway anything for a few second and it has me worried that he's disappointed in my choice. Then he smirks. That smirk again.

"Correct answer"

"Oh thank god" I sigh, which has him chucking.

With an agreement, we order dessert and when it comes we are presented with two spoons. It's tough to keep my eyes on the food and not on him as he licks stray chocolate from the side of his mouth. On the occasions in which I'm not staring at him, I catch him staring at me. Is he thinking the same way about me? Or is it one sided.

Once the last few pieces of cake are eaten, he asks another question.

"I'd love to know more about your Web Design job. What company do you work for? I may know it" he says casually, not knowing that his questions are about to ruin this lovely night.

What do I say? Can I tell him the truth? My face must be pale because he speaks again. "You don't have to tell me

Sofia" he soothes. Which is slightly funny because what he asked is completely normal.

Glancing at his patient gaze is my first mistake. Thinking about the fact that I'm not employed with a company is my second.

That's when it happens. When all of the defeat and despair of the last year comes crashing into me like a bullet train.

Is is because he's so kind? Because he's a stranger? Or because I haven't spoken to anyone about this yet? Whatever the reason, it all comes out.

"I want to tell you but I can't because there is no company" I confess.

Then I don't stop talking. I tell him that I lied on my profile, that I'm in fact merely an aspiring web designer. I tell him about university, about how I saved up to get there. My struggles of getting a job, my loans, my coffee shop interview, my portfolio, my lies to my friend and my parents. Telling them that I'm okay. I even tell him that I haven't had a proper meal in so long that I've forgotten what that's like. The only thing I leave out is the one thing not even my parents know. No one knows. No one needs to.

I'm ashamed. I'm horrified. I didn't want him to know because now it looks as though this was all on purpose. I look fake and needy. Desperate for money. Even though that's the last thing I came here for.

Why did I just say all of that? I don't have a real reason but it certainly wasn't to make him feel sorry for me.

Yet I'm sure he does.

I can't look at him. So I stare at my used dessert spoon. I'm a fucking idiot.

My hands wring nervously on the table, my heart in my throat. I'm not crying yet but it could still happen just so that I can embarrass myself more.

God dammit!

"Sofia…"

"I'm sorry. I didn't mean-" he cuts me off.

"Sofia, look at me" his voice is so soft and inviting but I still can't do it. I don't want to see pity.

Suddenly my hand warms as his fingers slide over my knuckles. My skin tingles from the touch, my heart thudding with new emotions.

"Please look at me"

This time there is authority in his voice and it has me looking up. I see no pity or annoyance in his gaze and it has me frowning. "You've been dealing with a lot haven't you?" He asks.

"Please don't feel sorry for me" I beg.

"Feel sorry for you? No. Sofia, I'm in awe"

What? In awe of me? I'm a mess.

"I was impressed before and now even more so. You came all this way on your own" he tells me, smiling softy.

"You're not mad I lied in my profile?"

"You didn't lie. You may not be employed by a web design company but that doesn't make you any less of a web designer"

"It just seems like a poor me story"

"It's not a poor me story, it's reality and you're so brave to face it" he comforts me, his hand now squeezing mine.

"I promise that I'm not here for your money even though now you probably think so"

"I don't think so but even if you were, you've still been a lot more subtle about it than most. I mean you haven't asked me for a car yet"

"What? Tell me that hasn't happened?" I exclaim.

"Of course it has. More than once"

"No, shut up!"

"I will not shut up, its true"

Just like that the conversation is easy again as if nothing was said. He tells me more stories of crazy sugar baby requests and I'm laughing so much I almost choke. His carefree expression is one I really enjoy seeing. To think he runs a huge company all day, no doubt with a serious expression, yet he's laughing right now.

I'm not sure what time it is but we've been here for a while and I'm worried he will need to leave soon. After all, he's a busy man and probably works at all hours of the day and night. I don't want this to end.

"How has your sugar baby experience been so far? Rate it out of ten" he requests, looking genuinely interested in my reply. Well, I can't be serious about this.

"Hmm like a five" I reply, shrugging nonchalantly.

"Ouch. I guess you still don't want a sugar daddy then?" The way he says it is like he's hiding a serious question with a joke.

"No, I couldn't ever take money from someone just for my time. It wouldn't feel right. Although I'm glad we did this. I've learned a lot" I assure him, wanting him to know I've had a good time.

"Okay, no sugar daddy" he states but it seems like he has more to say. His fingers play with the table cloth slightly.

"Elijah, what is it?" I ask, enjoying how it feels to say his name.

"I could still help you out you know, just until you get back on your feet-"

"Elijah that's sweet but no. Apart from the fact we've just met, it wouldn't feel right." I tell him, feeling incredibly touched at his offer. Why would he want to help a women he's doesn't really know?

"Okay, no help" he nods then continues, looking hopeful. "How about a second date just to make sure you got everything?"

"Why would you want to go on a second date with me? I'm not a sugar baby. I'm certainly no good to you" I tell him, letting a small piece of insecurity out. Do I want to see him again? Yes because this has been amazing. Not the fancy restaurant but talking to him. Getting to know him. It's had me feeling a certain way.

"Don't say that. You don't have to be a sugar baby. Maybe we could be friends or occasional dinner buddies. You could just give me your number. I'll take anything you'll give me"

I assume he's messing with me but the seriousness on his face suggests otherwise.

"Friends?" I smirk and he nods. For some reason I think now is a good time to mess with him. The intensity is getting to me again. There's something going on here, inside of me, maybe inside of him. It's terrifying so I'm just going to ignore it.

"Hmmm, I'll have to think about it. Thank you for tonight. I've really appreciated it Elijah" I continue and push out my chair.

I tell myself that I need to get out of here so I don't keep him but really it's so that I can collect myself and work out what the hell is happening.

The panic on his face is slightly amusing.

"Hold on, I'll walk you out. Or do you need a ride home?" He asks pushing his chair out too and signalling for a waiter.

"It's okay, I'll walk home"

"Walk? It's dark and you don't have a jacket"

I'm trying not to blush at his level of care.

"Oh no, how will I survive" I tease and give him one last long look before I get up. "Goodnight Elijah"

I begin to walk away knowing that he has to pay the bill before he can leave. Which makes me feel bad because I know that meal cost a lot. See? I could never be a sugar baby or take money from someone. Maybe when I get a job I'll pay a meal for him?

What are my intentions now? Never see him again? I already don't like that idea but I need to think.

Getting out into the fresh air, I shiver from the cold of the night. Maybe he was right.

Oh well. It's just a little breezy.

"Sofia?! Hold on" I hear and turn to see a frazzled looking Mr Everett. Did he run after me? I like that thought.

Stop it.

"You are determined aren't you" I laugh, then watch as he removes his suit jacket. What's going on?

"I don't like the idea of you walking home alone in the dark. Is that so bad?" He questions, placing the jacket over my shoulders. I'm instantly warmed, while I take in his white shirt that does wonders for his broad shoulders. I would like to see under that shirt. I wonder if I'm right about the lack of a six pack. Is he soft and inviting with a chest I can lie on? I've always found a less toned body more attractive.

No! Enough Sofia.

"You don't need to do this" I assure him but he doesn't stop there.

He steps to the side of the road and hails a passing cab. Before I can protest it's pulling up next to us. This man is irritating... and sweet.

"I may not need to but I want to. Not to be rude or bossy but you are going to get in this cab and let it take you home"

"But-"

"Don't argue or I'll lift you in" he says, tilting his head in challenge.

"What about your jacket?"

"I'll come pick it up some other time" he smirks and I glare at him. He's clever.

"You're far too confident that there will be a next time"

"Not confident but hopeful" he whispers, leaning down to press a kiss to my cheek like he did before. Also like before my body is set alight.

He opens the cab door and I try to argue once more for good measure. I don't like that he's going to pay for this too.

"Elijah-"

"You are stubborn aren't you. Please get in the cab Sofia. For my peace of mind" he pleads and I admit defeat.

Dropping into the cab, I pull his jacket around me. It smells so fucking good.

"Safe travels Darling" he says with a wink before he shuts the door and hands the driver what I assume is cash. God dammit.

He stands back as the cab pulls away, a triumphant grin on his face.

Asshole.

I'll get him back.

Giving the driver my address, I sit back and try to work out what the hell just happened tonight.

Also did he just call me Darling?

Darling.

I like that.

Pulling my phone out of my bag, I already know what I'm going to do. There's no way I won't see him again. I know that from the way my head is whirling. Too many things flying by.

Meet him for what? As what? I don't know but I can do one thing. Just to see what happens.

Opening the Sugar Rush app, I send him a message.

Sofia: I suppose I could just give you my number...

Elijah

The cab drives away, taking the sweetest woman I've ever met with it. She's beautiful, naturally so. The thoughts that entered my mind during dinner should be illegal.

Fuck.

When she ate her first piece of steak my dick had twitched at her pleasured expression. I want to give her that look.

Chill out!

What the fuck is wrong with me?

Only, it's not just her beauty that has me trying to figure out how the hell I can see her again. No, it's more than that.

Turning away from the road, I head in the direction of the valet.

I would have liked to have driven her home. Just to make sure she was okay. There's no reason that she wouldn't be. She's a grown woman after all but I still have the urge to ensure her safe delivery home.

Another urge just like before.

Sofia is unlike anyone I've ever met. I don't just mean the sugar babies I've had but literally anyone ever.

She's honest and real. Which is not something that I'm used to dealing with. I'm better at sensing deceit and lies.

None of which I felt from her. She trusted me with such personal information too. Is this what it feels like for someone to be themselves with me?

Her determination and intelligence is breathtaking. When I said I was in awe of her, I wasn't lying. She really did it all herself, from moving to Chicago to getting a degree. It's extremely impressive to me, someone who was handed everything on a plate.

Something else that's unusual was the way she wanted to listen to me. She wanted to hear what I had to say. Business partners listen to me but people in general only want to hear how much I can pay them.

Sofia doesn't know who I am from my company nor does she want to take my money.

When I get into my car, I have to take a moment to think about that.

What do I have to offer except that? It's all I know.

She doesn't even want to accept help. She'd rather do it herself.

I shouldn't be surprised by that. I'm technically still a random man. She probably doesn't trust me.

I certainly shouldn't trust her so easy but it seems my mind is already made up on that front. Even though I should know better.

Why am I feeling this way? Why do I already want to know if she's okay? Or what she's going to eat tomorrow, if anything.

Fuck I hate that she might not eat. It's clear that she's a little slimmer than she should be and that worries me.

I don't want to help her out of pity or to be the hero.

I want to help her because she doesn't deserve to be living the way she is.

She deserves a break for the stress.

To be able to take a breath. If this was anyone else would I care so much? I mean I feel compassion for other human beings in hard situations but this is more than that.

Is it a selfish reason? If I impress her maybe she'll let me see her again. Maybe she let me kiss her or do that one thing in my bio that I haven't actually done. Lay down on my couch, eating snacks and listening to music. I've never done that with anyone. Certainly not a sugar baby, so why is it suggested in my profile? A stray desire? One that I want with her?

Fucking hell.

What is going on?

Why do I feel so shaken up?

Usually I know exactly what to do and when to do it in all situations but right now I haven't got a clue. Do I message her? Leave her be?

This was supposed to be a date to get rid of my curiosity but now it's turned into something so much more terrifying.

In normal circumstances I have to fake my enthusiasm just so that I'm not alone. The faking it was worse than the loneliness. Which is why I was glad I'd given all of this up. Now I'm glad I took this chance because I got to meet her. None of my enthusiasm was fake.

None of the things I said were a lie.

Even if somethings didn't mean to come out.

She made me weak. Unguarded.

What's worse is I don't hate it.

Pulling my phone from my pant pocket, I intend to message her, only to find that she's already messaged me. I had put my phone on silent earlier so it didn't interrupt our meal.

My mouth pulls into a smile and I immediately try to push it away.

What is going on with me?

Sofia: I suppose I could just give you my number

Fuck, yes.

Calm down Elijah.

What would it mean if she I saw her again. She's never going to agree to be my sugar baby.

Do I even want that? It doesn't seem right. Although what else could she be? There is no other kind of relationship I've had. No friendships I can count on, no girlfriends, no proper family support.

What good am I to her?

Right now I don't care. I just want to answer her message.

Elijah: Please do.

Really Elijah? I sound so desperate!

Oh whatever!

Elijah: And tell me when you make it home.

Sofia

"Yes! Just like that Elijah. Oh god! Shit you have such a magical tongue" I cry as his mouth devours my pussy. My fingers have a tight grip on his hair as he looks up at me hungrily.

"This is the tastiest dessert I've ever had" he chuckles against my thigh, nipping at the skin there.

PING!

Huh? What's that?

PING!

No no no! Not yet!

The scene slips away around me, fading in my mind as I'm pulled awake from my fantastic dream and into reality.

I can't believe that's where my brain has taken me. One meal with the guy and apparently I'm a sex fiend.

A frustrated sigh slips from my lips as my eyes open to dull morning light.

The memory of me getting home, yanking off my dress and falling into bed a distant one.

PING!

For god sake! Who the hell is messaging me at this time! Come to think of it, I've no idea what time it is but I'm assuming it's early.

Feeling around the bed for my phone, my fingers grip it at the same time as I realise something else. My movements have caused me to notice that there's a certain dampness between my legs. Oh boy that dream was powerful!

Once my eyes adjust to the harsh light of my phone screen, I can make out that it's just after seven in the morning. Dropping my eyes lower I see a bunch of messages from the sugar rush app again.

Now that I think about it, I probably don't need the app. I'm not exactly planning on finding another sugar daddy to go see and Elijah now has my number.

Smiling at the memory of sending it to him last night during the cab ride, I also recall his desire to ensure that I got home safe.

Once I remove all of the sugar rush notifications there is room for the screen to display older ones.

Last nights date wasn't a dream and neither is this message.

Elijah: Good morning. I hope this doesn't wake you up. I have an early conference call and just wanted to send you a quick message

A conference call so early and on a Sunday. That sounds horrible.

Sofia: Sorry. Who is this?

Seconds later...

Elijah: Ouch! That hurts but I'll jog your memory. We shared dessert last night before I had to force you into a cab.

Sofia: Ah! Yes sorry, now I remember. You were my third date of the night ;) x

Oh shit. I didn't mean to add that kiss. He's gonna think I'm weird. I'm just so used to adding them when I'm texting other people. I'm surprised I didn't make the mistake earlier.

Elijah: You're a busy women. I better do my best to keep you interested. What happened to the other two dates? x

Huh. It seems my mistake wasn't a bad one. My thumb hovers over the little x at the end of his message. He's probably just returning the gesture but it's still cute.

Sofia: They are locked in my dungeon. You're lucky you're not with them x

Elijah: Maybe I wouldn't mind being in your dungeon. A beautiful women like you would definitely keep me entertained x

Sofia: Are you flirting with me? X

I hope he is. Against my better judgment.

Elijah: I might be. If you let me see you again then I can definitely flirt with you x

Sofia: If you close your eyes and wish really hard, you'll see me again ;) x

Elijah: I'll try that but I'm not sure it's the same as the real thing x

    Sofia: Wait, didn't you say you had a conference call? X
    Elijah: Yup, on it right now :D x
    Sofia: What? What are you doing messaging me while you're working? I don't want to be a distraction x
    Elijah: Well, I hate to break it to you but I'm thoroughly distracted. I can't even remember what I'm supposed to be talking about x
    Oh my god!
    Sofia: Stop messaging me then! X
    Elijah: No, you can't make me x
    Sofia: I could make you. I'll block you! X
    Elijah: Oh no please don't do that. This is so much more fun than what I'm being told from Japan x
    Sofia: You're on the phone to Japan? The really important deal thing you told me about x
    Elijah: That's the one x
    Sofia: Okay I'm ignoring you now until it's over x
    Elijah: No, come back x
    Elijah: Sofia x
    Elijah: Sofia x
    Sofia: Stop it, you're busy! X
    Elijah: I'll stop it if you agree to see me again ;) x
    Oh my fucking god. He's relentless.
    Sofia: I told you I don't need a sugar daddy remember x
    I'm only stalling. So that I can tell myself I at least tried to put up a fight. Obviously I want to say yes.
    Elijah: I'm not going to be your sugar daddy, just your acquaintance x

Sofia: Focus on Japan! x
Elijah: I can't until you answer me :'(x
Sofia: I'll think about it ;) x
Elijah: That's progress but not quite a yes x
Sofia: Fine! I'll see you again! x
Elijah: When are you free? X
Sofia: You're pushing it! X
Elijah: Okay, I'm going I promise! X
Sofia: Goodbye Elijah x
Elijah: Have a nice day :D x

Once again I have the urge to call him an asshole. Even though I rather enjoyed that. The thought that he felt the need to message me, to get an answer, while on a very important call, makes me feel somewhat special.

Don't be ridiculous Sofia! He probably does two things at once all the time.

Either way, it's still a nice feeling.

***

Something that never occurred to me before is that I could simply Google Elijah Everett if I want to know more about him. He runs a large company and I'm sure he's known to many people. Maybe I'd have known who he was if I'd paid more attention the going's on in the business world.

As I begin to research the 'Brew House' for my interview tomorrow, I contemplate just going for it.

What's wrong with a little research on him. It makes logical sense.

Closing some tabs, I open up a new one and bring up Google. My fingers type in his name but with every letter, I feel a sense of growing guilt.

Is this wrong?

Is it technically snooping on someone's life?

Yes.

Sitting back in my chair, I ponder what the worst outcome could be.

An array of images of him with different women? Information that would make me feel less excited to see him again?

Both are possible.

Seconds tick by but then I jab the search button.

Results appear in seconds.

A row of images appear but in most of them he's alone. A couple of women are present but I ignore those.

Taking in his handsome face, I enlarge a few pictures like the creep that I am. In every photo he's wearing a suit. Not one shows him in casual clothes.

The most obvious thing to note is the saddest.

No pictures of him smiling can be found. All serious expressions.

It's a complete contrast to the man I saw last night.

Not wanting to look anymore, I click off the images and read the first headline that appears.

'ELIJAH EVERETT: ALL THERE IS TO KNOW ABOUT THE RUTHLESS BUSINESS MAN'

Ruthless?

You know what? I don't need to do this. The internet is not the way that I should get to know him. Spending time with him myself is the only way to do that.

BUZZZZZZ!

I jump about a feet in the air as the intercom at my apartment door alerts me to a visitor.

Who on earth could that be?

Possibly Annabelle. She's the only person who really visits me in Chicago.

Striding to the door, I press the button to speak. "Hello?"

"So you are alive" is the pissed of familiar reply I get.

What the hell? My Mom is here!

Oh shit! She's going to kill me, this place is a mess.

"What are you doing here Mom?"

"Charming! You weren't picking up and you haven't called in weeks. I was worried. So here I am! Let me up!" She exclaims, clearly irritated. Oh dear.

Pushing the button, I open the door and wait for her to make the ascent up the many stairs.

As soon as I see her, my eyes well up a little. I've missed her a lot. It's been about six months since I saw her last and even then I was lying to her about my situation.

Which I definitely will be doing again!

She stops in front of me, shakes her head, tuts and then pulls me into a tight hug.

"You're going to give me a heart attack!" She exclaims before pulling back to squish my cheeks.

"Stop that" I laugh but she only does it more.

I'm basically just a younger version of my Mom because I haven't got a single one of my Dad's features.

Stepping aside, I let her walk in and instantly know what she's going to say. It's obvious with the way she glances around.

"Don't you know how to clean?" She sighs before sitting on the edge of my bed. I don't have the luxury of a couch.

I don't blame her for asking. Since the clothes that are scattered over the floor suggest I don't know how to.

"I'm getting to it" I reply, sitting next to her.

"So, how are you anyway. Is everything okay? Or is there a reason you haven't been in touch?" She asks, eyeing me up for any lies I might tell.

Sadly I've gotten good at disguising the truth.

"Everything is fine. I've just been busy. I've sent a lot of job applications out. In fact, I have an interview tomorrow morning" I explain and because only part of it is a lie, I think I'll get away with it.

"Oh that's great honey! Are you okay for money? I could-"

I cut her off because I hate that she feels the need to ask. I certainly won't take money from her. My parents can't afford much either.

"I'm okay Mom I promise. How's Bree doing?" I ask as a way to change the subject. Well, also because I genuinely want to know.

Bree is my younger cousin from my Mom's side of the family. She has visited me a few times here but mostly we video call. She's like the sister I never had. She was born when I was seven and as soon as she got old enough to annoy me, she took every opportunity and still does. I miss her too.

"She's doing good. She's getting ready to start college in a few months" she tells me and I know that means a college in Ohio. Bree's parents a.k.a my aunt and uncle are strict with her and they won't let her leave the city for education, that's for sure. I feel sorry for her. It's such a shame.

"What about Dad?"

"Oh you know what he's like, always onto a new hobby. You know he's building motorbikes kno-"

She pauses abruptly and I follow her line of sight.

Elijah's jacket sits on the back of my desk chair where I left it last night.

God dammit.

She's gonna ask so many questions.

"Something you want to tell me?" She asks, a sly smile on her face.

"I'm really into men's clothes" I reply, wondering if that'll work.

"Oh come one! Tell me. Do you have a boyfriend?" She almost squeals as if she's a teenage girl getting some gossip.

"No, not a boyfriend. Just a friend. He left it here last week, that's all" I lie smoothly but she doesn't buy it.

"Uh huh. Sure. What's his name?"

"No comment Mom. Don't be so nosey"

"I'm your Mother. It's my job"

Then at the worst possible moment, my text tone sounds. My phone vibrates on my desk and my face heats.

Probably Elijah.

My Mom takes one look at my obviously red face and gasps. Then to my horror she darts for my phone.

This women is insane.

"Mom! Put it down!" I yell and try to grab it off her.

She steps away and holds it out of reach.

"Who's Elijah? Is he your friend? Anyway apparently he's won some kind of deal. Oh he put a kiss. Are you sure he's just your friend?"

I might just kill my own Mom right here and now.

"Mom, give it back. Also why are you assuming he's the friend I was talking about? I could have multiple male friends" I sigh.

"Do you?" She questions, handing it back.

Thank god, my heart almost burst from my chest. He could have said anything. Something that would have given away that he's a sugar daddy. She'd drag me back home in seconds.

"No, I don't but that's besides the point"

"Fine, don't tell me. I'll find out another time though! How about we order some food? My treat"

With a bullet dodged, I spend the rest of the day with my Mom. We catch up on everything there is to talk about and I really enjoy having her here. It makes me remember the good parts about being at home.

I make a note to answer Elijah at some point but right now what's important is making the most of this time I have.

No matter how much I itch to read his message.

***

Monday.
The morning of my interview.
I'm nervous as hell.

My Mom had to leave early, apologising for such a fleeting visit but honestly I'm just glad I was able to see her. It means a lot that she came all this way.

I only managed to reply to Elijah to congratulate him on his successful deal twenty minutes ago. Since it's Monday, I don't think I'll be getting as many quick responses.

Finding the most formal outfit I can – a blouse and some black pants – I begin my walk to the 'Brew House'. It's about thirty minutes away but it's worth it if it means I could have some income soon.

When I arrive, I take in the cute design of the place. It gives off an outdoorsy feel and looks like it belongs in the middle of the woods. Even though it's placed in a row of modern looking shops. It stands out well. Wooden panels make up the exterior and ivy covers the door.

Just before I enter, I glance at my phone and smile.

Elijah: Good luck with your interview. You're going to do fantastic Darling xx

He called me Darling again and two kisses?

How can a man I've just met make me feel so calm after one message? It makes no sense but it's exactly what I needed.

The coffee shop is warm and inviting, just like the little old lady who greets me as I enter. As it turns out, she's the owner of the shop and the one who is conducting the interview.

Her pleasant manner takes away any left over nerves as she asks me to take a seat opposite her at one of the tables.

There are only a few other people in here so it's nice and peaceful.

When she begins asking questions, it's more of a casual conversation rather than anything formal.

She questions me on things that I hadn't expected her to. For example my hobbies and what I'm planning to do with my life.

Those are both easy to answer and I watch her scribble down some things in a little notebook.

All in all, it must only take about twenty minutes before she informs me that I'll find out within a week if I've been successful.

So I leave with a small sense of hope.

That wasn't so bad.

My first instinct is to take out my phone and message a certain man.

I really can't believe how he's affecting me.

Sofia: I think it went well x

He replies as I start walking home.

Elijah: I knew it would! Are you free tonight? We could celebrate? X

My body automatically screams yes while my mind tries to be more reasonable.

Why am I so eager to see him? I can't possibly miss someone I've met once.

Except the eagerness hasn't went away since he put me in the cab on Saturday. It's only been two days.

Sofia: Celebrate what? I haven't got the job yet silly! Besides, it's Monday. I'm sure you'll be busy and I don't want to mess up any schedules you have X

I'm genuinely curious about his answer. The reason he has sugar babies is because he has no time for anything else. Yet he's asking me out again. So quickly.

Which I'm more than happy about.

Elijah: You may not have it yet but you will soon. I'm sure of it! Well, usually I would be busy but tonight's meeting got cancelled. So I'm all yours if you want me ;) x

Shit. That's hot.

Want him? In more ways than I'm willing to admit. What I will admit though is that I do want to see him tonight.

Do I flirt back? Should I?

Or maybe I'd rather tease.

Sofia: I want you...to pick me up tonight because my feet hurt from all of the walking I've been doing today. Only if you can of course x

Maybe getting in his car isn't smart but my gut is telling me that I'll be perfectly safe with him.

Elijah: I'm so glad you asked. Is five pm good? X

Sofia: Yes. I'll send you my address. Where are we going? X

Elijah: It's a surprise ;) x

Sofia: Okay but at least tell me what I should wear x

Elijah: Whatever you feel comfortable in :D x

Sofia: You'll regret saying that x

Elijah: I bet I won't xx

***

Whatever I feel comfortable in huh? Well he asked for it.

After showering and shaving just about every inch of my body – just so that I feel good about myself, no other reason – I start the task of choosing such an outfit.

Finding my casual black skirt that sits just above the knee and my white long sleeve t-shirt, I add some sandals and my black leather jacket. I actually have to dust it off because it's been in my wardrobe so long.

Then I tie my hair up, pleating the back before tucking my bangs behind my ear.

There, this is comfortable.

I'm ready just in time.

Elijah: I'm outside :D x

Excitement shoots through me but I try to push it down. This is the second time I've met him. I shouldn't feel this way.

Not to mention I should be spending my time applying for more jobs rather than seeing a gorgeous man.

Oh well.

Hopping a little too happily down the stairs, I tell myself that I just haven't satisfied my curiosity yet. That's all this is. No sugar daddy.

As soon as I step outside, I see him.

He's leaning against a black Mercedes that's parked at the curb, his hands pushed into the pant pockets of his suit. He's wearing a black one tonight, all black. Even the shirt, right down to his shiny shoes. His hair blows a little in the wind giving it even more of a messy look. The first few buttons of his shirt are unbuttoned and he looks like a GQ model but without the annoyingly obnoxious gym body. He's so gorgeous!

When he sees me he pushes off the car, a lovely smile gracing his face. Oh there go the butterflies again.

"Sofia, I've been looking forward to this all day" he greets me, his hands lightly touching my waist as he leans down to kiss my cheek.

Fireworks!

Wow I'm gonna faint!

"How does one women look so good?" He muses.

"I think you need to get your eyes checked" I joke.

"Oh no Darling. I have twenty twenty vision and you're smoking hot!"

He wiggles his eyebrows and I feel my face turning into a bright red tomato again.

"Stop trying to flatter me. Its not working!" I lie.

"Ohh, that's a shame...I'll try harder then" he winks, opening the car door for me. I nudge him playfully before sliding onto the plush leather seat. Cars don't impress me but I can't deny this is lovely.

As soon as he's in the drivers seat, I can't stop my curiosity overflowing. He didn't tell me a thing about tonight.

"So, where are we going?" I ask as he pulls out into the traffic.

"I can't tell you that. Then it wouldn't be a surprise"

"Oh no, you're kidnapping me aren't you? I knew I should have Googled you more before getting in your car!" I exclaim.

"Google wouldn't tell you about all of the women I've kidnapped. I'm too good for that" he teases. I think. "Have you Googled me?" he questions, glancing at me briefly.

Should I feel guilty for doing so?

"Very briefly but all I saw were some lovely pictures and the words 'ruthless businessman'. I didn't go any further. I decided I should make my own assumptions about you" I reply, smiling as I catch his eyebrows raising.

"I appreciate that Sofia. Really..." he says softly before continuing. "I guess ruthless business man is rather accurate though. Some use less tasteful words" he grins playfully and my heart thuds.

"I can imagine" I state, wondering if he has a bad reputation with anyone.

While his eyes are on the road it gives me an opportunity to watch him in a totally non creepy way.

His hands grip the steering wheel, hands that I shouldn't be thinking about in the way I already have.

His side profile is obviously gorgeous, his nose perfectly shaped, his beard looking so soft I want to touch it.

It's like I'm in a trance until he snaps me out of it.

"So your interview went well?" He asks and I tell him all about it.

He listens, nodding and commenting on what I say. Which is obviously what most people would do but with Elijah it's like he's genuinely interested in hearing me speak.

Once I'm done, he asks something else.

"Have you eaten today?" His voice is wary, as if he doesn't want to offend me.

"No" I reply and look away out of the window, watching the streets whiz by in a blur.

This is awkward.

"I'll fix that Darling"

The car falls silent because I don't know what to say. I'd like to thank him but the words don't come out.

The radio playing quietly fills the quiet until I find a way to change the subject.

"Are you happy about closing the Japan deal?" I ask and this time when he glances at me, his expression is unreadable. Is he shocked? Confused? Maybe he's surprised I've asked?

"Yes! As well as swapping some databases they wanted to haggle me down on some industrial space I bought from them. For some reason they wanted it all back. So I charged ten percent more than I originally bought them for" he tells me, a little smile on his face. He's so pleased with himself. It's cute.

"You must have the magic touch. It's gotta be easy for you to say the right things" I tease and he glances at me out of the corner of his eye.

"Most of the time I do...not recently"

His sentence is followed by another look in my direction, his eyes glued to mine for a second.

"Oh come on...you're a very talented business man with an extremely handsome face. Mergers, Big Bosses, Women. They must all be easy to conquer for you"

"Darling flattery will get you everywhere but you'd be surprised by how easily a man like me can get flustered. It's a new thing for me though. As new as last Saturday" he confesses, very obviously meaning because of me.

"Hmmm, I'm not sure what you're referring to" I say casually, just as he drives the car into a multi-storey parking lot.

As soon as the car comes to a stop he turns to me, his hand reaching over to brush my bangs back behind my ear.

"You, my dear have made me less than sure of myself"

"I'm nothing special Elijah" comes out of my mouth before I can stop it. He shakes his head as if in disagreement.

"You're very special Sofia" he assures me, his voice a little deeper.

The temperature in the car rises and suddenly we're gravitating towards each other. My eyes flick to his lips involuntarily. I can almost feel how soft they'll be.

Knock! Knock!

"Sir?"

We both jump as a man appears at the drivers side window. His knuckles tapping the glass.

Elijah slams his finger on the window button in a frustrated manner.

Kind of like how I feel.

It's getting hard to remember the reason I'm here. Well why I'm supposed to be here. I think he's forgotten too.

"Yes, can I help you?" He asks.

The man who I now see is in a red velvet waist coat with a name badge attached, sticks out his hand.

"I'm Rodger, we spoke on the phone Mr Everett. The cinema is ready for you"

Cinema? Ohhhh! That's what we're doing. Yes!

"Thank you Rodger" Elijah quips, his voice perfectly calm with only a tiny edge of annoyance.

I think Rodger just gave away Elijah's surprise and he's definitely not happy about it.

When Rodger walks around the car to open my door, Elijah stops him as he jumps out. I'm not exactly sure what Rodger's job is but I think it has something to do with meeting and greeting guests. The poor man is all flustered and I feel a little bad for him.

I think Elijah does too, now that his initial annoyance is gone. He takes my hand, helping me out of the car and smiles politely at Rodger.

"Sorry if I seemed a little rude. It's just, this was meant to be a surprise for this lovely lady" he explains and Rodger looks mortified.

"Oh I am so very sorry Sir. Mam, I really do apologise" he exclaims, panicking a little.

"It's okay, I'm just happy to be here" I tell him. I can feel Elijah looking at me and when I turn my gaze to him, he whispers: "Me too"

With that Rodger leads us through the exit door of the parking lot and straight into a grand foyer. Huge pillars, titanic stair case, red carpeting and drapes...lots of drapes. Wow, I didn't even know cinemas like this existed.

There are a few other people milling about. I guess it isn't busy because it's the start of the week.

We are led down a corridor full of numbered doors that obviously lead to cinema screens.

Finally we stop outside one that reads 'Cinema 5'

Rodger leaves us there, scurrying away no doubt still embarrassed.

Elijah guides me inside.

When we're met with rows are rows of empty seats, I'm little confused.

"Where is everyone else?" I ask and he looks really pleased.

"It's just us" he tells me and gazes at me as if he's waiting to see how I'll react.

"You booked the whole cinema?" I breath and he nods. He booked the whole damn cinema! I am VERY excited!

"Yes, I just thought it would be something we can both enjoy" he explains, looking sheepish. I think I'm the first women that he's ever been unsure of. I assume most of his dates/sugar babies would tell him what they think he wants to hear. It's part of the package I guess, when you see someone for money.

I'm not his sugar baby and I'm no good at faking emotions.

They get displayed right on my face for all to see.

I think he's misunderstanding my awe for displeasure.

"We can go somewhere else if-"

"No, this is perfect! Thank you!" I cut in and his worry falls away, revealing relief.

My excitement has me stepping closer to him but I'm unsure on what I plan to do.

We're staring at each other, an eclectic current of excited adrenaline zinging between us. There's something else too. I don't want to admit it but I feel desire and with the way he's looking at me, he feels it too.

My eyes fall to his lips again and I wonder how they taste.

I think he's wondering about mine too and it only seems right to put us both out of our misery.

So when the feeling gets too much, I snap. Reaching for him, I grab his suit jacket and pull him towards me. He comes willingly, immediately leaning down so that our lips can meet. And boy do they meet.

For a few seconds, I'm in heaven.

Then my brain catches up and I'm surprised by my own actions. So I pull back abruptly.

"Sorry" I gasp, looking up at his flushed face.

He shakes his head, his green eyes dark.

"Don't be sorry" he breathes and cups my cheek with his hand. His palm warms my face, his gaze questioning. I know what he's asking.

I nod once and his lips slam into mine once more.

Any shock soon changes to pure lust as he wraps me in his arms. He presses his mouth to mine harder, a muffled moan escaping.

His lips are soft and plush, contrasting with the roughness of his beard as it tickles the skin around my mouth. It's a welcome sensation. So is the feeling of his tongue sweeping into my mouth as he deepens the kiss, making me grip his jacket tighter.

When we pull apart for air, his lips hover over mine. He gives me one more long kiss before properly separating our mouths. Our breathing is ragged and for a man who seems outwardly tough, he's very gentle with me.

I think there may be an animal underneath. I can tell by the way he looks at me. Hungry and wanting.

Taking my hand, he clears his throat.

"Shall we?"

"Yes" I squeak and he leads me to the best spot in the cinema. Back row, right in the middle.

"Is this okay?" He checks once we're seated.

"It's fantastic, thank you" I reply and glance at his fingers entwined with mine on the arm rest. My hand feels tiny in his but for some reason that's attractive to me.

When I look back up at him, he's staring at me again, his lips parted.

"Can I kiss you again?" He asks and my face breaks into a flattered grin.

"Of course" I whisper and lean closer. This time he kisses me slowly, his mouth moving over mine with tenderness and affection. My pulse quickens as I try to deal with feelings I've never felt before.

He said there was no intimacy when it comes to sugar babies. I'm sure that extends to me but this definitely feels intimate.

He only pulls back when the screen lights up, a soft smile on his lips.

"I could kiss you for hours Darling" he breaths, his fingers brushing over my mouth.

"Really? Is this part of the experience?" I ask, trying to hold back a grin. It's a serious question though. I need to know.

He frowns then and shakes his head.

"No, it isn't. This is...new" he explains and pecks my mouth once more.

Huh. Interesting.

"What are we watching?" I ask, trying to keep my mind out of the gutter. We're here to watch a movie, not make out.

"Lilo and Stitch" he smirks.

"Omg, I love this film" I gasp, squeezing his hand. "How did you know?" I joke and he shrugs.

"Lucky guess"

I'm so touched by this.

He did all of it for me. Maybe it's not a big deal to him but this is crazy.

As the film starts, he lifts the arm rest between us and wraps his arm around my shoulder, inviting me to cuddle into him.

This is such a contrast to what he's told me that I don't know how to feel.

It's like I'm seeing this movie for the first time too, in such an amazing situation. I can tell that Elijah is watching me when I smile or laugh because I feel him shifting as we're so close.

Because of that fact, it's hard to concentrate and soon my mind is focused on him rather than the movie.

It seems he is thinking of me too because I feel his hand gently, maybe even hesitantly covering my knee. He just leaves it there at first, his thumb drawing slow circles on my skin. Does he know what he's doing to me? Probably.

Tilting my head towards him, I see the desire there when the screen flickers light onto his face. My breathing is erratic at this point and I'm ashamed to say that I can't stop my legs from parting a little.

This is not who I am but maybe it is who I can be for now.

"I want to touch you Sofia...can I touch you?" He whispers, his lips tickling my ear.

"Yes" I say breathlessly and guide his hand further up my skirt with my own. He gasps at my actions, turning in his seat more to get better access. I can't control myself! Help!

"Open your legs further...spread them for me" he commands and I do as he says because I'm god damn desperate for him. I should be ashamed but that's the last thing I'm feeling.

His fingers tease the outside of my panties and I know he can feel my wetness through them. Especially when he growls in my ear.

"Fuck, is that all for me?"

"Yes. Elijah you make me so wet and needy, it's crazy" I whine while he slips his hand inside my panties, his thumb heading right for my clit. "Ahhh yes, touch me like that" I beg, my hand reaching out to his thigh. I wanna know if he's hard for me.

Shifting his hips, he shoves his fabric covered cock into my hand and groans gutturally. My god he's so big.

I rub my hand over the bulge in his pants while his fingers tease my entrance. I buck my hips to encourage him and he takes the hint, pushing his fingers inside me.

I can't believe we're doing this in the cinema. He's finger fucking me and I'm just about to try and tear down his zipper so I can give him a hand job. I've never done anything like this before in a public setting. It's so thrilling though. I don't want it to end.

    Running on pure lust, I grab his shirt and yank him to me, kissing him with all of the pent up tension he has caused.

    It doesn't take him long to gain back his dominance as he pulls me into his lap, my thighs on either side of his legs. My skirt rides up and his hands slip under the material, his fingers running over the front on panties.

    I gasp as he finds my clit again, rubbing his thumb in slow teasing circles.

    "You're all hot and bothered Sofia, all horny and breathless. Some men might see this as having all the control but not me. Because your flushed face and desire filled eyes have me under your spell. I've never seen so much expressiveness. I'm weak for you Darling.

    "Elijah, please...please touch me more! I want-"

    "What? What do you want? You can have anything Sofia" he growls, his thumb moving faster.

    My logical brain is gone and my body is in control.

    "Fuck me! Please fuck me now. I want to feel you inside of me...god I'm so wet" I pant and moan, feeling the dampness beginning to pool in my panties and drip down my thigh. He can feel it too.

    "Right here?" He asks, a hint of teasing in his rough tone. Yes. Right here in the cinema with Lilo and Stitch playing. I don't give a fuck.

"Yes! Yes please!" I call gripping his shirt and pulling on it wildly.

"Right now?" He continues, driving me wild.

"Ah Elijah, I'm gonna come if you keep this up. I can't stop it" I yell and immediately his fingers disappear.

"No....no! Please"

"Shhh, it's okay" he begins, cupping my face and making me look at him. "The only place I want you to come is on my cock. So if you want that too, unzip my pants" he growls, capturing my lips and slipping his tongue past them.

My hands drop to his trousers and pop open the button. Then they're fighting with the zipper as if they have a mind of their own. I feel like a sex addict because I want his dick so bad. I've never felt so needy. I'm glad I'm on the pill because fumbling with a condom right now would be too much hard work.

Just as I'm thinking that, the gentleman in him reappears.

"Sofia, we should probably use this" he pants, pulling his jacket open and producing a little foil packet from his inside pocket. "I know they suck but unfortunately they're necessary. I'd much rather have nothing separating us Darling" he gazes at me, his eyes heavy with lust. "Not that I'm suggesting we don't use it, I'd never-" he continues to ramble and it's so cute coming from such a confident man.

"Elijah it's okay...I'm protected" I whisper and he watches me for a second before deciding that's good enough for him.

"Fuck yes!" He groans, capturing my mouth with vigour.

When I finally manage to tear down his zipper, he lifts his hips and helps me pull down his pants and boxers. His cock springs free from it's confines, hard and ready. My hand reaches for it in seconds because apparently I'm now this mans personal whore. I've decided.

I'm okay with it.

Stroking him roughly, I watch him bite his lip. His hands hold onto my waist tightly and they clench as I move my panties to the side. Then I rub the head of his cock through my wetness and over my clit.

"You dirty girl. Do it again" he commands and I rub my pussy all over his dick, whining and moaning. My hips rock desperately as I try to get the friction I need.

After a few moments of watching me writhe on top of him, his grabs his dick and lines it up with my entrance.

Grasping my chin, he pulls my face closer, his eyes burning with need.

"Yes?" He pants and it's a question. One final question to make sure that I want him. How can he be so demanding, yet so sweet? I can't stop to think about that right now.

"Yes!" I exclaim and sink down onto him quickly. His mouth falls open on a broken groan as his hands grab my ass roughly.

"Fuck! Sofia! You feel so fucking amazing. You gotta slow it down or I'll come in seconds. I've never felt anything like you" he pushes out, watching me with fascination as I rise back up ever so slowly. His cock feels so good that my eyes are struggling to stay open.

"Ah...this is...so damn amazing Elijah. You...feel...ahhhhhh" I yell as he grabs my thighs and thrusts up into me, making my core pulse around him. Sweet Jesus!

"Yes baby girl, tell me about it! It's indescribable" he groans, his hands sliding under my top. "I wanna see all of you" he states but it's more of a beg.

Before I even know what I'm doing, I'm helping him take off my jacket and top and unclasping my bra. As soon as it's gone his warm hands meet my breast and I can't help but push my chest forward into him more.

"You too...shirt off" I command and he stops touching me momentarily to let me yank at his shirt. As soon as it's unbuttoned and discarded onto a seat with his jacket, I'm pulling him back to me.

He sucks on the skin of my neck, possibly leaving hickeys there. I don't care though...it's fucking hot.

Our hips rock together in a desperate rhythm as his lips suck on my right nipple. I tug on his hair with one hand, the other feeling the warmth of his chest.

As I begin to slow my movements, he does too. Perfect synchronisation between the two of us.

Dramatic, I know but so very true and amazing. I never thought this would be happening in my life ever. The gorgeous man, the sex, the cinema, the euphoria!

His teeth nip at my bottom lip now, his eyes boring into mine with such ferocity that I might come just from that.

"Elijah...I'm going to come" I yell, tugging on his hair again.

"Tell me how to make you scream. I wanna know exactly how you like it" he growls and I'm amazed by his words. No guy has ever asked that. Truth be told I've never felt this amount of pleasure so all I can do is tell him what feels right.

"Fuck me harder, grip my hips. I wanna feel you as deep as I can" I cry and he does as I ask, squeezing my hips while bucking up into me wildly. His face is a beautiful picture of pleasure, his throaty groans pushing me to new heights.

"Now kiss me" I beg and his lips meet mine. His mouth is rough now and it's everything I want.

"Sofia, can I come inside you?" He pants and that question is what has me falling over the edge into another universe.

"YES!" I scream as my body is thrown into worlds of ecstasy and heaven. "Come inside me please" I whine and this has him joining me in that heavenly place.

A chorus of our moans and whispers fill the cinema as the end credit song plays in the background.

Elijah is gripping me to him like a boa constrictor snake and I feel so at home in his arms. Jesus Christ Sofia! Don't think such stupid shit!

My head slumps onto his chest as I try to regain sanity, my hands fluttering over his stomach.

His fingers run through my hair that is no longer in a pleat but instead cascading down my back in a terrible mess.

"You are going to drive me insane Sofia. I already know it" he whispers into my neck.

"Oh you mean you're not going to block me and never see me again now? Wow, that's unexpected" I joke and he tuts glaring at me playfully.

"No, I'm certainly not. Are you planning on doing that to me?" He asks, raising his eyebrows while he reaches for my clothes, then helps me pull them back into place. Which really does surprise me. Not many men would help you dress after sex. But then he's not like many men.

"Well, I'll have to think about it" I grin and he pouts sadly before licking his lips.

"It's a shame that you have to put these clothes back on"

"I was just thinking that about you"

"Oh really? Do you like my untoned non existing abs?" He jokes but I feel like this is something that he genuinely isn't happy about.

"Yes. I'm not a fan of six packs. This is all much more sexy to me" I say looking him in the eye and feeling up his chest. It's gorgeous to me. I wanna kiss him all over.

He doesn't say a word in reply. Instead he grabs my face and shows me exactly how he feels about my answer with his tongue.

He's a very expressive man it seems but words aren't how he does it. He chooses actions instead.

Naturally I don't want to let go of him because then I'll have to come face to face with what has just happened.

It's a lot to take in.

We do eventually tear ourselves apart and try to make our clothes look somewhat normal and innocent.

I hope we look presentable as we walk out but I'm sure the bright red blush on my face gives away that we've been up to something.

The drive back home is filled with fleeting glances, blushes and silence that shows we are both unsure of what to say.

Neither of us expected what happened tonight and I guess it needs to be processed.

I'm confused when he pulls into a fast food drive through but then I remember our conversation earlier.

He's going to fix the fact that I haven't eaten today.

Once again I want to protest. I hate that he's already done so many nice things for me within two meetings. The thought of all the money he has probably spent, especially booking a whole cinema, makes me sick.

"Elijah you don't have to buy me food"

"Sorry, I should have asked. Do you want to go somewhere else?" He asks, misunderstanding what I'm saying. His desire to please me obvious as he waits for my reply.

"No, I mean at all"

"You mean to tell me you're not hungry, especially after what we just did?" He teases, making my face heat up.

"Well yes, I'm hungry but I don't want-"

He stops the car before the order window and turns to me.

"Where have you come from?" He asks, his eyes searching mine.

"What do you mean?" I reply confused. What kind of question is that?

"You don't want me to spend money on you do you? It bothers you? I've never encountered that before" he explains, his features expressing true disbelief.

"I hate when anyone spends money on me. I'm an adult, I should be able to pay for myself. It's not anyone else's job to fund me. Also there are plenty of people like me. You obviously haven't been hanging out with the right ones" I try to joke but he doesn't smile.

"I've hung out with many types of people and every single one of them were more than happy to take my money. The fact that you don't...I like it but also I really want to buy you some food. Please..." he takes my hand in his and kisses the back of it. Then he places it back and closes his eyes for a fleeting moment.

Shifting back to face the windshield, he says:

"I don't know what's gotten into me"

Maybe he's just as baffled by this as me. This uncontrollable need to figure one another out. To know more. To touch and be touched.

I haven't let myself think about it yet. To think of how crazy this all is.

"You can buy me food" I say, watching as his body visible relaxes. Does it bother him so much? That I haven't eaten. Or maybe this is the only way he knows how to do things.

Buying things. Spending money on others.

Maybe it's his form of affection. Whether he knows it or not.

"Would you like a milkshake with your food? A dessert? Snacks?" He questions, his face lighting up.

"Snacks? You really love snacks don't you?" I laugh and he nods enthusiastically like a big kid.

***

Once we've collected our food, he parks in a bay and eagerly sucks on a strawberry milkshake. Which has me staring for so long that he notices.

"You want some?" He asks, licking his lips.

"No thanks, I'll drink my own" I giggle.

In the middle of eating our tacos and fries, he stops to ask me a question.

"Will you take a look at my company website?"

He shoves some fries into his mouth casually as if he's asked what my favourite colour is.

"Why would you want me to do that? Don't you have a whole team?"

"Yes but ever since you scrutinised the Sugar Rush website, I've been wondering what you'd think of mine. I mean, I didn't create or design it myself of course but I'd still like to know. I'd like an outside opinion"

"I'd be happy to give you one" I reply, baffled nonetheless.

With an appreciative smile, he finishes his meal and waits for me to do the same.

"I like to see you eat" he confesses and I give him a strange look.

"Creep" I state, while he starts the engine once more.

"You got that right"

Too soon we pull up outside my apartment building. The atmosphere is thick with uncertainty and I'm not sure what to do now.

I should get out of the car.

"Thank you for tonight" I whisper.

"No thank you..." he begins and it looks like he's going to say something else.

Only he doesn't.

So I blurt out:

"Do you wanna come in? I mean, is that weird? It's probably weird. Sorry, I shouldn't have asked. I don't know what's-"

"Sofia!" He cuts me off and I glance at him warily. "I'm glad you asked Darling"

"You are?"

"Yes. I was hoping you would. But I don't want to overstep my mark. I understand if this is too much-"

"It's not" I reply quickly.

"Phew" he says, a small smile on his lips. I didn't expect that. I'm happy about it. Really happy!

Shit my apartment is a hideous mess and it's the size of a shoe box compared to his place, I'm sure.

"What's wrong?" He asks, no doubt because I've been staring into space for a bit too long.

"Ummm, I just...well my apartment isn't exactly..."

"You're worried what I'll think" he says, answering his own question.

"Yeah...a little bit" I mumble, staring out of the window. I'm a little embarrassed.

"Sofia, Darling look at me" he commands softly, his fingers brushing over my cheek. How is he so soft and gentle, yet so...well him! I know I keep asking myself that but it's crazy to me.

Turning to him, I take in his gorgeous face and wonder how I'm going to make it out of this situation with my fragile feelings in tact. A few days of knowing him and I already feel an attachment growing...a safe place.

No. That can't be true!

"There's nothing to worry about. Sure, I'm rich but I'm not a snob" he quips.

I burst out laughing at the way he says snob and his mouth steals my breath. When he pulls back he looks a little shocked at himself.

"Sorry, I just...I like it when you laugh"

He seems confused by his own actions. I don't say a word and begin to get out of the car so he doesn't feel embarrassed.

Grabbing his hand once he walks around the car, I lead him up the few flights of stairs to my little student accommodation.

I try not to cringe at my own mess as I shove the door open, close it with the same vigour then lead him into the middle of the room.

I've never felt so shitty for only having a bed, desk, kitchenette and a bathroom.

Oh Lord. This was a bad idea.

"No tour?" He jokes and I nudge him in the side, shaking my head.

"You want a tour of the one other room?" I question and he nods enthusiastically.

"Yes actually. I want to see where Sofia Westwood sits and contemplates life" he smirks, tugging on my top to pull me closer.

"Well you're looking at it" I gesture to the half made bed and grimace. What on Earth does a man like him want to do with me?

"Don't do that Darling"

"Don't do what?" I ask, curious as to what he thinks I've done.

"I can tell you're about to try and escape into your own head. I've noticed that you like to do that when you're unsure of the situation" he explains and it makes me feel a little exposed.

"You've known me three days smarty pants" I retort and he quirks his eyebrow at me as if to say 'oh really'.

"Yes and I've enjoyed every minute of it. Now... you didn't mention anything about snuggling in your bio. I'm not happy about that" he says, his voice stern.

"Is that right?" I ask crossing my arms while he takes off his suit jacket. The second one that's now in my apartment.

I assume he's going to fold it neatly and place it somewhere that it won't get ruined but no...he drops it on the end of my bed next to many of my own garments.

Maybe he's not a snob.

"Yes because I'd like to audition for the part of personal space heater" he says proudly, placing his hands on his hips.

"For a start you have too many clothes on for that. So do I actually. I'm going to need that good pure body heat if you want the job" I use my hands to express my wishes and he immediately begins unbuttoning his shirt. My eyes follow his fingers and I ogle every bit of skin that is revealed. We may have had sex but it was in a dimly lit cinema and neither of us have seen each other's goods properly.

Let me just say...he's a fine specimen.

When he gets to unzipping his trousers, he winks at me and I really try not to smile. I fail because he's a cocky asshole.

My eyes drag up his amazing thighs, widen as I take in his very nicely sized cock - that I don't know how fit inside me - and make my way up his lovely chest. There is a small amount of hair there that I want to run my fingers through. So manly.

When my clothes are gone and thrown to the side he stares at me too, stepping closer so that he can lean down to kiss me.

"You're fucking beautiful" he whispers while my hands finally roam his chest properly. Wow, I literally can't wait to snuggle this man.

Giving him a shy glance, I tug on his hand and pull him to my bed. Throwing the duvet back, I lie down and watch as he slides in beside me, his body glued to my side in seconds.

His arms wrap around me, while I live out my fantasy of being squashed to his chest. Our legs tangle and a contented hum vibrates in his throat.

"Are you a warm enough?" He asks. I glance up at him to see a small smirk on his face, his eyes looking tired and relaxed.

"I'm perfectly warm thank you" I reply and feel his hands rubbing down my back. This is lovely. So lovely. I'm putty in his hands...well arms. "Did you offer personal space heater services to any sugar babies?" I ask, smirking at his confused adorable frown.

"I've never offered this service to anyone" He replies, his fingers tracing over my arm. His voice wavers slightly.

"No? Not even an ex girlfriend?" I continue because apparently I have no boundaries.

He leans up on his elbow, his other hand moving up my stomach.

"I've never had a girlfriend Sofia" he replies matter of factly.

What?

Not possible.

"That has to he bullshit Elijah!"

"Why? I told you I've had sugar babies"

"Yes but only for five years of your life. What about before that?"

"I tried dating but most women were not interested in me personally. So it was difficult and I wasn't very interested either"

"I don't understand"

"Most people know I'm rich before they know me. So that's what they focus on. No one ever really wants to look past that. Which sounds so sad but it's not. I don't blame them. It's not just women either. It's men who have claimed to be my friends. I think it's just part of being born into money I guess. Which is not something I have any right to complain about. I'm not exactly forth coming myself. It's my own fault. I hate talking about this kind of thing because people actually have real issues"

He says all of this as if it's no big deal and I don't know how to reply.

How can this be?

"The sugar daddy thing makes it easier for me because at least I know what to expect. I know that the women want my money and there's nothing to leave to chance. Does that make sense?"

"Yes it does. Although don't you get lonely?"

"All the time but lonely is better than trying to pretend to like someone. Being a sugar daddy has its problems too. Having a woman with me helps for a while but because I know it's all fake on both sides, it's hard to keep up"

Well now it all makes more sense. The reason he became a sugar daddy so young. His eagerness to spend money on me. He assumes that's what everyone wants.

"I'm sorry Elijah" I reply because I really am sorry that he feels the way he does. It makes me want to change it. To make him feel like the person I'm seeing right now.

"Don't be sorry" he says, capturing my lips again. His tongue sweeps into my mouth and his hand grips my thigh, pulling it over his hip. He releases my lips and runs his nose along mine.

Then something occurs to me.

"I know I'm not your sugar baby but are you pretending with me?" I ask, worry eating me up.

"What? No Darling. I don't know what the hell is happening here but it's very real" he pauses and looks as if he's contemplating something. "Let me help you Sofia. Let me take care of you" he pleads and my mouth opens and closes again. "Even just a little bit. I won't be your sugar daddy I promise but let me give you something"

How could I do that?

"Why do you want to help me so bad?" I question, having to know what he's thinking.

"Because you don't deserve to live this way. To struggle. You're beautiful and intelligent. You say it as it is and this intimacy between us right here is real. We're not touching because we have to. We want to. I can't get you out of my head and for some strange reason, you seem to want me too. I won't lie and tell you that I understand it because I don't but I want to try. Money is all I know and the only way that I know how to care for someone. And I want to care for you"

Well...he said that huh. Fuck...that's intense. What am I meant to say to that. In typical me fashion I go for a fucking joke.

"Well, this has been great. I'm going to have to leave now" I state trying to keep my face serious. It's impossible when his mouth opens in shock and he pretends to be very wounded.

"Sofia how could you!" He growls. I pretend to get up, sitting and swinging my legs out of bed.

"I should go..." I giggle just as he pulls me back down onto the bed, pinning my arms above my head. Oh boy...

"You're not escaping so easily. Plus, this is your apartment. You can't leave" he grins from ear to ear. He's happy. It's beautiful.

"Shit! You're right! Well what am I supposed to do now?!" I exclaim. He releases my hands and pulls me back into his arms. I throw my leg back over his hip and bring my face closer. My lips brush over his, my fingers sliding into his hair. "Guess I'll have to stay and snuggle you"

"Guess so..." he breaths, his fingers teasing down my rib cage in a feather light touch. "I want you again Sofia" he pants and I can feel his cock hardening against me.

"Please answer my question...please" he begs shifting further between my legs. Oh god. This is not what I expected when I signed up to that damn website. I've gotten a whole lot more than I bargained for. A whole lot better too.

I still don't want him to be my sugar daddy. I couldn't live like that. I also don't want him to give me money.

However I could let him help me a little, if it means I can see him more. Then I'll pay him back when I have a job.

Oh fuck it! I have to suck up my pride.

"Yes...yes please take care of me. I want you. I want to be yours" I confess and watch the joy blooming over his lovely features. His lips smile, his eyes crinkle and soften.

"Mine" he sighs before gently pushing himself inside me. He fills me completely, his hips pressing into mine and his arms tightening around me like a vice. I do like being warmed up constantly and he ticks that box and then some. I've never felt this warm.

My whole body is cocooned in the protection of this strong, sweet man. His hips move slowly, driving his cock in and out of me while his mouth whispers dirty yet lovely things.

"Do you like having my cock deep inside of you Sofia?"

"I more than like it" I moan, squeezing my legs around him tighter.

He fucks me slowly until we're both close to the edge. I cry his name as he picks up speed and makes me come. It's earth shattering. Mind blowing.

If coming is my first gift then hearing him chant my name as he comes too is my second. It's glorious.

He kisses my neck and my breasts, all the way back up to my lips in a lazy sloppy fashion as our breathing slows. He slips from between my legs and the heavy feeling of tiredness begins to take over.

As my eyes begin to close, his arm secures around my waist, his body spooning mine from behind. I was never a fan before but this is heavenly.

"You got the part. You can be my personal space heater" I whisper lazily, my hand covering his on my stomach.

The last thing I hear is a soft joyful whisper before I fall into blissful sleep.

"I'll take my new role very very seriously Darling"

***

Did I just have another amazing dream about Elijah? It wouldn't surprise me if I'm honest. There's no way I actually got to live out last night for real.

No way in hell-

"Sofia..."

Am I still asleep? Have I gone mad? Oh god...it was real!

Fighting the affects of sleep, I wrench my eyes open to find a fully dressed Elijah hovering above me, his arms on either side of me as he leans on the bed. Have I time jumped? Did I miss something? Why am I asking myself all these questions when there's a gloriously handsome man above me?

"I'm sorry I woke you but I didn't want you to wake up and find me gone" he explains while I try to get my bearings. Reaching up, I run my fingers down the fabric of his shirt and curse it for being on his body.

"Why do you have clothes on?" I ask, glaring at the offending material. Bad shirt! Evil clothes!

"I have an early morning meeting that I completely forgot about. Actually I'm late to the meeting. Very late. I never sleep in but I guess I didn't anticipate that you would act as the perfect sleeping pill. I really struggled to get up" he smirks, smooching me loudly.

"I'm so sorry. I didn't mean to make you late. It won't happen again. I'll set an alarm or-" I begin, feeling somewhat guilty but he stops me.

"Darling it's okay. You are very much worth it. In fact I was very close to cancelling the meeting but I already did that for the previous one" he grins, his cheeky face lighting up. I look at him curiously because I feel like there's something I don't know.

"You said last nights meeting got cancelled?" I drawl suspiciously.

"Yes by me because I had a very important cinema date"

WHAT?!

"Elijah! You can't cancel things for me! You're gonna get in trouble" I exclaim becoming just awake enough to shake my head at him.

"I can't get in trouble. I'm the boss." He winks and plasters a triumphant kiss on my lips.

"That's not the point" I reply against his mouth.

"Shhhhh, kiss me Darling. I wanna remember how it feels so that I make it through the day"

"Elijah!" I warn as his hand caresses my cheek. How am I supposed to resist him. He cancelled a meeting to see me. Ahhh.

"Kiss me..." he whispers again and holy god I can't say no.

I put my best moves into the kiss to make sure that he does in fact remember how it feels. He groans, making me shiver and I wish that he was still naked beside me.

"I'll message you as soon as I can" is the last thing he says before he stands up, grabs his jacket and finally looks like he's in a bit of a hurry.

"What about your other jacket?" I call.

"Keep it" he winks and then he's gone.

The sound of my door closing behind him is my cue to flail around and squeal excitedly like a girl from a high school teen movie.

I lie there and stare at the ceiling for god knows how long. Going over every moment from last night. I'm only disturbed by a ping from my phone and I grab it excitedly thinking it's a message from Elijah.

When I see the notification, I give my phone a strange look. It is a message from the app. The bar displaying a statement I've never seen before.

'DEPOSIT REQUEST FROM E. EVERETT'

Squinting at the words I finally click on it. The app pops up briefly before a hyper link takes me to my bank account. The feeling that gives me is a sickly one.

I know I agreed to his help but I didn't think he'd just send me money. I thought we'd discuss it. So that I could tell him when I could pay him back.

My banking app requires my fingerprint to open it but it takes a while as my hands shake. I'm not sure why I added that feature when it doesn't have an amount worth stealing.

Well I didn't. Past tense. Now though I've no idea what figure I'm going to see and I'm terrified. I think I've made a mistake.

The loading circle appears and I watch it spin. It resembles what's happening in my brain right now. Thoughts going round and round.

Then up pops my bank balance in black bold jarring numbers.

Is he serious? That can't be right? There's no way that he meant to send me that much!

FIVE THOUSAND DOLLARS???

He pushed far too many zeros! He must have! Am I having a heart attack? Yes quite possibly. Goodbye cruel world!

Using my still shaking thumbs to type him a message, I jab at my phone angrily.

Sofia: THAT IS FAR TOO MUCH ASSHOLE!

I'd rather be screaming that in his face but screaming with the power of capital letters will have to do!

THAT MOTHERFUCKER!

Elijah

What. The. Fuck.

I have no idea what's going on. I'm usually so controlled.

I know what to do, when to do it and how.

Yet this women has my mind all over the place.

So much so that I can barely think straight.

I like being near her. Listening to her. Touching her.

Which is the most unfamiliar thing to me.

I should be more worried that this is all an act. That she's pretending to be this way with me for a reason. Only, unlike people who have done that before, I can't sense it from her.

It's all seems so real.

She wants to be next to…me.

And kissing her…

No words.

Dropping into my car, I contemplate going back up to her apartment, just so that I can kiss her again.

Oh fuck off Elijah! Focus!

Get to work! Do your job!

No, first I'll make sure Sofia can eat today. She said yes to letting me care for her. Which has really given me a sense of calm. I can ensure that she's okay.

That's not a desire I've ever had before.

Opening the Sugar Rush app, I choose the deposit option just like I've done so many times before. Only this time, as I click Sofia's name, it feels right. Like I'm doing something. Something I really want to do.

Sitting for a moment, I try to work out how much to send. I wonder how much debt she has, maybe I could help with that too-

Jack: Where the hell are you Elijah? You already put this meeting off. There are people waiting.

Shit.

Well a few thousand should do right now. I can send her more later if she needs it.

Completing the deposit, I drop my phone and stamp on the gas peddle.

Two things I don't do. Cancel meetings and turn up late. Yet I didn't hesitate to cancel yesterday. Seeing Sofia was more important and that thought has my knuckles turning white on the steering wheel.

I'm in trouble. I know I am.

Oh and I can't believe how fucking late I'm going to be!

***

The noise of the people around the boardroom table is like static to me. It seems I've left my mind in bed with a beautiful women. I wish my body was still there too and it could have been because this meeting is complete bullshit!

All of the men and women here are older than me and very much set in their ways. Everything that I suggest they shoot down. I think it's because they are all supposedly more experienced than I am, yet here they are meeting in a building I own. It's pettiness and we're going to get nowhere if this continues.

As a balding man named Alistair begins to chatter away about the stock market, my mind wanders off again. I'm picturing Sofia still sleeping, her lovely face relaxed and care free. I wish that she wore that expression all the time but unfortunately it's clear to see that she's going through a lot.

Her brow furrows and sadness creeps into her features in the moments that she remembers her own situation. I'm not sure how I've noticed all that from knowing her such a little time but she's the type of women that makes me pay attention.

Not just to her beauty but to her intelligence and passion.

Passion is something I lack in my work. I do it out of obligation. So it's surreal to hear her talk the way she does.

It's so endearing to listen as she tells me about about literally anything and then goes off on some completely unrelated tangent. I think I could listen to her all day and night. No, I know I could.

The closeness I'm already feeling to her is so unfamiliar that I don't know what to do about it.

That's something that baffles me too. Sofia really wants to be near me. The way she snuggled into me last night, her head on my chest, seemed more than genuine.

Everything about the past few days with her has just been perfect.

When she asks me questions about myself it's hard for me to answer. I don't know why she's even interested. I don't recall many people asking things about me. I like it that way.

Except I don't mind with her.

And the sex...was indescribable.

Sure, I've had decent sex. Good sex even but nothing like this.

With her all I cared about was wanting to make her feel pleasure like never before. I want to keep doing that for as long as she'll let me. I just can't help it.

The way she rode my dick in the cinema and called my name. Her grip on me as I fucked her a second time in her bed.

She wanted me deep inside her. All around her...just me. She cared about my pleasure too...

I can feel my dick getting hard as I remember how she felt around me. The passion, the sweat, the intimacy.

Shifting in my seat, I try to think of something that will make my erection die down but it's tough when all I can see in my head is Sofia moaning and writhing. I gotta see her again as soon as possible. Maybe tonight? Is that too much too soon?

Maybe she could come to my apartment and stay over. Which is something else that would be new for me. Just like sleeping in her bed. Staying the night.

I didn't want to leave.

"Elijah?" I hear and look up to find eight sets of eyes staring back at me. Clearly I've missed something and they apparently want my opinion. Well, I've no idea what the hell to say to these assholes.

"Sorry, can you repeat that?" I ask, covering up my awkwardness with the most casual tone I can produce.

"What should we do?" Alistair asks.

Good question because I've no idea what you're talking about.

***

A couple of hours and arguments later, I finally retreat to my office. Locking the door, I drop down into the leather chair behind my desk and sigh.

Usually I wouldn't feel so stressed out. Then again usually I wouldn't have anything else to occupy my mind.

Looking at my phone for the first time since leaving Sofia's apartment, I'm thrilled to see a text from her. Until I read what it says.

Sofia: THAT IS FAR TOO MUCH ASSHOLE!

Shit!

It seems I've fucked up.

I'm an idiot!

I should have told her that I was going to send her money.

Another distinction between her and other people is right in front of my face. Anyone else would have simply checked the money was there and happily went on their way.

But not Sofia. No, she doesn't seem happy about what I've given her.

Just like she wasn't happy about me buying her food.

I feel like such an asshole. I don't want to overwhelm her.

Is she mad at me? If she is, how do I fix it? Why do I care so much about fixing it?

The thought that she's angry puts a feeling in my stomach that I can't quite place.

If people are mad at me in normal circumstances, I'd tell them to fuck off because who gives a shit.

It seems that in this situation, I do. I give a shit.

I've overstepped my mark.

Tapping the call button, I watch as my phone dials hers.

Holding it to my ear, I feel a nervous sensation come over me. My palms sweating.

What the hell?

She picks up on the third ring, her tone confirming what I thought.

"Have you lost your mind? This is ridiculous Elijah. You need to take it back! Right now!" She yells, my ear stinging from the volume.

This is unfamiliar territory for me and my brain struggles to find words.

"Elijah?"

Her voice is softer this time and it relaxes my body.

Shit.

"Please don't be mad" is my first reply because I'm desperate to change her mood back to happy. I don't want to cause her upset.

Which means I'm weak.

Weak as hell for this woman.

Sofia

How can he ask me not to be mad? Does he even understand how much five thousand dollars is to someone like me?

I already know the answer.

To him it's merely a few cents.

"I can't just take it Elijah. I agreed to let you help me but not on this scale. Not without talking about it first!" I tell him, trying to explain how I'm feeling.

"I'm really sorry Darling. I should have discussed it with you this morning. I know it's a lot but I want you to have it" he replies, sounding as though he really didn't mean to upset me.

Of course he didn't. Everyone else would be thanking him for such a gift. It just doesn't feel right to me.

"I appreciate it. I really do but I can't keep it. Certainly not it all. Hell, I shouldn't keep any of it Elijah. I know what I said last night but I feel horrible. I've done nothing to deserve your generosity"

A feeling of inadequacy overcomes me then, realising just how crazy it is that this man even looked twice at me.

"Deserve it? Sofia if anyone does, it's you. Although the last thing I want to do is make you uncomfortable. We should probably talk about this in person. Like I should have done in the first place. I'm sorry about that, really"

He definitely has a point there. We should talk about it in person because over the phone isn't going to cut it.

"It's okay but you're right, we should talk about this in person" I agree, hating the unpleasant awkwardness between us.

Two people trying to navigate each other's emotions.

"What about tonight? I can make it up to you. I was thinking about asking you if you wanted to come to mine anyway. Only if you feel comfortable. You can tell me if it's too much"

He was going to ask me out tonight? Two nights in a row and to his place?

Butterflies swirl inside me and I can't help but smile. This is all so weird and I certainly won't admit that I've missed him since this morning. Nope. Not a chance.

"You're supposed to be a busy man. I assumed I wouldn't see you again for at least a week" I admit and hear him chucking.

Just like that the weird tension evaporates.

"Do you want me to wait a week? I could" he asks, his tone sounding mischievous.

"No...that's a long time" I breath, pissed at myself for saying it.

"Tonight it is then!" He exclaims and it's like I can hear his smile. "What kind of food would you like? I'll cook"

"You cook?" I ask shocked.

"Yup, not very well but I try" he laughs.

"Huh, I assumed you'd hire a private chef to prepare meals for you every night" I tease and he gasps.

"What other opinions do you have on me?"

"That you probably don't clean your own apartment? Do you live in an apartment? Or a mansion?"

"Okay you got me there. I do have a cleaning lady but no I don't live in either of those. It's a castle" he jokes.

"With a dragon?"

"I'm the dragon Sofia"

"Ohhh that was deep!" I tease.

"I know right. Tell me what you would like for dinner and I'll try to impress you"

"I'll eat any pasta. Any"

"And to drink?"

"Beer"

"That's hot Darling"

"What about snacks?"

"You know I'll have those. I'll have all the chocolate you can eat too"

"I'm very excited"

"As am I. I should be finished around five thirty if that's okay for you?"

"Does being done at that time include anymore meeting cancellations?"

"Hmmm, I can't tell you that"

"Elijah!"

"I like when you yell my name" he replies, his voice deepening. Oh.

"Maybe I'll be yelling it tonight" I tease, trying to sound somewhat seductive.

His breathing becomes more ragged and it seems I've done good.

Why was I mad again? Who knows?

"I sure hope so"

"Well, I guess we'll have to wait and see. Goodbye Elijah" I reply, in a nonchalant tone, purposely leaving him hanging.

"Sofi-"

Hitting the end call button, I smirk at my phone.

Take that! Hopefully he'll know not to mess with me in future.

PING!

Elijah: You are in trouble x

Oops.

***

Is this the first time I've properly cleaned my apartment in about a year? Yes...yes it is. Why? Because I'm a lazy hermit and I like living in a black hole. Now though, I actually have someone that I want to impress, so a little cleaning... or a lot of cleaning is necessary.

I just found a plate underneath my bed that may have been there for...let's just say a while. I think I just saw the weird black fuzzy lump stuck to the plate moving.

That's not possible right?

Wrong! My eyes widen as a bug breaks free from the substance and I launch the plate through the air.

Shit...there it goes. The sound of it flying through the air makes me tense waiting for the inevitable.

SMASH!

Well I guess now I have something else to clean up. Then I gotta shower and make myself look presentable for Mr Everett.

Although I have a feeling if I showed up in nothing but sweat pants and a hoodie like I'm used to, he'd probably still say I looked hot.

I'm not going with that outfit though. I'll wear some skinny jeans and whatever top I can find.

PING!

Ohhh hopefully that's Elijah!

Finding my phone in the carnage of my clean up, I'm surprised to see it's someone else.

Annabelle: Hey! When are we catching up again? I'm free on Friday if you wanna get some drinks Xxx

Do I wanna catch up? Yes. Have I ran out of excuses to tell her no anyway? Yes.

I guess I'll just have to go and drink water because I will not be spending Elijah's money. Hopefully that money won't be in my bank by Friday anyway.

Sofia: Hey! Yes! This Friday would be great! I can't wait to see you. Cheers ☐ X

Annabelle: Fantastic! Are you bringing anyone? I think Max might come too. Xxx

Max is her boyfriend and he's a lovely guy but do I want to be a third wheel? No, that'll be strange.

The only other option is to cancel...again.

Unless a certain CEO would like to come with me.

No, he wouldn't want that. We've just met and he certainly won't want to meet my friends.

Sofia: I'll get back to you on that one Xxx

Annabelle: No problem! It'll be fun either way Xxx

With tomorrow only being Wednesday, I still have plenty of time to change my mind. Plus, maybe being a third wheel wouldn't be so bad. I miss her.

After my apartment is put back into somewhat of a less chaotic order, I peel my disgusting sweaty clothes off and jump in the shower. It's roughly four thirty and I know that Elijah will still be deep in meetings and probably a lot of paperwork. Do CEOs do paperwork? I imagine they do.

I smirk as I think of him sitting at a desk typing on his laptop or leading a meeting of thirty other people.

I bet he'd be hot doing either of those things. I'm feeling a little frisky as my body remembers having him all over it. In the cinema, in my bed...GOD HE'S SO GOOD! I guess the rumours are true, older men do know what they are doing.

My hands slip over my wet skin and I try to imagine that they are his instead. It's a poor substitute but it's better than nothing.

Of course I'm touching myself before I can stop it and my hand slips between my legs, his name falling from my lips.

I wonder if he's thinking about me too and if he isn't, well I'm about to change that.

Stepping out of the shower, I grab a towel to dry my hands before reaching for my phone on the side of the sink. With my body wet and flush from being aroused, I open my camera and try to work out a good angle.

I can't lie, I stand there for a good twenty minutes changing my facial expressions and poses to get it just right. In the end though, I settle for one of me biting my lip. It's a genuine expression too because at that moment I was thinking about having his head between my legs.

I attach the picture and write a simple text underneath.

Sofia: Thinking Of You xx

That's cheesy but less so with the visual. Hopefully he won't be able to get me out of his head now. Cause I can't get him out of mine.

***

As I wait for Elijah to pick me up, I decide to do what he requested yesterday. Check out his website.

I'm still not sure why he wants my opinion.

His whole team will be much more experienced than me.

Although, I am able to give him an outside opinion like he said.

Typing in 'Everett and Son Industries', the first result that comes up is the one.

As soon as I click on it, the web designer in me is active.

A navy blue colour is prominent as a jumbotron displays the logo. Underneath are columns of information, stating what the company offers.

Everything from database management to entrepreneurship services.

Scrolling down, I click on 'About Us' and read the paragraphs provided. All good sized text, nothing distracting.

Right at the bottom of the page is founder information and a photo of that founder.

The picture shows a grey haired man. His green eyes intense and scrutinising. The wrinkles on his face suggest a life of stress and when I look a little closer his features look familiar.

Then the penny drops.

'Everett and Son Industries' as in Elijah is the son and this must be his father. I'm not sure why I didn't think about it before. Elijah must have taken over from his father. Which I think is really sweet.

PING!

Elijah: You really want me to go insane don't you? I'm on my way and you are in even more trouble now. Xx

Oh god!

When he arrives, I buzz him up and open the door.

I don't even get a chance to speak before he captures me, his arms squeezing me to him while his lips drive me insane. When he pulls back, he looks shocked at his own actions.

"I couldn't stop that" he breathes as I release him slightly. I'm now noticing that he's wearing a white shirt and a grey tie with matching trousers. He's left the jacket off today and it makes him look slightly more casual. So handsome.

Me on the other hand, I'm just in jeans and a t-shirt. Just like I expected, he still compliments me:

"You're so gorgeous... I like this" he tells me, referring to the graphic on my t-shirt. It's a Metallica logo.

"I forgot to ask you. What's your favourite album?" he continues.

"The self-titled black album" I reply immediately and cross my arms as I wait to see what he will say.

"I'm glad you said that. It's mine too"

"Phew" I laugh.

"That could have ruined us huh?" He smirks.

"Oh yeah, if you'd said anything else I would have slammed the door in your face" I tease and he acts offended.

Stepping back into my apartment, I grab my bag. I don't know if I'm staying the night with him and I don't want to assume but I packed my toothbrush just in case.

Once I'm ready he takes my hand in his and waits patiently as I lock my door. It's little things like the way he gazes at me while I do literally anything that make my heart thud faster and my emotions shoot through the roof. He's unlike anyone I've ever met and he makes me feel noticed and cared for.

I'm looking forward to tonight. Relaxing, getting to know each other better and definitely sorting out the money situation.

Hopefully he can make me feel more at peace with the large lump sum in my bank account. I need to send it back.

I've tried not to think about it all day but it's been tough. It's just sitting there making me nervous.

His hand rests on my knee as he drives. I can't remember how far away the Sugar Rush website had said he was from me or what to even expect. I keep looking at all the high rise apartment buildings and wondering which one could possibly be his. Or is he really in a god damn mansion?

"How was your day?" He asks, glancing at me quickly.

"You mean the short amount of time you weren't in it? Terrible, an absolute nightmare" I joke and he squeezes my knee, chuckling.

"I'm really sorry to hear that. I didn't know my presence was so powerful" he jokes back. I cover his hand with mine and watch him concentrating on the road.

"Yes, you make it all better"

It's meant to be a joke but I'm beginning to think that I'm not wrong. I feel a lot happier when he's around. I need to keep my emotions in check though, so I don't get hurt.

"Ditto" he says and I giggle at the word. It sounds funny coming from such a distinguished man. But I also love it.

Just then we pull up to an underground garage, the building it belongs to is so frigging tall that my neck doesn't bend backwards far enough. It's all glass windows and shiny metal. Very modern, very expensive.

Elijah presses a button on his keys and the garage door glides up slowly. I'm absolutely speechless as he drives into the pristine place. My eyes take in the rows of fancy cars and I wonder how many of them he owns. Hopefully not all of them.

He pulls into a space that is labelled on the wall with his name...nice! Then he looks at me warily as if he knows I'm having a mini panic attack caused by so much expense.

"Are you okay Darling?" He asks quietly. It's the only sound that can be heard because it's so quiet. If this was my apartment we'd be able to hear the two guys downstairs yelling at each other. Which they do a lot.

"Mmmhhh" I mumble finally looking back at him. He leans forward and kisses me softly and I wonder if he's knows that his touch calms me better than any drug.

"It's okay, it's just material bullshit" he assures me and I nod slowly, very much ready to get out of the car and get acquainted with his apartment. The quicker I get there, the quicker I can be flabbergasted and the quicker I can calm down and chill for the rest of the night.

Once I've unthawed and can move again, we make our way to the elevator that is also extremely pristine. How often does this place get cleaned?

As soon as we step in, I watch to see what button he's going to push. I really should have guessed he'd be in the pent house but maybe I was hoping for a nice even floor twenty or something. Seriously, what does this man want with me?

When the elevator begins to rise his arm slips around my waist and he steps into my side. Glancing up at him, I find him looking back and wonder what's on his mind.

"I'm happy you're here" he says simply and that one sentence means a lot more to me than anything has for a long time.

"I'm happy to be here" I reply and his cheeks pink ever so slightly. There's a very affectionate person underneath his strong indifferent facade. He's hasn't been cold with me but I can tell he puts on a front for the whole world to see. He wants to be known for nothing more than business and money. He thinks people see him that way, so has become that person. Yet with me securely squished into his side, he is dying to unleash his care and passion. It makes me feel so very special.

Once the elevator doors open, I immediately try not to be fazed by the huge expanse of open plan space, the leather couches and floor to ceiling glass windows. I try not to care about the massive staircase with yet more glass railings. I really really try not to care about the modern marble counter topped kitchen with multiple ovens. I even try not to think about the hallway opposite us that no doubt leads to even more stuff! Alas I fail.

"Holy. Mother. Of. God!" I exclaim and stand there next to him like a statue. My jaw is on the floor and I'm scared to step inside the place in case I break something I cannot afford. I don't think even the five grand now in my bank would cover many things in here.

Probably not even one of those wall mounted gorgeous guitars that hang on either side of the tv. Which is above a fireplace...and...and...it's all too much.

"Sofia? Are you still with me?"

"Nope...I've left...gone...wow"

"Come with me" he tugs on my hand and pulls me into the apartment or kings fucking manor. I'm like a kid in a museum looking at everything with my mouth open. Fancy art work - Check. Huge dinning table - Check. Fluffy rug- Niceeee.

I'm like a robot while he sits me down on a bar stool at the kitchen island. Hmm does this mean I get to watch him cook? Hot!

Opening the huge double doored fridge he pulls out two beer cans and hands one to me.

"Take a sip and breath" he says, smirking at me. I do as he askes and you know what? It actually works. Who'd have thought it? "Better?"

"Yes, thank you. Sorry for my freak out, I'm just not used to all of...this" I answer, gesturing around the room.

"I get it. I think it's all a bit much most of the time too" he tells me, going back to the fridge and pulling out some strawberries now.

"What do you mean?" I ask as he plucks one out of the little bowl. He holds it up to my mouth and I can't help but I laugh as I bite into it.

I hear a quiet "Damn" whispered as I lick my lips.

"Well, all of this is nice but it's not very enjoyable when I have no one to share it with" he explains, gazing at me a little too intensely. I feel the way it affects me, the desire it brings out in me and I'm a little scared of how quickly I'm getting attached to this man. So I try to distract myself.

Grabbing a strawberry I pop half of it into my mouth and then lean forward so he can take the rest from my lips. He does so with enthusiasm, biting into the fruit while making sure our lips touch.

"Mmmm, tastes sweet" he sighs, winking as my face blooms bright red. He makes everything sexy...EVERYTHING! I'll never look at a strawberry the same way again. Damn!

Clearing my throat, I try to shake away my need for him because yanking him over the counter could be dangerous.

"So what kind of pasta did you decide to make?" I ask as he rolls up his sleeves...yum.

"Ravioli, if that's okay with you?"

"That's perfect! I haven't had that in a very long time" I tell him, feeling excited. The reason I haven't had it in a while is because there are no tinned microwave versions sadly. He seems pleased, like he's even more thrilled to make it than before.

"Then I better make my best dish ever!" He exclaims, rubbing his hands together. Then he leans over to give me a long smooch before getting to work. I- I just...he's amazing.

Almost too good to be true...

While he cooks I have a fantastic time watching him. He even makes the ravioli parcels himself and helps me do some too. I've never made them myself so it's a lot of fun.

He instructs me how to fold the the pasta correctly around the filling and boy do I love hearing him praise me for doing well. It's kinda weird huh? But I find it hot as hell.

"I think that's the best out of all of them" I state, looking at my little ravioli neatly shaped.

He looks it over as if he's judging it, scratching his chin as he thinks about it.

"Hmmm...well I suppose so!" He admits dramatically. I smack his arm and he laughs, his eyes crinkling at the sides.

"I can't believe you've never made this and yet you've shown me up" he pouts covering his eyes with his hand as if in devastation.

"Awww now come on, don't feel bad. I'm just amazing that's all" I beam at him and he comes around the counter to pull me into his arms.

"You are very amazing Darling" he breathes, nuzzling into my neck.

He makes me laugh the whole time the pasta cooks along with the sauce. He teases me, declaring that I'll have to cook for him next to see who is the better chef. I hang on the two words 'next' and 'time' because it suggests he wants to do this again. As in, a lot more.

We should really talk about what's going on between us but I don't think I know myself.

I make a note to mention it when we're eating. Only I don't have to because he gives me a good topic to Segway into mine.

"So I owe you an apology in person for springing the money on you. I really should have thought about it more" he begins as we sit at the lovely dining table with a view of the whole city out of the windows. We're sitting across from each other, his foot subtly touching my ankle. I wonder if he's doing it on purpose or if he just subconsciously wants to touch me? Maybe I'm looking too much into it?

"It's okay. I know it isn't a lot of money to you but it's like a whole lottery win to me. It goes against everything I believe in to keep it. When you said you'd help, I thought you just meant a couple hundred dollars that I eventually could pay back" I explain and he looks really guilty.

"I promise it won't happen again and you can send me the money back if you like. However, it would mean a lot to me if you kept it. Also, if it makes you more comfortable, you could simply pay me back when you become a famous web designer" he says, his face giving away no jokes. He really means it.

Could I keep it? If it means a lot to him. If it's his way of showing affection? Or will it eat me alive?

"You think I'm going to be a famous web designer?"

"Absolutely you are" he winks, popping some pasta in his mouth.

"I'm glad someone believes in me" I sigh and then a question pops into my head. One I've yet to ask. "Is five thousand dollars the standard amount you give to sugar babies?"

I feel tense as I wait for his answer. I really hope he doesn't see me as a sugar baby.

His face goes a little pale as he chews his food and swallows.

"I have a confession..." he whispers, looking at me with a nervous expression.

"Uh oh..." I breath, giving him my best stern look. Who am I kidding? I'm not stern at all.

"I've never give that much to someone. Not in one go any-" he starts but I'm so shocked that I cut in before he can finish explaining.

"Elijah! Then why give it to me? Are you insane?"

"My mental state is debatable but I don't think I'm quite insane yet. It just felt right. I simply wanted to" he explains but I still have the same question.

"But why? You need to be careful with who you give your money to! I could be totally fucking with you. What if this is all bullshit. What if I knew who you were and decided to play you? You just gave me a lot of money!" I reprimand him as if he's a little boy. "I could leave here tomorrow and then never see you again" I try to reason with him. I see a small flicker of sadness in his eyes but it disappears in a millisecond as he covers it up.

"Are you planning to?" He smiles but it's a little less happy. As if he wanted it to come across as a joke but he's actually worried.

"No...of course not" I assure him, placing my hand on top of his. He links our fingers and kisses my knuckles. "My point is, you can't just give someone all that money. Who knows what they will do with it. I guess I'm just thinking about you. What I mean is, if you were to go out and get another proper sugar baby and you do the same thing, then..."

"Then what?" He asks, looking very curious.

"I don't like the thought of someone taking advantage of you...of anyone!" I finally get the words out. It's tough to say because I don't want him to know just how strongly I care for him already.

"That's such a nice thing to say Darling but I have to confess I'm not planning on having a sugar baby anytime soon. As for why... well I already told you I want to help you. I know most people want money to spend it on lavish things but I know you need it for more important stuff. I couldn't help it. It's not pity money Sofia I promise...I just...care. If I had it my way I'd be lavishing you in every single thing you could think of. Five grand would be nothing" he speaks with such determination that I'm unsure of how to respond. My heart is thundering.

Getting up from my seat, I walk around his side of the table to sit in his lap. He anticipates what I want and pushes his chair out, opening his arms to me.

The money really is his way of caring and for that reason alone I don't think I can send it back. On one condition.

"Thank you so much. You don't know how much it means to me. I will accept your money but you have to let me pay you back. Promise me" I whisper and his sweet relieved smile in reply is so lovely.

I still don't intend to spend the money unless I really need to. Only for rent and food. The essentials.

"You're very welcome and I promise you" he replies and leans in to kiss me. I stop him, placing a finger over his lips.

"One more thing. This... whatever this is between us...whatever we're doing...is it exclusive? Because I don't exactly plan on being with someone else at the same time. I guess I just don't want any surprises" I say sheepishly. It's an embarrassing thing to say. It seems wrong since we've know each other for such a short amount of time.

"I'm so glad you said that because I've wanted to talk to you about that too. I don't want to share you with anyone. I couldn't handle it. I can guarantee I won't be sharing myself with anyone but you. I'm yours Sofia. For as long as you want me"

That's it...that's all I can take. I kiss him with a passion I never knew I had inside of me. He tastes like ravioli and something that's just inherently him.

I'm not sure how long we kiss for but when we eventually lie down on the couch together, it doesn't stop. I don't want it to.

He brings a selection of different chocolates and puts Iron Man 2 on at my request. Marvel is second to my Disney obsession.

As soon as I'm snuggled into his chest, I just want to kiss him some more.

It gets a little bit messy when the chocolate gets involved. I steal one from him and pop it into my mouth but he tries to steal it back by tackling it from my lips with his tongue. It's hilarious and extremely sexy when he licks his fingers then grabs mine.

Sliding my finger into his mouth he sucks off the melted substance while I laugh my ass off.

He does the same with the chocolate that I've obviously missed on my lips and then trails that fantastic tongue down my neck.

"Am I your snack tonight?" I giggle and he hums in agreement.

"You definitely are. The sweetest of them all" he croons as my fingers brush through his hair. "I want to taste more of you" he tells me. "The picture you sent me today...it was beautiful. So fucking sexy. What were you thinking of?" He groans, his voice desperate.

"You...with your head between my legs. I've thought about you tasting me since I saw your picture" I confess, my chest rising and falling as my breathing deepens.

"Oh Sofia, I wish you'd told me that sooner. I'd have eaten you out on that table in the restaurant" he says, his hands running down my sides. "I'll give you anything you desire...anything" he whispers, his hand pulling my t-shirt out of the way so he can kiss my breasts. Oh lord I am sinning.

Speechless, I am speeches. Everything after that is just a dream like haze.

I watch completely enraptured by him as he unzips my jeans and pulls them down. They're thrown to the floor along with my panties and my thighs fall open in the same second. I need him so bad.

He gazes at me, his eyes flicking from between my legs to my face over and over.

"I swear you're a goddess pretending to be human" he breaths before his tongue drags a hot trail up my thigh. The feeling of his beard on sensitive skin contrasts, the roughness adding to my pleasure. I gasp at the sensation, the wetness between my legs growing by the second.

"Oh god...I've thought about this far too much and still I'm not prepared" I half moan, half laugh.

"Well you have to tell me exactly how you thought about this..." he smirks, his eyes almost glowing with desire, his tongue flicking out just to catch my clit. Evil evil man!

"You were much more naked to start with" I whine and lick my lips as he sits up and begins pulling his clothes off. His shirt and tie are first, his trousers and boxers next. I don't know what I want to look at first.

I don't get to stare too long because he's soon diving between my legs again.

"Tell me what you want" he commands and I throw up my whole damn fantasy.

"Start off slow, tease me. You'll know when to be more rough I'm sure. Use your fingers too...I love having you inside me in any way I can"

"Fucking hell Sofia...you're so hot"

With that he gets to work, doing exactly what I told him. I forgot to mention in my fantasy that I do a lot of hair pulling and that I like it when he looks at me.

I have nothing to worry about though because his eyes stay glued to me as I write and moan, my fingers gripping the plush couch.

When I tug on his hair it only makes him more enthusiastic and he moans too. He fucking likes it!

He teases me into insanity. His fingers move in and out of me at a slow pace while his tongue laps at my clit as if he's just casually licking an ice cream. It drives me mad and I'm soon begging him to make me come.

One of his hands reach up to slide under my t-shirt, squeeze my breast. It prompts me to tug the offending material off as well as my bra. Those get thrown away too as he continues his torture.

"You really are the sweetest thing" he growls and sucks on my clit roughly.

"Oh Fuck Fuck Fuck! Please Elijah!" I scream and he finger fucks me harder.

My hand curls tightly into his soft locks and his eyes flick back to mine.

"You wanna come Sofia?" He asks menacingly.

"Yes! Oh please!" I yell.

"You wanna come around my fingers or my dick?" He asks and then licks me again. Well that's an easy question.

"Your dick, baby please!" I yell and he shifts onto his knees and grips my thighs. He moves closer between my legs and leans over me.

"You sure Darling?" He whispers but I can't answer because I'm so desperate. I push my heels into his ass and his hips move forward, his cock sliding into me quickly. He groans in my ear and I come instantly, the feeling of him so deep setting me off.

"Shit! Elijah!"

My finger nails dig into his back and he circles his hips increasing my pleasure before I come back down to Earth. He watches, keeping completely still as I catch my breath.

He leans down and peppers kisses over my face.

"So beautiful. I've never seen anything quite like you Sofia" he croons, shifting slightly. I wrap my legs around him and run my fingers through his hair. I rock my hips and he groans softly.

"Why aren't you fucking me?" I ask, laughing at his flushed face. It's clear he wants to and boy do I want it too.

"I'm rather enjoying you keeping my cock warm" he smirks. "It prolongs the feeling Darling. Being inside you like this is like teasing myself. Plus if I give you a minute then I can make you come again. Which is ultimately my goal" he grins, very pleased with himself.

"You know I've heard of cock warming. I just never knew people actually did it" I confess and giggle as he winks.

"I've never actually done this before but it feels...right"

He's not wrong either. It does feel right. Not only does it feel right but when he finally does begin to move and fuck me slowly, the feeling building inside me again is so much more intense. I didn't think that was possible but it's like the waiting has made it even more pleasurable.

My second orgasm is off the scale and if his loud swearing and rough gripping hands are anything to go by, so was his.

"Mmmm, baby I can't get enough of you" he sighs, his hands still roaming my body.

"I'm glad to hear it because I think I'm addicted to you"

He snuggles back into me afterwards and then puts on another film. His fingers brush through my hair, making it hard to stay awake. The calm and solace I've enjoyed for the past four days is a feeling like no other. I am so relaxed even though I'm still in the same situation I was before. Still unemployed. Sure I have money now but I'm still not out of the woods.

The man breathing softly beneath me somehow takes away the worries I have. I don't know how or why all I know is it works. Maybe he's a wizard or maybe there's just something inside both of us that fits well together. Two puzzle pieces with jagged edges, sanded down with every touch to slot together. That's hella dramatic and far too fast for me to be thinking that way. Oops.

We begin to chat about anything and everything.

He asks about my home life and I swiftly dodge the topic. Instead I simply tell him about my Mom visiting.

I ask him about his parents too and just like I did, he evades the question.

He says he wants to tell me about them but he doesn't want to ruin our night. I'd love to ask more because I want to know even if it's bad. Although I can tell he really doesn't want to talk about it. Maybe another time when we know each other better.

However, asking about his parents reminds me of his website. So I change the subject.

"I checked out your website today" I tell him and his eyebrows raise curiously.

"You did? Was it up to your standard because if it wasn't I'll have it all rebuilt" he says, very seriously.

"You seem to think that my standards are high. Yet you haven't seen anything I've created" I laugh and he looks away awkwardly.

Huh what's this?

"I may...have seen your work and I may have been blown away" he confesses and this has me sitting up so that I can give him a very confused look. "I...I looked up your thesis"

I forgot that people could do that.

I'm surprised he even wanted to see it and touched that he's interested.

"And you liked it?" I question, just to be sure.

"Loved it. I'm amazed that people understand a whole computer language. Let alone use it to build websites. It means nothing to me but to you, it all makes sense. It's why I asked you to look at mine. I wanted you to like it" he explains, reaching up to cup my cheek.

"I did. It's exactly the right kind of site for your business" I assure him and he gives me an appreciative smile.

"Thank god"

With the atmosphere so lovely and a lot of feelings swirling inside me, I decide that it wouldn't hurt to ask him if he would like to come with me on Friday.

"Are you asking me out on a date?" He smirks, teasing me.

"Maybe...I totally get it if you don't want to. It's no big deal. It would just be nice if you did" I tell him shyly.

"I'd love to Darling, just let me shift some work stuff around and I'll make sure I'm free"

"Oh I don't want it to be any trouble"

"It's no trouble, I want to come with you. I really do" he assures me. "I'm a busy man but I'll always have time for you...whenever you need"

That goes against his whole Sugar Rush bio. It goes against what he said about his lifestyle. Did he lie? Or is he genuinely making time for me because he cares?

I don't know what to say? Apparently nothing. I bluff my way out of getting emotional or thinking too much by making out with him. What a cop out! Still, if he keeps up his sweet words I'm going to melt into a puddle.

We eventually head up the fancy stairs to bed and I collapse into his soft silk sheets. Sheets that are grey and match the decor of the room. That's as much as I can take in right now. I really wanna have him deep inside me again but my tired body won't let me. If he minds, I can't tell as he squashes his warm body to mine.

"I've already decided that I like having you in my bed" he hums, kissing my neck softly. Turning in his arms slightly, I kiss him for the thousandth time tonight but it's more of a thank you.

"I really like being here too...

What I really meant was being in his arms.

***

Staring out of the floor to ceiling glass windows, I see all of the tiny twinkling lights below. It's an amazing view and almost reflects the same kind of twinkling stars in the sky. It's very peaceful yet so far away from everyone else.

What must Elijah feel like being here alone?

I'm standing here because I woke up and couldn't fall back asleep. My mind is whirling with many different things.

The main thing being Elijah and I.

Is it possible to want someone as much as I want him already?

Is it healthy?

I don't know but it worries me. I'm worried because I already know he has the power to hurt me. My Mom warned me at a young age that life can be cruel and emotions are crueler.

Something else that is on my mind is how peaceful I feel right now. How calm and happy. Even though I still have worries, they seem muted right now.

"Sofia?" I hear my name spoken in a tired sweet tone and look over my shoulder to see Elijah walking toward me, still very much naked. Such a gorgeous sight.

"Hey, I'm sorry if I woke you. I was trying to be quiet" I reply, feeling guilty.

"I only woke up because there wasn't a beautiful women wrapped around me. I require that to sleep" he smirks. He looks so inviting with his bed head and warm gaze.

"Oh, I didn't know. I'm sure you could find a woman to do that no problem" I tease back.

He looks around as if he's searching. When his eyes land back on mine they widen and he gasps.

"Found her" he quietly exclaims, his face breaking into a triumphant grin. Two steps and he's wrapping me in his arms. Mmmm I don't know why I got up, this is much better.

Clasping my hands around his neck, I peck his lips and he gazes at me inquisitively.

"What's on your mind Darling?"

"Nothing...I feel completely content. Which is unusual for me"

"Yeah, I think I know what you mean. Usually I'd be up at this time, minus already having been asleep. I'd be scouring the playing field for something new to snatch up but with you here, I can actually relax. I like it a lot. What would you be doing at this time normally?" He asks while I try not to look too much into what he's just said. I help him relax...awwwww god damn!

"I'd be trying to find a job to apply for that I haven't already. Which I need to get back to doing. Even if I get the job at the coffee shop, I still need to keep searching"

"You're so very motivated. It baffles me that you don't own your own business by now. You know I'd be more than happy to do give you a job" he tells me and although I'm flattered it just wouldn't feel right.

"Thank you but I want to work for my position. It wouldn't be right if it were just given"

"I thought you'd say that" he smirks, a fleeting glance of that strange emotion in his eyes again. "You know, we could take things slower if you like? I can be overbearing when I'm really into something. That something has never been a person so I'm worried I'm doing this all wrong"

His small self deprecating admission has me shaking my head. He's perfect how he is. I wonder why he feels otherwise.

"You're just fine the way you are. Don't change for anyone. As for taking it slow...I think this is a great pace. You aren't the cause of my insomnia, I'm just adjusting. I'm sure it's the same for you. Trying to work out all of this" I explain.

His hand rests on my cheek and I can almost see the cogs turning in his head as he sorts through what I've just told him.

"Oh I'm very confused but I like it" he replies.

Then he's dipping his head to kiss me, his lips ferocious yet sweet.

Taking a few steps back, I pull him with me knowing that the dinning table is not far behind.

When my back hits the edge he helps me

up onto the hard surface, his hands gripping my hips. He steps between my legs and feathers kisses down my neck while I squeeze my thighs around him. Closer, I want him closer. Reaching between us I stroke his already hard dick, teasing him slowly. His eyes snap to mine, desperation clear in his gorgeous irises.

"Yes, touch me like that Darling. Feels so good" he moans.

"You're so hard...so thick...it drives me wild" I confess, stroking harder.

He takes my face in his hands, nudging further between my thighs, his hips rocking.

"I have no self control when you're around. I don't know what's happening to me" he growls, excitement mixed with panic in his tone. He looks at me as if begging to be saved and holy hell do I wanna save him.

"I don't know what's happening to me either. I'm usually so focused. Now I can barely think straight" I tell him, gasping as he teases my clit with his thumb.

"Darling it seems we're both having issues. Maybe this will make it better..." he sighs, shifting his hips while I guide his cock inside me. The talking stops immediately, replaced by moans and sighs as he thrusts deep.

I think he's right, this does make it all better. My mind is clear and all I'm registering is the amazing feeling of him in and around me. I can hear his whispers of pleasure and they only add to my own.

"Sofia, you feel so good...never felt anything so amazing...fuck...sweetest thing ever...mine..."

If I could record his breathless compliments I'd play them over and over. It's the most wonderful feeling to not only get pleasure from someone but to know you're giving it back too. It feels like more than that as his words become unguarded.

"...fucking hell...I'll take care of you Sofia...shit...beautiful..."

He already knows the signs I show when I'm close to coming so he picks up the pace. His lips smother mine for a few precious moments and when we pull apart for air I'm able to compliment him right back.

"Ah shit...you fill me so perfectly...I want you to come inside me again"

"Fuck, yes!" He growls, his rough final thrusts setting my orgasm off like a firework explosion. Honestly I think I'm shot off into the stratosphere as my body tries to deal with all of the euphoric feelings coursing through it because of this mans amazing skills.

"Oh Elijah! Yes! Mmmm baby you are fantastic!" I scream, my body going numb.

As he comes, his slumps into me, his face nestled in my neck. I hold him to me, my legs wrapping around him. Clenching my pussy, I try to draw out every last bit of pleasure from him. His muffled moans suggests that it worked and his arms slide lazily around my waist.

"Jesus Christ...that was out of this world" he gasps pulling himself up a little to lean his forehead on mine.

"Tell me about it" I giggle.

Nothing compares to this. Nothing. My little heart is trying to keep up with my emotions. He gazes at me in the low light and I can't find any words to say.

I know right then and there that I want to be his everything.

I just don't know if I'm enough to fill that spot.

He leads me back to his bed and with my mind pacified, I begin to fall asleep.

Only he must think I'm already in dream land because he whispers:
"I hope you stay Sofia. I know I'm not perfect but I really want to make you happy"

Elijah

We woke up this morning and are now having a lovely breakfast of different fruits. What's more lovely is watching Sofia bite into an apple while she wears only panties and my shirt.

I opted to sit next to her rather than across from her but this only makes it more difficult to focus on the food. I just want to touch her.

Having her in my bed was a fantastic feeling, one that I felt while sleeping in hers. Her body close to mine, her quiet breaths tickling my ear. It really makes it so difficult to get up. I'd much prefer to still be wrapped around her. The constant need to touch her, forever present.

I'm sitting in my boxers with my chest bare. It's not something I do very often, especially not if a women is around. Obviously I would get naked for sex but I've always made sure to get dressed right after.

I just don't feel comfortable but with Sofia I do.

No woman has ever stayed over either but with her it's all I want.

"So what's on your busy agenda today Mr Everett?" She asks, popping a grape into her mouth.

Even that is sexy.

Trying to put my business head back on, I remember back to what I saw on my schedule yesterday. Then I sigh as I realise today is not going to be fun. Not that it ever is.

"I have a meeting with a women from Russia. She has flown all the way here to try and sway me on something I've already said no to. She wants to buy a couple of my buildings here but I told her over and over that I'm not selling. It's getting a bit ridiculous" I explain, already feeling pissed off.

It's such an unnecessary waste of time.

"So she essentially wasted a whole trip to be told the same thing you've already been telling her" She replies, resting her chin in her hands.

Her soft blue eyes watch me, waiting for my reply. Once again her interest in my life baffles and beguiles me.

"Exactly, pointless as hell. I'd much rather spend the day with you" I reply and lean over to peck her lips.

Her fingers glide into my hair, the sensation making me hum in enjoyment.

"Make sure you tell me how it goes"

"I will"

"Good, now you need to go get ready or it'll be my fault you're late again" she sighs.

"I told you I'm the boss so it doesn't matter"

"You can still get in trouble"

"With who?"

"Me. Now go!" She commands, kissing my cheek before removing her touch. Then she sits back with her arms crossed.

"Fine but you need to get dressed too. So you have to come with me" I smile triumphantly and pull her out of the chair.

She squeals in shock and then let's me drag her back upstairs to my room.

It makes me sad to think about the fact that this thing we have right now could end. She may not want me for long. Or maybe she'll find someone more worthy of her.

Until then I'll try to make her as happy as I can. I'll look after her and let her infectious smile numb the feeling of loneliness eating its way through my heart.

The world is cruel. Matching me perfectly with a women that can never fully be mine.

For now though...I can pretend.

"So what colour of suit are you going for today?" She asks, perching on the end on my bed. Her bare feet running through my black rug.

"I'm not sure. Why don't you choose?" I ask and her face lights up with joy. She really likes that idea.

Jumping up from the bed, she bounces eagerly on her toes.

So cute.

"Yes I'd love to choose!"

"Come here" I say, holding my hand out for her to take. She links our fingers and I pull her into my walk in closet.

"Woah. This is a lot of suits" she gasps and I have to nod because she's not wrong. With the whole right wall covered in jackets and trousers, I may have gone overboard.

Letting go of me, she runs her fingers over the row of jackets, tilting her head as if to inspect certain ones.

She does this for a few moments before stopping.

"I thought this would have been difficult but I already have a favourite" she announces, tugging out an emerald green sleeve. "It'll match your eyes" she smiles, a blush creeping onto her cheeks.

Fucking hell. I like this woman a lot.

"White or black shirt?" I question.

"White"

"Tie or no tie"

"Tie. One that matches the green" she says confidently as if she's picturing it in her head.

"Okay now you have to go back out there so I can give you the full reveal" I tell her, wanting to see her reaction to me being fully dressed in what she chose. I hope she likes it.

She pouts, her fingers trailing down my chest. She then kisses me there before walking back into the bedroom. The feeling of her lips lingers on my skin and I have to shake my head so that I can focus.

Pulling on the trousers and shirt, I button it and tuck it in. I'm paying a lot more attention than I usually do, ensuring everything is immaculate. The tie is next and luckily I have one that matches the exact shade of green of the suit.

Phew!

Pulling the knot tight, I put on the jacket and do the middle button.

Then I step in front of my full length mirror and take a look. Brushing my fingers into my hair, I try to calm it down to a decent state and make a note to tidy up my beard later. It's getting a little scruffy.

I haven't worn this suit in a while but Sofia has made a good choice. She can choose everyday if she likes.

Here we go.

Stepping out of the closet and into view, I watch as her eyes widen. She then begins to nod enthusiastically.

I think that's good.

"Yes. Yes and yes" she sighs, biting her lip. Shit.

"So it's definitely a yes then?" I laugh as she steps forward, tugging on my jacket. I fall into her gladly and circle my arms around her waist.

"You look so sexy Elijah" she whispers. I try my best not to react but I know my face is turning red. Sure I've been complimented before but it's a lot better from her than it is from anyone else. I want to look good for her.

"I'm really glad you like it" I reply, leaning down to kiss her. She pulls me into her chest, her breasts pressing into me. I want to be naked again.

I could just pull off her panties, unzip my trousers and be inside her in seconds. The need in overwhelming. I've never felt anything like it.

"Mmmm, you need to get rid of that before you leave" she whispers against my mouth, her hand fluttering over my hard cock. "Sadly, you don't have time to let me help you" she continues, pulling away and stepping back. I want to whine at the loss of contact.

Unfortunately she's right. I shouldn't be late again even if I want to be.

When she pulls my shirt off so that she can get dressed, I feel disappointed. I liked seeing her in it.

I had collected her clothes from the floor near my couch last night and folded them on my dresser. So now I get to watch as she pulls her skinny jeans back on, her ass disappearing behind the denim.

So sad.

Although those jeans look fucking good too.

Once we're both ready to leave, she grabs her overnight bag and I lead her back to the elevator. I'm already wondering when I'll be able to bring her back here. Or when I can go to hers.

Fucking hell Elijah. Give the woman a break!

At least I'll see her on Friday.

I'll be meeting her friends too. I'm not sure how I'm meant to feel about that. Is it too personal? Too much to do so soon? I think that ship has sailed at this point and instead of dreading it like I do most social events, I'm looking forward to it. Then again the social events I go to are charity related and in large ballrooms with hundreds of people who try to make small talk. I hate those more than anything else. Even if I love what they stand for.

On the drive back to her apartment, I try not to stare at her too much. Mostly because I don't want her to think I'm crazy but also because I don't wanna crash the car.

"Will you promise me you'll eat today?" I ask her softly. I don't wanna sound controlling but I'm worried that she's gotten into the habit of skipping meals.

"I will. Thanks to you" she replies and reaches over, her fingers running over my beard.

"Good and I'll see you on Friday" I confirm and she nods.

"Only if you're sure you want to go" she replies, looking a little unsure.

"I do Sofia. I really do" I assure her and kiss her lips to drive the point home.

We pull apart and she pats my thigh, squeezing a little. With one more peck goodbye she says:

"Then I will definitely see you on Friday. Don't miss me too much Mr Everett"

"I can't promise that" I state. The worrying thing is I'm not joking. I'll miss her. I already know that.

What have I gotten myself into?

She pushes the car door open and gets out, waving a little before closing it again.

I wait until she enters her apartment building, so that I get to look at her for a few more seconds. An unfamiliar feeling of loss hits me as I pull away.

How fucking soppy I am?

It's embarrassing yet I can't bring myself to care.

***

Nadia Zoya...or as I like to call her 'the problem that won't go away'. She's a fucking nightmare and I can't believe it's come to this point. No matter how many times I tell her that I'm not selling any of my property, she just won't listen. I'm hoping that by telling her no to her face that she will finally get the message.

I'm already in a bad mood as it is. No one seems to be doing what they are told today and on top of that I really want to call Sofia. It may have only been roughly five hours since I dropped her off but I'm getting antsy.

Every time I go to pick up my phone to see if she's messaged, someone interrupts me. I think it's crazy how I'm acting with her. I guess it's not a surprise really, she's just...so... I can't even find the right word but I'll have to go with amazing for now. She's amazing and I want to be in her company as much as possible.

I wonder if she thinks of me as much as I think of her-

"Sir?" My wondering is cut short as my assistant Lewis walks in with Miss Zoya. He looks kinda nervous and it's obviously because Nadia is an intimidating woman.

She's typically good looking. I already knew this from our video calls so it's nothing special to me. She has legs for days, long black hair and the body of a super model. Her face is attractive too. It doesn't impress me one bit though.

As soon as I dismiss Lewis, he scuttles away and Nadia approaches me with a sway in her hips. I really want to roll my eyes but that wouldn't go down well.

"Elijah it's lovely to finally meet you" she greets me, shaking my hand before pressing plush lips to my cheek. It has my mind flicking to thoughts of another woman. I'd rather Sofa were greeting me right now.

Focus Elijah!

"And you" I reply, gesturing for her to take a seat in front of my desk. I walk around it and take my own seat, preparing to shut her down as quickly as possible.

"Now, I know we've been in disagreement but I'm hoping to change that today" she continues. The way she looks me up and down doesn't sit right with me.

"I'm not sure how we can change what has already been discussed. I told you multiple times that I won't sell my buildings. It's too profitable for me" I explain for the hundredth time.

"Yes well I can be pretty persuasive. Especially when I get to talk to someone face to face" she responds and that's when I notice her pushing out her cleavage, the top buttons of her blouse undone. Huh...I didn't think she'd stoop this low to try and win me over. Because of my glance at her breasts, she clearly thinks she has me. "Maybe I can offer you more than my money" she suggests, while I try to count how many minutes she's been in here. Maybe four but that's pushing it. So barely five minutes in and she's trying to seduce me into a deal. Someone is desperate.

Luckily I'm not.

"There's nothing else that I can think of. Money is all I care about" I state firmly until my brain reminds me that's not true anymore. I care about a gorgeous brunette women who screams my name and plays with my hair.

"Oh come now. You must care about something else. Something more personal..."she tries again. She must think that I haven't caught on to her game. That I'm dumb and I don't know she's offering me sexual favours of some kind.

So why not play dumb?

"What could you possibly be talking about?" I ask and enjoy the way she struggles to find words. I'm gonna make her say it and then throw her the hell out. Maybe then she will be humiliated enough to never try it again. I know it's mean but I have no time for shit like this.

"Me...I can offer myself" she pushes out, her cheeks flaming. Not so confident now are we?

"You? I don't understand" I say coyly and frown to add to my act. I'm going to enjoy acting appalled too. Why would I want sex from her when I can get that from someone who I want beyond belief.

"Sex! I want to fuck you! Jesus Christ!" She exclaims and I have to bite my lip so that I don't laugh.

"Miss Zoya that is highly inappropriate. This is a business meeting and there will be no sex" I tell her firmly.

She stands quickly and marches around my desk while I stay put to make sure she sees no weakness in me.

I'm not scared of her and she's about to know it.

"Oh come on Elijah. You know you want this" she whispers while leaning forward, exposing her cleavage again.

This is ridiculous.

"I don't want it and I suggest you leave before I call security!" I snap, shifting away from her slightly. She's pissing me off and her perfume is making me feel a little sick.

"Liar" she snaps and reaches for me suddenly. Grabbing her wrist, I stop her and stand. She's fucking crazy.

"Get out now!" I yell, letting go and marching towards my own office door. I yank it open and give her one more warning glare.

She huffs and stands up straight, her face now filled with embarrassment from my rejection. Good!

I think she's done but naturally she has one more thing to say.

"This isn't over" she sneers before marching out.

Wow. That's so very cliche. This isn't a film and it is in fact over. I'm gonna inform my whole company to make sure this women gets nowhere near me ever again. Quite frankly she makes me feel uncomfortable.

I don't like people who try to cheat in business or in any part of their lives.

Slamming the door, I move back to my desk and drop down into the chair. My fingers drum on the desktop as I glance at the clock on the wall. I have twenty minutes until my next meeting.

All I want is to hear Sofia on the other end of the line. Grabbing my phone, I strive to do just that.

My pulse is racing and my anger is still very much present. I want to punch something until...

"Hey Babe...hmm no I don't like that. I'll need to think of something better to call you. What about Honey? Actually no that sounds super serious" she ponders, reeling off more names.

Just like that, I'm calm again and my face is breaking into a smile.

"You can call me whatever you want Darling. Anything is nice coming from your lips"

"Oh wow that's a great compliment. Well done" she replies, her giggle echoing in my ear. So sweet.

"Thank you. It just came naturally to me. What have you been up to?" I ask and sit back in my chair to listen to her talk. She tells me about an interface design she's working on. Worries? I have none when she's speaking.

"So how was the meeting with the Russian lady?" she questions once she's finished. Naturally my instinct is to lie and say that it went fine. Being closed off is what I've practiced my whole life.

I never really give anyone details but with Sofia I feel like I can come out and tell her.

"She tried some rather strange persuasion tactics" I explain.

"What did she try?" she says warily.

"She offered me sex" I reply, hating that I have to say those words. How fucking ridiculous.

"What?!" She almost growls back. The tone of her voice is very obviously shocked but muted in some way. Like she's trying to keep her cool. She's mad for me and that's incredibly sweet. Like she has my back.

"She offered me sex in return for my buildings" I continue and wonder how she's going to respond.

"How dare she! Who does she think she is!" She yells, jealousy creeping into her voice. Don't worry my dear Sofia, you've nothing to be jealous about.

"I know, it's a disgrace. I was very appalled and I threw her out" I explain and the line goes silent for a few seconds.

"You did?" She asks quietly and I really wish I was with her so I could kiss her. I want her to know that I meant it when I said I won't be sharing myself with anyone.

"Of course Darling. I've no interest in her. Certainly not like that"

"Good..."

"Sofia?"

"Yes?"

"You don't believe me do you?" I ask and sit up straight, wondering why she thinks I'm lying.

"I believe you...it's just...well I'm sure you're used to a lot of beautiful women coming onto you. When I Googled you the other day, the women you were with in photos were glamorous"

Fuck! I should have known my internet reputation would bite me in the ass. I can see it now. Her pretty eyes taking in all of the pictures of me with different women. She had told me that she wanted to form her own opinion but I guess it's been sitting in the back of her mind.

The women in those photos are previous sugar babies or business partners. People who I was never romantic with and only some of them was I sexual with. When I go to events it looks better if I'm with someone. It's part of why I had sugar babies. In short, these photos mean nothing.

"It's not real Sofia. It's publicity and propaganda Darling"

"You don't have to justify it to me Elijah. It's none of my business. I'm sorry, I shouldn't have brought it up. I guess I just struggle to understand how someone like you could want someone like me. Its silly but I-"

"I want you Sofia! Please don't pay any attention to the internet. It makes me look like a monster" I pretty much plead with her. I'm not lying either. The tabloids paint me as the biggest asshole alive. It all comes from previous business partners who have tried to fuck me over. I take no shit from anyone but I'm fair. Sure I can be tough on my employees too but I'm not a horrible person.

I treat everyone with respect but I'm not going to be nice to someone if they are not nice to me. So if you're an asshole, I'll be an asshole back regardless of gender.

"You're not a monster Elijah. I know that for sure" she laughs but I can picture her troubled face in my mind. I wish I had the courage to tell her properly about the feelings she makes course through me. Maybe then she'd believe that I won't walk away. Unfortunately I'm a coward and I can't say it.

"I'm glad because I don't know what I'd do if you thought I was" is my response and luckily this seems to be enough for her.

"So tell me more about what you've got to work on for the rest of the day..." she changes the subject and I gladly comply.

I have to find a way to show her how special of a person she is.

I'll make it my mission.

Sofia

I'm an insecure idiot. Why did I bring all of that up? I know it was dumb. I guess seeing photos of him with beautiful women stayed with me and burned a whole in my mind, making me worry.

He pacified me well though. In fact, at the end of our phone call I requested something from him. Mentioning that none of the photos of him online showed him smiling, I asked if he'd send me one. Just for me.

He'd said yes but couldn't do it right away because he'd had to end our call when his assistant came into his office.

So that's why at one am on Thursday morning I receive a text with a photo attached.

*Elijah: Sorry this took so long. I'm still at my building because this is the only time that my partners in Australia could video call. Xx *image attached**

His face appears on my screen. Soft smile, tired eyes, rumpled hair, lovely beard and something new. He's wearing glasses. Shit that's hot.

Elijah: Are you gonna print out my picture and do some voodoo magic on it? Xx

Sofia: How did you guess? Xx

Elijah: There's no other reason you could want it ;) xx

Sofia: I want to look at it when you're not with me. When were you gonna tell me you wore glasses? Xx

Elijah: I didn't know it was vital information. Do you like them? Xx

Sofia: Yes. They're hot. Fuck me with them on? Xx

Well I guess I just went and sent that! Where is my shame? Gone!

Elijah: You can have anything you want Darling. You know that right? Xx

Sofia: In that case, I don't care how late/early you finish work, come to mine and make my dreams come true xx

Elijah: You got it Princess Xx

Oh yes! Elijah Everett at my service.

***

"Yes! Yes! Yes! Mmmm Elijah! That's it!" I scream as he thrusts up into me, his mouth open, glasses steaming up from our body heat.

He got here at about three thirty in the morning and I yanked him inside immediately. We've been fucking ever since and he's working me towards my third orgasm. Third! How did I get so lucky?

We're on my bed and I'm riding him like there's no tomorrow. It's heaven...bliss...perfect!

He's like a drug trickling through my veins. Making his way to the deepest parts of me. His firm grip is like an anchor, his beating heart like a siren call. The thrill is dangerous because I know that this feeling isn't just sexual. I know that the way his gaze makes me weak isn't just a reaction of crushing on someone.

Elijah is plucking my emotional cords one by one. I want to make some joke about being dramatically poetic, only this doesn't feel like a joke to me.

The perfectly constructed insanity that I've made inside my own brain is melting away. Chaotic is how my Mom would describe me but boy she hasn't seen anything yet. I'm going to lose myself to this man, I already know it.

"Sofia...look at me" he pants, reaching to cup my cheeks. My eyes meet his as he sits up a little, pressing his forehead to mine. "I'm yours okay? Please don't think otherwise"

Clearly I'm not good at hiding my emotions. He really does know when I'm retreating into myself. Not now though. Not with him between my legs, whispering sweet things.

If my orgasm had a theatrical display there would be fireworks going off that's for sure. I imagine his display would be something to do with a wild beast. The way he grips me as his hips still and his eyes glaze over reminds me of a lion being satisfied by catching his prey.

Weird analogy but it fits in this moment.

I'd gladly be his prey if he were a lion. There I said it! Sue me!

We're a sweaty mess as we collapse together onto the duvet. It's something I never imagined wanting. I never liked to cuddle with my previous sexual partners but with Elijah its almost essential for both of us. A period of time to come back to earth and appreciate the person who just rocked your world. Well that or we just really like cuddling each other.

I think that's enough emotional shit for one night Sofia.

"So you like the glasses huh?" He chuckles, pulling them off and dropping them onto the floor with a little difficulty.

"Meh, they're okay I guess" I smirk as he nuzzles into my neck.

"Any fantasy you have, please let me know. I want to fulfill them all for you Darling"

"Oh you're gonna regret saying that. What If I wanna fuck you up the ass with a huge strap on?" I joke. Well I think I'm joking. Hmmm.

"I'd give it a go for you my Princess" he mumbles and I'm extremely flattered, not to mention intrigued by his new pet name for me. That's twice he's said it.

"Princess is a new one. Alas I don't have a castle or a noble steed"

"I'll buy you a castle and a noble steed. You'd look great in a crown"

"What made you choose my new title?" I ask tilting my head at him. He looks a little shy.

"Well I guess it's to do with the tabloids painting me as a monster. You'd be the princess in this little story. I'm the big bad villain that steals you away from your prince"

Oh no. He thinks he's the bad guy but it's so not true. Still, I think he will like what I've just remembered.

"When I was a little girl, I never liked any of the princes. I preferred the villains. So I guess you wouldn't have stolen me from a prince. I'd have went with you willingly" I confess.

"In that case, I'll happily be your villain"

***

Elijah had to leave at about seven in the morning but told me he'd be back tomorrow afternoon to pick me up in time for our drinks with Annabelle and Max. It sounds like he's going to have a really busy day today and I definitely won't have any late night visits this time.

I actually thought he might cancel but no he's still coming. It makes me extremely happy.

Something else that made me happy is how I gained the courage to use some of the money he gave me.

I sat and thought about it for a long time, guilt creeping into my mind. Eventually though, I paid my rent and made a note of it. Four hundred dollars spend. One hundred percent guilt trip.

So the only way I could feel better was telling Elijah about it.

Sofia: I paid my rent. Thanks for ensuring I don't end up without a home. It means the world xxx

Two hours later...

Elijah: You don't need to thank me Darling xxx

How can he be so sweet?

With some time on my own, I text my Mom, apply for two knew web design jobs and video call Bree.

She's extremely excited to hear from me.

"Sooooo, I was told that you might have a boyfriend" she says, her joyful face filling my phone screen.

Oh for goodness sake!

"Let me guess. My Mom told you that?" I reply, knowing that my Mom loves to take any kind of gossip and run with it. She saw one mans jacket and suddenly I'm in a relationship. Well, am I in one? I don't know.

"Yup, my good old Auntie Lou" she tells me. I find it cute that she shortens my Mom's name. Bree and her are a lot closer than she is to her own Mom. Which is no surprise. It warms my heart.

"Well it's not true!" I exclaim and Bree shakes her head.

"Uh huh... sure it's not. You can lie to her but not me, remember? You're the one who taught me all of your tricks"

Shit, she's right.

"I may be seeing someone but he's not my boyfriend"

"What's his name?"

"Elijah..."

With that, I tell her about him. Of course I leave out the part where I found him on a sugar daddy website.

It's nice to tell someone about him. Someone who won't ask too many questions or judge me.

She also tells me that she's planning to study interactive media at college and pride blooms inside me. You could say that interactive media is like a sister to web design.

My little cousin, following in my footsteps...sort of.

She's really damn intelligent. I just wish her parents would see that.

Talking to her makes me feel like it always does.

Happy and sad.

Sad because I want to go to Ohio to see her. Even more sad knowing that I won't.

Maybe one day I'll have the courage to go back there. It's my home after all.

***

Friday afternoon arrives and I'm feeling really good. I get to see Annabelle - who was really happy when I told her I was in fact bringing someone - and I get to see Elijah.

I haven't seen him in over twenty four hours so that photo of him really came in handy.

It's been a week now since he came into my life and boy what a week it has been.

Opting for another casual look, I go for my skinny jeans again but this time I pair them with a slouchy white top and ankle boots. Leaving my hair down, I ruffle it a little and decide I'm good to go.

Annabelle had said we're going to a bar we've been to many times before. Delilah's is the name and we certainly frequented it while in university.

As soon as Elijah says he's arrived, I fly down the stairs, bag in hand.

Butterflies fluttering.

What I do not anticipate is his less than formal look. I've only ever seen him in a suit, so when he opens his car door to get out, I have to do a double take.

He's got his glasses on again, a navy blue shirt and jeans that are neatly turned up at the bottom, above some lovely black timberland boots. Fuck me.

I'm pretty sure the silence that is happening between us right now suggests he's thinking the same thing about me.

"Sofia my lovely Princess, you take my breath away" he croons as I wrap my arms around his neck to kiss him in greeting. How did I get so lucky?

"Have you come to steal me away?" I reply and he lifts me up in the next second, making me laugh uncontrollably.

"Yes, you're coming with me. No man shall stop me"

My laughing doesn't stop because he physically picks me up and pops me in his car.

I've been successfully kidnapped.

***

When we walk into the bar, Elijah's hand tightens around mine. It's really nice having him by my side. What I don't expect is to immediately become a jealous brat when I notice other women looking at him.

Eww, I am not going to be that person! Who cares if they look? I don't own him. Still, if emotions showed in colour on my face then I'd be bright green right now.

Apparently so would he because when a very drunk guy winks at me in passing, his arm moves around my waist, pulling me closer.

I'm actually trying to suppress a laugh but it's tough when I catch him glaring before he smiles down at me.

It seems he doesn't like other men flirting with me and I'm fine by that because I don't like it either.

I'm torn from my musings as a loud booming voice calls my name. I know it's Annabelle without looking.

"Sofia! You made it!" My eyes follow the voice and latch onto her shoulder length blonde hair. Sitting next to her is a grinning Max. They're so cute together.

Weaving through the crowd with Elijah attached to me, we finally make it to them. Annabelle jumps up and pulls me into a tight hug and I giggle at her enthusiasm. She is literally a ball of joy and happiness. A stark contrast to my usually pessimistic self.

Elijah shakes Max's hand as he introduces himself, then we swap our greetings to the opposite person. Max kisses my cheek while Elijah opts to shake Annabelle's hand. She smiles politely at him but I can tell she's already trying to work him out. The inquisitive face she now has on is something I've come to recognise quickly after being her friend for five years.

I pray she likes him, otherwise I'll no doubt hear about her disapproval. For now though, she doesn't say a word and sits down.

"What is everyone drinking? I'll get the first round" Elijah announces and there goes that guilty twang in my stomach again. I know he's only going to buy me a drink but it still makes me feel bad.

I think he can tell I'm about to freak out because his eyes soften when he sees my expression and he leans into me.

"It's okay Darling, you can buy me one back" he whispers, squeezing my hand.

He takes our drink order and walks off with a sexy swagger, that I can't take my eyes off of. And that ass...seriously I have a problem.

"Well he's new" Annabelle states, smirking in amusement.

"Yeah he's very new and dreamy too" I tell them and Max shakes his head, probably because he thinks we're going to break out into stereotypical girl talk.

"Why didn't you tell me sooner that you found a new boo?" She continues.

"Because it's very recent...very" I explain. I really hope she doesn't ask any awkward questions like she did when we first met because I will drop kick her ass. She asked me about my sexual orientation in about zero point five seconds and then went on to ask about my sex life. It was a lot. I guess it's the journalist in her. Nothing is too personal.

"Is he nice?"

What kind of question is that?

"No, he's an asshole but I'm just ignoring that part!" I smirk sarcastically and she rolls her eyes.

"You know what I mean!" She laughs and that's when Elijah returns. For some reason I thought she'd stop her questions but I really shouldn't have been so naive.

"How did you guys meet?"

What? Oh no! This was not on my list of prepared answers for tonight. For some reason I didn't think that this question would come up. I'm not sure why though, it's literally the most basic thing to ask someone when they first start dating. Or that's what Annabelle thinks we're doing. Are we dating? Honestly, I'm not sure.

I open my mouth in the hopes that something believable will magically start coming out but nothing comes to mind.

"Online dating website" Elijah states, saving the day. I mean I'm not sure why I couldn't have just said that because technically it's not a lie. Plus, it's a very common thing these days.

Annabelle smiles tightly as if she's trying to seem pleased for me but is really thinking that I'm a big fucking idiot. Yup she's really giving off judgmental worried vibes and I'm sure that it's not just me that can tell.

"And how long how have you guys been dating?" She continues her interrogation like questions and I subtly tilt my head at her, to let her know that I'm very much yelling "What the fuck?" in my head. I don't like being the centre of attention and she knows this. So right now I'm just drowning in uncomfortableness. Like there's a huge weight on my chest and I'm just sinking further and further to the bottom of the sea, unable to get any air.

Yikes, I'm a drama queen but I'm still sticking with the uncomfortable part. I'll leave the drowning metaphor for someone who knows how to use it better.

"About a week" I choke out.

If her judgy expression was extremely obvious then her widening eyes are like a neon sign that says "What are you thinking?!"

I'm sitting here like a statue. Not a well built one either because if she asks one more nosey question I'll crumble into dust. I know I shouldn't be ashamed or be trying to hide Elijah and I's situation but honestly I can't be bothered with the lectures or the disapproval.

Unfortunately, I think I'm going to have to deal with that anyway as Annabelle announces she's going to use the ladies room. Her eyes latch onto mine and she gives me a clear signal that she wants to talk to me. Once again, she isn't sly about it.

As she walks away, Max raises his eyebrows and lets out a laugh.

"You've been summoned" he smirks and I wanna throw a cup at him.

"I think you're about to get in trouble for online dating" Elijah says, sliding his hand onto my knee in comfort, while he gives me a sympathetic look.

"Oh I definitely am. Do you think I should remind her that I'm an adult and actually not her daughter? Or would that get me smacked?"

"She'll beat you until death if you sass her while she's berating you. It's best to just nod and agree" Max advises me, amused.

"Damn okay, hopefully I won't be too long. If I'm gone for longer than ten minutes, send help" I tell them and Elijah kisses my cheek in support.

Following the direction Annabelle went, I find her standing against the bathroom sinks with her arms crossed. I try to speak first.

"I know what you're thinking-"

"What am I thinking Sofia? Hmmm"

"That I'm an idiot for dating someone I met online" I sigh and she nods rapidly.

"Yah that's part of it. How about the fact that you can only get hurt from this relationship"

Huh? Why would she think that?

"What are you talking about?"

"He's older than you and probably only interested in a thrill for a while. He's probably married with kids too"

Well... she's definitely reaching for reasons to reprimand me. A wife and kids? Seems unlikely with the amount of time he's been spending with me.

"Annabelle just because he's older it doesn't mean he only wants a thrill. That's rather judgmental of you" I tell her and copy her serious stance, crossing my arms in defence. I think she's overreacting here.

"What about his previous relationships? Have you found out about them? You can never be too safe with an online fling"

Fucking hell. It's not a fling...at least I hope not. His previous relationships recently were sugar babies. He's also hinted at trying to date but it never working out. Getting to know someone takes time and isn't going to happen within a week.

"Why are you so weird about this? I thought you'd be happy that I've found someone?"

"I am happy Sofia. I'm just worried because of all the online horror stories. He does seem nice, I just want you to be wary"

"Well thank you for worrying but I am an adult and I think I can handle him" I wink and this changes her serious expression into a grin.

"He is hot though..."

"Oh god I know right. Honestly it's hard to think straight"

That's all it takes for us to actually do the stereotypical girl thing and squeal about overly romantic things he's said and done. She tells me about how Max and her are getting on too and then we realise that we should probably get back to the guys.

Elijah's questioning glance when we return, shows his concern for my well being. It's strange because I've never had anyone care in such a way. It's nice to watch his frown turn to a smile when he sees that I'm all okay. So sweet.

"I'll get the drinks this time" I state and Elijah pouts at me.

"I missed you while you were gone" he whispers to me and I actually don't know what to say. Is he real? He can't be? Surely he's a mirage that I've dreamed up! Maybe I'm actually in a coma and this is my fantasy.

"Come with me then" I suggest but Max changes the plan.

"How about a game of snooker Elijah?"

I see the panic in Elijah's eyes as he struggles. He wants to come with me but he doesn't want to be rude. So I mouth "go" to him and his pout returns.

"Whoop his ass for me please. I never beat him" I complain and this cheers Elijah up considerably.

"I'll destroy him in your honour" he smiles and presses a long kiss to my mouth. I end up with a tomato red blush and a teasing look from Annabelle.

Then I go to the bar and order drinks. I'm on a high. Feeling quite possibly happier than I've ever felt. Why did I think that would last for more than ten seconds?

"Hey baby, what's your name?" I hear and see the same drunk guy from earlier. The one that winked. He looks about my age and has clearly consumed his body weight in alcohol.

I ignore him because I don't know what else to do. I've never been able to handle being hit on especially not by drunk overbearing men, who don't know what personal space is.

"Did you not hear me?" He tries again and this time I turn to him and say softly:

"Yeah I heard you, I just want to be left alone"

He doesn't like that one bit and shifts closer to me. So I back up, fear trickling down my spine. No...not this please.

"You haven't even heard what I wanna say to you. Why do you look so scared?" He laughs but it's pretty terrifying. So is the fact that I don't think he can really see straight.

"Because you're scaring me..." I state simply and he frowns.

"Well you don't need to be scared. How about you come home with me tonight? I'll treat you real good"

"No thank you" I state more firmly, moving away once more.

Where the hell are my drinks? Why the hell won't he go away?

"Oh come on! You're hot as hell and so am I"

I want to scoff at his statement but I know better than to make the situation worse. You see as a women, it's ingrained in us from birth not to make a man angry. For me, it was also retaught over and over as a kid. On repeat.

My brain flickers with a long lost memory, dread filling me.

"Please leave me alone. I'm with someone" I try but he still won't listen. Fear continues to grow.

"He's not as good in bed as me I bet"

"I said, leave me alone" I reply one last time with a bit more annoyance.

I shouldn't have done that.

"Don't be so fucking rude!" He growls and shifts close again, his anger taking over in seconds.

Shit!

No!

When I try to move away from him again, he tries to grab my waist but he doesn't get to make contact.

A fist flies into his face, making a crunching noise against his jaw. I gasp in shock and jump back as my brain tries to process what's going on.

My eyes find a very angry Elijah. He's just as mad as the guy now crumpled on the floor was and I don't like how it all makes me feel. It's too much. Too many angry men around me.

Too much violence.

When the drunk guy begins to get back up, Elijah steps in front of me. Logically I know he's protecting me but I still can't calm down.

"You stupid fucking kid. You're a waste of space"

I tense from a fleeting flashback, knowing a slap or kick came next after those words.

Back in the present Elijah lands another punch. I watch his fist flying through the air and it makes me feel sick.

I have to get out of here.

"Sofia? Darling are you okay?" I hear as I begin to turn away.

Elijah tries to pull me back, his hand taking my wrist gently. It still makes me panic.

"Don't!" I yell and snatch my hand back.

"I'm sorry..." he apologises, letting me go. His anger is gone, replaced by worry and dare I say hurt.

I just need to go!

So I turn away and march out of the bar on wobbly legs. I can hear my name being called by multiple people but I don't stop.

The first cab that appears in my line of sight, I hail and jump in as if I'm being chased by a murderer. I don't know why my mind is muddled.

I'm not a kid anymore but I still get trigged this way. I can't be around men with quick tempers. Men who resort to violence so fast.

I was so sure Elijah wasn't like that.

Pulling out my phone when it begins to vibrate, I see Elijah's name. He's trying to call me. So with shaky fingers I decline.

Why did he get so angry so quick? How is that my only experience with men in my life? I hate it! I hate how I react and how it makes me feel. Maybe I should have told Elijah about my childhood but no one knows. Not even my parents.

I've been doing so well.

I guess I just never thought I'd have to encounter it with him. He made me feel so safe. Safer than anyone.

I'm an idiot! I don't know him! We've just met and I was so stupid to trust him so quick!

Who the fuck clicks onto a random link in an email and begins a relationship with someone who they have absolutely no idea about?! ME!

This is why I'm a hermit!

Fuck this shit!

When he texts, I block his number. Then I delete the sugar rush app for good measure. It all happens so fast, before I can really process what I'm doing. He was just trying to protect me...but it's so clear now that the whole thing between us was ridiculous! A few fucked up days of me being sucked in by a handsome man. How stupid!

This is a lesson well learned. Don't trust someone so easily. No matter how pretty the face is. My Mom warned me about handsome men.

I won't be fooled again, that's for sure!

Tears prick my eyes and I swipe at them angrily. I'm better than that.

I can't cry over a man I was never meant to have.

Elijah

"Sofia!" I yell for what must be about the tenth time. The cab she jumped into drives off into the distance, while I stand in the street willing her to come back. Except I know she won't.

If Annabelle hadn't stood in my way and told me to let her go, then maybe I would have been able to talk to her. I'm sure she's a great friend but right now I'm not her biggest fan. In fact, I'd go as far as saying that I very much despise her in this very moment.

I despise myself too. The look of fear on Sofia's face when I tried to stop her running away is ingrained on my brain. I feel like shit knowing that I've scared her. All I wanted was to help. To get that drunken asshole away from her.

When I saw him trying to touch her and the way she recoiled, I just lost it. I've never felt so protective over anyone and I acted on instinct. My temper can be quick sometimes but nothing like that.

I didn't expect her to recoil from me too. Did she think I was going to hit her? That I was a threat? The thought makes me sick. I'd never do anything to hurt her. I had wanted to pull her into my arms and take her fear away but how could I when I was the one she ended up being afraid of?

Should I go after her? Should I leave her be? I don't know what the right course of action is because I've never felt this way. I've never felt such a strong need to apologise to someone and to make it all better.

Oh Sofia, what do you want me to do?

My need to go after her and bang on her door is still very much present. I want to beg her to talk to me because right now I'm terrified that she won't ever want to see me again.

That shouldn't bother me as much as it does but I think at this point I should really just accept that Sofia has flipped my world upside down.

I think a more subtle approach than pounding on her door is suited right now. Maybe she will answer my call.

Dialling her number, I begin to make my way back to my car. There's no point in going to ask her friends for help because they will no doubt try to stop me. I understand that of course but it's still fucking infuriating. I feel helpless.

No answer...Fuck!

Slamming the car door shut, I sit looking out the windscreen, wondering what to do next. I have to fix this.

She probably won't answer any messages from me but it's worth a try.

Elijah: Darling you need to tell me what's wrong so I can fix it xx

I wait to see if she's going to read it. It makes me nervous, more nervous than being in charge of thousands of people.

She does see the message and I begin to sweat waiting for her response. Only it doesn't come.

Elijah: Please tell me you're okay Xx

I have to at least know that. Maybe she doesn't want me near but this is more important. She has to be okay.

I can't believe how stupid I've been. I want her so bad but I've ruined it with my temper. A temper that is about to rage with my own self hatred.

You can no longer contact this number.

No...FUCK NO!

Throwing my phone in the passenger seat, I slam my fist on the dashboard before covering my face in frustration.

Why do I care so much? I never care. I don't give a fuck! I'm better than that!

I don't do cute shit, I don't stay over and I certainly don't catch feelings. Well look what's happened now!

I should probably leave her alone. I'm pretty good at taking a hint but surely that can't be it done.

PING!

My eyes shoot to the phone in my seat and I snatch it up with a feeling of relief. Maybe I'm wrong.

Only I just feel even worse when I see what's on my screen.

Sofia Westwood has requested to transfer money into your account.

She's trying to send the money back. I don't want it though. As far as I'm concerned it's her now. She deserves it.

This women is so strange. Unlike anyone I've ever met. So what do I have to do to get her to talk to me?

I think giving her time to herself is a good idea. I don't want to make her panic again.

Then I'll go to her.

I have to at least try. I have to know if this is over.

That thought jabs at my insides violently, making the beer I drank swirl.

I can't stay away from her.

Sofia

Transaction Declined

What? Why won't he take the money back? I don't want it, certainly not now. Not after I embarrassed myself in front of him and ran from the bar like a lunatic.

Turns out, I'm able to think more rationally now that I'm in my apartment and my heart rate has slowed. It was hard to pin point where to place my fear when my instincts just wanted me to bolt.

I went from realising he was protecting me, to going back to worrying that I don't know him enough to trust him.

This isn't his fault though. It's mine. It's my childhood.

Since leaving Ohio, what happened tonight has only happened once before. In University a guy I'd been seeing got mad at me. Jake was his name. He punched a wall near my head and I was triggered, sent back to being seven years old. I'd ran then too. Only this is different.

Elijah isn't the same.

He wasn't going to hurt me. He wanted me safe. From the moment I began messaging him, I felt a sense of calm that no one has ever made me feel. The dull buzz of fear when being around men isn't present with him.

Which is why I need to fix this. I need him to know that he did nothing wrong.

The man has very evidently made a mark on my soul.

There I go again with the dramatics. Still, even if it's nothing to do with my soul, it's definitely emotional because I miss him already. I still think that I was crazy to get so involved with him so fast but I guess I can't control how I feel. We've only been apart for a few hours, yet I want him back.

Only, I'm scared to unblock his number in case he's done the same thing to me. He probably doesn't even care that I'm not speaking to him.

He's probably glad that he doesn't have to let me down gently-

BUZZZZZ!

Answer it...or ignore it...that's the question. There's a fifty percent chance someone has pressed the wrong button. That happens a lot. There's also a twenty percent chance it could be Annabelle. I haven't answered her texts either because I'm too embarrassed.

The other thirty percent goes to Elijah. I'm definitely hoping for that.

With my sweat pants and hoodie on, I walk to my door and hesitate. If it's him, how am I going to explain my own idiocy?

I guess there's only one way to find out.

Pressing the button to allow whoever it is in, I wait. Then...

Knock! knock!

Opening the door, I'm met with the worried green eyes of my lover. His face transforms with relief as he sees me. I'm staring so hard that I can actually see his pupils dilate and his cheeks flush.

"Sofia, you answered" he sighs. He seems surprised but then I guess I can't blame him. I did run from him in terror.

"I'm surprised you're here" I reply because it's true. He could have left things the way they were but he's came back even after my freak out.

"Of course I'm here. I need to know that you're okay. I really didn't mean to scare you"

"I know you didn't. You should come in so we can talk" I tell him, stepping aside to let him past. His face brightens up at my suggestion and he walks into my apartment, yet keeps his distance.

When we sit on the end of my bed together, the atmosphere is far different than the last time we were on it. I mean of course it is. We're scared to touch each other.

He angles himself towards me and waits for me to start the conversation. Only I'm not sure what to say.

"I'm sorry for how I reacted" I tell him, feeling so stupid.

He looks appalled at my words, his forehead creasing in a deep frown.

"What?! No, don't apologise! It's me that needs to do that. I didn't mean to scare you. I went too far. I'm really fucking sorry Darling" he replies, looking horrified that I felt the need to apologise.

I can tell he wants to touch me, to comfort me but he's wary.

"You were trying to protect me and I'm grateful" I assure him.

"I'd never hurt you Sofia. Never. My tempter today was out of order but I just saw red. I didn't want him to hurt you" he confesses.

"Yes, I know. I should have told you about-" I pause, not sure if I can get the words out. "Things happened, when I was a kid..." is the best I can get out.

His expression then is unreadable. He frowns, his lips pressed onto a thin line. Anger shows in his eyes then but a different kind. A kind that says he would rip someone to shreds in my honour.

"Did someone hurt you?" He says, deathly quiet.

My stomach swirls as I think about that someone. It makes me freeze.

"Remember when you didn't want to talk about your parents?" I ask and his eyes soften, immediately understanding. "I can't talk about this thing yet"

"Sofia I-" he stops. He's holding his hand out to me as if asking permission. Then he really does ask. "May I?"

Nodding, I place my hand in his and intwine our fingers. A feeling of calm washes over me and I can't stop myself from shifting closer to him.

He smiles softly at this and squeezes my hand. He's being respectful of any boundaries that I may have. It's unusual for me.

"You're safe Sofia. I won't let anyone hurt you" he whispers. "I'll keep you safe"

"You make me feel safe" I confess, flexing my fingers in his. He doesn't reply but his eyes light up at my words, his lips parting. "I usually don't with men" I continue, letting out another piece of the puzzle.

"I'm so sorry...for whatever it is that happened to you. I wish I could make it better"

"You are..." I breath and his fingers brush over my cheek.

"I think it's only fair that I give you something...some information about my parents. Since you've told me things"

"Only if you're sure" I reply, not wanting to push him.

"I am. I think...I think my temper comes from my Dad. I remember him shouting a lot. I know it's no excuse but I'm pretty sure that's the route of it. He was very ruthless and he taught me not to take shit from anyone"

I can tell it's hard for him to speak, as he thinks of his words before he says them.

"He sounds lovely" I joke a little and he smiles ever so slightly, shaking his head.

"Yeah, he was a little strict. He never had time for me or my Mom" he sighs.

"I'm sorry Elijah. What happened to them?" I ask but I think that's as much as I'm going to get from him tonight. I can see him shutting down.

"I'll tell you some other time" he whispers, his voice breaking. The sadness radiating from him tells me all I need to know for now and I just want to take it away. "I want you to know that if you do decide to tell me about your past, I'm here. Anything you want to talk about. I want to know you Sofia"

Slowly he leans forward and gently presses a kiss to my forehead. He's testing the waters, still unsure.

With a deep breath, I'm able to tell him about the previous time I ran like I did today.

As I talk, I only get closer to him. It's like my body naturally gravities towards him and he doesn't seem to mind. His arm wraps around my shoulders and I rest my hand on his knee as I tell him my story. He tenses when I mention the things Jake said to me in anger. The things that were so similar to what another angry man had said to me as a kid. When I mentioned him punching the wall, Elijah's arms tighten around me.

When I fall silent, his fingers tilt my chin so that he can look me in the eye. He caresses my cheek with a care that is so far from the angry man from a few hours ago.

"Thank you for telling me" he says, brushing his nose against mine.

"Are we okay? I don't want you to be afraid of me Darling. I want you to feel one hundred percent safe with me"

The way I feel about him hasn't changed.

"I still want you Elijah and I'm not afraid of you. I think we're both a little more complicated than we thought and maybe we should take things slow. In the emotional sense anyway. Get to know each other..." I suggest and he nods immediately in agreement.

"Yes of course" he replies while looking a whole lot happier than he did when he first got here. The colour is blooming in his cheeks and his warm eyes tell me so many different things. "I said I'd take care of you and I meant it" he continues, cupping my cheeks. His eyes flick to my lips and I know he's desperate to kiss me. To mend the rift between us.

"I'm really sorry I ruined tonight" I blurt out because everything is just hitting me at once.

"Don't say that. It wasn't your fault. Darling I loved being out with you and your friends. I loved seeing you laugh and relax. That asshole is the one to blame" he growls, his eyes heated.

Looking away from his gaze, I blush and then remember that I should probably contact Annabelle to let her know I'm okay. Only right now I'm a bit distracted.

"Oh and don't try to send me money back again or you'll be in trouble" he states, his stern expression making my body shiver.

Should we be seducing each other right now? Probably not. We should probably work on the getting to know each other part some more. Although I don't think we will get far.

I'm starting to get familiar with the crackling electricity that surrounds us when we're together. More specifically when we both really wanna be naked together.

"I'm sorry, it won't happen again" I whisper.

"Good" he breaths and runs his hands up my sides. It's tickles and I squeal in shock as he does it again, eliciting the same reaction from me.

"Elijah!" I yell as he laughs at my wriggling. Although I can tell he's still holding back, when I end up lying on the bed with him hovering above me. The desire in his eyes almost sucks the air from my body. Yet he doesn't move.

"We shouldn't have sex. You've been through a lot today" he says seriously.

Huh...such a lovely gentleman wrapped inside a freak in the sheets. It's a rare thing.

"Okay, we won't have sex" I reply, running my fingers up his arm. "We could just make out..."

What an ambitious thing for me to say. I'm not sure our bodies know what 'just making out' is. As soon as his lips are on mine, our hands begin to wander and clothes are tugged at desperately.

"No sex" he repeats as his lips move from my mouth to my jaw.

"No, of course not" I say breathlessly, my fingers gripping the back of his shirt. "But you could take this off" I suggest but it comes out as more of a beg.

"Yes, that'll be okay" he whispers and my fingers begin undoing the buttons in record time. He throws the material away like it has offended him and my hands feel his chest.

This must look like dry humping porn as he grinds his jean covered erection between my legs. His breathing is ragged and his hands are gentler than normal as they slide under my top.

"Elijah you don't have to hold back. I'm okay. I promise you" I push out between desperate moans that are simply from his hands on my bare skin.

"I don't want to fuck things up Darling" he responds, a sadness in his voice that makes me stop. This time its me grabbing his face to make him look at me.

"Why would you say that?"

"Well I almost ruined things earlier and I seem to do that a lot"

"What happened tonight wasn't your fault. You were protecting me and now that I think about it...it was hot. You did a good thing"

He burrows his face in my neck and breathes deeply as if he doesn't want to accept what I'm saying. Like it's unusual for him to hear anything positive.

"Darling you ultimately deserve better than me but I'm selfish and I don't want to stop seeing you" he whispers in my ear.

"Stop talking like that. I'm not so perfect either"

He gazes down at me, he eyes searching mine before he gives in and smothers my mouth again.

Is it possible to care so deeply for someone so quick? To feel like I've known him for years...strange but it's like he belongs right here in my arms.

Even though he's still very much saying no sex, somehow we still end up naked. Shocking I know. How did that happen?

"Ah Sofia, you're so wet" he groans as his cock slides through my pussy lips. This is going to drive me insane.

"Elijah please fuck me. I want to feel you inside of me" I beg and watch him contemplate it. He licks his lips and teases my entrance again.

"Are you sure? I don't want-"

"I'm asking you, no begging you to fuck me. I've never felt safer than when we're joined" I whine and rock my hips so he can feel me.

A bead of sweat rolls down his forehead. That's how hard it is for him to stay still. Poor man.

"You want me Darling? You're not scared of me? Tell me you're not"

"I'm not scared. I need you baby"

Finally he slides inside of me and my finger nails dig into his skin as he fills me up. Yes!

"Ah shit! I've never felt anything so perfect" he groans. Wrapping my arms around him, I spread my legs as far as I can and let him thrust into me slowly. It's sweet torture and I'm more than happy for him to take all the time he needs. It just feels so fucking good.

"Harder Elijah!" I yell and he slams into me with even more enthusiasm. His lips suck on my nipples and his hands reach wherever they can.

Maybe we're just obsessed with one another or maybe it's something deeper. People do say once you know, you know. Whatever the hell that means!

When he comes it sets of my orgasm and I'm pretty sure I'm screaming the place down. My poor neighbours.

I'm so glad that this evening is ended the way it has. I could have been alone and scared but instead he didn't just walk away from me. And I didn't just kick him right back out.

I think it's clear that even though we haven't said anything, we're very serious about our 'relationship'.

That night while he spoons me in bed, he informs me that he's planning to take me somewhere nice for the day. I don't think I've felt so excited for a weekend in a long time. I wonder where we're going?

***

In the morning he wakes me up early and we shower quickly, trying our best to keep our hands to ourselves.

As Elijah dries off, I lie on top of my bed half dressed and mess around on my phone, trying to beat the next level of my coding game because I'm a nerd. Then an email notification pops up.

My heart jumps in my chest as I see it's from the coffee shop. I don't even have to open the email properly to see what it says because the subject line reads:

'Congratulations! You got the job with Brew House!'

Oh shit! YES! Omg omg omg! Jumping up, I don't know what to do with myself but I'm super frigging excited!

"Elijah! I got the job!" I yell because the only thing I wanna do is tell him. He appears from the bathroom in his boxers with a grin on his face and pulls me into his arms tightly.

"Well Done Darling! I knew you would!" He praises, leaning down to give me a congratulatory kiss. "Oh that means I have an excuse to buy you a gift" he continues, looking just as excited as me.

"You better not spend-"

I'm cut off as my phone begins to ring now, Annabelle's name popping up. I assume she's calling to check that I'm okay. Oops, I should have really called. Side tracked again! I almost don't answer because I'm on a high and I just wanna jump around like a big kid. Then I think I should probably let her know my good news anyway.

"Hey! I'm sorry I didn't call you-"

"Sofia! Are you with Elijah?" She asks, her tone more serious than I've ever heard it.

"Yeah, we made up. Why?" I reply, my voice going flat because of how she sounds. If she's going to give me more shit, I'm just gonna hang up.

"You have to get away from him. He's not safe Sofia. He's really not safe" she yells down the line as his hands rub my back.

"Everything okay?" He asks, smiling softly.

Ummmmmmmm.

"What do you mean?" I ask her because I can't possibly begin to work out what she means.

"He was accused of murder last year..."

What. The. Hell?!

Sofia

What? She must be high or something? I'm not sure how to reply to that. It must be a joke.

"Plus, just yesterday a report was filed against him. Nadia Zoya or something. She accused him of assault" she continues, making my head spin. This surely can't be real.

"Annabelle, doesn't this sound a bit far fetched?" I reply but my throat is beginning to close up. It's one thing after another. First I'm having a god damn panic attack and fleeing the bar, now this. Is the world trying to tell me I'm making a mistake being anywhere near Elijah?

"How do you know it's far fetched? You barely know him"

She has a point.

Elijah sits on the bed next to me then, his hand sliding onto my leg. Am I sleeping with a murderer? And if I am, what exactly does she expect me to do right now?

"You'll have to give me more details than that" I reply, trying to keep my sentences normal. I haven't said anything that could give away what I'm saying but it'll be tougher soon.

"I'll send you links. Please get away from him as soon as you can. This is real Sofia!"

"Okay cool no problem, I'll speak to you later" I say cheerily and hang up, keeping my phone tightly clasped in my hand.

My first thought is to just come out and say "why did you get accused of murder?" because I want him to burst out laughing and tell me that it's a load of shit. Only, if it's true then I risk putting myself in danger. What if I'm supposed to be his next victim?

"Sofia are you sure you're okay?" He asks, looking at me with a concerned expression on his face. That's probably because I haven't said a word since hanging up the phone and I'm kinda frozen stiff.

Think! How do I get out of this?! I just need to get away from him until I can work out what the hell is going on?

"I don't feel very well" is the best thing I can come up with. The words fly from my mouth uneven and pathetic. It's not totally a lie though because I'm feeling sicker by the second. If this was a murder mystery, I'd be fucking dead, that's for sure.

"Is there anything I can do to make you feel better?" he asks, his hand resting over my forehead. "You are rather hot, I'll go get you some water" he says, pressing a kiss to my cheek. Really? How is this guy a murderer, he's so sweet? My god I don't wanna believe it.

What if this is part of his thing? To make me like him and get close to me so that the killing part will be more enjoyable.

Glancing down at my phone, I fumble to open the link that has the words 'accused of murder' in it and wait nervously as it loads. All that I can take in once it pops up is one simple sentence:

'Multimillionaire Elijah Everett Kills Lover in Penthouse Apartment'

His lover. Well shit that definitely makes me more of a target huh! Fuck! Fuck! Fuck!

I really should have googled him more. Fuck making my own opinions.

My ears ring as a feeling of dizziness overcomes me but I can make out the sound of his footsteps coming back.

Okay, not good.

"I'll go to the store and get you some painkillers or something Darling. What exactly do you think is wrong?" he says softly, appearing in front of me again. Fight or flight???

"I'm going to be sick" I exclaim and jump off the bed, dodging around him, I sprint into the bathroom. I slam the door shut behind me and lock it with adrenaline endorsed fear. I actually do feel the bile rising in my throat but I take a deep breath and lean against the cold tile to try and collect my thoughts.

"Are you okay? I'm sorry I'm so shitty in these situations but I wanna help Darling" he calls through the door. I wonder why he's so shitty? Maybe because trying to make people feel better is the opposite of his strong points?

"Um it's okay, maybe you should just go because I don't think I'll be up for much at all today" I push out, my voice wobbly. I don't think he will notice though considering there's a door between us.

I begin typing a message to Annabelle, my fingers shaking.

Sofia: What do I do? How am I supposed to get away from him? I'm stuck in the bathroom and he won't leave!

I hit send quickly as I hear him trying to comfort me. What a good act.

Then my blood runs cold as I hear Elijah's text tone over his voice. Looking at my phone in horror, I realise my mistake. I've sent him the text by accident! Annabelle and

Elijah are the two people I've texted recently so it's an easy mistake right...right!!!

"No!" I whisper under my breath with the power of a yell. I wanna scream the place down because of my own stupidly. If he kills me then good for him because I'm a fucking idiot!

"Sofia? What's going on?" I hear him say and keep well back from the door. Oops. I've fucked up royally.

I should call the police. Why haven't I done that yet already?

"Why are you afraid of me? Please Sofia, open the door Darling"

"You need to leave! Please, I saw the article. I know what you did. I know about Nadia too! What the hell is wrong with you?!" I yell, a little too confident for someone who could be stabbed any second. Or strangled. I wonder what his thing is?

"Fuck! I knew I should have told you about that earlier. I didn't kill anyone Sofia and I have no idea what you mean about Nadia! I promise you"

Of course he'd say that. He wants me out of here so he can end me violently.

"Please just go. I'm scared" I confess, hoping that this might help. I'm not sure why, surely he won't care if he's a psychopath.

"You don't need to be scared. I would never hurt you"

"That's what a murderer would say"

"If I were going to kill you, don't you think I'd have done it by now?"

"I don't know. I'm not a fellow psychopath. Not too sure how you guys think"

"I'm not a psychopath. Maybe I'm a little crazy but that's about it. Just come out and I'll tell you everything that happened. I'm not doing it through a damn door"

"No! I don't want to hear it! Go!"

"Sofia!" He growls, his frustration growing. "Open the door! This is ridiculous! If I had my hands on you right now the only thing I'd be doing is spanking that ass! Which I think you'd probably like!"

Is he fucking serious?!

"Get out!" I try again and this time when he speaks it's clear that he's realising how serious I am.

"Come on Darling. Don't do this. I'm not a threat to you. I just want to look after you"

"Please go Elijah. If you care about me at all you'll go" I beg and silence falls. Seconds pass and I can't help but press my ear to the door to try and work out what's going on.

I can actually hear him breathing. The rhythm the same as mine as I try to calm down.

"Okay, I'll go. If that's what you want. Promise me something though. Do some more research. You'll realise that I didn't do what you think I did. I hope you work it out soon too because I don't fancy the thought of not seeing you for any length of time. Sofia, I need you"

And I need you...shitttt. It's true.

Oh boy. There it is. The reason that I haven't called the police. The reason why, even though I'm filled with fear, I'm also still consumed with yearning for him. It's also why I let him in last night. Because I've never needed anyone the way I need him. He's like the X to my Y. CSS to my HTML. Ying to my Yang.

It's the strangest thing.

"See you soon Sofia" he says finally, the defeat heavy in his voice. I squash my ear to the door to hear him collecting his things and the sound of his footsteps retreating.

Through the fear and terror, my heart beats wildly as if it's punishing me for what I've just done. As if it's trying to escape my chest to follow him.

Unfortunately that doesn't change the articles on my phone. It's still bright and glaring at me. Was I sleeping with a murderer? Or have I made a huge mistake?

All I can do is try to find out...

Elijah

It's only after I left Sofia that I saw the email from my lawyer about Nadia. I've been so caught up in Sofia that I've hardly been checking anything, especially not my mundane emails.

Back at my apartment I'm lying on the couch where Sofia and I made love, with my phone in one hand and a glass of whiskey in the other.

Why can't I catch a break? Why does the world have to keep fucking me over? I don't blame her for wanting me gone. I'd be scared too if I found out the news that she did today. Only it's fake news and I really hope she realises it.

I'm not letting myself think of this as the end of us. She's too clever to think it's true once she actually looks into things.

I wish she didn't believe it in the first place but I know how convincing those articles are. Plus she has no reason to think it's fake. Maybe I am the monster everyone thinks I am.

She's different though. She sees through the bullshit. She sees me.

Closing my eyes, I try to fight the urge to call her. I want her to have a clear mind and come to her own conclusion.

Dropping my phone to the floor, my mind wanders to the dreadful night that warranted all the tabloid mess. The reason I haven't had a sugar baby in a year.

It was one of the worst nights of my life. I'd been working into the early hours of the morning. I was the only one in the office and it was about three am by the time I actually got home. I'd walked into my apartment to see her on the floor. Dead. I didn't know her well but that didn't stop me feeling sick at the sight of her body.

I didn't know what to do. I had stood there frozen for god knows how long, my mind trying to comprehend how it had happened. How was she dead on my floor?

Upon closer inspection, the needle stuck in her arm was a huge give away. Now why was she in my apartment? That question was a little harder to work out.

The women had been my sugar baby for a mere day and I had sent my standard payment for the time we spent together. I recall thinking that she certainly seemed more desperate for the money than the others. I mean they at least tried to pretend that they gave a shit. She didn't. She'd asked me for it right after we had sex and I'd complied, rolled over and went to sleep while she left.

The police investigation didn't take long but with the news of her death getting out and the sight of the officers leaving my building, the tabloids went mad.

It turns out she'd remembered the passcode to my elevator during her night with me and had come back to demand more cash. The video feed from the elevator confirms her entering my place but considering I had no other CCTV, there wasn't a clear view of what happened after that. Hence the suspicion from the press that could have gotten me arrested.

It's safe to say I'm more carful when entering my passcode now and I've got cameras in most places in my apartment.

The police came to the conclusion that she'd shot up and overdosed. I guess I was too indifferent to even notice she was a drug addict. Because I'm a selfish prick and if I'd paid more attention then maybe I'd have been able to save her life. Rest in peace Lucy. You deserved so much better.

Shaking my head, I pull myself up and drag my ass upstairs to my bedroom. I haven't even made my bed since Sofia was in it last and I really wish she was here now, wrapped in my black silk sheets.

Pulling off my clothes and dumping them on the floor, I make my way to the shower. Hopefully blasting myself with pipping hot water will make me feel better.

It's crazy that a week ago I'd probably be working right now. Sad and lonely with no hope of escaping my dreadful life. Now I'm sad and lonely in a new kind of way. Plus my work couldn't be father from my mind.

The only productive thing I've done since leaving Sofia's apartment was actually call my lawyer to tell him to deal with the Nadia thing. I'm not even going to bother looking into what she's said about me. All he told me in the email is that she's accused me of assault. What a load of shit. She clearly wants to get me back for turning her down. I should be the one filing a sexual harassment complaint.

Steaming water pours over my body as I drag my fingers through my wet hair. Right now all I'm hoping for is a phone call from my girl. I want to hear that she knows I didn't kill anyone, that she wants to see me.

Today started off so bright. I was going to take her away for the day. Maybe a quick flight somewhere.

Anywhere that she wanted to go in fact. Alas, here I am staring at my own reflection in the glass shower wall. I look like shit.

I wonder what she's doing. Erasing me from her life for real this time? Or researching like I suggested?

The worst part of all of this is I know that I'm bad for her. I know that in the end I'll only disappoint her but I can't for the life of me stay away.

I can't let go. She's my Princess.

Sofia

The email about the job stated that I could start on Monday. Which is tomorrow. Until then I plan to stay wrapped up like a burrito in my bed, while fighting back tears and confusion.

I could pretend that I'm okay. I could move on and let the past week disappear into my mind like a distant memory or a dream. Only I know that I won't be able to do that.

Curiosity is what got me here and it's the same emotion that has me googling Elijah's name at eleven pm on the day after I made him leave.

Maybe I shouldn't be listening to a possible murdering psychopath but if I owe him anything it's doing some proper looking into it. I'm not one to jump to conclusions but yesterday I was faced with a situation that scared the shit out of me. I had to make him leave.

Clearly I'm a psycho myself because his absence has left me feeling empty. He hasn't tried to contact me and I'm not sure if I'm grateful about that or not. I mean what the hell do I expect from him? I'm not sure.

The first article says much the same as the one Annabelle sent me. A young women found dead in his apartment. Which is really no good to me.

In fact, that's all the information lots of them give. Some say she was a random women, while others say she was his former lover. None of them mention the sugar rush website which is possibly because she wasn't anything to do with that.

A lot of the articles mention that he was found innocent but they also speculate that his wealth had everything to do with that. These blogs and news reports don't offer much insight. Nor do they offer evidence.

Which is why I find myself paying for a public police report. Yup I'm that desperate to know what the hell happened. The voice in my head is saying 'well you should have just asked him you stupid bitch' but I punch her out and keep going. There's not much I can do about it know. I've acted the way I have and that's it.

The report is dated a year and two months ago. The 15th Of April 2017. The first thing on the page is a picture of Elijah walking into the police station, his head hanging with very obvious sadness. I can feel sympathy rising in me but I stop it and continue.

After the photo is a brief explanation. Yet it still gives me more information than the shitty tabloids.

'A young women named Lucy Greyson was found dead in CEO Multimillionaire Elijah Everett's pent house apartment. So far it seems the pair had a recent one night stand but that's all of the information we currently have on the connection between them'

Another part further down the report mentions drug use but doesn't say how it fits into the crime scene. How does that even make sense?

There's a lot of information that I've already seen but there's also something new.

'Elijah Everett currently has no alibi"

That doesn't make me feel good but it also suggests that this report hasn't been updated with the final outcome.

Useless!

Throwing my phone down, I cover my face and scream...and scream...then scream some more.

I do so until my throat hurts and sadness plus frustration mingle in a way that has me passing out in bed.

Too much...it's all too much! I don't even have the energy to look into Nadia Zoya's claims.

***

I'm actually surprised that I make it out of bed and to the coffee shop on time. Considering I had woken up feeling emotionally drained and very much like a zombie, it's actually a miracle.

Another miracle is that I'm able to take in anything that the little old lady owner is saying. I arrived about five minutes ago and in those five minutes, she's thrown an apron at me and made three different coffees. Three!

"You with me so far?" I hear and nod quickly to show that I am in fact still on the same planet. Doesn't really feel like it though. I didn't sleep well and I think my sore head is now a migraine. Fantastic! First day at work and I'm not exactly in top form.

After half an hour of her firing out different drinks, she hands me over to another women that works here. She's lovely and obviously sees my tired state. She basically has to show me everything all over again but she's very patient with me.

Her name is Willow. She has red hair, many piercings and must only be slightly older than me. Oh and smiles a lot. Like a lot. It's nice though since I can't get my own face to do the same today.

I spill a jug of water, I burn myself on the fancy machine and even blow some steam in my eye. Here's some advice: don't ever do that. It hurts.

I keep looking at Willow nervously as I make mistake after mistake but her repeated response is: "You're doing great Sweetie"

She's a liar but I still like her. She has wise knowledgeable eyes. Ones that have seen and experienced more life than I have. Not much more but...more.

I kinda want to ask her if she knows how to deal with the situation that I'm currently dealing with.

"Hey Willow do you have any idea how to deal with falling uncontrollably for a possible murderer? He's super hot and sweet and I'm going insane"

Nah I don't think I'll say that out loud!

She does ask about me while we're on our break though. We sit in one of the brown leather booths near the back, our coffees on wooden tables. Fake moss coats them. Something I hadn't noticed during my interview.

I tell Willow about what I studied because it's the only thing that I deem worth telling anyone. I'm like a broken down record in that sense. I just haven't achieved anything better.

She asks if I'm single too and for a second I think she's hitting on me. Scratch that, she's definitely hitting on me. Well shit, I'm a catch these days.

Unfortunately I have to tell her that 'it's complicated'. Boy that's an understatement!

"Guy or girl?" She asks sipping her coffee with a smirk on her face.

"A guy" I reply and she laughs.

"Well then, that's your problem" she jokes.

Yup, I like this women. I think we're going to get along great which makes me so fucking happy. I was terrified that no one would like me here. It's like the first day of school all over again but now I feel a lot more relaxed.

Of course I'm never going to be totally at peace. Not when I start to wonder what kind of coffee Elijah would drink.

Which is literally what I try to work out for the rest of my shift, while I get the hang of the cappuccino machine.

When I get back, my feet ache and so does my head. The feet are because of all the running around and my head is because my brain won't stop working overtime thinking about Elijah.

Checking my mail box for the first time in a few days, I pull out lots of junk just like always, until my hand grabs a small package.

What do we have here?

Inspecting it on the way up the stairs, I try to work out who could have possibly sent me anything.

I don't even bother sitting down before I open it. I just shove my door closed and tear at it.

The first thing I see is a note with slightly messy handwriting. I'm confused at first but then I see the name signed at the bottom and my heart thuds in my chest.

'Congratulations on your new job! You're going to do great. Please accept this gift. You deserve so much more but I thought this was a nice way to motivate you to keep going. You're going to achieve your dreams... I know you will. Good Luck Princess! Elijah xxx'

God damn it! Why did he have to get accused of murder? I wish I could just brush over that fact and let myself feel just how much this means to me. I haven't even seen the gift yet but the note already has tears in my eyes. Why? Because no one has even written such a nice note to me. It really does show that you can know someone for years and never find a connection. Yet here I am just over a week in and Elijah has flipped my whole life on its head. Good or bad, I can't deny that he's made things more interesting.

    Finally I look at the gift in the box. It's a silver necklace. Pulling it out, I let it dangle from my finger and happy tears roll down my face.

    The pendant is in the shape of a forward slash and pointed closing bracket from html code and I'm pretty sure this would have needed to be custom made. Holy fuck!

    I so badly want to wear it but how can I when I'll only feel like a fraud. This is so meaningful and definitely expensive.

    Although it probably didn't cost much in his opinion. I hate the thought that he actually is a psychopath and this is one of the things he does to get a kick out of his victims. Of course it's possible but that would only hurt like hell.

    He's put so much effort into it.

    I spend an unhealthy amount of time staring at the necklace. Watching it dangle from my fingers and spin a little.

    It's so beautiful.

    Maybe I should put the note in the bin and hide this in a drawer but instead I shove the note in my purse and fall asleep clutching the necklace to my chest.

    Oh yeah...I'm totally fucked up!

***

    On day three of my job the machine buzzes and whirls, making noises that are definitely going to make my head ache worse. Oh yeah it's still present. Kinda worrying at this point actually.

I'm like a robot right now because most people order the same thing and this just isn't rocket science anymore. It's safe to say I've picked everything up at lightening speed and the repetition is testing my sanity. Still at least I'm going to earn some money now.

My mind wanders to Elijah because he's all I think about. It's pretty easy to fall into a fantasy when the job I'm doing doesn't take much out of me.

I glance up, hand the guy his coffee, smile and watch him walk away. Then I go back to cleaning the machine like I was before.

Does Elijah miss me? Or has he given up because of my shitty reaction? Or...is he a murderer and pissed off that I got away?

Its either the first one or the last one because when I look up from my cleaning duties, the next customer is the man that I'm obsessing over. Jesus Fucking Christ! Be still my beating heart...literally. Have my eyes popped out of my head? Am I still breathing? Fuck! Fuck! Fuckkkk! I almost drop a glass coffee pot in my panic.

Oh god I miss him! The sleepless nights give that away for sure. Maybe it's been the same for him. His eyes look a little tired.

"Sofia" he says softly in greeting. His voice swirls into my ears soft and warm, pulling me into a false sense of security. Today he's wearing a white shirt with a navy sweater vest on top, some dress pants and those glasses that do things to me. Which he probably wore on purpose.

I have visions of pulling him over the counter to kiss his soft lips. I wanna feel his beard scratching my skin but I snap out of it quickly.

"What can I get you Sir?" I ask flatly. His lips pull up into a small smile while I keep my face straight. He's not going to get to me.

"Maybe just a moment of your time would be good" he replies softly.

"I'm sorry we don't serve that here" I retort and he frowns deeply as if he's trying to think of something to say.

"Well how about black coffee then" is what he comes out with and I'm fine with that. Plus now I know what he drinks...what a relief to my wondering mind. Seriously, I'm not even joking, it's been driving me insane.

As I pour the piping hot drink into the cup, I can feel him watching me. It makes me tingle in a weird way.

"Here you go. That'll be one fifty" I state and watch as pulls out a ten dollar bill.

"Keep the change Darling" he replies and for some reason this really irks me. Maybe he's just being nice but I don't like it.

"You can't buy me Elijah" I snap as quietly as possible, so I don't draw attention to myself. He looks momentarily hurt but my words before he composes himself.

"I know that. I was just tipping you" he says, his mouth falling into a straight line of annoyance.

"It's a bit much don't you think"

"No, I don't think it is. Nothing is too much for you"

"Stop it! Why are you here?"

"To see you of course. I would have thought by now that you'd have realised the truth"

"I done the research you asked but I'm no further forward. I still don't know what to believe" I explain and stick out my hand with the cup in it. He reaches out to take it but covers my hand with his purposely, his fingers caressing my knuckles.

"Then let me explain" he says softer now.
"There's a queue forming Elijah. You need to go"
"Let me take you out after work"
"Go..."
"Fine! But I'm not giving up! You'll have to talk to me eventually"

That's the last thing he says before he walks away. I watch his retreating form in pain. I don't want to get hurt. Not emotionally or psychically and with the way he affects me, I know it's definitely possible.

Maybe that's why I'm telling myself I'm so scared.

"Um Mam..." the next person in line cuts through my thoughts and I blink back to the here and now. I can't think about this here.

What I do know is, I wish he were still standing in front of me. Arguing with him is still communicating and that two minute conversation has set me on fire.

***

Elijah wasn't lying when he said he wouldn't give up. He came to the shop every day after that. The same time too. About noon he comes in, orders a coffee and tries to talk to me. When I say no, he sits at a table and waits to see if I'll change my mind.

So far it's been a week of that and everyday it's been getting harder. Today though, there's no way I can ignore him.

I had to take my break early because the my boss began arguing with another member of staff in the back. For a little old lady she has a loud voice on her. Unfortunately the man she was yelling at did too and it made me rather uncomfortable. I witnessed the shouting and felt the fearful feeling rise within me again. Just like always. I'm not freaking out this time but I have removed myself from the situation so that no one else needs to find out about my pathetic fear of angry men.

So when Elijah arrives right on time, he looks very confused for a second. Then he sees me and skips the coffee, opting to come right over here. He's all suited up today. He must have lots of meetings. Hot motherfucker.

"Are you okay?" He asks as soon as he gets to the booth. He slides in opposite me while I stare at the coffee mug in front of me. If I wasn't being so annoying then I'd be able to take comfort from him but alas I'm weird.

"Yeah. Just a little bit too much anger going on in the back" I reply, sighing at myself.

"Was it aimed at you?" He asks, his own anger creeping into his voice. It doesn't seem to bother me though. How strange. It's also rather nice that he wants to protect me. But does he?

"No" I tell him and catch his hand moving over the table next to mine. He hesitates for a second before deciding that he's going to take the chance. He links our fingers and I let him because I'm a selfish fucking bitch. Okay! I really am and I just can't take it anymore! I don't want to be this way. I want him back but I'm now too embarrassed and ashamed to admit it. Fucking stupid whore!

"Darling, are you sure you're okay?" he asks again, his fingers squeezing mime. The sadness radiating from me has nothing to do with the yelling in the back.

"No" I puff out and shake my head. That's all it takes for him to understand.

"Then let me talk to you properly. I can tell you exactly what happened. Do you still think I'm a crazy murderer?"

"I don't know Elijah. Maybe you are. I'm too scared to be alone with you to find out"

It's not technically a lie. I'm worried that if I give in to what I really feel then I'll be wrong and put myself at risk. I don't know what to do.

"Do you have any idea how much that hurts me Sofia?" He asks and my eyes snap to his. Damn it! I never wanted to hurt him, I really didn't.

"I'm sorry Elijah. I just don't know what to do! I'm trying my best to make sense of everything but it's not easy to trust someone who has accusations of murder on their name"

"But I didn't do it Sofia! I thought you of all people would believe me. I thought we had something"

"I don't know what we had okay!"

Liar! Fucking stupid lying bitch! I'm a coward and I know it!

I get up and leave him there because any longer and I might just flip a table.

What I don't expect is Elijah to stay exactly where he is. He sits in that booth for hours as I work, giving me longing glances with puppy dog eyes. I kinda have the urge to go over and pat his head. And maybe kiss him a little and- NO!

My boss asks me to lock up the shop and one by one, everyone leaves. There's no staff but me and I expected to find Elijah gone the next time I look up after closing the register. Nope, he's still there. Now we're alone. Fuck!

"I'm closing up the shop, you need to leave" I tell him, trying to look him in the eye. Only I can't because that'll only make me fall under his dangerous spell.

"I just want to talk to you. I want to explain everything" he says, getting up and approaching the counter.

"I'm busy Elijah" I bluff and begin to walk away through the staff door to the back. This is where all the stock is and also where I exit once it's all closed up.

I expect him not to follow me but I should really have known better.

"Sofia, why won't you speak to me? Tell me the truth?!" He asks and I whip around to glare at him.

"I told you the truth! You scare the shit out of me! Which by the way isn't helped by you stalking me in here when no one else is around" I yell. The air crackles around us just like always and I curse the world for making me feel this way. Why do I miss him? Why do I want him when he could be so very dangerous?

He rocks back on his heels, staring at me after my outburst. He looks so very hurt by what I've said and I feel bad again. Seconds later his expression changes, a smile forming and it makes me wonder if he really is just a little bit crazy.

"What is it you think I'm going to do? Murder you right here? Tell me...what do you think I'm capable of?" He asks, his tone slightly menacing. Weirdly enough, I think I like it. What the FUCK is wrong with me? I need to go to a therapist.

"I don't know. Maybe you like to mess with your victims first..."

"Ah yes, that definitely seems like something I'd do" he continues. I know he's teasing me now, trying to get a reaction out of me for some reason. He's enjoying this.

"You're having fun aren't you?" I ask bitterly and he nods enthusiastically.

"Yes, I fucking loving it Sofia. You know why? This is the most we've talked in days. Not to mention I feel so much better knowing that you really aren't scared of me. If you were, you would have ran away by now. You'd be screaming the place down but no, you're right here feeding off of me"

Am I annoyed that he's technically right? You bet your ass. Will I admit it? Over my dead body! Maybe literally...

"You're wrong" I breath and watch completely frozen as he steps towards me. Just one step.

"Am I?" Another step. My heart rate accelerates and I'd love to prove him wrong by saying that it's because of fear but it's really not.

"What are you doing?" I ask, unable to move. He's close enough to touch. I can smell his gorgeous scent but I want to snap out of it. This could be bad.

"Murdering you apparently but how will I bring you to your end hmmm?" He ponders, raising his hand. His fingers brush over my cheek and I close my eyes instinctively. They trail down my neck and I don't know what the hell to do. "I think you know the truth Darling. We're very in tune with each other...you know I wouldn't ever hurt you"

"How can I know that? Whatever is between us, it's purely sexual" I blurt out because he's stoking something inside me. Something darker than I'm used to. I want to see his emotions. I don't even know what the hell I'm doing but it feels good. So very exciting. I want him to prove me wrong. I want him to show me what I already know. What he's already shown me over and over. This isn't just sex. Even the first time we fucked it was so much more and I need that right now.

"Is that so? If it's sex you want my love then sex you will have. I told you before I'll take you in anyway I can have you. So can I have you?" he growls, his voice rough with the emotion I so desperately want. I open my eyes just in time to see the passion in his. It's beautiful.

"Why don't you find out?" I tease, begging him to take action. DEAR GOD SOFIA MAKE UP YOUR MIND!

The next thing I know he's backing me into the nearest cabinet, my back making a soft thudding noise as it makes contact. He traps me against it, one of his thighs moving between mine to part my legs. Ah shit! The gasp that comes from me is once again not one of fear and it's over for me. I want him so bad. Honestly he can kill me if he likes, I'm not sure I'd care.

"Tell me to stop Sofia. Tell me and I'll never touch you again I promise" he whispers in my ear, his hands trailing down my body. His fingers tease the button and zipper on my jeans.

My hands flies up to grip his shoulders, keeping him there. I open my mouth to try and yell at him again because I don't want to give in so easy.

"Don't...don't stop!" Is actually what comes out. Well shit!

"You're mine Darling...all mine" he moans and with that he yanks down my jeans and panties, his fingers sliding over my clit in seconds.

He watches as he touches me, his face alight with lust. I writhe and moan against him. My logical thinking tries to fight through against my wild heart but it's never going to win. Of course this isn't just sexual. I know it. He knows it.

"You're so wet for me Sofia. You don't fear me Darling...no fear" he mumbles as if he's telling himself. The thought that I'm afraid of him really has cut deep and even though I still don't know the full story, I feel guilty.

It doesn't last long because soon he's sliding his fingers inside me. His lips devouring mine. Fuck I've missed his mouth. So gentle and rough all at once.

I'm being finger fucked by my quite possibly insane lover I can't stop wanting, in the back of the coffee shop I just started working for. That's a sentence I never thought I'd use to describe my life.

This is the most crazed I think I've ever been. Yanking at his clothes like I'm some kind of animal. My only success is having him almost shirtless but he helps with his trousers, shoving them down.

I'm stroking his dick and he's swearing in my ear, his fingers curling inside me. Should this be happening right now? Probably not and certainly not here but I don't think we can stop now.

The statement 'I'm a slut for this man' have never been truer. I was just accusing him of being a murderer, now I'm sinking to my knees to suck him off. Oh yeah, I've wanted to do this for a while.

"Fuck Sofia!" He growls as I lick the tip. The shock in his voice is actually a huge turn on as well as his fingers wrapping in my hair. When I look up at him he's watching me and I can't help but smirk before slowly letting his cock push into my mouth.

Which one of us has more of the control right now? It's hard to tell. My mouth controls his moans and his desperation but he controls the rhythm, holding my hair back so he can watch.

He's such a powerful man and maybe I like that more than I want to admit. It's not to do with the money or status, it's just something that flows from him as a person. So fucking sexy.

"Oh Darling, that mouth of yours is more dangerous than I could ever be" he groans, his hips rocking harder. There's the answer. I have the control but do I want him to come down my throat or else where?

Reaching up, I cup his balls and the noise that comes from him is so guttural, making me wetter than I already am. I think I know what I want now.

Releasing his cock from my mouth, I lick my lips and look up at him. He breathes deeply, his chest rising and falling with the effort.

"You little tease" he smirks, his fingers soothing the place where he gripped my hair.

"Well I'll do anything to get you to fuck me" I reply. He's grabbing me in seconds, helping me from the floor and lifting me off my feet.

I wrap my legs around his waist and he's pushing inside of me like there's no tomorrow.

He's fucking me against the stock shelves and if I was thinking straight, I'd realise how much of a bad idea this is. Just like gripping one of the shelves and causing a case of coffee beans to smash and fall over the floor is.

It would have been wise for us to stop then but I guess this just feels far too good.

I'm holding him to me with a death grip, hoping that this marks the end of all the bullshit. I made the mistake of believing tabloids. That won't happen again. He's no murderer.

He makes me come like a nuclear bomb going off because he knows my body better than I do but more importantly he makes me feel complete. Yuck...who do I think I am? Oh fuck it...it's true okay, I've never felt so whole! This is where I'm meant to be.

He comes inside me, his lips still moulded to mine, his hands becoming more gentle and sweet. Soothing me as I catch my breath.

He leans his forehead on mine, his eyes sparkling with happiness. I guess the thing that he's dangerous to is my heart.

I want to hear the full story so that I know all the details and most importantly the truth. However, whatever he tells me won't change how I feel. I mean it never really changed a thing anyway.

What is it that I feel for him? Of course it's more than lust. We've admitted that there's something between us. But what is that something? He's not my sugar daddy, not my boyfriend, so what? Does it need a label? Does he want more than this?

I'm so confused. Yet I have a never ending sense of clarity at the same time. The answer to my problems is in my arms. Any and all of my problems. He makes it all okay. No amount of money could match this feeling.

Once I've got my bearings again I'm able to take in the mess we've made. Oops! My eyes latch onto the smashed coffee case and then a horrifying realisation hits me.

There are cameras in here. Recording everything that happens...as in there are cameras that have just recorded us fucking in the stock room.

Uh oh!

Sofia

      Slowly but surely we pull apart but not until he's kissed every inch of my face. It's the only thing that has stopped me panicking about the accidental porno we just made.

      "Looks like we have some cleaning up to do" He smirks, eyeing the spilled coffee beans. I don't think he's noticed the CCTV just yet.

      "Yeah...not just that spillage either. We're going to have to work out how to get rid of the video footage from the past half an hour..." I reply, gesturing towards one of the cameras on the wall.

      He follows my gaze and I look back at him just in time to see his mouth falling open.

      "Fuck...that is going to be a problem"

      "Mmmmmhhhh"

      Pulling my clothes back into place, I wait for Elijah to zip up his trousers and of course blush as he winks at me.

      "I'll deal with this mess so that we have one less thing to worry about" he tells me, kneeling down before reaching out to the shattered glass. My eyes widen in horror.

      "Careful" I say abruptly as he begins picking up the larger pieces. I have visions of him cutting up his fingers. "There must be a brush here somewhere" I state, glancing around.

      "You're worried I'm going to hurt myself?" He asks ever so quietly.

"Of course I am" I reply matter of factly. He looks very vulnerable then. His expression is softer than I've ever seen it and I'm not sure what he's feeling but it's definitely something. I don't think he's used to people caring or looking out for him. Even in the simplest of ways.

It makes me so sad. It's clear he craves affection yet at the same time doesn't know how to handle it. I hope I can change that in some way.

Ten minutes later the brush is found and the mess is gone. Elijah doesn't ever have to clean. So I have a great time watching him sweep awkwardly, for me to then throw out the glass into the trash can outside. That way hopefully no one will suspect a thing.

No more glass. No more coffee. Part one complete. Now for the sex tape we just made. This is going to be a bit harder I think.

Locating the computer with ease, I notice how old it. Older than my laptop, which is well...really fucking old.

Sitting down at the metal desk, I curse in annoyance as the password screen pops up. Of course it's protected... old but still protected. Guess I'll have to put in a little bit of effort to get in here.

Elijah

Does she know how amazing she is? I know the answer to that is no. She doesn't think she's all that special and that baffles me every day I spend more time with her.

I watch her fingers fly over the keys as she cracks some kind of code. I've no idea what she's doing right now, the screen is just filled with lines and lines of words and symbols. It means nothing to me but she seems to get it. I'm beyond impressed.

"Ha! Got it!" She exclaims as the video footage pops up. In awe, I stand there with my hands in my pockets wanting to express exactly what's on my mind. Only I think if I did then I'd go over the top. It's so strange to feel this way. To feel so attached to someone so quickly.

Never in my life have I looked at a person and felt such strong emotion. It's foreign to me. So I do what I do best, shove it away and focus on the present.

She scrolls through the video file and finally we appear in the footage, our bodies wrapped together half dressed. Damn we're pretty hot. Well she is.

"You know what? I think we should make our own porno" she jokes, glancing up at me.

Walking behind her, I wrap my arms around her shoulders and press a kiss to her neck. Why? Because I can't help myself.

"I'm sure that can be arranged" I whisper and she giggles. The sound flows into my ears, making me fall more and more under her spell. She has power but she doesn't even know it.

Carefully she selects the time scale needed. From us coming back here until after the sex. Then with a few more clicks the video disappears frame by frame. A few more seconds and the computer is back to its original state as if it's never been touched.

Wow, she's brilliant! I'm so lucky to even know her. I'm even luckier that she finally believes me. I'm not sure what I would have done if she had cut me off. I never rely on anyone but apparently I'm very reliant on her. I need her. It's a weird thing to admit, even to myself.

Those days without her…well they weren't pleasant at all. I was going mad.

I'm pretty sure everyone that works in my building heard of my bad mood. Maybe it's because I did a lot of yelling. I suppose I have some apologising to do. Especially to Jack.

He noticed how unfocused I was and kept asking me questions. Which only let to more yelling. I really can be an asshole. Even more so when the woman I'm besotted with thinks I'm a murder.

I'm so glad that's over.

"Come home with me Darling. We still need to talk" I ask as she stands looking very proud. So she should be.

"I know. I was planning on it" she grins and I can't help but smile back.

"Oh good, so you don't think I'm a murderer now?"

"Well, I sure hope not. Otherwise I might be in trouble"

"Oh you're already in trouble. You're sweet and intelligent, so it's going to be a problem. Maybe I'll let you live a bit longer" I joke with her and I can see she's trying to hide her blush.

"What's happened to Mr CEO Multimillionaire Serious Face? You're being soft" she laughs at me, then her face goes completely straight as if to mock me. Little minx.

"Would you prefer I called you a dirty wench?" I ask, crossing my arms.

"No, I'd prefer you called me a nasty whore" she winks and grabs my hand tugging me to the exit.

I've got it bad and I don't think there are any signs of this thing letting up.

She collects her bag, locks up and puts the keys away. The bag by the way is silver and sparkly which for some reason to me, describes her personality perfectly. It also makes me very happy.

Usually the men and women I have to associate with in the business world or at events, wear nothing but designer items. Don't get me wrong, I like expensive things too so I'm not judging. The difference is, I buy things I like whether they are expensive or not. That's why I have a huge collection of action figures in my library. Actually, I think Sofia may like those.

My point is, she's not the same as them. She likes what she likes and she's not afraid of it. She's not showing off. Other people buy things to make themselves look good. Sofia looks good anyway.

Beautiful and brilliant and mine... for now.

Sofia

I've been a big soppy mess ever since I met him. You'd never have found me reading a romantic novel or crying over a romcom. None of that appeals to me but in real life I want to write poems and love letters. No not love letters, we're not in love. Come on Sofia don't be so ridiculous. Sure we care about one another but that's all.

Jesus Fucking Christ. I gotta keep myself in check before I confess some kind of undying love and make him run away.

Like right now all I'm doing is holding his hand while we walk to his car but it's so perfect to me. It makes me feel amazing. Plus he makes me feel safe in this dark alleyway at the back of the shop.

"Did you like the gift I sent you?" He asks, almost shyly. I hadn't put it on because of obvious reasons but my god had I wanted to. Now I can and I'm super excited about it.

"I loved it Elijah. I'm sorry I don't have it on, I was just... well I was rather confused" That's my subtle way of reiterating that I thought he was a murderer without actually saying it.

"I know, I understand" he smiles softly and opens the car door for me once we reach it. I slide onto the leather seat and watch in silence as he walks around the car. I know I'm being dramatic here but I can't help but stare for those precious few seconds. He's just a normal guy but he's flipped my world on it's head and then back around again. I'm not sure how. Maybe it's just the way he looks at me or maybe it's just him.

On the short journey to his apartment, he doesn't stop glancing at me. I can feel his gaze burning into the side of my face. I like it because it makes me feel special to him. Of course I'm probably very wrong but I can let myself think that for a little while.

The elevator ride is filled with tense silence and I can sense he's nervous to tell me about what happened. Being accused of murder is bound to mess with anyone's head and although I feel bad about making him tell me, I just have to know for my own sanity.

Elijah doesn't do awkward but he sure looks it now as he walks into his apartment, offers me a drink, almost drops the glass and tugs on his hair in frustration.

"Elijah...breath" I tell him, approaching his almost terrified form with a reassuring smile on my face. "If you don't want to tell me-"

"I do want to. I just don't want you to think of me differently" he confesses.

Great! I've scared him half to death with my tendency to choose flight instead of fight. I'm a fucking idiot and I don't know why he seems to care so much for me. If I were him, I'd have told me to get lost a long time ago.

Tugging on his hand, I lead him to the couch. I'm hoping here is a good place to talk. We surely won't get distracted right? Who am I kidding? It's very possible.

He keeps my hand locked in his as we sit for a few quiet moments. I never thought I'd see him this way but I guess I kind of like the vulnerability he's showing. It means in some way he really does trust me. Well I think it does. Sure Sofia, he totally trusts you! Keep dreaming.

He presses a kiss to my lips, his mouth moulding to mine quickly. I think it was only meant to be a peck but hey, that never happens.

When we finally pull apart, he seems to have more courage and with a squeeze of my fingers he begins to talk.

"She was my sugar baby for a whole day. I met her for dinner and we were attracted to one another. Well enough to want to come back here and have sex" he starts, cringing a little as he speaks. It's probably not pleasant to say those words in front of me. I don't mind though. "After the sex, she demanded payment for the night we'd spent together. I complied and then she left. I assumed that was the last I'd hear from her. She didn't mention wanting to meet up again and I was completely indifferent"

His eyes are focused on a spot behind me, glazed over as if he's far gone in the memory. Not in a good way though. It's more of a haunted look.

I'm trying to comfort him but I'm not sure my attempt at soothing touches are getting through to him. He's frozen. This has really messed him up and I don't blame him.

"I had given her five hundred dollars and I'm pretty sure she used all of it within the next day. That's why she came back to my apartment. For more money. She had obviously noted the elevator code and was able to get back up here. It was on the CCTV. I just remember walking in and seeing her body lying there. I didn't know what to do. Or what had happened. It made no sense and I just wanted to believe I was imagining things. Of course I wasn't. She was a drug addict. She had overdosed. Probably by using the money I'd given her"

He goes on to tell me about calling the police and how quickly the press and tabloids began to speculate and attack him.

I'm finding it hard to hold back tears as he speaks so openly about every detail of the events. It's such a shame. He was traumatised but still had to go through being accused of the murder. Not to mention I no doubt just added to his pain with my rejection and unwillingness to listen.

I feel so bad and I think he can tell.

"It's okay Sofia" he mumbles, his fingers swiping at my cheeks. Turns out the tears I felt have fallen and I'm bubbling like a big kid. I'm supposed to be comforting him.

"I'm sorry I didn't believe you" I croak out and instead of answering he cocoons me in his arms, his face burrowed in my neck. His hands run up and down my back and my crying stops as I listen to the steady rhythm of his heart.

"I guess I maybe should tell you about my parents too, unless you want to wait until another night?" He asks. There's no point in waiting though. It may as well all come out now.

So we keep talking and he speaks of his parents death. A car crash. He mentions how cliche it is with a weak laugh but then gets sad as he talks about how much they meant to him. How much he thought he needed them and how much he wanted to please them. Even if they didn't have much time for him in return. He was so young and yet he took over a whole empire in his fathers absence. He didn't get to college or university because of this. This is also when he tells me how much his company is a burden. One he doesn't want but feels he has to maintain out of guilt. He can't bring himself to give it up. Then he goes on to tell me how his wealth led to him being isolated. From being a kid with friends who only wanted him for the fancy things. To being an adult who couldn't connect to anyone for fear of being used for such wealth. Which led to the sugar daddy thing at such a young age. Obviously he's told me bits and pieces of this part but now it's all coming together.

"I hadn't been a sugar daddy in a year when I met you Sofia" he confesses and I frown in confusion.

"What? Why?"

"I didn't want to be. Not after Lucy. It was like a sign for me to stop"

"So how are we here?" I ask, trying to work out how this all adds up.

"I meant to delete the sugar rush app but I must have forgotten. So when you liked my profile, I got the notification"

"But it was a year of time. Surely you would have gotten a lot of notifications" I reply, trying to make sense of it.

"Not many sugar babies do the liking" he tells me, smirking a little.

"Why didn't you ignore the notification?" I ask, incredibly curious.

"Your profile was unlike one I'd ever seen. It made me want to meet you. I tried not to but I couldn't stop thinking about you. All from that profile" he explains and I don't even have a reply. This is crazy. It all seems like it was meant to be.

Oh stop it!

It's true though. If he hadn't looked at my profile we would never have met.

That thought has me kissing his lips in a panic!

He's been lonely as hell and yearning for someone to care for.

I'm literally speechless. It's a lot to take in but I'm so grateful. I want to know it all.

He even mentions Nadia Zoya's accusations and how his lawyer made sure they fell through quickly. He promises me over and over again that he didn't hurt her while I reply over and over that I believe him.

We get it all out. All of our thoughts and questions. I tell him about my parents a bit more. About the good parts of my childhood. How my Mom and Dad would much rather have had me stay in Ohio but supported me anyway. How I still can't bring myself to go back. He looks curious then, desperate to know all the details but unfortunately, I'm still not able to get it all out. I even tell him about the first boyfriend I had when I was about thirteen. When I mention that I'd been dumped for being boring, he doesn't look pleased.

"Do you know where this guy lives? Full name?" He says gruffly, his expression all serious and protective. He crosses his arms over his chest and sits back, looking at me.

"Why?" I question warily. I'm trying not to laugh though because I have a feeling I know what he's getting at.

"Oh you know I just want to pay him a visit. Maybe have a chat" he begins and I nod slowly, unable to hold my grin back. "Maybe punch him in the fucking face"

"Okay, I don't think that's a good idea. He was just a kid like me. Plus, I'd rather not see him again. So if you punch him I'd have to be there to stop you from straight up beating his ass" I laugh and Elijah's face breaks out into a grin.

"I'd be able to control myself" he states.

"No, he was super annoying so I don't think you would. You don't have to worry about what he said anyway. I know I'm friggin awesome" I joke and he nods in agreement.

"You are friggin awesome" he repeats and smothers me in kisses. He's playful now and I love seeing him this way.

He's a hard faced business man who takes no shit from anyone but with me he's just the sweetest man in the world. I'm so happy that I get to be his for however long this is going to last. I love this. Right here right now. I love- anyway that's enough of that.

"Okay I think we deserve some real greasy take out after all of that deep stuff" I laugh, biting my lip at his joy filled face. I think a weight is off his shoulders now.

"It's like you read my mind Darling. What am I thinking now?" He asks. Shifting closer I press my fingers to his temples and close my eyes.

"Hmmmm, well once I get past all of the dirty thoughts in here, I'm seeing pizza"

Opening my eyes, I find him looking back at me in mock shock. He's just the cutest. Wow...I can't deal with him.

"Amazing...pizza is exactly what I want. Pizza then hopefully you naked" he smirks and pecks my lips. "Maybe I could be naked too" Another kiss. "Maybe you could wrap those thighs around my head" Kiss. Dear god help me I'm melting!

***

The pizza was delicious and so was the taste of his skin as I kissed down his chest, his fingers wrapped in my hair. It's safe to say we did plenty making up and many romantic words were whispered in my ear. So many in fact I found it hard to remember that he's probably not the person I'll get to spend the rest of my life with.

There's no way I'll get to keep this man but I can't bare to think about that.

It's funny that a month ago I didn't even care about having anyone by my side. Now if he were to leave or reject me I'd quite possibly get put in a mental hospital because of the sadness it would cause. The heartbreak.

Maybe thinking about that before going to sleep was a bad idea. No it was definitely a bad idea.

In my turbulent dream state, my mind conjures up a fantastically vivid scene of Elijah telling me he doesn't want me anymore. It's so real that the tears that stream down my face actually feel damp as my hands touch my face.

"You can't leave me like this!" I yell. Horror filling my voice dramatically as his face breaks into a sadistic grin. Jesus fucking Christ.

"Of course I can. Did you really think I'd never get bored of you? Your ex was right, you're a fucking drag!" He shouts back.

Damn! Praying on my insecurities is just plain evil!

The dream- well nightmare changes to something new. I guess you may be wondering how I know it's a nightmare when I said it's so real. Well there's a distinct giveaway. Elijah doesn't look quite so perfect as he doesn't in real life. The only explanation is a dream.

Now I have to witness him with another women. I try to close my eyes but I can't. It's like they're glued open so that I'm forced to watch the one thing that has now became my worst fear. Three weeks of knowing this man and my whole life's ambitions and phobias have changed.

As he kisses her my mind can't take it anymore. Jolting awake I gasp for air in the dark room. My lungs fill just like normal but the panic inside me doesn't lessen. It only gets worse when I reach to my side for Elijah and find the space empty.

Oh god! Was it real after all? Am I all alone? Don't be ridiculous Sofia! He's probably just gone for a drink of water.

Taking a few deep breaths, I try to make the feeling of loneliness subside. My hands instinctively go to my face to rub my eyes and that's when I feel the dampness on my cheeks just like in my dream. I was crying in real life. My god what is wrong with me? I have to pull myself together!

Lying back down in bed, I swipe at my cheeks in frustration. I'm glad he's not here to see the state I'm in right now. It's somewhat pathetic! No it's extremely pathetic!

Glancing at the clock on the bed side cabinet I see that it's three thirty am. Sighing, I close my eyes and pray that I can fall asleep.

Of course that was never going to happen. Instead I stare at the dark ceiling wide awake. The next time I look at the clock it's just after four am. Still no sign of Elijah and even though logically I'm sure he's fine, I still get the urge to go look for him.

"No Sofia just fucking wait..." I say, then realise how crazy I am for talking to myself. Oh boy he should dump me now before I get really attached. Wait... too late for that!

Eventually I admit defeat and swing my legs out of the side of the bed. With some difficulty, I switch the lamp on and locate his discarded boxers and shirt to pull on. Cliche I know. Don't judge my romantic tendencies. Or maybe its just the person writing this lacks imagination. Either way, I like the smell of him, the scent hitting my nostrils quickly.

My plan is to go down to the kitchen because I assume that's where he will be but two steps outside the bedroom and a soft sound can be heard. Music? Singing?

Trying to be as quiet as possible, I strain to hear where it's coming from. My ears decide it's the room down the hall. A room I've never been in.

Maybe I should go back to bed. This is probably invading his privacy right?

Rocking back and forth on my heels, I think about what I should really do. Probably not go to the door and press my ear against it. Yet somehow my legs are moving all by themselves and I have absolutely noooo control over them.

Before I know it I'm squished against the door and it immediately becomes obvious that the noise is singing. Not only that but it's Elijah that's doing it. Holy shit!

"If I go, will you go with me? Don't leave now, let us just be"

Well...I don't even...what am I supposed to do now? The beautiful soulful words hit my ears and I've no idea what they're about but they actually bring tears to my eyes.

When the singing stops, a frustrated sigh follows and I step back to stare at the door, unsure of what to do now. My legs are useless at this point and obviously my emotions aren't going to help me right now. God his voice is amazing.

Before I can work out what to do next, the door opens and I'm caught red handed by a surprised Elijah. He stands in front of me in a t-shirt and sweat pants. I'm not going to lie, the sweat pants distract me for a moment because I've never seen him wear something so casual but soon my gaze snaps back to his unreadable face. Is he mad?

"Why were you standing out here?" He asks, slight annoyance creeping into his tone.

"Um, I woke up and you weren't there so-"

"So you thought you'd snoop around?" He cuts me off, glaring harshly. Shit. I didn't think he'd be this angry about me coming to find him.

"I'm sorry, I didn't mean to be nosey or anything. I just missed you and-" I have to stop because his face transforms, breaking into a grin. I watch as his shoulders shake from trying to hold back laughter. That asshole! He's messing with me! "You're a dick!" I exclaim, swatting his chest.

"I couldn't resist. When I saw your 'deer in the headlights' expression I had to!" He chuckles, stepping closer to yank me into his arms. "I'm sorry Darling"

"You will be!" I snap just before he brushes a thumb over my cheek. His laughter disappears, replaced by concern.

"You've been crying?" He asks, frowning at me. I'd completely forgotten about that.

"I had a shitty dream and I woke up crying. Weird I know but there it is" I tell him quickly, not meeting his eyes.

"Well let's see if I can make you feel better..."

I like the sound of that even though I'm dying to ask about his singing. I get the feeling it's something he might want to keep private for now.

***

Elijah had a lot of work to catch up on. Which is why I haven't been able to see him for a few days. Although earlier he had called and asked if I'd come to his building so that he could see me. His exact words were: "I miss you Darling and

I'd really like to see you, so if you can spare any time, why don't you come visit me"

His voice had been silky sweet and full of a desire that I obviously couldn't say no to. Let's face it, I miss him just as much but I don't want to admit that I've been lying awake unable to sleep because he hasn't been there. Surely that can't be the reason. I can't be that obsessed! Right?

Anyway, that's why I'm now walking over pristine marble floors, my sneakers squeaking a little with every step.

This is the top floor of the very tall skyscraper with his name imprinted on the front door glass. Oh and in a lot of different other places too. Everett and Son Industries.

A lady had greeted me on entrance, so that she could swipe the censor in the elevator to let me up here.

Glass, granite, shiny surfaces, white leather couches, big biggggg windows. Kind of like his apartment but even more neutral. It's very 'Fifty shades of Grey' and I wonder if that's where he got his inspiration. I'll have to ask him about it. I wonder if he has any desire to spank? I also think I'd actually quite like that. He did mention it once.

Clear your mind, you're in a professional place Sofia! Yet I couldn't look any less professional. I wish I'd dressed up a little but unfortunately I'm only in jeans and a t-shirt because why wouldn't I be?

This place screams class and importance but I'm not sure why I expected any different. Elijah is very classy and important. To my left there's a reception desk, to my right a seating area and a few doors which I assume lead to offices. Directly opposite me are two larger doors that are different from the others. I can tell from the sleek woods style and the logo once again imprinted on the frosted glass panels that those doors will lead me to Elijah.

Approaching the blonde haired man at the reception desk, I struggle to think of a sentence that would be appropriate. How do I introduce myself? 'Hey I'm Elijah's...what? What am I?

"Hi there, I'm here to see Elijah. I'm his...friend" is ultimately what I go with. Wow I'm awkward as hell and this guy knows it. It shows as he smiles back at me, yet looks unsure on how to respond.

"Do you have an appointment to see Mr Everett?" He asks, putting emphasis on Elijah's second name. Clearly I'm not supposed to say his first name but why not? I've never called him Mr Everett in a serious manner and I undoubtedly never will.

"No but he asked me to come see him" I reply, even more awkwardly than before. It's safe to say I'm actually becoming distressed by this interaction. I'm socially awkward at the best of times so I'm drowning in it now.

"I'm afraid you'll have to make an appointment" he says politely. I know he's just doing his job but I want to see my man. It's urgent really...I need...well I need to squish myself against him and have him wrap me in his arms. It's really important!

Turning away and walking to the seating area, I pull out my phone and call Elijah. He answers on the second ring.

"Darling, are you here?" He asks immediately, his voice sounding very much excited. How sweet, he really has missed me.

"Yes but I'm not allowed to see you without an appointment" I laugh and he sighs in frustration.

"I'm going to fucking kill him" is the last thing I hear before the line goes dead. Oh dear, I think I may have gotten the poor guy in trouble. Turning back around, I give him an apologetic smile which of course he doesn't understand until those fancy doors are yanked open.

"Lewis! This lovely lady is the very person I told you I would be expecting. So why is she still standing here?" He asks, slight irritation showing. Still polite though and that amazes me.

He comes to my side and wraps his arm around my waist. His body heat warms me up instantly and it's honestly a struggle not to just snuggle into his side. He looks good too because of course he does.

I can hear Lewis explaining himself. Something along the lines of not knowing what time I'd be getting here. That's all I can make out though because I'm too distracted by Elijah's gorgeous face and enticing scent. His beard is a little thicker than usual as he seems to have forgone his usual routine of trimming it. It's looks amazing though.

His navy suit fits him like a glove. My eyes drag all the way to his feet and back to his face before getting mesmerised by his lips as he speaks. Oh and those glasses... I swear he was only created to fuck me up really good. Let's face it, if someone asked me my own name right now I'm not sure I'd know the answer. I think it begins with S.

"In future, send Miss Westwood straight to my office. If I'm in a meeting then come and inform me that she's here please" I hear Elijah say, his slight irritation gone. He may be a hard ass to his employees but he's also respectful which I...well respect.

"Of course Mr Everett. I'm sorry Mam" Lewis apologises and I feel bad that I've gotten him in trouble.

"It's okay honestly. I guess I should have been clearer" I tell him and watch in confusion as Lewis struggles to reply. Maybe he's not used to such replies. It's quite possible most of the people he meets are less forgiving.

"Have a nice afternoon" is what he comes out with just before Elijah takes my hand and leads me into his office. Well I say office but it's bigger than my whole apartment. I think I'll just call it his space. Yes, that suits it better.

The warmth of his palm against mine pretty much eradicates the last few minutes of conversation from my mind and I'm back to only being able to focus on him.

Once the door clicks shut he turns to me, immediately dipping his head to press our lips together. Wrapping my arms around his neck, I pull him closer and we pretty much just stand there smooching. I imagine it would look pretty cute from someone else's perspective but I'm glad that I'm the one he's kissing and not simply watching.

"You're wearing it" he sighs happily as we pull apart, his fingers brushing over my necklace.

"Of course I am. I love it" I reply, trying not to gush even more about how much this actually means to me. No one has ever gotten me something so personal and gorgeous.

"I'm so glad Darling. How have you been?" He asks, tugging me over to his desk. I lean against it, taking him in as he stands in front of me. He already knows the answer to this question because we've been calling each other every day.

"Good. Working. Nothing exciting" I push out, getting distracted by him. "Got my first pay cheque from the coffee shop yesterday"

He steps forward, placing his hands on the desk on either side of me. This means he has to lean down, his nose almost touching mine. A zing of excitement shoots through me just like it has done every time he's been close to me previously. Even the first date. It's so hard to pinpoint what it means.

"Congratulations Darling. I'm proud of you" he replies, his lips brushing over mine. "Is there anything you need from me?" He questions and I actually think I could ask for anything and he'd give me it. It's a funny question, like he's trying ensure he's up-keeping his promise to look after me.

"Nothing material" I reply and he nods once, his eyes a little sad.

"I feel as though I haven't done enough for you. I don't know how to care for someone who doesn't want money" he breaths. "It's all I'm good for"

"Don't say that. It's not true. I want this from you…"

I lean forward and close the distance between our lips softly. "I want your time. You're company. Your affection. That's what taking care of someone is. I want to do the same for you" I tell him, making sure my voice is filled with the emotion I'm feeling.

"Sofia…" he sighs my name as if he doesn't know what else to say.

Then his lips hit mine. Hard this time.

Something I've noticed about Elijah is he's very gentle with me. Even in passionate moments when his fingers dig into my skin, he's still touching me with care. Gentle-roughness is how I'm going to describe it.

When our lips separate, he stays close and his hand trails up my arm. Our kiss seems to have made him remember something.

"I'd like to take you away. Wherever you'd like to go. Just the two of us. So we can do more of this" he pauses to peck my lips before continuing. "And so that I can spend the whole time finding out all there is to know about Sofia Westwood. In case you haven't noticed already, I'm very intrigued by you" he explains, the side of his mouth curling up. There isn't much more to know about me but hey I'll try to sound interesting.

For a man who stated in his bio that he didn't have time for a proper relationship, he really is making an effort for me. I'd be lying if I said this didn't make my heart beat faster and my emotions get so far out of control that I become speechless.

Which is why he's currently staring at me waiting on my answer. While I struggle to make my brain work. Come on Sofia. Say something...say literally anything.

Suddenly we're interrupted by a loud knock on the office door and Elijah throws a look of annoyance over my shoulder.

Standing up straight, he crosses he arms over his chest and yells.

"Come in!"

It's very clear he's pissed that our moment has been ruined and that only makes me more mushy inside.

Jumping off his desk, I stand next to him as Lewis enters. He looks flustered and kinda terrified too.

"I'm sorry to interrupt Sir, it's just Miss Zoya is attempting to enter the building and she won't leave" he blurts out.

Nadia Zoya. The women who Elijah banned from his building and oh yeah the women who accused him of assault. What the hell is she here for? I'd love to smack that bitch!

"Get security to make her leave" Elijah responds and Lewis shakes his head.

"They're with her but she still isn't budging"

"Fine, I'll fucking move her!" He growls. This makes my stomach turn but this time it has nothing to do with his anger. I know exactly what will happen if he goes down there. So when he goes to leave, I grab his arm.

"Elijah, this is what she wants. If you go down there and start yelling at her in front of the public eye, what do you think will happen?" I ask.

His angry expression is firmly in place as he looks at me. Then it's like it slowly drains away and gets replaced by some kind of confusion. He's not used to having anyone telling him what to do or even suggesting anything.

"You're right" he says softly before turning back to Lewis.

"Call the police. Surely they can make her leave" He commands. Lewis leaves to do just that immediately and Elijah turns back to me. "I'm sorry about that. The women is insane!" He apologises but I'm not sure why. It's not his fault.

He's right. This women seems to be absolutely crazy and that's coming from me. I may not be medically insane but I definitely think something happened to my brain during birth. Most people describe me as 'quirky'. That's just a polite way for weird but Elijah doesn't seem to mind.

"You don't have to apologise" I tell him and he relaxes, becoming rather animated again.

"I was saying something about taking you away wasn't I? Where would you like to go?"

"You're giving me the choice?" I ask, trying to squash down the shock and thrill all at once. I never thought I'd get asked such a question. I'm freaking out!

"Yes Darling, the choice is yours. Wherever you'd like to go..."

"Well what are my choices?" I question naively, even though I know the answer. I'm trying to process it. I'm not used to having so many options and possibilities but if I'm honest the most exciting thing about all of this is getting to have him all to myself. It's crazy how fast someone can become important to you. Well either that or I'm just crazy in general. Probably the latter.

"You have a choice of the whole planet really" he smirks. Where have I always wanted to go? That's a tough question. Everywhere, is the answer but I have to find somewhere to start. Somewhere realistic for a short break away. Outside of America may be a bit far but I guess there's no harm in gathering some intel.

"Where in Europe would you suggest? You do seem like a well travelled man after all"

"Well, I've been a few places. How about we discuss it over dinner? I want to get out of here and I want you out of here too. I can't be too careful especially with Nadia still lurking around" he explains and with that I grab his hand, pulling him out of his office.

I wave to Lewis on the way by and he looks shocked as I tug Elijah with me. He's probably never seen Elijah holding anyone's hand. I guess that's a win for me.

I'm rather happy with myself until we get outside and he drops my hand as if he's been burned. Huh? What's his problem? Maybe he doesn't want to been seen being affectionate in public. I'm trying not to let that hurt my feelings but I'm not that strong.

So I stay silent for the rest of the walk from the rear exit to his car. I stare out of the windshield while he gets in and the silence continues as he clicks his seat belt into place.

"I'm sorry Darling" he says gruffly, his gaze forward. Clearly he can tell I'm hurt. It's not surprise really when I'm sitting here with my arms crossed like a big kid. I'm so fucking dramatic.

"Are you embarrassed of me?" I ask, even though I probably don't have the right. We're.Not.A.Couple!

"Of course not! Quite the opposite Sofia" he turns to me but I don't want to look at him for fear he will see how weak I am. "I can't hold your hand in public in case people see...okay that sounds terrible but it's not for the reason you think. It's because if people know that we're a thing then you become a target. You become a news headline. Someone for people to harass. I don't want that for you Darling. You don't deserve it"

God damn it. Why does he always have to be so sweet yet so unattainable?

I can't help but turn to him now and see his soft pleading expression. I imagine he's begging me to understand. Which I do and it has me freaking out in the most terrifying way. I'm so fucked with this man. He's going to mess me up in the best way.

"I don't care if people harass me Elijah. I just want to hold your hand" Nope. I did not just say that. No. Yuck! I'm going to be sick. Uhhhhhhhh.

"Here" he whispers, taking my hand in his. Then he leans forward to seek out my lips. A perfect apology. Only our lips don't meet because of the harsh knocking on the car window! It reminds of the night we went to the cinema. The world really wants to interrupt all our best moments huh?

We pull apart from each other and turn to the irritating sound. I can't see Elijah's face now but as soon as he sees who it is, anger pours from him like a tangible aura. In my case, I'm in shock.

This must be Nadia fucking Zoya. I can tell because she's beautiful. Like a literal goddess. Why would I assume this is Nadia because of her beauty? Well because that's how much my insecurities want to fuck with me.

"Open the window!" She yells but it's slightly muffled because of the window she just mentioned. I like that window. It's keeping her out and away from Elijah.

He turns back to me, annoyance clear on his face.

"Let's get out of here shall we?" He asks, revving the engine.

"Let's!" I smirk and he grins back at me mischievously.

I have visions of him hitting the gas and us tearing out of here and away from the bitch. Only she opens her big mouth again.

"Hey Sofia! How are you doing honey? Why don't you tell your boyfriend to open the window"

How the fuck does she know who I am?

I watch as Elijah's hands tighten on the steering wheel and instead of slamming the gas, he slams the window button with his finger.

Oh dear. This won't be pretty!

Elijah

In normal circumstances I'd loose my shit and tell Nadia to fuck off and bother someone else. That's exactly what I want to do, especially since obviously she's been doing her research on Sofia. I thought I'd been careful. I thought that no one knew I was with anyone serious but I wasn't careful enough. To be honest I'd quite like to open the car door and smack the life draining leech with it. That's a bit violent though.

Having Sofia in the passenger seat has a certain kind of calming affect on me. She's here and safe. Nadia can't hurt her. So with my new found calming balm, I ask:

"What do you want?"

I'm not going to lie and say that I don't still sound as irritated as I feel but it's an improvement.

"You know what I want. Some of your property or maybe even shares in your business. That sounds better actually. Oh and the other offer still stands" she smirks and unfortunately I know what she means. Just like before I still have no desire to fuck her.

"I'm going to have to say no to both of those offers. Just like I have every fucking time you've asked. Take the hint"

"No one ever says no to me so you can understand why I'm having a hard time with it. How about we at least chat about it properly? Our last meeting was cut short by your manhandling. Do you remember? You were a little rough with me"

Her tone is teasing, her gaze shooting by me to the passenger seat . I'm about to open my mouth to tell her she better stop when Sofia beats me to it.

"You know for a women who at first glance seems really intelligent, you're actually pretty dumb. I mean if you were serious about doing business then you wouldn't try to seduce the person whom you wish to do business with. To me, all that says is you aren't actually a serious business women but instead an attention seeker with a little too much time on your hands. In future I suggest you use your brain instead of your tits!"

Holy fuck. My girl is on fire! And she's not done yet.

"And accusing him of assault was a shitty and stupid move too. Because let's face it, if you had achieved what you set out to do then you really wouldn't have won. What was the plan? He goes to jail, you wrangle some of his business? If it had worked then you'd be left with a bad taste in your mouth knowing that you didn't get those shares simply because of your intelligence. You got them by cheating the system. Work on your tactics Nadia and work out what you really want to stand for before you end up ruining your own life"

Nadia stands there with her mouth half open, unblinking in shock. It's hilarious in fact. Sofia just beat her at her own game and I really want to kiss the life out of her and fuck her with so much gratitude. She amazing.

With Nadia frozen in place I push the window button again, this time with glee as it glides up and shuts her out.

Then I finally hit the gas and wrack my brain to try and find the right words to thank Sofia. I'm truly grateful for everything she just said because not only was it true but it put Nadia in her place in a way that I don't think I could have. I don't think I'll be hearing from her in the near future which means neither will Sofia and I can relax knowing that she won't be harassed. One thing that Sofia does for me that no one else ever has...she supports me. She has my back. She puts my mind at ease and this is no different. She's literally a fucking goddess and I found that incredibly sexy. My hard dick confirms that.

One glance at her and I can see the tension rolling off her. A tension matching mine. She's still angry. I don't want to let Nadia ruin our night. I wanna see her smiling and have her laughing. I'm not sure that dinner is the right idea now and honestly the only place I want to be is between her legs. Just like she's reading my mind, she says:

"Can we go back to your place please?"

Sofia

  I don't even know where all of that came from. First I was just angry because of what she tried to do to Elijah then it escalated. She is so nonchalant about the things she does that it infuriates me. I work my ass off every fucking day to try and get to the places I want to be. To try to achieve my dreams and aspirations. While she takes her accomplishments for granted and lowers herself to sleazy underhanded methods. I want so much from this world in the way of achievements. She already has it all and doesn't give a shit. If I was in her position I'd be trying to better myself even further. Maybe that's why I connect with Elijah so much. He's driven and I think he sees that quality in me too.
  I can't shake the anger inside me but I can feel it turning into something else. It's stemming from an undeniable need to protect Elijah. That's what set me off after all.
  She tried to put him in fucking jail. That's where my anger began and it's came full circle back around. God I'm so invested in him that it's scary. Too many emotions flying around and I need to get them out.
  Beside me Elijah drives with a certain toughness in his jaw. His knuckles white on the steering wheel.

I do my best to keep my hands to myself but that was never going to happen. Reaching over, I slide my hand onto his thigh and he sucks in a sharp breath of air.

"Darling, if you keep that up I'll crash the car" he growls, while I smirk with glee.

"Concentrate then...eyes on the road" I reply and brush my fingers over the bulge in his trousers.

I can tell that he's struggling to keep his gaze forward, his body rigid with the effort. Something I've noticed about Elijah when we're doing anything at all, sexual or otherwise is he likes to look at me. Giving me his full attention and taking everything in. I'm not going to lie, it makes me feel pretty damn amazing.

Teasing him like this is quite possibly my favourite thing to do. The power is mine, I can make him squirm simply by fluttering my fingers over his cock. It's hard and straining against his trousers.

I guess you could say I'm a women possessed as I undo the button and zipper. It's a bit of a struggle and I can't imagine I look very glamorous glaring at the offending piece of clothing.

Elijah doesn't seem to mind, one hand on the steering wheel and the other reaching out to touch me.

"No touching, keep those hands on the wheel" I command and he whines a little in protest before following my order. Yes, I like this a lot.

He shifts in his seat and I take this opportunity to free his cock, stroking it as best as I can while leaning over the centre console.

It's gonna be ever harder to give head in a car but I'm going to give it my best shot.

It doesn't take Elijah long to work out my plan and his eyes shoot to me as I unclip my seatbelt (Don't try this at home).

"Sofia, put your belt back on! I'd much rather keep you alive to suck my dick many more times after this" he exclaims but I lean down and wrap my lips around the head of his cock anyway. "Shit!" He gasps. Hehe.

The cussing continues as I work my mouth over him and I get so carried away that I barely notice the rest of the journey. I'm too focused as the feeling of his cock hitting the back of my throat makes my eyes water.

The sound of him groaning is response is like music to my ears. It urges me on.

The car darkens slightly as he drives into the underground garage and I don't think I've ever been so happy. I want to have him all over me.

As soon as the car stops, he relaxes into the seat and slides his fingers into my hair, effectively giving him a better view of my actions.

"Fuck that feels good baby" he moans, guiding my head and rocking his hips ever so slightly. His obvious enjoyment has me soaking between the legs and I can't wait for him to be there.

"Sofia, I need you. Please..." he begs and I can't argue with that. I release him and look up, licking my lips.

His flushed face is a lovely sight, his eyes glazed over with desire...

The next few moments are a blur. Exiting the car, the elevator ride, the doors opening to his apartment, his hand tightly wrapped in mine...all a haze.

Once we're in the foyer he tugs me to him, his lips crashing into mine. It's amazingly animalistic the way we try to get each other's clothes off but it isn't very successful.

We end up trying to find the quickest way to be joined. Which means we're still half dressed as I bend over the kitchen table and reach back to yank him closer to me.

He grabs my hips and in the next second his cock is sliding inside me. I actually moan in relief which is not something I will ever admit to anyone. I mean I'm so desperate for him that I'm actually relieved to have him deep inside me. Wild! And kinda insane.

"Harder baby!" I beg him and he does exactly as I ask. He takes my hands and holds them behind my back effectively restraining me, then uses the leverage to thrust into me harder.

"Like this Sofia? Is this how you like to be fucked?" He croons bending over me to whisper in my ear. "Do you like being at my mercy?" He growls, his tone teasing now.

"I fucking love it, I'm not going to lie" I pant and hear him laughing darkly. Well fuck. Listen, if he asked me to call him Master right now I probably wouldn't say no.

"I love this Darling. All of this" he responds, releasing his grip on my hands. "I didn't know sex could feel this good"

I love that Elijah let's his feelings out during sex. I love that he can't stop himself. I also love that he's so right. I didn't know sex could feel this good either.

He glides his hands up my stomach, prompting me to stand up. With my back flush against his chest, I feel him bending his knees so that he can push up into me, a hand gripping my thigh to pull my legs apart.

"I need you closer" he groans. The first response that comes into my mind is 'You can have me closer forever if you like'. However I decide against that and just say the first part.

"Have me closer then"

He spins me around to face him and kisses me with so much passion I almost fall over. My body tingles, pleasure shooting out in every direction and that's just from touching him.

Lifting me in his arms, he carries me through his apartment while I work on getting the rest of his clothes off.

Somehow I remove his shirt and he steps out of his trousers properly. It doesn't take him long to do the same to me once we reach his bedroom. No more half dressed bullshit. Now I can touch all of him.

We land on the bed in a mess but I'm spreading my legs and pulling him closer before I can take another breath. He's quick to push inside me, his thighs warming mine as his cock hits deep.

"Good god Sofia! You make me fucking feral"

I feel the same as my nails dig into his back and drag down to his ass. He's got such a good ass.

Elijah is so expressive. He tells me everything he's thinking and it's amazing to me. He's not shy at pouring compliments and sweet dirty words from his mouth.

Passion. Overwhelming passion. That's what our sex consists of. Chemistry beyond belief. Every touch like heaven. Fireworks. Heat.

All of these things make us perfect together. We touch each other as if we're madly in love. The way he caresses me and takes care of my needs, scream admiration and devotion.

Yet we balance on the edge. The edge between a real relationship and one that we can't quite name.

I wish no money had been given. I wish he was really mine and that there was no possibility of him throwing me away.

Luckily that thought dies as quick as it arrived as Elijah stares down at me, eyes filled with affection.

Maybe we haven't labelling this thing between us but that doesn't stop the way he makes me feel. It doesn't stop the pleasure from tearing through my body or his name passing my lips in a chant.

When his own pleasure consumes him, his arms wrap around me and finally he collapses on top of me. Being sandwiched into the mattress by his satisfied body is a luxury I don't usually get. He's always careful not to fall on top of me like a sack of potatoes. Its one of his strange gentlemanly quirks.

This is nice. He mustn't have been able to stop himself tonight and I'm extraordinarily happy about it.

"Shit" he mumbles, his breathing ragged. "Sorry" he continues, pushing up onto his elbows to look down at me.

"What for?" I ask, running my fingers through his hair.

"Squashing you" he smirks and I shake my head.

"I liked it. You should do it more often"

I'm being serious when I say that. He doesn't have to be subdued with me in any way.

"Okay" is his one word response. It's breathy and kind of sounds like he's thanking me. I hate to think of the previous women he's been with, no doubt wanting him away from them as soon as the sex was done. It infuriates me that they might not have appreciated what they had.

In the silence that follows our passion, he shifts to my side, his fingers gliding over my stomach. His lips press to my cheek and my face breaks out into an uncontrollable grin.

Turning my head towards him, I can't help but comment on his soft relaxed features.

"You're cute" I whisper and he raises his eyebrows at me.

"No one's ever called me cute" he responds. "But I think I like it coming from you"

"What do people usually call you?"

"Asshole, Bastard, ATM" he replies with a smirk on his face.

"Surely not everyone has such mean names for you"

"Everyone except you it seems but I'm sure you'll get there" he tells me with a slight hint of worry shaking his voice. Without replying I trace my fingertips over his cheek and down, feeling the beard I love so much.

"Don't be so sure. Well, unless you start being an asshole to me" I pout, looking as sad as I can.

"I use all of my 'nice' on you and save the asshole for everyone else Darling" he chuckles, squeezing me to him.

"Lucky me" I whisper against his lips. It's a lighthearted comment but I mean it. I do feel lucky that I get the real him.

In the low light, I can feel him staring at me. I can make out the outline of his face. He caresses my cheek and I can tell from the shift in atmosphere that he's about to say something that maybe he usually wouldn't. Something he's not used to.

"No... lucky me. I'm so lucky that I get to be with you. That I get-"

His sweet confession is cut off by the sound of a phone ringing. By the proximity, it seems to be coming from my jeans on the floor.

I want to ignore it so that I can hear what else he has to say. I will the ringing to stop but as quick as the moment came, it's gone.

"You should get that, it might be important" he muses but it's just a way to change the subject.

I am so very pissed off at whoever just ruined what could have be a heart felt confession. It actually takes me a good few seconds to work up the energy and will power to untangle myself from him to get the phone.

After some searching, I find it and see the caller ID on the screen. It's my Mom and I think I already know what she's going to ask before I answer it. I haven't seen her since she visited, so she's probably going to do her monthly inquiry into when I'm going to be able to come home and visit. Every time, I say no but she never gives up.

Lying back down in bed, I hit accept and lean my head on Elijah's chest. His fingers go straight to my hair, playing with it softly. Maybe this isn't the best thing for him to do in case I fall asleep mid call.

"Hey Mom, how's things?"

"Hey Sofia! Things are the same as always Honey. How are things with you?"

"You know they're pretty good right now" I tell her, glancing up at Elijah who smiles down at me. "The job is going well and I'm starting to make some money" I continue quietly.

"Oh wow that's fantastic! I'm so proud of you honey!" She exclaims. "When are you coming home so we can celebrate?"

There it is.

Just like always a twinge of sadness hits me. Of course I want to be able to go home. I just can't.

Fuck. How do I get out of this?

"I'm not sure. Maybe once I'm able to save up a bit more" I bluff without thinking. I could afford it if I wanted to. I could use the money that Elijah gave me but I just can't go.

My Mom will buy this excuse but when I glance at Elijah he's frowning at me in confusion because well... he knows I have the cash.

My Mom expresses her sadness while I watch Elijah get up and walk out of the room. I immediately assume I've offended him somehow. Maybe he thinks I've spent all his money already.

He soon returns with his phone and I wonder why he's still looking so damn serious. What have I done? In silence he fiddles with his phone while the sound of my Mom's voice fades out. Not literally, in fact she keeps talking but I'm too focused on Elijah's sudden change in mood to hear. Selfish I know.

After a few moments he shows me his phone screen and my eyes widen immediately. Dear Christ I'm gonna faint.

"Now you can afford it Darling. You should have said you needed money. You can always tell me" he whispers while I sit there unable to form words. He's just deposited another two grand into my bank account, which is on top of the money I still have.

"Mom, I'll call you back" I mumble because I truly don't know what else to do. The reason he was all frowny and confused is because he thought I was too scared to ask him for money. So as soon as I hang up, I all but yell:

"Elijjahhhhhhh! I still have a lot of the money you gave me. Pretty much all of it in fact. I was just telling her that to get out of going home" I explain.

"Oh I see. Sorry Darling. I just...I can tell how much you do want to go. I know you said there's a reason you can't but what if I go with you? Would that help?"

Oh wow. I can't believe he just said that. Could that work? My mind ponders the idea, a sickly feeling slinking in just like always. Bile rises in my throat. Then I look at him and it all goes away. "If anything makes you feel uncomfortable, I'll bring you right back here" he continues. How can he tell how much I long to go home? Why does he want to help so bad? "That's if you'd like me to come? I understand if you don't" he continues a little shyly.

"You'd do that?" I reply with my own question.

"Of course Darling" he states as if it's obvious. Dropping back down onto the bed, he pulls me close.

"Can I think about it?" I question because even with him coming I still need to process. I still need to work out if it's a good idea. If it's worth it. All these years of staying away can't change just like that.

Plus, on top of that he would be meeting my parents. Wow.

"Think about it as long as you like. It's your decision Darling. I just want to make you happy"

Fucking hell. Shit. I can't with this man.

"You're very sweet you know that right?" I begin and then remember the extra money. "Too sweet! I'm sending that money back" I say sternly.

"Sofia-" he tries but I stop him.

"Elijah!" I exclaim in warning.

"It's yours-"

"No it's not"

"Don't argue with me" he croons, trying to distract me with his wonderful hands.

"Oh I'll argue with you alright!" I yell as he moves on top of me, holding my hands above my head. I'm trapped.

He gazes at me with a soft smile on his face and he seems so very happy.

"Please don't" he pouts, leaning down to peck my lips.

How is this man real? Why does he think that I deserve to be given so much money? It drives me mad because it goes against who I am but look at his pleading eyes. He's so damn supportive. I just want to be the same for him. I want to give him everything he deserves.

He has no idea what he's in for if we go to see my parents. They'll interrogate the life out of him. My Mom will go crazy with the confirmation that I do in fact have a man.

My god I appreciate him but how do I say that without it being weird.

"You're insufferable" I joke instead and he grins widely.

"Now that's more like it. Soon you'll be saying I'm an asshole. You still like me though right?" He pouts and I shake my head in response.

"No, I don't like you" I love you...GOD! No, I don't.

"Sofia! How could you say that?" he asks, feigning shock.

"I'm a bitch!"

"You're a goddess actually...and I wanna worship you"

"A goddess? Are you drunk?"

"Yeah, on you Darling" he laughs, blowing a raspberry on my neck. It has me squealing.

"Oh god that was a cheesy line! Never say that again!"

"You can't stop me! I'm a professional at cheesy comments"

As we throw shitty remarks at each other something occurs to me.

"Wait, what am I going to introduce you as to my parents if we go? No offence but I think my Mom will faint if I tell her I not only met you online but that it was from a sugar daddy website too"

He takes a moment to think about it, then says simply:

"Tell them I'm your boyfriend or partner... it's not technically a lie..."

Not technically a lie...boyfriend...tell them I'm your boyfriend...dear god.

My boyfriend? Partner? As in real relationship?

Pull it together Sofia! He didn't say it as a fact! He's just throwing out ideas right?

"My boyfriend?" I query, testing out the word. I say it as if I'm unsure and asking him for confirmation. What's really happening is my brain is short circuiting.

"Yes. I'll just say 'Hi I'm Elijah, Sofia's boyfriend. It's nice to meet you'. They won't think anything of it. I won't tell them I'm a creepy pervert who is so very lucky to have a women like you anywhere near me" he jokes and my mouth falls open in shock.

"Stop that! I happen to like being next to you...boyfriend"

I play that off as I joke too but really I just want to see his reaction.

"Hmmm, you know I quite like the sound of saying 'Sofia, my girlfriend'" he muses in response.

So do I! Too much! Fuck! I'm done for! Ruined!

"Elijah Everett doesn't do girlfriends" I tell him, hiding my hate for that statement.

He looks away from me, staring down instead. Is he nervous? Shy? Some kind of emotion that isn't natural for him?

"Maybe Elijah Everett wishes he'd written 'Looking for Sofia' in his bio" he says softly before pausing. His next words make my heart race.

Its not hard for me to tell how terrified he is saying those words. It's so obvious. It's in his deep frown and fiddling fingers that mess with the duvet. "Maybe I wish I did do girlfriend. Maybe I should try with you…"

Elijah

    I'm not sure why I thought asking her subtly to be my girlfriend would be a good idea. The immediate horror on her face says it all really. What was I thinking anyway? She said it herself, I don't do girlfriends and I should stick to that so that I don't ruin whatever we have right now.

    I guess I just got caught up in the moment. The thought of having someone that could truly be mine and want me back just the same has always been a desire of mine. A need that I have squashed and squashed until meeting Sofia. It seems I should keep it that way. I won't be her happily ever after but I can be her right now...

    Don't fuck this up Elijah!

Sofia

Shit. Fuck. Oh no! Say something! Anything! Make this okay! Say yes because obviously it's what I want more than anything. So why are my lips not moving?

Seconds tick by and the window of opportunity for me to answer is closing. He clears his throat and smiles me weakly. Then laughs in what seems like an attempt to brush it off as a joke. One blink and his neutral mask falls back into place.

"Hey, you still haven't chosen where we're going on vacation" he says, closing down in seconds and moving so quickly that I can't keep up. I still can't speak. "I have an idea to help you choose" he continues and leans down to take my hand, tugging on it.

In my messed up and confused state, I say something voicing the thought in my head in that second. Somehow I work it into what's happening right now.

"I still can't believe that we're going on vacation. You literally put in your bio that you don't have time for a relationship which to me meant you had no time to take a holiday" I reply, letting the words fall out of my mouth.

Which is what I always do and somehow it hasn't yet gotten me into any awkward situations with him. Well, until now I guess. It's quite possible I'm the only person who blurts these kinds of things out because everyone else seems to be intimidated by him.

My honesty and word vomiting twenty four seven may be why he likes me. I mean he has to like me right? He just suggested I be his girlfriend and now we're pretending it never happened. I'm like a robot as I get out of bed and walk with him. Are we gonna leave it there? I don't wanna leave it there. I wanna go back to ten seconds ago and say yes. Yet, I think we're both frazzled.

"I don't have time for a relationship but I have all the time in the world for you" is his reply, that he quickly pushes out without stopping. No glance in my direction, no eye contact but the tension that radiates from him suggests that wasn't easy for him to say. Oh and it wasn't easy for me to hear either. WHAT IS HAPPENING RIGHT NOW?

Girlfriend? All the time in the world for me? Excuse me while I faint.

He leads me down a corridor and opens the door in front of us. Another room I've never been in. I don't even want to think about how many rooms this apartment actually has. Hey, maybe he has a sex dungeon like in fifty shades too.

That would be interesting. Sorry, not relevant right now but I'd be open to that sort of thing that's all I'm saying. Anything for my man right? Except my willingness to please hasn't got anything to do with getting money but everything to do with wanting to see him happy. Ewwwww I hate myself.

It's a whole ass library. He has a friggin library in his apartment because why the hell not? Rows of book cases. Some brown leather couches, a fire place and the one thing he's leading me to: a huge map of the world. Clever. I like it. A map of the world should certainly help my dilemma.

"Close your eyes" he commands and I give him a questioning look. What is he going to do? "Don't you trust me?" he smirks but I guess this question holds a lot of weight due to our previous 'you thought I was a murderer' thing.

"Yes I trust you" I reply, smirking back at him before closing my eyes tightly. I feel his hands on my waist as he shuffles me forward.

"Okay, I'm going to guide your hand and your going to tell me when to stop. Wherever our hands land on the map, that's where we'll go"

"What if it's the ocean" I say smartly.

"Then we'll sail there or swim if you prefer" he replies, his fingers tickling my side momentarily. I grab his hand to stop his attack and hear the gorgeous sound of him laughing softly in my ear. This could be a god damn romcom.

Well it could be if I hadn't just accidentally declined his offer of being his girlfriend. An offer I may never get again.

Elijah

Not enough time for a relationship is what I wrote in that stupid fucking bio. Yet here I am guiding Sofia's hand over a map and wishing that I'd never wrote that. What else would I have wrote though? It wasn't a lie. I don't have time. Technically I don't have time to be standing here right now. I should be in my office, planning my next move.

I should be busy making more deals and investing in anything I see that's worth a few million. Except that doesn't excite me. This women does. All I want is to devote every second to her, no matter how pathetic that makes me look. I'm going soft but for some reason I don't hate it.

I think in reality I have always had free time, I just had no one to give it too.

Live in the moment. That's what my Dad always said. It was one of the few nicer things that came out of his mouth. Which is ironic because he never seemed to follow that rule. He was neglectful to those who he claimed to care for. I won't be the same.

I'll live in the moment right her with Sofia.

Her hair smells like some kind of fruity concoction from her shampoo. Her body is pressed against mine and she's so relaxed. She's so comfortable being here with me. My left hand is pressed over her eyes gently to make sure she doesn't peek.

"Am I on anywhere good yet?" She asks and I shake my head, nuzzling into her neck. Yeah I nuzzle now and snuggle. Those words and actions weren't part of my vocabulary or things I enjoyed a month ago.

"If I told you then it would defeat the purpose of the plan" I tell her just before she yells.

"STOP"

It almost gives me a fright because of the abruptness but I'm quick to recover. My eyes latch onto where our fingers are pointed. Just touching Hawaii. Wow. She did good.

"Is it bad?" She mumbles, sounding worried. "Do I have to get a new swim suit? I'm not sure how far into the ocean I'll make it. Swimming isn't my strong suit"

Taking my hand away from her face, I place it back on her waist and squeeze signalling for her to open her eyes. I hope she's happy with the destination because my mind is already filling with images of her in a bikini on a white sandy private beach. Sex in the sea, cocktails, her laughing-

"OH MY GOD HAWAII!"

She jumps around to face me and smiles with so much joy that it makes me speechless. Then it falls away and she shakes her head.

"Elijah you can't take me to Hawaii. That's too much. It's too expensive, I mean I know you can afford it but that's not the point. I just can't accept-"

"Darling, this is for both of us" I try to reason with her.

"I just don't want to be like...them. The thought of the things they asked you for and took from you is horrible. I'm not a sugar baby" she replies, looking petrified.

Oh Darling.

"You are nothing like them" I assure her, holding her face in my hands. She's so worried.

"Like I said before, I don't like the thought of someone taking advantage of you. I'm even more worried you'll think I am"

The last line rings in my head in an unfamiliar way. She's not going to take advantage of me. I know that wholeheartedly.

I want to take her on holiday. I want to spent time with her. Not because she's asked but because I want it too. I guess that's what I should tell her then. She's certainly not my sugar baby...she's so much more.

"You're not taking advantage of me Darling. I want to go away with you. It's for me too. To take a break. To spend time with a beautiful women on a beach and each copious amount of food that I shouldn't. Basically I wanna do what we do here together but in a different country" I explain and slowly but surely the lovely smile returns to her face. That's better.

In silence, she steps closer to me and wraps her arms around my waist. I'm not sure what to do as she pecks my lips then presses her head against my chest.

"Thank you. I appreciate everything you do for me Elijah. Honestly it means the world"

Well shit. It seems I do have a heart after all.

Sofia

While I'm cuddling Elijah in gratitude my eyes catch onto something on one of the book shelves. I take a moment to work out what it is as he squeezes me in his arms. Content and happy is the best way to describe how I feel right now. Like immensely happy. Happier than I've ever been. This man is gonna kill me one day and it's not because he's a murderer.

"Is that a Batman figurine?" I say slowly but not because I'm appalled. It's because I'm excited and I think I may have just unlocked another part of Elijah's personality.

Letting go, he follows my gaze and then looks back at me a little sheepishly.

"He's limited edition. One of five in the world" he mumbles. I feel my eyebrows raise uncontrollably in response to what he's just told me. No friggin way! I'm sure it's no surprise to anyone that I'm a geek. I mean I'm obsessed with staring at code if that didn't give it away. I like the back end side of building a website. Love it actually. I should point out that when I use the word geek, it's a term of endearment. Anyway, basically I love all this shit.

Comics, anime, superheroes, Doctor Who, you name it, I probably like it. My favourite Doctor is David Tennant and I'll fight anyone who argues. I should ask Elijah about his favourite Doctor in case I need to fight him. Oh and don't even get me started on Star Wars.

Elijah misinterprets my expression. I know this because he looks significantly embarrassed but I'm quick to correct him.

"That is awesome! Can I touch it?" I'm a child. I know that but Elijah doesn't seem to mind and nods, a shy smile that I've never encountered, forming on his face. A new type of smile.

I try my best not to run over to the unsuspecting Batman figure but end up doing a weird skip dance over to it anyway. I wonder if Elijah knows I'm insane yet? Yeah...he probably does.

For the next ten minutes I admire the amazing paint work on the figure and all of the detail. 'The Dark Knight' is the name engraved on the bottom by the feet. The simple and direct name suggests it's rarity. Am I drooling?

Do you like it?" Elijah asks, now at my side.

"I love it. He's beautiful"

"Do you want to see more?" He asks, excitement clear in his voice. I wonder if soul mates are real because if they are, he's mine.

"There's more?"

It turns out Elijah has a fantastically huge figurine collection. Which we spend the rest of the evening looking at. He's got first edition comics, memorabilia from Marvel films, including a life size iron man suit. That's my favourite I must admit. It's really cool to have rows of book and then have even more rows of geeky goodness hidden away at the back of a sophisticated business mans library. I find it rather sexy. This is what we're discussing currently.

"You think it's sexy that I'm a secret man child?" He asks as he pulls me into his lap on one of the brown leather couches. The fire that he just turned on throws shadows onto his features, making him look very mysterious.

"I think it's sexy that by day you're an amazingly cool CEO boss and by night you're an even cooler dedicated collector of whimsical fantastic things"

"When you put it like that, I feel less embarrassed"

"Why would you be embarrassed at all?

"Because I'm a grown man"

"And I'm a grown women who would have all of this kind of stuff too if it were possible. The best I have is a couple Funko pops that I cherish dearly. Didn't you see them on my desk?"

"I noticed but I didn't want to scare you off by seeming too interesting in them. Nice choices by the way, Wonder Women especially suits you. Since you're wonderful yourself" he winks and gives me a cheesy grin. Wonder Women and Baby Groot sit proudly on my computer desk.

"Wow, I think I'm going to throw up. That was a terrible compliment but I appreciate the effort" I laugh, sliding my hands up to his shoulders.

"You're welcome, baby cakes"

"No, no stop. Don't start this again!"

"What's wrong sugar plum?" He continues, throwing out remarkably bad pet names.

"You're killing me"

"Buttercup?"

"I'm never having sex with you again"

"Okay okay, I'll stop...love muffin" he teases.

"I'm leaving!" I shout dramatically and begin to get up.

I leave him on the couch, walking away out of the library. He follows me, moving faster to catch up. Obviously I'm not really leaving but teasing him is fun.

Taking my hand, he runs his thumb over my knuckles and leans into me.

"Don't go Darling. I can't do better"

I know he's referring to his cheesy comments but the way he says it holds so much weight that it seems like he's saying something else.

"You do just fine" I reply leaning up to kiss him. He meets me half way and presses our lips together. So very soft. Delicate.

I don't know what it is with the world but every time Elijah and I do something remotely meaningful, something interrupts us. Either it's a phone, a knock on a window or in this case the jarring sound of the apartment intercom informing us that something would like to visit.

Elijah sighs in annoyance and goes to the foyer, tapping the small screen next to the elevator. I don't want to invade his privacy so I stay where I am but I can still hear.

"Mr Everett, I really need to talk to you" A mans voice crackles over the intercom in a panic.

"I'm a little busy right now" Elijah replies. "You can talk to me tomorrow in my office"

I assume this person works for him and they've made a point of coming here to see him. It must be important.

"No Sir, this is terribly important. Your databases full of personal information have been hacked. The whole business is in jeopardy!"

Huh...that's pretty fucking serious!

Elijah

My whole fucking database has been infiltrated. All the clients I've ever worked with are now in jeopardy and my solid promise of privacy is too. No will work with me if my company becomes known for releasing personal details.

As Jack explains everything he knows about the situation, I try to take it all in and focus. I don't do well with all this stuff so it's difficult for me to follow. However the women sitting next to me, now dressed in my hoodie is completely opposite to me and my lack of knowledge.

Sofia had sat quietly for the first few moments but I could tell she was dying to say something. It was in the way she sat on the edge of her seat, her face focused and sure.

I'm glad she spoke up because she's asking questions and it's helping things make sense for me. I'm stuck between wanting to solve this problem and spending the rest of the night just listening to her talk about spreadsheets and confidentially. I'm in awe and watching her break down Jack's words and nod in all the right places does something to me that I don't quite understand. She's trying to help me. That's not something many people do.

It was rather annoying at the start when Jack had looked to me for permission to tell Sofia the answer to her first question. I know it's unusual for me to have anyone with me but I don't appreciate him looking at Sofia as if she's stupid.

Now though he isn't holding back and has clearly realised she is smarter than both of us put together. I'm glad because I don't want to have to fire him.

"Do you know the IP address of where the firewalls were infiltrated? That would lead you right to the source" Sofia questions and Jack goes slightly pale. Hmm what's that about?

"No Mam, we haven't checked that yet"

"Well you probably should" she replies in a polite tone but I can tell she's trying not to yell at him. Damn, I really shouldn't stare too long at her beautifully serious face. Or the small frown marring her forehead. I should avert my eyes from her jean clad crossed legs and my hoodie that's too big and creates sweater paws over her hands. She leans her elbows on her knees and places her chin in her palm, looking so very at home on my leather couch. My staring much be obvious as she glances at me, blushes, tucks her hair behind her ear then focuses back on Jack.

I love it when she blushes but I also hate it. Her blush suggests shyness or that she looks to me for approval. I don't want that. She doesn't need my approval for anything. I'm in no way above her. Its possible that she feels the same way when I praise her as when she does so to me. Anytime she compliments me on literally anything, I feel like I've achieved the highest award. It's hard for me to believe that I could make her feel that way but I hope that I do. I hope my words make her feel special and that she believes them fully. She's so god damn amazing and she needs to know it.

"Sir?" Is what finally snaps me out of my haze and I turn to Jack, a less pretty sight I may add. "Shall we go to your building to do more digging and get the IP address?" He asks and I nod once because I don't really know what else to say. I don't have control over this situation even though I pay hundreds of people to deal with this shit. I don't like how lost I feel.

My eyes snap back to Sofia as I feel her hand on my knee. She gives me a reassuring smile and I realise that I'm not hiding my panic well. I need to get better at that. Then again this situation in unique in many ways. Not only has it never happened before but I've never felt like I needed anyone's help.

Right now though, if Sofia got up and left I think I'd crumble under the pressure. I don't ever need anyone but right now I need her more than ever. I revel in her support, in her determination to help me. Should I bet getting off or feeling high because she's on my side, caring for me? Maybe not but I can't help it. I crave it from her.

Even so, I won't admit it and I don't want her to feel like she has to come with us.

"I can take you home first if you like?" I ask all the while hoping her answer is no.

Please come. Please come. Please come.

"I want to come with you. Well as long as I won't get in the way" she says completely neutral as if she's happy to do what's best for me. Dear god, where has she been all my life? And how could she think she'd get in the way?

"You won't get in the way" I assure her quickly.

Probably too quickly. She no doubt sees right through my nonchalance.

***

Silence pretty much deafens me on the elevator ride up to the top floor of my building. Sofia is sending me a reassuring smile right this second because clearly my panic is obvious to her. Jack on the other hand seems more awkward than panicked. Is it that weird for me to be seen with a women? Definitely not. Then again it's certainly weird that I'm being affectionate towards one. For some reason the clear impression that everyone has of me, bothers me a hell of a lot.

Sure I was never compassionate or all that caring but I've always been respectful and polite. Who am I kidding? I've been an asshole to most people in my life. I just can't act that way with Sofia, it's like all of that shittiness inside me evaporates.

Even now, I can't help but smile back at her. I mean look at her, look how cute she is. Her brunette hair is tied up in a drastically messy bun, while she still wears my hoodie. Her black jeans hug her in all the right places and all of this makes her look so cozy as well as sexy. Her slightly tired eyes make me want to take her back to bed so that she can sleep on my chest.

See, my mind is fucked. Why are we even here? Oh yeah, my database corruption.

The ping of the elevator doors signals our arrival on the top floor and Jacks walks out first. I take Sofia's hand as we follow him simply because I can. I guess I'm taking advantage of the fact that right now. I have someone to take comfort in. It's strange but addictive.

When we reach my office Jack unlocks the door. It's only him and myself that have a key. I'm actually not sure why we're in my office since the server rooms are a few floors down. I'm sure they mentioned the reason on the ride over here but I was too busy working out how I'm going punish the person who did this.

Publicly expose their sins? Maybe. Bankrupt them? Possibly. We all have something to hide so I think the first option would be more fun.

The lights flick on automatically and Sofia lets go of my hand to head straight for my laptop. I've been leaving it here more often these days. My work hours have been a little messed up.

"May I?" She asks, her hands hovering over the keyboard.

"Of course" I reply without hesitation and then realise how whipped I am. Sure Elijah just let someone have complete access to literally everything in your life.

Except it doesn't seem that big of a deal because...I trust her. Not sure how she achieved that from me but here we are.

"Can you type your password in please?" She asks waiting ever so patiently while I let my brain catch up. I'm usually so sharp but whoever said emotion is weakness was right. Although it's a weakness I'm happy to deal with.

"It's -" I begin, deciding that telling her would be easier.

"No! Don't tell me!" She exclaims, eyes wide and panicked. What?

"Why not?" I question confused by her reaction.

"Rule number one: the less people that know your password aka personal information, the better" she informs sternly as if she's reprimanding me. Well shit that's hot.

"But it's you. I'm assuming you aren't going to use it against me" I reason and this has her looking all soft and a little emotional.

"Well no of course I'm not but for all you know I could be lying to you. When it comes to this kind of stuff, trust no one. Not even the hot girl you're sleeping with, okay?"

It's ironic that what she just said only makes me trust her more. She seems to care so much about this that she doesn't even want me to trust her. I must admit I'm a little frazzled.

You know maybe it's a good thing I didn't tell her. It would embarrass me anyway. The thing is I have to change my password every so often for security reason (security my ass) and right now it's: Westwood45799

It's her ID number from the sugar rush website. Turns out it's perfect as a password and makes me smile every time I type it in.

Right now is the same as always. Sofia gives me a questioning look as I hit enter and my messy desktop of files appears.

"Jesus Christ Elijah! How do you find anything?!"

"There's a system" I defend myself and she gives an unimpressed glance. Oh dear.

"We can fix this disaster later"

***

Turns out the reason they didn't need to go to the server room was because it would be easier to do everything from the source of the data...my laptop. All of my clients information is obviously not simply kept on my hard drive but I guess you could think of my laptop as a master key to it all. There are back ups upon back ups but this is where it all goes through first.

I watch them work together at my desk, while I sit in one of the leather chairs. I never sit here but I don't want to disrupt what they're doing. Sofia is deep in concentration while Jack stands beside her observing. They have a common understanding of what's going on.

I'm obviously not an idiot by any means but it's actually nice to have someone know more than me for once.

What I don't like is the building feeling of jealousy inside me. I know it's completely uncalled for. I've nothing to be jealous of. They're just working together and I'm literally right here watching them.

Regardless, I'm surprised I'm not bright green.

I'm a fucking asshole.

Sofia

He's panicking. It's not super obvious but for someone who studies his features like it's a sport, it's easy to notice the signs. The slight twitch in his stone cold expression is a giveaway.

I'm planning on changing that though because I'm seconds from finding the IP address and the culprit. I'm so happy he's letting me help him.

Watching the screen load is driving me insane. Jack stands next to me looking just as tense. Finally though...

"Got it!" I exclaim and Elijah jumps up from his seat to join us. The location is only about thirty minutes from here. "I don't think any information has been tampered with yet and all I can do is put the firewalls back up" I tell them. I'm not qualified to do much more. "Sorry I can't do any more unless I've got more information"

Elijah's arm slides around my waist and he plants a kiss on my cheek. Naturally I'm blushing.

"Thank you. You've done more than enough Darling. You don't know how much I appreciate it honestly" he says softly.

"I'm assuming you can do more though with your team. You know research the location and put better protection in place?" I ask Jack and he looks at me with an awkward expression.

"I can't lie to you Mam, our team are rather useless. If they weren't, this wouldn't have happened in the first place" he explains.

"Are you kidding me? You're telling me I spend hundreds of thousands on a team that I was told were the best and you're only now saying that they're not any good?" Elijah raises his voice slightly and stands up straight. Oh dear, I think Jack is in trouble.

"Sir, I did most of the interviews myself. All the information and qualifications checked out" he tries but it doesn't appease Elijah.

"Well you clearly weren't paying attention!" He shouts. "What's the point of me having a fucking right hand man if I'm better doing it all myself?!"

"Okay you know what, this isn't solving the problem!" I cut in and they both fall silent. Jack looks sheepish and Elijah looks pissed. Which I must add that I find rather attractive, especially with his untamed hair and haphazardly thrown on shirt. Gotta love the crushed look.

"Don't look so grumpy, we'll fix this" I tell him and boop his nose. Childish I know but it has his cracking a smile.

"Mam" Jack begins again and I turn to him, hoping he's going to have a solution.

"Oh before you continue can you call me Sofia please. The Mam thing makes me feel old"

"Of course Sofia. I just wanted to ask, would you like a job?"

"What now?" I ask because I'm not sure I've heard him right. Glancing at Elijah, I look to see if I'm going deaf. He smirks at me and nods as if he's completely fine with the whole thing. Huh?

"I believe he offered you a job" Elijah reiterates and I end up with no words forming in my head.

"You'll get full training, although I'm pretty sure you'd be the one needing to train everyone else. We can talk about salary and stuff, I'm sure we can be flexible with that to meet whatever your needs are. You'll get a company car. Oh and you don't need an interview. Not with what I've just seen. However a background check will be required..." he keeps talking, going over a lot of different things from holidays to sick pay and I stand there unable to process it.

Except one thing does pop into my head. Elijah already asked me this previously. I said no and I still feel the same way. Plus, if I say yes then Elijah will ultimately be my boss. Not to mention this won't be something that I'd have achieved myself. It'll be through association and I'm not sure I could live with that. I guess I've actually answered the question.

"I really really appreciate the offer but I can't accept it. I'm more than happy to help but I can't take the job offer" I tell Jack sincerely then turn back to Elijah.

"I don't want you to be my boss" I begin and he raises his eyebrows. "I don't mean that in a bad way. I'm sure you're a fantastic boss but I'm sleeping with you and that kind of situation never ends well..."

Elijah

  Could I respect her anymore than I do in this moment? I don't think so. Really I should have known she'd say no since she's declined my offer before, although I thought that there was a chance she'd change her mind with Jack asking.
  But no, she confidently explains why she's declining and I get it. I desperately want her to have the job she dreams of and deserves but with me running things it's not that job. Jack seems shocked by her decline, while I want to ask her where she gets her resilience. She genuinely teaches me new things everyday and I didn't think that was possible in all my years of being alive.
  "Right well I think we've done all we can do tonight. I'll inform the team in the morning that they'll be needing some extra training and we'll get to the bottom of this. I'm sure it's nothing serious. Probably just some overly smart kids messing with us"
  I wish I could believe that but with all the unwanted attention from Nadia and the press recently, I have a feeling the person doing this is a little more vindictive. Only half an hour away from the building. I wouldn't be surprised if the address leads to some makeshift den for Nadia herself but maybe I'm jumping to conclusions...
  Right now my main priority is getting Sofia back to my apartment so we can get some sleep. We both gotta work

tomorrow and I know for a fact I'll fire more people than necessary if I don't get enough sleep. Sofia may be a buffer for my temper but I'm not sure I'll do so well tomorrow morning when she's not with me.

Sofia

As soon as I get into work the next day, I wish that I'd taken Jack's job offer. A new person is starting and apparently I've got to train him. Which doesn't sound like fun. Not only that but I can't even enjoy the fact that it's Friday because tomorrow is Elijah and I's trip to my parents.

I had thought about it a lot last night. Weighing up the pros and cons but ultimately, I realised that one day I have to face my fears. What better time to do it than now?

I've got a lot of mixed feelings about it. Joy because I can see my parents. Nerves...a lot of nerves. My Mom was ecstatic though. She even said she was gonna tell Bree so she could see me.

I am looking forward to the drive to Ohio. It'll be like a road trip which I'm not too fond of however being stuck in a car for over four hours with Elijah will be amusing.

My happy thoughts are ruined as the boss appears with a blonde dude at her side. This must be the new guy. He looks about the same age as me and is wearing an overly tight superman t-shirt. Oh dear, now I instantly don't like him. Kidding! But come on it's Batman all the way. I think Elijah would agree with me too.

If the superman top had me frowning then the next thing I notice has me squinting my eyes...

Okay I'm sorry but I have to point out that this dude needs to buy bigger sized t-shirts if this is the size he always wears. I can see every god damn part of his obvious six pack through it and it makes me feel very queasy. Look I'm not judging, it's just very unnatural looking and I'm worried that he's suffocating himself. Just to clarify for anyone who isn't following, abdominal muscles scare me. I'm pretty sure I have an actual phobia.

"Sofia hon, would you mind showing Gabe here the ropes?"

I want to reply sarcastically but I hold my tongue and agree instead. I can't afford to lose this job because I'm feeling like a smart ass today. I'm not sure why I'm grumpy but it could be something to do with lack of sleep or not having seen Elijah in like an hour. I sent him off to work with a good luck kiss and told him to go easy on his tech team.

"Of course!" I say cheerily and with that I'm left with Gabe.

"Hey! Thanks for doing this" he says, sticking out his hand for me to shake. I do so quickly because as soon as our hands meet I feel the sweat on his palms. I have to discreetly wipe it away on my apron.

Then I decide to stop being a little bitch and get on with on. Only six hours left and I'll be with my six pack free lover. Thank god.

***

Surprisingly Gabe isn't hell to work with. He's actually kinda funny and picks everything up real quick. Not that it's rocket science but I had some issues with the different machine parts on my first day. I don't know how many times I just filled cups with whipped cream. Yum.

The hours go quick and our boss leaves me to lock up. Not that I mind.

"You can go if you like" I tell Gabe who's still hovering as I clean tables. His shift is done so there's no need for him to be here anymore. I'd be walking right out that door.

"Oh it's okay, I'll wait until you're leaving" he responds and begins cleaning some tables too.

Well that's kind of him.

Since there's only a few tables left, I think my time is better spent taking apart the coffee machines and cleaning those instead.

We work in silence for a while until I feel like I'm being watched. I nearly jump out of my skin as I find him standing next to me.

"Oh sorry! I didn't mean to scare you"

"Dude! I was about to smash this mug over your head! Make more damn noise when you walk" I exclaim and he laughs. Like he really laughs...too much.

Then he doesn't say anything and just kind of leans against the counter as I begin draining the water from the machine. It's official, I feel creeped out. Plus it's dark outside now and I'm simply not getting good vibes from him.

"Damn that's a nice car" Gabe sighs in awe seconds later. Glancing up my gaze finds Elijah's black Mercedes pulling up to the curb. The street lights make it look rather shiny so I get Gabe's excitement I think. For me it's not the car that has my heart racing, it's the man that steps out.

Even in the limited light, I still try and take in all I can. He's wearing a dark grey suit tonight and it's perfectly pressed from head to toe. He buttons the jacket with a smoothness that has my mouth watering before he walks towards the shop.

His slight swagger has me smiling. I'm sure Gabe is talking to me but I'm just not processing his words.

All I can focus on is Elijah and now my eyes take in his black rimmed glasses. I think he wears them more than he did before he met me because I like them so much. His hair looks so soft and I know it feels that way too. I'm forever running my fingers through it. Or tugging on it when we-

"Sofia!" Gabe exclaims seconds before I feel instant pain.

"Fuck!" I yelp as my fingers burn from the stream coming off the coffee machine. Opps, clearly I should pay more attention.

"Are you okay?" he asks, moving closer.

"Yeah I'm good" I assure him, blowing on my singed fingers rapidly.

"Here let me see" he gasps.

Before I can blink, he grabs my hand and begins inspecting it. It makes me feel incredibly awkward and even though I'm trying not to look at him weirdly, I'm pretty sure I'm frowning.

I pull my hand away as politely as I can and step away from him with a thankful nod. I know he's only being nice but well...I don't like it.

It's then that the sound of the door opening hits my ears and Elijah walks up to the counter. He smiles warmly at me before he shoots Gabe a certain kind of look that I can't make out.

"Hey Darling are you-" he begins but stops when he sees me clutching my fingers. He's close enough now that I can smell him and his scent almost has me forgetting the pain. "Are you okay?" He continues, his expression turning to a worry in seconds.

"Yeah I just burnt my fingers" I explain. He sticks his hand out over the counter and I place my sore fingers his palm. He inspects the damage which is very minimal. It was more shock than anything else.

He presses my fingers to his lips and I can't help but giggle.

"Wow, now they're all better"

"I'm magic" he smirks, winking at me playfully.

Gabe is still watching our interaction and the only reason I know this is because I have a horrible icy feeling on the back of my neck. Like my instinct is telling me something is off with him. Well I'm safe now anyway.

"My mouth hurts too" I whisper so that Gabe doesn't hear and Elijah gasps mockingly.

"Oh no, let me fix that for you"

He leans over and presses his lips to mine before purposely running his cheek against my skin, his beard tickling me.

"Stop that!" I laugh and pull back to escape his attack.

"Sofia? Ummm, I'll go now if that's okay?" Gabe cuts in and I really want to say "I already told you to go" but that wouldn't be very nice I guess. Also it's probably uncomfortable for him to watch Elijah and I's PDA.

"Yeah of course" is my choice of reply. I feel weird saying it because I'm not his boss.

"Thanks, I'll see you soon" he grins rather widely and winks at me too. What the fuck was that?

When I glance back at Elijah he's glaring at Gabe as he leaves. I immediately feel better with him gone.

"He seems...nice" He says very slowly with gritted teeth, which makes it obvious that his words are a complete contradiction.

"Yeah, he's alright I guess. Kinda weird if you ask me. However he said he liked your car" I mention and watch as Elijah crosses his arms over his chest.

"It's not my car he likes Darling, it's my girl" he pushes out gruffly. What now?

"Huh?" I question, genuinely confused.

I have to push aside my joy at him calling me his girl because what he's just said is so ridiculous.

"He clearly wants what's mine" he states, looking pissed. Really? Are we doing this?

His, huh? Is he calling me an object? I mean I really doubt it but I'm still gonna call him out. He needs to stop being such a baby.

"Oh so you're saying I'm an object to you? A possession?" I ask, making sure I look just as pissed. I'm not all that mad just confused as to why he'd act this way.

To my amusement his face goes white.

"No, no that's not what I meant. Of course I don't think of you as an object" he says quickly, his arms uncrossing and his brow furrowing. Worried are we? I'm not going to lie, I do love having the ability to make this controlled strong man quiver. Although I'm not mean enough to keep it up for long.

"Well that's what it sounded like. Maybe you should choose your words carefully in the future so you don't sound like a possessive animal"

"Sofia, I swear that's not what I meant. I just don't like the way he was looking at you" he explains and walks around the counter to me.

"I didn't like it either" I sigh. "Oh and I know you weren't calling me an object, I just didn't like the way you said it"

"I am sorry" he pouts and tugs on my apron to pull me closer and well...I'm powerless to resist.

"I was messing with you so that you'd realise how ridiculous you sounded. I mean I've no idea if Gabe is attracted to me and I don't care"

"Darling I just hate the idea of another man anywhere near you and I know that's absurd but I can't help it. Plus he gave me a strange feeling and I want you safe. I don't know how to deal with jealousy right" he confesses softly. He's jealous? Of Gabe? That's ridiculous! And he wants me safe? Okay Sofia breath.

"Just because I'm talking to a person of the opposite sex that isn't you, doesn't mean I'm gonna run off with him. Unfortunately Elijah there are men all over the world and I'll have to come into contact with them at some point. Can't avoid them all you know" I smirk and he glares playfully.

"As long as it's not too much contact" he growls.

This has me laughing and shaking my head. Still I want to assure him of where I stand.

"I said I wanted to be exclusive with you and you agreed. Even if we weren't I'd still only be sleeping with you because I'm not about that shit. One man is hard enough to deal with" I sigh and widen my eyes at him.

"I really am sorry for making it sound like you were an object" he apologises again and I realise that he thinks he's done something extremely awful.

"It's okay silly, you already said sorry"

"Is it?"

"Of course. What did you think was gonna happen?" I ask because I'm genuinely intrigued to hear how his mind works.

"Well I assumed you'd stay mad for a bit longer and maybe you wouldn't talk to me, that you'd leave..."

What the fuck? I hate that he immediately thinks that. So many people clearly have got up and walked out on him. Both friends and family.

"Woah! I'll stop you right there! Did you think I was gonna leave you because you said one thing that wasn't so great? Elijah, it's not that deep. I was messing with you and even if I were really mad, we'd talk about it and resolve it. That's what people do. That's what I hope will happen if you're ever mad at me too"

"I messed up a little and I don't wanna do that to you. I don't want my overbearing personality and control problems to ruin this"

I did not expect this to become so serious. My man really needs to be taught the basics when it comes to relationships. Not to mention he needs affection more than ever.

Squishing myself impossibly closer, I reach up to touch his cheek. He likes this kind of small contact I've noticed. Like he enjoys having my undivided attention.

"You didn't mess up but even if you did or do it's normal. It's okay. Hell I'm surprised I haven't messed anything up yet. I'm a walking disaster. Unfortunately as humans that's what we do but there's no need to panic about it. If this is how all our arguments are gonna go then I'm very happy about it. I'm more used to yelling and not getting a chance to speak" I tell him, recalling certain arguments with people I dated. Well I never really dated properly but it still counts.

"Why didn't you get a chance to speak?" He asks looking confused.

"Well I guess most people aren't as respectful as you. It's hard to get your side across when someone is yelling in your face you know? Arguments never get resolved like that"

"Well I promise to always let you have your say and you can yell at me if you like" he says softly. Right now he looks so needy. I don't mean that in a bad way. I mean that he's showing me that he needs me. He's letting me in. I can't believe this minor thing turned into such a meaningful conversation. This man has layers and layers of complexity and I'm really enjoying getting to know them all I must admit.

"I appreciate that but I have no intention of yelling at you. You gotta have your say too you know. Respect works both ways baby" He looks extremely grateful for what I've said and wraps his arms around my waist. "I am yours though. You know that right? I said it once before and I still mean it. I have no interest in anyone else" I assure him.

"Then you should know that I meant it when I said it before too. I'm very much yours. I'm not sure if that's a good thing for you or not" he jokes but I can't laugh at that. Self deprecating is something he does that I hate.

"Oh it's good trust me" I breath and slide my hands up his chest. Gripping his shirt, I pull him forward and tease his lips with mine.

He holds me somewhat gently in his embrace as we stand in the middle of the coffee shop. His lips mould over mine and everything is so lovely until I realise that if we keep this up we're going to have to delete another video from the CCTV.

"We should probably get out of here. We can't have sex here again" I laugh and he immediately looks thoughtful.

"You're right. We could however have sex in the car" he muses and gestures outside.

"Yes!" is all I say before I'm rushing around and closing things up. My apron is thrown off, my bag grabbed, door locked, shutters down, Elijah all but shoved into the back seat of the car by yours truly.

Thank god for his tinted windows.

I straddle him and he works on unzipping my jeans immediately. I laugh my ass off as I have to wiggle out of them. He's tugging on one jean leg and laughing just as hard. When he throws off one of my shoes, his fingers begin tickling my feet.

I'm sure if anyone can hear us from outside the car they'd be concerned about the high pitched screaming and strange sentences.

"Elijah nooooo, not my feet oh my god!" I beg.

"Ticklish feet, I wish I'd known earlier" he says mischievously and grabs my other shoe to pull it off. Well I guess my jeans will come off easier now.

"I'm gonna get you back for this! Just wait" I yell.

"Sorry I can't hear you" he responds before tickling my other foot relentlessly.

"Elijah! I'm gonna murder you!" I scream and try to grab his hands to stop him.

"Oh shit so sexy. I love it when you threaten my life" he teases before I'm finally able to capture his hands. I pin them to the back of the seat on either side of him and grin. I know he could break free if he wanted but he lets me hold them there anyway as our ragged breathing slows.

"You're evil" I sigh and his eyes light up.

"I'm your villain remember?" He whispers, running his nose along mine.

"Yes, you are" I agree, then I move one of his hands between my legs. He bites his lip as I press his hand with mine against my now wet panties. I want him to feel it. To know what he does to me.

He presses his fingers against my clit and I gasp.

"Use me Sofia. I'll give you whatever you want" his voice comes out breathless. "Take what you need"

I'm gyrating against his hand like it's a sport while he watches me with hungry eyes.

"Touch me more" I beg and he pushes my panties aside and slides his fingers inside me. His free hand sliding under my top to cup my breast.

"Yes, yes, there"

This goes on for some time, his fingers pushing me close and closer to the edge. However I'd much prefer to have his cock inside me.

I fumble with his zipper but soon I'm able to stroke him, making his eyes flutter shut.

"I want this to be about you Darling" he whines but is unable to stop raising his hips.

"Oh this is for me" I pant and kiss his neck. My lips move to his ear and I nip on it with my teeth. He loves that.

"Fuck! Sofia h-how do you do thi-s to me?" He asks, his words broken.

"I could ask you the same thing" I laugh before running the tip of his cock through my wetness. He grips my hips tightly, his nails digging into my skin and finally I sink down onto him.

We haphazardly remove the top half of our clothes because the more skin touching the better.

He pushes up into me while his lips kiss my breasts. My fingers tug his hair while his hands roam my back. They drop lower and squeeze my ass. It's strangely sweet to have his head against my chest as he fucks me. I guess my breasts make a good cushion.

Arching my back, I lean against the back of front seats and rock my hips. His hands glide up my stomach, over my breasts and into my hair. He tugs gently sending shock waves through my whole body. Now I get why he likes it so much.

The car heats with our passion, the windows steaming up. This is crazy erotic and I have a feeling every time I get in the car from now on all I'll be able to think about is this.

***

Turns out I was right about that. Elijah stayed over at my apartment last night and once we'd got in the car this morning, we both smiled at each other knowingly. Yup we've checked this off our list.

Before our drive to Ohio we stopped for some supplies which consisted of a copious amount of junk food. This included pop corn because Elijah loves the mixed sweet and salty flavoured bags.

Since the drive is about five hours I'm currently occupying both of us with a messy game of 'how many pieces of pop corn can Elijah catch in his mouth?'. It's probably dangerous but Elijah is good at it and my laugher is uncontrollable as one piece gets stuck in his hair.

"You can eat that bit later" I giggle.

"I think I'll keep it there for you in case you get hungry" he replies and I reach over to take it out of his hair and pop it in my mouth.

"I'm hungry now" I state and this has him laughing so happily that it makes my heart flutter.

Easy there heart. You need to tone it down.

The lightheartedness is good for me. Especially as we get closer to my home. It helps take my mind of things.

Just before we arrive at my parents, Elijah tells me that he listened to my words of advice when firing some people. Apparently he wrangled it down to two weakest links as he calls it. I'm rather proud because I've heard him fire about six people before just over the phone.

"Any luck with finding out who hacked your database?" I ask leaning against the head rest, enjoying his lovely side profile.

"I had a private investigator go to the address but they didn't find any helpful information. Jack said he might need your help again but please don't feel like you need to, it's not your responsibility"

"Of course I'll help" I respond and he glances at me softly.

"I'm so lucky I found you..." he sighs dreamily.

"No I'm lucky" I retort.

"No I am"

"No-"

His right hand reaches out to cover my mouth and I stick my tongue out to lick his palm to freak him out. Only it doesn't work.

"You think that's gonna bother me? Darling we've swapped a lot more bodily fluids than saliva" he laughs. I tug his hand away from my mouth and hold it in mine.

"Fine, you win"

I knew this drive would be fun but I didn't know it would be this wholesome.

Elijah

We arrive outside what must be her parents house at about three thirty. This is where the navigation guided me but if I were unsure if it's the right location, the way Sofia tenses gives it away. It immediately has me on guard, making sure there is nothing around that could make her uncomfortable. I wish the I knew the whole story. It's not hard for me to put some of the pieces together. Someone hurt her here and that thought has my blood boiling.

"We can drive back home Darling. If you don't want to go in. It's no big deal" I tell her but she shakes her head.

"No, it's okay. I have to do this. I've been gone for so long it's ridiculous. I need to get over myself. You're okay with being introduced as my boyfriend right? I mean I'm not sure what else to say?" She asks looking slightly worried.

Does she think that I wouldn't want that.

"Of course I'm okay with it" I reassure her and give her a long kiss to calm to her down. Also to give myself a hit of my favourite drug because we'll no doubt have to be good this evening.

I rest my hand on her back as we walk up the gravel driveway. The house is white with grey shutters on the windows, the door matches. Some greenery surrounds the front lawn and all in all it looks very homely and welcoming.

Sofia takes a deep breath as we reach the door.

She knocks and I grab her hand in support.

I know she told them that she was bringing a guest but the two people who open the door still look somewhat surprised.

The women pulls Sofia into a tight hug while the man stares at me unsure. So these are the people who created the best thing in my life. I should be thanking them immediately.

"This is Elijah, my boyfriend" Sofia says happily, introducing me to her parents. Now is not the time for me to lose composure but here I am with the word boyfriend ringing in my ears. I know it's just because she can't tell her parents the truth but I still fucking love it.

Why does it have me feeling this way? Why do I care? No idea. Nevertheless, as her Dad shakes my hand I almost miss his scrutinising look because my mind is stuck on that one word.

Almost. He gives me a stern nod in greeting and I kind of want to laugh. I know he's obviously trying to play the tough father role and show that he's defensive of Sofia. Still, it doesn't affect me. We're not teenagers and Sofia is an adult. I'll be with her for as long as she wants me and this guy ain't gonna change that. I wonder if he will try and give me the intimating "don't hurt my daughter" talk later.

It would be interesting, considering I'd never hurt Sofia. I'll always take care of her.

Okay Elijah, snap out of this shit!

Her Mom greets me next, kissing my cheek and patting my back. She seems to be less fazed by my presence. I can see that Sofia got most of her features from her.

"So when you told me that Elijah was just your friend you were lying huh?" Her Mom asks, giving Sofia a knowing look.

"If I'd told you when you visited I would never had heard the end of it" she replies, while her Mom shrugs and accepts it to be true.

"You're right honey. You know me so well" she says stepping aside. "Come in please"

One glance at Sofia and I'm glad to see that so far she seems completely happy with what's happening. Although we have only arrived. I'm gonna be watching everything like a hawk to make sure nothing makes her feel uncomfortable.

Sofia

Introducing Elijah as my boyfriend has got to be the best feeling in the world. The fact that he seemed to like it too only makes me happier. Remind me why I didn't say yes when he asked me to be his girlfriend? Oh yes, I panicked like a fucking idiot and couldn't speak.

Anyway the joyous feeling makes it easier for me to be here. I feel just fine. No panic just yet.

In fact, I'm kind of having the time of my life since my Mom and Dad are right here. Wow I've missed them and they clearly missed me too because they give me another tight hug once we've been led into the front room.

Having them visiting me every now and then just doesn't cut it. This is better. Much better.

"Oh myyyyy goddddddd!" I hear as my Mom lets me go. My joy pretty much over flows because I already know who it is.

I turn around just in time to see Bree charging towards me.

"I missed you so much! You need to visit more, I can't survive it here without you!" She yells right before she collides with me. Bree is very much the same as me when it comes to ambition. I told her a while back to get out of this town as soon as she could. I may not be doing so well since I left but I'm doing better than I was here.

"I missed you too! Like nothing else" I reply and squeeze her tighter. When I pull back to look at her, I realise how much she's changed since I saw her. Not in a psychical way. It's the way she holds herself with such confidence. Her brown eyes are glowing with the determination I had at her age. I hope she keeps it. She's going to do so well.

I lost a little of my excitement for life due to being rejected by pretty much every job I've applied for. Still I'll get there, I just know it.

"Sorry to break up all this hugging but dinner is ready" my Dad calls. Bree lets me go and turns to Elijah with a huge grin.

"Well you must be a pretty awesome guy to put up with Sofia" she jokes and I shove her playfully. Elijah can't help but laugh and I glare at him.

"You're gonna get yourself in trouble with me" I tell him and he holds up his hands in defence.

"I didn't say a word Darling"

"Oh my god he calls you Darling. I'm gonna die, this is so cute" she squeals before feigning seriousness. "However I will kick you in the balls if you hurt her!"

"Bree! Manners!" My Mom yells and I shake my head at this natural disaster.

"I won't hurt her I promise" Elijah assures Bree before we head to get dinner. She seems happy enough with that.

"Are you regretting this yet?" I whisper to him and he shakes his head, leaning down.

"Not one bit. This is great. I like seeing you like this" he whispers back and kisses my cheek. I catch Bree pretending to be sick and stick my tongue out at her.

"Seeing me like what?"

"Interacting with your family. Smiling, laughing, all of it"

"I smile and laugh with you too" I state, confused.

"Yes and it's the best thing I ever get to witness. Being here makes me feel even closer to you. Like I'm part of your life and it makes me feel very special"

"That's because you are part of my life Elijah. A huge part"

Uh oh. Why are we doing this here? We should talk about this later because making out in the hallway in front of my family would not go down well. I think he notices this too because he squeezes my hand and gives me a very heated look before blinking and clearing his throat.

We compose ourselves and finally take a seat in the dinning room.

All of the food is already laid out curtesy of my Dad. He loves to cook and today he's went all out for his guests, creating a full spread of burgers, bbq chicken, salad (no thanks) and an array of meat and potatoes. How many people did he think were coming?

Regardless I'm pretty happy to take a bit of everything and my Mom widens her eyes. Oh no, here we go.

"Sofia, could you try and be a bit more classy?" She asks, her voice a little high pitched. Maybe I don't miss her as much now...kidding. My Mom is rather proper. She's very feminine and delicate and is probably worried I'll scare off Elijah.

The irony is Elijah has mentioned before that he loves that I don't hold back. He also said he's never understood why women eat less to seem appropriate. That was a fun conversation. He gave me bedroom eyes while I chomped on a pizza.

"I like food" is all I can say with a shrug. I purposely ignore her look of disapproval and dig in anyway. Elijah shoots me a sly smile as I shove a piece of chicken into my mouth.

Naturally when Bree does the same as me she gets in trouble too.

"Honestly, you girls are ridiculous" my Mom sighs.

"Leave them alone Honey!" My Dad pipes up and this prompts her to listen. Only she then turns her attention to Elijah. Oh boy!

"So where did you guys meet?" She asks, glancing between us. Shit. We did not discuss this before hand. Shit. Fuck. Damn it!

"We met online which may have a bad reputation but it worked for us" Elijah answers before I can even think. He places a hand on my knee for affect and I try not to burst out laughing. He's laying this on thick but she's still not gonna like that.

"Ah well isn't that lovely" she hums and smiles genuinely. What? How is she okay with that? She doesn't stop there though.

"And what is it you do?"

There it is! The question I've been waiting for. Hey I'm surprised she isn't grilling me like expected but I guess Elijah is more interesting right now. I'm glad and worried all at once.

"I'm the CEO of a multinational company" he says a littler quieter than before as if not to gloat and just like I imagined my Mom's eyes widen.

"Holy shit! Like you own the company?" Bree asks excitedly.

"Yeah. My father set the foundations of it then I took over after he passed away" Elijah explains and unlike my

Mom who is no doubt planning our wedding, I'm looking at Elijah with so much respect. When he first told me this story I was in awe then and I can't help but feel that again.

"That's so lovely Elijah" she says and my Dad nods in agreement.

"That is really impressive" He states and I'm sure if he could he'd give Elijah a hard manly pat on the back.

If my parents weren't gonna like Elijah before, I have no doubt they will like him now. I think Bree likes him too but she keeps giving both of us a strange look. Maybe I'm imaging it.

With the burning questions out of the way, dinner goes smoothly. Elijah is a hit with everyone as he recalls stories of his years in business and I almost cry with laughter as he talks about a disgruntled client who threw pink paint over his car. Apparently Elijah caught him in the act, grabbed the paint bucket and dumped it on his head. I wish I'd seen that.

I'm also pleased to say that I survive the whole meal without any of my parents asking me any tough life questions. So I'm safe for now.

Once we're all done, I'm finally relaxed. Right up until Bree offers to clean up and asks me to help. Seems innocent enough apart from the weird look she gives me and the 'come here' gesture she acts out frantically as she exits the dinning room.

What's that about?

I feel bad leaving Elijah alone with my parents but he smiles at me as if to say he's okay while I leave.

I follow Bree and I almost squeal as she grabs my hand and pulls me into the kitchen faster than my feet can move. She then stops so quickly I crash into her.

"What on earth are you playing at?" I whisper yell at the same moment she crosses her arms and gives me a 'really?' stare.

"I could ask you the same thing!" She exclaims, raising her eyebrows.

"What do you mean?" I ask completely clueless.

"I mean that not so long ago I got an email from this weird dating website. I mean it happens all the time you know it's junk mail..."

"Yah I know what junk mail is"

"Well sometimes I sign up to these dating website things so my friends and I can have a laugh and-"

"Get to the point Bree! Please you're killing me! We've all joined dating websites!"

"Well, as soon as you introduced me to Elijah today I knew I recognised him from somewhere. So I searched his name and sure enough he's on the dating app thing!" She explains before shoving her phone in my face. My eyes are met with Elijah's sugar rush profile and when I glance back at Bree her eyes are wide.

"Your boyfriend is a sugar daddy!" She says a little too loudly for my liking. God forbid Mom or Dad hear! Luckily they're probably too engrossed in the conversation at the dinner table to pay attention.

How do I respond to this? Deny it? Act shocked? Tell her the truth? None of those actually. I'm more concerned about her being on this website. She may be eighteen but she's still a kid in my book!

"Never mind that Bree. What in gods name are you doing on that website?!" I know I'm a hypocrite but I don't want anything bad to happen to her. I just happen to have gotten lucky.

Her cheeks turn red immediately now that the heat is on her.

"L-like I said...it's for fun"

Now I'm crossing my arms and raising my eyebrows.

"Okay, that's fine but please tell me you haven't spoken to anyone...pleaaasseeee"

"Ummm..." she mumbles and looks away.

That's when Elijah comes to find me. He appears at the kitchen entrance looking like a snack and I'm momentarily distracted. Those rolled up shirt sleeves are gonna give me a heart attack.

"Everything okay?" he questions and suddenly I'm struck with an idea. Time to give Bree a quick life lesson.

"Yeah, I'm just chatting with Bree about dating websites. Oh and she told me something about you actually" I say in mock annoyance. I catch Bree flinching beside me. Heheheh.

"Oh no, honestly it's nothing" she tries. I send Elijah a quick wink and he smirks, realising that I want him to follow my lead. His face falls then transforming into a stone cold pissed off expression. This will be fun.

"Why don't you tell him what you found?"

"Honestly it's nothing" she squirms.

"No? She says you're on a sugar daddy website. Is that true?"

"Fuck...I'm sorry baby I didn't want you know that"

"I can't believe you would do that! Am I not enough for you?" I push out, trying my best not to laugh. A quick glance at Bree and she's pale white, watching our fake argument.

"Of course you are...I'm sorry Darling. I'm really sorry!" Elijah pleads, stepping to my side. I pretend that I can't look at him and turn away.

"Oh my god! What have I done?! I'm so sorry!" Bree cries.

"I think you should go!" I snap at Elijah and Bree's mouth falls open.

"No, baby just listen to me" Elijah pleads.

"No, no don't make him leave. I'm sure you guys can fix this-" she rambles on, her panic and fear so clear. I think that's enough of that.

Finally I let my laugh out and she stands there looking like she's seen a ghost.

"It's okay Bree. I know he's on a sugar daddy website" I tell her before she really gets upset. Elijah slides his arm around my waist and chuckles too.

"What? What do you mean?"

"That's how we met. Now I'm telling you this because I trust you okay? Please don't tell Mom or Dad. You know how they will react"

"You...you have a sugar daddy?!" Her mouth falls open in shock before she grins and shoves my shoulder. "Sofia! This isn't something I expected from you. What happened to making it on your own?" She teases and I glare at her.

"He's not actually my sugar daddy. It's just how we found each other" I explain and she nods but in a way that shows she doesn't believe me.

"Sureeeee. Does he buy you fancy cars?" She teases.

"No! It's not like that! Also stop that shit! Where the hell did you learn to be a smart ass?"

"You, you idiot. I learned everything from you"

"Then you learned from the best" Elijah states and I glare at him too.

"I will smother you while you sleep" I threaten, nudging him.

"That's okay, I'd die happily with you on top of me" he whispers but Bree still hears him.

"Okay ewww, stop that. I don't want to hear about your weird kinks" she cringes but recovers. "So I know you said he's not your sugar daddy but surely he's bought you cool stuff. He's a millionaire" she continues and I want to flick her on the forehead for not knowing when to stop.

"I told you, it's not like that" I state and she sighs.

"Not even a trip to Bali? If you haven't been yet you should go and take me with you. Elijah can we go to Bali?" she asks and I have to admire her for trying.

"If we're going to Bali, you better get your own sugar daddy to treat you" I joke, only her face goes red again. That's right, she's on the sugar rush website and she hasn't yet told me if she's talking to anyone.

"Bree, please tell me you haven't went and got yourself a sugar daddy? I know I don't have the right to tell you what to do but it can be dangerous. It was a stupid thing for me to do too but luckily I didn't go on a date with a murderer"

"I mean, I don't technically have one. Well, I haven't met him but he..." she stops talking and shoves her hands in her jean pockets looking sheepish.

"He what?" I ask already feeling sick at the thought of something being untoward.

"He won't leave me alone Sofia. Like I said I was on the app for a laugh and I messaged some guys. I didn't know it would end up so serious"

"Tell me everything..."

***

Bree, Elijah and I end up in the front room with her divulging the whole story. Luckily my parents went to bed so we don't have to make anything up to tell them.

It's crazy how easily these dating websites can be dangerous.

She tells us that he sent her cash just for sending a picture of her face. I asked why she even did that but I already know the answer. When you're lonely and insecure and someone says nice things to you it's easy to get caught up. So as the story goes, more money and more pictures got exchanged. Intimate pictures. Then Bree began to feel uncomfortable and tried to get this guy to leave her alone. So he threatened to leak the pictures. Which means she's essentially trapped.

I'm sitting here feeling powerless. Angry. Frustrated. Scared too because it could have been me. In fact I wish it had been me if it would have meant that it wasn't her. Yeah she's an adult but to me she's still my baby cousin.

Elijah must sense my distress because he takes my hand, his thumb soothing me with soft movements.

"I'm going to fix this for you Bree. I don't how yet but I will I promise"

"I second that" Elijah says sounding as pissed as I do.

"Thank you guys so much!" She exclaims and jumps off the couch to hug me. I stand in time to catch her and hold her closely. She must be terrified and by the sounds of it, we're the first people she's told.

She also hugs Elijah when he stands up and it's a amusing to watch him hug her back awkwardly. He isn't used to so much affection in any sense of the word. I don't think he's had as many hugs in his life as he has since meeting me. Sometimes a hug fixes everything. He's been neglected in that area.

After divulging all of the information to us she looks exhausted, so it's no surprise she heads to bed too. This leaves us standing alone in the front room.

"Thank you for offering to help Bree" I tell him.

"The whole thing makes me mad Darling. The poor girl doesn't deserve that. I kept thinking what if it had been you and that just drives me crazy. I can't even think of what I'd do if something like that happened to you. I'd kill the guy"

Grabbing him, I pull him to me and smash my lips to his. His arms wrap around me immediately, his body pressing into mine. I've wanted to do this all day.

"I wanna protect you Darling and that extends to protecting the people you love. I never got to protect my parents from their death and the rest of my family don't want to know me so I'm putting all that effort into someone who does care"

Wow he's just admitted that he's finally allowing himself to believe that I care about him. I'm- wow!

"That means everything to me"

Elijah

And you mean everything to me.

I've said many telling things to Sofia. Most of them giving away the feelings that I can't fight. Sometimes my admissions are interrupted. Sometimes she says those things back to me yet we still try to act like we don't know what's going on between us.

It's the lie we both seem to tell ourselves. It's the fear of getting hurt that seems to be engrained in both of us.

We're both broken and damaged souls. Desperately trying to find our missing puzzle piece. It's quite possible that we're staring the answer in the face every time we're together. Yet neither of us will admit it because we're afraid to mess up this bliss. It's very fragile, yet I can't bare the thought of losing her for any reason, especially not because I got too attached and freaked her out.

So instead of saying what I really need to, I just kiss her soundly and try to show her what I'm thinking.

I kiss her as gently as possible and for god knows how long. Instead of pulling apart, we just hug each other, her arms securing around my waist, her head on my chest. My face in buried in her neck, my arms holding her so tightly I'm worried it may hurt.

"Hey boyfriend, you wanna see my bedroom?" She whispers in my ear after some time.

"Are you allowed boys in your room?" I tease taking her hand.

"Probably not but if we're quiet we can sneak upstairs"

"Oh how naughty of you. I love it"

She leads me up the stairs and I take in the family photos on the wall. I catch a cute little picture of a small rosey cheeked Sofia.

"Oh lord don't look at that" she sounds horrified and tugs on my hand harder.

"That is the cutest thing I've ever seen" I sigh, glad I caught it.

"God, you must need your eyes checked, I was an ugly kid. Not much better now to be honest"

"You're beautiful Darling" I tell her as we make it to her bedroom. She flicks on the light and my eyes take in the double bed with purple duvet. The walls are covered with posters of everything from iron man to some boy band I've never heard of. I don't think her parents have changed her bedroom since she left and to be honest I'm so glad. Every little thing I learn about this women excites me. Everything right down to what I assume was an attempt to learn guitar, since an acoustic one with broken strings sits in the corner.

I should play for her some time, come to think of it. I'm not great but I can strum a few tunes.

"Welcome to an expression of my younger self. Please ignore...well all of it!"

"Not a chance!"

***

Sofia hates every second I spend looking at her walls but I love it more than anything.

Eventually though I can't resist joining her in bed. I'm really touched that I get to be here. I never imagined she'd want me somewhere so personal. Her family home, her old bedroom, pressed against her body like I matter to her more than anything else.

I know that can't be true but right now I want to believe it. Just for a little while.

She's wearing my shirt to sleep in because she forgot to pack pyjamas. I used to be a pyjama guy before we met but now I prefer to sleep in my boxers or completely naked. I like to feel her against my skin.

"You know I actually never brought a guy up here" she informs me. "Mom and Dad would never have let that happen so this is really nice"

She trails her fingers up my arm, a content and happy expression on her face. I feel those same emotions. I'm scared to admit that I've never been this happy.

"Now I feel really privileged. The first guy in Sofia's bed huh?" I joke and she nods, playing with my hair. It's so nice. My hand moves over her hip and under the shirt to her waist, feeling her curves. So fucking sexy...all the damn time.

"Yeah you're my first so you better be gentle with me" she teases, biting her lip. Oh I see what we're doing.

"Are you sure you want this baby?" I ask, trying my best to sound like an eighties rom com.

"You know I always hated that line. Women are always made to look so unsure and scared of sex in films when in reality..."

Her hand slides down my stomach and into my boxers to wrap around my cock. Yesssss.

"We just want dick" she finishes the sentence and her face breaks into a cheeky grin.

This women is it for me. There I said it! How can I deny it? No one will ever make me feel this way. So I better enjoy it while she still wants me.

That night I am so very gentle with her. I'm not sure how long we move together, our bodies in perfect synchronisation but it's not long enough. It could have been hours and I'd still want more.

Unfortunately I'm only human and after giving her as many orgasms as I possibly could, I had my own and slumped onto her like a dead weight. I promised I'd never do that again but she said she liked it.

So here I am, too exhausted to move. Her hands still roam my back and occasionally playing with my hair. Mmmm yes, this is where I belong. There's no where else I need to be.

Right here in my girls arms is my home.

Sofia

I didn't think that anything could ruin my high. The feeling of being on cloud nine stayed with me all night and into the morning.

Waking up and gazing at Elijah's cute sleeping form only made me happier. I'd brushed my fingers over his cheek before pulling some clothes on and getting up to go to the toilet. What could possibly go wrong right?

Apparently a lot can change in a matter of seconds.

A matter of moments.

Walking out of the bathroom, I head downstairs for a drink. I open the fridge, pull out some juice and grab a glass from the cupboard.

The juice is poured and the glass is pressed to my lips.

"Well, what do we have here then?" Hits my ears in a horribly familiar rough voice, that has me whipping around in shock.

A voice that has given me nightmares. One that is making it impossible for me to move.

There in the doorway stands my older cousin Brian. Shouldn't really be a big deal right? Wrong.

Ice pours into my veins. My heart pounds and my feet itch to take me far away from here. It's the same feeling I got when I ran from Elijah in the bar. Only a thousand times worse because this man is what has caused it all. All of my pain. The fear I have of men, angry men. It's all because of him.

Brian is the whole reason I don't want to be here. He's the reason I feel sick when I think of coming home. He's the route of my fear. Fear I try to forget has a hold of me.

My hand shakes so hard that the glass slips from my fingers and falls to the ground.

The smashing sound hurts my ears and it replicates the shattering of my bliss.

Well, there goes all my happiness.

I shouldn't have come home. I can't be here.

"You are you going to pay for being so clumsy"

My brain drags up a sentence long buried, my mind trying to pull me back into my childhood. Only I don't have to go there to feel fear.

This is happening now and I can't fucking breath.

The coldness in his eyes is so familiar as is the sick smile on his face.

He takes a step towards me and laughs when I flinch. "You're still a little coward huh? Clean up the mess"

Help.

Please.

Someone help me.

Elijah

     I'm having a lovely dream about Sofia and I cooking together. It's extremely lucid and I feel like I actually have control of my own actions. The only reason I know I'm dreaming is because every time I try to touch her, I can't reach. It's torture...no it's hell. In fact, it's quite possible that this is a nightmare. However I do want to try and remember to cook more with Sofia in the future. I think it'd be fun.

     SMASH!

     "Fuck!" I jolt awake as a jarring sound hits my ears.

     Sofia mentioned last night that we'd have to be quiet because of the thin walls in this house. She wasn't wrong because whatever I just heard didn't happen in this room but it sure sounded like it.

     Turning to my right, I look to see if Sofia is awake too but I find the space next to me empty.

     I might be overacting but waking up without her there is a horrible feeling. I'm so used to having her beside me now that it actually scares me a little. I know it has nothing to do with simple company or dependence because the thought of anyone else in bed with me is very unappealing. I've picked apart my feelings for Sofia so much that I've decided I can't crack the code. Guess I'll just have to go on clueless and blissfully happy.

     Now where is my girl?

     Sitting up, a wave of drowsiness hits me. My body is still so relaxed from our passion last night that I can barely get up. God I just wanna go back to sleep but I can't do that without Sofia.

Lazily I pull my jeans and shirt back on. I'm sure I look like a mess but I don't really care. I'm kinda worried about that smashing noise and the lack of a women in my arms. Boy I'm mushy these days. Funnily enough I don't hate it.

Scratching my beard, I realise that it's gonna need a tidy up so I don't give my girl beard burn. That's what I'm thinking about in my dazed mind as I saunter down the stairs. I'm sure everything is okay, I mean I don't think anything could ruin my high.

Really that's a stupid thing for me to think. I should know better.

"You really have grown up huh? Not that it's much of an improvement but at least you don't look like a little brat anymore"

I hear those words as clear as day and they don't sound like anyone I've met yet. In fact, they sound harsh and cold.

Walking towards the kitchen, I hear no reply. I'm hoping that this dude isn't talking to Sofia like that and that she's somewhere else in the house.

The first thing I see is obviously the owner of the voice I heard. One quick glance is enough time to notice his almost bald head, unwashed look and menacing smile. Who the fuck is he?

I don't really care to find out because in the next second my eyes find Sofia.

She is crouched over broken glass, picking up the pieces. Much like I tried to do in the coffee shop with the broken jars. Just like she panicked at my attempt, fear fills me instantly.

"Darling, be careful!" I almost yell and dart to her, crouching down to grab her hands. I'm instantly angry as I realise that asshole over there was just watching her do this! I also realise that his harsh words were aimed at her and my anger turns to rage.

I have to close my eyes and take a deep breath because I can't loose my shit here and I don't want her to be afraid of me.

It hasn't gone unnoticed that she hasn't said a word yet. Which is certainly not like her.

"I'm sure she can clean it up herself. No need to pity her" I hear and my blood boils. What the fuck is wrong with this man?

I've never seen Sofia so subdued. She's so quiet and looks so small. She's terrified. I hate it.

"Sofia?" I question and she looks up at me, fear prominent in those gorgeous eyes.

"I'm fine" she states robotically as if she's programmed to say those exact words. What has he done to her?

"Hey dude, who are you anyway? What are you doing in my aunts house?" the asshole asks.

"That's none of your business Brian!" Sofia snaps her voice weak but defensive.

"I think you'll find it is! He's in a family members home and has yet to introduce himself. He could be a danger"

Seriously? I'm a danger?

At that exact moment Sofia's Mom walks in and saves the day. Or rather she saves Brian from being thrown across the room by me.

"Oh Brian honey, I didn't know you would be paying us a visit-" she pauses when she sees Sofia and I crouched on the floor. "What happened here?"

"I dropped a glass" Sofia responds, once again like a robot. I really don't like it. It doesn't seem right.

"Ah you're still as clumsy as ever then" her Mom comments with a little laugh and Sofia looks back at the floor. I still haven't let her hands go and I don't plan on it either. Standing, I tug her with me and step away from the mess on the floor. "You guys go get ready for the day, I'll clean it up" she continues and I use that as a perfect cue to nod in thanks and remove Sofia from the situation.

Brian doesn't say another word and I'm glad because I'm not sure that I'd be able to stop myself from punching him. Which wouldn't help at all.

Sofia is quiet all the way back up the stairs and I worry she may never speak again. Only as soon as we're back in the room, she throws her arms around me and snuggles into my chest.

Oh baby girl, what's wrong.

"Sofia, talk to me. What just happened?" I ask but instead of giving me any more information, she pulls away from me and mumbles.

"I dropped the glass..."

"Yes but why do you look so spooked? Is it him? Brian or whatever he's called? Did he say something to you? Is he the one that hur-"

"I just got a fright" she cuts in before trying to fake a smile. She's lying but I don't want to keep asking in case it makes her feel worse. "I'm going to take a shower, I won't be long" she continues, her voice a whisper.

I watch her walk away, fighting the urge to go after her. She wants to be alone.

While I want to go downstairs and beat the shit out of that man. If he's the reason she didn't want to come home, if he has hurt her, I'll kill him.

Sofia

Shit. Fuck. Bastard! I knew I shouldn't have come home. Why did he have to pop by the one weekend I'm here? Unless my parents told him I was coming and he decided to come and torment me.

He instils the fear of god in me. You know when you meet someone and they just give off bad vibes? Well it's like that except worse because I've experienced the output of those bad vibes. I dealt with it for years. He's scares me more than I'd like to admit and my skin crawls whenever I'm around him.

I want to leave and never come back. Maybe another five years away will do the trick. Yet I can't make a scene. I can't walk out because then my parents will ask questions. They can't know about him. They can't know he beat me black and blue well into my teenage years. It would destroy them.

I still have no idea why he hates me so much.

Shutting myself in the bathroom, I shake away flashbacks of the past that involves him. I don't want to think about that right now. I gotta put my game face on. Be brave.

Elijah has probably worked it all out now but I don't know what to say to him. He should know the full story. I need to tell him.

Stripping out of my clothes, I hop into the shower and stand under the intense spray. The heat seeps into my body and helps me forget the nasty feeling inside me.

Poor Elijah. I must have looked like a psycho. What if he thinks I'm a coward who's scared of her older cousin?

Because that's the truth of it. I don't have the guts to fight back.

Running my fingers through my hair, I let out a sigh so loud it's like I have a world of problems. When in actual fact my life is better than its ever been.

This weekend is special. Elijah is with me and I've finally gotten the courage to be here. I can't let Brian ruin this. I'm an adult now. I can hurt him back.

The sound of the water running and hitting the shower floor is all I can really hear, which is probably why I don't notice anyone entering the bathroom. Well not until the shower curtain is pulled back and I shit myself.

"What the fuck?!" I scream, trying to cover my naked body. My heart rate soars until I see who it is.

"Sorry Darling, I did knock...and call your name. I was worried" Elijah says sheepishly as I relax against the cold tile, dropping my hands and closing my eyes again.

"That was like a scene out of psycho. Turns out I wouldn't be very good at defending myself in that situation" I tell him, cracking my eyes open to see him looking up and down my body. "Heterosexual men really are useless when faced with a naked women huh?" I joke and he nods as if he's in a trance.

"Sorry again...I can't help it. I do still want to know if you're okay or not?"

"I'm okay, I promise. Are you?" I laugh, feeling a little better already. Magical.

Maybe Brian will be gone by now and I can pretend this didn't happen.

"Yes I'm okay..." he begins, looking wary as if what he wants to say next is tough for him. "Will you...will you tell me about your childhood one day? I want to know so that I can protect you from things. From anyone..."

Oh Elijah you're the sweetest.

"I'll tell you soon. I promise baby" I assure him.

"And you want to stay? You feel comfortable?" he checks and I nod because speaking right in this moment is too hard. I guess comfortable would be lying but I don't wanna go. Brian won't chase me away this time.

"Okay Darling. Just let me know if you don't feel okay at any point"

"Thank you Elijah. I really appreciate you coming here with me. I couldn't have without you" I confess and he smiles softly.

"I really want to join you" he breathes, biting his lip.

"You know shower sex is dangerous right?" I ask, imagining all the different ways in which we could slip and crack our heads open. Shower sex, not for me.

"Who said anything about sex? Maybe I just wanna hold you? Or wash your hair? You know like in those ridiculous romance movies?"

"Ewww no thanks, that's sickening" I smirk and scrunch my nose in disgust.

"Well, can I touch your butt?" He asks, shrugging nonchalantly. His cute casual demeanour and hopeful expression has me laughing probably more than necessary but it makes him laugh too. Is this what it's like to find your person? Someone who can make you feel better? Happy? Someone who can take away a lifetime of fear and reverse the effects of childhood trauma?

"You can...you can touch my butt"

"Yes!" He exclaims and fist bumps the air. I shake my head at his childishness as he starts pulling off his clothes too. I love it...I love him.

NOPE! I DON'T!

Don't catch too many feelings Sofia! That can't end well! He certainly doesn't love you! This is just a good time for him, a distraction-

My inner pity party is cut off as he steps in the shower with me, his arms immediately snaking around my waist.

He squeezes my butt while looking rather pleased with himself. Smug asshole.

I squish myself against him and pull him under the spray so I can watch his soft hair get wet. It's weird the things that I now enjoy because of this man.

"Is it still a no for the kissing?"

"I guess, maybe a little kissing won't hurt" I sigh dramatically and roll my eyes for effect.

He leans forward and I anticipate his lips on mine, only they touch my cheek instead.

"I think I missed my mark" he chuckles and presses a kiss to my neck now. "Oops"

I hate that he's so good at this. The way that he can make me feel so free and floaty because it means he can take it all away. He could make me feel like I'm in hell too if he wanted.

My hands move down his chest to his stomach, feeling his wet skin. His breathing deepens, his hands moving around my back to secure me against him.

"Darling, I think I have a problem" he breathes in my ear. "Every time we're not touching, I feel like something's missing. It's kinda scary. I don't know how to control it"

Fuck. I think I need my hearing checked or maybe he's just so aroused that he's saying random shit but fuckkkkk.

I want to help him but I can't because I feel the exact same thing. Sometimes I wish he wouldn't say these kind of things because it gives me a false sense of hope.

Elijah

Well I guess I said that out loud. I certainly didn't intend to but with her hands on me it's practically impossibly to think straight. I'm surprised I don't jizz the second she lays a finger on me.

Does she feel it too? The electric sensation that pulses through my body with every touch. I wish I could say it was simple lust but I've experienced that and it's nothing compared this. The way she looks at me, the way she talks, the genuine affection I can see and feel. It's all so overwhelming and so easy to drown in. I'd stay here forever if I could.

"Elijah what are we doing?" She asks, yet its more of a whine. Like she's begging for an answer.

"Showering" I answer, even though I know that's not what she's asking.

"No, I mean-"

"I know what you mean Darling"

I pull my face away from her neck so that I can see what she's feeling. She looks confused and a little lost. A bit like myself.

"I don't have an answer for you. I just know that I need you" So very desperately. How could I let myself become so weak? Maybe I've always been this way but no one ever broke me down.

"You had sugar babies. You didn't have any girlfriends. You had no free time. Yet this...this is not the same" she reminds me. I don't know why we're having this conversation in the shower at this random moment.

Except maybe I kind of do. This happens every so often when we both don't know how to deal with our emotions. When the fear is routed so deep that it has to come out sometime. It's random and there's no way around it. The first time this happened we had only been together a few days. I'd woken up in the middle of the night and stared at her so hard she woke up too. I'd asked her what she'd done to me. She didn't know how to answer.

Just like I don't right now. I don't know why I act this way with her. I still don't know what she's done to me but maybe it's just because she's so...everything. The beauty, the brains, the attitude, the care. All of it is a perfect cocktail of heaven to me.

"And you wanted to know about the sugar lifestyle. You weren't looking for this. You weren't even looking for a fling. So what are we doing?"

"We're definitely ruining sugar rush's perfect reputation of carefully constructed sugar relationships. You know I deleted the app. I should really remove myself from their mailing list. I keep getting emails"

Huh? She is? I deleted the app too and I requested for my profile to be removed. I guess it hasn't worked yet if Bree was able to see it. It better work soon, I don't want anyone to think I'm available. Not as a sugar daddy or as a boyfriend. Put it this way, if this all goes to shit, I don't want anyone else. Certainly not a sugar baby.

"What do they say?"

"They keep asking me to 'Review My Daddy' and to 'Recommend My Daddy To Other Sugary Sweets'" she grumbles, not pleased at all.

"And why haven't you?" I tease, more eager to hear her answer than I wanna admit. "Would you not recommend my services?" I smirk.

"No! Of course I wouldn't!" she scowls and my mouth falls open in shock. What have I done wrong? Haven't I been good enough for her?

"Why not?" I ask alarmed and worried that I've not done enough.

"If you think I'm going to encourage other women to message you, then you must be crazy! You're mine"

Woah! If I wasn't already rock hard then I would be from that statement alone. I actually shiver in delight as she shows off her possessive side. I may lean towards a dominant nature but I'll bow down to her that's for sure.

"Yes, I am Sofia" I confirm. "You got me baby girl. Besides, no one could message me. I deleted the app too"

"You did?" She asks a little surprised.

"Of course. I'm not a sugar daddy now. I don't wanna be ever again. All I wanna be is yours" I confess then panic at my words.

Was that too much? Have I scared her?

I don't have to wonder for long because grabs the back of my head and pulls my lips to hers fiercely. It's funny how life goes. I really am hers because no matter how this ends, I know I'll never want another women. I know I'll never let another women touch me. She's got me and I hope to god I have her.

Sofia

God he's got a way with words. I don't know what about me keeps him so interested. He didn't have to agree to monogamy but he did. How do I fascinate such a powerful and successful man? I'm not so special.

Yet he makes me feel that way as he massages shampoo into my hair. The smell of it reminds me of my childhood because it's still the same stuff my Mom has always bought. All my childhood reminds me of is the desperate need to get out of this town. It's kinda making me nauseous so I'm glad when Elijah begins to wash it back out.

I wonder what people would think of him if they could see him being this way. From the few tabloids I've seen, they always introduce him as 'Elijah Everett, CEO Multi-Millionaire who takes no shit from no one and has a mean streak'.

Sometimes they say billionaire and to be fair I actually don't know which one is correct. It's not something I've ever asked and I don't think I want to know.

I'm sure they'd take away the mean streak part if they knew how gently he is currently touching me.

He doesn't stop touching me in fact, even while we dry off and get dressed. His hands slide under my t-shirt as I try to pull it down and I can't help but laugh as he tugs me close.

"You sure you're okay?" he asks.

"Yes, I'm okay. Now are you going to be able to keep your hands to yourself at breakfast?" I tease and his lips turn down.

"Maybe...I mean I'll try my best but it's gonna be tough"

"I'm sure you'll be just fine" I smirk and peck his lips for good measure. Maybe he'll be fine but I don't know if I will. I can still feel the ache between my legs that he created and I still want more. Nevertheless, I guess I'll have to be good until we go home tomorrow.

***

No such luck. Brian is still here. So I do what I did as a kid. I hide how I'm feeling with perfect finesse.

Even if he does sit opposite me at breakfast. I'm not even sure why he's still here, surely he was just popping by.

I don't want to let him bother me considering I need to enjoy my time with my family. Especially with Bree because she'll probably be going home right after breakfast.

I relax a little when the conversation is fairly normal. Bree talks about her future aspirations, my parents mention their holiday plans for next year. It's sweet and free of disaster right up until Brian opens his mouth. SHOCK!

"So Sofia, you've been gone for a few years now. I'm surprised you haven't settled down yet" he muses in a completely normal manner. Now most people would think this was an okay thing to bring up but I know better.

He knows that mentioning me settling down will spark my parents dire need for me get married and have kids. Two thing I don't want...ever.

"I'm only twenty five. I've plenty of time for settling down"

Really I should have guessed my answer would not go down well.

"Oh Sofia, you really do need start thinking about the future though. Twenty five isn't that young when starting a family is concerned" my Mom is quick to remind me. Is she serious?

One glance at Brian and I can see how smug he is. Fucker!

"I am thinking about the future. My ideal life is marriage and baby free, travelling the world and not getting my money sucked dry by some stinky kid" I reply dramatically which has my Mom shaking her head.

I can feel Elijah's hand sliding onto my knee under the table. He must be able to tell I'm hella uncomfortable with this topic.

I'm surprised he isn't terrified by what's being said.

"Although there is one thing marriage can give you" Bree mumbles obviously afraid to bring it up. If she's got something to say about this then it must be worth listening to. She's about the only person at this table (and Elijah of course) that's worth listening to all together.

"And what's that" I smirk, letting her know I'm not mad. I'm aware my marriage views aren't the same as everyone else's here.

"Security and the fact that if the person you do choose to be with gets into a serious accident you may not be allowed in to visit them in the hospital because you won't be considered family"

Huh? I guess I've never thought of that. Probably because I've never had anyone I cared about enough. Now though, if Elijah were in an accident and I couldn't see him, I'd be going ballistic.

There's an awkward silence rising now and I can tell Elijah is staring at me. When I turn to him, he looks away and clears his throat.

"Well, let's hope no one gets into any accidents huh?" I try to brush the subject off and luckily it seems to work.

Phew.

Elijah

    I hope no one noticed the colour leave my face when Bree brought up the whole security in marriage thing. I know it's ridiculous but it really bothered me.
    It bothered me because: Sofia in an accident? Unthinkable. Which is why I've never thought of it. It hurts

me to think of her being in any kind of pain. Although I know for sure that if anything happened to her, I sure as hell would not be stopped getting into a hospital to see her.

"And how is the job hunting going?" Brian asks Sofia once again forcing her to talk about a subject that makes her uncomfortable.

I know how she feels about her job status and not necessarily because she's told me but because it's not hard to see. She feels like a failure because she hasn't gotten the job of her dreams yet. The longer it takes her the more it bothers her.

So when I say that I really don't like Brian, what I really mean is I fucking hate him with everything inside me.

"It's going" she mumbles and bites on a piece of toast to end that line of conversation. Something I've noticed about her parents is that they are a tiny bit judgmental. They go from supportive to not so much really quickly.

I'm surprised her Mom is like this considering she genuinely seemed pleased that Sofia has gotten a job. It's a strange dynamic and I don't blame my girl for wanting out of here. Even though I know her parents were not the reason she left.

Brian tries a third time to knock Sofia off, only this time he doesn't do well at all.

"Still as geeky as ever with those comics and shit? You probably still have action figures too!"

"Oh don't be silly Brian of course she doesn't" her Mom exclaims while Sofia turns red. Don't worry Darling, I've got this one.

"What's wrong with action figures? You should see my collection, it's crazy" I say enthusiastically and Brian frowns in my direction.

"Are you kidding? You don't have to lie to save her feelings dude. It's okay if you want to run a mile. I told her she'd never keep a man with all that childish shit"

"Stop being an ass Brian! You're so fucking rude!" Bree yells at him causing Sofia to cut in.

"It's fine Bree honestly. Elijah does have an impressive collection though" she says smugly and turns to me. "It's amazing"

"What can I say? I'm a geek too" I grin and can't help but stare at her beautiful smiling face. I think we won this one.

"Oh god get a room!" Bree jokes, while I catch Brian scowling. He clearly has something against Sofia but I can't even begin to imagine what that might be.

After that, everything settles back down and the pleasantries continue.

Sofia

Before Bree leaves, Elijah calls some members of his team. He asks them to see what they can do about the guy who won't leave Bree alone. I had thought up some ways to block the creep completely from her life but I'm not yet experienced enough to do that myself. Which is why it's better that Elijah's new and improved band of hackers - I mean tech team - do it instead.

You see this particular sugar daddy obviously knows what he's doing, since Bree blocking his profile and number didn't work.

"I've been informed that in about twenty four hours he shouldn't be able to contact you again. If it doesn't work, let Sofia know and we'll try something else" Elijah says while we're in the front room. My parents are currently making a quick trip to the shops so that's how we're even able to talk about it. Brian went for a midday nap because apparently he's had a hard week. He really needs to fuck off!

"Thanks so much! I really appreciate it! I'm glad I have a good sugar daddy on my side" she laughs. I have to remember to thank him too later.

"It has nothing to do with being good. It's just a decent thing to do" he shrugs and I lean my head on his shoulder. Bree looks suddenly happier and mischievous as she sits across from us, cross legged on the couch.

"You still haven't told me what he's bought you!" She exclaims joyously. She really doesn't wanna believe that he's not actually my sugar daddy huh.

"Oh you know, just a Ferrari and stuff" I lie and her mouth falls open in shock.

"Shut up! No way!"

"Exactly, no way! Why the hell would I want or need a Ferrari?!" I laugh and she glares at me.

"There has to be something you've always really wanted?" She asks. Elijah looks at me then as if he's desperate to hear the answer too. I guess I don't blame him. He's so used to buying things and funding people that it's probably tough for him not to when it comes to me.

"I don't know. I guess I'm not very materialistic" I tell her and she rolls her eyes.

"Come onnnnn Sofia! You must desire something? What's your dream car?"

"I've never thought- oh wait actually. I do like Chevrolet Camaros ever since bumblebee was one in the Transformers. Although yellow isn't my colour"

"You like Bumblebee?" Elijah asks and I nod enthusiastically. I loveeeeeee Bumblebee. "So do I, he's my favourite"

"Dear God you guys are literally so good for each other. You're both so nerdy, I love it! This is legitimately a love story, I can't with you guys" Bree gushes and I don't know what to say.

In that moment it's like we both get triggered by the mention of love and look away from each other. It isn't a love story even if I'd like it to be. Elijah sure doesn't want that.

"So what's your plans for the rest of that day?" I ask her to change the subject. She's not dumb so she notices what I'm doing. Still, she goes with it.

"I'll probably catch up with some friends and try to find myself a new boo since as you know the last guy didn't work out"

"But not on that website right?"

"Of course not. I'm going to try the whole meeting people in real life thing for now. Oh and I think I'll be staying away from men for a while. I always feel a lot safer when I'm dating women anyway"

"Good idea. It's nice you have the option. Me on the other hand, I just love dick" I grin and she shakes her head. My parents, nor her own, know that she's bisexual. Which is probably why she likes being around me so much. She was terrified to tell me a few years back but when I told her that it didn't matter to me, she was so much happier. I hate to think that she thought I would care.

We've kind of been there for each other through everything.

"Sorry I should rephrase. I love one dick" I giggle and pat Elijah's leg for good measure.

"You're lucky you said that. Otherwise you would have been in big trouble" he growls, sending shivers through my body. Oh boy.

"I love being in trouble with you" I breath.

"Ohhhhh-Kay! That's my cue to leave!" Bree laughs and stands to say her goodbyes.

I'm not going to lie. I wish she'd stay longer so that I didn't have to deal with my insane family alone. Luckily I think Elijah will help me make it through.

***

After Bree's departure, I decide that it would be nice to show Elijah around town. My parents still aren't back so I don't see any harm in it.

When I say it's the nicest feeling ever to walk down the street with his hand in mine, I mean it. I know that we hold hands in public normally now but it's usually just from a building to his car and then his car to one of our apartments or a restaurant. With both of us working, doing much else is hard. So this, this is great! Plus, he's gotten over his fear that something bad will happen to me if we're seen together.

It's also great that he's wearing casual clothes. Dark jeans and a grey t-shirt covered up by a black jacket, is a look that has my mouth watering. I don't look any different of course. I always wear jeans and a t-shirt. Come to think of it, he's only seen me dressed up a handful of times. Not that he seems to mind.

"So a Chevrolet Camaro huh?" he questions as we walk by some little shops. Uh oh.

"Don't even think about it!" I warn him.

"What? You don't want a car? You'd look sexy driving a Camaro that's for sure. Then again you'd look sexy driving a Fiat Panda so I guess I can't use that to fight my corner"

"It's not that I don't want a car, I just don't want you to spend a ridiculous amount of money buying me one. I wouldn't spend so much money myself therefore I can't expect someone else to do so"

"You know, I could give you anything and everything. All of your hearts desires, you could have" he tells me, his voice full of dramatic wonder.

"Anything?" I ask and he stops me, placing his hands on my arms. He looks down at me, his eyes lit up like a kid on Christmas.

"Anything" he repeats. He looks so excited as if he's dying to give me anything that comes out of my mouth.

"Hmmm, well then I know what I want"

His face breaks into a grin but my answer isn't anything of monetary value.

Tugging on his jacket, I pull him closer so that he knows what I want. His eyes soften when he realises just how simple it is.

He presses his lips to mine and just like every time before it's like I've never felt such passion. I literally can't think of anything that I'd want more than this. A fast car might give me a thrill for a while but nothing would compare to this.

When he pulls away from me, he still looks determined.

"I won't give up you know. There has to be something else. Something you'd let me buy you"

"There is"

Oops that's a lie. Which is not something I'm good at.

Idiot. Now what are you gonna say huh? You just wanted to see his face light up again and now you're stuck! Stupid Sofia!

Glancing over his shoulder, I see a window full of cakes. That'll do.

"Cake" I state.

"Cake?"

"Lots of cake"

Gesturing behind him, he gets the idea and turns around.

"Oh yes, lots of cake"

I'm glad Elijah is as enthusiastic as me when it comes to sweet things. I'm even more ecstatic when he's keen to share hot chocolate brownies and ice cream with me.

"That's my one!" I complain as he digs his spoon into my half. The audacity!

"Oops guess you're too slow!" He teases. So I steal a bit of his and it's like some sort of spoon battle.

I end up cheating a little, gliding my leg up the inside of his. This distracts him long enough for me to eat the last mouthful.

"I win!" I grin and he looks at me in shock as he realises what's happened.

"I can't believe you played me. You'll pay for that"

"Will I?" I question, looking at him with innocent eyes, while licking my spoon. Then I get another idea.

Dragging my finger through the chocolate sauce on the plate, I then hold it up to his mouth. He smirks and wraps his lips around my finger before closing his eyes. Damn. Guess this one actually got me rather than him.

"Maybe I could forgive you" he muses, linking our fingers once he's done.

"I sure hope so. I can make it up to you"

Did we then sneak to the tiny bathroom in the cafe a few minutes apart and fuck like animals? Maybe...

Did he have to cover my mouth with his hand when someone tried the door handle? Also maybe...

Guess I'll leave it to your imagination. Although I will say that Elijah forgave me rather quickly when my lips were wrapped around his cock.

***

When we get back we enter the house in fits of laughter. I almost can't control it. Well that's until we walk into the front room.

My parents are sitting there as if someone has died and Brian is looking more smug than normal. This can't be good.

"What's up?" I say causally, hoping I've read the situation wrong.

"I think we should be asking you that Honey" my Mom sighs. Huh, this outta be interesting.

"Ummmm okay? You'll have to forgive me. I'm a little confused" I reply and fight the urge to cross my arms and become immediately defensive.

"Is it true?" she asks and I genuinely don't know what she's on about. I shoot a quick glance at Elijah and he seems just as confused as I am.

"Is what true?" I ask back and Brian rolls his eyes.

"Is he your Sugar Daddy? Like does he pay you and shit?" he questions.

Shit. Fuck! What am I meant to say?

My Mom tuts at Brian and I'm assuming it's because of the way he's asked but she wasn't too concerned about his tone earlier.

"Yes Honey, it's just Brian overheard you earlier talking to Bree and we're just concerned is all"

Fucking Brian! Of course he wasn't napping! Of course he was snooping around, listening to our conversation so that he could find something to use against me. I gave him the perfect ammo too.

"You ever heard of a joke?" is my best sarcastic answer.

"Didn't sound like a joke" Brian grumbles. Fuck sake.

"I just want to make sure you're safe Sofia. Surely if this is true then it's not a healthy relationship to be in" my Mom continues.

I don't know what she thinks she knows about a healthy relationship. I'm pretty sure Dad and her have been on the edge of divorce for years.

"Our relationship is perfectly healthy" I state and feel Elijah taking my hand. Yes, good! That'll reinforce my words. We've done nothing to suggest we're in an unhealthy relationship.

"That doesn't answer our question" My Dad hits back. Damn. They're really going for this one.

"Just admit it! He's your sugar daddy and you're with him because he pays you" Brian inputs, stirring shit up again.

Fine, if they want the truth they'll get it.

"He doesn't pay me. We met through a website that caters to sugar daddies and sugar babies but he isn't my sugar daddy. I promise you that. I'd never be with anyone for money and Elijah means a lot to me" I tell them and my Mom look immediately guilty. As if she feels bad for believing Brian.

"Oh bullshit! You couldn't make it on your own! So you had to find someone who could bail you out of a shitty situation didn't you?! You're practically a prostitute!" Brian sneers and this triggers a world of anger inside me.

Apparently it does the same to Elijah because through the sounds of my parents reprimanding Brian, Elijah shouts:

"THAT'S ENOUGH!"

I squeeze Elijah's hand tighter and he pulls me into his side.

Silence falls. For about two seconds.

"I'd like it if you didn't shout in my household" My Dad snaps at Elijah and I actually have to laugh. "What's so funny?"

"It's funny that every one of you have been nothing but disrespectful to me since I arrived and the second someone sticks up for me, you don't like it" I push out through the tight squeeze of emotion in my throat.

"Disrespectful? How have we been disrespectful? You're the one who has brought this random man into our home, who apparently is not simply your boyfriend!" My Dad continues. Did he not just hear what I said? Or I guess he doesn't believe me. His own daughter.

"What did you expect? Did you think she'd actually ever find someone proper?" Brian adds.

Then finally my Mom:

"He may not be your sugar daddy but this still isn't okay. I was right about you leaving this town Sofia. It was a bad idea. You've changed. You've become someone we don't even know!"

Ouch. That one hurts the most.

Beside me Elijah is close to losing his shit for real. I can tell because of the tension hitting me in waves. Me on the other hand, I'm just done.

"Of course she's someone we don't know. She's changed so much she's with someone who literally pays to fuck her?!" Brian laughs. This doesn't bother me but his next words do. In fact they set off the anger I've been keeping at bay. "Basically what you're saying is he doesn't really care about you. He just sees a young dumb women who is willing to do anything for money. You're playing right into his hands"

Implying that Elijah doesn't care about me was not the way to go Brian. It really fucking wasn't.

Before I can loose my shit, Elijah beats me to it. He dives forward and grabs Brian by his shirt, pulling him from his seat. Uh oh.

Brian's anger is immediate and quick like it always has been and just like that fear hits me like a tidal wave. It isn't because of Elijah, it isn't because of my yelling parents. It's because of Brian and the rage he displays as he flails against Elijah.

I want to step in and stop this but I'm rooted to the ground by terror. Brian throws a punch that connects with Elijah's gut and I have to close my eyes. I can't see this.

"Stop it" I whisper as the commotion goes on around me. Maybe my parents are getting involved but I wouldn't know. I'm blocking it all out.

"Stop it!" I say a little louder. My fists ball at my sides and I feel the need to run consuming me.

Cracking my eyes open, I see another punch landing near Elijah's face but not quite hitting the target. I see him flinch in pain. That's all it takes to snap me out of my haze. My anger comes back and my need to protect takes over.

"STOP IT NOW!" I scream and lunge forward grabbing Brian's arm to stop him from attacking my man. It doesn't do much good but when Elijah sees me getting involved and my general horrified state, he shoves Brian off with all his might.

Brian stumbles backward and falls to ground. This gives Elijah enough time to grab my hand and pull me away. My parents are still yelling.

"Sofia wait! We have to talk about this" my Mom calls as I turn to leave. "We have to talk about your behaviour..."

My behaviour? Mine? I can't fucking do this anymore. I won't go on having my parents think that I'm the bad guy. So I do something drastic...

"You want to talk about bad behaviour? Sure. How about we talk about his" I begin, shooting my gaze to Brian. My parents looks confused but they're about to look worse. "How about we talk about his anger? His violence!"

"You shut the hell up bitch" Brian yells but it only helps my case. It shows his anger.

"Quiet!" my Dad yells, stopping Brian from saying anything more. He stands there with rage in his eyes.

"He had a tendency to beat me black and blue at every opportunity. All of those times he told you I fell over. That I'd been clumsy...it was him Mom. He hurt me. Every time he was meant to be looking after me when you were away. The only reason he stopped was because eventually I got too big. So then he started to verbally abuse me so much more. I didn't want you to know. So if you think I've changed because I left home, then I'm so very sorry but if I'd stayed here near him, I probably wouldn't be alive today"

Silence. You could hear a pin drop.

My parents both look horrified. Brian looks like he could kill me at any moment.

"Is it true Brian?" my Mom asks but the answer is written over his face. Of course it's true.

Then he says something I didn't expect.

"I couldn't stand her. I still can't!" he begins and this has me frozen. "She was a little brat who everyone thought was perfect. All my parents talked about was perfect little Sofia. While I was never good enough!" he growls.

What? Really? That's it? That's the reason he hurt me so much? Because he was fucking jealous of a kid?! I really can't believe it!

"You hurt my daughter?" my Dad breathes, rage slowly growing.

Everyone is completely still. Then all hell breaks loose...

My Dad lunges for Brian, my Mom tries to stop him. They all struggle while I'm still stuck to the spot. Shit. I caused this.

My cheeks feel hot and it doesn't take long to notice it's from my tears.

"We're leaving Darling. I'm taking you away from here" Elijah whispers, pulling me into his side securely. He pulls me out of the front room and down the hallway.

I think I can hear my Mom begging me not to leave but surely I'm imagining that. Surely it didn't take this terrible ordeal to make her see how shitty she has been. Looks like it though.

"Sofia! Come back!" My Mom yells but I ignore it.

Elijah leads me out to his car and squeezes me tight.

"I'm gonna get my keys and our things okay. I'll be two minutes. Just two minutes Darling" he assures me before kissing my forehead then jogging back inside.

For the whole one hundred and twenty seconds it takes for him to reappear, I'm worried. I wouldn't be surprised if Brian tried to attack him again.

All of this is going on in my head yet I can't seem to bring words to my mouth. I'm silent and afraid.

When Elijah reappears and opens the car, my Mom comes out of the house, still yelling after me. I look away and jump into the passenger seat. I'm so relieved when Elijah pulls away from the curb.

"I'll find a hotel okay?"

"Okay" is all I can say. Which I hate because I don't want to feel this way. I'm so embarrassed by what just happened. So sad. I didn't want my parents or Elijah to find out this way.

***

It takes us about half an hour to find a hotel. It's the nearest one to my parents house and I'm so glad when we arrive.

Elijah hasn't said a word since we left and I'm worried about what he's thinking.

I wish I could shake this horrific feeling but then my family just blew up so I guess it's no surprise that I'm so empty.

Hopefully I'm not too much of a burden right now. Elijah does the checking in and leads me to our room. I'm on autopilot. I couldn't even tell you what the lobby looks like.

Once the door closes behind us, I finally feel like I can breath. Turning to him, I watch him set our stuff down. He looks so very worried about me when our eyes meet.

"I'm sorry that this happened" I finally push out and he frowns as if he's confused.

"Do not apologise" he replies, moving closer. He pulls me to him and holds me close. We just stand there clutching each other. His hands move up and down my back, his steady breathing soothing me. "I'm so sorry for what he did to you Darling. So fucking sorry. I won't ever let anyone hurt you and you won't ever have to go near that man again"

His determination makes me so emotional. He really wants to keep me safe.

"I wish I'd told you before. I hate that you found out like that"

"It's okay Darling. We can talk about it whenever you're ready. You can tell me however much you want" he breathes.

That's when I remember that Brian got a few hits in and my sadness turns to worry.

"Are you okay? Did he hurt you?" I ask, pulling back to look him over.

"No, I'm totally fine don't worry about it. Honestly I've been through worse" he explains and winks playfully. I can't stop my lips from pulling up slightly as the cold feeling inside me begins to subside. I can't believe one man can make me feel better so quick.

Wrapping my arms around him again, I lean in close and close my eyes. Which is a bad idea because all of the shitty things Brian said rush back.

"I can't believe he called me a prostitute. Is that what I am? I mean you did send me money. Oh my god!" I begin to ramble, my mind working faster than my mouth.

"No! You are not a prostitute! And even if you were it wouldn't make a difference Darling"

"What do you mean?"

"I mean that I like to think regardless we'd still be here...well not here exactly but I like to think we'd still have met and you know...that we'd be together"

"Hmmm, how much would you pay for a night with me?" I ask, wondering how he's going to answer. This line of conversation is actually distracting me too. Which is great.

"There is no amount of money that would suffice Darling. You're that good" he smiles and pecks my lips. Good answer.

"Wow, I'm flattered" I respond, playing with the buttons on his shirt. Even though he's made me feel better, I still hate what Brian said. Elijah gave me money because he wanted to help me. He isn't paying for the sex we have but I still feel strange now.

I guess I better tell him how I feel right now.

"I feel weird about having sex with you now" I confess, looking down at his shoes. God I hate that Brian has gotten to me this way. He's made me feel dirty and wrong.

"I understand Sofia but you know it's not a requirement to keep my attention"

"So if I decide right now that I never want to have sex with you again, you're telling me you won't dump my ass"

I expect him to laugh but his face stays completely serious.

"Do you remember what I said the first night we had dinner?"

"Hmmm it's a hazy blur. I remember thinking wow this guy is hot!" I joke. Actually I still think that every time I see him.

"Well let me refresh your memory. I said that we could be friends or dinner buddies. That I'd take anything you'd give me. I meant it. I will take you any way I can have you Sofia" he reiterates sternly. Damn, that's hot and my body reacts like always. Still, I don't think sex is a good idea tonight anyway.

"I thought that was just a line" I admit.

"No Darling. I've never lied to you. I've never used a line or a move. I was automatically honest because you made me want to be. I didn't have to be fake"

"Stop saying nice things, it makes me want to have sex with you! Well it makes me want you all the while feeling very conflicted. I'm not sure why"

"You feel conflicted because Brian has made our relationship seem cheap"

"Wow you got that a lot quicker than I would have. I guess it really is that simple. I hate that he's done this" I snap and burry my face in his chest.

"Don't worry, I know how to make you feel better. No sex tonight. However, I would like to propose ordering room service, watching shitty movies and lots of snuggling"

Elijah saying snuggling is my favourite thing. It seems so out of place and strange coming from his mouth. Yet it also feels special to me. I like to think he's never used that term when speaking to anyone else.

"Wow, I've never heard anything so perfect"

I guess intimacy comes in all forms.

Elijah

I've seen a lot of shitty people in my life. It's part of being a business man. However, I haven't seen someone with quite an evil look in their eyes as I did with Brian. Nor have I wanted to kill anyone so much.

The thought that he hurt her, makes me want to hurt him. I want to match every single bit of pain he gave her and give it to him right back. It would give me great pleasure to see him wheezing in agony.

The one punch I landed on him felt good but it wasn't enough.

He's the reason she's so afraid of men. Angry men. He's the reason she ran from me. He has made her petrified of life and he deserves to rot in hell.

I'm so privileged that she has let me into her life. Even more so now. It must have taken her a lot to even meet me. Yet here we are. She's let me so close to her. She trusts me.

The only thing I want to do is make her happy. So knowing she's hurting right now is driving me mad. I want to take her pain away but I know that all I can do right now is be there for her.

Like right now as we take advantage of the luxury bath. She filled it with so much bubble bath liquid that it over flowed and is currently making me a bubble beard.

Her brow is furrowed as she concentrates. Gently she places a handful of bubbles onto my face, covering my real beard. This gives me a lot of time to study her beautiful face and the way she's focused on completing my new facial hair.

"Does it look good?" I ask and she glares at me as some bubbles fall.

"Don't speak, you're ruining my work. But yes, it looks fantastic"

I wait for another few moments, following her order to stay quiet. I'm at peace, my hands resting on her thighs under the water as she straddles me. Naturally, I'm aroused because I can't help it but I ignore it because this is just as good as sex.

"I'm done" she whispers as if speaking at full volume will disturb the bubbles.

"Thank you Darling" I mumble and she grins at my attempt to keep the new beard.

"You're welcome" she replies before destroying her own work by kissing me. I smile against her lips then rub my cheek against her, mushing the bubbles onto her face.

"You look good with a beard too" I laugh and she pouts, raising her eyebrows as if to pose.

"I actually think I'd be able to pull off a beard you know" she giggles.

"You would. It'd be very sexy" I confirm and she smiles before the room falls silent. Her smile falls too and she wraps her arms around my neck and cuddles into me.

I know that she's upset about today and that she probably wants to forget it happened. I think talking about it might help but I'm not so sure if I'm good at that stuff. I want to be. For her. Like when I told her about my parents and she comforted me.

"You can tell me about Brian if you like. All of it"

"Brian is an asshole. The End"

"Hmmmm, Nope. Tell me more" I coax as she keeps her face hidden.

"He's a bully and a coward all at once" she sighs. "I didn't know the reason why he hurt me until today and I can't fucking believe he beat the shit out of me because he was jealous. It doesn't make any sense. I know it must be hard when your parents don't pay attention to you. I understand that part but to take it out on me...why? I was a kid. I wasn't any better than him"

As she speaks her voice shakes. I instinctively hold her tighter, wishing that I had the answers to her questions. I'm just as confused as her. His reasoning is pathetic. Not that it would matter, there's no excuse for beating someone up. Especially not a kid.

"I used to wonder what I'd done to him. Now I know that I didn't do a thing. The older I got, the less he would hit me which is how I know he's a coward. He only had the balls to kick and punch me when I was too little to fight back. I think I was fifteen the last time. It was only a slap. After that he used his words which honestly was sometimes worse. I just remember his rage. How quickly he'd get mad. Which is probably why I always assume that I'm gonna get hit when a man is angry"

My fists are balled on her thighs now, my breathing deep. With every word she speaks I'm so very grateful but I'm also livid. I want to go back to that house and break all of his bones. I want to time travel and save her from his fists. Maybe I'll end up being a murderer after all. That's okay, I'd do the time!

"I never told anyone about it. He didn't even have to threaten me. I just automatically lied to my parents. I knew it would hurt them. So I made it my mission to leave town and I succeeded"

Pulling her back a little to face me, I look into her sad eyes and cup her cheeks.

"I'm so proud of you Darling. So proud of what you've overcome. You've achieved so much despite of what he did and all you deserve is happiness. I meant what I said earlier, I will keep you safe. You won't have to go near that man again. However, I will make him pay if you want me to...I can do that" I tell her, a little afraid of my own admission.

"Thank you baby. I really appreciate that but I don't want revenge. I just want to move on with my life. I want to be better. If I keep on like this then he's won. I'm going to have to speak to my parents again before we go back to Chicago though. They were being assholes but I can't imagine how they feel now" she explains and I completely understand. They were being assholes but I know she will need to mend the rift between them.

"I'll be with you every step Darling. I promise"

Every step, for the rest of your life if you'll let me. That thought in my own head should scare me but I'm done being shocked at the truth. I want to say it out loud but I worry it'll be too much. I'd probably scare her away.

Having her here with me makes me feel powerful. Like I could do anything having her by my side. No one has ever made me feel that way.

She's amazing and so strong.

I want to be the one to make her feel the same. I have no doubt that she could conquer the world on her own but I need her to know she has me. That I'm her partner in whatever way she needs me to be.

I'm so fucking useless. I can't tell her how I feel because I don't know how. I've never been in a relationship...not a real one anyway. It's hard for me to even admit that I want to be in one.

Sofia isn't useless like me. She can see that I want to say something more. She reaches out and touches my cheek, my inner struggle warring on inside my own head.

"Thank you, that means a lot and I get it Elijah...I get it..."

Sofia

I get it. I see the way he's looking at me like he wants to make everything better. Like he wants to snatch me away and protect me from the world. It's hard for me to believe but I guess for once I can't deny that he might just care about me a lot more than I've been thinking.

"So, no marriage or kids huh?" he muses, changing the subject onto something a little less jarring. I didn't think he'd care about my marriage views and such but apparently he does. Either that or he's just making conversation.

"Definitely no kids, it's never appealed to me. As for marriage, well I don't think it stands for what it's supposed to. It's meant to be about love and commitment but in actual fact it's just a legal agreement. Which makes it very cold to me. It's just a piece of paper and I strongly believe that if you love someone and want to be with them, then you'll show that person so. Getting married doesn't prove shit"

"Wow..." he breathes and I wonder if he thinks I sound crazy.

"What?"

"I've never agreed with anything more. As a man who deals with many many contracts, marriage comes across as exactly the same as them all"

"I'm so glad we agree. Don't get me wrong I completely understand commitment and monogamy. I just don't think you need a contract to achieve those things. I mean most married people cheat anyway"

"Cheating is something that baffles me. I know I'm not exactly known as the prince of romance and I haven't ever had a proper relationship but the idea of it just pisses me off" he tells me and I appreciate it. I love hearing about his life in any way.

"I did try the dating thing before I sold myself to the sugar daddy industry. I wasn't very good at it. Never showed up for dates you know. One women I knew from when I first took over my father's business. She didn't like it when I fucked her and left during the night" he says awkwardly.

"Elijah! That's so mean" I reprimand him because all I can do is imagine it being me. How would I feel? Like shit is the answer.

"I know. Sorry Darling, I told you I'm not a very nice guy. I don't even have an excuse for it. I mean sure I was exposed to greedy people from a young age so I assumed no one really wanted my company, just my cash. Still it's not a reason for my shitty attitude"

He takes my hands under the water as if he needs some comfort.

"Then why are you so nice to me? I don't get it. I'm sure plenty of women have wanted you for you but you never let them in. Yet you seem to let me in"

"I can be mean to you if you like?" He asks, dodging my question. Hmmmm.

"Go on then, I'm intrigued" I smirk, ready for a challenge. Only his expression softens and he looks very incapable of hurting my feelings.

He opens his mouth but no words come out.

"Well?" I prompt and he shrugs.

"I've got nothing, maybe if you start" he suggests and I hum as I think about it. He's right, it's tough being mean to someone you worship like a god.

"Sometimes you snore a little but honestly I actually like it...damn it!" I growl and he chuckles at my frustration.

"Oh dear, my feelings are hurt baby" he pouts. I can't resist kissing those lips.

***

I'm so grateful for him. I'm so grateful that he ordered us pizza and chicken wings, that we devoured in about five minutes. Emotions make me hungry.

I'm grateful that he gave me his t-shirt to lounge in and pulled me close. His fingers glide up and down my leg that's thrown over his hip and I sigh in contentment. I've almost forgotten about today's shitty outcome.

"You know I wish I'd faced my fears of coming home sooner. I wish I'd faced Brian sooner. Maybe I'd be over it by now. I feel so weak"

"I'd say you're doing amazing already Darling. You stood up to him"

"Barely" I sigh.

"All that matters is you did. Even if you hadn't, it doesn't make you weak. Sofia, you're the strongest women I've ever met" he informs me, his fingers brushing over my cheek.

"Not possible" I reply stubbornly, pretty certain that I'm right. Elijah has met too many women in his life for it to be true.

"Do you wanna argue about it?" He asks, quirking his eyebrow at me.

"Maybe I do" I smirk then glare at him.

"I've never seen anyone stand up to someone like Nadia Zoya the way you did, for example. I wasn't able to do it. You stood up to Brian even though you don't believe you did. You don't take any of my shit that's for sure. Not to mention you don't try to act like you're the most amazing person ever like most people I know. Which baffles me because in my opinion you are the most amazing person"

"You're sweet"

"No, I'm really not but I'm glad you think so"

Naturally I can't stand not making out with him. I'm pretty sure that by tomorrow our no sex rule will be lifted.

Of course I don't get to enjoy his lips for long because like most times throughout our time together, a phone call interrupts us.

It's Annabelle, which reminds me we haven't spoken or seen each other in a while. The first thing she says is:

"So how are you doing? Over that psycho murderer dude yet?"

Uh oh! I just realised that I didn't tell Annabelle that Elijah wasn't a murderer. I didn't tell her that we got back together. In fact, the last bit of communication I had with Annabelle was texting her to tell her I was okay and alive.

Well...this is gonna be a fun conversation.

Sofia

"Ummmmm, funny story. Turns out he's not a murderer" I inform Annabelle. The line of conversation has Elijah propping himself up on his elbow and raising his eyebrows.

I look back at him with a tired expression because let's be honest, I'm sick of people judging the person I choose to be with. That's all I've gotten from today and I'd love it to stop.

It's not her fault though, she was only trying to save me from ending up in a grave.

"What? Dear God, Sofia it was very clear that he was a murderer. Are you still with him? Oh my god are you with him right now?" She questions, her words firing out one after the other as she panics.

"Yes and yes. I promise you he isn't going to kill me. Well not unless I make him mad" I joke and Elijah shakes his head at me. "I might steal too much of the bed covers and get stabbed for it. Who knows?"

"Sofia! That isn't funny" Annabelle continues. I can't lie and say that she has my full attention. Not when I'm much more occupied with dragging the fingers of my free hand over the hairs on Elijah's chest. I draw patterns on his skin as his arms wrap around me tighter.

"Let's talk about you instead. How's things?" I ask, taking away the heat from myself.

"Oh no you don't!" She whisper-hisses.

Well that didn't work.

"How do you know he isn't a psycho?" She continues.

"Because I did more research. It was fabricated by the media. I also let him explain everything to me and I trust him. I know it might not seem ideal to you and I understand but I just want to move on" I tell her and hope it's enough. I just want to sleep now.

"If you trust him then I'll give him the benefit of the doubt. Just be careful though yeah?"

"I'm always careful" I laugh and I can almost hear her shaking her head.

"That's a lie" she grumbles.

"I know but I really appreciate you looking out for me. It means a lot"

"Of course, that's what friends are for. I'm going to let you go, you sound like you've had a rough day" she says and I'm not surprised she's noticed. Maybe it's from the tone of my voice or something else but Annabelle always knows when something is up.

"Hmmm yeah, that's another story for another time" I explain, not wanting to get into it.

"Okay well, I'll pretend you didn't say that. Speak to you soon" she sighs. I know that she's probably gonna question me on a later date.

"Goodnight Annabelle"

After dropping my phone down, I lie flat on my back and let out the longest sigh I can produce.

"She still thinks I'm gonna kill you huh?" Elijah asks, tilting his head towards me.

"She seems satisfied for now but don't be surprised if she sends out a hit man for you. Always keep vigilant" I giggle as his eyes widen.

"Dear god, what have I gotten into?" He gasps.

"You don't wanna know Elijah…you don't wanna know…"

Elijah

Did I just enjoy her defending me? More than words can describe. It also made something inside me very happy when she shut down what Annabelle was saying. It shows she truly believes me and I'm so fucking glad. There's so many people out there who still think I'm a murderer.

But not her.

I sense that Sofia is the more submissive friend where Annabelle is concerned. So I'm glad that she stuck up for herself on the phone. I get the feeling she'd usually go along with whatever Annabelle said. Sofia likes peace and therefore doesn't like conflict.

It wasn't hard for me to be selfish before I met Sofia. Now though, all I do is think of new ways to make her smile. I even care about the people around her.

Right now she's trying to keep her sadness at bay and I hate that she's feeling that way.

Her emotions are all in her eyes and even though she's trying to hide it, she can't from me.

"You know I'd never hurt you right?" I ask just like I've done before. With Annabelle bringing up the murder accusations I'm afraid to say its made me a little insecure.

"I know that Handsome. I just wish everyone else did" she tells me softly. I think I'm actually blushing. She's never called me handsome like that before. Okay get a grip Elijah! You're a grown man. "I bet you didn't have this much bother with sugar babies? You know, no protective friends or crazy families"

"I guess you could say that no I didn't but I've also never been in this kind relationship. There's not much that can happen when you meet someone a handful of times. If you're suggesting that your family and friends are a bother to me then you're wrong. I don't care if they don't approve of me Darling. You do so that's all that matters"

"Thanks, I really do approve" she smirks before her face becomes serious and she seems to be deep in thought. What's going on in that beautiful brain?

"Everything okay?" I probe because I'd hate to think that she's still thinking about today. I want her to forget it all. Forget her parents, forget Brian and forget Annabelle. I know these are all things she will have to deal with at some point but right now she needs to relax.

I see it as my duty to make her happy. To give her everything she could possibly want. Right now though I don't know what she desires.

"Mmmhhmm, everything is fine. I just can't believe how complicated my life got in one whole night. I liked it better when my parents weren't judging me, when Brain was a distant memory and when Annabelle was too occupied with her man to bother about mine. I like peace and quiet" she explains and it's just as I thought. She worrying.

Is it bad that my go to distraction is the one thing we agreed not to do tonight? Surely I'm better than that? Surely I can help without resorting to something sexual.

Maybe I can tell her about the lyrics that she inspired. I am by no means a song writer but from time to time I mess around. Like that time she almost caught me singing when she woke up in the middle of the night. I was signing about her but the thought of her knowing that terrified me. It's less scary now and I think I'd benefit from her hearing it as much as she might. Finally letting it out. Surely singing to her is too weird? I could try it a little. No, no signing.

"Peace and quiet huh? I like that too. You wanna know what I do when my mind is going a hundred miles an hour?"

Maybe she will say no. Maybe she won't care. Maybe this is a bad idea all together. What if I don't really want her to know?

"Yes I do wanna know, very much so" she says excitedly, her expression brightening quickly. Of course she wants to know. My inquisitive girl. I'm already glad that I've flipped her mood again. I want to be an expert at taking away any of her worries.

"I sing or write songs. Not very often but sometimes I'm inspired"

"I was wondering when we were gonna talk about this. Don't think I didn't notice you dodging the subject before. I caught you and you distracted me" She teases, rolling over a little and leaning up on her elbow. Fuck, there's no going back.

"It's nothing special, so don't get too excited. I'm not sure how my most recent song is gonna go but I have some lyrics down...if you wanna read them"

Her eyes light up as if I've told her the most exciting thing ever. Is this really that interesting to her? Does she actually care about something that I do on the side?

I guess I'm about to find out.

Sofia

Elijah takes a few moments finding the lyrics on his phone. He must randomly type them whenever they come to him. I find that incredibly cute.

I catch the nervous look on his face before he hands me it. Immediately I notice there are a few different lines, that must be from different songs or maybe he just doesn't have a place for them yet.

He has written:

You're the best thing and the worst. I can't take it but I can't let go. You drive me to the edge, your voice echoing in my head.

If I go, will you go with me? Don't leave now, let us just be.

Worst of all, I know the truth. You'll never stay but maybe I could hold your attention for just one day.

How am I supposed to feel? What am I supposed to do when everything I want centres around you...

I take my time reading every line. I try to work out what they could mean and who they are about. It actually makes me jealous when I think of him writing these things about someone who isn't me but unfortunately they simply can't be about me. It's just not possible.

He's staring at me, I can tell. He must be waiting for my answer but how do I cover up my innate curiosity? How do I stop myself from asking? My heart is beating irregularly, my skin covered in goosebumps because every line that I've just read is beautiful.

"Sofia? What do you think?" He finally asks after what must have been about ten minutes. I didn't notice the time passing because my mind is moving too fast for me to keep up.

"I...I think that all of this is beautiful. I've never read lyrics like those or heard anything similar. It's all fantastic" I tell him, looking back at his shocked face. Clearly he wasn't expecting praise. He really does hide behind a confident facade.

"Really?" He questions as I hand him the phone back.

"Really" I confirm and peck his lips to show him I mean it. My burning question is on the tip of my tongue so I'm glad when he kisses me harder.

He hovers above me when we pull apart, his expression full of warmth and what I can only describe as acceptance. I wonder how long he's been waiting to show someone his talent. I wonder if he's ever sang them to someone.

No Sofia, don't go there.

That can only make me more jealous.

Elijah

She liked them...she really liked them. Wow. The way that makes me feel is hard to explain but her genuine praise has me feeling all fuzzy inside.

We're silent now but I have a feeling there is something she wants to say. It's in the way she keeps frowning and looking away from me. She's thinking too hard about something and her frustrated expression would be cute if I didn't know something was bothering her.

"Darling? Whatever you wanna say, you can say it" I prompt her and her eyes widen a little as if she's shocked.

"How do you know that I wanna say something?"

"Because I spend a god awful amount of time staring at your beautiful face. I have now come to know when you're unsettled" I explain and she glares at me playfully.

"Creep" she mumbles but I'm not gonna let her change the subject.

"Yes I'm definitely a creep but I'm also correct aren't I?"

Her loud sigh of defeat tells me I'm right.

"I don't wanna seem nosey or anything" she begins, taking my hand and playing with my fingers. Oh dear, she must really wanna know something desperately.

"Wanting to know something isn't nosey. I've always been honest with you this far and that's not going to change. I'll answer anything Darling"

She lets go of my hand and covers her face. She's embarrassed, really embarrassed.

She finally speaks but I can't make out what she's saying because her words are muffled by her hands.

I know how to get her to speak.

"Sofia, tell Daddy what's wrong" I say sternly and immediately her hands fall away to reveal a disgusted face. Bingo.

"Never say that again Elijah. I swear to god!" She exclaims and I can't help but laugh at her. The use of the word daddy is never endearing

"I won't if you tell me what's wrong"

"Nothing is wrong. I just wanna know who you wrote the lyrics about but it's none of my business. I really don't have the right to know. I mean it's probably personal…"

She keeps going, letting more and more words fall from her mouth. She obviously thinks she's overstepping some line but she really isn't. I assumed she knew they were about her. I thought that's why she liked them so much but it turns out she has no idea and now I'm nervous again.

Regardless I have to stop her panic.

"Sofia, they're about you!" I say loud enough so she can hear me. The room falls silent again and she looks at me with real shock this time.

"Me?" she breathes and my stomach flips. Is this bad? Is this too much?

"Yes, they're about you Darling. Of course they are. I've never felt the need to say anything like what I've written about anyone. You mean a lot to me Sofia"

She sits up and I do the same because I'm so worried I've done something wrong. Only in the next second she's grabbing my face and kissing me like never before. It seems I've done a good thing after all.

My body tingles...yes tingles...shut up! My heart flies in my chest and for the first time in my life I feel...complete.

Do I love this woman? No, I don't. Love is bullshit. Love is something people throw around too easy. I can't use the word love to describe how I feel because it would be disrespectful to her in my opinion. However, I would walk through the fires of hell for her. I would do anything in my power to make her happy. I don't know what that means but I don't care right now as she covers her body with mine.

Are we going to have sex? I don't think we should, we agreed not to. Then again, how could I resist her?

"Elijah" she breathes and it's music to my ears. "I...adore...you" she pushes the words out. It's as if she's struggled with them. Maybe she meant to say something else but couldn't. I can't think about that though. Not when her hands roam my chest.

Her lips disappear and her forehead presses against mine. Our breathing is far too wild to speak but I can hold onto her tightly. She grips my shoulders and kisses me once more.

Sorry, I know we said no sex" she sighs.

"That's okay, this is perfect" I assure her. I'm not lying either. Having her wrapped around me like a vine is heavenly.

In fact, that's how she falls asleep. On my chest she lays with her arms holding me. I hold her back as she sleeps and do the one thing I wanted to do while she was awake.

I sing.

"How am I supposed to feel? What am I supposed to do when everything I want centres around you"

Sofia

In the morning, I knew that I wouldn't be able to go back to Chicago without talking to my parents first. So after finding endless missed calls from both of them, I called back. I told them that I wouldn't come if Brian was still there but I was assured that he wouldn't be setting foot in the house again. That statement from my Dad really made me happy. It soothed something inside of me. It means they believed me.

When Elijah and I arrive they both greet us. The atmosphere is awkward until I'm pulled into the tightest hug imaginable by my Dad.

"I'm so sorry Sweetheart. I'm so sorry we didn't notice. That we did nothing" he tells me, his voice almost pleading for forgiveness.

I don't blame either of them one bit.

The only person to blame is Brian.

"You don't have to say sorry. I wasn't your fault or yours Mom. I'm sorry I told you the way I did" I reply, feeling guilty for the emotional way it all came out. I should have sat them down and told them delicately.

"I wish you'd told us sooner" my Mom cries, hugging me once again. I feel at peace as she squeezes me because I think now we can move on.

"I didn't want to hurt you both"

"You silly girl. We're supposed to be here for you" she sighs, guilt once again evident.

"And you have been. When I needed you the most. You've been supportive…for the most part" I joke and luckily that makes her laugh. "Oh and you should know I wasn't lying. Elijah isn't my sugar daddy"

"I believe you. It shouldn't have mattered anyway. I'm sorry that I'm tough on you sometimes. I know I can be judgmental but I just want what's best for you. You're my only baby" she gushes, crying into my shoulder. Which only sets me off.

The three of us all hug at the entrance of the house while Elijah waits patiently. I'm so lucky to have him. To have had him through all of this.

To my surprise my parents both apologise to him too. My Dad pats him on the back and my Mom hugs him like she did me. Once again he looks a little awkward, unsure of how to receive such a normal gesture of affection. It's so cute.

"Will you stay longer?" she asks but unfortunately we can't. We both have work to get back to.

"We can't but I won't be staying away so long this time. I'll be visiting you as much as I can" I assure her.

"Thank god Sofia!" She exclaims, then her joyful expression changes. Oh. "What should we do about Brian. Should we report him to the police?" she asks and my mouth opens and closes as I try to think.

"I don't want to have to do deal with him anymore. If we go to the police then there will be a trial no doubt. He was still a minor most of the time it happened. I'm not sure there's much they can do. The only person he's a threat to is me and I won't be near him ever again" I explain. There may not be much resolve here but what can I do? Regardless of his wrong doings, maybe he deserves a chance to do better. To realise that his parents always loved him.

They seem happy with my choice and wave Elijah and I goodbye.

I feel so much lighter on the drive back that I did on the way here. So I guess even though it's been an emotional two days, I'm glad it happened. Now I can get on with my life and try to overcome my fears.

***

We got back to Chicago a few days ago now and all I keep thinking about is those lyrics Elijah showed me. I find myself thinking about them when I'm supposed to be working. I almost spilled coffee over someone because I was so lost in thought.

Right now however, Elijah is on his way over to my apartment and I couldn't be more excited. I'm always excited but considering he's been catching up with a lot of work, I've seen him very little. We still haven't had sex so I'm a little...needy.

The no sex thing has nothing to do with me not wanting to. I no longer care about what Brian said.

I think Elijah is missing me too.

Yesterday when I finished work he had a driver sent to pick me up and take me home before I could call a cab. When I got in there, there was a box of chocolates, a DVD and a note on the back seat.

The note read: *I really wish I could come watch movies and eat chocolate with you tonight but I'm unbelievably busy with a possible new client. I'll tell you more about that when I get a chance to call you. In the mean time please enjoy one of my favourite movies and the chocolates tonight for me. I'll see you soon Princess xxx*

The movie was 'The Princess Bride' and it made me smile. He literally acts like the least romantic man to the outside world but actually he's super soft on the inside and adores romcoms.

So I thanked him in the form of a long voice note detailing just how much I missed him.

His voice note in return informed me that he had an update on the hack situation. Nothing much just that the apartment in which the hack happened doesn't belong to anyone.

Which is weird and I wanna talk to him about it more when I see him tonight. Preferably after he fucks me senseless. Hmmm for some reason using that term doesn't seem right anymore. Maybe it never did. It doesn't feel like he ever fucked me in a derogatory way. Even when he's rough, it's never seemed uncaring.

That's the thought that is currently in my head. It's only when the buzzer goes that I'm snapped back to reality.

Thank god he's finally here.

When I open the door I'm ready to grab my man but unfortunately I'm halted when I see it's not who I expected it to be.

"Hey! Sorry to stop by unexpectedly but I just thought we should catch up in person " Annabelle says cheerily. She's right, we should talk face to face.

"Hi! It's good to see you. Come in" I reply and step aside to let her in.

She walks in and stands awkwardly in the middle of the room. We've never been awkward with each other. I guess the lack of communication recently has made things weird. We really should update each other on our lives more often. I also think she's still worried about me even after our phone call.

"I have to apologise to you" she begins and my eyes widen. She never does that. "You're an adult and I shouldn't try to meddle in your business" she continues. I'm not mad at her at all. Sure I was a little pissed that she wouldn't let the murder thing go but that's behind us now.

"It's okay. I really appreciate that you care about me so much to meddle. It's just that I'm really happy right now" I tell her and she smiles as if she's happy for me.

"You deserve to be happy. I'm glad you've found someone"

"Thanks. How's things in your love life?" I ask and just like that, everything goes back to normal. We sit on the end of my bed as she gushes over all of things her and Max have been up to. It's nice to just listen and watch her hands fly all over the place. I contemplate telling her about Brian and then decide that maybe not everyone needs to know. It has to stay in the past.

She only stops when the buzzer sounds a second time.

I try my best not to run to the door but I'm sure Annabelle will have noticed my rushed walk.

This time it is Elijah, thank god.

My eyes are immediately blessed by my gorgeous man. My man? Yes my man. I'm saying it and accepting it. He's my man.

My man is wearing a lighter blue suit today. Underneath the shirt buttons are popped open at the top revealing a little bit of his chest hair. Yummy. His beard is nicely trimmed. Add in tired affection filled eyes, behind black rimmed glasses and I can tell he's had little time away from work over the past few days. I already knew that but seeing the affects just makes me wanna take him to bed and cuddle him to sleep.

"Hey Darling, I've missed you so much" he groans as if it's psychically been painful for him. It feels like it has been for me too.

I'm about to tell him Annabelle is here but before I can open my mouth, his lips cover mine and well I simply can't help kissing him back. His kiss expresses the same frustration and need that I feel.

When he pulls back I'm all hot and bothered. Nevertheless I still notice he's holding one of his hands behind his back. Which is certainly strange. Why didn't I notice that at first? Oh yeah...because he's so gorgeous I got distracted.

"What do you have there?" I ask as I step back into my apartment and he follows me. He's smiling down at me, almost grinning in fact.

He opens his mouth, I assume to tell me but he's stopped by Annabelle, who appears at my side.

"Hey Elijah, sorry to interrupt but I just want to apologise for accusing you of being a murderer" she says with an awkward smile on her face. I imagine that's because such sentences aren't said very often. Not to mention she seems to feel guilty too. I don't want her to feel bad anymore, she's apologised to both of us and we're all good.

"That's okay. I know you were only looking out for Sofia. Which is something I can't be mad about" he replies. .

"Well yeah, she's pretty special" Annabelle says, nudging me playfully.

"She really is" Elijah agrees and I can feel a blush making its way to my cheeks. That's enough of that!

"I'm so glad we all agree that I'm crazy amazing. Now let's move on okay?!" I try but Annabelle crosses her arms.

"There's just one more thing I have to make sure of" she states. "Does he treat you with respect? Because that's all that I care about now"

Elijah stands next to me silently as we essentially talk about him. A quick glance in his direction and I see his warm gaze.

"Yes, I'm not sure that anyone has ever treated me with as much respect as he does. Plus, I think he really likes me..." I laugh.

"Great! Then I won't stay any longer. The sexual tension in the room is strong enough to knock out a thousand people" she smirks and squeezes me into a tight hug. I hug her back and feel so thankful that I have someone like her in my life.

"We'll have a proper catch up soon. You can tell me more about how great he is" are her parting words before she winks at me and leaves. The soft click of the door shutting behind her signifies that we're now alone.

"For the record, I do really like you" Elijah says softly as my eyes land back on his handsome face.

"I hope so or things are gonna get awkward" I giggle and wrap my arms around his neck. Of course he can't put his arms around me because he's still holding something behind his back.

"I should give you this now before we get distracted" he says and I step back so he can show me. He holds up a large fancy bag with a very obvious Apple logo on the front. Immediately I'm excited and worried all at once. I don't know why but I don't think I'm ever going be good at receiving gifts. I already feel bad that he's bought me something. Fuck.

I stare at the bag warily because I know whatever is in it cost more than I could possibly justify if it were me buying it myself.

"Please take it from me before my arm goes dead" he laughs and I snap out of my haze. Regardless of my wariness I'm actually being quite rude by not taking the gift from him. Well that's the logic I'm going with.

Taking it from him, I feel the weight and it makes me worry more.

Really Sofia?! You gotta pull yourself together. It's a gift. He's allowed to buy gifts for god sake!

"Darling, you really do amaze me" he muses, no doubt seeing the way I struggle with what to do next. Logically opening the bag would be a good idea. "I've never met anyone who looked so terrified when given a gift. I've never met anyone who wouldn't be tearing it open as quickly as possible" he continues, a small smirk on his face.

"I'm sorry. I am excited, I promise you" I reply, sulking a little. I really do suck.

"I think you're perfect. I can tell that you genuinely appreciate anything anyone gives you and that is something I'm not used to. It's very refreshing" he tells me, his hands sliding onto my arms in comfort. "You need to know that there's no shame in accepting a gift. You don't have to of course. I can take it back. I don't want to make you uncomfortable" he says soothingly. I do contemplate giving him it back but then I also realise that he's probably spent time picking this for me and that's why I want to keep it.

"I do want it and I already love it" I laugh and he raises his eyebrows.

"You don't know what it is yet" he grins getting excited. I think he's gonna enjoy seeing me open this.

"Doesn't matter, I still love it"

Finally we go sit down on the bed and I place the bag on the floor. With my shame gone, excitement fills me and I yank off the bit of tape keeping the bag shut.

As soon as I pull it open, I see the shape of the box inside and I become a women possessed. Pulling the box out I'm met with the lovely image of a brand new MacBook Pro. Holy fuck. Not only that but a small sticker labels this MacBook Pro 'Custom'.

Which I know means he didn't just go out and buy me a laptop, he chose all of the specifications and got it built for me. Double holy fuck!

"Oh my god Elijah! This is... I don't even know what to say"

"I know that you need a new one and I also know that you wouldn't buy it with the money I sent you" he begins. He's right, I wouldn't have spent his money on this. I've barley spent it on anything. Only the essentials. I can't bring myself to do anything else with it because I feel bad.

"Did I do good? I asked Jack for help on the specs and stuff. I know a thing or two but I wanted to get it right" he informs me. One glance at the specs on the back of the box and I can confirm he did do good.

It has an i9 Processor Turbo Boost with 2TB SSD Storage and 16GB RAM. The graphics card looks to be out of this world. This is something I could only ever dream of.

"It's amazing Elijah, I've never seen anything so perfect" I exclaim, pulling the plastic off the box. I gotta see it for myself. With much care I pull the lid off to reveal the silver laptop. My fingers glide along the top and I can't actually believe I'm touching it. "I don't deserve this" I mumble.

"Of course you do Darling. You deserve the world" he breathes, his hand rubbing my back.

I can actually feel tears pricking my eyes because of this gift and because of his words. This is all really crazy.

"There's an inscription on the bottom" he whispers as if he's afraid to overwhelm me. Too late for that. I'm done for. I swear to god if this says something sweet I'm gonna ball my eyes out.

Gently picking the MacBook up, I turn it upside down to find the tiny words written there.

'You are going to take on the world and succeed!'
Well fuck...my heart.

"I know your old laptop limits you too. You're so fucking good at what you do Sofia and now nothing can stop you" he breathes, his fingers squeezing my shoulder.

When I say that I throw myself at him, I literally mean it. I pretty much knock him back onto the bed as I wrap my arms around him tightly and bury my face in his chest. He squeezes me to him, gladly accepting my sneak attack.

When I look up at his gorgeous face, all the carnal feelings that I had before Annabelle arrived come back with a vengeance. If I was horny before then I'm not sure how to describe what I am now.

The amazing gift and lovely engraving probably didn't help my situation. So sweet, yet all I can think about is him spreading my legs and pushing inside me. Fuck!

"Can we have sex now? Turns out I actually don't care what anyone thinks, especially not Brian" I blurt out because apparently my now porn filled brain thinks it's best to get to the point.

"Hmmmm, maybe I like the abstinence" he teases, a mischievous look in his eyes. Evil man. The worst! Yet so damn sexy I can't stand it.

"Huh in that case I guess I'll have to get myself off" I sigh dramatically and roll onto my back. Two can play this game. He may be able to mess with me but he can't hide what he really wants.

I count the seconds until he moves up the bed beside me. I only got to eleven. Someone didn't waste much time changing their mind on abstinence.

"Can I help you?" I ask, crossing my arms.

"I've changed my mind" he replies giving me his best puppy dog eyes. I mean I wasn't going to turn him away anyway but if I were then my plans would be ruined. So damn cute and hot all at once.

"What do you want?" I question, wanting him to say it.

"You Sofia. I want you" he says in a rather pleading tone. Wow, things have changed in the last few seconds.

"What do you want to do to me?" I continue to question him with glee.

I watch in fascination as he removes his jacket then unbuttons the cuffs on his shirt sleeves before rolling them up. Once that's done I have to focus on keeping my mouth from dropping open as he gets up and kneels on the floor in front of me. My mouth goes dry when he places his hands on my thighs, tugs me to the edge of the bed and spreads my jeans clad legs. He then shifts between them to get closer. Dear god help me.

"What do you want me to do to you?"

"Anything...everything" I blurt out. Wow it's really tough to make sentences with a God between your legs I guess.

To put it simply, I got everything and anything I wanted. Boy I'm lucky.

***

Even though I'm now glad that I have a job and some kind of income, my dream job searching hasn't stopped. I want a career and a future. I don't want to have to depend on anyone for my money.

I'm still not having much luck in the career department though. Oh and there's another reason I want a new job. To put it quite simply...Gabe.

He's strange. I don't mean that in a quirky way either. Ever since the first day he started when he did a lot of staring, it's gotten worse. I catch him doing it quite a lot.

I'd love to brush it off as him simply finding me attractive but that seems unlikely. Not even someone with a crush stares so much.

He's also somewhat interested in Elijah. More than would seem normal. He asks a lot of questions to which I give vague answers. After all it's none of his business 'what Elijah earns' or 'where he came from'.

I thought the questions would stop but currently I'm standing with my mouth hanging open. I have one hand on the coffee machine and one hand free ready to slap this guy!

He literally just asked me how many women Elijah has been with. Of course I can't answer that anyway but I'm still in shock. I think it's about time I actually told Elijah about Gabe's inquisitiveness. I haven't yet because I didn't think it was a big deal but honestly now I'm just pissed.

"I don't know Gabe. I really don't know. I'm also not sure that's an appropriate question to ask me" I almost spit out.

"Why not? Doesn't it make you insecure?" He says casually and I really want to throw a mug at him. Does it? No.

"It doesn't matter to me. He's with me now and that's all that counts" I reason with him.

Surely it's almost time for my shift to end. One glance at the clock confirms this and my eyes shoot outside to see if Elijah is here yet. He's picking me up because, and I quote "I want to be with you sooner rather than later". Yeah, he's so soft and so am I.

"Yeah but surely the thought of him fucking other women bothers you..."

WHAT THE FUCK!

I'm out!

"Gabe, I'm leaving now. Please don't talk to me in the future unless it's about work. You can lock up!"

What is wrong with him?! I really wish I had more shifts with Willow instead.

"Wait! I'm sorry-" he tries but I don't wanna hear it.

"I said I'm leaving" I snap.

As if by magic Elijah arrives and I dive around the counter. As I exit, my whole body shivers as if expelling Gabe's weird vibes.

Holy shit, there is something wrong with that man!

Sofia

As soon as I get in the car with Elijah he asks me what's wrong. My rushed jog from the shop must have given away the fact that things weren't normal.

I actually have to take a deep breath and reach over for his hand before I can begin explaining. Gabe just really freaked me out and I'm still not one hundred percent sure why. His questions were out of line and his staring was just wrong but my reaction feels weird. I literally want to go take a shower and bleach my brain to forget the creepy vibes he gave off.

After ranting without taking a breath for a good two minutes, I finally suck in a huge gulp of air. Elijah is squeezing my hand, his forehead marred with a concerned frown.

Although the look in his eyes tells me he's more than concerned.

"Do you think I'm overreacting? Maybe I am? I do that sometimes I guess. He just creeped me out" I sigh, worrying that maybe I'm just being dramatic.

"No Darling, you are not overreacting" he answers cooly. So cooly in fact that I'm really confused when he lets go of my hand and unclips his seat belt.

"What are you doing?"

"I'm going to have a little chat with Gabe. I don't care if he asks shit about me but I won't have him making you feel uncomfortable" he growls. If that isn't enough to signify that he isn't just going to chat with Gabe, then his palpable anger is.

When he goes to exit the car, I grab his arm and pull him back gently. There doesn't need to be any conflict here. In fact, I'd much rather just forget about it. I'm sure Gabe is nothing to worry about. He's probably just nosey.

"Please don't go in there. I'd much rather you just help me forget about the freaky feeling I have right now" I tell him, pouting more than is probably necessary. That's all it takes for his mood to change, his anger disappearing. He leans over the centre console and silently asks for a kiss. It's possible we both have too much power over one another. I don't know if that's good or bad.

"I'm sorry. I tend to overreact when I feel strongly about something...or someone" he whispers against my lips.

"Don't be sorry. I appreciate that you're willing to fight my corner. I just don't like literal fighting" I smirk and kiss him properly.

When we pull apart he looks like he's just had an epiphany. His face lights up and he looks really excited. There go the butterflies.

"I know exactly how to make you feel better Darling. I think it's about time we took that trip to Hawaii don't you?"

Oh my god! I'm not going to lie, with everything that's been going on lately and with us generally trying to navigate our relationship, I may have forgotten about our holiday plans.

Now though the excitement that I felt when my finger landed on Hawaii returns. I can't believe he's really going to take me on holiday. I honestly feel like I'm living a dream. Although just like always, a feeling of uneasiness comes over me. I don't deserve all of this.

"You must be busy though Elijah. Your work is important. Of course I'd love to go but I don't want you to plan this just for me. I can wait. In fact, I don't ever have to go" I say casually because I hate the idea that I'm taking him away from his job.

"Sofia there's something that you need to understand. My work important sure but there's nothing more important to me than you. No matter how busy I am, I always have time for you..."

He's told me this before but just like last time, I find it hard to get my head around. I'm really not that interesting, yet he seems to find me fascinating and worth giving up his precious time. So I really only have one response that will keep my emotions in check.

"Fuck it! Let's go to Hawaii!"

***

"Is that cake?" I hear and almost drop said cake on the floor in shock.

"No...it isn't" I try to say around the mouthful of joy. Naturally I have to hide it behind my back because that way he will never know I have anything! Never!

"Hmm it looked like cake" he muses.

We're at the airport and while Elijah went to the toilet, I acquired a slice of chocolate cake from the five star cafe. I never knew a cafe could have five stars but here we are. You know he actually apologised to me earlier because there's been a delay with getting his private jet ready! You know just a causal private jet. Did I mock him dramatically? Yes. God forbid I have to wait an extra half an hour in a VIP lounge that only accommodates people who own the private jets. GOD FORBID!

"No cake here!" I lie, looking away from his glaring eyes.

"Then what are you hiding behind your back?" He asks, crossing his arms sternly.

"God damn it! Fine! It's cake! I can't believe I always have to share my cake with you now" I sigh and show him the chocolate heaven. Of course, I'm kidding. Part of the reason I bought it was so that I could offer him some and enjoy watching him lick it off his lips.

"That's part of my special requirements. All snacks must be shared" he grins smugly, breaking a bit off and popping it into his mouth. Yummy. He then proceeds to lick his lips and I can feel myself smiling involuntarily. Bingo!

"I'm a snack, does that mean you have to share me?" I tease and his glare returns with vengeance. Oh dear.

"No. You my dear, are just for me. Only me" he answers, his voice rough with meaning. Oh damn, that's hot but I'm not about to let him know that yet.

"Did you just objectify me again?" I snap and his face goes white.

"What? No of course not! I'd never do that, I just...I just-" he stutters, his hand running through his hair nervously. Okay, I'm mean.

"Wow, you're so easy. I thought you were a tough guy? An asshole? You seem pretty considerate to me" I laugh and he shakes his head at me.

One day my teasing is gonna get me in trouble. I can just tell.

"You want me to be the man I am in the boardroom? I can do that Sofia" he tests me, taking the rest of the cake and finishing it off. Lord, how dare he?!

"Oh hell no! Is boardroom you greedy?!" I whisper as he throws the napkin the cake was on in the trash. Dick!

"No, he's assertive and takes what he wants" he whispers once he's back in front of me. His voice is like silk and I think I might wanna jump on boardroom Elijah.

"He sounds pretty hot actually. Is he always available or do I need to make an appointment?" I query as he slides his arms around my waist.

"Always available to you Princess"

***

His private jet is simply a modern gem. It's painted fully black, the only contrasting colour coming from the 'Everett and Son Industries' logo emblazoned on the side in a bold silver font.

I'm in a trance as he guides me up the steps. This seems to happen a lot around him especially when he's showing me new things.

I'm pretty sure the captain greets us as well as an air hostess but I'm too busy gawping at everything to be able to do more than smile politely. I do however catch Elijah's sly smile as he sees me with what I imagine looks like childlike wonder.

White leather with silver threading covers all of the seats. All of the other furniture including the small bar near the back is black with silver accents. Masculine but not too much.

I'm somehow able to sit down in one of these seats and not ask many many questions. I don't know how. Considering I really want to know how such elegance is capable of being in an aircraft.

Elijah sits opposite me and suddenly a flute of champagne appears in my line of vision. Where did he get that?

"Would you like some?" He smirks, still enjoying my curiosity and joy.

"Yes thank you" I take the glass from his fingers and finally calm my racing heart by looking at his lovely face. He leans over and squeezes my knee gently before clinking his glass against mine.

I try to listen to the captain's voice over the speakers and watch the air hostess' demonstration but in order to keep grounded, I have to keep my gaze on Elijah. This is fantastic but it's a lot.

"I feel so fancy" I admit, sipping on my champagne.

"I'm not overwhelming you am I? I just want to show you and give you everything" he asks concerned. Oh no, my tendency to freak out at lavish things has made him worry. I'm an idiot! Getting out of my seat, I step over to him and he automatically opens his arms for me.

I sit in his lap and curl my knees up so that I'm completely cocooned by him when he wraps me in his arms. It's one of my favourite things to do because it makes me feel safe.

"No I'm not overwhelmed. I appreciate every second of this. It's different but amazing. Thank you Handsome"

He relaxes visible and his cheeks pink a little. I've only called him 'Handsome' twice as a pet name but he seems to love it. It makes my heart pound when he looks all bashful like he does right now.

"You're welcome Princess"

Although I had to return to my seat for takeoff, I'm quick to jump back into his lap once the seat belt signs are tuned off. I can't help but snuggle into him, feeling weightless because of the altitude and because of his closeness.

I worry that I might be getting a little too addicted to this man.

Elijah

As Sofia sits in my lap, I think about all the flights I've taken before. I've sat here so many times, laptop open, my mind consumed with plans and schemes to better my business. I never thought that I was missing anything. Now when I think about it, I was painfully lonely. Yet the thought of having someone else in my lap to soothe the loneliness doesn't appeal to me. It's only her. Only Sofia who can sate the need for companionship.

I don't think I'll ever understand it but that's okay.

"What are you thinking about so hard?" She asks, tapping her finger against my nose.

"You of course" I reply truthfully.

"Hmm, I doubt that but it's a good answer" she smirks before leaning her head on my shoulder. She snuggles into me, while I squeeze her closer. I can smell the sweet scent of her shampoo that comes from her hair and I have to refrain from sticking my nose in it. That may seem strange.

She's falling asleep and my eyes are growing

heavy when the sole flight attendant appears at our seat.

"Can I get you anything, Sir? Madam?"

Jesus Christ, I had forgotten she was here. Then again she's been sitting behind the screen-door at the back of the plane in the work station for most of the flight so it makes sense.

There's a different attendant most times I use my jet and they are usually good at gauging when to ask or offer their services.

"No thank you" I tell her and focus back on my sleeping girl.

"Well if you change your mind just let me know" she continues and when I glance back at her, I catch her winking at me. Really? Is she seriously trying to flirt with me when there's a women in my lap?

I'm happy to say that I've never fucked any of the flight attendants so it's not as if she's assuming that'll happen. Unless she's just hoping I'm a sleaze ball. Unfortunately for her I'm not and I wouldn't be even if Sofia wasn't here.

"I won't change my mind" I confirm making sure my voice tells her she's being inappropriate. Just then Sofia stirs and shifts in my lap. She sees the flight attendant and immediately asks: "Oh could I have a glass of water please? I don't wanna be drunk during the day" she laughs but the flight attendant doesn't laugh back. In fact she scowls slightly before nodding and leaving. Jesus Christ! I'll be making sure I don't have her on any of my flights again. Rude!

"Did I say some thing wrong?" Sofia asks, wrinkling her nose in a cute frowning expression.

"No Darling, I just think she's in a bad mood"

When she comes back, Sofia thanks her for the water and then asks: "Are you okay?"

It's a genuine question, said without any malicious intent. She genuinely wants to know even though the woman has been rude to her.

"Um yes Mam. I'm fine thank you. It's just been a long day. I apologise if I don't seem fully up to it" she replies, her tone now completely different. It's as if she appreciates Sofia's concern. Which makes sense since I doubt many people ask. I know I never have. Maybe I should have done.

"Sit down for a bit. We don't need anything right now anyway" Sofia suggests and the flight attendant is truly shocked. God I don't deserve this girl.

"Oh that wouldn't be appropriate" She says awkwardly.

"It's okay, we don't mind" I add because she's looking for my permission since it's my jet. I kind of hate the thought that I can override Sofia in this kind of situation but I guess it's okay because I'm asking the flight attendant to do the same thing she is, not the opposite. Just like that, the flight attendant changes completely. Thanking us profusely before taking a seat a few rows back, still giving us privacy.

"You're so lovely Darling" I gush in awe.

"I feel bad for her. Plus the only reason she was being snooty is because she assumed I would be. All she sees all day is women and men flashing cash, being rude to her and a lot of the time they haven't earned the cash themselves. Like I haven't"

"Just because it's not your jet doesn't means you don't have the right to be here" I assure her.

"I know handsome, but she deals with stuck up idiots all day, so I get why she thought I was one"

I suddenly worry that I come across as snooty. I didn't care before but now I certainly do.

"Am I stuck up? " I ask, a little paranoid.

"No, you're polite. I've never seen you being rude. Sure, you're assertive because you're a boss and sometimes you yell but you're not snooty or stuck up. If you were I wouldn't be here. Because then you'd see me as a peasant " She jokes, her grin growing wider.

"A peasant? You? Never! You're a goddess my Dear" I confirm, brushing my fingers through her hair.

"I don't know about that but you're definitely a God"

"Now Darling, I'd be careful what you say. You don't want to boost my ego too much. You also probably don't want me to give an erection here"

My hands tighten on her impulsively and I think it might be too late to stop myself getting hard.

"You mean this erection?" she muses, shifting her ass against my hardening cock. Damn!

"I don't think you want me to fuck you right here in front of prying eyes either, do you?" I whisper, nipping at her ear lobe.

"Not right here but there is a lockable bathroom. I'm not in the mile high club yet. Are you?"

"No but that's about to change Darling"

"Thank god you agree" she squeals before glancing over the back of the seat. What is she up to?

"The flight attendant is asleep. Come on"

Oh I forgot about her again! This woman really takes up my whole brain and thought process. Which I love!

She takes me by the hand and pulls me all the way to the toilet. Upon opening the door we discover the small space. The size of the toilet has never occurred to me before. Maybe I should get it made bigger for any occasions like this in the future. Or maybe I should just throw this entire jet away and get a new one with a bedroom!

"We can make it work!" She states with determination, yanking me in and sliding the door shut. The soft click signifies that it's locked and I can't help but laugh as we're squashed against each other. No complaints here.

Moving my hands around her, I palm her ass and pull her impossibly closer. She gasps breathlessly and tugs on me too.

"Oh yeah, we can definitely make this work" I confirm smiling gleefully at her.

"I'm so glad you're on board with this idea"

She shifts her leg and somehow hooks it around my hip, her foot slamming against the opposite wall.

"Oops, sorry about that" she cringes.

"I don't care Darling. Do what you have to! I need you so bad!" I growl because fucking hell its true. The speed at which she affects me is absolutely unbelievable. It's like I'm wired to be ready for her whenever she desires.

Literally every breath we take is causing our bodies to push together and the desperate look in her eyes has me dying to please her.

"Then take me" she whispers and that's all it takes for us to go wild. We're all limbs, tugging at clothes. Some elbows are banged but we do manage to get our jeans down. She tugs my boxers down enough to free my cock and strokes it roughly. This has me gasping as I try to push her panties out of the way.

Her hand is so soft and warm gripping me tightly while my fingers are finally able to get the fabric out of the way and find her wetness. The moan she produces as I slide a finger inside her has me feeling carnal and needy.

"More Elijah please!" She begs and who am I to deny her?

Kissing her neck, I add another finger and she pants my name. Her hand strokes me quicker and I have to lock my legs so that I don't fall over.

"Feels so good Darling, I love it when you touch me"

"Can I have you now? Please baby!"

Damn, I love it when she begs. I think she knows I can't say no to her.

"Always" I croon, trying to ignore the deeper meaning of that singular word. Have me forever. Have me always. Fuck!

I remove my fingers from inside of her and grab her thighs, hoisting her a little higher. God my cock is weeping for her. She guides me to her entrance and I do as she asks, pushing inside her quickly.

"Fuck! Yes! Elijah, don't be gentle I need to feel you!"

"You got it Princess!" I groan, finding it hard to keep my eyes open as I slide out of her tight wetness. Dear god she is literally heaven. Slamming back into her, her heads hits the wall and her mouth opens in ecstasy. She squeezes me to her, one hand on my shoulder, the other sliding into my hair to tug hard.

She's beautiful and I'm so damn lucky to be the one who gets to give her pleasure. She then grabs my shirt as I drive into her and I can't help but close the final gap between us to kiss her senseless.

My hips move hard and quick, hitting as deep as I can. My balls tingle as she uses her thighs to squeeze me.

"Sofia you feel so good!" I practically whine against her mouth and she cries my name as I shift my hips. She leans her forehead on mine now, passion consuming her eyes. I'm sure I look the same. It makes me shiver. I've never felt a connection like this.

"Elijah, I love how you fill me. It's like you were made for me!" My heart thuds at her words.

"I think we were made for each other" I agree because I don't care how cliche that sounds. Or how important. All that I care about is that it feels true.

We're swearing and moaning, in fact she gets so loud at one point that she tries to muffle her noises of pleasure in my shoulder. I wish we didn't have to be quiet. I love to hear everything she has to give. I crave it.

I know that I won't last much longer and by the way she writhes against me, she won't either. Honestly I wish sex never had to end. Correction, I wish sex with Sofia never had to end.

Reaching between us, I tease her clit with my thumb and it drives her wild. Oh my beautiful girl.

"Yes! Yes! Yes!" She yells.

"You like that baby?" I croon, knowing she likes to hear my voice too.

"YES!" She screams.

I'm all smug about making her loose her mind but I should know by now that she can have me just as wrecked. With that thought in my mind and without warning, I feel her hand caress my balls. Oh sweet Jesus!

"Ahhhh fuck!"

"Do you like that Elijah?" She smirks as I struggle to find words.

"Yo-u haaave no idea how much!"

It doesn't take much longer for both of us to find release. With my hips jammed against hers and our lips locked, I come inside of her while she comes around me. Her walls pulsate and pretty much milk every last drop of pleasure from me. I don't know how we haven't passed out yet.

One glance at the mirror next to her head and I see that it's all streamed up. As our breathing slows I drag my finger through the condensation and draw a very cheesy love heart because that's exactly how I feel right now.

My bones are like liquid and my emotions are shot to hell.

"Awww, you are just the cutest" she teases when she sees my art. She pinches one of my cheeks playfully, making me grin from ear to ear. I then watch as she adds a E+S under the heart, completing the masterpiece. How lovely.

"Gorgeous work. We make a great team" I tell her.

"That we do Handsome. That we do" she responds pecking my lips.

After our bodies are capable of movement again, we pull apart. Grabbing some tissue from next to the toilet, I gently wipe between her legs, cleaning up the mess I've made. She blushes, her cheeks rosey.

"So considerate" she giggles.

Then we try to reassemble our clothing. I'm not going to lie, it's not easy but somehow we do it. Then we practically fall out of the tiny bathroom as soon as I open the door.

On the journey back to our seats, it's clear that we weren't very quiet as the flight attendant is no where to be seen and must have retreated back to her section. Oops! Sorry not sorry!

"Hey, high-five! We're now part of the mile high club" Sofia grins, looking rather pleased with herself. I don't blame her because I am too. High-fiving her waiting hand, I link our fingers and pull her back into my lap because I much prefer her here than in the seat opposite me.

"Thanks for initiating me into it!" I smirk.

"Oh you're so welcome! Thank you too!"

With a kiss to my cheek she snuggles back into me like before. I hold onto her as I realise that she is the most important and precious thing ever. I hope she never gets bored of me because I'm not sure what I'd do if she didn't want me anymore.

Sofia

When we land in O'ahi Hawaii it's midday and the instant heat that hits me is amazing. Elijah takes my hand once we're down the airplane steps and the level of freedom and happiness I feel should be illegal. There will be no judgment here. We're just a couple on holiday and no one is gonna ask me weird questions or give us strange looks.

After our luggage is offloaded we go in search of a cab and I take in the beautiful landscape. I don't know where we're staying because Elijah said everything is a surprise. I think he must have some things planned for us and I can't even describe how excited I am about that. He really spoils me.

On the ride to our accommodation all I do is use a selection of words including "Wow" and "Oh my god LOOK!"

Remind me again why Elijah doesn't find me super annoying?

I'm reminded why when he says "Sofia, look at that!" excitedly while tugging on my arm. He's just as enthusiastic as me and as silly because his excitement is due to a funny looking palm tree. God, I wish I'd met him sooner.

I feel like a kid who is being given gift after gift, especially as we pull up to a lovely villa. It's very private as the nearest villa next to it is quite a bit away. Plus each one is cozily nestled within bushes and palm trees. The sun beats down on the thatched roof with matching fence. Oh and as soon as we get out of the cab, the distinct sound of the ocean hit my ears. It's a beach villa which obviously is kind of to be expected but the reality of it in front of me has me jumping for joy. I can't believe it.

Elijah tips the driver and comes to stand next to my frozen form.

"Do you like it?" He asks, pressing a kiss to my cheek.

"Elijah, I have no words" I reply, cuddling into his side. When I look up at him with gratitude, I notice a bead of sweat rolling down his forehead and it makes me realise just how hot it is. We're not dressed in the correct attire for this heat and I can't wait to rectify that.

If I thought the exterior of the villa was nice then it's nothing compared to the interior. A lounge full of wicker furniture, chairs with soft cream cushioning and deep bay windows, opens up into a wonderful kitchen. Marble counter tops remind me of Elijah's apartment.

A wooden sliding door separates the bedroom on the right. Inside a huge king size bed - with cream duvet to match the lounge furniture - sits opposite yet more huge windows which means the sun is beating down on the bed.

Through those windows my eyes catch a round swimming pool glistening in the light. Wow.

There's more too. Behind the swimming pool is a little pathway, partially surrounded by bushes. I assume this leads directly to the beach and that fact makes me even more excited. Is it weird that I have a sudden urge to go build a sand castle?

The bathroom is as grand as the rest of the place with a huge tub and two person shower. I'm pretty sure we'll use that!

It all leaves me in shock like on the private jet and I only snap back to myself when Elijah wraps his arms around me from behind, leaning his chin on my shoulder.

"It's pretty isn't it?" he sighs, kissing my neck. That sigh sounds like he's expelling all frustration or worries that the outside world has created. I feel that way too. Being here with him in this place just feels so...good. Freeing.

"That's an understatement" I breath.

Squeezing his hands that rest on my stomach, I tilt my head back to nuzzle closer to him. I don't know how long we stand there in the middle of the lounge, staring out of the window at the greenery outside but it doesn't matter.

It soothes my soul.

***

We eventually peel off our sweaty clothes and change into more appropriate attire. I choose a simple light blue sun dress that causes Elijah to stare at my legs every two seconds.

To be honest I can't blame him because as I'm slipping some matching sandals on, I see that he's showing some leg too. I honestly didn't think he could get any hotter but boy was I wrong.

He's wearing a white short sleeved shirt that shows off his lovely arms. His bottom half is covered with navy board shorts, so like I said... I can stare at his legs too. I've never seen him in shorts before so it takes me a minute to remember where I am. In fact its very rare to see him in any kind of casual clothing but I feel so privileged that I get to..

On his nose sits a pair of black ray ban sunglasses and as my eyes shoot to his feet to take every detail in, I see the flip flops on his feet. Yes, he even has nice feet. I mean I've seen them before but I guess I've never stared.

"I can already tell that we're going to find it hard to leave this villa" he chuckles, his eyes glinting with lust as his gaze washes over my whole figure. Wow, that does things to me. "Although I guess I find it hard to leave anywhere if you're there too" he continues stepping towards me.

"I guess this is a little different since you're used to seeing me in sweat pants and oversized t-shirts all the time" As I say those words I realise that maybe he'd like me to make more of an effort. I mean he's used to the women around him being primed and plucked and in designer dresses 24/7. So maybe he'd like that from me too.

As if he's reading my thoughts he says:

"You're beautiful no matter what you wear Darling. I don't know how you do it but damn...you do it" he grins.

"Well, I am the lounge pant queen after all. I guess I'm a natural!" I reply, winking at him.

"The lounge pant queen huh? How about being the queen of my pants"

As soon as he says the words, he cringes and I try to stifle my laughter.

"That wasn't my best line was it?" he pouts sadly.

"No Handsome it wasn't but don't worry, I'll still sleep with you" I tease, tugging on his shirt to pull him closer.

"Thank god" he sighs in relief before hiding his face in my neck.

"There, there. It's all gonna be okay. You're still a god to me" I laugh, rubbing my hands over his back in mock comfort. "Come on, all of this can be forgotten. Let's take a look outside shall we?"

"Yes please"

He takes my hand and pulls me towards the sliding glass doors that separate the lounge from outside. As soon as he opens it, heat once again hits us, only this time we're prepared. Stepping into the sun, I take in the pool in more detail now. It also has a jacuzzi attached to the size. That will also be getting used.

As we walk around the pool a terribly mischievous though enters my mind.

"You can swim right?" I ask and Elijah glances at me with a curious expression on his face.

"Yes, I can. Why do you ask?" he says warily, already putting together the pieces. I wish I was better at being subtle but unfortunately I need to work on my poker face if I wanna be better at this kind of stuff.

I can feel myself grinning like a lunatic which solidifies what I'm sure Elijah has worked out.

He's going in that pool.

"Don't you dare!" he exclaims, letting go of my hand and stepping away from me quickly.

"What? Where are you going? I just wanna talk to you!" I bluff, following him slowly as he backs away. "I just want a hug"

"Funnily enough my dear, I don't believe your mischievously cute face" he glares, stepping back again.

"Baby, come on. I would never hurt you" I call and he moves quicker.

"No, you won't hurt me but you will push me in that pool. I know your plan!"

Crossing my arms over my chest, I sigh as if in defeat.

"Fine you're right. That was my plan. You can run but you can't hide. Before this holiday is over, I'll be dunking you in that pool. Mark my words"

His expression changes from shock to something darker as he marches back to me.

"Not if I dunk you first. You've just started a war Darling"

We glare at one another and excitement fills me. This is completely ridiculous but totally what I've always wanted from a partner. I'm not a serious person and having fun and playing with each other is pretty much at the top of my list when I think about the words soul mate. I mean, I don't believe in that shit. I don't even know if I believe in love but right here, right now...I believe in him.

Wow...deep.

***

We decide that our little game will commence properly tomorrow and agreed on no foul play for the rest of the day and night.

Elijah hinted that the first thing he has planned is tomorrow night, so we have today and most of tomorrow to do whatever we like. We decide on a leisurely walk on the beach to explore our surroundings.

Because I'm a child I splash my feet in the sea, kick some of it on Elijah and run away. He chases me, I surrender and end up engulfed in his arms.

I take pictures of the sea and the darkening sky as sunset begins. That's when it occurs to me that Elijah and I have no pictures together. So we spend a large amount of time in the fading light posing together for many many selfies.

As soon as I start taking pictures, I can't stop. I'm obsessed with capturing Elijah the most and snap some of him looking out to sea. When he notices me singling him out, he pulls his phone from his pocket and does the same to me. It's obvious that the same addiction over comes him as I sit down on a lonely rock. His camera flash snaps my attention to his open legged, tilted head stance as he tries to play photographer.

I think we may be just a little bit obsessed with one another.

Elijah

    Why didn't I think of this before? Why have I never taken any pictures of my beautiful girl? Is it because I've been worried that one day she might leave me? That maybe our relationship isn't as serious as I think it is.

    Well whatever the reason, I don't care about it now. I know for a fact that these pictures of her are going to soothe me when I'm working long hours and miss her like hell.

    She laughs at my continuous snapping and brushes her hair behind her ear. Her dress blows slightly in the breeze and I'm mesmerised by it. Snap. Snap.

    I should probably stop.

    "Are you satisfied?" She giggles, getting up and padding over the soft sand to me.

    "No I'll never be satisfied. I want all the pictures of you that I can get"

    "Or you could just have the real thing" she wiggles her eyebrows and immediately my phone is forgotten. She's right after all. No photo can do her beauty justice.

    "Yes, I think that's a better idea" I murmur before circling her waist with my arms and lifting her off the ground. She squeals in surprise and grips my shoulders for support.

    In this very moment, something I've been missing slots into place. I never thought this was the kind of life I

wanted but with every second of Sofia I get, the more it becomes my dream. A dream that I don't want to let go of.
    It's happening now and I'm going to hold on tighter than I've ever held onto anything.

Sofia

The next morning once I'm dressed, I sit in the lounge and eat some apple slices that I found in the fridge. I'm wondering why Elijah has taken quite a bit longer than me to get ready but I don't have to wonder for long.

He walks out of the bedroom and I have to do a double take. Something is missing. His beard is no longer present and in its place is a lovely smooth shaven face.

Gorgeous.

Moving towards me in a black t-shirt and matching shorts, he looks a little nervous.

"Do you like it?" he asks as he stops a few inches away.

"Do I like what?" I question, pretending that I haven't noticed a thing. His eyes widen as if in shock and confusion but when I grin he shakes his head.

"You're mean" he pouts dropping down beside me.

"I'm sorry, I couldn't help it. You look extremely handsome. I love it" I tell him, reaching up to stroke his smooth cheek.

He's never not had a beard since the day I met him. Whether it's been thick or trimmed neatly it's always been present, giving me sweet beard burn on my face or my thighs. I love it but I also love this new look and I hate that he seemed worried about my opinion.

"I'm glad you like it" he sighs as if in relief.

"Why were you so worried?" I question, thinking it's such a normal thing for men to do. Why would he think it would bother me?

"Well some women have strong opinions on facial hair and I just didn't want you to think I looked terrible without it. I was gonna keep it because personally I like having a beard more than not but the heat here is too much for me to –"

I stop his ramble, pressing my lips to his, trying to shove all of my feelings of affection into him. He's fucking gorgeous no matter what.

When we pull apart he nuzzles his nose against mine.

"Okay, I'll shut up. You clearly still think I'm hot stuff" he chuckles, returning to his confident cocky self.

God I lov- really like him...

***

With our free time today we opted to explore a wider radius around the villa. Walking down busy streets, past some shops and to a lovely market full of trinkets and other cute things. This is the place that finally answered a question or rather a desire I've had for a while now.

What do you buy a billionaire? What can I buy a billionaire?

It's hard to find something to give a person who either has everything or the means to buy anything. In fact it's pretty impossible.

I even thought about making something but craft is not my strong point. I'm not even sure why I'm so obsessed with finding a gift for Elijah. Maybe it's because no one ever gives him anything and he deserves so much. Jesus that's deep. Regardless I've been spending a lot of time trying to work it out. Whether it's during my break at work, tapping away at my phone while he sleeps beside me or lying awake wracking my brains.

It's been the most frustrating thing ever. Until today...

I found it. The perfect gift for Elijah. It's somewhat a novelty and only cost me ten dollars but boy am I pleased with it. Maybe I can say it's pretty ironic too.

It was tricky to even buy it without Elijah noticing. I had to wait until he was occupied, browsing the stalls. Then as quickly as humanly possible I picked up my gift, dived to the make shift till point and all but spat my idea at the poor unsuspecting stall owner.

So...it's a coin. A silver mental coin with the word 'together' engraved on the front. Nothing special I know but to me it's perfect. He can't do anything with it and I doubt it's lucky at all but I'm hoping the sentiment behind it will get across what I want to say. It has no monetary value. Giving him a coin that isn't money but so much more.

What do I want to say you may ask? What does a metal coin tell someone?

I want him to know that no matter how lonely he feels or when he thinks he has no one, he will always have me. Even if this thing we have ends, I'm still going to be there for him. Maybe the coin won't just be a representation of my care for him. Maybe it'll represent other people in his life. Work associates that he thinks are just acquaintances probably like him a lot more than he thinks. He has people who love him and he just doesn't seem to notice. Maybe this will help.

    Elijah has all the money in the world but he doesn't have this currency. He can't sell it. He can't spend it. All he can do is hopefully keep it and when our time together inevitably comes to an end and we don't see each other all that much, he can look at this coin. It'll represent that not everyone only wants his money. That when he's lying in bed with a women that doesn't care...I still do. That's a horrible thought but there's no way this man won't want more than me one day. Okay, I want the coin to represent fucking everything! I want it to be super ironic too. Someone giving him money...crazy!
    I should also mention that on the back of the coin I requested another engraving. An engraving that he almost caught happening when he returned to my side but I pretended I was just watching the stall owner work.
    I literally held my breath as he turned away to look at the shelf behind me. Then I finally was able to scoop up my little coin and pop it in my pocket. Mission complete.
    My blood pressure returned to normal and we walked off hand and hand as if nothing had happened. I don't think I've sweated so much in my life.

***

    For the rest of the afternoon we decide to lounge on our private beach. We did a lot of walking and god my feet hurt.
    When I appear next to him lying on the sun lounger, he drops the book he's reading as soon as he sees me. He then lifts his sunglasses as if to get a better look. Sure he's

seen me naked more times than I can count and I'm sure that's his favourite way for me to be. Saying that, I'm also pretty sure he currently loves the bikini I'm in.

"I just want you to know that I mean my next words in the most respectful way possible...you're so fucking hot" he growls, which makes it hard for me to keep my composure. My eyes are still hidden behind thick sunglasses so he can't see that I'm loosing my mind.

If he looked good before in his t-shirt and shorts well he looks fucking fantastic now. Shirtless, a little sweaty from the sun. God I wish I had water right now. Then again no amount of water can solve my issues.

I'm obsessed...there I admitted it! Send me away!

"Wow I feel so disrespected. How could you?!" I say dramatically, glaring down at him.

"I'm so sorry Darling. You're just so sexy. I've never seen such beauty" he replies with just as much drama. I love it.

"I guess I could forgive you...maybe" I tease. This causes him to sit up and reach for my hand. He tugs on it and I lean down to kiss his gorgeous lips. He takes this opportunity to grab me and pull me into his lap while I squeal all the way in surprise.

"Got you" he whispers in my ear as I move to straddle him. Sorry I can't help it. He sure has got me though, in fact I think we're as bad as each other.

"Or maybe I've got you" I smirk squeezing my thighs against his. My hands rest on his shoulders, my nails digging into his skin a little. He bits his lip and swallows, his hand going to my hips. Hehehehe.

He shifts beneath me and I become very aware of his erection, only covered by thin swim shorts. Perfect, I do have him.

"Damn. I can't resist you Sofia, you drive me insane" he growls and captures my lips in one swift movement. His tongue invades my mouth almost immediately, one of his hands slide into my hair. He tugs a little and I love it. These little things are his attempt to gain back some dominance partly because he knows I like it and partly because he wants me to submit to him. I think it's tough for him to choose which he prefers. He's used to being in charge in all aspects of his life so it's natural for him to want the control. On the flip side when I make him do what I want he loves it...sometimes even begs for it. He seems to thrive on letting me win. We tend to know which role to take. We know what the other person needs.

I'm going to go out on a limb here and say that maybe I even make him feel safe. He's never trusted anyone so with me he can actually let go. I'm glad I can be that for him.

Today I'll be the submissive one and I let him know this by dropping my hands from his shoulders and placing them on his chest gently. Tilting my head back, I give him access to my neck and he immediately kisses and sucks on the skin there. His arms wrap around me tightly, pulling me close before he rocks his hips up into me.

"I think you need some sun tan lotion on Darling" he groans, moving quickly go grab the bottle he left in the sand.

Before I can blink he's tugging on the strings that keep the top part of my bikini in place. It falls away and exposes my breast to him. I watch in fascinating as he squirts some of the lotion on his hands and rubs them together. A second later his warm palms cup my breasts, massaging roughly.

"Oh Elijah, that feels so good!" I moan pushing my chest into him further. He breathes deeply and pinches my nipples between his fingers. This sends shock waves through my body making me dripping wet for him.

"You're all mine Darling" he pants squeezing once more.

"I've never belonged to or with anyone before" is what I accidentally let slip out of my mouth. Oops. Well it's true. I don't just mean in a possessive manor. I mean I've never felt like I've belonged in general. Not really. No ones ever made me feel part of them. Until him.

He cups my cheeks with his lotioned hands to make me look at him. His eyes are full of desire for me and it only makes me feel more alive.

"Well you belong with me okay?" he growls and my replying nod isn't enough for him.

"I need to hear it!" he snaps, rocking into me again this time as more of a punishment. I whine and writhe, needing him inside of me. For some reason I can't speak. It's like I'm worried if I confess what I feel that it'll disappear. That he will! "Hmm it seems I have to persuade you more" he says menacingly.

With that statement he grabs my hips and lifts me slightly, then the heel of his hand presses right against my clit through my bikini bottoms. YES!

"Say it Sofia! Tell me"

No words fall from my mouth. He pushes his fingers inside of me and I am consumed by ecstasy. I fucking love it! But he's on a mission and he knows how to play me. So he stops when I try to ride his fingers.

"No...more please" I beg and he chuckles darkly.

"You'll get more when you do as I say" he assures me, leaning forward and sucking my nipple into his mouth. His tongue swirls and drives me mad. Then he's reaching for my chin with his free hand and his eyes blaze with need and determination.

"Why can't you say it? What's the matter?"
His eyes do something to me. They hypnotise me. So I can't stop my confession.

"I'm scared I'll lose you. I don't want to lose you" I push out, my voice filled with agony. He shakes his head, totally dispelling such a thing as if it's impossible.

"I'm not going anywhere Darling. I'm right here. So please...tell me. Tell me who you belong to"

Now he's begging and pulling his hand from between my legs. He shuffles his shorts down and frees his cock, waiting for me to follow through with his demand. He leaves me wanting as he strokes his length and I can't help but watch.

"Say it!"

He's not touching me now. I'm just hovering over him desperately. All that is connected is our eyes as they lock together. I see that he means what he says. I see that he doesn't want to leave me.

He stops torturing himself and grips my hips. All I have to do is pull the string on my bikini bottoms and the agony could end.

"Fuck! Sofia you drive me insane. I want to be inside you but I won't do it until you believe me"

Looking at his tortured face, I let go of my fear. Not because I need to be joined with him so much it hurts but because he's showing it to me. He's showing his vulnerability. He won't leave me.

"I belong to you Elijah. I belong with you"

In a millisecond we both snap, yanking off my last piece of clothing. He pushes inside of me and the relief it's catatonic.

"Aghhh Sofia! Shit! Yes! Fuck, ride me!"

The sun beats down on my naked back and I sink down onto him. His hands caress my hips as he fills me and it's such a glorious feeling. A feeling that I don't think I ever want to live without.

We get lost in the sensation, moving together like one being. It's glorious. Fantastic! Wonderful! Okay there aren't enough words to describe how it feels.

In fact, we're so far gone that it takes a good amount of time for us to hear the chitter chatter of other people to hit our ears. When it does though my eyes shoot open and I gasp in horror rather than pleasure. Elijah sits up straight immediately and my head whips around to see a couple strolling hand in hand on our 'private' beach.

They notice us the same time we notice them, stopping dead in their tracks and staring. I jump off Elijah with super speed as embarrassment fills me. We're completely naked and as that thought enters my mind I try feebly to cover myself with my hands.

Elijah jumps in front of me, hiding my body from them.

"What the hell are you doing? Get out of here?" he roars, vibrating with anger. Obviously he's naked too and finally instinct kicks in. I grab the towel from the sun lounger and reach around to cover his glorious manhood. I don't want anyone to see that but me.

I think he feels the same way about me as the couple continue to stare.

"This is public indecency" the man yells and Elijah takes a step forward, a sound coming from his throat that simply isn't human.

"Get the fuck out of here" he shouts again and moves forward once more. I have to step with him to keep the towel in place and he reaches back to keep me close. Elijah's advance seems to scare off the guy and make him realise he won't win even if Elijah is the naked one.

"We'll report you! What mind kind of people do that? Is she a whore?" The women finally speaks. How fucking dare she?!

"What the fuck did you just say?" Elijah growls as the couple start to walk away.

"I'm no whore, I'm just not a friggin prude" I yell, unable to stop myself.

Wisely the couple don't reply this time and keep walking.

"How fucking dare they!" Elijah continues while I drop the towel and pull him back around to face me.

"It doesn't matter. They're gone. Thanks for protecting my modesty" I smile softly looking up at him through my lashes. His eyes go dark with possession.

"You're mine Sofia, I'm yours and this thing between us in special. I don't want anyone to see it but us" he explains, saying exactly what I'm thinking.

"Then we better finish what we started because you're making me even more desperate"

He searches my eyes then latches his mouth onto mine. We fall into the sand and in seconds his still throbbing cock pushes into me roughly making me cry out. My nails dig into his back, dragging all the way down to his ass. Urging him on, I watch his lovely face looking blissful with pleasure. I do this to him...only me. His forehead presses into mine, his eyes glued to me.

We share all of our feelings without speaking. Our breathless moans and groans are enough. We cling to each other pushing ourselves to the edge of glory.

"Remember when I told you that I don't have a type?" he pushes out, his words breathless. He told me that on the first date we had.

"I remember" I gasp as he cups my cheeks, his hips rutting wildly.

"Well you're it. You're my type Darling. Just you"

Fuck.

"Elijah..." I whine because I don't have a response that will do his words justice.

Grabbing the back of his head, I pull his lips to mine and kiss him with all of the passion I can. I can't deal with all of the emotions that war within me. It's getting more difficult every day.

As the sparks in my lower stomach explode throwing me into heaven and his head buries into my neck while he comes too, something occurs to me.

I guess it's a little childish but we've just had sex on the beach.

***

Finally I get to find out the first thing Elijah has planned. As the cab pulls up next to a harbour with many many boats docked, my eyes take in all the different types. Catamarans, large fishing boats and glamorous yachts all lined up.

The one we stop by looks like it may have been used for sight seeing tours around the island at one point but is now docked and stationary. It's large and through the windows lots of table are visible. It's been made into a restaurant. Oh my, this is lovely.

Elijah watches my reaction as we get out of the cab and walk towards it. I think the look on my face says it all.

"You really spoil me" I sigh and he shakes his head in disagreement.

"There's so much more I want to do for you and with you. You have no idea"

He links his arm with mine, guiding me onto the ramp that leads to the boat. Its roof and railings are covered in fairy lights. The gorgeous white vessel almost glows in the moonlight and I feel so at home by Elijah's side.

The feelings inside me are only growing and it's as if they are bubbling and about to burst out of my chest. I'm just not so sure what that'll mean when they do.

There are lots of couples here and we are simply one of them. It's so refreshing and welcoming.

"Madame, Sir" the waiter greets us politely. I find it rather funny yet fantastic that this is a relatively fancy restaurant but everyone here including us, are dressed pretty casual. "Follow me" the waiter continues, walking off. Elijah takes my hand, his thumb drawing soothing circles on my knuckles. I think he's enjoying this experience as much as I am.

We meander through white clothed tables with candles flickering softly, until we reach our table near the back of the boat. It's right next to the window and I can just about make out the black swish of the see. It's quite mesmerising and such a different view to a normal dinner. Elijah really is spoiling me.

The reflection of the moon hits the water which has me staring for a bit longer than is probably socially acceptable. When Elijah pulls my chair out, I'm snapped from my trance and blush as I take my seat.

The waiter gives me a knowing smile that kind of says "girl you're lucky" and I give him a silent reply of "oh I know."

As Elijah takes his seat opposite me, I smirk and say "Such a gentleman" in a teasing tone.

"For you, yes" he replies winking devilishly.

"What can I get you both to drink?" the waiter asks and I immediately crave some gin and lemonade. I haven't actually drank in a while apart from the odd wine here and there and the champagne on the jet but since we're on holiday I guess it won't hurt. So yeah I go for the gin and Elijah surprises me by choosing the same.

"I want to see if you have good taste" he teases, smirking at my "oh really" expression.

"Huh, I thought by now you'd know that I have good taste. I'm with you aren't it?" I hit back and this makes him look far too smug.

"Actually some would say I'm a terrible choice. After all I'm not nearly as tall or as fit as the average man that is deemed attractive. Plus I can get terribly sweaty" he says totally nonchalant as he flicks through the menu. Huh, it seems there are some insecurities here.

"Well I'm far too outspoken and 'quirky' for societies liking. I don't wear make up and every time I look in the mirror I wonder how anyone could find me attractive. Yet here we are" I retort and look at the menu with the same casual uninterestedness. The point is we may try to act casual about our worries and downfalls but it bothers both of us. I really do wonder how he could want me. It seems he wonders the same about how I could want him. Which is crazy to me.

My confession makes him stare at me just like I was staring at him.

"Stop that" he says softly reaching for my hand.

"Stop what?" I ask as if I'm completely obtuse.

"Putting yourself down"

"Why? That's what you just did"

"Yes but" he pauses struggling to answer and I look over at him, his forehead creasing in a frown. Maybe I can answer for him.

"It's easy to mock yourself isn't it but when I do it you don't like it" I finish for him.

"Yes exactly" he confirms, squeezing my hand.

"Well I don't like it when you put yourself down either. You are quite frankly the most gorgeous man I've ever met. So please shut up about being below average or I'll kick you under the table" I say seriously giving him a stern look. He gazes at me strangely then, as if I've said something he's never heard before.

"Thank you Darling. That was sweet. Now I won't threaten to kick you but I will-" he pauses and leans closer so he can whisper. "I will spank you if you ever say those things about yourself again. You're fucking stunning with a sharp tongue that makes me hard. If anyone says anything about you being outspoken you send them to me so I can punch them into next year!"

Wow! I took a lot from his speech but honestly my mind got a little stuck on the spanking part. Does he know I kind of have a fantasy about that?

"How about I don't put myself down again but you still spank me?" I whisper back and his eyes light up. Bingo!

"That can definitely happen Darling. Anything you like" he hisses, looking like a wolf in human skin, his eyes almost glowing yellow. Damn.

"Anything?" I test.

"Anything-" Just then the waiter comes back with our drinks and we're snapped out of our little sex fantasy. Oh shoot! I still haven't looked at the menu properly.

As soon as the gin is in front of Elijah, he sips it and I immediately want to know his verdict.

"Well? Do I have good taste?"

"You have wonderful taste Darling. This is fantastic" he bites his lip before sipping some more. Win!

Actually this gives me an idea. A way to get out of not looking at the menu yet.

"How about you pick my food and I'll tell you if you have good taste" I suggest and he nods happily, his eyes skimming the menu and settling on something in seconds.

"The salmon please. For both of us" he tells the waiter with a coolness that I imagine he uses in the boardroom. Only when the waiter nods and leaves his face transforms as he grits his teeth and laughs.

"I'm not going to lie Darling, that was chosen on a whim. Sorry if it sucks"

I shake my head at him.

"I expected more from you. I expected better. Maybe I will look for a new man. Hmmm maybe someone else here so I can ask him to give you tips" I joke, pretending to glance around. Elijah crosses his arms and glares.

"Fine, I'll help you..." he breathes before his eyes shoot around the room too.

A few seconds into my scanning and I see a couple that looks to be into a certain lifestyle. One that Elijah knows well.

"What do you think about them?" I muse glancing at the couple across from us. Elijah takes one look and leans into me.

"I think that I'm not the only man here who has relations to the sugar lifestyle"

The man looks to be considerably older than the younger woman who is laughing at little to loudly for it to be real. Now obviously I'm not one to judge, I mean I literally can't judge but this definitely seems like a stereotypical Sugar couple. Like you'd see in the movies. Either that or he has no idea she wants his cash. Or hey! Maybe it's his daughter who knows!

Now that we've probably incorrectly judged an innocent couple and forgotten our original conversation, I nudge Elijah and tilt my head the other way.

"Okay, what about them"

Two women sit together, their hands linked on the table top. All I see is a cute couple but Elijah seems to notice something else.

"I think they're on a secret getaway because she's married and that's her lover" he explains.

Upon closer inspection, I notice the wedding ring on one of the women's hands.

"Ah but maybe the other lady just doesn't wear her ring" I try to defend but in the same second the ring wearing women's phone begins to ring. When she answers it she immediately looks concerned. It's clear within a few moments of the conversation that she's lying and Elijah raises his eyebrows at me triumphantly.

"Damn, I was wishing for a better outcome"

"Me too Darling" he agrees looking a little deflated.

"What's wrong?" I ask concerned.

"I hate when people are betrayed by the ones they care for" I don't think Elijah has experienced this in a romantic setting but I'm assuming he's experienced with friends and family.

"Because why be with someone if they don't make you happy? Why hurt someone else?" I state.

"Exactly. I've not been much of a caring guy in the past but I've never cheated or committed to someone I didn't want to" he confesses sincerely. I have a feeling he may need to hear the same thing from me.

"I haven't either" I tell him truthfully and take his hand again.

"Good to know" he nods and clears his throat as if dispelling any unwanted emotions. Maybe that's another insecurity he had, that I'll end up not wanting him and cheat. The very thought makes me sick. My confession of no previous infidelity seems to have settled something within him and for some reason his confession of the same has settled me. It's not because we don't trust one another, it because we both think we're not good enough to be worthy of each other.

Changing the subject, I pick one final victim.

"Okay, last time. What about him?" I ask, gesturing to the table diagonally across from us. The man is alone.

"He has no date but he keeps telling the waiter that someone is coming" he guesses but as he finishes his sentence, a tall blonde women appears and takes her seat. Ha!

"Looks like you got that one wrong big guy" I laugh and pat his hand.

"Shit! That's my reputation ruined! How will I ever live on now?"

"It's gonna be tough baby but I'm sure you'll make it through" I sooth, picking up his hand and kissing the back of it. He blushes which is becoming more of a common thing. I love it. He leans over and presses his lips to mine ever so gently.

"With you by my side...I'll get through anything my Dear"

***

That night after dinner we headed back to our extravagant beach house. Elijah is now pouring me wine as I sit on the stool at the kitchen island. We're both a little tipsy from the drink during our meal so I decide now is the perfect time to give him the gift.

Here we go...yup...just give it to him...no big deal.

I've kept it close to me all day, contemplating just forgetting it. I can't do that though. I really want him to have it.

So I take a gulp of my wine as Elijah comes around the counter to sit on the stool next to mine. I set down the glass and turn to him.

"I love this" he mumbles, his fingers reaching out to glide down my arm. Okay, that's distracting. Focus Sofia.

"You love what?" I ask, blushing without even knowing his answer.

"Having you all to myself. I know I have you to myself back home but it always gets interrupted by boring life stuff and I have to spend hours of my day without getting to do this"

Well...tipsy Elijah is even more forth coming that sober Elijah. Tipsy Sofia better keep her mouth shut.

Which is easy to do as he leans into me and brushes his lips against mine. A small but meaningful question of 'can I kiss you?'. The answer is always yes but this is another of his unusual gentlemanly touches. For a man who gets called an asshole so much, he's the most respectful human I've ever met.

I give him permission by pressing my lips into his fully and his responsive moan echoes in my ears. I get caught up in him because how could I not?

We make out until his lips trail down my neck teasing me. The thought of gifting him the coin knocks at the back of my head and it's a crazy struggle to try and focus on it.

"Elijah...I-I" I try to get the words out but they end up fading out into a sigh of joy as he nips at my skin.

Still my half assed sentence is enough to stop him. His face appears back in my line of sight, his eyes flitting over my face.

"Are you okay Darling? I'm sorry, I just can't keep my hands off you"

"Oh no, it's not that. I'm fine" I assure him and peck his lips. I'm more than fine. I'm on fire but I can't have him put me out until I get this part over with first. "I have something for you"

"For me?" he questions, his eyes lighting up with joy at my words. It's so heartwarming. Here he is gazing at me with bright eyes. His cheeks are flushed from the alcohol and our antics. His shirt crumpled from the crazy day we've had. The top three buttons are undone which is a sure way to show that he's on holiday. Back home he's always buttoned up unless his work day is over. His hair is a chaotic mess and his goofy grin is throwing me off my thought process.

"Yeah for you" I confirm and watch in fascination as he becomes almost confused.

I reach into my pocket and he follows my every movement. Finding the tiny paper bag the coin is in, I get even more nervous. What if he thinks it's ridiculous?

"Hold out your hand"

He does so in wonder, lifting his palm in my direction. I place the tiny bag in it with my own sweaty hand. God! I'm going through it.

I sit there and watch him stare at it. It takes him a few seconds before he opens it up and lets the coin drop into his hand. It lands with my personal engraved message facing up. I'd hoped he'd see the side that says 'together' first so that I'd have a minute to collect myself. No such luck...how ironic!

I don't know what he's thinking but soon he's tracing the engraved words with his index finger.

"You have me, asshole" he reads out loud the words I selected so carefully. All that time going from women to women, never connecting has to have been soul destroying. My statement also conveys that not everyone sucks. He has me and I won't ever betray him or lie to him like he thinks everyone does. I know it's pretty deep but at this point I've given up on hiding how much I care for him. The asshole part was meant to make him laugh but his serious expression has me worried.

"Oh god you hate it. I'm sorry. It's stupid. I was just trying to be cute" I begin, trying to bluff my way out of it. "I'm so bad at gifts, it's ridiculous"

"Sofia-"

"Let's forget this ever happened. The level of embarrassment I'm feeling right now is crushing. This is why I never do meaningful things...oh god"

"Darling I-"

"I'm not sure anyone has ever done anything so cringe worthy. Why am I like this? See this is why no one wants to actually date me because I'm fucking weird"

"No, you're not-"

"A coin, a fucking coin. What a ridiculous idea!"
"SOFIA!"

His loud yell finally cuts through my melt down and my cheeks warm as he reaches out to touch me. With the coin firmly grasped in his other hand, he gives me a stern look before speaking.

"Darling, no one has ever really bought me anything. Let alone something so...meaningful" he begins, his voice wavering as he struggles to get the words out. It must be tough for him to admit. "So you'll have to excuse me because I don't know how to react. I don't know how to express how I feel right now but please don't think that I don't like it. I love it. I love it more than I can put into words"

"Well in that case, you're welcome" I say as casually as I can and he smiles warmly at me. "As for expressing how you feel, what are your instincts telling you?" I ask, trying to make light of the situation and brush over my embarrassing moment.

"My instincts?"

"Yeah-"

I'm cut off by his mouth smothering mine, his arms snaking around my waist. He pulls me from the stool and stands, holding me flush against his body. His lips nip at my ear and his breathy response has me reeling.

"My instincts tell me to thank you. They tell me that having you is too good to be true"

He pulls back to look at me, his eyes glassy. Fuck. I'm not sure I can take all this.

"Well you do have me. The coin says so. The coin doesn't lie" I laugh and he gives me a small smile yet stays serious. My heart thuds in my chest and I wonder if this is actually happening or if I'm imagining his vulnerable stare.

"I have you..." he whispers as if he's finally accepting it. Wow, big moment.

"Yes Elijah"

"And you have me" he breathes and I wonder how I'm still standing. Probably because he's holding me up.

That's it! I'm done for!

Grabbing his shirt, I pull him to me and wrap my arms around his neck. I don't want to ever let go. This is so out of hand and crazy. I never thought these emotions and feelings existed outside of a crappy romantic novel. Yet here I am. A puddle of goo in his arms.

Then...well then I make a mistake. I do the one thing I know I shouldn't. When we stop hugging, I look back into his eyes and I can't stop the words that slip out of my mouth.

"I love you Elijah"

The sheer panic that I feel immediately becomes displayed on his face too and I know I've fucked up.

I know I've ruined us.

Elijah

What? Did she say those three words? Three words that I've learned throughout my life mean very little.

I'm a businessman. Which means I've seen pretty much everything. I've seen the married couples sell each other out. New lovers murmur 'I love you' before sitting in my office and flirting with me.

Cheaters and liars say those words and now my Sofia. What do I do? What do I say? Everything that 'I love you' has taught me is becoming twisted as she stares at me with no lies in her eyes.

Could she feel that way about me? Do I feel the same about her? I certainly don't love her because to me that would not be doing justice to how I feel. I'd be stupid to try and pretend that my feelings for this women don't completely surpass the word love.

She is everything to me. My world. I adore and cherish her but I won't disrespect her by telling her I love her.

As her face crumbles with sadness and pain, I know that she truly believes her feelings. Maybe she's the one and only person on this planet who could say 'I love you' and mean it with all her heart. I'm floored and honoured to have her love. I don't deserve it. I should tell her that but all I want to do is find some way to explain all of this to her without her thinking that I don't feel what she feels.

"Ummm, sorry. That was silly. I shouldn't have said that. I'm just gonna go for a walk" she barely whispers and everything inside of me is dying to speak. To stop the rejection she feels but my mouth won't move. I can barely breath.

I watch her pad away from me and my feet itch to follow. I should stop her.

My throat closes up as I try to call her name but it doesn't work and she exits the villa through the glass doors and off to the beach.

"Sofia..." I push out, my vocal cords finally obeying. Fucking asshole! I really am. I've finally lived up to the name everyone gives me.

Suddenly the coin in my hand feels heavy and I wish the metal would heat and burn my palm in punishment. She gave it to me and it said everything she held in her heart. I don't deserve it either.

Do something idiot! Fix it! Because if you don't, she will never look at you the same way!

Sofia

I tried not to cry. I really did. Because what's the point in crying simply because someone doesn't feel the same way. I can't change it or fix it. It is what it is. So I need to pull myself together.

Well...maybe not quite yet. I think a little more time sitting on this rock will be beneficial for my heart. Although considering it's the same rock we took pictures on yesterday before I ruined things with my stupid confession today...maybe I should go.

I can't sit here all night but how am I supposed to face him? He's probably plotting a way to let me down gently. He'll say that it's time for him to find someone else and I won't even blame him. I suck.

The breeze blows hot air at me even though it's getting late. My tears become damp streaks on my face rather than wet drips of total sadness. I'm wondering if walking into the sea and floating away will save me from this humiliation but I know that's ridiculous. Or is it...

Just as I'm about to test my theory, my skin prickles like it always does when Elijah is close and I try my best not to accept that he's come to find me. Is that worse than me going back to him or not? I'm not so sure.

It's a struggle to stop my head turning to face him. The sand must have muted his footsteps or maybe I'm just so consumed by my own turmoil that I didn't notice.

"Sofia"

One word. My name. It holds so much distress and pain. Why is he in pain? Why does it sound like I've hurt him? Regardless I immediately want to apologise and fix it. No matter how silly that sounds. I don't want him to feel hurt.

"Sofia, please. Come inside and we can talk about this" he continues and I grit my teeth to stop more agony overflowing. Talk? All he's gonna do is break up with me. I'll make it easier for him.

"It's okay. We don't need to talk. You don't have to let me down gently or anything. I'm a big girl, I'll get over it" I mumble. I feel him moving closer, his aura chaotic. Aura? Who the hell do I think I am? I ain't spiritual and I'm not even sure what an aura is but I feel something coming from him.

"What? I don't understand?" he questions and finally I have to look at him before my own neck snaps with the temptation. Fuck it Sofia! You really have it bad. You also have it wrong.

His forehead is creased with a confused frown. His eyes wild as he tries to understand something. I don't know what he doesn't understand. Anyway he's gorgeous and I'm a mess.

Those wild eyes widen when he takes in my tear streaked face and in seconds he's reaching to cup my cheeks. Warmth. Passion... but not love on his part.

"Don't cry. I'm not worth it Darling" he assures me but it certainly isn't assuring. I can't help but laugh bitterly.

"Well I apologise for crying. It just sucks to know I've been incredibly stupid. I knew from the beginning this shouldn't be anything serious and now I've ruined it. Now you're going to leave me and-"

"What?! I'm not leaving you!" he yells, pulling me from the rock and capturing me in his strong arms. God why is he doing this to me?

"You're not?" I squeak and he shakes his head frantically. "But you don't feel the same way? So why would stay with me?"

I'm trying not to hold onto any hope. I don't want to think anything will change. He's not going to suddenly love me.

"Come on, let's go inside and I'll tell you exactly how I feel. It may not make any sense but I'm praying it'll be enough" he explains, worry evident on his face. Is he worried that I'll leave him? This is all so confusing.

My mind is reeling. I don't know what to say or do. I don't know what's going on. All I can do is let him drag me back to our little holiday house in silence.

We may not be saying anything but our insides rage and war. There's a lot going on and I'm not sure how we'll survive it.

His hand tightens in mine as we make it back. He slides the glass doors shut and guides me to the sofa where he lets me go and I panic.

Should I be doing something? Saying something? He said he's not leaving me but he's pacing back and forth as if he's working up the courage to let me go. It frightens me more than I want to admit.

"Elijah...whatever you feel, just tell me. I can't promise not to be upset but I won't hold anything against you if that's what you're worried about"

"I'm not worried about you holding a grudge Darling. I'm worried about the same thing you seem to be worried about" he breathes hard, his hands shoved in his pockets deep as he burns a hole in the ground.

So I was right? I think. He's worried I'll leave him? What? Why? My head is spinning, my heart thudding and grasping at the tiniest bit of hope that we'll make it out of this together and not torn apart.

"Okay...I'm just...I'm just gonna tell you"

Shit. This is a horrible. He stops in front of me and then kneels there too, his face level with mine. He takes my hands and looks as terrified as I feel.

"I don't love you Sofia..." he pushes out and I'm immediately struck with complete pain and horror. Is he purposely trying to hurt me? Because it's working. I can feel my own face contorting with agony and anger. Is this a game to him? "Wait! Let me finish!" he exclaims, seeing my reaction. I want to pull away from him for the first time since we met. His touch is making me feel sick because right now it just seems like he's messing with me.

Yanking my hands away from his, I sit back to get space. His face crumbles as I reject him and he stands again stepping back.

"Sorry. I really am trying to explain. You see I don't love you because to me...love doesn't mean a thing. Sofia, I've seen people who claim to love each other and I've seen the very same people betray one another too. I've seen those three words get thrown around and hold absolutely no meaning. People use those words to lie. To cheat. People say 'I love you' and then they end up 'loving' someone else. My parents did it. Many many business partners I've encountered have done it. It's fake and I won't say those words to you. I won't disrespect you or the feelings I have for you Darling"

He breathes deeply as he lets his words flow. I process them delicately and with precision. My heart begins to pick itself off the floor. Maybe this isn't the end...

"Because you see I have never felt what I feel for you. I don't know how to put it into words but I won't use those words to describe it. I worship you. I adore you. I'd walk to the ends of the earth for you but I don't love you. I know it's messed up. I know that when you said them to me that you meant it. I've never felt such happiness and confusion all at once because you said it. You...the one person who I trust and can't possibly imagine could betray me. So I'm a little frazzled. I'm not leaving you Darling and I hope to god that you won't leave me because I don't love you...I...I...fucking...I don't know! I hate that there isn't other words to use!" he yells the last part, his fingers tugging on his hair wildly.

    I'm like a statue. I can't believe what I'm hearing. It makes no sense and complete sense all at once. Okay...he doesn't love me but whatever he does feel is stronger than I could ever imagine I'd be worthy of. This gorgeous, intelligent, passionate man adores me and all I said was 'I love you'. He's right. There needs to be better words.

    My whole body tingles. My blood pumps in my veins so loud it's vibrating in my ears. Everything in me is yelling "go to him".

    So I do.

    "I understand if you don't want-" I cut off whatever self loathing sentence he wants to say and pull his hands from his hair. My lips seek his out and I pull him to me as hard as I can. He gasps in shock but catches up quickly, his arms squishing me to him desperately. God! I do fucking love him. Maybe other people don't mean it but I really fucking do!

    "I do mean it Elijah" I confirm against him mouth and he nods with eyes half open.

    "I know baby. I know you do" he growls and attacks my mouth again. Yessssssss! That's my heart by the way! It's soaring.

My fingers latch onto his hair the way he had done not so long ago, yet when I tug he moans. Those sounds are all that fill my ears for the next hour? Two? I'm not sure because time isn't a factor.

All I know is skin on skin. My back on the soft couch. Completely naked. Him inside me and all around me. Almost falling off the couch. His legs tangling with mine. His lips kissing my cheeks and his tongue removing any left over tear stains. I'm not sure how many times we have sex but in the times in between he never stops kissing me. Soft words are spoken. His fingers trail my skin before desire takes over again. I think he actually might enjoy making me come more than he enjoys doing it himself. His face sets with determination as he pushes me higher and over the edge. He tells me I look beautiful. I tell him he does too.

By the time we come back to Earth and finally accept that our bodies can't go on any longer, we're on the floor sprawled out as if we've been through the worst events possible. Only it's been the best.

Everything aches. In fact everything definitely hurts but not in a bad way. So so good. I'm not sure I'll be able to move ever again but I think I'm okay with that.

"Darling I want to ask you something. I asked you before and maybe it's silly but I'd like to ask again" he whispers in my ear and I rack my brains trying to think of what he could say. What has he asked before? Why does he need to ask again.

"Go on then. Ask away" I prompt, turning my face into him and pressing my lips against his chest. Ah heaven.

"Now don't laugh" he smirks, tilting my chin with his finger.

"I would never laugh at a distinguished man like you" I reply feigning seriousness.

"Hmm that's lie"

"Fine you're right. I'd laugh at you a lot but I'll try not to right now" I assure him, my lips curling up regardless. He glares at me, his fingers tickling my thigh.

"It's quite simple really. I just want to know if you'll be my girlfriend. I know it's silly like I said. I know labels don't matter but for some reason I just really-"

"Yes. I'll be your girlfriend" I say immediately which actually shocks me. The first time he asked I'd wanted to say yes but we'd been interrupted and the moment was gone. I also wasn't sure if it would be a good idea to say yes even if I was going to. I didn't know what it meant. I didn't know if I wanted to make any kind of commitment that could break my heart. I guess I still don't know but my heart made that choice itself when it shoved those three words out of my mouth. I've been committed to him without even deciding to be. I've been telling myself that it's not that serious and that it won't last. I've been stupid! He wants me in his life for the foreseeable future. Which I've struggled to believe before but not now. He could still wake up tomorrow and want me gone regardless of what he's said today but then so could anyone. I can't let that stop me from going all in with this man.

I love him and I'm going to have to accept everything that comes with it. Even the terrifying vulnerability.

Elijah

Girlfriend. One simple word that technically sounds juvenile but holds so much weight to me.

I've never named any women I've been involved with my girlfriend. Sure I've dated and tried to commit before my sugar daddy lifestyle but it never worked out. I was too busy...except now I see that wasn't true. I could have made time for those women. I just didn't want to.

The woman lying naked beside me, snoring lightly however, can have all of my time as far as I'm concerned. I've never wanted to be with someone so damn much. It's like an uncontrollable need that if I don't sate it I end up angry and irritated.

Is this what people feel when they say I love you? Surely not? Because then they wouldn't leave or cheat. I can't even think of another women. It's literally impossible for me ever since meeting Sofia. Oh and if someone tries to flirt with me - which happens a whole damn lot in staff meetings - it makes me really fucking mad.

A small mumble hits my ears and I can feel my girl shifting while she sleeps. In the dark my eyes adjust and I can just about make out a frown.

What is she dreaming of? Or is it a nightmare? It's none of my business but I can't help but want to know every single thing surrounding this women. Including her amazing brain.

Hoping to comfort her, I pull her into my arms and hold her close. Maybe I'm being cocky assuming that this will work but she immediately turns her body towards me as if accepting me in her sleep. Fuck.

If someone told me I'd be feeling these things and doing this a few months ago I'd laugh. I'd tell them to fuck off. I feel like an entirely different person. I'm compassionate and caring. I have more time for people in general. I've noticed this at work when I don't lose my shit when my employees ask questions I've answered a thousand times.

I don't understand Sofia's power. Maybe she's a witch. A beautiful witch.

Sofia

Sun beats down on us as we stroll hand and hand to the next excursion Elijah has planned. Yesterday after my slip up/confession I was convinced I'd be on a plane back home and very much single. It turns out I'm happier than ever.

Elijah may not have said those three words to me but he didn't need to. He used other beautiful words to make me feel like the most cherished women on the planet. I don't want to analyse it any further or I'll drive myself mad. His explanation was pretty detailed. Clearly he's been exposed to the worst of human kind and I don't blame him for finding hate in love. For him to care about me at all is an amazing thing.

"Did you sleep okay last night?" he asks glancing down at me through his sunglasses. His clean shaven face is now slowly becoming replaced by stubble and I can't decide which look I like best. He's so gorgeous.

My mind shoots me back into the weird dream I had and wonder if he really can read my mind.

"Sure I did, why do you ask?" I reply trying to hide what had my mind turbulent last night. I had images of him rejecting me torment me all night. So I guess it wasn't a dream... it was a nightmare. I'm not sure why it happened considering I feel like our relationship is stronger than ever. I'm assuming it's just left over anxiety at his initial reaction.

"You were a little restless is all. Is anything bothering you?"

"I'm probably just restless because I haven't checked my emails for a few days" I lie quickly, coming up with something, except it isn't really a lie. I haven't checked my emails because we're on holiday but I really need to. What if I have a job interview for my dream job? I can't remember the last time I've went a day without checking them so maybe there's some truth to it.

I assumed he'd laugh at my ridiculous answer but instead he simply says "you should check them then Darling. It doesn't bother me"

"I just don't want to seem rude. After all I'm pretty sure your emails are more important than mine and I haven't seen you on your phone" I quirk my eyebrow at him and he smirks.

"You've kept me thoroughly distracted. Anything work related can wait" he winks and leans down to kiss my cheek.

"Then so can my emails" I sigh breathlessly forgetting my anxiety and the nightmares I had.

Luckily he asks no more questions and we arrive at a little peer with a small selection of boats. Much less than all the boats that were at last nights dinner destination. It's beautiful and cute. The clear blue sea looks warm and inviting.

Which is just as well because it seems that's where our next activity is going to be.

"We're going snorkelling" Elijah announces as if he can't hold it back anymore. Now I understand why I'm wearing a bikini underneath my sun dress.

A zing of excitement shoots through me. Hell yes!

Finally my chance to see a mermaid...they're real! I swear!

***

I'm not going to lie, I was a little terrified at first. Having so many marine animals all around me was scary but soon I settled in, becoming fascinated by every movement. I think Elijah was a little shocked too but he got used to the swoosh of tiny creatures just like I did.

We stay close to each other, keeping our snorkels above the water and our eyes glued to the rainbow of colours down below. Coral, sea weed...is that a shark?

No...just a large fish. Phew!

In the sea with nothing to worry about but the possible sting of jellyfish, I feel at peace. The sensation of being underwater blocks out all sound and seemingly any worries I could ever have.

Although at this stage of my life I have very little to worry about thanks to the lovely man swimming a little bit away from me. He's just the cutest thing. I know I should be concerned with the fish and other tropical life beneath me but instead I'm watching his hair floating around his head like a make shift halo.

He reaches out to touch a passing clown fish that darts away as soon as he gets too close. He turns to me then, bubbles flowing from his snorkel. He swishes his arms to move closer to me, his eyes crinkling with happiness through his mask. He may be thirty four but somehow he looks barely thirty. Especially when he smiles.

I grab his floating hand and pull on it so that I can try and show him the crab hidden in a shell that I saw a moment ago. As we bob next to each other I motion for him to stay still. Seconds later it appears, peaking out of its hideaway before scuttling across the sea floor.

I almost pass out in fright as a large creature catches my eye and appears in front of us. A sea turtle. It's actually really cute once my panic subsides.

It comes super close and I wonder why it isn't afraid. Then it occurs to me that all the sea life along this reef are probably used to humans invading their home by now.

I'm mesmerised by the dark green shell of the turtles back. Elijah and I both reach out to touch it at the same time and the lovely creature doesn't seem to mind one bit. It's kind of slimy but tough. Wow. Look at me, casually touching a sea turtle. I never thought I'd do this, that's for sure. This is such an unreal experience.

There's just so much to take in! Time goes fast when you're surrounded by a whole new world.

After a flurry of sea horses and many more marine sightings, exhaustion sets in and it's clear Elijah feels it too. Swimming with so much inquisition is tiring. I assume we're about to go back to dry land but before we do Elijah pulls me to him.

I try to communicate my confusion but it's tough when there's a snorkel in my mouth. He stares back at me, our air supply even and strong. Peace forms around us once more and it's like he's simply taking me in. Then he pulls his snorkel from his mouth and my eyes widen in shock, my hands moving to make him put it back.

Silently he asks me to do the same. I don't know why or how this could be a good idea. Yet in a moment of blind trust I do the same and remove my snorkel from my mouth. Insanity. As soon as my snorkel is gone he tugs me closer quickly.

Immediately he kisses me and it's like nothing I've felt before. With the world shut off and silence around me, all I can do is feel him. I'm weightless in his arms, we're floating and it's so damn magical.

Of course it can only last a few seconds. We come up for air with our lips still touching.

"How did you know that would feel so...wow" I breath deeply.

"I didn't. I just saw you there and I had to kiss you. I couldn't help it"

My need to say those three words again is strong and I almost do but somehow I squash them down at the last minute. Does he want to hear them again or would he prefer I kept them to myself?

Elijah

Say it. Please. Say it. I want you to. I can't tell you that and I can't say it back but my god I want to hear it. I'm selfish, I know but I can't help it.

How crazy that I went from being disgusted by those words to craving them overnight.

Unfortunately she doesn't say anything more and instead blushes and begins to swim to the shore as if trying to stop herself from spilling anymore secrets. Damn it! I want all of those secrets.

Following after her, we reach land together and dry off with the provided towels. However I didn't think about a change of clothes. Cursing under my breath I realise we're going to have to walk back to the villa in clothes that will get wet from our swimming attire.

I'm usually so organised. I never forget to think ahead but here am I with no excuse except with Sofia I'm so very relaxed. I barely think of anything but her so I guess it makes sense.

When she realises the same thing I do, all she does is laugh and pull her sun dress back on. Immediately wet patches show through it where her bikini sits underneath, highlighting her breasts. Well...shit.

"I'm sorry Darling. This really isn't ideal" I breath, trying to focus on her face rather than the soaked parts of her dress.

"It's okay, you're gonna look a little strange soon too" she smirks and as I pull my shorts on I know what she means. Sure I could have taken my swim shorts off but where would be the fun in that.

So I end up walking back with a wet patch over my crotch and together I guess we look like a really strange couple. It doesn't matter though because Sofia's laughter takes away any embarrassment I might feel.

"So shall we cook tonight?" She suggests as we continue squelching back to our holiday home.

"Absolutely! I think we'd make a good team in the kitchen" I muse. I'm an okay cook but Sofia is skilled. She told me she had to learn to cook while living on her own for college. Not so long ago she was cooking a meal for us at my apartment but I never got to eat it. Which pissed me off. I got called into my building at eight pm because of another emergency. It was much like the hack situation only by the time I got there everything was under control. It's beginning to worry me. There seems to be a lot of people trying to steal things from me lately.

I hadn't brought Sofia that night because I didn't want to keep involving her in my shitty work stuff. Although I wish I had. I'd called the police that night to investigate more but they found nothing. I'm still no further forward with the first hack. It making me crazy. The last thing I told Sofia was that no one lived in the apartment that the hack came from. I haven't told her that I need her help. She shouldn't have to deal with it.

"Yes! We definitely will make a good team. What shall we cook?" she says breaking me from my straying mind. I should talk to her about it.

"Oh well, when I was booking this trip, I did a bit of research on the food and asked some of my business partners who've been here what they'd recommend. There's a dish called Poke that seemed to be the most popular all round" I explain, picturing the images I'd seen in my head.

"Ohhh sounds interesting. What is it?" She asks beaming up at me.

"It's sea food with any sauce you like. Pretty simple but it sounds yummy"

"I hope we have the ingredients in the villa" she hums as if trying to remember what was in the cabinets.

"I'm sure we do, they certainly stocked it well and if not we can go catch some fish ourselves" I joke and she raises her eyebrows at me.

"Wow...like caveman times. You know I'd pay good money to see you dressed in some leopard print with a big spear" she sighs.

"A big spear...hmmm I think I already have one of those" I wiggle my eyebrows.

She stops walking to look at me, her face bright red.

"Yes. Caveman Elijah. Big spear" she gives me her best impression of a cave person, her words coming out in chunks instead of smooth sentences. So fucking cute. Her rosey cheeks are a little fuller than when we first met. She was just as beautiful then as she is now but it was very clear she hadn't been eating. Now though, she looks healthier and it soothes something in me, knowing that I can ensure she never goes hungry again.

"Cavewoman Sofia. Want. Big spear?" I mimic her impression and suddenly my shorts feels incredibly uncomfortable.

"Okay, you know what, this conversation is not going to end well right here. We should get back first" she suggests, no doubt worried we will get arrested for public indecency. She had a good point.

"You're right...cavewomen Sofia"

Sofia

We squash our cave antics long enough to get changed and cook the meal we decided on. I prepare most of the food as Elijah watches, fascinated. It's not because he doesn't want to help but because I really want to cook for him. He did the odd chopping before settling on distracting me at any opportunity.

He currently has me trapped against the counter as I create the sauces we have chosen, his erection digging into my ass.

"Do you want this food?" I ask, shoving back against him.

"Hmmm yes. I want food and other things"

"Which one first? Food or other things" I ask him, reaching back between us to squeeze his bulge.

"Fuck. You're evil" he breathes and steps away from me. "Food! We should choose food or we won't have energy for anything else"

"So very wise of you" I taunt and wiggle my butt for him to see. I guess the fact that I decided to just wear panties and a t-shirt doesn't help him.

"Caveman Elijah is struggling my dear"

"Good, that's what I like to hear"

***

The food went down a treat. It was delicious and refreshing. We ate it outside as the sun set and Elijah's moans of appreciation hit my ears, making me feel very much achieved in my goal of cooking for him.

"It's so fucking good Darling" he groans eating the last few bites.

"I'm glad you like it" I smile, my chest filling with so many happy emotions. Yes I do like pleasing him. Oh no. I've become that women...the women I could never stand. Pleasing a man's every whim! But is it so bad when he pleases me in return? Surely not-

My thoughts scatter as he stands and collects our plates. A sudden memory of me promising I'd throw him in the pool renters my brain. This is our last night. My last opportunity...

Gazing innocently at the sunset, I wait until he returns. He stands for a moment by the pool gazing at the view just like me. It makes me wonder if the world is purposely giving me this perfect chance.

Very carefully I stand and tiptoe up behind him. He's stronger than me. I have to catch him off guard.

Seconds tick by and my heart rate sky rockets. You got this Sofia!

"This is such a pretty place. I'd never have thought of coming here before. Although I'd never have enjoyed it without you" he says softly. His words distract my plan but only for a second.

"I wouldn't have enjoyed it without you either. That's why I'm sorry for what I'm about to do" I whisper.

"What?-"

Lunging at him, I push hard and watch as he stumbles forward. It's like a slow motion effect. He's going in that pool! What I didn't factor into my plan was him twisting slightly as he falls and reaching behind himself to grab my arm.

Fuck!

SPLASH!

Guess that's karma huh!

Water surrounds me for a second time today and I surge to the surface gasping for air.

"You mean women!" he shouts as he surfaces too. Both of us splashing wildly.

"You're just as bad! I can't believe you got me! You're far too skilled! DAMN IT!"

We splash and splash, taking revenge out on each other. All that I can hear is our laughter and joy.

I try to jump on his shoulders to dunk him but he's quicker and grabs me around the waist.

"Let me go!" I yell, thrashing some more.

Oh no. I can't do that...caveman Elijah wants to touch" he half laughs, half growls. "Does cavewomen want it too?" he asks immediately after, his eyes wide searching mine.

"I'd go as far as saying that cavewomen needs it. Use your big spear" I giggle and oh boy does he use it.

Bracing me against the wall of the pool he slips my underwear off and let's the material float away. He keeps up the caveman façade, manhandling me with just the right amount of roughness. His hands disappear from my body for a second, for him to push his shorts off before he's grabbing my thighs and spreading them.

My legs wrap around his waist as his arms circle me, crushing me against him. He holds me up in the water, keeping us afloat.

He watches me like a hawk as if making sure I'm okay. Always making sure. While all I can do is push into his touch, writhing and moaning. I can't even think of ever not wanting this, wanting him. However he's always using the last shred of his sanity to make sure I want every second of it. He's the most attentive man alive even as he tugs on my hair to give him access to my throat.

"Please Elijah. Take me. Fuck me!" I yell, begging him. Yet he takes it slow, teasing my whole body.

We get rid of the top half of our clothing and those float away too. When our chests push together, our breathing rough, that's the last straw for him.

He pushes inside me quickly, my body accepting him instantly. He swears and groans, worshiping words making me fall for him even more.

We may be desperate but Elijah makes it last. He slows down his movements and I savour every feeling. It's glorious and perfect, which is why I end up saying those three words all over again.

"I love you" comes out of my mouth once again before I can stop it. Only this time he doesn't look at me in shock or confusion. Instead he pauses for a second before driving into me harder, his hands grabbing my face so that he can look at me.

"Sofia...I..." he struggles. His face says it all. He can't say it back but I'm not sad this time. I know how he feels and that in turn makes me feel whole and somewhat powerful.

"It's okay. It's okay!" I comfort him and he buries his face in my neck, whispering to me all of the things that he's prepared to admit. All of the things he can say. Words that to him, describe how he feels better than 'I love you'.

His breathless "you're my everything" does it for me and I'm screaming his name so loud I'm sure our neighbouring holiday makers hear it.

He's going to destroy me. I know that already.

***

On the outdoor seating I rest my head on Elijah's chest and curl my knees up. Throwing my arm over his stomach, I cuddle into him and resist the urge to close my eyes and fall asleep.

Instead I gaze up at the stars while Elijah plays with my hair. He seems to love doing it and I love it in return. We're both in sweat pants and t-shirts after showering to warm up. It's super cozy and perfect.

"Have you had a good time?" he mumbles nuzzling into my neck.

"The best time" I reply and smooch him rather loudly. God I wish I could thank him in so many ways. Not just for this holiday but for everything.

"Me too" he whispers, kissing me back.

We settle against each other again, silence falling once more. So I decide that now would be an okay time to check my emails just to put my mind at ease.

Pulling my phone from my sweat pants, I scroll quickly through my filled inbox, hoping to check them all and be done with it. I see no job interview offers and deflate sadly. When will I get my chance? All I want is to work in a proper company! To have a career.

On the plus side I've gotten no more emails from sugar rush since I removed myself from their mailing list.

My sadness turns to confusion when my eyes land on an email from the landlord that owns my apartment.

Unfortunately it isn't anything good. In fact, it's very very bad.

They're evicting me.

No!

The owner needs their apartment back due to unforeseen circumstances.

Fuck.

What will I do now?

Where will I go? Back to my parents? God no.

I have a week to leave.
A week to work out what I'm going to do so that I don't end up homeless.

Sofia

"Anything Darling?" I hear Elijah asking, referring to the reason I actually checked my emails.

Do I tell him? I don't think I can. Although I'm not sure why. My first instinct is to lie and to hide my utter sadness at being homeless soon behind the fact that I've no job interviews.

"No nothing yet" I sigh and shove my phone back in my pocket as if to punish it.

"It'll happen, I promise you" he croons encouragingly, his lips pressing into my hair. Fuck! I don't wanna lie to him.

There's a simple option to fix my problem really. Use Elijah's money to rent a new apartment. Easy! Except when I think about doing that my stomach twists into knots because I feel like that would make me the same as the rest of the women.

I don't want to spend more than I already have. No, I want to be able to support myself so that I can send it all back to him.

The worst part is I know he'd tell me to use the money. He'd want me to. Have I brainwashed him? Is that what's really happening? Or would he have given any women the same amount of money if they'd stuck around?

I already know the answer to that. No he wouldn't have. He wouldn't have trusted them enough. Yet here I am, gifted with his delicate trust.

He doesn't seem to notice that anything is amiss so I stay quiet and snuggle into him to try and forget about my impending issue just for a little while.

That's the same attitude I apply the next day as we pack, head to the airport and fly home. I try to act as normal as possible, plastering a smile onto my face whenever Elijah gives me a strange look. Of course he knows there's something wrong now. I'm like an open book to him.

He doesn't ask me if I'm okay. It's as if he knows that I don't want him to but he never stops glancing at me.

Especially as he drives me home after I declined to stay with him. I told him I was really tired and feeling unwell after the flight, which really wasn't much of an excuse. If those things were true I'd want to stay with him.

Nevertheless, he goes along with my lie with a concerned frown and kisses me goodbye.

As I'm closing the door of his car he calls after me.

"Is there anything I can do to help you feel better?"

There's an underlying tone in his voice as if he's asking something else. Of course he wants to know if he can help me...with anything. Right now I hate how perceptive he is.

"I'm okay, I promise you" I say softly, turning back to face him with a reassuring smile stuck to my face. He doesn't buy it for a second but he nods anyway.

"I'll call you tomorrow morning?" he says but it's not a statement, it's a question.

"Yes of course. Thanks for the amazing holiday. I'll see you soon" is the last thing I can say before I turn away, my face crumbling. I know I must seem flakey. I told him I loved him yesterday and now it seems like I don't want to be around him. In actual fact I just don't know how to deal with this new development and I'm too proud to ask for anymore help. Especially not him. He's done enough for me.

I hear his Mercedes tyres screeching as I enter my apartment building. It's the only thing that gives away his frustration at my silence.

Shaking away some of my sadness, I enter my apartment as if everything is normal. I make the mistake of glancing around and taking in all of the things I could loose. No apartment means I don't need any furniture and I

- 465 -

probably won't have anywhere to put any of my personal belongings.

  A shower helps me feel better as does using my brand new super laptop. I stare at the screen and apply for yet more jobs. I spend hours coding a new website to use in my portfolio. It's a thousand times better than my last laptop so I'm able to finish much quicker.

  Then I apply for a certain job that I know I could never get. Head programmer? Why did I even bother? I'm not experienced enough.

  Flopping onto my bed, I stare at the ceiling and contemplate just calling Elijah to talk to him. I don't need to tell him anything. We could just talk. I only got out of his car five hours ago but apparently when you're obsessed with someone, mere hours feels like weeks.

  I don't really want to be away from him. I just don't know what to do.

  Go home and stay with my parents, spend his money or become homeless? If I'd had more time I could have saved my own money up from my job but time is not my friend.

  This is a disaster.

Elijah

  I tried not to call too quick. I wanted to give her space because it was clear she needed it. I'm not sure what's wrong but I think that her lack of job interviews are getting to her. I don't understand how no one has snapped her up. I wish she could see what I did. That she was more than qualified for so many things and every company that turned her down were losing out big time.

Distracting myself from her was hard but I tried to get some work done after arriving home. I dealt with everything that needed to be done, everything that was urgent and needed my attention. Unfortunately that only took a few hours and I was left with nothing to do but wonder what bothered Sofia so much. I should have demanded she stay with me so that I could look after her. I think she really does feel unwell but it isn't to do with normal sickness bug symptoms or the common cold or even jet lag. No it's something that's happening in her mind.

I'm twiddling my thumbs in my home office when an idea pops into my head. I could kill two birds with one stone. I need to tell her how worried I am about all of the hacking that's been going on. I also need to ask for her help. Maybe if I tell her what I need to, she will tell me her problem in return.

Elijah: Can we talk? I think I might need your help with something-

I type out the text message but something stops me half way. What if asking for her help makes her issue worse? What if it puts pressure on her to do something she doesn't want to? Shit!

I said I'd call her in the morning and that's what I'll do! Give her space Elijah! Don't be a dick!

Placing my phone onto my desk, I push it away from me a little. God it's tempting. I could just call her now. What if she's really unwell? God! Stop it! She's fine!

Pushing my chair back I get up and walk out of the room, leaving my phone behind. There has to be something else for me to do. I did plenty of things on my own before I met Sofia. Well, I worked. I worked until I passed out but now I have no motivation.

There has to be something good on tv.

Lying fully dressed in my shirt and jeans, I flick through the channels and settle on some crime drama. Another wife killing her husband or some shit. Huh, he probably deserved it.

Glancing at my coffee table as the wife on tv cries uncontrollably, I notice my wallet that I threw there when I got home. Snatching it up, I find Sofia's gift wedged into one of the card spaces. The silver coin glints in the light as I pull it out and drop my wallet on the floor. I move the small piece of metal through my fingers, occasionally flicking it in the air with my thumb and catching it again.

My eyes settle on the word engraved on one side. 'Together' is reads boldly, the other side telling me that I have her.

Damn it.

Sitting up quickly as if I've been shocked, I realise that both of us are going against everything this coin represents. If we're supposed to have each other then why are we not *together.*

Sofia

I went to work the next day after Elijah called me in the morning. I'd refrained from calling him the night before but the sigh of relief that left my lips as I heard his voice at seven am was incredibly ridiculous.

He had asked if I was okay and I lied to him again. I'd said I was fine. He'd taken my lie even though I knew he didn't believe me.

His tone changed after my fib. From soft to commanding and determined as he told me that he'd really love it if I met him at his building after my work. He was going to find out what was wrong with me no matter what, that much was clear.

When I asked him why he wanted me to come to his work, he told me that he needed my help which changed my mood entirely. He needs me? Then I'll be there. I still haven't worked out what I could possibly help with that his very experienced team can't but I won't turn down his request. In fact a zing of excitement and confidence has followed me all day. I felt this way before when I found the IP address of the first hack.

My shift goes by in a blur and I'm actually able to forget that I'm getting evicted soon. I'm also able to ignore any questions that Gabe asks because apparently he still doesn't know what boundaries are. I'm able to shut him down with one word answers but I'm so very close to reporting him for being a nosey harassing mother fucker.

Finishing at four pm, I hail a cab and ride to Elijah's sky scraper. This time I'm met by Lewis in the foyer.

He greets me with a wide smile, holding out a lanyard for me to take and escorts me to the elevator.

"I was wondering when he was going to give you one of these. Makes it easier for you to access him whenever you want" he smirks as the doors slide shut.

"Does this make me special?" I joke as I swipe the card over the scanner beside the buttons like he demonstrates.

"Oh very special. That's an access all areas pass. I think about ten people in this whole building have one. Including me of course" he explains, grinning like a maniac. What is up with him?

"Why are you all smiley?" I ask, unable to stop my returning smile.

"I'm just glad Mr Everett has someone now. Especially someone like you. You're good people Sofia and he really really needed that. I've never seen him so relaxed or happy and I've worked here for six years" he gushes and I immediately want to pick his brain. What was Elijah like when he was younger? Has Lewis seen the revolving door of women? "No..." he says suddenly. What the hell? "I know what you're thinking. No other women that he has been intimate with have been here. Just you"

"Thanks" I mumble super appreciatively as my awkward jealousy settles.

I'm about to ask more but the elevator doors ping open and Lewis guides me out.

"He's still in a meeting right now but he won't be long trust me. He's never late for anything, especially where you're concerned" he informs me and gestures towards the seating area. He takes his place back behind his desk and I suppress the urge to ask so many things.

Glancing at the time on my phone I see that it's four-twenty-five pm. I wonder what time his meeting will be over-

The doors to his office open and Elijah walks out with a red haired women in a pant suit. They shake hands and she smiles politely at me before walking away.

"Another deal done" Elijah announces, his expression bright as he takes me in. I do the same in return and my chaotic brain settles and calms. "Hi Darling" he continues, his voice like silk.

"Dear god, please go into your office before I choke on the sexual tension" Lewis quips and Elijah shoots him a glare.

"Oh I'm sorry, I wasn't aware that you were able to give orders in this building" he replies sternly but there's a layer of mirth in his voice that lets Lewis know he's not being serious.

"Not an order Sir just a simple request. Or I'll be very upset as I'm excruciatingly single" Lewis pouts turning his gaze on me.

"You're single? No, I don't believe it" I gasp dramatically and Lewis sticks his tongue out. We've only met a couple times before but somehow we've formed a kind of friendship. He's the type of person anyone can get along with.

"I know, I'm amazing" he sighs and holds his head up high.

Making my way to Elijah, I take his outstretched hand and give Lewis one last grin.

"Get some work done" Elijah orders him, still with the same half serious tone. I think Elijah quite possibly sees Lewis as his friend but the employee/boss dynamic makes him unwilling to admit it. Which is a real shame. Maybe I'll ask him about it.

As his office door shuts behind us, I'm reminded that I'm here to help him. So my mind immediately screams for the answer to my question. Help him with what? My own issue pops up as he looks into my eyes, as if trying to search my soul but I squash it down. This isn't about me right now.

"What can I do for you Mr Everett?"

Before he answers, he steps closer to me and leans down to press his lips against mine. It's a greeting and a way to tell me that he's missed me over the last eighteens hours or so. I cling to him as if he's my only life line because like I've admitted so many times before I'm obsessed and well...in love.

"Come sit" he says and guides me to the seat opposite his desk. He then sits in his chair and I sit up straight as if I'm about to be interviewed. He quirks his eyebrow at my formal position. "This doesn't feel right does it?" he asks, glancing at the space between us.

"I don't know what you mean, this is perfectly okay. After all we're going to talk business aren't we?" I laugh because I simply can't keep a straight face.

He clears his throat and crosses his arms, relaxing into his seat.

"I guess you're right. Would you prefer it if I called you Miss Westwood for this meeting?" he asks, perfectly serious. Oh goodie! I get to see him in business mode. Love that.

"Yes I would prefer it actually" I confirm and make my face go straight.

"Right then Miss Westwood, I need your help with a certain case of database hacking. I'm sure you're familiar with what I'm talking about. You see my team and I are no further forward with either situation. The first invasion or the second. Both are very similar but we've been unable to get any more information regarding both occasions. No traceable addresses apart from the one you already know about. No one lives there and no one has been seen there since well before the first attack happened"

Woah! His professional tone and wording has me glued to the seat and almost distracts me from the seriousness of the issue at hand. I knew he was still dealing with this but I assumed his new and improved team would get to the bottom of it. I didn't know he was as worried as he now seems. Every time he mentioned it to me or updated me he seemed confident it would all be okay.

Now though I understand what's happened. He's done the same thing I'm doing right now. Keeping his worries from me. He probably hasn't wanted to bother me with it. Shit!

"How long have you needed help?" I reply quietly, already a hypocrite.

"Umm, not too long" he states. A lie. His professional persona falls and he grimaces. "Okay a while"

"And why do you think that I can help? I know I did a little before but surely there are people here more experienced than me" I have to ask him this because it doesn't make sense to me.

"I know that if I tell you that you're amazing, you won't believe it. I know that if anyone tells you how talented you are, you won't believe that either but Sofia...you are! You more than rival the people I employ. I've never met anyone smarter than you and I'm not just saying that because we're together. If you'd applied to work here before we met, you would've been given an interview and then a job immediately. You know that's true because Jack offered you a job within half an hour of meeting you. So even if you don't understand it, I really do need your help"

I want to argue. I want to say that he's right because I don't believe him. At the same time my chest constricts with an unfamiliar feeling of acceptance. He thinks I'm good enough to help him. Then I'll help him.

What if I fail? I guess the only way to find out is to try.

"I'll help you" I reply in a whisper and the relief on his face nearly bowls me over. It's like a weight has been taken off of him.

"Thank you Darling. If it's okay with you I'll get Jack and a couple of my other employees to tell you everything we know. They'll do a better job at it than I will. I'm not good with the technical terms remember?" he laughs a little and I smirk at his bashful face. He's very intelligent. Definitely more intelligent than me but web tech stuff isn't his forte. However it's my only forte.

"Of course I don't mind and yes...I remember" I giggle and his eyes soften. He reaches over his desk to cover my hand with his and searches my gaze once more. Suddenly his mood changes to concerned.

"Darling, I know something is up but I won't push you to tell me. Although I really hope you do because whatever it is I want to help you too"

Well shit. He makes it sound like he could take away all of my worries. I know he could in fact. I just have qualms about letting him do it.

"I'll tell you soon" I mumble, turning my hand and linking our fingers. "Let's deal with this first"

And I will tell him soon. I just need to swallow my pride.

***

Countless amounts of paperwork and notes cover the boardroom table. It's hard to keep track of all the information that I'm being told and trying to read at the same time.

There are two other members of Elijah's staff, one women and one man in the room with us, as well as Jack.

Elijah sits beside me and listens too, while my mind works a mile a minute. Two laptops sit in front of me displaying video footage of the apartment as well as back end code that runs a programme to search any linking data to the address.

The women - who I learned is called Amelia - sits opposite me and she speaks a language I very much understand. I already like her a lot as she tells me how she designed the programme I'm looking at. Brilliant.

The man named Marvin tells me more of the investigative side. Which is harder for me to understand but I get the idea. He talks about private investigators and planting microphones and cameras.

Jack interjects information that they forget to add and soon I'm caught up on everything they know.

My eyes flick between video recordings and code. Naturally I'm more interested in the latter. I'm afraid to look at Amelia's code in case I find something wrong. I don't want to tell her that she's made a mistake in case she thinks I'm trying to act better than her.

Unfortunately my eyes latch onto something quickly and I glance at her apologetically. Her programme is searching for anything related to the apartment. Previous owners and tenants, work that's been done on it, any crime that's happened in and around it recently. However there's nothing to cross reference Elijah's company with the area. Nothing that searches for anything about previous crimes or attempted hacks against the company.

The code also doesn't run within a twenty four hour time frame. So it could have missed something within its dormant hours.

Looking up at the women across from me once more, I cringe inwardly. I don't wanna be that person but I have to tell her.

"You need to add some cross-referencing and run the programme to search more things to do with this company specifically. Maybe adding a wider time frame would also help" I tell her softly with as little order as I can. I don't want to seem like I'm commanding her.

To my surprise her face lights up as she becomes excited. Oh thank god!

"Yes! Wow, I can't believe I didn't do that" she exclaims and takes one of the laptops before typing furiously.

I can feel Elijah staring at me and when I look back at him he's all starry eyed. He's impressed and that makes me even more confident. I want to impress him, I can't deny that. Blushing, I turn back to the remaining screen.

Nothing about the apartment gives anything away. I mean why would it.

"Oh, do we know what brand of computer or laptop was used? I know it sounds unimportant but it could help" I ask and Marvin shakes his head.

"How could we find that out?" he questions.

"It's similar to finding the IP address but all you gotta do is add a little bit of code on" I explain and do that exact thing on the laptop. I download an application I've used many times before and once again find the IP address. Then I insert another tiny piece of code anddddddd... boom! There we have it.

"The laptop is a HP Envy. It's silver. High end" I state.

"Are you sure you don't want a job?" Jack asks for the second time since I met him. With a polite smile I shake my head.

"No thank you. I really appreciate it though"

Elijah stays silent for the whole meeting, simply observing. We go through more information but nothing else comes up.

Amelia tells us that she's going to need some time to code the new programme and that she will have it done later tonight. By then maybe we can get more results but for now we're once again at a dead end.

Elijah announces that the meeting is over in his formal tone and thanks everyone for attending. Jack, Marvin and Amelia all thank me while I barely know how to respond. They leave the boardroom, the door clicking shut behind Jack.

I'm really surprised that I was able to help at all. I'm super glad I could though. At first when Elijah had introduced me, telling them that I was his girlfriend, I worried that they wouldn't take me seriously. I assumed that they'd think I was trying to sleep my way into a position of power. However I was wrong. Oh and I blushed like a tomato when Elijah had said the word girlfriend. It's the first time he's introduced me as such and now I know how he felt when I introduced him to my parents. Wow, how fulfilling. I feel like I belong with him.

Elijah gets up from his seat in silence and I'm relieved because I haven't been able to read him right through out the whole meeting.

Suddenly I'm pulled from my seat as well and encased in his strong arms. Oh lord.

"Thank you so much. I really appreciate what you've done. I appreciate you even being here. You didn't have to do this" he breathes. All I can do is squeeze him back and refrain from saying "I'd do anything for you"

"I just hope it actually helps and there are new results" I reply as we pull apart. He holds onto my waist and my hands rest on his shirt covered chest as he looks at me.

"I hope so too but even if nothing comes up it doesn't matter. I'm still so grateful Darling. So thankful you helped me"

"It's no bother really" I say shyly, feeling a little overwhelmed with all this praise.

"Speaking of helping...will you tell me what's wrong yet?" he asks. I can see the desperation in his eyes.

"It's not a big deal" I try but he doesn't look convinced.

"I think it is. I think something happened in Hawaii when you checked your emails and for some reason you don't want me to know"

Damn him and his all knowing brain.

"It's not that I don't want you to know. I just want to deal with it without having to ask for assistance. You've done so much for me already and-"

"And I want to do more. Whatever it is, I really want to help" he implores me, sucks me in, makes me feel like nothing is too much to give.

Closing my eyes, I try to summon the courage to tell him no. To tell him that I'll be okay and that he shouldn't worry. But then if the roles were reversed, if I'd known how worried he had been about the hack, I'd have wanted to know immediately. I'd have wanted to help like I did today. So how can I deny him that right?

"Okay...I got an email" I begin and I can tell he's focusing on nothing else but me. Giving me all of his attention.

"What did it say?" he prompts, his voice encouraging and soothing.

"It said that I'm getting evicted. They need my apartment back and I don't know what I'm going to do about it" I push out quickly, my voice almost breaking into a sob.

I assumed he'd take in this information and think about it for a minute but he replies immediately.

"So come stay with me until we can find you another apartment. Or just...stay with me and we won't find you another apartment" he whispers the last part as if he's scared to say it. My gaze shoots to his to see if he's being serious. "Shit I'm sorry. I completely understand if you don't want to stay with me. It's maybe too much. You probably like your own space. Well we can go look for a place right now. You don't have to worry about paying for it-"

I clamp my hand over his mouth as he says the one thing I knew he would eventually. I'm still stuck on the first part of his speech but I have to make something clear.

"You are not paying for an apartment for me. The money you've already given me is more than enough to rent a place but I don't want to do that Elijah. I know most people would love spending your money but I just don't. I won't. I won't be like them" I express my feelings as best as I can.

"You're not like them Darling. I know you don't like spending my money. Whatever you want to do, I'll help you with it. Whatever you decide, I'll be here" he replies, leaning his forehead on mine. I breath deeply, thinking about his first option. I guess I could stay with him for a while... could I? Do I want to? YES! Woah!

"My only other option is going home to my parents and that really isn't an option at all" I say, throwing out the worst suggestion so I don't eagerly agree to stay with him. Or beg to stay with him.

"Not that it's up to me but I hate that option" he breathes.

"Me too"

"And do you hate my first suggestion?" he squirms a little as if he really wants me to choose it.

"No I don't hate it. I love it in fact but I just don't wanna seem clingy you know" I whisper and he grins, shaking his head slowly.

"Please feel free to be as clingy as you want. I'm sure I've told you that before. I'm mad you didn't take me up on my offer of being super duper clingy" he chuckles.

"You're gonna regret saying that" I warn.

"You said that before too and I'm still not regretting it"

After a long pause...I agree. Let's be honest, I'd be lying if I said I hadn't thought about if far too much.

"Okay, I'll stay with you...for a while" I smirk and he nods.

"Yes, for a while" he repeats but I can tell he's thinking the same thing I am. He very much doesn't want to put a time limit on my stay.

"Thank you..." I sigh as the panic I've been carrying all day disappears. I hug him like he hugged me a few minutes ago.

"You're welcome Darling. So welcome"

***

"I HAVE A NEW RESULT!" is yelled as the conference room door bursts open. Amelia darts into the room, her face flushed from excretion. How far did she run?

Elijah and I had stayed in here a little longer after our problem solving. Just you know...chatting and stuff.

It can only have been an hour or so since the meeting ended. Amelia is good...fantastic! Fucking brilliant!

I jump off Elijah's lap and clear my throat while he subtly shifts in his seat. Light petting may have happened between us. That is all.

"What is it?" Elijah asks, his voice rough from desire. It changes quickly back to professional.

"Well a lot of new stuff came up but nothing all that interesting. Then a few names popped up so I ran them through our back up database and well...one of them matched!" she explains in a rush. Oh boy this could be it! This could be the answer.

"Who was it that matched?" Elijah asks urgently, sitting up in his seat.

Amelia looks like she's going to overflow or combust with information and excitement at cracking the crime.

Come onnnnnnn!

"A women that goes by the name Nadia Zoya?!"

OH FOR FUCK SAKE! THAT BITCH NEVER GIVES UP!

Elijah

The moment Amelia says that name my blood begins to boil. At this point I'm just so fucking done with Nadia's bullshit. She isn't getting a penny from me and she certainly isn't getting any of my hard earned business. I've met plenty people like her before. She's a leech and she no doubt only wants my company to sell it for assets. Or for the simple joy of saying she won. She's the worst kind of business partner and I feel sorry for all of the people who have fallen for her shit before.

"Call the police. I'm going to give them all the information we have. What she's done is illegal and I'm not going to let her get away with it" I tell Amelia, who nods and leaves the room swiftly. I'd called the police on her before for harassment when she wouldn't leave my building but that never seemed to get the message through to her. Maybe if she's actually charged it'll ensure she will stop.

Next to me Sofia looks pissed, her beautiful face marred with anger.

"I can't believe she's still trying to get to you"

"It's okay, she won't be able to for much longer" I assure her, slipping my arm around her waist. I wouldn't have even been this far ahead if it wasn't for her. God I'm so grateful. I want to make it up to her but I know something materialistic won't do. I'll need to think harder.

I'll start tonight once we're back at my apartment. I'll worship my princess...or I should probably say my queen.

***

When the police arrive, I gather everyone that has worked on this hack situation. I want to make sure the police get all of the information they possibly can.

We spend a good few hours being questioned and handing over our evidence. I get pissed off when the police officer in charge tells Sofia that she doesn't count as a witness and since she isn't involved in the company cannot give any information.

I inform them that she's met Nadia and was there when that horrible women harassed me. Well she harassed us in my car. That changed their tune and Sofia was taken away to be questioned.

By the time everyone is finished with it's about ten pm at night.

Sofia and I head to her apartment to get some essentials before going back to mine. I assure her that we can get everything out of her apartment within the next couple of days.

The thought that she's staying with me warms me inside and as we walk into my foyer I feel a sense of completeness. Is this what I've been missing my whole life? A partner? An equal? A best friend and lover?

Yes, I think I might have been missing her. Maybe she was put on the earth for me but that would be ridiculous right?

Sofia

The next few months of my life are the happiest I've ever lived. I settled into life at Elijah's apartment as if I'd always lived there. Obviously I'd stayed before but having my stuff there and going back every night after work was different.

Different but right. I was worried at first that Elijah might regret his choice of letting me stay but he seemed just as eager as me. I caught him smiling at me one morning as I brushed my teeth at the sink next to him. When I'd asked what he was smiling at he just replied "You". Later he told me that he loved seeing all my things around his place.

Well he said our place and I almost melted. It was very obvious early on that we had no plans to look for a new apartment for me.

We put all the stuff that I couldn't bring with me in a storage unit. I wasn't sure if I'd ever need any of it again, so I thought it best to keep it just in case.

I found out quickly that my favourite part of the day is when Elijah gets home. I finish work before him so I get to watch as exits the elevator looking slightly tired, yet so inviting.

If I'm not in the great expanse of his front room when he arrives, he seems to always make it his mission to find me first before doing anything else. His appreciative sighs ring in my ears when he kisses me in greeting. It's what everyone calls mundane life but it's not boring to me. And apparently it's not boring to him because his passion only seems to grow stronger.

Of course we haven't just been working over these few months. Oh no, many other things have been happening.

Apart from me trying to keep my 'I love yous' to a minimum, I surprised him with an event I knew we'd both love.

SanDiego Comic Con was a crazy experience. Neither of us had been before, so when he worked out where we were going he was ecstatic and I was pleased that I'd chosen right.

Apparently Elijah Everett being at an even such as this was unheard of. So within an hour of us arriving the paparazzi did too. Which was quite amusing since Elijah was dressed in a Spider-Man suit. Yup. And I didn't even have to persuade him very much. The tight lycra suit came in handy though as he donned the mask and hid from flashing cameras in the crowds.

Me on the other hand, I'd chosen a Harley Quinn outfit much to Elijah's pleasure. The booty shorts, tight t-shirt and heeled boots made him stare a lot. I think he chose to walk behind me just so he could stare at my ass. I couldn't blame him though, his buns were very much on display too in that super hero outfit.

Spider-Man and Harley Quinn are definitely a strange coupling but it sure made things fun. My only complaint was the blonde itchy wig.

We entered into a costume competition just for fun. I really enjoyed watching Elijah work the mini stage with many different typical Spider-Man poses.

When it was my turn, I used my paper mache baseball bat to strike my own moves. That has been a team effort to create and I remember Elijah's disgusted expression as his hand got covered in glue.

Anyway the mess was worth it because the bat added the final touch to my outfit. I swung it behind my back on stage. Elijah cheered and I blushed bright red.

Neither of us won the competition. The winner was a cute little boy in an iron man suit. Which we both agreed was well deserved.

At one point Elijah spent some time browsing a Funko POP stall before presenting me a couple of figures.

"What do you think Darling?" he had asked holding up a mini Spider-Man and Harley Quinn.

"It's a yes from me!" I nodded enthusiastically, my heart swelling.

Those two figures now sit together on the dresser in his bedroom. Sorry our bedroom. That's hard to get used to but when I do remember that I can now call this place home I'm amazed at how far we've come.

He also tries to buy me far too many gifts.

 I don't feel as guilty anymore because he's also my partner. I give him things in return and he knows that I'd never take advantage of his generosity. The other day I bought him a new shirt simply because I knew it would look good with a suit and it was like I'd given him the best thing ever. He'd admitted immediately after wearing it that it was his favourite shirt. It makes me sad to think that no one bought him anything before. I mean his reactions are priceless and it makes me want to buy him everything I can possibly think of.

Oh! I should definitely mention that I met one of the women that did take advantage of his wealth. It was not a pleasant time...

Elijah asked me if I'd accompany him to a charity event. He had said "I understand if you don't want to. It's all snobby people pretending to care about something they actually deem to be beneath them. Although it would be much more bearable with you"

"How many of these things have you been to before?" I asked, wondering how many times he'd went alone.

"I've lost count Darling. I like to go to these things to actually donate money and do my best to help. It's not a fun environment but it means I can do my part" he explained, while I tilted my head at him trying to work out how he could ever think badly of himself.

"Of course I'll go with you. Have you had to go alone to all the other events?" I asked casually but let's face it, I was just being nosey. Did he take other women before? That should not bother me! We hadn't met when he went before.

"Most of them I was alone at yes. However I did try a couple of times to take a companion. Which made things worse, I have to admit"

That gave me all the answers I needed.

"Well maybe I can help you enjoy it just a little bit" I smiled and made a deal with myself that I'd ensure he had a good time.

I had no idea what I was gonna wear but a few days later before I could ask Elijah about it, he took me to his large walk in closet and held up a dress bag.

"So, I hope you won't be mad at me for this. I bought this a while ago for you when there was another event scheduled but it got cancelled. I know it's a little weird for me to choose a dress for you too but I saw it and I couldn't help it" he told me, looking more than guilty. I'm still not sure why he thought I'd be mad? Maybe because picking a dress for me could seem controlling?

"Can I see it please?" I asked and he looked a little wary as if he was unsure about my reaction.

"Of course" he replied before pulling down the zipper to reveal an absolutely gorgeous black body con dress. I noticed it would sit far enough down my thighs to give it the respectable formal feel for such an event, however the swooping neckline gave it a little more of a sexy effect. Wow. "Oh and these too" he interjected, bending down to grab some matching heels.

"I guess I can't be mad when faced with such good taste" I smirked and his face brightened as he smiled.

"I'm so glad you like it"

I really did like it. Even more so when I put it on and found it was a perfect fit. It contoured around my body perfectly. Adding the heels, light make up and a slight curl to my hair and you know what? I looked kinda alright.

After I'd finished making sure I looked okay, I'd caught sight of Elijah in the mirror and turned around with my mouth watering. Dressed in a black tux, his hair slightly styled and his beard neatly trimmed, I'd almost fainted just from looking at him.

His eyes had widened upon looking at me too and we stared at each other with feverish desire.

"You. Are. Beautiful" he breathed, stepping towards me slowly.

"I could say the same about you. Well I am going to. You are just as beautiful" I laughed and he'd wiggled his eyebrows.

That's when I noticed the box he was holding and knew immediately I was about to be gifted with something expensive. Wonder filled me. Not because of the price tag I knew would be attached to the box but because every gift Elijah had given me had been thought about and meant something.

"For you" is all he said as he handed me the velvet box. Upon opening it with shaky fingers, I found a bracelet that I immediately noticed matched my necklace. Silver and delicate, yet the pendant was not a bracket. Instead dangling from the chain was a crown. "I don't want to say anything too cheesy right now but let's just say I very much see you as my queen"

Yeah, I'd wanted to rip my heart out and hand it to him. Instead I'd grabbed him and kissed him silly. I'd wanted a better way to show my gratitude but it had been tough to process my emotions.

He'd clipped the jewellery into place before kissing my wrist where it lay. For the first time in my life, in that moment I'd thought that marriage wasn't such a bad idea.

I'd slapped the thought away and let him take my hand, pulling me to the elevator and down to the waiting black SUV. He explained as we got in that the car is arranged as soon as a guest confirms attendance which answered my incoming questions.

He'd held my hand on the journey to the event location. He must have known I was nervous. I'd never been to any kind of fancy ball and I knew that it would show in my inexperience.

So he'd spoken to me about the charity. Letting me know that this particular event was to help children who got lost in the adoption system. I felt immediately sorry for any such child. I may have rather annoying parents but at least I have them.

Elijah doesn't anymore and I could tell that this meant a lot to him.

When the car pulled up outside a large brick building that looked like something that could only be found in the UK or in a fairy tale, I almost lost my nerve.

Outside the car door were paparazzi ready to photograph us on a very red carpet.

"We can go right back home Darling? We don't have to be here" he'd soothed me, his hand squeezing mine, his thumb rubbing small circles.

"I want to do this. I'll be okay, I promise" I reassured him, leaning to kiss his lips.

"Okay but if at any point you want to leave just let me know"

Just then the car door was opened by a man in a grey suit, who held out his hand for me to take. With a deep breath and a little bit of hesitance I'd taken it and stepped out of the vehicle. Elijah followed quickly and pulled me safely into his side as the cameras went off.

It was terrifying and so very daunting. I could barely move or see as flashes blinded me. I tried to relax and smile while my hand gripped Elijah's waist for dear life. The only reason I made it into the building was because he guided me.

After that the night was lovely for a while. I gawked at the interior of the building, a huge ballroom and marble floor greeting us. Chandeliers hung from the ceiling and the place buzzed with activity.

Elijah introduced me to some of his business partners and we had plenty of lovely conversations. I was relaxed and actually quite comfortable. I wanted to tell him how wonderful he was when he donated a cool one million dollars to the charity. Okay I almost fainted as I heard the sum of money but mostly I was in awe.

It was great. We sipped champagne. We were about to dance together for the first time ever but naturally we got interrupted.

A dark haired women approached us. Slightly older looking than me, her face set in a fake smile. Her blue dress swished behind her.

"Elijah my dear, how are you?" she crooned. As soon as he locked eyes with her he stiffened at my side. He became even more icy as she rested her hand on his arm in greeting.

It wasn't hard for me to realise that something had happened between them. Something...not so good.

"I'm fantastic. How are you Lauren?" he asked in return, his voice strained and cold. It was awkward.

"I'm good yes and who is this?" she replied in her high pitched tone, turning to me. I wanted to speak. To seem confident but my tongue wouldn't move.

"This is my girlfriend Sofia" Elijah answered for me with the strength I was lacking.

"Girlfriend?" she questioned as if she wasn't sure she'd heard him right. Oh dear. I knew then that the conversation was gonna go bad. Bad like stale milk.

"Yes my girlfriend" he confirmed, his fingers tightened on my waist. He felt the need to be protective and that worried me.

"Are you sure? You don't do girlfriends" she laughed and a chill went through me. Who is she?

"I do now" he snapped.

"Does she speak?" she taunted and I wanted the ground to swallow me.

"I speak" I had pushed out and watched her eyebrows raise.

"Well, what a relief. Here's a word of advice from women to women...don't stay with him for long. I mean I'm sure he met you on that sugar daddy website right? That's how he met me. I did what you should do. I got the money I needed and left. I did it to the next guy too because honey, rich men ain't shit. They think they're gods gift and don't give a damn about anyone else. So please don't fall for any of his crap"

What...I...did she really just say all of that? For some reason the only thing I took from her 'advice' was that she had been Elijah's Sugary Sweet at some point. He'd obviously given her money and I assume she'd never spoken to him again.

"That's enough!" Elijah snapped just loud enough for the people around to hear.

"What's wrong? Are you mad because I'm telling her the truth?" she paused then turned to me again. "I bet this is actually the first time you've met him. Did he pay you to act as his girlfriend?"

"I'm done with thi-" Elijah began but I had cut in.

"We've been together for roughly five months, not that it's any of your business. As for his money, I don't want it. I love him for who he is. So I'd really appreciate it if you stick your nose else where" I told her, my skin prickling with annoyance. How fucking dare she? She never knew a thing about Elijah and she certainly didn't know a thing about me.

Her face went white at my reply and I saw the moment she backed down. Her shock turned to jealousy fast and her parting words were:

"He'll get bored of you soon!"

I had to roll my eyes. Such a stupid statement and even if it were true, I couldn't let it bother me. Our relationship isn't a fling.

"I am so sorry about that Darling. I've never seen an ex-sugary sweet at any one these events. Please don't listen to what she-"

"It's okay, it's not your fault and I'm not listening. You can tell me all about her later. Come on, you owe me a dance" I butted in to stop his rising panic. His eyes searched mine as if he was trying to find any unwanted emotion in me but I honestly felt okay. I understand jealousy and I understand selfishness. Elijah isn't selfish and he's worth so much more than his money. She just didn't stick around enough to see it.

"Yes I do owe you a dance. Many many dances"

Gliding onto the dance floor, I'd wrapped my arms around Elijah's neck and he'd held me gently. We swayed to a soft song, my arms covering in goosebumps from how special it felt. He rested his forehead on mine, his arms moving around me to pull me closer.

For a moment I'd wondered what it would have been like if we'd met under normal circumstances. If we'd met in a bar. Would he still have wanted me? Would we still be here? I certainly wish we'd met in a way that didn't involve any money being sent to me. Every time I think about it, I feel bad. Nevertheless, we're here now and I'm happier than ever in his arms.

"I love you" I reminded him and watched as his lips trembled. He breathed deeply and I could feel his heart thrumming wildly.

"Fuck" he growled as if to himself, closing his eyes.

"You'll get there one day and even if you don't, I'm not saying it to hear it in return. I'm not saying it to cause you pain. I just want you to know"

"I know Darling. I just hate my own fucked up emotions. I hate the way I am" he sighed roughly.

"Stop it. Don't do that" I commanded and he nodded.

"I'm sorry baby, come here"

Maybe making out on the dance floor was inappropriate but I guess no one seemed to mind.

We danced for a while, even when the songs became faster. He threw me about as I tried to keep up, my laughter echoing through the building. It was glorious.

"So have I made this event bearable?" I'd asked and he'd beamed brightly at me.

"It's been fantastic Darling. Thank you so much" he admitted and I was so pleased I'd helped him enjoy it. I'd had a great time too. I was glad I'd went.

Once our feet got sore and we'd sat through an auction of expensive gifts – Elijah bid on a guitar and won, even though he said he wasn't the best at playing - we decided to head home.

We said goodbye to his business partners and I couldn't help but feel like they'd somehow accepted me.

Then we got taken home in the SUV while Elijah told me a little more about Lauren. They'd matched on the website of course. They met a couple times for dinner. No sex was involved. He said that they got along well. Although as soon as he'd sent her money, she'd never spoken to him again, apart from sending him one nasty message. Apparently she hated rich men and simply wanted to mess with them. Elijah wasn't hurt by this but instead was pissed off that he'd been so stupid.

It reminded me of the story he'd told me on the first night we'd met. I thought he'd been dramatising his stories but it seemed women really did act that mean.

The conversation somehow changed to focus on me and my past lovers. To which I tried to be as open as he had been.

"What do you wanna know? How many men I've slept with? When I lost my virginity?" I asked, grinning at his suddenly stone like features.

"Whatever you're willing to tell me" he'd replied gruffly to which I couldn't stop my grin.

"Oh no, are you grumpy now? It's not so fun hearing about your partners past conquests is it? I haven't even said anything yet" I teased and he glared playfully.

"Come on then, get it over with" he promoted as we arrived home. We rode the elevator back up, I grabbed his hand and pulled him to the sofa, kicking my heels off on the way.

"Soooo, I lost my virginity when I was seventeen. Wasn't great. Actually it was terrible. I hated it and never wanted to have sex again" I told him and he looked sad for me.

"I'm sorry about that. I was sixteen when I lost my virginity to a girl in school but it was great. I'd never felt anything like it. I guess there's a few perks to being a man" he grins and I stick my tongue out at him. "Come on tell me more. When did you start enjoying sex?"

Uh oh. I hadn't expected that question. You see I'd had plenty of sex and it had been okay but it had never been good or fantastic or mind blowing...until him.

"Ummmm, well I had a decent amount of sex in college. I did a lot partying so one night stands were pretty frequent. I dated a few guys too and that was nice..." I explained trying to avoid answering the other question.

"Nice? Just nice?" he queried, tugging me into his lap.

"Elijah it's not as easy for a women to enjoy sex. In fact it's frustratingly hard" I sighed remember the anger and annoyance at not being able to orgasm during sex. Then I noticed his face going white.

"So does that mean you don't enjoy sex now?" he breathed so softly I barely heard it.

"What? No that's not what I meant! Elijah what I'm trying to tell you is I didn't enjoy sex at all really...until I had sex with you. Boy I bet that's an ego booster huh" I laughed and he stared intensely.

"Shit! I don't know whether to be mad that you didn't enjoy sex or ecstatic that I can give you the pleasure you wanted for so long" he pretty much panted, his hands going to my thighs.

"Be ecstatic. Because I am" I laughed until his hands moved higher, making me gasp instead. Pushing me back onto the sofa his body covered mine, his hand going between my legs to tease over my panties.

"Like this?" he breathed deeply, rubbing over my clit.

"Yes, oh yes"

My sighs and moan got cut off though by the shrill sound of a phone ringing. We ignored it the first few times but finally Elijah had to rip himself from me to answer the annoying sound.

That's the night we found out that Nadia hadn't gotten charged. The police couldn't tie her to the hack even though there was some evidence. Elijah had hung up and used every bad word in the bad word book. It sucked big time but surprisingly after his outburst of swearing he became somewhat positive telling me: "Maybe she didn't get arrested but hopefully having the police pull her into custody will be enough to ward her off. Surely if she keeps this up they will have to put her in jail"

I'm not sure if he brushed it off because he truly believed what he said or if he just was so desperate to continue what we'd started that he decided she wasn't worth the worry. Either way she didn't show up in our lives over these past months. There were no more hack attempts either.

As well as our comic con event and fancy charity thingy we also went to visit my parents again. Which was more pleasant than the first time. There was no Brian and we all got along.

My parents were also the ones to show Elijah and I our paparazzi taken pictures from the charity event. My Mom dropped the magazine in front of me at dinner and smiled softly.

"You both look very lovely" she'd told us and she was right. Our picture looked fantastic. It made me blush seeing Elijah's tight grip on my waist and our fancy formal attire. There was one particular picture of him looking at me rather affectionately. I found it online later that day and saved it to my phone. I'm pretty sure Elijah did his own picture hunting too. It's possible I look at those pictures and the ones from Hawaii far too much to be healthy.

Anyway, the fact that my parents clearly seemed to accept Elijah and I as a couple was a great feeling.

Not to mention Bree stopped by and told us that she hadn't had any more bother from the harassing sugar daddy. Which was fantastic.

A few weeks ago, I spent time with Annabelle and a few of my old university friends. Which was lovely. Annabelle didn't hold back on telling them about my new man. So I spent most of the dinner and drinks answering questions.

I pulled her aside at one point to tell her that I had moved into his apartment after being evicted. Which is how I remembered that I hadn't told her about that.

"YOU GOT EVICTED?! What? How are they allowed to do that?" she had exclaimed, her hands waving wildly.

"Because it wasn't my place to keep" I explained and she huffed dramatically. "It worked out anyway, now I get to see my man a lot more" I smirked and she gave me a knowing look.

"You love him don't you" she assessed my no doubt bright red face and I had to nod in admittance.

"Yeah, I kinda do"

"And does he love you back?" she'd asked and I'd cringed because how was I supposed to explain it to her?

"It's complicated on that side but not in a way that bothers me" I tried to help her understand. She didn't seem to like it but clearly saw my happiness and let it go.

"Well as long he keeps treating you right, I have no complaints. I'm happy for you Sofia" she grinned and hugged me tightly before we went back to the table and the questions resumed.

"Where did you first have sex?" Rang in my ears as I took my seat. Kasey from one of my interactive design classes had asked. She is sweet and innocent. More innocent than anyone I'd ever met in my life, never mind at university. Apparently with some alcohol that changed.

"In the cinema" I laugh and her face becomes a image of shock. The others had laughed but I had been worried that my words would have her fainting.

"No way!" she'd exclaimed.

"Yes way" I'd replied and luckily at that point it seemed all of their questions were sated.

Elijah went out with some business partners one night too, who are obviously his friends but he won't call them that. It's just like his relationship with Lewis.

He had only been gone for a couple of hours before I received a text.

Elijah: I'm not sure I'm the same man I used to be. Talking about sports and who's sleeping with who just isn't doing it for me tonight. Can you come and save me? Xxx

I had dropped him off earlier so that he could drink and he'd said he'd get a cab home if he was gonna be really late. I'd told him that I'd pick him up no matter what time.

Sofia: You poor thing. It must be a nightmare. I'm on my way xxx

I'd driven his Mercedes into town to the fancy bar, putting a little too much pedal to the metal. I couldn't help it, I loved driving his car.

When he got in the car a little tipsy, he seemed to love me driving it too.

"You're so hot. You handle this car better than me" he'd pretty much moaned as I'd pulled onto the street.

"Why thank you! It does suit me doesn't it?" I joked.

"It really does. Do you want one? Your own car I mean. I'm more than happy for you to drive mine but it's just occurred to me you'd probably like your own" he said quickly, very animated.

"Oh no Elijah, you're not buying me a car"

"No? Not even the Chevy Camaro you really adore?" he teased seductively as if trying to entice me.

"No! Don't even think about it. This is fine. Maybe I'll buy my own car one day once I've made enough money of my own" I explained, glancing at his grinning face.

"You're an enigma Sofia. You really do have my utmost respect" he'd replied, his hand moving to cover mine on the gear stick.

"Thanks, that means a lot"

When we'd gotten home, I'd taken much pleasure in helping him undress. He fumbled with his shirt buttons, swearing at them as his fingers couldn't complete the task.

"You know I wasn't meant to drink much" he confessed.

"That's okay, you deserve a break from all your hard work" I'd told him, pulling his shirt off.

He'd kissed me then, his tongue sweeping into my mouth tasting of sweet liquor. God it was hot.

"Sorry I really want to make love to you right now but I'm not sure I'm in any fit state. I don't want to flop around all over you like a teenage boy" he admitted and I'd laughed.

"You can make it up to me in the morning" I'd smirked and helped him get the rest of his clothes off.

It was so nice snuggling into his warm chest, his fingers soothing over my body.

"You're so lovely" I'd told him as we were falling asleep.

He did wake me up early in the morning, his more sober voice whispering in my ear.

"Do you still want me to make it up to you?"

"Oh yes, I do" I'd moaned and pushed back against him. He'd quickly removed his underwear and my sleep shorts before giving me what I desperately wanted.

Good times.

Something else I've enjoyed is getting voice notes from him late at night when he has to be at work until ungodly hours. His soft voice has helped me fall asleep on many occasions. As well as his actual phone calls that have brought me to orgasm. I'm not ashamed to say we've had phone sex more than once while he's been in his office.

Using FaceTime so we could watch each other touch ourselves was a very fun thing to do. Even more fun when I told him once not to come until he could come home and do so inside me.

"Shit! Sofia I'm going crazy" he'd whined, while I'd grinned triumphantly.

"You better not come. I'll know if you do. Keep that beautiful erection for me" I'd demand. I knew it was tough for him, having to continue working with a bugle in his pants.

However it had been worth it when he'd gotten home. I'd put him out of his misery by dropping to my knees, unzipping his pants and sliding his cock into my mouth. He'd came instantly with his fingers tangled in my hair.

Oh then he'd thrown me on the bed and shoved his face between my legs. I was a lucky girl.

When we've had free time and we've been too tired to go out we have often lay in the library/nerdy stuff exhibit. Reading in silence while Elijah types softly on his laptop is not something I ever thought would be that exciting. Although it really was.

It was so lovely one night when he closed his laptop and rested his head on my shoulder. He fell asleep there and the only reason I noticed was because of his change in breathing. I lay there with him for hours, unable to fall asleep too but more than happy to be his pillow.

Of course just like any relationship there had to be some arguing. I know how rubbish. No one wants to hear these parts of the love story but hey it has to happen. So deal with it.

"There's something not right about that guy!" Elijah exclaimed in reference to Gabe. To me Gabe has become normal again. He never bothered me or asked me any questions. He became almost invisible to me. Although apparently one night as Elijah waited to pick me up, Gabe finished his shift before me and approached Elijah's car. He'd said some not so nice things about me which Elijah didn't want to tell me at first. I eventually got it out of him. Hence the arguing.

"He's weird! I'll give you that but all he's trying to do is get under your skin. Maybe if you told me what he said then I could settle your mind!" I huffed in annoyance.

"I don't want to repeat it" he'd snapped, turning away from me to march down the hallway. He'd drove us home in silence and it was only when he'd gotten to the front room that he'd told me about Gabe. He got pissed off when I brushed off his worries because to be honest I'm pretty sure Gabe is just eccentric. He refused to tell me what he said since.

"Really?! That's mature!" I'd yelled after him. I wasn't going to follow the big baby if he wasn't going to talk to me. So I left him to do whatever he wanted and tried to ignore the annoying voice in my head to go after him.

I had been triumphant in staying away. Elijah however had not.

He was waiting for me as I exited the shower, a towel of truce hanging from his finger.

"I'm sorry for being an asshole" he whispered. Instead of taking the towel from him, I let him wrap me in it so that he could cuddle into me. I know! I'm weak! Don't you dare judge me.

"I'm sorry too" I replied and he frowned at me.

"Why are you sorry?" he asked.

"Because you might be right. He might be unsafe. Please tell me what he said"

He swallowed thickly and shook his head but finally let me know.

"He said that you are playing me. That you're lying to me. That you want my money-" he started but I couldn't even let him finish.

"Fucking bastard!" I yelled. "How dare he?!"

"I know Darling. That's why I was so mad. I still am. I told him to fuck off and I'm going to do something about him" he promised me.

"No, I'll do something. I'll report him tomorrow"

And I did report him. That's all still up the air as far as I'm aware.

Okay so you could say that wasn't much of an argument but it still kind of counts. That night turned out to be amazing though because he showed me that he'd learned to play a song on guitar. I knew he could play a little but nothing like he did that night.

He sang me a song. A mix of the lyrics he'd once shown me on his phone. Coupled with new ones. His voice rang in my ears and brought tears to my eyes. I'd heard him sing months ago but only through a door and he'd changed the subject. Only that was nothing compared to this song.

I'd been sitting opposite him in his makeshift studio as he'd strummed away, his voice filling the room. I couldn't take my eyes off him as he sat in his boxers and nothing else, the guitar strapped to him and his fingers moving diligently. It was beautiful and kind of erotic.

The song said the words he couldn't say. It was his 'I love you' and I've never been the same since.

As soon as he'd put the guitar down, I was on him faster than he could blink.

"So you liked it then?" he'd asked and I'd been unable to speak for a good few moments.

Then I'd admitted:
"It's the most beautiful song I've ever heard"

So there you have it!

The last few months of my life compacted into some paragraphs. I think that's all the important parts. Now you're all caught up!

Well maybe I should add that things are different now. Things have changed. My happiness no longer exists.

Within the last few hours or maybe even just less than twenty four hours, my happiness has been stolen. We've been torn apart and I'm sitting here in an abandoned warehouse talking to myself in my head, over and over.

My bruised ribs make it hard to breath and my burst lip keeps me from speaking. I can't keep track of time.

I left work yesterday? Two days ago? Well the time is irrelevant. I left work and was waiting on my cab home when the sound of tyres screeching caught my attention.

In the next second a black van raced down the road while I stood there with my mouth open, confused about what was happening. My own confusion stopped my instincts from kicking in and it was too late for me to react.

The van door opened and I was grabbed, blindfolded and thrown inside. I tried to scream but my mouth became stuffed with some fabric, my nose picking up a sweet scent that stung my eyes under the blindfold.

Fear consumed me before I blacked out...and woke up here. I haven't seen anyone or heard anything. The chain on my ankle keeps me shackled on the dirty ground and I wonder what I did to deserve this.

I don't know what I did wrong. I don't know what will happen next. I'm terrified of all the unanswered questions yet my body doesn't tremble. My fear level is reasonably low for the time being but when I think about a certain thing it spikes.

That certain thing is Elijah. What if I never see him again? What if he never finds me? What if he doesn't even try to?

Elijah

When I get home from work I'm looking forward to finding Sofia and hearing anything she has to tell me. It's the best part of my day because she settles my mind, her soft voice is much preferred than anyone else's.

Maybe we can watch the rest of Avengers, since we fell asleep last night.

I go in search of my girl, throwing my jacket off as I move through the apartment. Checking our bedroom, I find nothing. Our bathroom...nothing. Office, studio, kitchen, library...nothing.

Maybe she's gotten held back at work. Sometimes she has to clean the coffee machines at the end of her shift. Although I hate the idea of her being alone with Gabe. I know she reported him but nothing has been done in response yet. It bothers me every time she goes to work.

Maybe she went to the store or to see her friends. There's plenty of explanations. Yet I feel strange about this.

Pulling out my phone, I dial her number just to check she's okay.

I let it ring for far too long but there's no answer. I know that I shouldn't immediately panic but it's hard to squash my worry.

In order to act like a normal person and simply wait for her to get home, I go for a shower and then watch the news. I can't focus on it though, my eyes keep flicking to the foyer, my ears straining to hear the ping of the elevator.

An hour passes and I call her again for the third time. God she's going to think I'm insane when she does get home. All the missed calls. I need to chill out. She's okay...she has to be okay.

It occurs to me that maybe she can't answer a call if she's still at work. So I send her a text in the hopes that she can send me a quick one back.

Elijah: Hey Darling, are you working late? What would you like to eat tonight? I'll cook something for us or we can order in xxx

    I try to make it sound casual, like I'm not freaking the fuck out.

    When in actual fact I'm really freaking the FUCK OUT!

Sofia

    After some more time that I can't keep track off, I hear the distinctive sound of heels on hard ground. It sends unwanted chills down my spine. I've been holding it together pretty well considering my situation. I've held back tears...just but I'm still frigging terrified.

I'm finally going to find out why I'm here. Well I think I am. I'm not sure if I want to know and as all of the different possibilities flash through my mind I become even more scared. It may be cold in this empty building but my fear induced adrenaline is keeping me warm.

The clicking footsteps get closer and soon my captor comes into view as they walk around a pillar. My fear turns to hate and disgust as I take in the immaculately dressed and primed view of Nadia Zoya.

Of course it's her. Of fucking course! I'm now deciding that she's insane. There's no other explanation.

Oh hey my fear is gone...because this women is a joke. I actually find it hard not to laugh at her smug face. What does she think she's achieved by doing this?

My eyes catch another person walking behind her. A man dressed all in black with a ski mask on. That's sinister. I guess he's her muscle.

The large warehouse lights shine down from above them, casting them in fake light and making them seem more creepy. Well this is gonna be great fun for me.

"Oh dear, it looks like my men were a little rough with you. I'm sorry about that" Nadia begins, her voice dripping in mock sympathy. I swear this bitch needs help.

"No you're not. So can you skip the boring taunting part and get to the reason you've accosted me. Oh actually wait! I know why! You're still obsessed with getting your greedy hands on Elijah's business shares" I keep my voice calm and controlled but make sure to match her own mocking tone. She thinks she's better than me but she should know that not everyone will bow to her. Certainly not me.

"You should be careful how you speak to me. You do realise that you're here at my mercy. I can hurt you if I like and believe me...I'd like to" she retorts, his eyes flashing with evil intent.

Nope still not scared.

"Go on then. Hurt me. It's not gonna change a thing for you"

"I can't hurt you yet. I need you to do something for me first" she grins maniacally and reaches into her jacket pocket. Her hand reappears with a mobile phone in it. My phone.

Of course I'd wondered where it was. I'd spent a good few minutes looking for it when I'd woken up but it wasn't in my pocket. So I didn't have many other places to look. I'd come to the conclusion it had been taken and well I was right.

Staying silent, I watch as she scroll through my phone. It drives me mad because it holds everything personal to me. Every text from my parents, every photo, every voice note from Elijah.

"Aww look, he's been worried about you" she sighs and my heart beat picks up. It's obviously visible on my face too because she tuts and shakes her head. "You're so cute. Why do you care so much about him? I don't know why you waste your time. He's a man and he'll only hurt you in the end"

"That's your opinion. Are you going to tell him that you have me? So that he'll give you what you want?" I ask, coming up with the most obvious answer to my kidnap. God I want to contact him. I want to tell him I love him in case this ends badly.

She only laughs at me, the sound echoing through the warehouse.

"Where would be the fun in that? Sure I want the business shares but I want to have a good time too. He's turned me down far too many times. So he has to pay for that"

Her words make my blood boil and my fear returns. Hurting me is something I can deal with but hurting him is not.

"Don't hurt him!" I yell viciously. It may show my weakness but I don't care. I can't help it.

"Don't be silly. I'm not going to hurt him" she assures me but I can tell she is playing me right now. It's in the way she tilts her head as if she's really looking at me. Looking at me so she can watch my reaction to something.

I'm about to ask what the hell her plan is. If she's not going to hurt him then what's her revenge plan? What does she need from me?

After a long ominous pause she steps closer to me, leans down then whispers a short sentence that shoots me right in the heart.

"You're going to be the one to hurt him"

Elijah

I can't sleep. She hasn't answered. She hasn't come home. It's midnight. I need to call the police. Am I overreacting? Maybe. But I don't care.

I'd rather overreact and have her safe than do nothing and have her in danger.

So I dial 911 and tell the operator what's wrong. I assume that they're at least going to send a cop car to me so that I can explain my worries. Yet the man on the other end of the line informs me that someone being missing for a few hours doesn't actually count as missing. He even suggests the same things I tried to tell myself, that's she just busy.

"Sir, is it possible that she may just need some space? Usually if someone doesn't answer the phone it's simply because they don't want to. No need for panic"

Is this guy serious?! I'm pretty sure giving relationship advice doesn't fall under his job description.

"I'm positive that she doesn't just need space" I grind out, my anger and worry growing.

"Well I'm sorry, I can't do anything right now. If she's still missing in forty eight hours call us back"

Hanging up, I almost throw my phone into the wall. Then the seed that the operator planted blooms in my head. Does she need space? Have I been too clingy as she would call it? Fuck! What if I've scared her off?

Sitting on my couch, I try to go over the past few weeks. I can't recall ever thinking that she seemed different or as if anything were wrong.

What do I do now? I'm faced with the fact that maybe she doesn't want to be around me right now. Or maybe she is in serious danger and I'm sitting here sulking. How am I supposed to choose the right path? If I look for her now and find her, it would only make things worse if she needs space from me.

Then again if I don't look for her and something bad has happened I'll never forgive myself.

Fuck it! If she doesn't want to be around me then I'll respect her choice but I have to make sure she's okay first. I have to make sure she's safe.

Sofia

"I'm not sure what you have planned but if you think that you can make me do anything to hurt him, you're severely wrong" I spit back at Nadia's annoying mocking expression.

"Is that so? I'm pretty sure I know exactly how to make you do as I say" she replies, far too confident for my liking. Its unnerving.

At first I think she's going to have her henchman beat me up some more and force me to do whatever she wants but he makes no move to approach me.

Once again she looks at my phone, purposely not giving me any answers to all of the questions I have.

Suddenly my phone rings in her hand and she rolls her eyes. While I try not to show the desperation on my face. I know it's Elijah calling and my need to answer that phone has my guts twisting up inside me.

"He really doesn't know when to quit. You know he called all last night and all of today. It's ridiculous" she sighs as if it's causing her some sort of problem.

She's given away a piece of information though. I must have been kidnapped last night. A day less than I assumed. Whatever drug that was on the cloth that got shoved in my mouth must have helped warp my perception of time.

The fact that Elijah hasn't stopped calling gives me hope. Hope that he knows something is wrong. Hope that he will find me. Regardless I have to try my best to escape too. Maybe if I give her what she wants then I'll have a better advantage. Do what she says and make her feel as though I won't attempt to run. First I need to get this cuff off my ankle.

"Not to worry, he will be getting a call back soon. Then we won't have to worry about him calling ever again huh" she teases and I try to work out what the hell that means.

"Why won't he call again?" I breath, trying not to panic.

"He won't have reason to. You see Sofia, you're going to call him back but not just for a chit chat. You're going to break up with him. You're going to break his heart. I don't care what you say or how you do it. Just do it. I'm sure you'll know what to say to hurt him most won't you?"

My own heart breaks. My skin prickles. My blood runs cold.

No! No there's no way I can do that. I can't possibly break his heart. I can't break his trust. Not to mention I don't have the ability to lie at the best of times never mind lying to him that way.

"I can't do that" I tell her. I'm not trying to taunt her, I'm simply telling the truth. I just can't. I won't cope.

"Well, let's see if I can give you some motivation. If you don't break up with him. If you don't tear his pathetic heart out then I'll make sure you never see him again. I'll make sure he goes to jail. Don't think I can't do it. I mean he's been accused of murder before so it would be pretty easy to pay some people to accuse him of other crimes. A few women coming forward and saying he abused them. A few men saying they've done illegal business deals with him. Once a criminal always a criminal. The press would eat it up"

I don't know what to say. I can't think of any witty come back because I know she's right. The media would have him locked up with or without evidence. The police would love to pin something on him because he got away with the previous accusations. He's not a murderer or abusive but no one will care. The press are vultures.

I can't let that happen. Yet I don't know how I'm going to lie to him either.

"Do you think he's going to believe that I've just suddenly decided to leave him?" I ask her because truly I'm at a loss.

"Like I said, I'm sure you can think of something" she shrugs, holding up my phone.

"What does this achieve? What does this get you?" I have to ask. I have to know why she wants to cause so much pain. I know she wants revenge but that can't be all.

"If you break his heart and he believes you've left him and don't want him anymore then he will become weak. He will become reckless and uncaring where his business is concerned. He won't care if I try to strike a new deal because all he had to live for will be gone" she explains. It makes a lot of sense and maybe she's right. Maybe he'd get sad for a while but he would never be weak. He also certainly doesn't live for me.

"If you believe that I'm all that matters to him then I don't know what to tell you. He cares about me sure but that's as far as it goes. I really don't think his business stance will change" I tell her, partly because I want to throw her off and party because it's true. He cares deeply for me but he won't risk his life's work just because a girl he adores walked away. That company is his father's legacy.

"Stop trying to fuck with me. He's besotted with you. It's going to work. So I suggest you prepare your breakup speech"

Do I have a choice? I could use the phone call to yell that I need help before she would inevitably snatch the it from me, but then she'd get him locked up and no doubt leave me here to rot so I couldn't help him.

Or I do as she says and hope he sees through my lies. He's too smart to believe it right? He has to be.

I can do this. I can lie to him to keep him safe. Even if he does believe it and he hates me forever at least he'll be okay. He won't go to jail and hopefully he won't give up his business to this nasty bitch.

"Fine, give me the phone"

Elijah

I drove around most of the night as well as driving myself insane. I didn't know where to begin looking.

I'd driven past her work just in case she was there. No signs of life showed in the empty coffee shop. So I drove past her old apartment. I don't even know why but I had to keep myself doing something.

Nothing, nowhere. She didn't call back and my mind worked a mile a minute to try and piece together where she could be. I contacted her parents at three in the morning and her Mom picked up, her voice groggy from sleep.

When I'd asked if she'd heard from Sofia she'd said no and asked what was wrong. I tried not to worry her but had to tell her that I didn't know where Sofia was. She replied, saying that she'd try to contact her and get back me.

So I waited for her call in my car on a random street. My fingers gripped the steering wheel, my knuckles white as I struggled to cope with the fact that there was nothing for me to do.

I should have went back to the apartment then but instead I ended up calling her over and over until falling asleep, my head pressed against the freezing window.

It was a tortured sleep. Filled with nightmares and flashes of Sofia in danger. Her crying. Her running from me.

When I finally woke up to the sunlight and people milling around the streets, it was early morning, I could barely remember where I was. My head pounded and my body ached from sleeping in an ice box but the first thing I did was check my phone.

My heart jumped as a text displayed on the screen but I deflated when I saw it was from her Mom, letting me know that Sofia didn't pick up. She said she'd call the police and I didn't tell her I already had because maybe they'd listen to her.

Shaking off my all round sadness, I had to force myself to stay positive. What was my next move? Maybe she's back home? I decided that I should definitely check and if she wasn't there then I'd start contacting more people. I'd start my own investigation if I had to. She may not want me to find her but I planned to anyway.

Pushing away the thoughts of her in pain or distress, I drove home.

That's where I am now. There's no Sofia. Just emptiness in the apartment and in my heart. Where are you Darling? What's going on?

In my office, I open up my laptop and prepare to search the whole fucking world. Only my fingers barely touch the keys when my phone rings.

Fumbling to pick it up, I finally grab it and almost cry with relief as her name and photo covers the screen.

FUCK YES!

Smashing the answer button with my thumb, I put the mobile to my ear and prepare to hear her voice.

She's okay! My girl is okay!

"Sofia?! Where are you?!" I exclaim, desperate to go get her or to know that she's on her way home. With my heart in my throat I wait for her reply. The line crackles for a few seconds before I hear a deep inhale, then finally her voice.

"Elijah...hey" she says softly, the shake in her voice obvious. Something's wrong. She's not okay.

"Yes, what's wrong? What is it baby?" I ask quickly. I'm barely able to breath waiting for her reply. I need to know. What's going on? Is she hurt? I need to get to her now!

"I'm okay, I'm fine. It's just... w-we really need t-o talk" she stutters and my world stops.

The relief at hearing she's okay quickly changes to worry all over again because I don't believe her. She doesn't sound okay.

Also what could she possibly want to talk about while sounding as if she's being held at gun point?

Nothing about this seems right.

"What do we need to talk about?" I ask softly trying to keep my voice even. I want to try and sooth her because I can literally feel her fear through the phone. It kills me but if she is in danger the worst thing I can do is not go along with her conversation.

I need to keep myself in check. All of my instincts are telling me to curse and swear at whoever made her feel this way. To yank her through the phone and into my arms so no one can hurt her but I can't do that.

"Us" she breathes, destroying me with one word. Us? She wants to talk about us?

All of my insecurities rush back and I bite my lip so hard that I can taste blood on my tongue.

It seems I'm the one making her feel this way. I'm the one that's making her voice shake and tremble.

I've never hated myself more in my whole fucking life.

Sofia

"What do we need to talk about?" he asks and bile rises in my throat. I wanna throw up. His voice breaks me into pieces because I know that soon his adoring tone is going to change.

Nadia stands with her arms crossed and her lips turned up in a small smile while I struggle to breath. She can hear every word of our conversation because she forced me to put it on loudspeaker.

Come on Sofia. Do it for his sake.

"Us" is all I can get out. How am I going to do this without crying? I can feel the tears threatening to fall already.

He doesn't respond. I can just about hear him breathing. It's like he knows what I'm about to say. It's like he's afraid to speak.

"What about us?" he finally pushes out and I close my eyes, letting the tears fall. If I just get it over with maybe it'll hurt less. Who am I kidding? This is gonna fuck us both up.

"I can't be with you anymore. I'm sorry but it's just all too much too fast" I lie, thinking of the shittiest excuse ever.

"I don't...I don't understand. I thought you were okay with staying with me. I thought you wanted to be with me like I do you" his words slice me into pieces. The agony that already coats his voice is strangling me.

"I thought I did too. I really did but I feel like I can't breath"

I can't breath. I'm not lying but it's for a different reason than I'm saying.

"Why didn't you tell me this in person?" he asks, sounding a little more suspicious now.

Nadia then raises her eyebrows at me as if she's telling me to convince him better. I honestly wish I could stab her.

Swiping at my tears, I try to pull myself together enough to get this done. I'm going to have to hurt him. I'm going to have to make him hate me so that he doesn't work this out.

"You smother me Elijah! I feel like I can't ever get away from you! I didn't want to have to say that to you but there it is!"

Every part of myself that I held high and strong since being kidnapped dies with those words. I hate myself for not being clever enough to avoid being taken. I hate myself for not being smart enough to work out how to stop this phone call and I hate myself for even being able to say those sentences to the man I love. I kind of hope I die here.

"Right I see. I'm so sorry for making you feel smothered. Except I don't believe a word you're saying" The tremble in his voice lets me know that he's so very close to losing it. I don't know if he's going to go crazy with anger or crumble with hurt. "I think something else has happened. Darling you are fantastic at many things but you are a terrible liar"

Shit! Fuck! DAMN IT! My fingers tighten around the phone and I feel as though I might crush it in my palm.

I don't want him to believe me but I also do. I want him to be safe. I want him to be a free man and not imprisoned.

What do I say now? How do I convince him that we're over?

"Sofia, just tell me where you are and I can come and get you. I won't let anything hurt you baby" he pants, the emotion in his voice seeking out mine.

It comes to me then. The answer. The horrible sickening answer. I know how to hurt him. How to break him.

"I don't want you to come and get me. I don't want to see you at all. You want the truth Elijah? Do you want to know why I'm not with you right now?" I grind out, pulling all of my anger at Nadia and putting it into my words so that he believes me.

"I'd love to know the truth..."

"I'm bored now okay. I'm done pretending to give a shit about you. I saw an opportunity to live a better life and I took it but there's only so much acting one person can do! I stuck around after you sent me the money you did because I wanted to see how much you'd give up. I now have enough in the bank to get me through. I didn't want to tell you that. I wanted to spare your feelings but Elijah you were right. All those women only wanted your money and I'm no different from them. I played you and now I've gotten what I wanted and left. So do yourself a favour and leave me alone"

So now I'd very much like to go to hell and be punished for my sins. I want to hurt myself for hurting him. My tears return and stream down my cheeks uncaring. I have to slap a hand over my mouth to stop the sobs from escaping.

I want him to yell at me. I want him to say the worst things in the world back. Yet he doesn't. Even when I deserve it.

"I'm glad you got what you wanted. I hope you enjoy the money and eventually find what makes you truly happy. Just tell me why you have to tell me you loved me? Why did you have to go that far?"

He sounds so emotionless now. Ice flowing through the phone to freeze my ear. He's went cold on the inside just like I have.

"I just thought it was the right thing to say. I thought it would make you feel special"

This has to end now because I'm losing it.

"You did. You made me feel something I've never felt before. Congratulations. Goodbye Sofia"

"Elij-"

The line goes dead. As does my soul. Dropping the phone from my hand, I don't look up to see Nadia's triumphant grin. Instead I wrap my arms around myself and squeeze to hold all of my pain in. I want to scream but that'll only please her more.

"Bravo! That was moving! You know I didn't think you'd pull it off" she taunts before I catch her grabbing my phone from the ground. "Now then, I'll keep you here for a while just until I get what I want then we can talk about setting you free. There will be terms of course. The most important one being, don't go anywhere near Elijah. We'll work all of that out later though. Have a nice night"

I hear her footsteps walking away and glance up to see her leaving with her muscle man in tow. She then turns around again, joy on her face.

"I just thought you should know that you got an email about a job interview today. Something about head programmer? Sounds pretty impressive. Shame you can't go to it"

Aside from murderous thoughts I can't help but think how interesting that is. It's really funny how the world works. The one time I'm not available and a company finally decides to give me a chance. Maybe it's just karma punishing me for hurting Elijah. I mean that's the job I never thought I'd even have a chance at getting.

SMASH!

I jump at the sudden noise that's followed by a crunching sound. Nadia has thrown my phone on the ground and is now standing on it with her heel. Is that supposed to bother me? I've no one to call now. I've nothing to feel.

"Just in case he has a change of heart and tries to track your location" are her parting words. I'm glad to see her go.

I never thought of the tracking thing but the thought that Elijah wouldn't even attempt such a thing now is what has me finally letting out the most agonising scream ever.

He won't care now. He won't want me. He probably hates my guts.

Elijah

"FUUUUUUUUUCKKKKK!"

All my body is capable of is breaking. Smashing. Tearing apart anything in my line of sight. My mind is paralysed from the torture my stupid heart is putting me through.

I want it out of my chest. I want to destroy everything and everyone. How did I let this happen?

I was so sure when she began to talk to me that she was lying. That something or someone was making her say all of that shit to me. I thought I knew her so well. That I knew when she was trying to hide something from me.

When in actual fact she's been hiding things from me from the beginning. She's just like the rest. NO! FUCK!

The coffee table is flipped, everything on top of it flying through the air. The smashing of glass should shake me from my rage but it only spurs me on.

Was any of it real? Her hopes and dreams? Her favourite colour? Fuck was her name even real? How much did she lie about?

Her face flashes in my mind and I slam my hands over my eyes as if I can dig far enough into my skull to pull the images out. Every smile, every laugh torments my mind with no escape.

I'm being torn in two. One half of me is consumed by rage and agony. While the other tries to make its way into my consciousness to convince me that something still isn't right. That she couldn't have faked it all.

"AHHHHHHHHHH"

What do I look like right now? A monster? A psychopath?

I throw the next thing my hand touches. I don't know what it is but the echoing crack suggests it's broken now. Good.

I still want to know where she is. Who gives a fuck?! She doesn't care about me so I have to do the same with her.

When I find nothing left to smash in the front room I move to the kitchen, my body itching to strike out. I've never felt so violent in my life.

The first thing I find is a fruit bowl which I toss and smash. My fist punches the wooden cabinet which gives up a good fight but eventually cracks under a third blow. My knuckles howl in pain but it's nothing compared to my insides.

With my good hand I grab my next target. I go to launch the object across the room but when I notice it's a vodka bottle I decide there's a better use. I'm not a hardcore drinker but I guess that's about to change.

Yanking the cap off, I tip the bottle to my lips and take far too many gulps. My throat burns and my eyes water.

It should have taken the edge off immediately but another surge of anger attacks me and the bottle meets the same fate as the previous objects.

She took me to see her parents! She invited me into her life! She told me her secrets! Well now I'm guessing they really weren't her secrets.

For the first time in my life I'm not pissed off that I was used for my money. That's actually the least hurtful part.

I'm being torn apart by the fact that she used all of me. She convinced me to trust her. I let my guard down even though it went against all of my beliefs. She listened to me tell her about everyone who'd fucked me over all the while planning to do the same.

She's the worst type of human.

I fucking hate her!

Except I don't. I can't stop my heart from bleeding. I can't stop myself from wanting. If she walked out of the elevator right now what would I do?

Would I curse her out? Would I yell at her?

The crushing blow is that I know the answer.

I'd fall to my knees and beg her to give me more time with her. That's now fucked up I am. That's how addicted I am.

Well fuck that!

Grabbing another bottle of god knows what alcohol, I find my keys and thrown away phone in the mess. Somehow it's not broken. I don't really need it anyway. I just need to get away from this apartment that is filled with her stuff.

Then I make my way to the garage and into my waiting car. Pulling out onto the street, my unstable head space has me slamming on the accelerator.

I don't know where I'm going. I don't even care. All I know is I need to get out of here. I need to get away from a town that she quite possibly still in.

Pushing my car to its limit, I drink down some of the alcohol. It burns just like the last bottle but still my mind won't settle.

This is stupid and dangerous but it doesn't matter. She doesn't care about me.

No one cares about me and really I've nothing to live for.

So if I end up wrapping my car around a tree then it won't make a difference.

Fuck it! Fuck the world. Fuck everything!

Most of all, fuck Sofia Westwood!

Elijah

    Drink. Push the pedal harder. Repeat.
    I don't know where I am. The alcohol is taking effect and my blurry vision tells me that I should no longer be driving. I don't give a fuck. So I go faster.
    Maybe I should worry about getting arrested for drink driving. It's something I never thought I'd do but here I am.

I'm consumed with the need to go faster but at 150 mph my car can't cope. The engine revs far too much making me even angrier.

"Fucking piece of shit!" I growl, slamming on the breaks. The tyres skid on the tarmac brining me to a shaky stop at the side of an empty road. Fuck knows where I've ended up. On either side of me are some houses spread rather far apart. A couple shops I think and maybe a gas station. There's no sign of life even if it is only early evening.

The silence and lack of distraction doesn't help me. So I beat the shit out of my steering wheel.

My already aching knuckles scream and bleed but it doesn't register good enough.

It's only when my phone rings that I stop and I glare at it as if it's my worst enemy. I don't want to talk to anyone.

A quick glance only makes me want to smash it. Sof- No I don't want to think that name. Her... her Mom is calling. Probably to ask me if I've found her yet.

Snatching it up I answer it so I can tell her that her daughter is perfectly okay. She's just a bitch!

Even thinking that word about her hurts me. I should want to call her all the names under the sun but I ache with every bad word. It's too ingrained in my mind to protect her from all of that kind of stuff.

Fucking hell I need to get a grip. She's not who I thought she was.

"Elijah? Are you there? Listen I called the police but they said -"

"That you'd have to wait until forty eight hours before reporting a missing person. I know. Look I got a hold of her, she's fine" I drag the words from the depths of my brain because being civil is not something I'm good at right now.

"Oh thank god! Where was she?" she asks cheerily and I cringe. I can't do this. So I hang up. I've done my part. She can call her Mom herself now surely.

I try to gulp back some more alcohol but nothing hits my lips. I've drank it all. Fuck! Guess I'll have to go find some more then.

Some more aimless driving takes me further away from my town, away from her and finally I pull up into a random hotel parking lot.

The neon flashing sign above the entryway hurts my eyes as I try to read it. I simply can't because my vision is far too impaired. God knows how many stars this place has but honestly it really isn't important. The bar in there will have more liquid to twist my mind enough to breath. I hope.

As soon as I exit the car an unpleasant smell hits my nose. Where the fuck am I?

Stumbling to the shaking front door of the hotel, I step through the threshold only to have to clutch the wall for balance. I don't think it was the door that was shaking.

As I squint my eyes, I'm met with peeling paint and odd coloured carpets. I can just about make out the ware and tear of the beaten up reception desk as I try to reach it without falling over. Wow I'm more of a lightweight than I thought. Or maybe a whole bottle of whiskey is a lot. Who the fuck knows? I probably should but I don't know anything anymore.

The fuzzy man at the desk does not look pleased so my plans of telling him this place needs a lick of paint and new furniture are put on hold. This is definitely two star. Maybe just one.

Look at me and my snobby ass picking on someone's business. Maybe that's why Sofia left? Am I too snobby? Too rich? What?! No! That's what she liked. The money!

"One room for the night please" I force my lips to move and don't miss the disapproval on this guys face.

"Sure. That'll be three hundred dollars" he replies and I know even with my foggy brain that he's exploiting me right now. Do I look rich? Probably. Oh whatever, I can't blame him for taking an opportunity when he sees one. Guess that means I shouldn't blame Sofia either...I wonder what she's doing?

STOP IT!

"No problem" I snap using my black American Express to pay far too much for this sort of place.

"Enjoy your stay" he almost sings gleefully as he hands me a key. I've probably just paid triple the normal price.

"Point me in the direction of the bar" I demand and his eyes light up, probably guessing that I'm going to spend more money.

"Right that way" he points left and I'm moving before he can say another word.

Let's get this party started. This pity party.

I'm not sure when I last had shots. Maybe when I was a teenager. Anyway that's the first thing I order. A whole round of absinth shots all for me.

Not that anyone else would be able to drink them anyway since there's probably about three people here in total and that's including the bar attendant. Who also doesn't look too pleased with me. I must be a very annoying drunk. Sofia didn't seem to mind though...

Leaning my cheek in my palm, I stare into an empty glass as my mind takes me to a happier place...

"Okay, yellow or red?" she asks while sipping some red wine. I watch her lick her lips before she raises her eyebrows at me expectantly.

"Red" I reply, telling her what my preferred colour is. We're playing 'This or That' in the midday sun. Facing each other on the lounger situated on the balcony. I've lived in my apartment for years but I've rarely used the space accessible through the large glass doors attached to the kitchen. It never occurred to me that it would be relaxing to sit in the breeze with thousands of people far enough below that they look like ants. I also never thought I'd ever sit here with my legs entwined with such an amazing person. She makes me happy just by being here.

"Your turn" she prompts, her cheeks rosey from her alcoholic beverage. I'm nursing my own glass of whiskey and am at the tipsy stage. She's there too I think but I don't need alcohol to make me feel so floaty. She does that to me everyday. Wow, I gotta stop thinking about cutesy things and focus a little on what I wanna ask.

"Hmmmmm, let's see. Cats or dogs?" Is the best thing I can come up with and she answers immediately.

"Dogs. All day long! I've always wanted a dog" she tells me, her eyes slightly glazed over as if she's somewhere else in her mind. Maybe with a bunch of puppies. Maybe I'll surprise her with one...

"Tits or ass" she laughs and my mouth falls open in shock.

"Oh come on now. You can't expect me to choose one" I shake my head genuinely thinking that it's impossible.

"Think about it. Tell me your reasoning"

"Okay well, your ass is great to grab when partaking in certain...activities. It's also really fucking sexy when I get to watch you walk away. However your tits are just the holy grail now that I think about it. They fit perfectly in my hands and I really do love sucking on your perfect nipples-"

"Elijah this is meant to be a general question. Not about me!" she giggles and I shrug unapologetic.

"I can't help it. I guess my answer is I'd prefer to grab your ass while shoving my face in your tits"

I love seeing her blush. Her pink cheeks do something to me. They mean that I've said something she likes. I love that no matter how many times we talk about dirty things or the dirty things we partake in together she still blushes. We've done a lot. We know every inch of each other. We've asked questions about each other's bodies simply due to curiosity. I may have asked for too many questions about her time of the month but really I just wanted to help make her feel better.

"I'll let you off but you can't choose both next time" she grins sipping some more wine.

"Thank you Darling. Music or movies?"

"Oh god, that's a tough one. I'm gonna have to go with movies. I feel like they are more entertaining over a longer period of time. Although if you're the one providing the music then I'd pick that"

She's so damn sweet. I'm not sure how I got so lucky but I'm not going to question it.

"That's a lovely answer. You really do have to be careful about stroking my ego. I've warned you about that" I tease and lean over to peck her lips. She meets me half way and then pulls back, keeping her hands on my cheeks.

"You deserve all the compliments in the world Elijah"

I want to stay in my memory for longer. It's nice there. There's no pain or anger. Only happiness.

Unfortunately I'm pulled from my heaven and back into my head spinning reality.

I'm back in the bar with blurry vision and a growing headache. It seems more people have showed up and there's now quiet chatter all around.

As soon as I'm back to being aware of my current situation, I end up biting the inside of my cheek to stop myself to roaring in anger. My stomach churns and my knuckles go white on the glass. Shit, shit, shit! It hurts!

"Sir? Are you okay?" I hear an unfamiliar voice and realise that's why I'm no longer locked inside a fabulous memory. Someone has sat down next to me at the bar.

Turning my head ever so slightly I can just make out the women beside me. Blonde hair, pale skin. She's wearing a blue top...but that's all my brain can process.

"I'm fine" I reply and go to order another drink.

"Don't you think you've had enough?" she stops my attempt and I automatically glare at her. What the fuck is her problem?

"Don't you think you should mind your own business?" I snap, signalling to the bar tender to give me more. More of what? I don't care what it is.

"No I'm not going to mind my own business. If you drink anymore then you'll pass out and then you'd be no good to me" she continues talking to me, her voice changing from casual to something else. My irritation only grows.

"Excuse me?" I question, not really having enough brain capacity to have this conversation. I wonder if Sofia told me the truth about anything at all. God I really want to know.

"Well, I think you might need some kind of help. Help to take your mind of something...or someone?"

Oh great she's still talking. You know in the two seconds in between my reply and then hers, I'd forgotten she was there. Two whole seconds for my brain to change direction and go back to the only person I want to talk to. I am so fucked.

Although something does nip at my brain...

"Why do you think I have something or someone on my mind?" I ask because it's weird that she'd suggest such a thing from just seeing a random guy at a bar.

"I see it all the time. If someone is drinking alone is usually means something isn't quite right"

Never mind. Whoever she is obviously takes pleasure in prying into people's lives. I don't have the energy for that.

"Well how very clever of you. Goodbye" I reply in a mocking tone. I think it's time I retire to my room. Or rather lock myself in it and hopefully drift away to a more bearable time.

With a lot of difficulty I get up off the barstool and dig my hand in my pocket to find my room key. Trying to work out the number on it is extremely difficult but eventually I make out the two and one.

Okay room twenty one. Let's see if I can make it. One foot in front of the other.

The corridor in front of me wobbles as I drag myself along the wall. Fuck this is hard work. If Sofia were here she'd help me. She'd help me undress and put me to bed.

Except she's the reason I'm in this state. So I'd very much love it if I could shut off my whole mind. Please. Please. Please.

I don't know how long I hold onto the wall for support, my feet shuffling as if I'm carrying weights on my ankles. Eventually though, I see the number twenty one on a far away door.

Well one second it's far away and the next I'm falling against it. Woah!

The more I try to focus on the key hole, the harder it is trying to insert the damn key.

"Fuck sake!" I growl, jabbing randomly and hoping for success.

"Need help with that" hits my ears and I whip around to see the same women from the bar. I want to yell at the fucking ceiling. Can she please go away? Is this women okay? Is she lonely or some shit?

"No I don't!" I shout and go back to my task.

"Seriously, I can help you with that. I can also help you with other things too. Maybe I can relax you? Give you some sort of pleasure to soothe your pain"

In an instant I realise what's going on. I've heard that tone and similar words so many times before. Seductiveness coupled with vindictiveness coats her voice. She's flirting with me but not because she's simply attracted to me. Oh no, she wants something from me.

I recognise this technique because it's been used on me on many occasions. From business partners to previous sugar babies. I've never fallen for it and I won't start now.

Sofia didn't use that technique. No she hid it so fucking well. That's why I'm so messed up. I didn't see it coming and I never would have.

My heart squeezes, sending another wave of torture through me. I can't do this! I can't take it. I want it to stop...

FUCK!

With my heart spilling blood I finally get the key in the door and I can taste freedom from the outside world.

"Is it a women that's hurt you? I can make you forget her?"

Forget her?

That's hilarious.

"Nothing you could possibly do would make me forget her" I breathe, bracing myself against the wall.

"I'm sure you'd forget real quick with me naked beneath you" Her words don't even phase me. In fact they make me laugh. My dick certainly wouldn't rise to the occasion. Not for her. Not for anyone but Sofia. That's the reality of my situation.

"No thank you" I state, my teeth gritted. Stepping back into the room, I intend to happily slam the door in her face. What a weird woman.

Unfortunately I don't get the chance because in the next second she's launching herself at me.

WHAT THE FUCK?!

Elijah

Stumbling backwards into the room, the crazy lady grabs my shirt. Because of my intoxicated state she's able to push me further.

"What the fuck are doing?" I yell, trying my best to shove her off. My whole body revolts at her close proximity. I try to step away but she keeps advancing.

"Giving you what I know you want" she snaps back before trying to yank my head closer to her.

Oh hell fucking no!

Twisting my face away, I'm able to grab her arm and yank her away from me.

"Get the fuck out!" I shout and step forward, trying my best to intimidate her.

When she notices that I'm somehow able to stand on my own two feet it seems to change her confidence. Stepping forward again, I watch as she backs up. That's better.

"You're making a mistake. This would be good for you" she says, looking a little more scared. Good.

"You don't know what's good for me. Now get the hell out before I throw you"

"But-"

"GET OUUUTT!" I roar. Her eyes widen in fear and she moves quickly, exiting the room before disappearing down the corridor.

I immediately slam the door shut, lock the dead bolt and thump the wood over and over. I kick at the door in anger, beating the shit out of the inanimate object. With one final punch, I lean my head against it and clutched my sore knuckles.

"Why did you do this to me Sofia?" I cry to no one and slid down the door until I crumpled into a sobbing ball. If she could see me now I'm sure she'd have cringe. Or laugh.

My whole body shakes as if trying to dispel the wretched touch of another women. Sickness threatens to overflow rises within me. Part of it is the alcohol but the other part was is disgust at that women's touch.

I have to let the sickness out.

Stumbling and tripping all the way to the bathroom I fall next to toilet. As soon as I lift the lid, the whole contents of my stomach spills out of my mouth.

I wretch violently and try to gulp down some air but there's far too much still to come. I haven't ate a thing all day so the only substance I can throw up is the liquid I've consumed.

It feels as though I'm throwing up everything that matters to me. It hurts like a bitch and tears sting my eyes. Not from the wrenching pain but from my overall situation.

She's walked away and abandoned me and I feel like a little boy lost and alone with no one.

After some time on the cold tile floor I pull myself up with the little energy I have left. To say I flop onto the bed is an understatement. I land on the duvet like a starfish before rolling over onto my back.

Deep breaths. Count to ten. Pretend everything is fine.

The room spins wildly and it doesn't seem to stop when I close my eyes.

Searching for my phone in my pocket, I pull it out with the intention of turning it off. I don't want to see any work emails, texts or phone calls. I don't want anyone to be able to get through to me.

The only person I want to hear from wants nothing to do with me. Not to mention I should have no desire to speak to her either. I can't fucking help it. Having someone be there everyday, giving you joy and then having them take it all away can destroy a person.

It's destroying me.

Holding my phone in front of my face and wrenching my eyes open I do something I know I shouldn't. Something I know can only hurt me more.

I bring up the pictures of us. The pictures of her. In Hawaii, at the charity event and so many other occasions in which I'd snapped a shot of her beauty.

One in particular makes me stop scrolling. It's her in my shirt, grinning at the camera. Zooming in on her beautiful face, I trace my fingers over the screen.

I haven't cried in a long time but here and now with no one to see or hear me, I sob and sob with her face staring back at me.

That's how I fall asleep, with my phone clutched to my chest.

***

It's now roughly eleven am on the next again morning. I slept far longer than any normal person needs to sleep. My head throbs and my stomach churns from the left over alcohol in my system and I feel emptier than I've ever felt.

I've no clue what to do with myself. I should be at work right now but that's the last thing on my mind.

I'm still fully dressed, lying on top of the hotel bed, my eyes glued to the ceiling. I know for a fact that I smell hideous. My mouth feels like cotton and my body feels as though I've never drank water in my life.

I'm not ready to get up and face the world. I'm not ready to accept that this is how I'm going to be for the rest of my days. I'm trying to hate her but how can I when all of the memories I have of her are amazing. The only exception is the phone call that began this hell.

So I close my eyes and once again get lost in my mind.

"You know it's actually in the 'Sugar' agreement section" I tell her, trying to hide my smirk.

"What? Are you serious? There's no way that's true" she says, crossing her arms.

We're at the shopping centre not far from town and I just remembered one of the requirements of being a 'Sugar Daddy'. So now we're discussing the weird and wonderful rules of the Sugar world.

"I swear to you. It states that a Sugar Daddy must take his Sugary Sweet on a shopping spree at least once a month to buy her any essentials needed"

"You're making that up!" She laughs and I shake my head, holding my hands up in defence.

"No I promise it's not. I'll show you when we get home"

Even though our relationship has never been of the sugar variety it's still fun to talk to her about it because her reactions are hilarious. It's fun to tease her and she does the same to me.

"I think when we go home I'm going to look at the whole damn list. It just can't be real!" she exclaims animatedly. I can't help but chuckle.

"I'm gonna need to have an ambulance on stand by because you may faint when you read the worst ones" I tell her and she opens her mouth to speak but shuts it again. Instead she shakes her head baffled. It's clear she never did get around to reading any of the sugar rules.

During our shopping trip we'd both bought some new clothes. I'd tried to swipe my card before her but she was too quick and stuck her tongue out at me.

"I win" she grinned which started an all out war on paying for things. I'd won when we got some lunch. She'd won when I picked up some new cuff links. It's a game that

I'm pretty sure no one else has ever played but man it got competitive.

"Do not pay for that!" I almost yelled as she leaned over the counter to tap her card for the third time today.

She's found some lingerie and another object from Victoria's Secret that she wouldn't show me.

The cashier looked between us with a confused expression then raised his eyebrows.

"Is someone gonna pay?" he asked and I used the moment of distraction to beat her to it.

By the time we were done we had so many bags that we could barely carry them between us. Once we got back in the car she turned to me with a triumphant smile.

"How's that for a shopping spree hmm?"

"I've never experienced anything like it. Thank you for the cufflinks" I hummed happily, leaning over to kiss her sweet lips.

"Thank you for the lingerie" she replied, kissing me once on the lips then on the nose.

"What else did you get?" I ask because my curiosity is killing me.

"You'll find out later. First we're going to check out the 'Sugar' rule book. I just have to see it for myself"

So that's what we did. We went to our library with her laptop and had the fire roaring. She snuggled onto my lap and brought up the offending page. Then we began going over the worst and most ridiculous requirements of the website we met on.

"The Sugary Sweet much meet all requests of their Sugar Daddy within reason" she read, her voice laced with annoyance. "I hate it already. You never told me about this one"

"Of course I didn't. I'm not a monster. I have never expected anyone to do as I say. Well apart from my employees" I reply resting my hand on her knee.

"The Sugar Daddy must receive enough sexual intimacy to keep him satisfy" she continues to read, her voice now deathly quiet. "That is messed up!"

"It is definitely" I agree, cringing as the list gets worse.

"This website may as well just call it prostitution and be done. I never knew it was that bad or sordid" she breathes.

"It's bordering on that profession yes. I have tried to ignore those sections. It's very old fashioned" I tell her, hoping that she knows I hate these rules as much as her.

"Have you received enough sexual intimacy? Are you satisfied?" she then asks, turning to face me. Is she serious? I've never been more satisfied in my life.

"You're not my sugar baby Sofia so none of this applies to us. In fact it never has for me. Although if you do want an answer to your question...I don't think I have to give you one. Surely you know. Surely you know just how much you drive me wild" I tell her, squeezing her to me. She has to know.

"Hmmm, I guess I have some kind of idea" she smirks.

"Good. Anyway, it's not just about me is it?" I question nuzzling my cheek against hers.

"No it isn't but I do like to please you"

"And I like to please you too. Look at this section" I reply, scrolling to the part that's more about what the Sugar Daddy needs to give.

"The Sugar Daddy must ensure his Sugary Sweet feels safe in his company" I begin, wrapping her in my arms. "He must also ensure all sexual contact is enjoyable"

"Well I'm so glad that it's in there, although I'm sure some people love to skip over it" she grumbles. I can't help but squeeze her tighter to try and take away her obvious distaste for these statements.

"Yes but it's the most important one isn't it"

"It's definitely not the most important one to most men" she laughs bitterly.

"It's the most important one to me" I assure her, my lips pressing against her neck.

She squirms against me, her hands moving to cover mine on her waist.

"I have to hand it to you. Enjoyable doesn't cover the way you make me feel Elijah" she sighs, closing the laptop and placing it on the side table.

Turning in my lap she straddles me, her hands holding onto my shoulders. I look up at her completely consumed by her soft wanting stare. All different emotions swim in her eyes and I know exactly what she wants.

I know when she wants me to be rough and I know when she wants me to be gentle. We always seem to be in tune with each other, wanting the same thing.

Like right now its very clear we want to go to bed and make love for hours. We want to take our time and drag it out. Make the pleasure last.

"How do I make you feel? Tell me"

I grip her hips, squeezing to control my need for her. She takes a few moments as she thinks about it, a smile turning up her lips.

"You make me feel like the most cherished women on earth or in the whole universe. I feel like I've transcended this planet and been taken to heaven when you're inside me" she whispers. My dick becomes even harder than it already is and my blood pumps faster in my veins. Most importantly my heart soars with joy because I make her feel that way. I make her feel the way she makes me feel. "I know it's super dramatic right?" she blushes.

"No it's not dramatic. I feel it too"

I carry her to bed and we explore every inch of each other's bodies. It's magical and out of this world and that's just the beginning. I haven't slid inside of her yet.

"I guess now I can tell you what I got today" she sighs, coming down from the orgasm I just gave her with my tongue.

"Oh yes, please tell me. I'm dying to know" I reply, nipping at her collar bone with my teeth.

"Wait here" she grins and shifts off the bed to retrieve her purchase. I can't even begin to work out what it is.

When she comes back, she's holding a plastic packet. She returns to bed and holds up the item for me to see. It's a red vibrating cock ring. Well shit I have no complaints.

"I've always wanted to see what these things feels like" she explains. "Apparently it'll be good for both of us"

"It'll definitely be good for both of us" I agree, biting my lip to stop my groan as she tears open the packet.

I lie back so she can straddle my thighs and slide the cock ring down my length. The pressure has me gripping the sheets as it rests at the base of my cock. It's a strange sensation but oh so good.

When she switches it on the vibrating has me gasping, my need to be inside her unavoidable.

"I think I could come just from watching you squirm" she moans as she rolls onto her back and pulls me on top of her.

"Please feel free to come at every opportunity. It's my favourite thing to see" I breath deeply, settling between her legs.

"Don't worry, I'm so fucking close again" she pants and I can't take it anymore. Pushing inside her deeply, the ring presses into her clit and she falls apart beneath me instantly. Fuck she's so beautiful. "Mmmm fuck, yes!" she screams, her fingers digging into my skin.

She feels so damn good around me and my own mouth hangs open in ecstasy. I pull out achingly slow and slide back in the same way. She whimpers in my arms so I stop my movements in case she's uncomfortable from overstimulation.

My fingers clench on the pillow as the ring continues to vibrate keeping me on the edge of my own release. It's like the most lovely torture.

I want her so bad but I won't move an inch until she's comfortable again.

Peppering kisses over her cheeks and down her neck, I soothe her. Even this is blissful heaven.

"Elijah...don't stop" she begs wrapping her legs around my hips, urging me forward.

"Are you sure Darling? I can wait if you need me to" I ask, in case the sensation becomes too much. Too much stimulation can end up painful.

"I'm sure. I promise" she breathes, her fingers moving to the back of my head. She tugs on my hair and seeks out my mouth. My hips jerk in response and I push back inside of her.

God it's so good. She's so good. So amazing. So everything. I fuck her. I make love to her. I could do this forever. I wish I never had to stop...

Opening my eyes, I glare at the bulge in my pants. Of course I'm hard right now. I'm only human and everything in me is attuned and aligned perfectly with her or so my body still thinks.

Throwing my arms behind my head I force them to stay there. I won't jack off to thoughts of her. I can't. I'm not that weak.

Breathing deeply, I clench my fists. I have to pull myself together. I have to ignore the pain.

How many hours has it been since I last saw her? How many hours ago did I believe she loved me? It'll be two days soon. I'd kissed her goodbye and told her to have a nice day at work. If I knew that was the last time I'd see her, I wouldn't have let her go.

Who am I kidding? If she'd told me to my face that she didn't want me anymore I'd have fought for her but I wouldn't have made her stay. My main priority is her happiness...was her happiness! Was! Not now! No!

My dick throbs as I roll over onto my front and smother my head in the pillow. Maybe I'll suffocate and this will all end or maybe I could just relieve the strain in my pants. Will it make me feel better? Probably not but it might take away my nightmare for just a brief moment. I can pretend everything is fine. I can pretend she wants me.

Accepting the inevitable outcome of my desire for her, I roll back again and sigh at the state I'm in. I'm pathetic and desperate...so desperate.

Palming my cock through my trousers, I shut my eyes and think of her. Her beautiful face, her soft inviting body.

"Ah fuck. Sofia..."

I feel no shame in tearing down my zipper and pulling out my cock. My fist immediately begins to move before I can even make the choice. I need this.

My eyes squeeze tighter as I try to fall into a fantasy. My hand is a shitty substitute but my memories of her gorgeous figure help me on.

I imagine her riding me. Her hands on my chest, her eyes full of desire for me. I imagine her moaning my name and smothering my lips with hers.

"Yes, shit!"

My hand moves faster, my hips rising off the bed, thrusting.

My biggest mistake is imagining her saying those words. Telling me she loves me, that she will never leave.

So when I come hard and quick, instead of pleasure it feels more like pain because reality comes crashing back.

I let out an agonising cry and breath deeply trying to pull myself out of such a horribly dark place.

Sitting up quickly, I notice the mess I've made on my own fucking shirt and clamber off the bed. My chest tightens and my head spins, my breathing struggling to flow.

I need to get out of here. I don't want to be here in a random hotel, fuck knows where anymore.

Buttoning my jacket to cover the evidence of my desperate masterbation, I dive into the hallway gasping for air.

What is happening to me? For some reason I'm in flight mode and my legs can't carry me fast enough back to my car.

I'm definitely still not in a good enough state to drive but I get in anyway. Only once the door is locked does my heart rate slow and breathing settle. Running my hands through my hair, I give myself a slap on the cheek.

I'm still alive but what's the point in that?

Turning the car around, I drive in the direction I came from until I recognise how to get home. Only that's not where I end up.

For some reason I pull up to the coffee shop. Okay, I know why I'm here. I want to see if she shows up. I want to know if she actually fucking works here. Or was that a lie too?

Most of all I'm here because I have a crushing need just to see her.

So I wait. It's just past lunch time and I know that if she was at work she would have gotten here hours ago. Yet I don't see her. She doesn't show up either. I held out hope that maybe she would just be in the back and any moment she'd appear for me to see as I sulk in my car.

I'm well aware of how creepy I look but naturally, I don't care about that either.

Seconds before I'm about to give up, I see someone I recognise walking towards the shop. It's fucking Gabe.

It takes everything in me to stay in the car instead of charging towards him so I can beat him within an inch of his life. I need to remember that she may have lied about him too. Only I saw first hand what he's like. After all he tried to fuck with me too.

Well he told me that she wanted my cash. He was right. So I guess he wasn't fucking with me after all.

Before he goes inside he notices my car and I wish I could become invisible. That's impossible though and he turns around and begins walking towards me. Oh fuck. I really don't need this right now. I don't know how much more I can take before I break more shit.

When he reaches my window I reluctantly press the button so it descends.

"She isn't here" he informs me nonchalantly and I already wanna stab his eyes out.

"No shit" I snap.

"Then why are you here?" he asks, making my blood boil.

"None of your business"

"Oh shit. Did she finally do it? Did she finally leave you?" he asks.

In the next second I'm shoving the door open and stepping out. He has to move out of my way but he doesn't get far. Grabbing him by the t-shirt, I slam him into my car. I don't care if people see. I'll kill him.

"What do you know? What did she say to you?" I demand answers, desperate to have something make sense.

"Hey! Dude! She just told me that she didn't wanna be with you no more. That you were overbearing. She's been talking about it for a while" he explains quickly, holding up his hands.

"Do you know where she is now?" I ask, fully aware of how crazy I sound. I sound like an asshole. Like a controlling asshole.

"No I've no idea I swear"

I'm about to let him go but something bothers me. Something doesn't add up.

"You just said that she isn't here. How do you know that if you just arrived?"

The panic in his eyes flares bright and he struggles to push words out.

"Tell me!" I yell, slamming him against the car once more.

"Ummmm, I...I know her rota. She's off today" he struggles and I glare at him trying to work out if that makes sense. She usually has a Tuesday and a Sunday off. This is Friday.

"You're lying! She's not off on a Friday!"

I'm gonna kill him. I'm going to snap him in fucking two! He's a sneaky little prick and I have a feeling that he knows more than he's trying to reveal.

"She changed the day this week! So she could make plans"

"What plans?" I ask even though I already know what he's going to say.

"Plans to get away from you"

Yup. There it is.

Letting go of him, I step back and he scrambles to get away from me. Just like she seems to have scrambled to get away. She wanted to leave so bad she changed her day off. She was desperate to get out.

"Look I'm sorry dude. You seem like a decent guy. Sometimes women are selfish. They don't think of us" I hear but I don't turn around. I'm done with him now.

"Or maybe us men are too self absorbed to notice when we're being far too fucking much for someone" I push out, yanking open the car door and getting back in.

Maybe if I'd payed more attention she would still be with me. Except that doesn't make sense because she's all I paid attention to. So maybe that was the issue. Either way I shouldn't want her now. She didn't want me for me.

Gabe walks away then and I'm really glad. I don't want to hear anything else from him. He's told me enough to add to the hurt I'm already swimming in.

My phone rings and I answer it without looking. I assume it's going to be work related only it's not.

"Elijah? I've still not been able to get hold of her. Have you spoken to her?" It's her Mom again. Fuck sake!

"No I haven't and I probably won't ever again" I reply coldly.

"What? Why? What's going on? I'm worried" she sighs loudly, her frustration obvious. I wonder why Sofia hasn't answered her?

"We broke up. So I can't help you. Please stop calling" I go to hang up again but she stops me.

"Wait! Why did you break up?" she asks, sounding confused.

"Because she didn't want to be around me anymore. She wanted my money and she got it. So she left" I tell her the cold hard truth about her daughter. I mean she probably already knows right?

"Why the hell would she want your money? She doesn't give a shit about money. Never has"

"We met on a sugar daddy website remember? Did you forget that part?" I snap.

"Oh shut up! I know that! That's not what I'm talking about! She really cares about you Elijah, I've never seen her so happy in my life. I know we have our differences and I can be hard on her but god it was so good to see her smile the way she does with you"

What the fuck is going on here? Did she lie to her Mom too?

"Well obviously it wasn't real because she's gone. I haven't seen her in two days. She called me to tell me she was bored of me and that I smothered her" I repeat the words Sofia said, her voice ringing in my memory.

"Men are so fucking dumb I swear" she replies and I'm shocked to hear her cursing. It almost makes me smile because it has me thinking of Sofia obviously. She must have gotten her fiery attitude from her Mom. "Look I don't know what she said to you but I know my daughter better than anyone. She would not use you for money. She wouldn't leave you without telling you how she felt to your face. Trust me!"

I don't know why a zing of hope shoots through me. Hope that I've been wrong. What would it mean if I've been mistaken? What is Sofia doing? No! Her Mom has to be wrong!

"You obviously don't know her as well as you think. I'm sure she will contact you soon enough. Good-"

"Elijah! Don't you dare hang up on me again. If my daughter is in trouble and you are being stubborn and stupid, she will only get hurt more!"

I can't take this anymore. I can't take the way my brain is ping ponging back and forth with different feelings.

"It's not my problem anymore! So kindly fuck off!" I roar and throw my phone in the back seat. I can't do this! I can't!

Clutching my head in my hands I double over as different scenarios play in my head. Has she left me? Or was it something else? Did she lie to me? Is there another reason she had to leave me?

Is she lying to everybody?

Grabbing my phone back, I scroll through my contacts. I have Annabelle's number because she insisted I take it now that I'm part of Sofia's life. Was part of her life...

I'd thought it was weird at the time but now I'm grateful to have such a number.

I wonder if she has spoken to her. Someone must have?

Tapping Annabelle's name I only have to wait a couple of rings until she picks up.

"Heyyyyyy! What's up?! You need my help buying something for Sofia?" she says in greeting and I frown in response. First of all, who asks so many questions upon answering a phone? Second of all, she obviously hasn't spoken to Sofia.

"No, I'm calling to ask if you've heard from her" I reply, pinching the bridge of my nose in frustration. I feel like I'm on a merry go round that won't stop. Pain. Anger. Hope. Disappointment. Over and over.

"Umm nope. I haven't. Why what's wrong?" she asks and I immediately regret calling her. She's gonna ask so many questions. I don't wanna have to explain what happened again.

"Nothing, it doesn't matter. Just let me know if she calls you okay?"

I don't even wait for her to reply before hanging up. Wow, I really am getting rude. I'm the asshole everyone thinks I am. Perfect.

I'm also a weak motherfucker because I know that I won't be able squash the little voice in my head. It keeps repeating how weird it is that Sofia hasn't spoken to anyone close to her in two days. Almost three in fact. Not to mention she isn't answering any calls.

If she needed to leave me and wanted to get away, it would make sense that she'd go to someone she was close to. Then she'd feel safe. Then she could vent and yell about the man who smothered her.

Maybe she wanted a completely fresh start and has used the money I gave her to leave the country? Would she do that without telling anyone? Am I so sure that she hasn't already moved on with someone else?

I hate her. I despise her. I don't want to ever see her again. Except there's nothing more I want than to see her again. Because I need her. I need her to be safe. To be happy even if she took my money and ran.

I have to find her. I won't stop until I do. She needs to be safe.

Sofia

I'm not sure what time it is now. I have to keep guessing. When I'd called Elijah yesterday it had been morning but I'd spent the rest of the daylight crying and falling further and further into a spiralling breakdown.

The hunger pains had come as a welcome temporary distraction from my brains torment. All I could think about was him. What was he doing? Was he okay? What was going on?

I hadn't slept at all. I'd started to count the cracks in the ceiling and tried to do anything to make the pain stop. It never did. It only grew worse with time. My breathing was the only thing that helped me believe I was alive and not in some kind of hell. I just lay there and shivered in the fetal position.

I haven't moved since. Daylight once again creeps through the cracks in the blacked out window above me.

I wish I could close my eyes and fade away or at least fall asleep to forget the way my mind won't stop replaying his voice. There's no chance that'll happen though. Apart from the rock hard cold ground being the only thing I can lie on, I'm simply not able to settle enough.

My brain is still constantly going over and over the dreaded conversation with Elijah because it's the only thing I have left of him now. It's very possible that I'll never speak to him again. Never see him again. Even if I did, he'd only look at me with hate.

That thought has me clutching my sides again, squeezing myself to keep the pain away.

The chain on my angle clinks with my movements and I stare at it in rage. I could just break my ankle to get out of here. I've no idea where I am but I could hobble to find help and get back to Elijah before he does anything stupid like giving that bitch shares in his company. If he hates me fine but I don't want her to take advantage of him. I want to protect him from everything but I can't while I'm here.

I don't even want to think about other stupid things he could be doing. Is he sitting at home hurting? Is he dealing with it better than me? Or is he being reckless?

He may have never admitted his love for me but I know he cared enough to be hurt in some way. Or maybe all he feels is betrayal and I'm nothing to him now. I wouldn't blame him. I used his worst insecurity against him.

I can see his face crumbling in my mind. I can see him cursing the world for fucking him over yet again.

Yanking my ankle hard against the cuff, I pray the chain will break. The metal digs into my skin as I pull and pull. There is nothing here that could aid me in breaking a bone. I know it's an extreme measure to take but I'm fucking desperate.

Not to mention I'm weak from lack of food and water and my pulling power is pathetic.

"GOD DAMN IT!" I scream, the sound echoing through the warehouse. "WHAT DO I DO?!"

I've no idea why I'm shouting at nothing and no one but it feels good.

Turns out I'm not actually alone because those heels start clicking on the concrete floor. Oh great she's back.

"Now now, you don't need to shout" I hear before I see her. God there are many horrible things I want to do to this women.

Around the pillar she appears again, this time on her own. My eyes immediately latch onto the things she's holding because I'm desperate for any kind of information.

A bottle of water, a chocolate bar and an envelope? I think.

"You don't look so good. Rough night?" she asks, her voice sickly sweet. I wonder if she'd sound so cheery if I gouged her eyes out with a spoon? "Not talking to me today?" she muses, then shrugs. I wonder why there's no back up today. She must not see me as much of a threat anymore. I doubt she ever did.

Shuffling with great difficulty from my balled up position, I sit and lean against the wall. Every part of me aches. The same pain in my side that I woke up to the first day flares up. I wonder if someone kicked me in the side while I was passed out?

"Come on it's not fun when you don't speak" she taunts before throwing the water bottle and chocolate bar at me. God I want to guzzle that water but I know that's only going to add to the pressure already in my bladder. I really gotta pee. "Look I don't like you one bit but I have no intention of letting you die. Drink the water and eat the chocolate. You'll get out of here soon. I think"

I don't trust her at all. So I stay silent. I've nothing to say to her. There's no point in asking questions because she won't answer them. I want to know if she's contacted him yet but I doubt he'd have replied so quick.

"Fine. Don't talk. Just listen. You'll be pleased to know that Elijah is already acting rather recklessly like I suspected. I've kept tabs on him for a long time and well now it seems like he's lost his mind. He really must have cared about you" she sighs, shaking her head a little.

I can't help it. I have to ask.

"What has he done? Is he okay?" I bite out quickly, my breath becoming short from my lack of energy.

"Don't worry your pretty little head. Apart from driving drunkenly like a maniac he seems to be just fine psychically anyway"

Oh god no. Drunk driving? Shit! He's going to hurt himself. I can't bare that thought. Why couldn't he have stayed at home and drank?!

"He actually seemed to have a little bit of fun last night" she laughs, dropping the envelope in front of me. "Go on, take a look. He may be missing you but he's definitely trying to get over you quickly. Typical man really..."

That's all she has to say before she walks away, leaving me alone with the envelope. What does she mean he had fun? Something tells me it's not my idea of fun.

Snatching up the envelope my desire to know has adrenaline pumping through me. I rip it open and pull out what's inside.

I don't know what I expected to see but it wasn't pictures. It certainly wasn't multiple pictures of him and another women.

My eyes scan over the photos even though I try to stop looking. No. No way. Really? Already? Did he really care so little about me that he'd fuck someone else so quick? I know I hurt him but wow. WOW!

Bile rises in my throat and I choke on it. It feels like my heart has stopped beating.

The first image is of him outside a hotel room with a blonde women. They're not too close for it to seem inappropriate but that quickly changes. The second one she's grabbing his shirt. I can't look at the third one anymore because my tears and blurring my vision. I saw it though, before I began crying. They're half way in the door and I don't need anymore photos to tell me what happened next.

I don't need to see anymore evidence to know he fucked her. It's obvious.

A tiny voice in my head tries to send hope back to me. It says he's not touching her with his hands. He's not initiating it. But it doesn't matter he's still doing it. He still did it!

In a surge of rage I tear at the images. I'm vicious in my actions making sure they can never be pieced back together.

I lied to him to save his ass! I hurt him to make sure he didn't go to jail. I'm sitting here mentally and physically dying and all he's doing is fucking another women. He's moving on while I'm stuck.

I'm mostly angry because I can't blame him. My tearing stops and my body slumps to the ground again.

I can't breath. I can't think. All I can do is pick up a tiny part of one of the photos. All that's still visible is his face. I can just about make out his blood shot eyes from the drinking.

I want to crush this part in my palm but against my better judgment I clutch it to my chest and cry. I cry and cry until my cheeks sting.

He hates me. He really hates me. Did he ever care? Maybe not if he's moved on so quick.

I don't drink the water or eat the chocolate bar.

Instead I bathe in detrimental agony at knowing that he was never going to love me. He was never truly going to be mine. He never truly cared. He never wanted me.

And he never will.

Sofia

My state has deteriorated more than I want to admit. All I'm capable of is staring at my little picture of Elijah and drifting off into what I assume is sleep. It doesn't feel like sleep though. I just relive memories and have nightmares.

I had to resign myself to relieving my bladder but because of my chain, it's not as if I could move that far from where I sit. So yeah I won't describe the unpleasant smell.

I'd gave in and drank some water earlier this morning. Well I think it's morning. It's getting harder to keep track of the light. This must be day three of captivity but honestly I don't think I'd know the difference between three days and ninety.

Somewhere in the back of my mind I'm aware that if I don't eat soon I won't survive. Although it's not my main priority.

Slipping into a coma and living in a dream world with Elijah is more important. I miss him so much and because I'm so deprived right now it's easier for me to close my eyes and live a fantasy. He doesn't even care about me anymore. I mean that much is clear from those photos. He's probably glad to get rid of me. Yet I still yearn for him. I get jabbed with the reality of my situation and pain courses through my veins. So I keep shutting it off and fading away.

He drove us to the suburbs of Chicago and has yet to tell me why we're here. I know he's planning a picnic because he didn't hide the fact that he was preparing it this morning.

"Come on, I have something to show you" he says, jumping out of the car and retrieving the picnic basket from the trunk. Oh yeah he even got a fancy basket. I know! I love it.

With his free hand he links our fingers and leads me down a street full of houses. After a short while we turn left onto a gravel path and become surrounded by trees.

Through the forest we go as birds chirp and sun shimmers on leaves. It's really beautiful and calming.

Eventually the trees separate to reveal a large expanse of grass. On the right there's a river and beyond that far away houses. Fancy houses.

A few other couples and families are here, their kids running around playing.

I'm dying to ask questions but I try to hold my tongue as Elijah pulls a blanket from the basket and finds a nice stop to put it.

Lying down together with the basket between us, I watch as he begins pulling out lots of yummy food.

Sandwiches, cookies, fruit, CAKE!

Snatching a cookie up, I take a bite while he munches on a sandwich.

"Thank you for doing this. It's lovely" I tell him and wait for him to elaborate on our location.

"You're welcome Darling. Although I wouldn't describe this place as lovely. I spent a lot of time here as a kid trying to escape my fathers' business lessons. That man knew that I'd have to take over his business one day and he made sure I'd know how to deal with it" he explains and all I can do is blink as I take in what he's telling me.

"You lived here as a kid?" I ask dumbly because obviously that's what he's just said. He finishes off his sandwich while my cookie is left hanging between my fingers.

Yes, if you look over there you'll see my old house. The one in the middle" he replies and my eyes follow in the direction he points. The houses I noticed, the fancy ones that are three stories high. The one in the middle is white with black rimmed windows and by the looks of it a black wrap around patio. It's hard to make out from so far away.

Wow he brought me to his childhood town. I'm beyond touched.

"I spent most of my childhood being groomed to become a CEO. I didn't have many friends because of it. This isn't a sob story by the way. I'm sorry, I didn't bring you here to tell you about my sad upbringing. I just wanted to show you because-" he pauses then and looks away as if he can't find the words he's looking for.

"It's okay, I don't mind what you tell me Elijah. I love hearing anything about you. It makes me feel closer to you" I confess and this helps him continue.

"I'm glad you don't mind. You see I was lonely as a kid. I was lonely as a teenager and I've been lonely as an adult too. I was used to it. Then you came along and made my life so much brighter. You've showed me what happiness actually is because I'm not lonely anymore. I'm not sure anyone else could've taken away that feeling except you because it runs deep inside me. The emptiness of no connection...yet you warm me up. You take it away"

I wasn't ready for that. I don't think I could ever have been.

"I'll never let you feel lonely again I promise" is all I can say and I mean it with all my heart.

"I promise you the same. I don't want you to ever feel what I've felt. I want to make sure you're happy...for the rest of my life"

"I love you Elijah" I breath, trying to keep my tears at bay. Can you blame me? This is damn emotional!

"God I can't even explain how it makes me feel when you say that" he sighs leaning into me quickly.

He kisses me then, his lips smashing into mine. I feel his sadness and happiness all in one. I feel his gratefulness and passion.

"You've changed my memories of this place already. Now I can think of this picnic instead of hiding from my father" he laughs, brushing a stray piece of my hair behind my ear. He then cups my cheek, looking far too soft for me to cope with.

"I'm glad I could help you out with that" I smirk and grab a cupcake. I drag the cream all over his mouth and cheeks much to his surprise.

"Mmmm, if that was meant to be mean it really wasn't" he chuckles, licking the cream off his face. Shrugging I swipe some off too and pop it in my mouth.

Taking a can of Coke from the basket, I hand him one too. Then I propose a toast.

"Here's to many more happy memories"

We tap our cans together and I truly believe my statement.

I had no idea I'd be forced to break my promise. I had no idea I'd leave him lonely again.

When I snap back into reality my eyes struggle to focus. They're stinging from the tears of my memory. God I'm so mad that I broke my promise. I despise myself.

When my eyes eventually do focus, I get the fright of my life.

"Oh good you're alive! I thought I'd killed you for a second" Nadia says, inches from my face. She taps my cheek and I flinch as my whole body aches from the slight movement. "Eat! Now! I'll sit here until you do" she snaps, backing away after dropping something in front of me. A sandwich.

I'm not capable of much strategical thinking but I do realise one thing. She needs to keep alive for some reason. I think she's worried she won't be able to hide my body. Or maybe she's worried that Elijah will kill her if he hears on the news that I'm dead. Then again, would he care?

He cared enough before to try and have her charged multiple times for interfering with his company. Would he do something drastic if he knew she'd hurt me. Or would he brush it off?

Either way I think I might be able to barter for some information.

"I'll eat if you tell me how Elijah is"

She rolls her eyes but answers me anyway.

"He's fine" is all she says, so I don't pick up the sandwich. I raise my eyebrows expectantly. "Fucking hell, why do you care? He left the hotel yesterday morning after his...session"

My whole body cringes as I'm once again bombarded with images of him with another women. I'd tried to forget but it's impossible when the remains of the photos lie on the floor. She hasn't commented on my mess yet. I've kept the part of Elijah tucked in my jean pocket. I go from anger to hurt at his betrayal. Even though I have no right to call it that. I broke up with him.

Nadia obviously enjoys my pain because she smiles eerily.

"Then he went home" she finishes and I glare at her. She has missed something out. I know it. "Eat!"

Reluctantly I open the sandwich packet and take a bite. My stomach automatically growls but as I swallow, a bad taste is left in my mouth. It actually makes me feel worse.

So I focus on getting more information before she leaves again.

"Have you contacted him yet?" I ask hesitantly. I don't know if I really want an answer. What if she has? What if he's so upset he's given her what she wants? Or what if he's so uncaring that he's told her to fuck off again. I hope it's the latter even if it means he's already forgotten me.

"I have" she replies before her features darken. She suddenly becomes angry, pacing away from me before pacing back. I've no idea what has just happened but her quick change of mood is extremely scary.

She then reveals something I don't think she meant to.

"He hasn't replied. I sent the email yesterday. Why hasn't he replied? This should have worked! He should be upset but not so fucking upset that he can't work! He's meant to have nothing to live for so why isn't he throwing everything away? He's a fucking mess! I know he is so why hasn't he-"

"I told you he wouldn't give you a fucking thing" I smile. I can't help it. I can't stop the psychotic laugh that breaks from my chest. It's probably partly to do with my fucked up starved and dehydrated brain. The other part is just pure joy at knowing she's failing miserably.

I can't stop laughing. I don't even know how long I keep going but this is the only piece of happiness I'm going to get.

"Don't act so cocky. If he doesn't answer me soon then I'll have to use my plan B" I hear through my cackling and it shuts me up immediately.

I want to tell her that it's technically her plan D. She's tried a few times to get shares already. Or has she forgotten? It wouldn't surprise me because she's crazy.

"What's plan B?"

She doesn't reply. She takes her turn laughing.

"Hopefully you won't have to find out. See you soon"

She walks away and to be honest I'm sick of seeing that sight. Every time she leaves she has always given me something else to be angry or sad about. There's only so much a person can take. I'm shivering. I'm starving and past exhaustion. I'm emotionally ruined.

Yet the only thing that worries me is that plan B could hurt Elijah even more than he already is.

"WHAT'S PLAN B?"

Elijah

Arriving home, I walk past all of the mess I made last night and go straight to my office. Dropping down into my chair I try to work out what my first move will be. How do you find someone that either doesn't want to be found or is in desperate need of help?

I keep going between thinking she doesn't want me to worrying that I'm wrong about it all and something isn't right. I know it's probably the first reason. I'm too scared to wonder or hope that she didn't really want to break up with me. In case it all comes crashing back down.

At the same time I can't hope for that because then it means she's not safe and she hasn't been safe for almost three days now. Fuck!

What I need to do is call the police again then phone Jack. I can ask him to track her phone which is maybe what I should have done to begin with.

I've been so stupid! The moment I felt that something wasn't right I should have tracked it!

My overactive brain chooses this exact moment to remind me of her phone call.

"I'm bored now okay...I'm done pretending to give a shit about you"

Taking a deep breath, I shake my head and try to forget it. I can drown in agony later. Once I know she's safe then I can let all of the hate consume me. I can curse her out.

"All those women only wanted your money and I'm no different from them"

FUCK! YOU WERE DIFFERENT! You never meant that! You wouldn't use me!

Banging my fist on the desk my eyes catch how messed up my knuckles are. Dried blood and peeling skin. My gaze quickly shifts to something else.

An involuntary smile tugs at my lips. The mini figurine of a knight stares back at me. The suit of armour isn't silver like a traditional knight, it's black. It was a gift from Sofia. She said that since I'd told her many times that I'm her villain, she felt that it represented me best. A villain disguised as a hero.

Why the hell did she buy me things? Why did she buy me things that held meaning if she was using me?

None of it makes sense and it seems that I may have to change my MO. I may have to become the hero and save the girl. Or maybe she'll turn out to be the bad guy like my heart is currently feeling is true.

I have to ignore it! I have to push on!

It's time to work this out! It's time to be the hero for now!

***

When I call the police they finally decide that enough time has passed. Now there is need to worry. They tell me they have to get all the information possible which I gladly agree to.

Next up is tracking her phone and Jack is quick to tell me it shouldn't be an issue. I send him her number and let him get to work.

Trying to find her makes my heart less heavy. It helps me forget a little bit about her tearing my heart out. It gives me purpose.

I spend the rest of the day going through every email, text and phone call I have received in case someone has contacted me about her. I call people who owe me favours to do some digging. After all I have no idea how to track someone down apart from the most basic logical ideas.

Her Mom had called me a few times as well as Annabelle, so I spend some time updating them on everything I know. Both parties said they'd help with anything they could and both also called the police to help motivate the situation to urgent in the laws eyes.

I worked well into the early hours of the morning because sleep wasn't possible or needed. I left my apartment at about seven am to go back to the coffee shop. I wanted to catch hold of Gabe again to interrogate him properly. Unfortunately he wasn't anywhere to be found.

My phone constantly floods with new notifications but most of them are work related. I ignore any business calls and try to once again sift through my emails.

Before heading back to the apartment to meet the police officer who is scheduled to question me in a hour, I notice one email that has me stopping.

It was sent last night but I hadn't thought it was strange then. It seemed to be work related. So I hadn't opened it. Now actually reading it, I don't like it one bit. I've no idea who the person is. I've never heard the name but the wording is similar to something that I've read before.

This person wants shares in my business. Someone named Amy Grace. Is that even a real name? The hairs on the back of my neck stick up as a horrible feeling comes over me.

What has Nadia Zoya been up to lately? It's been a good while since she once again escaped arrest for hacking my database. Although I know by now that her being quiet and staying away means nothing. She'd waited a while in between meeting me and the hacking.

I don't like what my gut immediately tells me. This email is rather similar to many of Nadia's...there's no way. This can't be her. She wants my business and that has nothing to do with Sofia. Yet there's a building panic growing inside me.

Calling Jack again, I try to keep my voice even and not panic. As soon as he answers I'm yelling.

"Find out what Nadia Zoya has been up to lately! Make that a priority!"

"Sir, what does this have to do with her?" he questions and I want to crack my phone in two.

"Hopefully nothing but I'm not taking the chance. Find out!" I shout before hanging up and shaking my head wildly. No. It's not her. Just calm down.

I contemplate answering the email but I don't know if that would benefit or hinder Sofia if Zoya is somehow connected. Honestly I'm pretty sure I'm being paranoid but I can't help it. Not when Sofia is involved.

For the next hour I'm at home talking to the police. I do my best to remember every detail. I tell them everything possible about Sofia. I don't want to mention her break up call in case they decide that's the reason she's gone. Of course it more than likely is but if there's a tiny chance I'm wrong then I'm not going to waste it. They have to help me find her even if she's okay. She's okay...

I have to keep repeating that so I don't lose my mind. Then I end up spiralling into the pit of agony right after.

She doesn't want me...

DAMN IT!

I so badly want to believe that she still wants me but I don't want to believe she's hurt. I'm like a fucking yo-yo. One minute I'm trying to hate her for using me and the next I'm fighting rage at the thought of someone laying a finger on her.

When the police officer leaves, Jack calls with bad news. He can't track her phone because it's either turned off or broken. Which only sends chills down my spine. It has me pacing like a mad man. So once again I leave and get in my car. I don't think I've ever been back and forth this much in my life. Staying at home too long makes me crazy especially when all of her stuff is everywhere. Going out makes me feel lost because I don't know what to do.

I feel useless.

Something I hadn't thought of before comes to me this time though. The storage unit... it has all of her things apart from the personal belongings that are in the apartment.

If she's left me and moved somewhere else or went somewhere to start fresh then surely she'd take something with her. My stupid heartbroken brain couldn't function before. It couldn't think about these things but now with a little hope blooming I'm able to get shit done! Just...

That heartbroken brain is just waiting to take control again as soon as I find her happy and moving on. Which is ultimately what I want. I want her to be happy and if I can't make her that way then someone else needs too.

Why? Why am I still thinking this way when she literally told me she wanted my money...fuck knows. I'm insane.

Reaching the storage unit, I have to take deep breath as I walk to the allocated space. What if it's all gone? What will I do?

It takes a huge amount of effort for me to put the code in the padlock and pull up the shutter. I actually brace for what I'm going to see.

Only the air leaves my body in shock and relief with a side of panic as my eyes take in the completely untouched items. It's exactly the same way we left it.

She has taken nothing. Maybe she just wanted to leave in a hurry? My insecurities spike and I'm thrown into sadness all over again. Was I that bad that she didn't even wanna stop to collect anything? I can't have been. I can't...

Slamming the shutter back down with the frustration of one hundred men, I march back to the car.

Positive thinking! This is a good sign isn't it? Well no actually it isn't. No matter what the outcome of this situation, it's gonna be bad. There is no positive thinking or ending to this because she either hated me and ran or she's been forced to leave.

Before getting back in my car, I lean against the wall and look up to the sky.

"I hope you've left me Darling. I hope you're just starting fresh somewhere because if you're not, if you're in pain...I'll tear the world apart to avenge you. I make everyone pay"

***

With nothing else to do I head back to the apartment for the last time. All I can do now is wait for information from the police, Jack, or one of my other contacts. Jack hasn't gotten back to me about Nadia's activity and sitting here doing nothing is going to kill me.

So I focus on tidying up a little. I sweep up some broken objects and pick up things that have survived. To my surprise the Funko Pops are still in tact so I end up standing in the middle of the room examining them. I don't know what I'm doing.

Dropping the Spider-Man figure onto the coffee table, I take the Harley Quinn one with me to the bedroom. I put her on the dresser so she's safe from the rest of the rubble.

Then I lie on my side of the bed and try my best not to shove my face in her pillow. Fuck, I miss her so much. I miss everything about her.

The way she smiles, her voice, her smell. I miss her warmth next to me. I want to hear her talking about the new drink she tried to make while at work. I want to hear how pissed she is that the latest series we watched had a shitty ending.

It's funny how she's the person I'd go to for help in a situation like this. I may act like a powerful man by day but by night all I want is my girl to be here and to tell me everything will be okay.

Pulling out my phone I find our text conversations. Scrolling a little I get to the last voice note she sent me. God this is gonna hurt but I wanna hear her.

With a think swallow, I press play.

"Soooo, the answer is no. She wasn't the murderer. Who would have thought it?! Certainly not me! Oh! I made pancakes for no particular reason but I've kept some for you when you get home. To answer your question, work was as amazing as ever. That's sarcasm by the way. I made coffee. A lot of coffee. I hope you don't have to work too late tonight, I'd very much like some cuddles. Okay, please drive safe for me. See you soon"

That night I was supposed to have two other meetings after I received that voice note. I think it was about six pm. Sure they were important meetings that I knew would be hard to reschedule but I'd cancelled them anyway. My girl wanted cuddles and I had to make sure she got them. I didn't tell her what I'd done because I know she'd tell me off. She'd say she wasn't worth it but dear god she was so worth it!

She will always be worth it. It's quite possible that she could tell me she hated me everyday for the rest of my life and I'd still answer the phone to hear her say it.

It doesn't matter if she's used me because I can't stop feeling what I do. I'd go to the ends of the Earth a million times even if it was just to have her look at me in disgust.

That's how bad I've got it. That's how much I need to be in her presence.

I know it's pathetic. I know it's wrong.

I know that if I find her and all her words were true then I'll have to let her go.

And I will let her go. While keeping her in my heart.

With that thought I roll over onto her side of the bed. I'm hit with her scent and immediately it brings me a little bit of peace.

It may be just a little bit but it's enough to lull my exhausted body to sleep. While my mind keeps very much awake.

All I see is her. All I dream of is her. All I need is her.

Darling, please don't leave me.

Sofia

Day Four. Am I dead? Am I asleep? I hope it's the first one. I mean what's the point in living. There's only pain and sadness. There's only men who claim to adore you but move on two seconds later. There's only me being stupid enough to have been made to hurt one of those men.

It's all pointless and I want it to end.

I'm not sure when I last opened my eyes but honestly I don't think I can anymore.

I wonder how much longer it'll take for me to die? I've heard dying of starvation is painful and slow. Perfect! How reassuring.

Is dying of a broken heart any easier? I doubt it.

Now and then I remember Nadia talking about a plan B. I'm never able to think about it for any length of time because my train of thought keeps changing rapidly. So therefor I can't even begin to work it out.

Drip. Drop. Drip. Drop.

What is that?

Cold. Wet.

I feel something tricking down my face. That trickle turns into a full splash of water that shocks me, my eyes wrenching open. I groan in pain as my body jerks.

A sharp sting hits my cheek as I struggle to become aware of my surroundings again.

"Get up! Get the fuck up"

Angry. Male. No thank you.

"GET UP!" he yells. This time my brain registers something. The voice is familiar...

My eyes lock onto Nadia's muscle man as he takes a hold of my shoulders and yanks me into a sitting position. My bones scream.

He's still wearing a ski mask but there's something about him that I recognise. Something I can't quite pin point with my tired mind.

He's going to hurt me.

There's nothing I can do. Coupling my condition with the icy fear that fills me, I've no chance of fighting back.

Only he moves away once I'm leaning against the wall. He squats down to my level and holds out a phone in his palm.

What is going on now? Is this not enough? Has Elijah given up his business yet? I hope not.

"Sofia, listen up" Oh great Nadia. "Unfortunately for you I'm having to go to plan B. I wish I could say I feel sorry for you but I don't. I feel sorry for myself that it's gotten this difficult"

I wish I could feel something but my fear is gone and it's replaced with my now constant emptiness and indifference.

"The lovely man with you now is going to do me a favour. He's going to make you look worse than you already do. Then he'll take a nice picture and send it over to me. You see this is all I have left. I'm ashamed to say that this plan failed and Elijah clearly is more obsessed with you than I thought. So obsessed that he hasn't been able to accept you've left him. So obsessed that he can't answer his fucking emails. Therefore I'll give you back to him. I'll call him personally and send him the picture with it. I'll tell him that if he ever wants to see you again then he'll have to give me the shares. If he agrees then I'll give him your location and you can live happily ever after. If he doesn't...well then you'll be left there to rot and die. Sorry about that"

Well that's changed my attitude. Very slowly her words sink in. I'd rather rot. I'd rather die here if it means everything he's worked for is safe. I'm not worth it. I'm really not. Also...does she realise she's messed up?

Clearing my throat, I attempt to speak.

"You d-o realise th-at..." wow I have to stop just to breath. "You've ma-de him hate m-e. He won't...he won't c-come for me. Not now"

God that was far too much of an effort. Weak does not cover how I feel.

"You're so stupid. You think that one phone call was gonna make him hate you? He seems to love you. I know that makes him a fucking idiot but it works in my favour"

"Jokes on y-ou. He doesn't l-love me"

Sucker! She really has messed up. She's assumed that Elijah fell in love with me. That he still loves me. Well that's not possible. It never was possible and I was stupid to think I was the one that could help him love.

Being with him felt better than love though...

"We'll see about that won't we. It was nice spending time with you Sofia. Maybe we'd be friends in another life. Good luck, I kind of hope you don't die. Actually...that's a lie. One more thing...you'll be pleased to know that you're already acquainted with my friend who's with you now...have a nice life"

The line goes dead and the very man she mentioned drops the phone. My blood runs cold, my eyes squinting to try and make out any of his features. All I can see is his eyes and mouth.

Only not for long. In the next second he reaches up and every so slowly pulls the ski mask off.

My breath is stolen from my body. My world crumbles. With the tiny piece of energy I have left I try to shift away from him.

Brian...

"My whole family no longer speaks to me because of you! You ruined my whole fucking life because you couldn't keep your mouth shut!" he sneers. "Well now I'm going to ruin yours"

I open my mouth to scream but no sound comes out. Seconds later there is a sharp pain in my stomach and my eyes widen in shock. Brian pulls back his fist and there's nothing I can do to stop the impact.

I guess it's over for me.

Elijah

    For some reason having slept all night hasn't made me feel better. I still feel exhausted. I feel wrong. Maybe waking up at five twenty six am and immediately snatching my phone up doesn't help.

All I can think about is pushing forward. Needing more information. The desire lives in my veins.

The first thing my eyes latch onto is an email sent by one of the business contacts I called yesterday. They specialise in CCTV and other types of security so I'm not surprised to find a video attached.

No not surprised. Terrified. Sick. What is it? Have they found a video of Sofia in her new life?

The milliseconds the video takes to load drives me fucking insane. My fingers twitch and my heart beats out of my chest.

Then I stop breathing and it plays.

There she is. Outside of the coffee shop four days ago at five pm. The low quality video doesn't do her justice. I can't help but devour every part of her I can see. My heart does somersaults in my chest.

Where you waiting on a cab to take you away from me?

Suddenly a black van appears in shot and I shoot up off my bed.

"No!" I shout at the screen as my girl is manhandled and thrown in the van. "NO!"

I can't breath. I can't move. I'm consumed with self hatred and ground breaking regret. I'm filled with rage and agony.

"WHERE IS SHE?!" I yell at no one, my hands pulling on my hair as if to pull out all of my thoughts that bombard me. I have to find her.

I was all wrong. It's all been wrong. This is all my fault! I should have believed the wrongness in her voice when she told me I smothered her. I should have kept her safe but no, I had a break down and wallowed in self pity when god knows what happened to her!

"NOO! FUCK!"

I'm about to launch my phone at the wall and tear the universe apart to find her. I'm about to kill anyone that gets in my way. Only the phone rings.

The number is unknown and I waste no time answering it. I don't care who it is but it could be something that I need to hear. It could be one of my connections calling to tell me they've found her.

Please! Please!

"Hi Elijah" The sickly sweet voice rings in my ears and my human exterior cracks, leaving behind a monster. A primal beast who's mate had been stolen. It's her! Nadia! Again! I know immediately she's taken my girl. I didn't think she'd ever go this far but clearly I've underestimated her.

"WHERE THE FUCK IS SHE?! I WILL KILL YOU IF YOU'VE HURT HER DO YOU UNDERSTAND ME. I WILL BE THE MURDERER EVERYONE THINKS I AM!" I shout, my fingers almost breaking the phone.

"Oh easy there tiger. I don't really like your tone. I'm kind of annoyed that you seem to think I've done something wrong. Maybe I'm just calling to ask how you are"

"I'D HAVE TO BE INCREDIBLY STUPID TO ASSUME YOUR CALL IS NOT RELATED TO SOFIA. I DIDN'T THINK YOU'D STOOP THIS LOW. THIS IS NOT ABOUT HER"

"Okay fine. I took her. I wanted to be the one to break the news though and make you shit yourself. I'm pissed I didn't have that privilege and I'm annoyed you worked it out. Anyway... of course it's about her! She matters to you and that means she's leverage. You should have given me what I wanted to begin with"

"You want the shares? Fine you can have them. Just let her go" I growl, my whole body crackling with aggression.

"I want it all now. Your whole busin-" she begins but I cut her off not giving a fuck what she wants. She can have it all for all I care. I just want Sofia back!

"DONE, JUST LET H-" I shout but she cuts me off in turn.

"Wow, that was easier than I thought. Meet me at your building in your office in twenty minutes. No police, no nothing. Just you. When you sign all the documents to hand over your business I'll tell you where she is but not a moment earlier" she replies sounding far too triumphant. It only makes me less sane.

"FUCKING TELL ME NOW!" I rage but she only tuts down the line.

"Do as I say and stop shouting or I'll leave her where she is. I'll tell you nothing. Meet me like I said and do nothing I don't like and you'll get her back. Oh just in case you have a change of heart, you should check your emails. It'll motivate you to keep on track"

I don't get a chance to shout anything else because she hangs up.

In seconds I'm opening a new email in my inbox. The photo I'm met with has me stumbling backwards and falling into the bedside table.

It's Sofia. She's passed out against a dirty wall, her face bloody and bruised. Tears stain her face and her arms lie by her sides limp and unmoving.

A sob breaks from my throat as I thud to the floor. I don't want to look anymore but I can't tear my eyes away.

"No no no no no"

My own tears cascade down my cheeks. She looks dead. She can't be dead. Nadia didn't say she was alive though.

I've never felt such a surge of terror. I've never wanted to die so much myself.

The thought of her no longer being alive...no longer breathing, has me clutching my sides. I psychically feel the overwhelming grief rip through me.

My eyes catch the caption attached to the photo seconds before I lose myself.

'Don't worry. She's breathing...for now'

Elijah

I'm at my building within six minutes and I don't even bother to park correctly before getting out of the car. Ramming my passcode into the keypad, I enter through the back door.

There won't be anyone here yet because it's six am and the first employees start at nine. Forty floors and thousands of staff. Yet it's empty, just like I feel.

It's actually quite eery as I step into the elevator. Everyone who works here and in other buildings I own now have uncertain futures because soon they will work for Nadia.

Maybe I should feel guilty. Maybe I should care that I'm going to give away everything my father worked for but I don't. Not one bit. Nadia can fire them all and burn the place to the ground and it still wouldn't faze me. Not when Sofia is in danger.

Stepping out on the top floor and into the lobby I walk to my office. Probably for the last time.

Losing my company means losing my assets and my millions. Only that doesn't scare me. What scares me is losing Sofia. I won't survive that.

What will I be without my money anyway? Useless. The only thing I'm good for is money. That fact is still true.

My heart swells as I realise that she didn't mean what she said. She doesn't want my money. I don't know what happened exactly but I'm going to assume that Nadia made her say it.

I feel ashamed that I believed it. I feel like the worst human on Earth now that I know my girl was suffering while I cursed her out.

She might not want me after this. She might blame it all on me like I do. However, I will spend the rest of my life trying to make it up to her. Nothing will be enough but I have to try.

I'm not even contemplating another outcome than me finding her alive. I simply can't think of any other ending. I can't cope with it.

If Sofia wants to beat me until I'm bloody and bruised so that I get to feel the pain she has felt then I'll gladly let her. I want that pain. I want to take it all away from her so bad.

In my office I fall into my chair and immediately get the pile of papers I need. I know these documents should be kept in a safe but instead they're merely in a locked drawer. That's because I've always wanted them next to me. They're my failsafe. They are meant to be there to be signed by someone who I deem good enough to take my business over when I no longer can run it.

I hadn't decided who that person would be yet. I haven't ever thought about it too much. Although if I really am honest with myself I'd have asked Jack one day. He's the only person I trust besides Sofia. I'm fairly certain she wouldn't want to run a business so it would have to be him.

I guess even as Sofia said those horrible words to me, it really never broke my trust at all.

I wish Nadia hadn't said twenty minutes. I wish she was here now so we could get this done. I need to be with Sofia. I need to take her to the hospital.

I've no idea how Nadia is going to get into the building but I'm assuming that she's worked that part out. If she can hack my database then she can crack the door codes. Well she better have cracked them because I don't want to waste another second messing around.

As I click a pen to use the office door opens and my eyes snap up. I see her and want to kill her instantly, however she's not alone. The person she's with I may actually want to kill more because he tampered with my chances of getting to Sofia quicker. He told me he didn't know where she was. He lied to my face while she suffered immensely.

Gabe.

I've no self control.

Leaping from my seat, I step around my desk and march towards him. My fist pulls back and he tries to move away from me. He has no where to go.

I punch him right in the jaw, twice in quick succession. It's not enough. I want to hurt him more. He whimpers in pain and makes no move to fight back. It seems his cowardice isn't a lie.

I almost get to hear his face breaking again under my knuckles but Nadia pipes up, reminding me that she has the power.

"Cut it out! Or I'll have those punches repeated on that women of yours"

"She's had enough!" I roar turning to her with more rage than I've ever felt. I've never hit a women before but I'd gladly beat the shit out of her.

She looks afraid for a nano second before she recovers.

"Do as I say!" she snaps and it takes everything in me to stop. The image burned into my mind of Sofia is what makes me return to my seat.

I watch as they approach but stay at a reasonable distance. Wise choice.

"So yeah, Gabe is working for me. I sent him to get close to Sofia. I wanted him to find out all he could about her and anything about you that I didn't already know. My original plan was to have him seduce her but that's simply impossible when she's so obsessed with you. What did you do to the poor girl? Brainwash her?"

I'm not even going to bother answering her question. I need to use all of my energy to keep myself from getting back out of this seat and killing them both. I'm not actually that shocked that she planted Gabe into our lives. It makes perfect sense. Now I understand why he acted so weird with my girl. The fact that he was there to seduce her drives me mad. Yet the thought that she wasn't interested makes my heart thud faster. I can't help the primal need to yell 'she's mine'. Because she is. Just like I am hers.

"I don't care about any of that now. I'm going to sign these documents and so are you. Then you're going to tell me where the fuck she is!" I growl, my fist tightening on the pen as I grab it.

"Now now, this won't be any fun for me if I don't get to tell you all the juicy parts" she puts on an annoying whiny voice and the pen snaps in my hand. I'm going to break any second. "What else do you need to know? Hmmm...oh yes. That women you fucked at the hotel...I hired her to seduce you too"

Jesus Christ. She really is insane and desperate. What was the purpose of that?

"I didn't fuck her. So I guess that failed" I push out, shivering in disgust as I remember the woman who pretty much attacked me.

"What? Of course you did. I know you did! I had you followed. She went into your room" she gasps and I smirk at her dismay. Ha, aren't happy about that are you?

"She pretty much tried to assault me before I was able to make her leave. I guess she lied to you huh? Bet that sucks! What did you think you'd achieve anyway?" I question before regretting asking. I don't have time for this.

"I wanted to know how reckless you were. I needed to know if my plan was working. If you were weak or not. I also wanted to see if using Sofia for leverage would work. I assumed if you fucked someone else then it would mean you didn't care"

"If you thought I fucked someone else then why are you still using her as leverage? Why not let her go?!" I yell again, slamming my hand on the desk. "And how the fuck did you get her to lie to me? What did you do to her?"

I can't take this. I want to know everything all at once. I want to know what crimes I need to avenge.

"You didn't answer your emails. You didn't give me what I wanted so I had to resort to this anyway. As for your second question, it was really simple. I just told her that if she didn't do as I said then I'd make sure you got locked away. Apparently she couldn't bare that thought"

If I thought my feelings for Sofia couldn't grow any stronger then I was wrong. She did it to protect me. She lied to me to keep me safe. No one has ever protected me...

FUCK!

"Are you done now? Can we get on with this?"

The next voice I hear is Gabe's. He hasn't said a word until now.

"It's really sexy isn't it? How intelligent she is?"

Does he have a death wish? He must have. Gritting my teeth, I glare at him without a word. Where is he going with this?

"She knew there was something wrong with me. She knew that I was a threat. I could tell. It was fun to hear her talk about you too. She's so in love it's sickening. She'd do anything for you. She didn't give me any information about you. Not a word. Yet, what did she get in return for her loyalty? A man who wasn't there to save her from danger. A man who so easily believed she wanted his money even after all you've been through" he mocks.

The self loathing that I've felt all my life manifests in that moment. It turns into a living breathing being swirling it's way around my organs. I have no come back. I have nothing to say that could possibly be good enough.

Because he's right. I wasn't there to save her and I did believe what she told me. I believed she wanted my cash all because she used one of my insecurities against me. I failed her.

I'm not good enough for her. She deserves so much better than me.

Gabe says nothing else. He doesn't have to because he's succeeded in his goal of torturing me.

I sign the papers. No words are spoken. In fact the rest of the exchanges are done in silence. Nadia doesn't need to say anything more to hurt me because she seems pleased with Gabe's achievement.

Usually in cases like this there would be plans made and boundaries set but I don't give a fuck what she does.

Nadia takes the pen and signs in her designated spots. She takes her copy of the contract and moves away from the desk.

My icy glare asks all the questions I need answers too without any sound.

"Pleasure doing business with you. Here's Sofia's location" she says simply, holding out a folded piece of paper. Really? Is that it? I don't trust her. "Oh I forgot to mention. That cousin of hers, Brian? Yeah he really loved beating the shit out of her. I've no idea what he's got against her but it worked out for me" she smiles.

What? No! How the fuck does she even know about Brian?

Oh Sofia baby, I'm so sorry! I'll hunt him down too!

"You're going to hell Nadia. I'll make sure of that" I growl but she only rolls her eyes.

"Look, you can waste more time making empty threats or you can go now. I don't actually want her to die even if it would mean you'd be in the worst pain imaginable.

Oh and covering up my tracks would be much harder if there's a dead bod-"

I don't wait for her to finish. I snatch the paper and run out of the office as fast as I can. Then I stab the elevator button. The stairs would take far too long.

I'd love to call the police and have Nadia arrested right now but I don't want to risk anything until I have Sofia safe in my arms again.

Although I will need to call them about Sofia's location and for an ambulance.

As the elevator arrives, I unfold the paper and read the address.

2505 S Pulaski Road
Industrial Estate
Building 27

I've never heard of such a place but that's irrelevant.

As soon as I've descended to the ground floor I call both the police and for medical assistance so that they will both be there when I arrive too.

In my car I input the address into my navigation system and curse in annoyance as it tells me that I'm forty two minutes away.

I'll cut that time in half if it's the last thing I do.

I'm an absolute wreck as I cut people off and hop lanes line a maniac. It's still early morning but soon it's going to get busy and the last thing I need is traffic.

"FUCKING MOVE!" I shout as the car in front of me does thirty in a sixty. Not that speed limits matter to me right now. I'm once again pushing my car to its limit. Only this time I'm not being reckless. No this time it's really fucking important.

The navigation ticks down the time left between me and Sofia. It's so slow, too slow.

So I try not to look at it.

Instead I focus on the directions it gives and pull off the freeway by cutting over three lanes. The horns of angry motorists don't faze me one bit. On the best of days I'm not a polite driver.

Sofia always tells me off for it. If she were here right now she'd be telling me that I'm a dick. Which I love and I wouldn't have it any other way.

Sweat drips down my back but not because of the heat. It's because I'm so tense and terrified. I'm scared to see her in person. I'm scared that she's worse off than I think. Which would be bad considering she looks extremely unwell.

But she's alive! She's alive...

I keep that mantra going in my head as the estimated time of arrival clicks down.

Fifteen minutes...

Ten minutes...

Five...

Then my car is skidding into an industrial estate that looks like it hasn't been active in years.

My eyes catch onto the blue flashing lights in the distance and I shove on the accelerator harder. The police have gotten here before me.

But where the hell is the ambulance?

As I jump out of the car with my heart in my throat, a police officer uses bolt cutters to snap the chain keeping the huge sliding doors locked.

The building is half collapsed at one side and the windows are all broken. She's been in here...for days. I want to be sick all over again like I did in the hotel room but I swallow back the feeling.

"Are you Mr Everett? The person who called us? You also reported Miss Westwood missing?" The police officer asks and all I can do is nod, desperate to get inside. "I suggest you stay out here until we check out the situation" he continues and I almost laugh in his face. That's never going to happen.

Yet I stay quiet as if I'm agreeing. I'm practically bouncing on my toes with the need to run to her.

Two officers pull at the rusty doors and they open with a loud rattling noise. As soon as there is a gap big enough for a human, I'm running through them.

"Sir! Stop!"

Not possible.

My eyes search frantically as I fly through the beaten up warehouse. Nothing but rubble, rusted metal work and pillars are visible.

"SOFIA!" I yell and it echoes through the place.

Where are you?!

I can hear the footsteps of the police officers coming behind me but I keep going deeper into the building. Right to the other side.

Here there is less rubble and a lot of empty space. My running slows down and my eyes continue to scan.

Passing the last pillar on the left I'm about to lose my shit thinking that Nadia has given me a false address.

Then I see her.

My sanity disappears. My feet pounding hard concrete to get to her.

"Sofia!" I shout as I reach her. My breathing catches as I take in her injuries in real life. It's horrifying. Unlike the photos she's lying down instead of sitting up. It's makes me panic more than ever.

What do I do?!

"WHERE THE FUCK IS THE AMBULANCE?" I scream knowing the officers will hear me because they're just arriving behind me.

My eyes latch onto her chest desperate to see it moving as she breaths. I collapse to my knees next to her and hover my hand over her mouth.

"Come on baby, you're going to be okay" I say out loud but I think it's more for my own damn comfort. My other hand presses gently behind her ear.

God awful seconds pass but suddenly I can feel her pulse and the slight air that feathers over my hand as she breaths.

"Oh god, thank you!"

My need to really touch her, hold her and keep her away from harm is so fucking overwhelming but even I know that I could do her more damage if I move her.

So instead I brush my fingers over her cheek. My skin tingles and I want to sob with relief. I never thought I'd see her again.

"Sir, please step away from her. We don't know what injuries she has" an officer calls from behind me.

"I'm aware of that!" I snap before softening my voice once more. "Can you hear me Sofia?" I ask even though it's pretty clear she's unconscious. I just had to try anyway.

Leaning down I press a kiss to her forehead then force myself to move away.

My fists clench at my sides and I want to scream at the paramedics for taking so fucking long.

Only they arrive in the next five seconds and my nerves calm a tiny bit.

It's hard to watch as they work around her. They also try to get a response like I did but there's no reply. They attach things to her and put an oxygen mask over her mouth and nose.

All I want to do is ask questions. I want updates. I need to know what's going on. Yet the only question I get out is the most terrifying one.

"Is she going to be okay?"

With a sympathetic look the female paramedic says:

"We can't confirm that right now. What we know so far is she has broken ribs and a fractured wrist. We don't know if there is any brain damage or internal bleeding. More tests can be done at the hospital"

I almost faint right there. She didn't deserve any of this. I did this to her! The only thing that keeps me upright is that I need to make this right. I want to nurse her back to health and make those who hurt her, hurt worse.

As she is pulled and strapped onto a stretcher I vow that Nadia will feel that pain. She will feel it and then some.

I've probably vowed this one hundred times over in my head already. Every time I've meant it. The desire to hurt her growing stronger each time.

She's going to pay.

And my girl has to survive because if she doesn't...if she doesn't then...well I simply can't go there.

I'm the problem in Sofia's life. If she hadn't met me then this wouldn't have happened.

As soon as she's well again I'll make sure that I'm not around to put her at risk again. I'll make sure she never has to worry about money ever again. I'll set up a saving account before I go bankrupt.

Because the only thing I want more than Sofia being with me, is her being happy. I want her to live and dream and discover.

If I'm a danger to her life then she needs to leave me behind. It'll kill me but she has to do it.

I want to watch her thrive and shine. Even if it means I'll live the rest of my life in hell.

Sofia

It's loud. Far too loud to make any sense. Beeping. Voices. My own breathing that confuses the hell out of me.

I don't know if the reason my eyes are shut is because I can't open them or because I haven't tried.

I can however move my fingers and wiggly my toes. Where am I? Where was I before? It's hard to tell.

Although my brain seems to be coming back to life slowly. So far it's enough to do a full body assessment. The conclusion...everything aches. I can feel something on my face but it doesn't stop my ability to breath.

There's something in my arm, something that isn't usually there.

"She should wake up soon. Try not startle her with too many questions. She may need a little while to understand what's happened" I hear and I wonder who this person is talking about.

I don't recognise the female voice or maybe I do and I've forgotten.

Oh! She! She is me. The beeping is coming from a machine. A machine in...a hospital? Yes! That sounds correct. Well it seems that I may actually be alive or this is a passageway to the afterlife.

"If she tries to get up please reassure her that she's okay. She's going to be in quite a bit of pain from the broken ribs especially. I'll come back later with more painkillers"

"Thank you so much"

Huh. That voice. The second one. I know it.

Mom? How can my Mom be here with me? She lives hours away. Why is she visiting? Beep beep. Oh yeah... hospital. I'm injured.

A flash of memory overloads my brain and my fingers squeeze against my palm. Brian...he kept hitting me. God it hurt. I never thought he'd stop.

Why did he hit me? What did I do? Nothing. He did it because he's always enjoyed making me feel pain.

But why was he there? Who else was involved?

Come on brain. You can do this.

The harder I think, the higher the wall in my brain rises. So I stop thinking and focus on the sound of my breathing.

"Come on Sofia. You need to wake up. It's no fun without you to talk to"

This voice is different...oh my god. Bree?! What is going on? Have my whole family came to see me? All because I've been beaten up. Honestly I don't think I'm worth the bother.

My line of thought is interrupted as more memories zip across my minds eye. It's too much all at once.

Nadia. The warehouse. The pain. The blackmail. A conversation. Lies. Leverage. Shares. Business. Tears. Photos...photos of someone.

ELIJAH!

My eyes fly open and I immediately squint against bright white lights. Jesus Christ!

Automatically my hand flies up to remove the obstruction from my face. Which I now realise is an oxygen mask. That I clearly don't need anymore. I hope.

"Oh Honey, you're awake!" I hear as my eyes start to adjust. My Mom comes into view, her cheeks slightly red. Her watery eyes give away that she's been crying and I wonder why.

"Are-" I try to speak but my throat is hoarse. So it takes me a minute but I finally get the words out. Lifting the mask I say:

"Are you okay? Why are you crying?"

Her expression changes then to shock.

"Am I okay? Of course I am. You should be worrying about yourself" she smiles, her hand reaching out to stroke my hair.

I don't ask why I should be worried. I just flick my eyes to the right a little and find Bree's grinning face.

"You are badass! Girl you went to war with a villain!" Bree exclaims her hands animated. I don't feel badass. I feel a little broken. Plus there's something I've forgotten again. My brain doesn't have the mental capacity to focus on more than one thing right now. So as they talk to me it takes up all the room. What was it?

"I'm so glad you're okay. You terrified us. Apparently you're lucky to just have some broken ribs and a fractured wrist. The CT scan came back clear. No internal bleeding just a hell of a lot of bruising to add to the broken bones" my Mom explains. That's when I glance at my other hand and see it wrapped in a supportive splint. Kinda like a cute little glove with Velcro. Not bad.

It occurs to me then that if I'm in hospital that means that Nadia revealed my location. If she revealed my location then that means...that means...damn! What does that mean?

It's like the cogs in my brain need oiled. They're a little stuck right now.

"How long has it been since I was found?" I ask trying to put the pieces together.

"About twenty four hours now. You arrived yesterday at about eight am" my Mom answers.

"Who found me?"

I feel like I should know the answer to that. It feels important.

"I did"

My eyes snap to the new voice in the room and I see a dishevelled looking man. His gaze bores into mine, guilt coming off of him in waves.

The final pieces click in my head and I'm overcome with a tsunami of emotions. Tears prick my eyes as I try to focus on the most prominent feeling. It's really fucking hard when I'm going through a wheel of hurt, anger, relief, joy, worry, desire and undeniable happiness. He's okay! And he's here! He came for me!

Elijah!

Dear god I've missed you so fucking much!

Elijah

Waiting...I hate waiting for anything. So having to wait for the most important person in my life to wake up is something that I haven't been coping with well.

They hadn't let me in the ambulance with her so I'd followed it to the hospital and stayed with her as far as I could. Until I was separated from her and she was taken to get all the necessary tests done. I'd demanded the best doctors possible, which only earned me a disgruntled look from one of the nurses. She took great pleasure in shutting me out of the room where Sofia lay.

She hadn't moved or shown any sign of life other than breathing. It made me crazy. I'd have done anything to see her open her eyes.

I wanted to smash the window that gave me a view of her being poked and prodded. I knew it was for the best of course but that didn't stop my desire to protect her from such inspections.

My eyes stayed glued to her until the blind was pulled down and I was completely cut off.

I'd just gotten her back and I was losing her again. I had no idea if she was going to be okay and that made me frantic and terrified. So I tried to distract myself. I paced the corridors outside of the room and called all of the necessary people. Her parents said they were leaving immediately and Annabelle told me she was only ten minutes away. There was probably more people who would need to know that she is in hospital but I hoped her parents could deal with that. I had no more points of contact.

Sitting twiddling my thumbs, I was relieved when the police officers asked to question me. It meant it could focus on getting Nadia locked away and ensure my girl could never be hurt again. Hopefully it meant Gabe and Brian could pay too.

With Sofia as safe as she could be I'd told them everything. Even stuff that they probably didn't need to know. It felt good to speak to them because this time the police seemed a lot more interested than the previous times I've tried to get Nadia charged. This time she'd done a lot worse.

Of course I wanted to do a lot more than put her in jail but aside from killing her myself that's the best I had. I didn't want revenge for myself, I wanted justice for Sofia.

Upon finishing the interview the same nurse from before informed me it was good news. To say I almost collapsed with relief is an understatement. I felt the lightheadedness swim through my brain before I collapsed into a chair.

She hadn't sustained any serious injuries apart from broken ribs and a fractured left wrist. There would be bruising but there was no internal bleeding or brain injury. In that moment I thanked a god I didn't believe in.

Naturally I'd asked when I could see her? When was she going to be awake? What can I do to help her?

The nurse then replied that she didn't know when she would wake up. Only time would tell. She also mentioned that it's possible part of her unconsciousness was due to lack of sleep. So she needed rest.

I'd rocked back and forth from heel to toe waiting for her to answer my other question. That's when Annabelle had appeared next to me asking the same thing.

"Yes you can see her now but only one at a time" she'd told us. I didn't wait for Annabelle to make a choice, I had to see my girl.

The rush of emotions that hit me as I opened the door and saw her looking far less ill was intense. She looked so peaceful and pretty. No, beautiful. The bruises that marred her face slightly made my hands clench on the bed rail with anger.

I'd ended up talking to her in order to calm myself down. In had to get everything out. I wanted her to know just how bad I felt and hoped she'd forgive me for putting her in the position she was in. Because let's face it, everything that's happened is due to me. She wouldn't be here if it weren't for my tyrannical business lifestyle.

I said everything I wanted to say to her even though she was sleeping. So many apologies fell from my tongue. It never felt like enough though and I'd have to make sure to say it all over again when she could actually hear me.

I'd brushed my fingers through her hair and held her hand. It made me feel guilty in case she didn't want my touch anymore. Which reminded me of how much I put her in danger. Of how much I could put her in danger in the future too.

That realisation had me backing out of the room. I disguised my leaving as wanting to allow Annabelle time with her.

I hadn't been back in since. I simply sat outside and waited as her parents and Bree arrived. They'd went in to see her and even when my turn rolled back around I didn't move.

I spent the night on the plastic chairs, trying to work out how the hell I could justify staying with her when I was the one who put her in here in the first place.

Now though, a whole twenty four hours later I'm even more stuck than before. You see when I was told she had woken up, I had bolted from my seat to see her.

All I had to do was hear her voice and look into her eyes. My plans of letting her go evaporated.

How can I leave you?

That's all that's going through my mind right now as she stares back at me.

"Elijah" she sighs my name, her voice a little hoarse. Well fuck. "You came for me.." she sounds slightly surprised and it tears me apart. She didn't think I would?

Her Mom and Bree make a swift exit at that moment and my feet carry me to the side of her bed. I'm in a trace, needing to be next to her.

"Of course I came for you" I reply, imploring her to understand just how desperate I was to find her. Even before Nadia's call I was going mad without her. Nadia...the police better not fuck up time or I really will be getting charged for murder.

"But those things I said...I was so horrible. I didn't mean it. You have to know that-" she speaks quickly as if she's dying to get the words out.

"It's okay. I know Darling. I do" I assure her but she shakes her head.

"But Nadia told me you didn't react well. She told me about the drink driving. I was so fucking worried but I couldn't do anything. I couldn't get to you" she cries, tears coming fast down her cheeks. More guilt hits me then as I think about believing her so easy. My insecurities ate me up as soon as she told me she was using me for my money and it took me far too long to realise it could never be true. She'd never use me. After everything we've been through I still fell for Nadia's tricks and manipulation.

God I want to touch her but what if I hurt her? I can't do that.

"I didn't react well no but that wasn't your fault. It was mine. I've spent far too much of my life believing that everyone was out to get me. I shouldn't have believed it Darling but you have to know that it didn't last long. I began to realise that something wasn't right but it wasn't quick enough. I'm so fucking sorry that I didn't find you faster, that I didn't prevent you from being taken in the first place. I'm the only person to blame for all of this and I understand if you don't want to be around me" my words come on in one breath, my nails digging into my palm as I try to stay upright. I want to fall to my knees and beg for her forgiveness. What if she doesn't want me at all?

I said this when she was asleep but I need her to hear it all. I need to spill out the guilt inside me.

When I go to speak again she stops me.

"No more talking, my turn" she breathes and I nod wanting to hear anything she has to say. I want to feel all of her emotions. "First of all, I'm sorry too. I'm sorry I couldn't have been smarter and gotten free. I'm sorry I got kidnapped in the first place" she cries.

"No don't be silly. This isn't your-"

I go to stop her apologies but she holds up her good hand to halt my interruption. Why is she apologising? This isn't her fault.

"I'm sorry that you no doubt had to give up some of your business to save my ass. I hate that so much Elijah. I wasn't worth that"

I think I've heard enough. I've also had enough of hovering next to her, my hands itching to touch her. I'll be gentle.

Reaching up I wait for her to accept my request. With her good hand she grabs mine, placing it on her cheek for me. The warmth of her fingers nearly burns me alive in the best way possible. God I've missed her touch, I've missed everything. She brings me back to life.

"I never want to hear that you're not worth it ever again! You are the only thing that matters to me in this world. My business shares are nothing. I don't care about any of it. Do you hear me?" I push out the words, leaning closer to her, my heart leaping at her proximity. I want to be honest with her and let her know about me signing over my whole business but that will only make her feel worse right now. I will tell her but only when she sees how important she is...the most important thing...worth everything...worth more than I can even describe. So much more important than a stupid company. I wonder if she will still see value in me if I have no company? Fuck, of course she will. She wants me for me. I need to learn to accept that better.

"I hear you, I just feel so guilty" she replies shutting her eyes tightly.

"No, look at me. Please" I beg, trying to coax her gaze back to mine. She does as I ask and lets go of my hand on her cheek, brushing her fingers into my hair. I'm done for. "There is nothing for you to feel guilty about. Tell you me know that..."

"I can't yet. I can't change how I feel. I know you feel guilty too. I can see it"

"Sofia I'm the reason you were put in danger. I'm the reason you're hurt. If we'd never met then you'd be safe. You wouldn't have been in this situation" I confess the worst thing that's eating me alive.

"No! That's bullshit and you know it" she growls her fingers tightening in my hair. She tugs me closer. "Is that what you wish? That we'd never met?"

"No I want you. I want you forever"

Truer words have never been spoken yet I know I shouldn't have said them. Because it's not something that's possible. My need to keep her safe flares up once more and I'm able to think clearer as she winces with a small movement. My thoughts from before come back. I can't stay with her. I'll put her at risk.

Yet I can't seem to do anything else but shift impossibly closer, my forehead leaning on hers. It would be so easy to press my lips to hers and feel the undying connection we have. I can tell she wants it too.

Maybe one kiss wouldn't hurt. Just one.

Her tongue flicks over her bottom lip as if in anticipation and I close my eyes to put us both out of our misery.

Only our lips never get to touch.

"Oh fantastic you're awake" I hear and jolt back from her as if I've been doing something wrong. The nurse appears next to me, smiling at Sofia who hasn't taken her eyes from mine.

It's like she's looking right into my soul. Pulling out all of the things she wants to know. She can see my fear, my pain, all of it.

Sofia

I feel like I can already see my own future. I can tell that Elijah is going to leave me. Whether he truly believes that he puts me in danger or he's using that as an excuse, he's going to leave. I know it's weird to say but it's like I can feel it. He's trying to pull away from me.

As the nurse checks all my vitals he stands quietly in the corner. I want to ask him if there's something else. Someone else...

Shit! The machine next to me beeps faster as it monitors my heart rate. That's because I've just remembered one tiny little thing. Something I've been shutting out because I was so happy to see him.

He slept with a women the night I broke up with him. He thought that our whole relationship had been a lie and decided to make himself feel better by fucking the first women he found. I mean that's how I'm interpreting it. Isn't that what men do? They get hurt and try to fuck the pain away. I can't blame him, I really can't but the image of him with someone else is haunting me. No it's eating me up like poison inside. I can't believe he did that?!

I shouldn't be mad at him. I mean he didn't cheat on me. Yet I feel just a little bit betrayed. Surely even though he thought I'd used him he'd still have feelings for me? Surely he couldn't just jump into bed with someone else so quick but he did.

"Are you okay?" the nurse asks as a sickly feeling swirls inside me.

"Yup. Fantastic" I breath deeply, to expel the nausea. It's hard to hold onto any other emotion other than guilt. Except part of me is angry. Angry at him when I have no right to be. Which is why I can't look at him.

I really shouldn't hold it against him. He did think everything about our relationship had been fake. I'd made him think It because of that bitch!

If I were to think about this whole thing logically I wouldn't blame myself. I certainly wouldn't blame him. No I'd blame Nadia because it's all her fucking doing.

There's a small pang of upset inside me now. I hate that all of these things are now coming to the forefront of my mind.

I'm hurt that he believed it. Part of me wishes that he had seen through my lies. Although a bigger part is happy he didn't because it prevented him from going to jail. So I guess I'd do it over and over again to ensure he'd stay a free man. I'd welcome him hating me. I'd welcome him sleeping with someone else to make sure that he didn't get locked away. He doesn't deserve that. He deserves to be happy.

God dammit Sofia make up your mind! Are you mad at him or not?

What a mess. I guess my real issue is that it feels like he never believed anything I said. Did he ever believe my 'I love yous'? Or what he waiting for me to let him down? I know he's insecure but I thought he trusted me. I thought he believed that I wanted him for him.

"Everything is looking fantastic. We will keep you here for another few hours but you should be able to go home tonight. As long as you have someone to stay with you" the nurse informs me. My first instinct would usually be to look at Elijah. This should be a happy moment. We should be able to go home and be together again. Only my previous thoughts hit me along with something else. What if he doesn't want me to go home with him? Do I want to go with him?

As the nurse leaves, my parents enter. My dad comes to my side, emotion making his eyes watery.

"I'm so glad you're back with us. I don't like when you're not being a smart ass" he grins and leans down to hug me gently.

"Sorry my unconsciousness was inconvenient to you" I laugh. Then my face falls as I notice Elijah leaving.

My Mom notices my reaction and sits on the edge of the bed.

"He's been going mad without you Honey. I've never seen a man so chaotic. He sat with you for hours last night then he spent the rest of the time making sure you were getting looked after correctly. He didn't come in and see you again until today. Which I assume means that he's dealing with some kind of self loathing. Sometimes people like to pull away from everyone when they think they've done something wrong. Don't worry though he'll get over it. Men are more complicated than us a lot of the time"

She looks up at Dad and he is dumbfounded.

"Not true at all. We are very simple creatures. Tell us what you want us to do and we'll do it. However we are sometimes very dumb though. I have a feeling whatever is going on in Elijah's mind is going down the dumb route"

"Well guys thank you for your advice. I'll be sure to tell him he's dumb" I smirk and my Mom shakes her head. I'm making fun of them but what they've said actually helps settle me. "Oh I'm getting discharged in a few hours as long as someone is able to stay with me to keep an eye or something" I update them.

"That's fantastic. You are more than welcome to come home with us. Although I think I know what you'll choose" she says with a knowing smile. Huh, am I that transparent?

"Maybe you don't know what I'll choose. Maybe I don't know either. I'm not sure if he wants me to go with him or if I even want to. A lot has happened in the last few days" I tell them, picking a non existent piece of lint from my bed cover.

"Talk to him. Sort it all out. I guarantee that whatever you're worried about won't be as bad as your brain is telling you it is"

"You make it sound so simple" I huff.

"It is. You love him don't you?" she asks and automatically I feel my blush rising. I shift a little in the awkwardness and my ribs scream at me. Well shit that hurts.

I haven't told anyone that I love him apart from him. So it's weird to hear my Mom say it.

"I love him so much" I admit and she takes my hand.

"Then don't let him make any stupid excuses. Don't let him hide from you" she replies before taking a different route. "Oh and he told us about that Nadia bitch. Let me tell you that if I ever see that woman she won't be breathing for much longer" she growls and my eyes widen at her sudden rage. Wow.

I'm going to assume Elijah didn't say anything about Brian. Which I'm glad about. I should be the one to tell them about his involvement. Nadia really must have dug deep to find him.

In the next second my eyes snap to the doorway to find the very man I'm missing, holding a glass of water. He didn't leave or run away from me. I didn't realise how much I was worrying about that but hey it feels like I can finally breath again now he's back. God this love shit is difficult.

"Elijah my daughter would like to ask you something" my Mom announces. What is she doing?

"Of course anything" Elijah immediately responds, walking further into the room. He holds out the glass to me with an apologetic look on his face.

"I would?" I question, feeling a little embarrassed that I have no idea what her move is here. Elijah smirks at my expression and we both look to my Mom for some help.

"Dear god! It seems not only men are dumb! You're getting discharged soon and you need to be with someone who can take care of you. I know for a fact that Elijah is going to want to be that someone. As for you, well you can tell me over and over that you're not sure what you wanna do but I'm your Mom...I know you. You'll act all tough and beat about the bush but you already know the answer"

I sit there in shock at being told off by my Mom at nearly twenty six years old.

"Can you believe the abuse I'm getting right now?" I pretend to be appalled, looking at Elijah for an answer.

"It's terrible I know. Although she is right about the first part. I do want to be that someone. As soon as the nurse mentioned you could go home I really struggled not to beg you if I'm honest"

"So you went to get me water?" I ask trying not to smile. He makes it so hard for me to be angry or any other emotion apart from happy. Even if I still don't know what happened with the women in the hotel. Even if I still don't know if he plans to leave me.

"Yes. A peace offering. I think we need to put our guilt aside at least for now. Both of us. That means also you" he replies, his stern commanding voice shinning through. "I want to look after you. I don't know what will happen after that. I won't assume anything. I just know that we need to do this together...remember?"

Together. The coin I gave him. The promise I made to always be with him. Shit. He's right.

"I remember"

"Oh thank god! We're getting somewhere here! I mean I've no idea what you're talking about but it sounds positive" my Dad butts in, dropping a hand on my Mom's shoulder. "Time for us to go. Our work is done"

All I can do is give them a strange look as they exit. They're usually telling me everything I'm doing is wrong but here they are trying to help my unconventional relationship. I guess that's what you'd call character development...in life.

I sip the water but end up taking large gulps when I realise how thirsty I am.

"I promise I'll take care of you" Elijah says softly taking the empty glass.

"I know. You've been taking care of me since we met. You've made me feel safe and endlessly happy. Not because of your money or the fancy things you have but because of you" I tell him trying to take away his insecurities. I thought I was doing a good job at that but it seems he's still got a long way to go.

"You take care of me too you know. You make this whole being alive thing worth it" he breathes shifting closer to me.

"Come here" I state, hoping he won't turn me down. I just want something simple. I want to be held by the person who has held me before in my time of need. He makes me feel so much better just with a touch.

Gently he leans down and puts his arm around my waist as best as he can. He barely touches me, very aware of my ribs. I put my hand on his chest and he plants a firm kiss on my forehead. I can hear his breathing shake as if such simple things are affecting him. Which makes sense because I can barely breath myself, my need to squish him to me so very prominent.

I'm not sure how long we stay like that but it's more healing than any medicine. I've missed him so much and this is like heaven. He talks to me softly about how much he missed me. How much he wanted me to come back to him even when he thought I didn't want him.

His voice quivers the more he talks and his line of conversation turns to things he did when we were apart. It's hard to hear him being reckless. He could have gotten hurt. Like the drink driving, the smashing of many objects, him being unable to move any of my things, checking the storage unit...then he begins talking about going to the hotel and I don't know what to do. I don't know if I can hear it. He thinks I don't know about this and he's going to tell me. That's something right? That he wants to admit it to me.

I'm not sure I can do this. There's no anger in this moment only hurt. The thing is, if he tells me right now that he's slept with someone and confirms what I already know, will I stay with him? The sad thing is I think I probably would. My thoughts of him not wanting me are now conflicting and confused. He wants me to go home with him. Everything he's doing suggests he does still want me.

Maybe he just wants to make up for his guilt.

"I had a lot of shots at the bar. I don't know why that was my choice of drink. Anyway um then a women sat down next to me and she started talking to me-"

"Sorry to interrupt. Mam, I'm just wondering if you're well enough to answer a few questions"

Both of us look up to see a police officer in the doorway. Of course I need to be questioned about Nadia and everything else.

I'm kind of glad our conversation was interrupted and I'm more than happy to tell the police every single thing Nadia did.

"Do you want me to stay?" Elijah asks as the officer takes a seat on the other side of the bed.

"Please" I reply and take his hand. I need him here so that I'll make it through reliving the ordeal. I'm mentally sound right now but something tells me the moment I'm alone I'll be having flashbacks about being beaten and tormented for days.

So I divulge everything I can remember. From getting shoved in the van to waking up today. I mention Brian and feel waves of anger coming from Elijah. I'm not sure if knows about that part yet. I'll have to ask him later.

The only thing I leave out are the photographs of Elijah and the women. I don't want to talk about that now or here. Plus it could be damaging information if Nadia tries to flip this whole thing on Elijah. I won't let that happen. She could try and say he got her to kidnap me. She could use the photos to show that he doesn't really care about me. That he's with someone else. There are so many things she could lie about.

Then it occurs to me that I still don't know if he is actually with someone else. I haven't asked. I don't want to.

No that's ridiculous. He wouldn't be here if he had another women. Would he?

The more I talk the more I can feel Elijah becoming rage filled. So when the officer finally leaves I turn back to him and see his livid expression.

"She fucking let you starve and humiliated you for fun. She had you beaten BY BRIAN! How the fuck did she even know about him? He deserves to be suffer! When she told me about him I didn't know what to do! She made you break up with me knowing that she was then going to leave you there for fuck knows how long while I pissed about wallowing in self pity instead of finding you! She had no idea how long it would take for me respond to a fucking email. I don't think that was ever her plan. She just wanted to drag it out longer! I'll fucking kill her. I don't give a fuck if I go to jail-" he yells into the room without looking at me.

"Enough! You can't do anything stupid. You can't go to jail! I did what I had to. To prevent that from happening. Plus! You can't fucking leave me okay?!" I yell back, my worst fear showing. "Not unless you want to..." I say quieter because I don't want him to stay with me if he doesn't want it too.

I'm so fucking confused. Is he here for me because he cares? Or is he here because he feels bad? Is there any chance of us being together or is he just being nice for my sake? FUCK!

He looks crazy now, his eyes blazing with so many different things.

"I don't want to leave you! Not now, not ever. But I also can't let her get away with what she did to you"

We're going back and forth. First we feel guilt then we agree to put it aside and now it's back again.

I don't know how we're going to work this out. How can we when we're both being torn apart by our own self hatred. I won't ever forgive myself for being the reason he gave up his shares or for saying those horrible things and it seems he can't forgive himself because he thinks it's his fault I was taken.

We may be back together in terms of distance but not in an emotional sense. Nadia is still winning.

***

After Elijah's outburst he left again. Only this time it was for much longer than before. Annabelle came and went, my parents and Bree did too. I told them about Brian and all three of them cried. My Mom couldn't speak will my Dad looked as though he was about to smash the room up. Bree simply held onto me for dear life. I wonder where he is now? I wonder if Nadia has paid him for his work?

Elijah never came back.

Not until I'm being discharged.

He steps into the room looking so very lost. While my heart rate sky rockets once again at seeing him. Is that normal? To go all heart eyes every time the man you love walks in the room?

The nurses help me swing my legs out of bed in the least painless way possible. Yet I still hiss and say ouch many many times.

Now sitting on the edge of the bed all I have to do is get up. They have a wheelchair on standby in case I find it too painful to walk.

Elijah's face says it all. He hates seeing me in pain. I think it might actually be hurting him too. I wish I could convince him to stop blaming himself.

"Okay just take it easy. Go slow" one of the nurses instruct as I shift forward.

My bare feet touch the ground, the hospital gown hindering my movement a little. I can feel Elijah watching me like a hawk.

Taking a deep breath, I push on my hands and try to shift my weight to my feet. The nurses hold onto my arms and I really do try. Only it's fucking agony and I fall back down. I hear Elijah gasp and when I look up he's closer, one of his arms out stretched as if he imagined having to catch me.

"Maybe you'd be more comfortable with your partner rather than us?" The nurse suggests and my heart does happy flips that she's called Elijah my partner. I guess I'll never get used to that. I hope that I won't ever have to.

"Yeah if that would be okay" I breath, trying to psych myself up to try again. I'm not just asking the nurses, I'm asking Elijah if it would be okay too. I don't want him to help me if he doesn't feel comfortable doing so.

Although as soon as they leave, he's moving in front of me, holding out his hands. He doesn't say a word, he just keeps me trapped in his gaze.

Grabbing his hands, I nod and he grips onto me tighter. Another deep breath and a push from my feet and he pulls me upright while I scrunch my face in pain. He catches me as I fall against him and for some reason that's the moment that everything catches up with me.

Elijah wraps me in his arms as if he can't stop himself and my chest heaves as tears spring in my eyes. I can't stop myself from leaning my head on his chest and wrapping my arms around him.

He holds me, one of his hands reaching to stroke my hair.

"It's okay, you're going to be okay Darling. I promise you" he whispers, burying his face in my neck. I inhale his scent - that is slightly different from usual, there's no aftershave and a hint of sweat, I love it - and it calms my racing heart.

I pull back slightly and pay closer attention to his scruffy beard. It tells a story of the way he's struggled.

I've no idea what's going on between us. Are we still together? There's a certain awkwardness that I'm hating but mostly we're still the same. I'm clinging to that.

"I told your parents and Bree that they are more than welcome to come stay with us for a while. So you can see them whenever you like and to settle their minds. I mean there's plenty of rooms for them. I hope you don't mind"

Oh that's really frigging sweet of him.

"Of course I don't mind. Thank you" I smile softly, pressing a kiss to cheek. "Although you don't need to ask me, it's your apartment"

"No it's our apartment Darling" he assures me and I can't help but ask:

"Are you sure you still want that?"

"I do. I'm maybe not the best option for you but I want it anyway"

I hate how sad he looks. I hate that I can't take away his self doubt but I'm going to make it my mission. I won't let him wallow in it. I won't let this awkwardness continue. I want him back.

"You are what's best for me"

I want us back.

Sofia

With much difficulty I'm able to leave the hospital. Elijah helped me back into my clothes then holds onto me as I walk and wince with every step. I opted not to choose the wheelchair, determined that I could make it.

My parents, Bree and Annabelle follow behind and Annabelle says her goodbyes with a soft hug once we reach the parking lot. My parents and Bree are going to get a cab to the apartment while Elijah and I will go in his car.

We all get in our respective vehicles. Well I don't simply get in, Elijah has to help lower me onto the seat so I don't thud down and damage myself further.

Every time I groan in pain his eyes snap to mine to check that I'm okay. So once I'm safely in my seat and Elijah is in his, the first thing he does is take my hand without a word.

He starts the car and keeps his eyes forward but doesn't stop running his thumb over my knuckles.

For the first time in days I feel...okay. I think there's a possibility that I might be able to feel like myself again. I didn't think that would happen.

"I know that you'll say I don't need to thank you but I want to anyway. So thank you for coming to get me" I say because I really am just so grateful.

He tilts his head towards me slightly, still making sure he's watching the road.

"Thank you for still being with me. I'm so glad you still want something to do with me. You could have told me to fuck off" he says, a small smile tugging up one side of his lips. Oh there goes my heart again.

"I have plenty of time to tell you to fuck off. I'm just waiting for the right moment" I joke and he presses his lips against the back of my hand.

For the rest of the journey I try very hard not to keep staring at him. It's a privilege I've been without recently but studying him is quite possibly one of my favourite things to do. He glances at me every so often as if he wants to look at me too.

Pulling into the underground garage we wait until the cab arrives outside so we can let my family in. All three of them are wide eyed as they take in all of the other fancy cars next to Elijah's.

"Holy hell, are these all yours?" Bree asks Elijah as he helps me from the seat. He watches my every movement as if he's trying to judge if I'm in too much pain again. It's far too sweet.

"No this is my only car. I've never understood the need for more than one" he replies and Bree looks surprised.

"You know I really respect that" she hums looking rather pleased.

I've never been so grateful that Elijah's parking space is nearest to the elevator. Sure it's been convenient in the past but now it's a life saver. Perks of the penthouse I guess.

The fancy elevator ride up to the top floor also impresses Bree and my parents. So when we step out into the foyer of the apartment, complete silence falls. They're all in awe.

I understand that feeling. I'm used to the grandeur of this place now but it took a while for me not to gasp at everything. The view still gets me though.

Entering the front room I end up gasping for another reason and Elijah stiffens beside me.

"I told you I smashed a few things" he whispers to me as I take it the broken pieces of glass bottles and ornaments.

Shit. I really hurt him.

Elijah must sense my line of thought because he pulls me closer into his side and guides me around the mess before I can think about it any longer.

"I'll be back in a second to show you to your rooms" he calls over his shoulder as I grip the back of his shirt.

"I'll help you clean that up" I mumble as he leads me to...our bedroom. Yes he still wants me to call it ours. Which makes me really friggin emotional and relieved.

"No you won't Darling. I'll call a cleaning service tomorrow. Please don't worry about it. It's just a display of my ridiculous temper"

"It's not ridiculous. I hurt you"

He stops just as we get inside the bedroom and steps in front of me. His hands rest of my arms, his expression so very soft.

"You protected me and I'll be forever grateful" he says, his eyes watery. "I don't deserve you"

Immediately I reach up and place a finger over his lips.

"If you don't deserve me then I certainly don't deserve you. So I guess we're even huh?"

This would normally be a time for yanking him to me to kiss him with all the passion inside me. Only we're still so unsure of our situation. We still have a lot to talk about and we both still feel guilty as hell.

So instead all that happens is he rubs his cheek against mine softly, his beard scratching my skin before he squeezes his eyes shut and pulls away. God this is torture.

"I'll go show everyone to a guest room. Do you want to go to bed or stay up? Is there anything you'd like? I have the painkillers the doctor prescribed. Do you want those?" he asks quickly shoving his hands in his pockets. Dear god he's never looked so unsure of himself. I hate that we're both feeling this way.

I just want us to be normal again. To be able to communicate without feeling like we're terrified of messing something up.

"I'm going to take a shower because I haven't had one in far too long" I reply and he runs a hand through his hair and cringes.

"Me either. I smell bad don't I? I'll help you shower. If you want? I mean if that's okay? I'm sorry I'll be back in a minute, don't try to walk too far without me Darling" he rambles.

Then he's gone, his footsteps echoing down the hallway.

This is torture.

Elijah

As I escort her family to a couple of the many guest rooms all I can't think is: I'm an idiot. What's wrong with me? Why am I acting this way? It's just Sofia, the person I'm closest to in the whole damn world. She's my happy place.

Yet I'm terrified that I'll hurt her or that I won't be there and she'll hurt herself. She's been through enough because of me and I just can't handle her being in any more pain.

We've never been this awkward around one another. Not even on the first night we met. It's crazy.

I'm going insane. I want to kiss her and give her all my affection but then I feel guilty. I don't know what we are right now? I don't know if she really wants me like before?

Can I even be with her? Will I put her at risk?

I just don't know a thing. What doesn't help is the obvious tension between us. There may be things we haven't spoken about and things that aren't as easy between us as before but that constant electricity that crackles between us is stronger than ever.

We need to talk soon. We need to get it all out and purge whatever we are both keeping inside. The guilt we both feel has to go. Obviously we've said small pieces but it isn't enough. We're always honest with each other and that can't change.

I hate that she feels bad about me giving shares...well my whole company to Nadia. I wish I could go back and deny that I gave anything to Nadia at all but then I'd be lying and she's too smart not to know. I need to convince her that it really doesn't matter. That I would have given away thousands of companies to find her. But of course she feels guilty. She's Sofia. She puts everyone else before herself. She thinks that the company was my world and that by giving up shares to get her back, that I've jeopardised my happiness.

She should know that she's my happiness.

She's my world.

I would literally like to revolve around her forever.

Sofia

While Elijah is gone I begin trying to pull off my top. It had been really difficult to get on after I'd spent a good amount of time getting out of the hospital gown.

This is no easier but I successfully yet slowly pull it up over my head and drop it down with a huff. Everything is tiring me out.

I'm about to try getting my jeans off too when I hear Elijah's voice.

"I brought you the painkillers and some water. Your parents and Bree have all decided to go to bed and-" He stops in the doorway, his sentence stopping too.

The look he gives me then is one I know well. Desire. Need. Desperation. His eyes flick over the parts of me no longer hidden by clothes before he clears his throat and recovers. Not before I notice the small flash of anger too. Which is probably because of the bruising over my rib cage. I get it. I'd be livid too if I saw him marred with evidence of him having went through pain. Livid maybe doesn't cover it.

"And they said to wake them up if you need anything"

Did he really just check me out and then pretend it didn't happen?

"Thank you for relaying the message. Eloquently done" I tease. "What's the matter? You never seen a women in a bra before?"

"I guess I've seen my fair share but well...I...never mind. Here are the painkillers" he holds out the pills and the water for me to take. He's struggling not to drop his eyes from my face.

"What were you going to say?" I ask before swallowing the tablets. "You don't usually stop yourself"

He looks a little shy as he steps closer, finally letting himself look at my breasts and down to my stomach. His gaze sets me on fire, stoking flames inside me. Shit. We really are tuned to one another.

"I was going to say that I've never seen a women as beautiful and sexy as you but I didn't want to make you uncomfortable"

"Being adored by you could never make me uncomfortable. I'm really glad you still find me attractive"

I hadn't realised I was worried until I said it. The last thing I should be caring about right now is whether he finds me attractive or not. I should be worrying about whether he wants to be with me in general, not just psychically. Which I am terrified about by the way. I know he said he does but I'm still scared. We're still not right yet.

"Why on earth wouldn't I Darling?" he asks, sounding appalled that I'd think his attraction to me has changed.

"Well I'm in a bit of a mess right now" I shrug. That's partly true but I'm also concerned his affection for me has changed because of the past few days. I don't know if he sees me the same way.

"You're stunning" he sighs as if I'm dreamy. Naturally it causes me to blush. "Let me help you"

Dropping my hands from my jeans, I let him do the rest. It's a strange feeling to have him pull them down, his fingers brushing over my thighs, when we're acting so awkward together.

He crouches down and asks me to step out of them. With a hand on his shoulder for balance, I do so and stare down at him with a bit too much intensity.

His face is level with the worst of the bruising across my ribs and stomach. So he pauses and glances up at me.

"I wish I could take your pain away"

"Thank you. I'll be okay though. It'll all heal"

He nods in agreement but stays where he is. I watch with rapt attention as he flutters his fingers over my stomach. My breath catches in my throat as his skin warms mine. Then he presses his lips to the biggest bruise above my hip.

I don't know what to say or do. So I just stay still and watch as he takes his time kissing every mark he can reach as if he can heal it. In a way he does heal me because in this moment I feel no pain. Only adoration from this gorgeous man.

My eyes are watery as he finishes his task and rises back up to full height.

"I want to talk to you about something if you'll let me" he mumbles, focusing his attention on the fabric Velcro cast on my hand and wrist.

Uh oh. I know what he wants to talk about. I still don't know if I'm ready to hear it.

"Can I shower first?" I say awkwardly because it's a clear evasion tactic.

"Of course Darling. Come on"

He helps me hobble to the bathroom and turns on the shower. Then stands behind me to unclasp my bra. This is a new kind of hell.

In order to save myself from insanity, I push down my panties and kick them away. I can hear his deep breathing as he moves from behind me.

Taking my hand he ensures I get into the shower safely, tension making his body rigid. I'm going guess that something else is rigid too. Which is not what I should be thinking about?!

God damn it! I gotta pull it together.

Shutting the glass door I stand in the large space as multiple jets of water spray. As soon as I step into them, I let out a rather guttural noise of relief. That is heavenly.

It then occurs to me that Elijah said he needed a shower too. I'm not sure what to do with that information at this stage.

"Do you need help washing or anything?" I hear through the noise of raining water.

I feel bad that he has to do so much. It shouldn't be his job. Then again I know I'd do the same for him.

Testing my ability to move, I reach for the shampoo on the little shelf, only to be jabbed with pain. Fucking hell.

"I'll be okay" I lie and try to stifle my yelp of agony. Trying again, I grab the bottle only to have it slip from my fingers and hit the floor. Normally this would be no big deal but there's no way I can bend down to get it.

"Are you sure?" he calls, obviously hearing the clatter.

"No I'm not sure" I huff in annoyance and look at him sheepishly as he opens the door.

"Do you mind if I come in?" he asks, shyness showing again.

"With your clothes on?" I giggle and he smirks so cutely.

"Well no but I don't want you to feel unc-"

"Elijah please stop saying that. I'm not uncomfortable. We've been naked together many many times. It's okay I promise you baby" I tell him in order to try and ease whatever weirdness he's feeling. I know he probably just doesn't know what to do just like I don't but I can't stand this walking on egg shells thing. It's driving me mad. I want him closer in body and mind. Also did I just call him baby? See?! I can't help it! "Of course, I don't want you to be feel uncomfortable either. It's okay if you don't want to. I'm sorry that you're having to do these things. I can call my Mom" I add, worried that maybe he's not acting this way for my benefit like I thought. How selfish of me. Maybe he doesn't want to do all of this intimate stuff. Shit. Fuck! I'm an idiot.

"Uncomfortable is not what I'm feeling Darling. I want to help you. I'm...desperate to be close to you, I just don't want to overstep my mark" he confesses, causing my heart to race. My body heats up but not from the water. Well that's a relief.

"Get in here" I demand and he immediately begins unbuttoning his shirt.

Sofia don't stare the whole time! At least try to pretend you're not frigging obsessed with every inch of him.

No such luck.

I eat up every piece of skin that becomes available for me to see.

He steps in beside me and into the spray of the water jets. I see the same kind of relief that takes tension away from his body as he relaxes, his eyes closing.

"Better?" I ask, trying not to melt or cry. I can't even imagine how crazy he's been. On top of hurting him I caused him stress and out right insanity.

"Much better" he agrees and and grabs the shampoo bottle from the floor. "Let's wash away the last few days hm"

"Yes please" I sigh as he begins massaging the shampoo into my hair. I watch the water run down his body and try my best to keep my hands to myself. I shouldn't touch him in case he doesn't want me to.

Then my hand is moving before I even realise it, my fingers trailing over the hair on his chest.

As I tilt my head back to let the shampoo wash back out of my hair, my hands keep moving, drawing patterns on his stomach. When I move a hand back up and over his heart I feel it beating wildly.

"Are you okay?" I ask, searching his blazing eyes. He swallows and nods but stays quiet, reaching for the sponge to wash me.

"I'm very okay Darling" he smiles brightly then, genuine and care free for a few seconds. "Having you safe makes me feel very okay"

"I'm safe because of you" I reply trying to drill that into him. He moves the sponge down my collar bone to my breasts, his breathing picking up.

He doesn't answer me. He focuses diligently on the task at hand keeping his eyes on the sponge.

Once he's satisfied he finally meets my gaze.

"You're beautiful and strong. You blow me away" he sighs and I feel like I might melt into goo and slide down the drain with water.

"You know that I still feel the same about you right? That hasn't changed" I assure him and he looks lost.

"I don't deserve that-"

"No. Don't say that"

I won't let him do that. Not now. Not ever.

Silence falls as he washes himself too.

That's when I notice how messed up his knuckles are. I'm not sure how I didn't notice before in the hospital but I can't stop myself from grabbing one of his hands.

"What did you do?" I gasp and he shrugs.

"Punched my steering wheel. Punched the kitchen cabinet...punched a lot of things" he explains and I want to scream. I hate that he's hurt himself. So I do what he did earlier to me and kiss each knuckle, one by one.

Then we stare at one another, silent adoration moving between us as the water flows. We stand there for a long time, until the water runs cold.

He pulls me back out of the shower and helps me dry, running a towel over my body. I can't help but giggle as he tries to wrap it in my hair to make a towel hat like I've done many times before. It doesn't quite work and falls off.

"Sorry about that" he smirks before going into his closet and coming back with some of my sweat pants and a t-shirt.

He throws on his own clothes and I try to tug on mine. Unfortunately I don't get far and he has to help with that too. God I hate that. He really shouldn't have to do this for me.

Glancing at the bed I wonder if wants me to sleep here tonight. Maybe he doesn't? So I stand awkwardly next to it until he holds out his hands to help me lie down.

Thank god.

The soft duvet and mattress is so welcome after the hard ground I've been used to for almost five days. Internally I feel so much better too because I was given plenty of fluids and classic bad food at the hospital. Although I'm still so friggin tired.

He lies next to me like so many times before only it's different. There's no touching, he's careful to keep a few inches between us as he leans on his elbow.

I can't do the same because it'll only hurt so I stay on my back, tilting my head towards him to hear what he's going to tell me.

"Are you comfortable?" he asks, his eyes moving over my body as if to check everything is okay.

"As I can be yes" I reply, smiley softly. He looks away, staring at the duvet before taking a deep breath.

"I just want to finish telling you everything that happened before I found you. You know I went to the hotel to drink"

I still don't think I can listen to this. I don't want to know the details of him fucking someone else. It's only gonna hurt.

So when he goes to start talking again, I stop him.

"I know what happened" I confess and he frowns immediately. No doubt sensing the change in my voice. I think I'm actually scared. Terrified to know. I think I might be sick.

"You know what?" he asks then, his eyes boring into mine. Guilt once again comes off him in waves and that doesn't help me at all.

"Nadia showed me photos" I whisper, tilting my head back to stare at the ceiling.

"Photos? What photos?" he sounds suddenly alarmed as if he has no idea what I'm talking about and that's making him petrified.

"I'm sure you can guess" is all I can say because forming the actual words is too much.

"I'm not sure I can Darling. I went to the hotel. I drank. A random women I've never met before started talking to me. Then I went back to the room because I didn't want to be around anyone, let alone a women asking me if I needed help. When I got to my room she followed me and-"

"You slept with her. I know..." I push out, throwing my arm over my eyes to hide from him. I don't wanna know!

"WHAT?! No! I didn't sleep with her!" he exclaims and I feel the bed shifting as he moves. I'm kinda disappointed he's lying. I wish he'd admit it and we could be done with this part.

"It's okay Elijah. I understand" I mumble before he takes my arm and moves it away from my eyes. He hovers over me, his gaze sad yet pleading.

"Listen to me. I did not sleep with her"

"But the pict-"

"I don't care about pictures. What was in them? Because it wasn't me sleeping with anyone!" he implores me to believe while I think back to the images I was given. They didn't show him touching her. In fact, all I've been doing is trying to fill in blanks.

"Tell me what happened" I ask willing...no desperate to know what he has to say.

"She propositioned me. Said she could help make me feel better. I told her that wasn't possible and I tried to get into my room but she lunged at me. She tried to kiss me and I immediately felt sick. I could only think of you and any one else touching me makes me want to wretch. Which I did. I threw her out and then threw up in the toilet"

"You didn't want her?" I ask but I don't even know why. I think it's shock.

"No Darling. Of course not. It's only you Sofia. It'll only ever be you"

He was hurt so much that he tried to drink away the pain. He thought I'd played him. Left him. Yet he couldn't even kiss another women.

It makes me realise how much control we have over one another. He thought I'd betrayed him yet he couldn't betray me back. I know it would be the same for me. God! I feel so much better now. The sadness inside me evaporators with the truth he's just told.

"I thought you hated me. When she showed me those photos. I thought you didn't care-"

"I could never hate you Darling. It's simply not possible. I'm so sorry. I'm so sorry I believed what you told me. I should have known better. You should never have been made to do that. You shouldn't have protected me. I don't deserve to be put first. I'm sorry I made you think that I could move on so quick or that I didn't care. I'm sorry you were taken. I'm sorry you were hurt. I'm sorry..." his voice is full of the apologies that he's speaking. Reaching up I run my fingers over his cheek and try to make him understand.

"There's nothing to be sorry for. The only person to blame is Nadia. Who I'm hoping will be locked away for good. Then she can't hurt us anymore"

"If she comes anywhere near you I'll kill her" he growls, his fingers gripping the duvet. I'll kill Brian too!"

I think he actually would kill them. Which is terrifying but then I think about him getting hurt and I decide that I'd kill anyone for him too. In a heartbeat.

Elijah

She's so strong. Stronger than I'll ever be. She could have told Nadia no. She could have screamed down the phone to me but she hadn't. She'd done as she was told so that Nadia wouldn't unleash a hurricane of fake news to put me in jail.

I've put myself in her position over and over trying to think of how she felt. Trying to feel her pain to punish myself.

Would I have done the same? Could I have lied to her knowing that I'd hurt her. Yes. Yes I would have lied to her to ensure her safety. I would have because she's worth everything. I'm not.

It isn't funny how we both think we're not worth it?

Is this what people call love? Putting someone else before yourself. Before everything. Wanting them to be happy even if it's not with you.

Love. It still isn't enough to describe the chaos and calm that Sofia makes me feel. It's not enough. Yet it's true. I love her. I love her so fucking much.

I hate that I can't make up a word that's better. I hate the shitty connotations that the word has. Love...too many people don't mean it. They don't use it right.

I always will. I'll make sure she knows when I say those words that I mean it. I more than love her.

I now live for her. Which maybe isn't smart but it's true. I know as she lies before me with her hands playing with my hair that I'd die for her too.

So very dramatic but... is it?

"What else happened while we were apart?" she asks shifting slightly, her face contorting in pain. I hate that.

"Ah right the next morning when I woke up in the hotel..."

Yeah, I tell her what I did. I watch her blush and her face go sad at my pain. I tell her about Gabe and his involvement which gains a response of multiple bad words and a promise to "beat his ass if he doesn't go to jail too". I let her know that when I met with him and Nadia at the office that I got a few good punches in. She seems pleased with that.

I tell her that Nadia sent the women in the hotel to seduce me and about Nadia being annoyed that her plan had failed. The only thing I miss out is the fact that I gave Nadia my whole company. I wonder how that's going for her? Hopefully she's too occupied with police interviews to really take her role as CEO.

Sofia becomes sad when the topic of business shares comes up. I tell her over and over that it doesn't matter. I hate that she thinks it's somehow her fault. She tells me that she wishes she could have stopped it. I tell her I don't care about it. It's nothing to me and that it really isn't her fault. It could never be. I tell her the truth. That I've never loved that company, I only built it up to try and make my father proud. Even while dead he still had a hold on me. It seems he doesn't anymore though I guess. She doesn't seem satisfied unfortunately and still expresses how bad she feels.

I would have given anything to get her back. She apologies for being kidnapped again and I tell her how crazy that sounds. That earns me a glare and a tug on my hair. Yet I'm right. She doesn't need to apologise for something that I should have stopped. So I apologise back and she tells me how crazy I sound in return.

I guess we are both crazy.

God, I want to kiss her. I can't remember the last time we went a day without having that intimacy. I don't want it actually, I need it.

My lips have been longing for hers since the second she went to work on the day of her kidnap. It's so simple but so important.

I guess we still don't know what we are right now. There's a certain distance between us that wasn't there before. We both know it. Yet I don't know what it is. Are we both afraid that the other person no longer feels the same way?

"Elijah" she sighs tugging me closer. "Please"

I know what she wants and fuck I can't say no.

I try to pause. I try to control my breathing but it's impossible.

As gently as I can, I lean down and press my lips to hers. The instant they touch its heaven. It's like we were never apart and there's nothing else to focus on but the way she feels. The was she makes me feel.

She opens her mouth for me, deepening the kiss. She moans and I find it hard to catch my breath. It doesn't matter. I don't need air. Just her.

Her hand inches under my t-shirt as I hover over her, her fingers splaying over my stomach. The warmth shoots all over my body. I slip my tongue into her mouth. I move my hand to her hip to hold her closer.

I forget she's injured.

I kiss her neck, she sighs my name. My fingers flex over her waist. I squeeze.

I hurt her. She yells in pain.

I'm two feet away from her in seconds.

"Fuck! I'm so sorry. I didn't mean to do that. Shit!" I yell and she breathes deeply, her nostrils flaring.

"It's okay! I'm okay. It was an accident" she gasps but I can see the pain on her face. Which only brings back my previous thoughts. I'm bombarded with images of her being in pain. Her suffering because of me.

"Shit!" I yell again as I try to stop it. She's in pain because of me. The ribs, the wrist, the guilt, the emotional agony. All caused by me.

"Elijah it's okay. Please come back"

This is why there's a distance between us. Because I know that I can only hurt her! I'm no good for her.

"I can't. Are you okay? Do you need to see a doctor again?" I ask desperately trying to access the damage from where I stand.

"Yes I'm fine. You just touched a sore spot. It's not serious" she answers, her features now back to normal. No pain. It doesn't matter. I could still make that happen again.

I have to get out of here.

"If you need anything let me know or maybe you should ask your Mom. She'll be better at this. I'm going to sleep on the couch. I don't want to hurt you during the night" I blurt out quickly before turning around and darting from the room.

She's calling after me but I can't go back. Not yet.

How can I do this? If I stay with her, I'll hurt her. If I leave her, I'll hurt her too.

What if I have to break my promise? What if we can't be 'together'?

Sofia

I've never slept here alone and I really don't like it. No I hate it.

I also hate the image I now have in my head of Elijah's terrified face. It makes sense now. The uncertainty I feel from him is fear, while the uncertainty he will feel from me is confusion.

We're going back and forth far too much for it to be healthy. First he says he's not the best option for me then we shower together and make out. Now once again he's riddled with the thought that he's bad for me.

I had no idea what to think when I woke up in the hospital. Did he still want me? Was her angry? Could I be okay with the fact that he'd slept with someone else and believed my lie so easy?

Now I know the answers. He still wants me more than anything and the last he thing is, is angry. He didn't sleep with anyone and I can't blame him for believing what I said because it's clear now it has nothing to do with his faith in me. He never doubted me or my feelings. He doubted that I could love someone like him. It's self hate. It's horrible. I want to take it from him.

My eyes droop with exhaustion and I pray that my body will finally give in. I want this strange lonely feeling to go away. This bed is too big and with Elijah's scent all around me its only more obvious that he's not here.

I count my own breaths and try not to think about anything in particular but that's impossible.

This isn't going to work.

It's probably a bad idea to get up on my own but if I'm honest, I'm a walking bad idea. Because good ideas are never fun.

Shifting to the side of the bed as slowly as possible, I bite my lip to keep a yelp escaping my lips. With one swift and painful movement I'm able to switch on the lamp on the bed side table. Sucking in a deep breath I try to get over the fact that it feels like I've ran a marathon just from doing that.

"Okay you can do this! Just gotta get up!" I mumble to myself, clutching my side.

My feet touch the ground and I count down in my head.

3...2...1...

With one hand on the bedside table and a lot of inner yelling, I hoist myself to my feet. I immediately stumble a little but am able to stay upright. I find it crazy that there's nothing wrong with my legs apart from the odd ache and bruise but my ribs cause every movement to hurt. Every step twinges.

Wobbling and shuffling out of the room I make my way to the kitchen. A journey that usually takes about five seconds takes roughly three minutes. Which isn't easy in the dark either but I don't want to turn on any lights in case I wake Elijah in the front room.

Considering the open plan nature of this apartment there's nothing to really separate the two rooms.

I'm not sure what I'm planning to do right now. I just don't want to be in bed.

Glancing into the living room I can just about make out the couch and I squint to try and see Elijah lying there. I can't make anything out but that's probably because I don't have night vision.

My stomach rumbles as I reach the kitchen island, so now I know what I can do. Eat. Anything.

How am I going to open the top cabinets? Or even the fridge? I can't exactly cook anything but there will definitely be a chocolate bar around here somewhere.

My slow and steady searching begins and I pull open the drawer that Elijah usually keeps all the candy. Yeah he's got a candy drawer. If I ever doubted he was my soul mate then finding this a few months ago only confirmed the fact.

My hand hovers over the drawer as a sudden sickly feeling overcomes me.

A shiver shoots up my spine as I sense someone behind me. I freeze before my mind throws me back into that warehouse. The fear, the psychical and emotional pain. The loss of Elijah. Brian beating me over and over.

I blink to try and escape the illusion created by fear but it doesn't disappear. My breathing picks up, my heart races. I sweat.

Suddenly a hand is on my shoulder and I'm jumping away from it, scrambling to avoid any more pain.

"No, please no!" I yell, my back hitting the kitchen counter as I try to escape. Pain flares up worse than before and tears prick my eyes.

"Sofia! It's okay! It's just me" I hear, the voice cutting through the fog just before I try to sprint away.

With wide eyes, I take in my surroundings. I'm back in the apartment with a worried and terrified Elijah in front of me. His hands are held out in front of him as if to show me that he's not a threat.

My body relaxes again and I suck in large gulps of air in relief.

"It's okay" he repeats as I stay slumped against the counter unable to move in fear of falling or getting lost in that place again.

He takes a hesitant step towards me, his face a perfect picture of need. Not sexual need. Affectionate need. Need to comfort me.

"I'm sorry" I breath and he shakes his head as if he doesn't accept it.

"You don't have to say sorry Darling. Where did you go just now?" he asks staying where he is instead of coming towards me.

"I just got a fright. It wasn't you" I assure him but he knows there's more to it. I'm afraid to tell him because I know he will once again feel guilt. "Why are you up anyway?" I try to change the subject.

"Couldn't sleep. You?" he asks back tilting his head.

"Me either" I reply and he nods in understanding. We're not good sleeping apart. It's almost impossible.

"How about we go sit and you can tell me what just happened? I just want to make sure you're okay Darling"

I knew he wouldn't let it slide. Although I'll tell him happily if it means he'll let me be beside him and not scurry off again.

Hesitantly he takes my hand as if I could break any minute but his hold is tight and strong. How I've missed it. The small things really do mean the most huh.

He leads me to the couch where a blanket is laid with a pillow. I hate that he even tried to sleep here. Not because it's not comfortable but it's just not right. He belongs in bed next to me.

When we sit, he's close but not like he'd usually be. I hate it...so fucking much. He keeps hold on my hand though which is probably the only reason I can breath right.

"Tell me what happened?"

"I just had a teeny tiny flashback of shorts. I guess getting beaten up really sticks with a person huh" I try to make light of it. I don't want it to a big deal or an issue.

Like before when I recounted my tales of being in that warehouse to the police officer, Elijah's face flashes with anger.

"No one is going to hurt you ever again. I promise" he assures me, his tone determined and sure. It's sweet but it's not a promise that he should make. He can't control the world around me no matter how much he'd like to, to keep me safe.

"I appreciate the sentiment" I reply and he smiles softly, the promise of protection still strong in his gaze. Then a yawn falls from my mouth and he's quick to pull me to him...still ever so gently. The warmth of his body against mine is so damn amazing. He snuggles me into him, his chin leaning on top of my head.

"You have to try and get some sleep Darling" he whispers and I nod without a word and close my eyes. "Do you want to go back to bed?"

"No I'm fine here for now" I reply because I know that I'll have to go without him if I get up now.

He doesn't seem to mind, in fact he holds me tighter as if he doesn't want to let go. That's should make me feel so much better but for some reason it leaves a worrying feeling in the pit of my stomach. Why does it feel like he's saying goodbye when we've just found each other again?

I don't have time to think about it because my body is truly exhausted and there's no way I can fight sleep while in his arms. Finally I drift away peacefully for the first time in far too long.

Elijah

Having her sleep in my arms once again is the best feeling ever. It soothes me right down to my bones. I can't really explain it. I've never been able to and maybe I don't want to.

I wish I could sleep like she is but instead I'm wide awake because closing my eyes means I can't see her. I'm worried I'll wake up and she won't be here. That finding her has been a dream.

It's strange that I feel this way considering eventually I'll have to let her go. Once she's well enough she will need to leave me for her own good.

Although I can't think about that right now. It causes me too much pain.

I should tell her how I feel. I should let her know that our relationship can't continue because she means far too much to me to put her at any more risk. Yet I can't do it.

I'm being a horrible person I know. But I want her to look at me with love for a little while longer. My god do I want her forever but how can I have her when there's every possibility that she could get hurt or worse...killed.

A world without her in it isn't bearable so I'll have to settle for coping with her being with someone else one day.

Thousands of miles from me.

For the rest of the night I drift in and out of sleep. One minute I'm in dream land and the next I'm jolting awake to make sure she's okay. I'm constantly holding onto her and trying to ensure her comfort. I worry that the couch isn't the best place for her with her injuries.

Although when she wakes up in the morning with ruffled hair and the cutest blush ever she seems well rested. Naturally I spend far too long getting lost in her eyes. The only reason that I snap out of it is because of the rumble in her belly.

Shit. She must be starving!

I'm not exactly a great chef but after helping her onto a bar stood I being trying my best to cook up a storm in the kitchen.

Gradually more of her family appear in the kitchen, all taking their turn to ask if she's okay.

I end up burning some sausages because I get so distracted watching her laugh with Bree. I love that Sofia acts as her big sister. Her compassion and support for the younger girl is so lovely. Not to mention they bring out the silly side in each other and seeing Sofia's wide smile and full body laugh has my heart lurching faster.

Happiness. I want that for her forever!

Sofia smiles and laughs like that with me too. She's comfortable with me. Trusting. Loving. I don't want that to ever go away. I want to make her happy.

Yet I can't.

With the food ready we all sit at the dinning table to enjoy it. I watch as my girl appreciates every bite and thanks me profusely for my chargrilled sausages.

"You'd be a very talented house husband" she laughs and I can't help but grin back at her. I've missed this free feeling that only she can give.

To be honest, it's not a bad thought. I'd gladly be her house husband. I'd gladly cook for her everyday but then again I also love to watch her cook too. Maybe it's the way she bites her lip when she concentrates or her frustrated sighs if she messes something up. Either way I want both. I want it all.

I can have none.

Snatching my gaze away from hers, I focus on my half empty plate as the rest of her family chat away. I can tell she's looking at me. No doubt seeing right through me. Oh god.

My phone begins to ring in my pocket suddenly and it makes me jump a little in fright. It's not the phone I'm scared of. I'm scared that Sofia is seeing the pain inside me. I'm scared she sees that I already know how this will all end.

Glancing at the screen I catch Jack's name. I don't wanna answer but I also need to let him know what's going on. I owe him that.

Although I don't want to leave Sofia's presence. I don't want to be away from her gaze even if she is currently putting together some puzzle pieces in her head. Does she know what I'm thinking? That I intend to let her go?

Fuck! Ouch! There goes the pain in my gut again. God I can't take it!

Excusing myself from the table, I march to my office ready to get this phone call over and done with. I don't want to deal with a company that is no longer mine, I want to focus everything on Sofia. It's selfish of me I know because thousands of people depend on me but I guess I can't help it.

Hitting the answer button I'm immediately slammed with the angry voice of my second in command. Jack.

"Where the fuck have you been? Do you not answer your phone anymore? There's so many important things that you have already missed and that need your attention! We can't sign anything off without your consent!" he yells and I have to admit I do feel guilty. It's all I seem to feel these days.

"I'm sorry Jack but I'm not your boss anymore. There's certain things I had to-"

"WHAT?! What do you mean your not my boss? You're the fucking CEO of the company!"

"Not anymore. Nadia Zoya is. I signed over the company to her" I inform him with gravel in my voice. I hate that bitch. I hate having to say her fucking name.

"What the hell would you do that?! Have you gone mad?" he shouts and I really wish he'd tone it down to save my already growing headache.

"She had Sofia. Jack, she took her. She hurt her. I had to do it" I barely get the words out. I'm met with silence on the other end for a few long seconds.

"Fuck. I'm so sorry man. Surely she can't get away with this?" His voice is now immediately sympathetic and understanding. He's a really good man. That's for sure.

"She won't if I have anything to do with it! I really am sorry for leaving you in the lurch like this but it had to be done. I'll make it up to you one day. So the only thing I can recommend is working like normal until she says otherwise. Although I wouldn't count on her giving out any new orders because I'm sure she will be up to her eyeballs with law enforcement. She better wish that the outcome is prison too because If she gets away with this I'll take her down anyway I can. Even if it's with a fucking gun. I've got my best people on this. Every bit of information and evidence is currently being fed to the police. She may have my whole damn company but she will never touch my girl again" I growl, seeing red at the mere thought of that women near Sofia.

At the same exact moment I finish my angry speech my ears catch the sound of soft footsteps. Then my eyes latch onto a very pale looking beautiful women.

Shit. Fuck! She's heard me. She knows I gave Nadia my whole company.

Damn it! I can already see the guilt on her face and it kills me. No baby this isn't your fault!

"Jack, I have to go!"

Sofia

    Something isn't right. Elijah isn't right. I already knew that but the look he just gave me before he darted away with his phone has me really worried.

    I shouldn't go after him because maybe he wants to be alone. Yet everything in me is begging me to move. To ask him what's going on.

    Without a word I push myself out of the chair, gasping only slightly as I go.

    I hear my parents offering help but I assure them that I'll be okay. Which isn't a lie. A few steps away from the table and I'm able to manage the pain. I'm already working out how to breath through it.

It takes me a few minutes to get to where I assume he's went. I can just about make out his voice.

As I get closer to his office, his words become clearer. I feel bad that I'm ease dropping on his phone call but that doesn't stop me hobbling closer.

Naturally if a person ease drops, they are going to hear something they don't want to.

"...Even if it's with a fucking gun. I've got my best people on this. Every bit of information and evidence is currently being fed to the police. She may have my whole damn company but she will never touch my girl again"

After that I can't hear anymore because my mind is too busy putting the pieces together. Not that there are many pieces. He gave up his whole company...to get me back.

No! He has to get it back! I can't be the reason for such a great loss.

My heart thuds with regret. So much regret at bringing this upon his life.

Rounding the doorway into his office, I make sure my footsteps are heavy and my presence known.

Immediately he looks up from his spot leaning against his desk, his mouth hanging open as if he was midway through another sentence.

I shake my head at him as my own face crumbles into sadness. I did this to him.

"Jack I have to go" he snaps gruffly and ends the call, immediately dropping the phone to his desk. He looks panicked, stepping forward to come to me.

I hold up my hand to stop him. Not because I don't want him near me but because I don't deserve to be near him.

"You gave her it all..." I breath deathly quiet, the words making my tongue feel heavy.

"It's doesn't matter Darling. It really doesn't matter, I swear to you" he consoles me, taking another step towards me.

"Don't! Just stay there" I exclaim, my hands balling into fists.

"Sofia, it's okay-"

"Stop saying that! It's not okay! You threw away your entire life's work and for what?! Me?" I laugh almost manically, bile working it's way up my throat. "I'm just a silly little girl Elijah and you're going to end up resenting me"

There it is. The truth. My real fear. That he will one day hate me for what he done to save my life. That he won't ever be happy again without a business to grow and conquer.

"Don't be ridiculous! I'd do it again! Over and over to get you back" he growls, closing the distance between us regardless of my protests. "I could never resent you. It's just a company. You are everything" he sighs ever so sweetly. In that moment I see the same look in his eyes that I've seen many times before. I've always told myself it isn't love because he told me that he wouldn't ever believe in love. He hates love. Yet that's what it is. The same sickness and disease that I have. Love.

Why doesn't that make me happy? Probably because its my love for him in return that makes me want to give him everything. Instead I've taken it all away.

"You need to get it back. Now. Do whatever you have to Elijah" I implore him and he frowns deeply, his eyebrows coming together to darken his features.

"Why? I don't need it. I need you" he whispers, reaching up to touch my cheek. For some reason his sweet statement doesn't make me feel good. His words contradict the way he's been acting.

I swat his hand away before it can make contact, my ribs screaming in protest. Because here's the thing...I know that he's bullshitting me right now. I can't ignore it anymore. The way he's been so off with me yet still saying all these sweet things.

Saying he needs me. That I'm everything. It's lies. I don't know why he bothered to give up his company because ever since I woke up in hospital he's been preparing to let me go. I can tell.

It's in every guilty look he throws me. He didn't tell me about his company because why bother? I won't be around much longer for it to matter.

"Sofia...please believe me. It's not an issue. I don't care about it-"

"How could you not care?! It's all you've ever known. It's your empire!"

"It was my father's empire. Any desire I had to maintain it disappeared when I found out that other things are more important"

"Like what?" I ask because I want to see if he will lie again.

"A life with you"

Fucking asshole!

"A life with me? That's funny. I doubt we can have a life together when you aren't planning on keeping me around are you? I'm not stupid Elijah!"

"What? Of course I'm keeping you around. I'm going to look after you and then when you're better-" he pauses and swallows because he knows that's I've seen right through him.

The way he bolted from the room last night when he thought he hurt me. The constant restraint he uses every second he's with me. It's all telling. Just like he can't convince me that him selling the business is nothing, I can't convince him that he won't put me in danger. It's so clear on his face.

"Then what? Hmm? We start a life together?"

He closes his eyes then, his jaw clenching as he tries to come up with an answer.

"That's what I want more than anything" he whines, his eyes opening to spill out the darkest fears inside him.

"But?" I snap getting angrier and more hurt by the second. How dare he throw me pieces of affection knowing he's going to turn it right back off when I'm well again.

"But I'm no good for you. I caused all of this. I put you in danger. I hurt you and all I'll ever do is hurt you. You deserve better"

It's like I've been kicked in the gut. It's like he's lashing at my heart. All we've been through together and it's going to end up being for nothing.

"You don't get to decide what's best for me! I'm a grown women. That's my choice" I growl but he shakes his head.

"This is a choice I'm taking for you because I know what's better. I know how to keep you safe-"

"What will keep me safe? Mediocre sex with a gentle man who never talks dirty because he thinks it's disrespectful. Is that safe?" I taunt, my temper flaring into dangerous rage.

His anger rises too. Quick and sudden. He doesn't like the vision of my new life. I don't let him speak, I only taunt him more.

"Maybe I should settle down with a guy who will provide for me and tell me I don't have to work. And when I do try to work he tells me it's not my place. What do you think Elijah? Are any of them best for me? Or maybe I should get married and have countless kids to a guy will no doubt end up cheating on me when my body goes to shit-"

"STOP! he shouts, his whole body quaking with bright green jealousy.

"Why? It's going to happen. Something similar is my new future. If you don't want me then what's the point? I don't love anyone else. I love you"

"And you'll love again. Someone else will make you happy" his voice is quiet now but it holds ice from a thousand glaciers. I never thought I'd be the one the try and tear him apart but he's doing the same to me.

"What about you? Will you be happy?"

"That doesn't matter. All that matters is you are safe and alive. You'll get over me"

That's the last straw for me. He's making it sound so simple. 'You'll get over me' Ha! Yeah, sure totally. Maybe it is simple for him? Maybe he doesn't really want me anymore and this is his way out. Maybe he so badly wants a way out that he was willing to give up his whole business to get me back and end all of this guilt free.

Well fine. I'll give him his way out.

I'm not waiting to get better though. Like hell will I be around him for another second if he doesn't want me to be. Or if he plans to throw me away.

"You're right. I'll get over you" I say ever so softly as tears well in my eyes. I don't let them fall though. I won't give him that.

My statement has him looking at the ground, his body frozen as if he will never in unthaw again.

"I'm going to start now. I'm leaving because I can't be here any longer"

His head snaps up in blind panic and he moves closer to me again. I step back, wincing as I go.

"You can't go yet. You're not well" he states, his eyes begging with me. He's not just afraid that I'll hurt myself, he's afraid that he'll never see me again. He wanted more time to process my leaving by making me better. All the while he left me believing we would be together. Well fuck that.

"I'll be fine. I don't need you. I never really did it seems" I push out a lie to hurt him purposely this time.

Suddenly the necklace he gave me feels heavy as does the bracelet. I want them off.

In a quick and stupid movement I yank at the chain on my wrist and I hear his audible gasp.

"Stop it. That's yours and you're hurting yourself"

"Believe me, nothing hurts right now Elijah. Nothing more than you"

I catch him trying to come closer to me again and once more I step back, and then turn to keep walking away. All the while the chain bites into my skin.

"Fuck!" I yell. My ears pick up his quick footsteps behind me and as soon as he tries to touch me. I lose it.

His fingers touch my waist as if he's trying to help me walk and I spin around, ignoring the agony in my body.

"Don't touch me! Ever again! Do you understand?!" I all but scream. His face goes white, his panic transforming to horror and desperation. Is he finally realising what he's done? How much he's ruined us.

"I understand but that doesn't mean you should be hurting yourself" he shouts his voice echoing through the hallways.

Ignoring him, I give one final tug and the bracelet snaps leaving a red angry mark on my wrist. I do the same to the necklace which to my joy and dismay breaks a lot easier.

He watches me with a hollow gaze as if his world is crumbling before him. Well good because so is mine!

"Please keep them Darling. The reason I gave you them hasn't changed"

Holding his gaze I drop both rather expensive chains to the floor, turn on my heal and leave him behind. I do catch his broken look as I go. The twinge it causes me almost makes me stop but I can't stop. I can't feel sorry for him.

Clutching my side, I go as fast as I can but obviously he's still going to catch up with me.

"Please stop! I don't want you to get hurt" he begs once more and all I do is laugh.

"Too late for that don't you think? How about you make yourself useful and help me pack my things? When I say mine, I don't mean anything you've bought me! I don't want the laptop, I don't want any clothes you got me! Oh and you sure as hell better accept the money back that you've given me! As soon as I can I'll transfer it to you. I want nothing that came from you!" I yell as I enter his bedroom. His, not mine. It was never mine. None of this was mine. He just cleverly disguised it all behind fake affection that he never intended to fight for.

"You don't mean that" he says so quietly that I almost don't hear it.

"Yes I very much do. If I could go back in time and have you never touch me, believe me I'd do that too. This whole thing has been bullshit! Ever since I met you, you complained that you could trust no one. That everyone wanted your money. Well look who turned out to be the one untrustworthy huh? You! You've shattered my trust into a million pieces. You're a coward! Poor you! I don't think this has anything to do with keeping me safe. I just think you can't be bothered dealing with me anymore. Am I too caring for you? Too selfless? Does it annoy you that you can't complain that everyone is out to get you now?"

As I finish my rant I find it hard to breath. He just stands there staring right through me. With a nod so powerful it cuts me in two, he speaks.

"I deserved all of that but I am trying to keep you safe. You can think what you want of me. I can live with you hating me. However I can't live with you thinking that I'm doing this because I don't want you. I want you so fucking much. There is nothing I -"

"Spare me. I've heard it all before. Maybe I've been mistaken about you. I thought you were a man who'd fight for me through everything. You proved that to me by saving me from Nadia but it seems when it comes to more emotional things you just don't have the same commitment. I was never going to really have you was I?"

"You always had me-"

"Can you leave me alone to pack?" I cut him off and look away. I decide in that moment that I won't ever look at him again. I don't even feel bad. I'm only doing exactly what he planned to do as soon as I got better.

This is it. The end. I've had enough.

I can't do this anymore.

Elijah

    If I thought that I felt pain when she called me to tell me she used me for my money then I was sorely mistaken.
    This emotion transcends anything I've ever felt. Having her scream in my face knowing that she means every word has ruined me forever.
    I was being selfish. Trying to keep her here while she got better. Not telling her that ultimately I planned to let her go. I wanted more time with her before I knew I'd never see her again.
    Pretending that everything was fine while showing her how much I wanted her, needed her, is truly the harshest thing I've ever done. It's because I didn't want to accept my own choices. I wanted to pretend that we could be fine. That I was good for her and that I'd keep her safe. All the while my

mind whispered the truth. I was so wrong for her. So dangerous.

Which is the only thing currently keeping me from falling to my knees and begging her to stay. For forgiveness.

I stay as still as possible as she struggles to pack her things. Every thing she does I watch like a hawk. I want to help her all the while I don't. I can't help her leave me even if I'm the one who's making her leave. I once again caused this pain. Maybe if I'd been honest with her as soon as she woke up in hospital then this would be easier.

Bullshit. This could never be easy.

My nails dig into my palms to stop myself from scooping her up and holding her in my arms. I've never had to exercise such self control.

The monster inside me is waging a war. Common sense and this beast always battle for victory within me. The beast wants me to keep her. She's mine. I'm hers. Nothing can stop or change that.

However common sense is winning. My heart is more powerful than some ancient instinct of possession. She's not mine. She's no ones and she deserves happiness and safety that I cannot give.

How am I still sane right now? How can I be watching my girl packing her things to leave my life for good?

It doesn't seem right. It's all wrong but there's nothing that can change my mind. She will be happier with someone else. She will be!

She has to be.

Right now our constant field of chemistry is buzzing like a live wire between us. She may be furiously stuffing clothes in a bag while my heart shatters but that doesn't make anything stop. It doesn't take away how much I worship the ground she walks on.

It also doesn't hide the fact that while she is actively trying to hate me and be disgusted, it isn't working. I hate that. I hate that I hold as much power over her as she does me. I wish I could change that for her.

I wish I could make her forget me so she feels no pain. While I want that pain. I want the punishment I deserve for hurting her all over again.

"If you happen to come across anything else that's mine, send it to my parents house...please" I suddenly hear, her voice shaking as she turns to me. She stares back at my still frozen body, her anger now sadness. Complete desolate sadness. Yeah Darling I feel it too.

"Of course" I mumble unable to take my eyes off her. God I love everything about her. I glance over every part of her, from head to toe. She glares back and I welcome it. The red mark on her wrist and the less angry one of her neck make me itch to somehow heal her. As well as the gaping whole in my heart that was caused by her tearing off the jewellery I gave her. They weren't just materialistic gifts. They came from raw emotion.

I don't blame her for not wanting them now.

"Elijah..." her voice wobbles. My stone form turns to liquid ready it give her any request she may have. Except staying in my dangerous presence.

"Sofia" I breath and watch in agony as tears spill down her cheeks. I bite the inside of my mouth as her distress calls to everything inside me. If soul mates exist. She's mine.

"I promised you I'd never leave you lonely. You promised me the same in return"

One simple statement. Yet it makes me hate myself far more than I ever have. She's right, we did promise that to each other. Yet here I am breaking it.

"I'm sorry Darling. I really am" is the best I can do.

What I don't expect is for her to completely shut down there and then. It's like the last part of her that held out hope has died. I can't stand it. There's no feeling in her eyes. Nothing. She's not angry or upset. Just indifferent and she walks by me as if I no longer exist to her.

I can't explain or use words. I'm in limbo. I'm nothing.

My mind registers the sounds of her telling her family that she's leaving. They ask her what the shouting was about.

She just repeats thats she has to leave. I can hear it all from down the hall.

Everything in me is begging me to stop her but I can't do it. Not when I've betrayed and broken her trust. Not now. Not ever.

Forcing my feet to move, I follow the sound of voices to the front room. Everyone but her looks up when I enter. All of them angry and disappointed. Bree even makes her displeasure known.

"You're an asshole!" she yells, while I stare back at her blankly. No one needs to tell me that. I already know.

"Bree lets go" Sofia prompts gently. I cling to the sound of her voice. She hasn't even told them what I've done but they know it's my fault.

Her parents only glare but I know they're ripping me apart in their minds. Quite right. I've hurt their child. I've hurt the most important person to them. To me.

"Will you be okay getting home? Do you want me to send for a car?" I ask feebly, trying one last time to be of any help. I don't know why I thought they'd accept.

"We want nothing from you" her Dad snaps and guides his daughter to the elevator.

My panic rises. She's leaving. I've known this for the last half an hour but I've managed the psycho inside me. I've kept it at bay.

Now as they step inside the metal box my heart thuds so fast I think I might be about to have a heart attack.

No. No. No. She can't go. We can't be apart.

Those words repeat over and over as a dark cloud descends over my entire being. I knew this is how things would end for me eventually. I deserve to be on my own.

All of the feelings of loss I felt before coming crashing back tenfold. I knew it would hurt. Worse than before. I know I'll have to live in this pain forever but I thought that I'd find peace in knowing she will be safe.

Nothing is giving me peace right now.

"Don't stay alone forever" I hear her beautiful voice beg me. A storm rages inside me. My eyes latch onto hers for dear life. I can't do this. I can't go through it again.

Not without her.

My feet move, she frowns in confusion. In hope.

The elevator doors begin to slide shut.

I can't take it.

They my mind is bombarded with images of a life we could have together. A life that could end with her early death if I make any more enemies.

Stopping dead I give her one last look. One that I hope tells her that I love her. One that begs her to know I'll never want anyone else.

The last thing I see is her mouthing those three to me before the doors shut completely and she's gone.

Gone.

Sofia

  I don't think I'll ever truly believe what just happened. He didn't even put up a fight. He really was planning to leave me.
  What was all of this for? Nadia won and we got nothing out of it. We simply lost everything.
  I wish I could understand better. His self loathing is bad but I never knew it was so bad that he'd tell me he wasn't safe for me. That he'd sever our relationship because of it.
  Now I really do wish I'd died in that warehouse because then he would still have his business and I'd never know that he had the ability to let me go.
  My parents and Bree don't say a word about my current situation on the six hour train ride home. It occurs to

me that I haven't even asked if I can stay with them again. I'm just hoping they'll let me until I get on my feet again.

I'm not sure how long that will take. The thought of a completely new future isn't something I can stomach thinking about.

The normal things that many people worry about don't even enter my brain. No money. No job. No aspirations...who gives a fuck about any of that. Definitely not me.

In fact I can't wait to send all of Elijah's money back to him so that I can relieve myself of the crushing guilt I feel. I wish I'd never accepted his money. I wish he hadn't bought me a thing because no matter how desperate I am for cash, I'll never be okay with spending someone else's money.

In fact, staying in his apartment without paying him a dime drove me mad too. I guess I felt pacified by the fact that I felt like I belonged at his side. That maybe one day we'd get a house together and I'd be able to pay half of everything. Silly me.

I'm still grateful for everything he's done for me, all the while wishing it never happened. I should have dealt with it all on my own. I'll never again let anyone pay for my life.

The money I have earned from working in the coffee shop will be used to pay my parents rent.

I may not desire getting a job right now because I simply desire nothing. Except I'll have to. I need a distraction from the excruciating pain flowing in my veins. I need income and to grow the fuck up.

Fall in love they said. It'll be fun they said... ha!

My strong bravado crumbles as the train pulls into the station. God I don't want to be back home. I feel like a failure. A complete mess.

My tear stained cheeks don't help one tiny bit.

The simple fact is I don't actually care about my future. Deep down I don't care about tomorrow or the next day. I don't care if I stay jobless and end up on the street...not really. Because none of that matters. None of that hurts me.

The thing that scares me most about my future is the fact that it's not going to have Elijah in it.

Elijah

One Week Since Sofia Left

"Do you plan on fighting for your fucking company or not?" Jack yells down the line causing my headache to pound harder.

"No I don't plan on that. Currently I'm planning on waiting until my residual income stops getting deposited into my bank account. I don't know why I'm still getting paid when I don't own the fucking company! I don't want it!"

"Well until that bitch Zoya takes some kind of action it'll keep happening. She may have her name on the contracts and documents but these things don't change within a week Elijah!"

It takes a lot of effort for me to care about anything right now. Like a whole fucking lot. Although I am baffled as to why Nadia hasn't started lording over her new business. I like to think it's because she's scared to move a muscle in case she runs into the law. From my last update she's had three different interviews with the police. She's a good liar though and it's going to take more time to pin this on her.

Even with the evidence and both mine and Sofia's statements...oh and with Sofia's injuries, they still can't fucking arrest her.

However they have arrested Brian. I'm waiting for an update on that part.

Squeezing my eyes shut I do my best to ignore the slideshow of thoughts and images that bombard my brain. No. Don't think about her.

Silly of me to even think her name. She's fine. Probably better than ever!

"Elijah?! Hello!"

"Yes I'm here. I keep telling you I can't do anything about it. It's out of my control. Why do you care so much anyway? You're still getting paid and doing your job" I sigh, sitting up on the couch and shielding my eyes from the sunlight beaming through the floor to ceiling windows. When did it become morning again?

"I care because you are my boss Elijah. You have been for years! Not be mushy but I look up to you. You've taught me a lot and I don't want you to throw it all away"

That's touching but not enough to get anywhere near the barricade slammed around my emotions.

"It'll all work out okay for you and hopefully for the rest of the staff. You don't need to worry about me because apparently I'll have enough money to stay filthy fucking rich for the rest of my pointless life. You know I was kind of hoping I'd go bankrupt soon. Maybe I'd have to get a normal job. Do you know how much money I've given to charity over the last week?"

"I don't want to know Elijah. You're being incredibly stupid! Look I know you're heartbroken but there's any easy way to fix that! Just go get Sofia back-"

"Stop! Stop talking. I don't want to hear that. Just stop calling too okay! I've had enough of your whining" I snap, standing up to relieve the constant state of irritation and desolation I live in.

This has me catching a glimpse of my reflection in the windows. Fuck I look like shit. I'm not sure how many different foods are staining my sweat pants or why I'm not wearing a shirt but who really cares? No one can see me.

"You need to pull it together! Seriously! If you're not going to get her back then find someone else. Or even just fuck someone please-"

Oh hell that's also not something I want to hear. Remember when she thought I slept with someone else? I hate that she even had an image of that in her head. I could never do that. I don't think I ever will again.

"Goodbye Jack-ass"

Ending the call and dropping my phone, I contemplate what to do now. My days consist of sleeping a lot. Occasionally eating whatever is in the cupboards and even more occasionally trying and failing to not think about Sofia.

Soon I will actually have to leave my sanctuary to buy more food or maybe I'll buy everyone else food too and try to put a dent in my bank account.

Apparently my new hobby is called: Trying To Go Bankrupt As Fast As Possible.

Which is really fucking tough!

My bones creak as I walk aimlessly around my apartment keeping my eyes straight ahead in case I see anything that may crush my heart even further.

We should be together right now. If I was a better man and less known to the world we could be happy.

I wish my selfish gene was stronger. I wish I could have said fuck it and held her close but then I wouldn't deserve her.

I still don't but at least giving her a better chance without me is something.

Hopefully she's already feeling happier. Hopefully she's forgetting me.

No that's a lie. The thought of her forgetting me is crushing. Maybe she will always hold me in her heart a little. I think I could live with that.

The ping of my phone once again enters my consciousness and I glare in the direction of it. Why can't anyone leave me be for a while? I need time. A lot of time. Like until the end of time!

Marching back to the couch I snatch it up, ready to send back an angry email or text to whoever has dared bother me.

Only it's a notification from my online banking. Great, have I been paid again?

Upon closer inspection the information I read seems to come out of the phone and slap me right in the face.

'Miss S Westwood has requested to transfer $5405.34 into your account'

Fuck.

My legs wobble slightly. I'd hoped that she would forget to do this. How sickening is it that although I don't want the money back, I'm far too happy just to see her name. Even though I was the one to ensure our relationship was severed, I can't help but want to communicate with her. Even like this.

Would she be mad if I declined?

Yes you asshole! You did this so just do what you know she wants you to do!

Will she be okay without the money? Does she have a new job? Are her ribs a little better? Is her wrist still sore? What did she eat today?

Running my hand over my face I try to expel all of the questions. It's none of my business anymore.

Opening the notification I see that she's added a note to her transaction that completely slays me.

Senders Reference: Please take it back. I can't bare to have it now. You've helped me enough. Thank you and Goodbye.

Sofia

Two Weeks After Leaving

    At first when I sent the money back, I'd felt so much relief. I'd felt happy that I wasn't taking anything from anyone anymore.
    Now though in my parents bathroom as I assess all of my faded bruises, I realise that the money was the only connection I had left to him. It's almost as if our relationship never happened because my parents act as if it didn't. Everyone around me pretends life is normal and that I'm not rotting inside.
    I could say that I miss him but that would not do justice to how much I want him to show up at the door.
    My anger at his plans to let me go has died down considerably. Now I just feel like a walking black hole sucking everyone's happiness away.

Being around other people just makes me sadder because when they smile, I can't.

I do try not to be in my parents house too much. I go for walks which actually have became rather addictive to me. It gives me free time to think about Elijah. He never leaves my mind.

My walks are often short. Even though the pain in my ribs is slowly dying down, they're obviously still broken and will take a long time to heal properly. My wrist feels stronger but my spirit feels weak.

Yesterday was my birthday. Not that it's significant or that I really celebrated it. In fact I requested that no one mention a thing about it. It's just another day. Another year closer to death. Hooray!

My parents did however leave a neatly wrapped gift on my bed. A new phone which I really wanted to protest about. I did try to actually but they ignored me and said that I'd need it to keep track of my life.

What life?

I suppose I should mention that after using my Mom's laptop to send Elijah his money back, I also used it to once again begin my crusade at finding a new job.

Since I've applied for so many in the last year of my life it's been really easy for me to robotically input my information. There's no joy to it anymore. Only the slight hope that one day I'll be able to make enough money to rent my own apartment for real. Then I can cry myself to sleep without anyone hearing me through thin walls.

There's a little bit of progress been made come to think of it. I have an interview for a small upcoming web tech business. Terrible pay but at least if I get it then I'll be able to get out for more than an hour.

Not so long ago I'd be jumping at this news. However I don't feel any excitement. Just borderline insanity at wondering if I'll ever be able to feel anything at all again.

I wonder how he is? I wonder if he's gotten his company back? Has he moved on?

With a deep breath I leave the bathroom and go back to my bedroom. God I really do hate it here. The last time I was in this room I was with Elijah.

On our last visit here he plucked my already broken guitar and accidentally snapped another string. His shocked and guilty face was so cute.

Lowering myself onto the bed, I think about a small triumph that has occurred. My Mom told me about Brian's arrest. Any information on Nadia's case is passed to my parents because I don't want to deal with having to talk to anyone.

Grabbing my phone I do the one thing that I do far too many times each and every day. Opening my banking app, I look at Elijah's reply to my transaction reference note.

Receivers Note: Of course I'll accept it back. I'll do anything I can to ease your mind Darling.

When I'd first read it I'd had to resist the urge to throw my Mom's laptop across the room. I was still very angry then.

Now I just find it hard not to send back a couple of dollars just so I can type another message to him.

"Sofia! Honey, there's a letter here for you!" I hear from downstairs, followed by footsteps. A letter for me? How could that be?

My Dad enters my room with a soft knock and holds out the almost impossible letter. The last address I was registered at was the student flat. I'd never changed it to

Elijah's apartment because I hadn't gotten around to it. I was too distracted by being you know...happy.

"It looks important" he muses as I take it and see the Chicago PD stamp on the front. Now that makes a little more sense. The police would have sent the letter to my old apartment but would have then been informed by the landlord that I no longer stay there. Logically the next address is the one previous to that.

So here it is.

My Dad leaves me to it as a sinking feeling begins to rise inside me.

Is this going to tell me that Nadia was arrested? Or maybe that she got away with it? Dear god it better not be the latter! I've tried not think about my kidnapper getting free but it's always at the back on my mind. I don't just want justice for myself, I want it for Elijah more.

With shaky hands I open up the letter and yank the sheets of paper out. More than one for some reason.

Upon scanning the pages with quick desperation I discover its good news. Fantastic fucking news!

This is a letter of invitation.

An invitation to testify against Nadia in court.

She has been arrested!

Elijah

    A letter to testify against Nadia. A way for me to ensure that she gets put away for a long time. Fuck yes!
    A way to ensure she can never get near Sofia again. Or anyone for that matter. Double fuck yes!
    For the first time in two weeks my face breaks into a smile. A crazed psychopathic smile. I can finally make her pay for hurting the most important person in my life. Okay so she may not be in my life anymore psychically but she will always be the most important person to me.
    I also know that this court date and all of the accusations will eventually make any of the contracts she's signed null and void. She can't own the company with a criminal record.
    Therefore very soon, no one will. It's irrelevant to me of course. I don't care who owns the company next. Okay, I care a little bit. I want Jack to be okay. I want all of the employees to have better management and the thought that this can now happen has a little bit of joy sliding through the dark cloud above my head.

It evaporates as quickly as it appears, eaten up by other thoughts. If I have this letter then so does Sofia. She's going to have to face Nadia all over again.

It's not fucking fair!

Maybe I could be enough to prove that Nadia is guilty? Maybe they won't ask Sofia to take the stand.

Except that outcome is inevitable. She will have to do it. She will have to once again feel pain because of Nadia.

We're apart so that she's safe yet it seems I can't protect her from everything like I very much want to.

"Shit!" I yell and tug on my hair with my free hand. What can I do? How can I stop this??

Even as I ask myself these questions I know that I can't. I can't save her from this.

There's something else too.

We're both going to court. We're going to be in the same room.

My heart immediately flies at the thought, my breathing becoming sharp.

God I want to see her. Once again that's selfish but this time there's nothing I can do. We both need to testify to ensure Nadia gets put away.

I'll keep my distance. I'll try to make it as painless as possible. I'm sure she's still angry at me and I don't blame her.

I pushed her away.

Sofia

Three Weeks After Leaving- Court Date

  I may be a fully grown woman but that doesn't mean that I don't need moral support. Which is why as I travel back to Chicago, my Mom sits next to me.
  She told me that I didn't have to do this. That I could let the court know it was too hard for me but how could I not go? The only thing that I have left right now is putting that bitch in jail for a long time. She deserves it and I don't want her to hurt anyone else in the future.
  Wearing the only partially formal dress I have with matching baby pink pumps, I feel as though it's some kind of armour. It makes me look more confident than I feel. My insides churn as time ticks on, brining me closer to the city I left. Closer to a certain person that I never thought I'd get to see again.

My fists clench as my hands rest on my thighs and I look out of the train window. The lack of pain shooting up my arm reminds me of how I've healed.

My ribs only twinge now and then while my wrist is basically back to normal. Any bruising on my face and stomach is barely visible and I feel a lot stronger all round. Well not so much on the emotional side.

Inside my head is a whole other story with one person in the spotlight.

Elijah.

If I think about him too long, I cry. Which always happens because I'm never able to remove him from my thoughts.

I've tried really hard not to think about the fact that he's going to be here today. Well I assume he's going to be. What would I prefer? Not seeing him? Honestly I'm not sure what would be more beneficial.

For some reason I think I'd be disappointed if he didn't show up for this. She's hurt him just as must as she's hurt me so a no show would really tear me apart.

I just hope that I can get through this trial without bursting into tears. It's not going to be easy especially when I'll have to look at Nadia's no doubt smug face. Maybe she's less smug now I guess? Maybe not.

For the rest of the train journey my Mom tries to encourage me to eat. Only I simply can't stomach any food. I feel sick already and when I stand as the train arrives at the station, my legs wobble.

I can do this!

I have to!

"You okay?" she asks as we become engulfed by the crowds of other people exiting the train.

"I won't lie and say yes but I will be" I confess as she puts a reassuring hand on my shoulder.

One foot in front of the other. That's all I can do. In fact that's all I can tell myself over and over as we hail a cab to take us to the court.

I don't say a word as I get inside the far too hot interior. The cab driver asks where we need to go and my Mom has to answer. Becoming mute is not what I need right now.

A bead of sweat forms on my forehead and trickles down the side of my face. Is it actually hot or am I just nervous?

Pressing my head against the cold window, I close my eyes. Just breath. All you gotta do is tell your story. Let the world know how much of a horrible person she is and it'll all be okay.

You have done nothing wrong. She can't hurt you anymore!

My Mom nudges me gently and my eyes wrench open.

If I thought I was somehow keeping myself under control, well I was lying to myself because the cab journey is too short. The grandeur of the court building comes into view and I want to throw up.

As the vehicle stops, I try to pull myself together. It doesn't really work.

My hand reaches for the door handle to help me escape out of this hot box only it freezes as my eyes latch onto something that distracts me.

The sight doesn't just distract me, it has my breathing stop and my blood pumping in my ears.

The man that has been filling my every waking thought and my dreams gets out of his car across the street.

He stops for a moment to frown at his phone and it gives me a chance to devour every inch of him. He's dressed in a crisp navy suit, his hair unruly and his beard is full. With a shake of his head he crosses the road and passes in front of our cab. He looks so confident, completely unfazed by the reason he's here.

Completely unfazed by the end of our relationship too by the looks of it.

My eyes automatically form a glare as he begins to walk up the steps to the large entryway doors. I'm about to get out of the car just to curse at his nonchalance but then he stops his ascent.

In a few quick movements he's leaning a hand against the wall by the door. He bows his head as if he's going to be sick. Now it's me who's frowning and wondering what just happened to him. Is he really going to be sick?

His hand runs down his face before he loosens the tie around his neck.

"Sofia? We're here" I hear my Mom inform me as if she thinks I'm completely unaware of my surroundings. I don't blame her. I'm as still as a statue, staring out the window.

I must look a little mad.

My attention never leaves Elijah's rigid form as he stands back up straight and runs both hands through his hair. He takes a deep breath before shoving his hands in his pockets.

I guess I was wrong. He is very much struggling. Why do I want to take away that struggle so much? After he pushed me away? After he gave us up?

I don't know what to do, I'm trapped gazing at him like a love sick fool. I should be angry. Yet the only emotion I feel is crushing need. Need to be with him. To be next to the person that my soul has chosen as it's other half.

    I miss him so fucking much. Yet we won't ever be together. How unfair is that?!

    My eyes don't leave him until he disappears through the front doors of the building. Immediately I want to see him again.

    Which I think is the only reason I'm finally able to exit the cab.

    My Mom follows suit and I can tell she's staring at me as we cross the road. She's probably wondering how my mood changed so quick. I guess it's hard to focus on the terrifying events to come when I'm so clearly still in love and obsessed.

    I can't afford to be love sick right now though.

    Which is why I try my best not to search for him when we enter the court foyer. It's a ridiculous thing for me to try and achieve because I'm naturally drawn to him.

    My eyes snap to his nervous looking form as he sits on one of the plush benches outside the actual court room.

    There's lots of people milling around but I don't notice any of them.

    Really I should be going over the exact words that I need to say. I should be recalling all of the shit Nadia put me through so I don't miss a thing but my mind is foggy because of this man.

    "Now I get why you pretty much ran here. You knew he'd be here though right?" my Mom asks softly as if she's worried I'll have a breakdown or start yelling.

    "Yes, I assumed he would be. He's just as much a part of this as I am. In fact probably more so. He's the one she really wanted to hurt" I explain, blinking back a sudden wave of sadness. I hate that this is where things are now. That we aren't fighting this together.

He vowed to keep me safe and this is his way of doing so. Or maybe he just wanted a fresh start without me?

Snapping my gaze away from him with a lot of difficulty, I focus on why I'm actually here. It's going to be tough to sit on the sidelines and listen to someone trying to defend Nadia. It's going to be more difficult hearing her lie through her teeth.

"Come on, you gotta sign in" my Mom prompts, tugging me in the direction of a booth with perplex glass on the front. The man that sits behind it looks pissed at the world and his serious expression makes me nervous.

He asks mundane typical questions and I answer as if I'm on autopilot. All the while my head whirls with far too much information. Far too many thoughts.

I'm not sure that I can comprehend how important my role in today is. If I think about it too much then I'll go insane.

The fact of the matter is, most of the charges that are being held against Nadia today are crimes she committed...against me. Blackmail, kidnap, assault. One count of blackmail against Elijah is also on that list. Which pisses me off because she should also be getting charged with stealing a whole fucking company! Oh and in general harassing Elijah for months!

My fists ball at my sides as I become angry at the things she did to him and not me. My Mom is talking again but I can't take it in this time.

My breathing is far too deep, my body far too rigid. My eyes scan the area around me once I'm done signing in, trying to grasp at something that will make me feel better.

Naturally there's only one thing I want to see. So of course I end up staring back at Elijah who is now standing a few metres away, his gaze looking right back at me.

Fuck.

With his eyes firmly taking me in, his face is a mixture of shock and pain. Exactly how I'm feeling. How crazy is it that not so long ago we were closer than ever and now it feels like we're strangers.

Still his warm struggling gaze is familiar and the world falls away around me. He opens his mouth as if he's going to say something and I'm desperate to hear it. What will he say? Am I ready to hear his voice? My body tenses as if preparing to take every word in.

"Court is in order!" Is the next thing that fills my ears and disappointment leaves a bitter taste in my mouth. My head snaps to the formally dressed man that the words came from and I want curse him out for ruining Elijah and I's possible moment.

Quickly I glance back at Elijah but he's now focused on the man too.

Now all I can do is wonder what he was going to say. Was it nice? Mean? Completely heart wrenching?

As people start to file into the court room, Elijah included, I realise that it's quite possible I'll never know what he was going to say or ever have him speak to me directly ever again.

And that...that kills me.

Elijah

    Have you ever felt like your heart was going to burst or that the world is so unfair you are very willing to tear the whole earth to pieces?

    Well I have.

    The second I saw her.

    My constant wonderings of her well being were answered instantly as I noticed how little bruising was visible on her face and arms now. She's healing. She's okay.

    She didn't look to be in pain like she was a few weeks ago and I wanted to punch the air because that fact makes me so happy. God I wanted to ask her how she is. I need to hear that she's okay.

    However, if I thought I felt empty before then I was wrong. Having her so close, yet so emotionally far away left a huge cavernous whole inside me.

There's so much I could have said. So much I should have said. I've never felt such yearning. Such agony from not being able to be close to a person.

She's so beautiful. Yet to see the emotional strain on her face matching mine, only ingrains more hurt onto me. Because I caused that strain.

Trying to do the right thing sometimes really doesn't seem worth it at all. Keeping her safe? Yet making her hurt...

It that justified? I'm not so sure anymore.

Now all I get to do is walk away from her and into another hideous situation that I don't want to face.

I could face it if I had her. She makes me better. I can't help but want to know if she still cares about me. Not having her is my fault too though and she may hate me now.

Yet even having her in the same room as me, whether she hates me or not, somehow gives me strength. Here I am again being selfish. Using her to make myself feel better.

With that thought, I steal a glance at her once more as I take my allocated seat in the court room. She's a couple of rows behind me and she catches my stare.

It makes me snap my head back around, embarrassed that I've been busted. I really need to get myself under control.

Self control is something I did once have. Then she blew all of that to smithereens in the best way possible. I didn't need to censor myself with her or hold back. I could be me.

Right now though, as the court room fills up and silence falls, I realise that I'm going to have to fight really hard to keep control in a different manner. Where she let me be free, she also had the ability to help me breath in difficult situations.

Sofia has this magic about her that keeps me calm. She can't take my hand now. She can't kiss my cheek and she can't whisper in my ear and tell me that it'll all be okay.

Have I always been so unhinged? So angry and ready for violence? Or is this a new thing?

Suddenly I hear the judge being announced and stand robotically as he enters. My legs wobble slightly throughout the seconds before I can sit again.

The back of my neck prickles with a feeling that I'm familiar with. I may be wrong but I think Sofia is staring a whole into the back of my head.

Which is why when more announcements are made, I can barely make them out because my head is swimming.

Wiping my sweaty palms on my dress pants, I take a deep breath and glance up just in time for the accused to be ushered into the court.

I feel my jaw clenching as rage fills me. She walks by confidently, led by two police men. I'm glad she doesn't look in my direction because that may tip me over the edge. If she's smug about this I honestly don't know how I'm going to stay put.

It's like a dark cloud consumes the whole room. Much like the feeling inside my heart. I want to kill on sight.

Yet I also want to turn around and snatch Sofia up to protect her from this. From that horrible women!

How can I sit through this? I want to scream. I want to tear her limb from limb.

It's very possible I won't make it through today without getting arrested myself.

Sofia

    The sickness that I felt earlier begins to creep back inside of me as Nadia is taken to her seat. The sight of her has memories of pain and terror flashing before my eyes.
    I actually forget to breath until my chest constricts desperate for air. I'm all but gasping to fill my lungs.
    Next to enter the court is the jury but I can't focus on that because Nadia isn't just sitting there facing forward. Oh no that would be too easy on me. Instead she scans the area and much to my dread, her gaze stops when she finds me.
    Instantly a glare forms on her face. This changes my fear slightly. I expected her to be smug. For her to be so confident that she will get her freedom but apparently that's not how she's feeling.
    Regardless that doesn't give me much joy. I don't enjoy other people's pain like she does.
    I'm white as a sheet. I know that for a fact. I also know that regardless of my formal attire, I look somewhat

run down. While she still looks so primed and proper. How is that fair?

Clearly she hasn't had any trouble eating or sleeping like I have. There's no remorse in her eyes as I hold her gaze as best as I can. It's like a test of nerves. The first to look away looses. Sadly it's me because those vicious eyes make me petrified.

What if she doesn't get put in jail? What if she comes for me again? Just out of spite?!

Staring down at my hands, I wring them together as if I'm the one on trial. Nadia is no doubt still looking at me and I wish I had the courage to look back and show her that I'm not scared.

I can't. I'm frozen stiff with fear.

That's why I'm endlessly glad when the judge begins to introduce each sector of the court. Oh and the list of crimes Nadia is being tried for.

"One count of blackmail. One count of abduction. One count of assault with intent of serious injury or death. One count of fraud and to top it all off, one count of failing to comply to the commands of a police officer..."

Huh. That last one is new. I guess she really didn't want to be questioned or interviewed. Maybe she's losing her smooth touch. Which I really hope is the case.

Maybe she's been taken down a peg or two. Although a second look at Nadia shows she looks very focused.

She's probably ready to spill lie after lie.

In an ideal world she'd just confess and we could all go home but this world is messed up and broken so I guess we'll all have to endure this hell.

For the next twenty minutes or so, I really don't understand much of the legal jargon passed between the judge, attorneys and jury. Mostly it seems to be to do with helping the jury understand each accusation and their role in all of this.

Then the real fun begins, except it's the opposite of fun.

"The count of blackmail is from Mr Elijah Everett."

Who you will hear from soon. The other more serious counts of abduction and assault are from Miss Sofia Westwood" the judge explains to the jury. Upon hearing my name and being pointed out from everyone else, I feel my face go bright red and fight the urge to run away.

Maybe a meteor will hit this exact spot and I won't have to deal with this.

Fuck. Fuck. Fuck.

Having multiple pairs of eyes on me is extremely intimidating. I want comfort. I want safety. I want out of here but mostly I want to be next the person a couple rows in front who looks more rigid than ever.

Come on Sofia. You did just fine before you met him. You can do just fine now.

I repeat my little pep talk in my head as the judge gives the jury even more back story to the accusations.

Then it happens.

"Miss Westwood, would you kindly take the stand"

Okay. Oh god.

"It'll be okay" I hear and my eyes snap to my Mom sitting next to me, who I pretty much forgot was here. That's how distracted I am.

As I stand, I put on the fakest confident expression. Which is pretty much just a poker face that could crack at any moment.

My cool exterior is contrasted by my racing heartbeat and held breath. Even though I only have to take about twenty steps to get to the stand next to the judge, it feels like a mile. A walk of shame even though I haven't committed a crime.

It's silent. So fucking silent.

I turn to face the rest of the room as if I've got a steel rod in my back. Even though I'm now looking at a whole crowd of people, I make sure my eyes don't focus on any one person. That would be too much.

"Miss Westwood, do you swear to tell the truth and nothing but the truth?" the judge asks.

This part is easy. I have no problem with telling all of my truths.

"I do"

Those two words are like a starting gun for Nadia's defence attorney and immediately my gaze snaps to a red haired women in a pant suit with a cool gaze.

Sweat trickles down my back. My hearing turns hyper sensitive and everything I know as fact becomes blurry as she asks the first question.

"Miss Westwood, is it true you engaged in a romantic relationship with the other person testifying today. Mr Elijah Everett..."

What? Isn't that fucking obvious? How is that going to help Nadia's case.

Instinctively my eyes snap to Elijah, who stares back with a pained expression. It's as if he's remembering every intimate detail of our relationship.

Then something changes and he sits up straight and nods ever so slightly at me. The room is waiting for my reply but I can't speak.

Well not until I see him mouthing 'you can do this Darling'. It's not hard to make out the words. I've studied his lips far too much not to know.

Okay...

I can do this. I will do this.

"Yes that's true" I reply cooly. Am I supposed to say more? Who knows?

I don't get much time to think about it because she moves on quickly. Quicker than I expected. Which actually isn't too bad because I don't want to linger on that sore subject.

"And your relationship with him started in a less than conventional way correct?" She fires the second question out and it makes me wonder how she knows this. The answer is obvious. Nadia would have divulged anything to make us look bad. She would have known about his sugar daddy background.

I also realise that I don't have to elaborate. If she keeps asking me questions this way, then I don't have to give any details. "That's also true" I respond. This prompts her to give me a somewhat strange smile. She knows that I've worked out how to answer on my own accord. I'm assuming she didn't expect that to happen so quick. So she's going to have to work harder to try and defend a demon like Nadia.

"In what way was it unconventional-"

"Off topic" the judge cuts in and I'm so damn grateful. She was about to try and humiliate me. "Ask relevant questions related to the accused"

"Your honour, I believe it's relevant as Miss Zoya-"

"Enough! Relevant questions or stand down"

Well...I'm certainly glad the judge thinks the specifics and intimate details of Elijah and I's relationship isn't relevant.

The defence attorney looks pissed but nods and faces me once more. Deeeeppp breathes Sofia. You got this.

My eyes flick to Elijah for a millisecond to find him still watching me closely. In that moment I'm reminded of how much I have his support. No matter what's happened between us.

"Did you have any issues with Nadia prior to your allegations?" Is the next question.

"I met her briefly when she stopped El- Mr Everett's car to ask him a second time about acquiring part of his company" I state, trying to sound somewhat professional. Which just makes me sound ridiculous.

"Was there any tension between the two of you?"

"Yes a little. I told her to back off. I imagine she didn't like that" I recall. Remembering when I sassed the hell out of Nadia. I'm still proud of it and I'd do it again.

"Is it possible that you were jealous of Miss Zoya?" she asks, her eyebrows raised. Ha, that's funny. If that was meant to bother me then she's failed. "I'll elaborate. Where you worried she may attract the attention of Mr Everett?"

"No, not at all. Mr Everett made it clear that she was trying to get part of his business and nothing more. I had no reason not to believe him. I trust him" I say casually. Except it isn't casual at all. Because apparently I'm still talking about Elijah in present tense as if we're not both broken hearted. I trust him. I think I'll always trust him.

"Miss Westwood, would you agree that your relationship with Mr Everett began with the exchange of money?" she quickly continues on and I'm shocked that she's back to this line of questioning.

She must notice the judge going to object and holds up her hand.

"It'll be relevant..."

Turning to the judge for some moral support, he nods at me.

"Please answer the question Miss Westwood"

Damn it. Shit!

The small piece of calm I was beginning to feel disappears. Yet I have to hope that the jury will understand and not judge. I shouldn't be ashamed of this.

In fact I'm not.

"No, it didn't start that way. Money was exchanged later on" I tell her with my chin held high. If anyone thinks bad of me for that then so be it.

"So maybe you made all of this up to ensure Mr Everett wouldn't give money to another pretty women. Maybe you wanted all of his money for yourself"

I'm sure this would work with other people. Yet it won't with me. Elijah and I broke up because of his desire to keep me safe. Therefore I still have the utmost respect for him. I also would be stupid to believe that I don't still...lo- care for him very much. The wounds are still fresh and so are my affections.

So when I answer I don't look at the defence attorney. I face the jury and show them all of my emotions.

"If Mr Everett wanted to give Miss Zoya money then that would have been none of my business. Any money given to me was a gift of kindness. One I was very grateful for but it wasn't why I entered into a relationship with Mr Everett. In fact, money isn't important to me at all" I explain truthfully.

"But didn't you meat Mr Everett through a sugar daddy website?"

Fuck. Well this looks really bad now.

"Yes, we met through a sugar daddy website due to my curiosity about the lifestyle but I was never his sugar baby. By the time my curiosity was sated, I already had strong feelings towards Mr Everett. So our relationship continued. In short, Mr Everett's money wasn't of interest to me. I don't enjoy spending other people's money"

I can tell Elijah hasn't stopped gazing at me. The intensity of it is burning my damn skin. I guess my last few sentences heightened the tension.

Tension between us in a courtroom...probably inappropriate huh?

The attorney clears her throat to gain my attention again.

Her next few questions are quick and I answer them without even blinking.

"Was Mr Everett ever violent towards you?"

"No absolutely not"

"You say Miss Zoya was the one behind the kidnap, yet she didn't psychically hurt you herself?"

"No, she just hurt me verbally and gave the orders"

"Are you and Mr Everett still in a relationship?"

I won't lie. This one has me pausing for a second. A zap of pain shooting through my system. Don't lose it now Sofia.

"No we're not currently in a relationship"

"Why is that?"

Okay, she's really going for it huh.

My broken heart beats haphazardly in my chest, begging for a way out of this question. I don't get one.

"Sometimes people come into your life and ruin any chance of happiness. In my life that person was Nadia. Mr Everett now believes he isn't safe to be with. So we have separated" I choke out. My eyes shoot downward so that I don't have to look at anyone and I notice my hands shaking slightly.

"One final question-"

"Give her a moment" the judge cuts in once more. Sucking in a breath, I look back up and smile gratefully at him.

"Thank you. I'm okay" I mumble.

I haven't looked at Nadia this whole time and that isn't going to change now. She will definitely knock me off. If she was glaring before then now she will be trying to shoot lasers from her eyes.

"One final question Miss Westwood before we show some evidence given by Mr Everett. You will both be asked about the evidence. First, did Miss Zoya tell you that she was going to blackmail Mr Everett for your freedom?"

"Yes, she told me exactly what she was going to do. I imagine to antagonise me or hurt me further"

"Thank you Miss Westwood. Can you now please take a look at these images"

Much to my surprise a police officer wheels in a tv screen on a stand. Immediately to my horror there are images displayed on it. Images of me beaten within an inch of my life.

These must be the photos she sent to Elijah. To use as blackmail.

An audible gasp comes from the jury and to be honest I don't blame them. I look unrecognisable. How must Elijah have felt? How would I have felt seeing him that way? Sick. I'd have felt sick and determined to get him back just like he was with me.

I can't help but look at him again. His eyes are on the screen, his face white and hollow. This must be brining back unpleasant memories for him. I wish I could erase it from his mind. As well as the guilt he feels.

My stomach churns. Brian really messed me up. Yet I survived.

Not without some serious violent flashback and creaky ribs though. The nightmares have been horrible recently. About being hurt. About Elijah.

Right then I run my finger over my previously broken wrist. It's okay now but undoubtedly it'll be weak.

Did Elijah think I was dead? I sure look that way. Maybe I shouldn't want to hug him right now but I really do.

"Can you confirm who that is in the photos Miss Westwood?"

"That's me" I state. I'd say state the obvious but it's actually hard to tell with all the blood and messed up features.

"And who did that to you?"

"My older cousin Brian. Nadia really must have done her research to know she could use him against me"

"I see. Can you tell me how long you were held in that location?"

"Three days...four...five. I actually can't tell you. I was in pain, sleep deprived and barely given any food or water. Not to mention I was extremely terrified for my life. I was petrified I'd never see anyone I love again" I confess. Yet the only person I love that I was worried about not seeing was Elijah.

I still love him. That's not going to just disappear. Maybe it never will.

"Thank you Miss Westwood. I just have one final question before you sit back down" she says, her eyes gleaming with some sort of mischief. Oh fuck. "In Mr Everett's statement he mentioned that Miss Zoya demanded his entire company in exchange for your location. He obviously chose to give up the company to save you. Do you believe he did the right thing?"

"Objection!" The other attorney yells while I feel the colour draining from my face.

"Objection granted. What did I say about relevant questions?!" The judge responds, clearly pissed off.

"It's okay I'll answer it" I begin because I really want everyone to know how bad I still feel about that. I know that Elijah doesn't seem to care about his business but I'm not sure I'll ever live it down in my own head. "I would have preferred that Mr Elijah had kept his business. He worked hard for it. I don't think I was really worth it-"

"Stop it!" I hear from the rows of onlookers and find Elijah standing out of his seat. He looks so broken and I wish I could take back my words so that I didn't hurt him. Yet he knows that I feel this way. He knows I wanted him to fight for his company.

"Mr Everett sit down!" The judge commands and he does so with a face of stone.

I realise then that I didn't want everyone to know how bad I felt, I wanted everyone to know how much of a good person Elijah is. How much he didn't deserve any of this because I want to protect him. I know they'll try and use his past in Nadia's favour. I hate that.

God I fucking hate that!

"No more question Miss Westwood you may leave the stand"

Which I do so on shaky legs.

As I get back to my seat, my Mom tells me how good I did but I'm not so sure that's true. I can't look at Elijah again because I'm not sure I can take it. He's hurting just as much as I am.

"Mr Everett, please take the stand"

As soon as he has said his oath the questions begin in seconds. It's like the defence attorney has renewed vigour with a new victim to attack.

"When Miss Westwood was kidnapped, why did it take you so long to realise it?"

Fucking bitch. That's only going to make him feel more guilty. Which becomes clearly displayed on his handsome face.

"I received a phone call from Miss Westwood that I assumed she made on her own accord. She told me she was leaving me. Later I found out that call was orchestrated by Nadia. So regrettably it took a couple of days to realise something wasn't right"

"Well that seems awfully strange doesn't it Mr Everett? I thought you were in a romantic relationship with Miss Westwood? Did you just accept that she was leaving you"

If I see this women on the street, I will fight her.

Right now if you looked up the definition of guilty in the dictionary there would be a little picture of Elijah's face next to it.

It wasn't your fault baby.

I try to mouth those words to him much like he did for me but his eyes don't meet mine. His mind is else where.

"Of course I didn't want to believe that she would leave me but I also knew that it could be possible. I don't really see myself as worthy of someone's affection. My reason for believing that Miss Westwood wanted out of our relationship wasn't because I questioned her loyalty. It was because of my own insecurities. I should have trusted my gut. I should have known she wouldn't just leave. If I could change it I would"

The raw emotion in his voice has tears pricking my eyes. I want to yank him away from this. This really isn't fair.

Once again the same images that were shown for me are shown for Elijah. As well as a short video that I've never seen.

It's me getting shoved in the van. Well...that isn't a nice sight. Apparently the jury don't think so either because they are once again gasping and mumbling between themselves. Yup take a good look. This is what she did to me. Only she isn't in this damn video!

"Before receiving the images and the video we've just shown you, when was the last time Miss Zoya contacted you?"

"The same time Miss Westwood mentioned. A few months prior when she stopped me in my car. A little while later when my database was hacked it became apparent she was linked to that event too. However she wasn't charged for that"

"Right and is it correct that you willingly signed over your company to Miss Zoya?"

"It's correct that I agreed to sign the contracts after she threatened Miss Westwood's safety"

"Yet there is no CCTV footage of her in your building on that date"

"I'm sure it wasn't hard for her to wipe it. She would have had access to everything" Elijah grinds out the words this time, his expression angry.

He's a clever man. He knows she's trying to mess with him. Yet he's not good at keeping his temper in check.

God damn it Elijah, you can do this!

I wish he'd look at me.

"Did you and Miss Zoya ever have any romantic or sexual moments?" The attorney keeps going, probably seeing that Elijah is cracking under the pressure.

"No absolutely not"

"I find that hard to believe. A beautiful women enters your life who is intelligent and willing. You have a track record Mr Everett"

"A track record of what? Dating women? Being an asshole?!" he exclaims. Fuck no!

"Please watch your language Mr Everett" the judge warns.

I see his fist clenching on the stand, his breathing deep.

Then as if he's heard my pleas, he finally looks at me and I'm able to return the favour.

You're okay. Just breath.

I mouth the words to him and watch as he sucks in a large gasp of air. Seconds tick by and I see the effect I have on him. He regains his composure and begins his answer again.

"I didn't care that a beautiful women had entered my life as you put it. I already had the most beautiful women in my life"

Okay Sofia, try not to swoon.

"Hmmm how sweet. Except Miss Zoya tells us differently. Why should we believe you? Why should the jury believe that a lady's man like yourself wouldn't take the opportunity? That he wouldn't try to have two women fighting against each other? That maybe it all back fired on you?"

Oh my fucking god! Is she kidding? Holy fuck. If Elijah looked angry a second ago then I must look like I've just been dragged from the pits of hell. How dare she? Why isn't the judge stopping this?!

"Mr Everett?"

Elijah is completely frozen. An ice berg on the outside. Which undoubtedly means he's an inferno on the inside. Please stay calm. Don't let her get to you.

"Because..." he begins but the attorney wants blood.

"Because what Mr Everett? We're all waiting" she taunts. No wonder this women is defending Nadia. She seems to enjoy people's pain too.

Elijah doesn't look at her. Nope, instead he almost melts me with his gaze. Ummmmmm. What's happening?

Seconds tick by. One. Two...

Then he says it:

"Because I love Miss Westwood. No other women matters"

Excuse me? Am I dreaming? Hallucinating? Have I ascended to a parallel universe where Elijah Everett says those special words.

Apparently so.

Fuck. Shit. That's all I've wanted to hear for so long and it hits me like a tidal wave. My pulse quickens, tears spills from my eyes so suddenly it scares me and I itch to say it back. Is this what he feels when I've said it to him before? This overwhelming need. This absolutely catastrophic realisation that we can never be without each other.

What am I supposed to do? We're in court! We've broken up! I'm supposed to be angry at him! Hell, I'm meant to be getting over him too! Oh and to top it all off we're trying to put the she devil in jail and he just throws those words out there as if they aren't going to drive me insane?

God he really is an absolute asshole!!

Elijah

    Well...that wasn't how I'd planned to confess my love. I wanted it to be better than that. More special. Preferably in a situation in which I could actually talk to her. Fuck! I guess I just couldn't stop myself.

    Sofia seems as shocked as I am. Is that good shocked? Bad shocked? Hopefully the former one. I don't think I'm going to get to find out right now.

    All I want to do is focus on her. To explain myself further. To apologise. Yet I can't do any of that right now when I'm supposed to be answering questions. I don't think I'm doing a very good job of keeping my emotions together...evidently.

    "Mr Everett?" The defending attorney says as if I've completely ignored one of her questions. When I tear my eyes away from Sofia's lovely flushed face, it becomes clear that I have in fact missed something.

"Sorry, what did you say?"

"I said, was there any sign of Miss Zoya when you found Miss Westwood in the warehouse?"

"No, there was no sign of anyone apart from Miss Westwood" I state, so ready for this to be done. With the way the attorney is questioning us, it doesn't make Nadia look very guilty and I fucking hate it.

"So there was no sign of her at the scene and no CCTV of her at your building. Mr Everett are you sure you don't want to change your story?" she asks, once again trying to mess with me. Not gonna happen.

"I'm sure"

"It's also very strange that the man we have in custody for beating Miss Westwood up, claims that he's never met Miss Zoya"

Fucking Brian! I'd love the torture both him and Nadia!

"Of course he'd say that! The man is a psychopath!" I growl. The attorney smirks at the emotions I can't control. Damn it!

"I don't think I need to ask many more questions now. Maybe just one..." she muses, pacing back and forth in front of the stand. I know whatever she says it's going to piss me off. "You were previously accused of murder and more recently you were accused of assault by Miss Zoya herself. Both acts against women. Is that correct?"

It's hilarious to me that Nadia accused me of assault for removing her from my office. It's even more hilarious because she just about sexually assaulted me by propositioning me.

"It's correct that I was accused of murder. Those accusations were dropping. The woman in question overdosed. As for Miss Zoya...her accusations are false. I did not assault her. I escorted her from my office after she offered me sex"

The attorney raises her eyebrows as if she didn't expect me to say most of that. I wonder which part shocked her.

"I thought there were no sexual encounters between the two of you? Are you taking that back?"

For fuck sake!

"There wasn't. Like I said, I removed her from my office after she offered me sex. I declined her offer. Therefore there were no sexual encounters"

To my joy, she looks exasperated and shakes her head.

"Very well Mr Everett, you make take your seat"

I'm relieved but I also feel like I should have said more. I feel like between Sofia and I, the attorney didn't really let us give our sides fully. Which makes sense I guess. She's trying to defend Nadia. What a shitty job to have.

Walking back to my seat in disappointment, I give Sofia another glance or a stare rather. In fact I almost trip up on someone's foot as I shuffle through the row.

I have no idea what's going to happen when we get out of here. Will she talk to me? Will she even acknowledge my presence? God I hope so. I can't go on like this. Without her there isn't anything that can make my life worth living. Before I met her I was lonely but I hadn't experienced anything to make me realise what I was really missing. So I was able to convince myself I was happy. Now I know what making her laugh feels like, what making her grin from ear to ear feels like. I'll never be the same again.

She makes me see everything in colour. Which is so fucking cliche. I didn't know what that meant before her.

What if I'm too late? What if I've messed up too many times? If she doesn't want me then I'll understand. I'll let her go but not until I've tried. Not until I've apologised and told her how much she means to me. I'll kneel at her feet if I have to.

I'm still not safe to be around but I'm going to do everything in my power to change that.

I should never have let her go.

Sofia

Elijah saying those words shouldn't completely knock me out of my own sanity. It shouldn't be an easy way to fix everything. I should know better than to immediately want to forget the past.

Yet I'm only human. I love him. So naturally hearing him say it back is going to mess me up. Not to mention he was extremely apposed to love not so long ago. The thought that I've changed that has me feeling all sorts of different ways.

There's also part of me that thinks I shouldn't have needed to hear those words so much. I should have only needed to feel it. Which I did. Every day I was with him. I still feel it now.

So what's my verdict? What should I be thinking and feeling? There's no hand book for this kind of thing but my god do I was there were.

An instruction manual for the heart.

Maybe I needed to hear it because I'm insecure. Maybe I've always thought he was too good for me. No, that doesn't make sense. He's never acted better than me. Never tried to be superior.

It's probably something psychological or something to do with society making everyone believe they need to hear those three words to feel complete.

Regardless, I can't think about it any longer right now. Because it's Nadia's turn to try and defend herself.

As soon as she begins to make her way to the stand, I know she's about to put on the best show ever. Even the way she's replaced her confident walk with a more demure one suggests she's trying to make the jury think she's someone she's not.

She's the biggest snake in the grass I've ever met. Even the way she gently rests her hands in front of her makes me angry. She should win an Oscar.

"Miss Zoya, please repeat the oath" the judge asks and I twitch in my seat as she begins speak.

"I promise to tell the truth and nothing but the truth" she speaks softly as if she's shy and I can feel myself glaring. I wish my glare could burn her!

This is probably going to be the hardest part for me to get through. The lies that she's about to tell probably feel like liquid on her tongue before she speaks. Black poisonous liquid.

When the prosecuting attorney steps up to her with his hands in his pockets and relaxed stance, it gives the feeling that he's confident in what he's about to do. Please be confident. Make her slip up!

"Miss Zoya, can you tell us your account of everything that happened please?" The attorney asks politely. I have a feeling he's pretending to be nice to lull her into a false sense of security. Good!

Nadia's sweet expression changes but probably not enough for many people to notice. I do though. Her lips twitch slightly as if she's been dying to speak her lies this whole time.

When I say that it takes about zero point two seconds for her to make me livid, I'm not being dramatic. She literally opens her mouth and I feel rage consume me.

"Sofia seemed threatened by me from the very beginning" she starts. Threatened? Not a chance. "I think she must have noticed how Elijah acted with me. The first time we met he asked me for sex, not the other way around like he said. When I denied he threw me out of his office with far too much force than necessary" she sighs as if remembering the situation.

Do you think I could hire someone to murder her myself? I think I'd get away with it!

"The database hack was a misunderstanding. I had been researching the company and that's why I must have been linked to the it. Since the event of stopping Mr Everett's car, which is true, I have had no contact with Miss Westwood. Which is proved with the lack of evidence. I'm not linked in any way to phone calls or emails as they claim. Miss Westwood was kidnapped by some horrible man but I wouldn't be surprised if she set it up to frame me"

I don't know how she does it. How can she just pull a fake story from thin air? I guess it's not so hard to twist things around and play the victim when it seems that's all she's been doing her whole life no doubt.

"You say there's no evidence, yet a burner phone with your finger prints was found near Miss Westwood's location. How do you explain that?"

"Again they must have set it up" she replies exasperated. Oh is this hard for you? Didn't you expect there to be any evidence?! What a shame!

"Did Mr Everett give you his business willingly?"

"Yes he wanted to get rid of it but didn't want Miss Westwood to know of my involvement"

I literally have to grip my seat so that I don't run up there punch her in the face.

That's now I feel for the next half an hour as she is asked question upon question. She's up there longer than Elijah and I put together.

It doesn't matter though because she lies flawlessly. She doesn't even flinch as she delivers every line.

She's so good at it. Weaving a web of fake truths that are so believable I almost start to question my own reality. There's no way this will work in our favour. She has the jury enraptured with her story.

Near the end of her questioning she is asked to plead guilty or not guilty. I'm not even sure why I'm surprised when she chooses not guilty. Maybe it's because I could never lie like her.

When her time is finally up, she has the cheek to sashay from the stand. She even shoots a wink in my direction as she passes. Bitch! She knows how well she has done. Oh god!

She's gonna get away with it. She's going to come after me.

I don't feel confident about this at all. There's no way they will find her guilty. There's just not enough evidence.

I can't stand the thought of her walking free. How will I sleep at night? I'll be looking over my shoulder with every step I take!

"We've heard from everyone. The man accused of assaulting Miss Westwood under Miss Zoya's command is unable to give a statement. He has been committed to a mental institution after an assessment he undertook yesterday. It's time to make a decision. Can the jury please leave the room to discuss their verdict" the judge asks. While I sit there dumbfounded. Brian has been admitted into a mental hospital? He's not insane! He's totally played them to save himself going to jail. When I glance at my Mom she has the same disbelief on her face.

"That bastard!" she grumbles, taking my hand in comfort. "He better be held there for the rest of his fucking life"

I sure how so too.

The jury begin to leave, only in the next second a police officer bursts suddenly through a door on the right. She scuttles towards the judge, her face flushed as if she's been running.

She leans down to whisper in the judge's ear, who only nods a couple of times. It gives nothing away and I wonder if this is just something routine.

Well that's until he makes another announcement, calling the jury back to their seats. What's going on now? Is something wrong?

"It seems we have a latecomer to today's festivities. There is a young man wishing to testify against Miss Nadia Zoya as well. Please bring him in"

A young man? Who else was involved in this? There's no one else that would want to test-

Oh. my. god. No way!

Entering through the same side door, the police officer escorts someone in. Someone I know. The very person who stood beside Nadia and helped her with all of this! No! He can't be here?! He will only help her again and he should be going to jail too.

Fucking Gabe!!

Testify my ass!

My eyes shoot to Nadia to see her reaction. I want to know if she's planned this too!

She looks white as a sheet. So white that I'm convinced this reaction isn't an act. Could he actually be here to spill all her secrets? What's changed?

Gabe is immediately led to the stand and both attorneys begin chatting to each other. They've probably been thrown off completely. Like everyone else.

"Please introduce yourself to the court" the judge commands, seeming rather annoyed at this intrusion. I guess this makes this session longer for him.

"Um I'm Gabe Bradshaw" he mumbles, looking petrified. I've never seen him like this before. I also didn't have a clue what his second name was.

"Mr Bradshaw, how do you know Miss Zoya?" The judge continues, his wrinkled face becoming more irritated by the second.

"I met her a few years ago. I worked as an intern at one of her companies" he explains. This is all new information to me of course and I'm starting to think that maybe...just maybe this might work for us. It seems that Gabe is feeling guilty himself and for some reason he wants to throw Nadia under the bus.

"Why are you here today Son?"

"To tell the truth. To tell everyone about Nadia. I can't take it anymore! I can't do this!" he cries, his hands shaking. It actually makes me feel sorry for him just a little bit. This could all be fake I guess but it doesn't seem so. Maybe he was manipulated by her like many others.

"Very well. You may tell your side of things. The attorneys have the right to question you at any point. Is that understood?"

"Yes...I understand" he breathes deeply and runs a hand over his face. Man he really is scared. I can't say I blame him. Nadia probably threatened him to keep his mouth shut.

"Swear the oath, then begin"

As soon as Gabe is given permission, everything comes tumbling out of his mouth faster than could ever be thought possible. He recalls how Nadia asked him to help with more personal matters. How she's had him hack so many different companies that he's lost count. I sit enraptured by his tales.

He goes on to mention how she made him get the job next to me in the coffee shop. That he was sent to keep tabs on me and report back. Apparently this isn't the first time he's been asked to do this kind of thing either.

"There were others too. Other women that Nadia wanted me to get close too. Sometimes even sleep with if I had to. I tried my best. I wanted to make her happy..."

Oh no. It makes sense now really. Gabe was her pawn. He did everything she asked to please her.

"But then I saw what happened to Sofia. It went too far. Nadia showed me some photos of her. It made me sick to see how beat up she was. I tried to go along with it and put on the best act ever when we met Elijah in his office but I couldn't keep it up. I didn't want anyone to get hurt. It showed me how vicious Nadia really is. She doesn't care about me at all" he cries. He's so unhinged he can't keep up with fancy formal words. In fact it seems he can't keep up with his own mind.

He is clearly in pain. Betrayed by someone he thought cared for him. Poor thing. It really must hurt. Especially when I know how good of a liar Nadia is. She probably made him think he was special to her.

"I hate you!" he yells suddenly, tears streaming down his face. "I fucking hate you!!"

"Calm down Mr Bradshaw" the judge warns but Gabe doesn't listen. He hurls insult after insult at Nadia, who just sits there with a blank expression. He gets so angry that he's pulled from the stand by two policemen and get dragged out of the room kicking and screaming. My hand shoots up to my mouth to stop a horrified gasp escaping because it's so hard to see. It's so jarring to watch someone breakdown that way. Although most people would react the same.

I'm so sorry for what happened to you Gabe. If Elijah had been manipulating me throughout our relationship, would I still be sane? There's no way.

As silence falls, I don't even know how to process what just happened. First of all Gabe wasn't the villain I thought he was. He was actually a victim too. What will happen to him now? Surely he will get some help.

"Ladies and gentlemen, I'm sorry for that scene. Mr Bradshaw will taken to another room to calm down" the judge pauses as if he needs a second to gather his thoughts. "This time there will be no more surprises. Would the jury please take some time to think about the new information presented and then leave the court to discuss their final decision on Miss Zoya"

Oh my god! This is it! Soon we will know the verdict. I'm not sure if I'm excited or terrified.

My head is all over the place. I'm not even sure what to try and focus on first. Did Elijah really say he loved me or did I dream that part? Maybe I'm just hallucinating because I'm so nervous.

The clock ticks on the faraway wall. It's actually quiet enough that I can hear it clearly. I watch the seconds pass for a moment and realise that time is bringing us closer to either bad news or good.

Shaking my head to stop myself from watching it any longer, I move my gaze to Elijah. Obviously I can't study his features because he's facing forward but I can study the back of his head like I never have before.

Has his hair always looked so soft? His shoulders are rigid as he sits completely still. He has strong shoulders. Perfect for me to hold onto when- no, stop it. This isn't the time or place.

I wonder if he's as scared as I am. Does he have the urge to turn around and given me his full attention much like I want to give him mine?

This is all driving me mad. I wish we were somewhere else. So we could talk. I don't know what the hell would happen if we talked but I feel like whatever the outcome of our relationship, it needs to happen.

I'm about to think way too far about what I'd say to him but suddenly the jury are entering the room again, the noise level turning to a soft whisper as people speculate.

My stomach drops. The clock seems to tick louder and I don't know where to look.

Tick. Another second goes by.

"Have you all come to an agreement on your verdict?" the judge asks.

Tick.

"We have" a blonde women states.

Tick. Please. Please.

"Please stand and announce if you find Miss Nadia Zoya guilty or not guilty"

Tick. Tick. Tick.

I can't breath. How can anyone handle this?!

The same blonde women stands. She must be their spokesperson. Okay Sofia, it's okay!

"We find Miss Nadia Zoya..."

SHIT. SHIT. SHIT.

"...Guilty...on all counts"

OH MY GOD!

My breathing stops, my heart flies and it feels like years of fear gets stripped from my soul in seconds.

I have to stop myself from shouting "YES" at the top of my lungs and jumping from my seat.

She's not getting away with it! Thank you! Oh my god thank you! I don't even know who I'm thanking! Probably every one in the jury who saw through her lies!

Instinctively I want to cheer and run to Elijah. Yet I stop myself just in the nick of time. It wouldn't look good for me to do so right now. In fact, I guess it wouldn't even be appropriate once we get out of court.

We're still not together. Even though so much has happened today! Soooo much!

Which feels so weird. We should be celebrating this!

Suddenly I feel my Mom's hand on my back and I glance at her with a smile.

I think I might actually cry. The tears are already welling in my eyes.

Which is probably a good thing because it means I can't fully make out Nadia's death glare as she is taken away.

Still it gives me a slight chill. I fully believe if she were to get free any time soon she'd definitely try and kill me.

When she finally disappears, I shake it off. I won't let her ruin this. She deserves to go to hell, not just jail.

"Thank you everybody, this case is now closed. You all may leave" the judge says with finality. Wow that's it? It's done. Obviously I'm grateful I don't have to wait around but it just seems so abrupt.

People begin to stand and I follow suit melding into the crowd. I don't think it's all sunk in quite yet. It's over? How is it over so quick? I mean we've been here for hours but still. It's done.

I really didn't think that she'd be put in jail. I was so convinced she'd weasel her way out of it like every other time she's been accused of something. But no. She's going to do time for her crimes. She won't be out in a long time.

Brian is gone too and he won't be able to get to me. As for Gabe...well I don't think he was ever really a threat.

All I can do is follow everyone else out of the room because I don't know what to do with myself. I don't know how to feel.

It's like there's a ball of happiness and joy inside of me just waiting to erupt.

So when we make it to the foyer and the crowd begins to disperse, I have to take a minute to just stand still. This is huge.

"Are you okay?" my Mom asks, looking more concerned than when we entered this damn place.

"I'm fantastic" I breath and grin from ear to ear. Nothing could possibly ruin this feeling.

Nothing except the memory that I'm still not going to be with the man of my dreams. Doesn't matter if we won. That doesn't change.

Just like that my bubble bursts then consumes me all over again as my eyes catch Elijah approaching me. He looks just as baffled yet gleeful as I feel.

"Sofia..." is all he says as he stops in front of me. The way he says my name has my body tingling in a way it shouldn't, so I squash it down.

"Hi" I reply, hoping that this time he's going to say more to me. I mean he has to right? Everything that was silently and verbally spoken between us in court can't just fade away...right? RIGHT?!

"We did it. She's gone. They're all gone" he whispers as if he's too afraid to say it any louder. Having him confirm it almost has me squealing.

"Yeah we did it" I repeat and have a sudden urge to jump up and down. Only that urge transforms into something else.

Something that Elijah clearly feels at the exact same time because suddenly we're both stepping forward and throwing our arms around one another.

Oops...

He squeezes me to his chest and I grip onto his suit jacket for dear life. His scent fills my nose and for the first time in weeks I feel like myself again.

Shit. This is heaven.

His hand rubs my back and I just want to melt into him and pretend everything is okay.

The sound of someone clearing their throat ruins the moment and I pull away from his hold to see my Mom looking less than pleased. Yeah...she still doesn't approve of his actions.

"Do you think you should be doing that?" she whisper-yells and I blush in an instant.

I really want to say yes I should be doing that. Am I being stupid? Am I letting the fact that he said those special words cloud my judgment? Yup. Can you blame me?

"She's right. I'm sorry Sofia. I shouldn't have done that" Elijah responds brining my attention back to him. He looks so defeated in that moment. What do I say?

"It's okay. It wasn't just you" I assure him and he nods gratefully, his forehead creasing in a frown.

"Maybe we can talk though..." he suggests, his gaze shooting to the floor. It's clear he's nervous. God I wanna hug him again.

We really do need to talk.

"Sofia" My Mom snaps. "We have to go"

Is she right? In feeling the way she does? Should I still be mad at him? I know that my Mom is probably assuming that I'll only get hurt again. Maybe she's right. What's changed? What will stop him from one day deciding he's not safe again? Does he even think he is right now? I'm confused.

It's very possible that we will talk and we'll only end up worse off. I don't think I'd survive that. At least right now there's still something keeping us connected. If we say anything more maybe we'll ruin even that.

I can't. I can't do that. So even though it makes no sense, even though it's selfish, I just can't bare to talk to him. In case we lose what little we have left of each other.

With immediate regret I say:

"I'm sorry, I'm not so sure that's a good idea"

Elijah

"I'm sorry, I'm not so sure that's a good idea"
Her words slay me. I didn't just expect her to agree right away of course but it still hurts to know that she won't talk to me. Even for a little while.
I can't blame her. She probably holds no trust in me now. I just gave her up. I broke that trust. Like an idiot claiming to do the right thing. Now here I am asking for her time. I'm an asshole.
My body still feel warm from her hug, my heart thudding...and begging me to realise how fucking stupid I was. Except I already know.

I've known for a while and been too scared to admit it. Been too terrified to think that I made the wrong choice. Now I know I did.

It was silly of me to think I could ever promise her safety with or without me. No one can achieve that. No matter how much I want to make sure she never feels sadness or pain.

However if we're together I can try my best to ensure it. I can do everything in my power to make her happy and keep her safe.

Letting that sink in has me sucking in huge gulps of air. It's like a wrecking ball hitting me. There was no way I was going to get through today with the same mindset as before. Not with the way she looked at me. The way she's looking at me now.

I want to say it again. I want to tell her how much I love her but it's not right. Not here.

I shouldn't have let her go and having her staring back at me right now, her face a beautiful picture of confusion...I just might faint.

"Are you okay Elijah?" she asks, her eyes moving over my face as if taking in every detail. Does she still care?

Please care.

"Yes, sorry. I understand. I shouldn't have asked" I reply, not wanting to make her uncomfortable.

All the while the cogs in my brain are turning. Finding a way to fix all of my mistakes.

She may not want me back but I have to at least find out.

She just said she didn't want to talk to you...

Fuck! Okay so that should probably indicate to me that she doesn't want anything to do with me. However there's something else.

Something that won't let me accept it. Maybe it's wishful thinking but I saw how she reacted when I confessed my love. She felt it too.

I have to try. Really try to make her see how sorry I am. How much I didn't mean to let her go. I have to tell her...tell her how much I love her in person.

I've tried so long to convince myself that saying those three words wouldn't be enough. Maybe they will never explain what I feel inside but if Sofia will feel the same thing I feel when she says them to me, then it's right. So fucking right.

I've been wrong about love. Love isn't fake. How can it be when I'm melting inside with every glance she gives me?

If she ends up rejecting me, I'll let her go for real. I won't ever bother her again. I want her to be happy. Endless happiness is my wish for her in fact. If I can't give her that then someone else better do it right!

For now though as she hesitates in front of me, I think I know what to do. I think I know how to make her happy.

A memory of a conversation we had once fills my mind.

I've got a plan.

Now I just need to put it into action.

Sofia

How can I just end this conversation and walk away from him? We've just achieved an amazing thing. We put a person who caused us both so much pain in jail.

Neither of us know what to say or do now. The awkwardness is choking me. I hate it. Awkward is something we've never been.

"Sofia, can we go now?" I hear my Mom's voice for the third time and I want to turn around and glare at her. She could give us some privacy?!

I do turn around and plaster a tight smile on my face.

"Can you give us a minute please? I won't be long" I ask and pray she just gives me this moment with him.

She raises her eyebrows and shakes her head in annoyance but huffs and then begins to walk away. Well, I'm going to get one hell of a talking to as soon as I get out of here.

"Sorry about her" I sigh as I turn back to face Elijah. Who now has his hands shoved in his pockets and his shoulders slumped.

"You don't have to apologise. It's understandable. I hurt her daughter, so naturally she's going to be wary of me. I honestly don't blame her" he replies and smirks as if he's trying to brush it off as a joke. Except I know he means it

Even though I should still be mad at him, all I can think is how I don't want him to put himself down. I'm a sucker.

"Well, I'm a big girl. I can make my own decisions" I retort. Even though I just made the decision not to speak to him properly. Idiot!

"Yeah you can Darling" he says so softly that I barely hear it. Every time he says Darling my heart skips a beat. This is no different and I can feel my cheeks heating. "How are feeling? Are your ribs better?" he then asks quickly as if it's something he's been dying to know but wasn't sure when would be the right time to ask.

"Yeah they're much better actually. Still a little twinge here and there but it really isn't that bad" I reply and he immediately looks relieved. Was he worried about me? I guess that makes sense.

"I'm glad you're feeling better. I hated the thought that-" he stops and shakes his head. "Never mind" he whispers, his Adam's apple bobbing slightly.

"You hated the thought that what?" I ask because now I want to know. Which is nothing new. I wanna know everything he wants to tell me. I really have it bad...for him.

He looks terrified for a fleeting moment before he recovers.

"I hated the thought of you in pain. That you were hurting. I know you were hurting in other ways because of me but I was hoping the psychical side of things were getting better. I'm really glad they are"

I want to tell him that it's not his fault. Which is true, the psychical pain isn't but I can't say he didn't cause me pain. That would mean I was lying. He did break my heart. Yet I don't think he should feel guilty. He tried to do what he thought was best no matter how angry it made me.

So I go for the best statement I can think of that won't be lying.

"We're both hurting Elijah"

That earns me a swift nod as if he can't bare to say anymore. Then he changes the subject.

"Who'd have thought Gabe would have saved the day huh?" he raises his eyebrows, a bemused expression on his face.

These are things we need to talk about but they're also being used as small talk. So that this conversation is prolonged. Neither of us want to let go.

I'm just realising that when I walk away, I may never see him again. Which has me looking away from his intense gaze so I can blink back yet more tears. I think I've cried enough to fill the sea.

"Yeah, it definitely wasn't expected but I'm glad it happened. I don't think we would have had the same outcome without him"

"Maybe not but if I ever see him again I'll still beat him black and blue. The same with Brian" he responds, his expression completely serious. I know he means it too.

"Me too" I agree because I'd love to punch Nadia, Gabe and Brian in quick succession.

After that, we can't seem to find anything to say. Which is crushing because it has never been an issue before. Not only that but we now have no excuse to stay standing here, so close.

As if there's a timer on our conversation, my Mom comes back into the building, her stance very obviously pissed off. My ears are already stinging.

"Um, I guess I should go" I mumble in the least enthusiastic way I've ever spoken. I don't wanna go.

Then again, I guess this is what break ups are like. This is how it feels. I have to be a big girl and deal with it for both our sakes. We can't keep going back and forth.

I want him more than anything, yet we're very likely to tear each other to shreds by trying to do what we think is best.

Elijah doesn't say a word as I begin to turn away. It's selfish of me but I actually wish he would.

Each step I take in the opposite direction feels as if I'm pulling on a tight rope that keeps me close to him.

Then...

"Wait Sofia!" he calls and I'm whipping back around in seconds because he's given me a reason to be around him longer. God dammit, this is torture for both of us.

"Yes?"

What is he going to do? I'm not so sure I can keep saying no to him. Maybe we'll crash and burn but this is all too difficult.

"Can we stay in touch? Just by text or phone calls if that's what you're comfortable with. I just...I want to..."

"I know Elijah, me too" I answer because I don't want to see him struggle. I know what he wants. He doesn't have to say it. He wants that tiny bit of connection we have left. The bit I'm too scared to break if we get too close again. "Of course we can stay in contact" I continue without a second thought. I can't help it. The thought of never talking to him again has been eating me alive. So now at least we have this.

"Thank you" he smiles so sweetly and it makes me wanna cry.

"Don't thank me Elijah. It's not a privilege to be able to text me. I'm just...me" I tell him because I feel like he is walking on egg shells. I don't want him to feel bad for anything. I wish he'd never let me go but I won't stay mad at him for it forever.

"I think it is a privilege. Everything I got to do with you was" he states, his face completely serious.

When I think about it, I feel the same way about him. Every little thing, every moment I had with him, that no one else got to was a privilege. Yet how can he feel that way about me? I'm just not that important.

"Do you need my number again?" he questions but all I can do is blush in response. No I don't need it again. I have it memorised. Maybe I shouldn't tell him that. Or maybe I should.

"It's okay, I know you're number" I tell him shyly and he ends up grinning knowingly.

Why does my chest feel lighter already? Have we just inadvertently given each other hope?

That we're not actually over? Dear god this is a disaster.

"I'll call you soon. If that's okay?" he asks nervously as if expecting rejection.

"Yes, that's okay" I nod and try to suppress my smile.

Maybe I could hug him goodbye...

"Sofia, we're going to be late for our train" my Mom calls and It's like I'm dancing on a tight rope.

"Okay, I really have to go" I tell Elijah, who doesn't looks as sad anymore. In fact he looks how I feel, lightweight and full of possibilities.

"One more thing...Happy belated Birthday Darling" he states as a farewell and I'm so touched that he remembered that I decide to give him that hug.

He looks pleasantly shocked as I throw my arms around him and I try to brush it off as a totally casual thing. In reality I'm memorising how he feels.

How it feels when he holds me tight. I also get to memorise how it feels when he kisses my cheek because his lips touch my skin and they linger there far too long for it to be friendly.

Naturally I'm as red as a tomato as we pull apart and I step away for real this time. My first few steps are actually taken backward so I can keep looking at him for longer.

He holds my gaze until I have to turn away and focus on keeping my eyes forward. Which is a huge task.

"You need to be strong Sofia" my Mom says as soon as I reach her but I don't have any kind of reply.

I'm a little bit high right now.

Which probably means I'm barrelling towards disaster.

***

As the next two days pass, my high subsides and I'm back to feeling alone. Elijah doesn't call and I don't feel like I should call him either.

It's like I'm in limbo and I don't know what to do with myself.

The only good thing about being so beaten up inside is that I have no nerves when it comes to my interview. I'm complete unfazed by everything. I enter, I'm polite and I try my best to sell myself and my skills. I guess it's because I don't care if I get the job now. There will be another. What there won't be is another Elijah.

So in all honesty I think it was my best interview yet. I shake the women's hand, smile super fake and then make my way back home to do more sulking.

Only when I do get home my Dad greets me with an envelope in his hand. He seems to enjoy delivering my mail to me. Maybe it's because it's the only time he gets to really interact.

"This one seems less official" he states before hovering awkwardly in the hallway. I don't think I've ever received so much mail since coming back home.

"Thanks Dad" I reply, giving him the best smile I can.

"How was the interview?" he asks, leaning against the wall.

"Pretty good I think"

"I'm glad. You know we're both proud of you right? We aren't great at showing it but it's true. You've already achieved so much" he tells me and even though I don't agree with his last statement. It's touching.

So I squeeze him into a tight hug that surprises him before darting back up to my room. That's enough socialising for one day.

I'm so unbothered by the envelope that I don't even look at it right away. I mean it can't be that important.

Boy am I wrong.

When I finally glance at it, my eyes are widening.

As soon as I see the writing I know exactly who this is from. How could I not when Elijah's handwriting is so distinctive. It's slightly messy and rough but for some reason to me it's like looking at the neatest writing in the world because it's so very him.

I remember the first time I saw his handwriting too when I'd watched him work one night. He'd been extremely busy but insisted that I stay the night. So I'd sat next to him as he sorted through all of his unattended business.

While on a phone call he'd scribbled down some words on a torn piece of paper. Then he'd slid it along his desk to me with a soft tired gaze.

It read: *Shouldn't be much longer now. Then you'll have my full attention, I promise. Can I have a kiss?*

Of course I'd leant over and pecked his waiting lips eagerly which made him grin with joy.

Now though, he's not here to kiss and I'm more desperate than ever to read his words. So I tear open the envelope like it's Christmas and pull out the white lined paper. In the bottom right corner his 'Everett and Son' logo sits, embossed and bold. My finger immediately runs over it before my eyes devour the messy words in front of me.

Dear Sofia,

I know I should have just sent a text. Maybe that would have been a better way to do this. Though I felt it would be more personal this way. And personal is what you always deserve from me.

You'll always have it too. Which is not something I've ever been with anyone. Only you. It's like you walked into my life and woke me up from the worst nightmare. Then I went and messed it all up.

So maybe I don't have the right to ask anything of you but I'm going to try my luck nevertheless.

I need to see you. I need to talk to you properly. I just want to spend time with you because I simply can't take how we left things. You were angry at me when you left my apartment and then we were awkward and left so many things unsaid after the court hearing.

So please, give me one more night. No rules or expectations, just us.

I'll understand if you choose to decline my desire and if that's your choice as you read this then I wish you endless happiness and joy. I know you'll achieve all of your dreams and I want you to always know that I support them. Don't ever doubt yourself Darling. Don't ever look back or have regrets and for the sake of every person who loves and adores you, be safe.

However I really hope that those words aren't the last you'll hear from me. I hope you choose to see me tonight. There's a bar about twenty minutes from your house. We've passed it a few times when we visited your parents. You know which one. I'll be there at eight pm.

I don't want you to feel uncomfortable Darling. So please don't feel like you have to do this. I want to see you but only if it's what you want too.

Hopefully you'll let me buy you a drink. I'll wait for you Darling.

Forever yours,
Elijah xxx

P.S. You have me, Beautiful.

    A drop of water hits the page and blurs a few letters. That's how I know I'm crying.

    This man is going to be the death of me. How can I say no to this? How could anyone? He wants to see me like he already asked but now I get to make the choice that I wanted to in the first place. Which does bring up my worries from before. I really don't wanna ruin what little we have left of each other, yet I can't bare the thought of passing on this opportunity. Especially with the amount of regret I'm holding about saying no to him after court. God I wish I had went with him.

    Just us. Together again for a little while.

    As soon as realise that I've made my decision already, that I'll see him and don't overthink everything, my spirit automatically lifts. Amazing how that happens.

    He wants to me meet me tonight but how did he know the letter would reach me in time? This suggests he probably delivered it himself and not by post. He's probably already in town.

    The thought that he's come all this way makes my heart swell. In fact I feel giddy or like a teenager who's about to go on a date with her crush. Only this isn't me going to see my crush, it's me going to see the love of life and try not to lose myself in him all over again. Its not a good sign that I'm already seeing that as not so bad.

    I fall back onto my bed and crush the letter to my chest. Would it be so bad? To just let go?

    Maybe this will be the last time I'm going to see him, so I better make the most of it. In fact I can't even think about that because it hurts too much. It also hurts to think that he still sees himself as dangerous for me. That when he asked to talk to me after court he probably wasn't even thinking about us being together again.

Because if I thought that's what he wanted then maybe I'd have said yes. Or maybe I'd still have said no. Especially with my Mom in my ear reminding me that it's a bad idea. That he could let me go all over again.

There's no point in thinking about that. I said no then but I'm saying yes now. I should enjoy tonight. Yup that's exactly what I'm going to do.

My Mom will no doubt try and talk me out of it but there's no way I'll let her.

I better find something to wear and soon. I want to look half decent.

I probably shouldn't be thinking this. Yet I want him to want me desperately because I know I'll feel the same way about him.

He's going to drive me insane. Just like he always does.

Elijah

    I don't think I've ever felt so nervous. This is my last chance to tell her how I really feel. I've said those three words but I need to say more. To explain everything, apologise and hopefully convince her that I won't ever hurt her again. Does she even want to be with me again? God I hope so. I wonder if she knows my plan. Does she know why I've invited her to a bar?

    I'm not even sure this will work. She once told me that she wished we'd met under normal circumstances. So that's what I want to give her.

    As time ticks on, I only feel more terrified. I asked her to meet me at eight. It's ten to now. I'm sitting at a small table that has a perfect view of the door so I can see when...or if she arrives.

What will I do if she doesn't show up? Well I'll probably drink myself into oblivion. I'm in the right place for it after all.

Five to eight.

I think it's possible that I might wait here all night in case she decides to show up late. No matter by how much.

Sipping my beer, I check my phone for the hundredth time in case she has texted or called. Nothing.

One minute to eight. Come on. Darling please.

My eyes shoot to the door as it opens but I'm only hit with disappointment as a couple walk in. The man takes the women's jacket and they go find a table.

It makes me so jealous. Which isn't something I'm used to. I would never have cared before. Now every couple I see being affectionate to one another has me turning green with envy.

When the clock hits two minutes past eight, I'm ready to down my beer and order another five. My heart sinks. My hope fades.

Glancing down at my phone again, I slouch in my seat and stare at my screensaver sadly. Sofia's laughing expression looks back at me. Maybe I should have changed it but I just can't bare it. I definitely should now.

The sound of the door opening again piques my attention once more. I look up expecting to see another couple or someone wanting to drown their sorrows.

Only my breathing stops with shock.

She came. Fuck...she's really here.

A smile almost breaks my face as I take her in. Dressed in a navy cami, black above the knee skirt with denim jacket on top and a black handbag, she glances around the place. Her gorgeous hair has a slight wave and she looks a little wind swept, her cheeks pink.

Beautiful. Gorgeous. Breathtaking.

I drink her in as if it's the first time I've ever seen her. From her black flat pumps on her feet, up her smooth bare legs, all the way to the top of her head. God I'm a pervert.

I need to stop before my imagination runs wild.

Taking a deep breath, I try to slow my heart rate. I gotta be confident. Put my plan into place. Pretend we just met. That we're meeting in this bar. Like normal people do.

She doesn't notice me and walks up to the bar, taking a seat on a stool. How convenient that the one next to her is free.

What do I say to her? What would I say if I really had just seen her? How would I hit on her?

Wow, Elijah you are going to need to pull it together. I just have to act normal. When I met her on the sugar rush website I still didn't pretend to be someone I wasn't. I was me. So why change that part? She likes me.

So let's do this!

Sofia

    I'm not sure what to expect when I walk into the modern revamped bar. I've seen it many times but never entered. I just remember that not so long ago it had signs on the windows about an overhaul of interior design. They did a good job too with new leather deep purple booths and single tables that match the aesthetic. While they've kept the wooden vibe all around the place, specifically the bar.
    It's lovely. Yet I'm more interested in the person I'm here to meet. All I know is Elijah wants to spend time with me. Apparently that's the only reason I need.
    When I don't see him right away, I make my way to the bar in case he's just late.
    I'm feeling so many different things right now. I can't think of the negative side of it so mostly I'm excited. Oh and terrified!
    As soon as I'm settled on the stool, a bar tender approaches me quickly. His purple waist coat matches the colours of the seating and I realise that they really have put

effort into the revamping of this place. Or maybe I'm just trying to distract myself.

"What can I get you?"

Should I drink or is that a silly idea? Probably but oh well.

"Can I have a red wine please?" I ask and he nods once before moving away.

While he gets my drink, I glance around again but there's still no sign of Elijah.

"Here you are Mam" the bar tender announces with flare as he places the glass in front of me. I pull out my wallet from my bag but a very enticing voice has me pausing.

"You can just put the ladies drink on my tab"

Immediately I'm turning and find the man I've been looking for as he sits on the stool next to me. He looks so very nonchalant. Confident and cool just like the first time I met him. Which has me shivering in a delightful way.

My eyes take him in as if I'm a dog in heat. Hungry and desperate. It's a rare sight to see him in casual clothes but tonight he's wear a deep grey shirt and black jeans. Jeans...yummy.

His beard is trimmed and neat now. His hair begging to be touched.

Like always it's his eyes that take my breath away. He looks at me as if I'm his last meal, his only saving grace. I wonder how I ever survived being with this man?

"Come here often?" he asks with a sly smirk on his face. What's he up to?

"No actually. First time" I reply and smirk back at him. I'm not sure what to expect from tonight but I've decided going with the flow is the best option.

"Where does a beautiful women like you usually like to drink?" he asks, his eyes twinkling with all of the things that I don't know. It's strange for him to be asking questions that he already knows the answers to, however maybe he's just being playful. That doesn't seem like the vibe he's giving off though.

"I don't drink much. Usually just special occasions or nights like these" I state before sipping my wine so that I can break eye contact with him. It's hard not to just pour adoring words out of my mouth while he sits so close. I can almost feel the heat from his body. Yet I'm wary of what's happening right now.

"Nights like these?" he repeats and I shrug.

"Well I'm not really sure what this is all about to be honest. Maybe you can tell me?" I fire back, hoping to crack whatever composure he's holding. It's so strange.

"I was just sitting over there when I saw you come in" he begins, gesturing over to one of the tables. "I wondered if you were alone and if so, how that could be possible. I came over here because I was curious about the girl alone at the bar. I'm still baffled. So I'm not sure that I can help you out with your question" he finishes and I tilt my head at him as if he's a damn alien. Did he get a lobotomy in the last few hours. "Oh I'm Elijah by the way. Elijah Everett" he then introduces himself as if we've never met before and that's when it all clicks.

Ohhhhhhh. Yup. Now I get it.

And I really like it.

This is us. If we hadn't met through Sugar Rush. This is us meeting randomly one night because we happen to be in the same bar.

Clever.

He seems to notice the second that I catch on because his strong gaze becomes a little softer as if he's calming down slightly. So with a smirk on my face, I place my hand in his.

"Sofia Westwood. Nice to meet you Elijah Everett" I laugh slightly before pushing it down. I guess I'm not the best actress but I can try for tonight.

His fingers squeeze mine gently before he lets go and leans his chin in his hand. Already my skin is tingling from the loss.

"It's nice to meet you too Sofia. That's a lovely name by the way"

"Is it? I've always thought it was pretty boring" I tell him and lean my head on my hand too. Now we're facing each other and to say that the rest of the world disappears, is an understatement. He's going to eat me alive.

He'd definitely would have won me over if we'd met like this. Hell it doesn't matter how we met, he'd always win me over.

He's confident. Maybe a little cocky. Like he knows what he's doing. This isn't new to me though. This is who he is. It shines through and makes me squirm. He's an enigma to me really. Strong and brilliant. Intelligent. Yet also really affectionate with a thousand layers of emotion. I shouldn't admit this but the fact that he's so gentle with me and so caring while he looks like the devil in disguise to a lot of people on the outside, somehow makes me feel incredibly special.

Maybe it's true that every women wants to bring a strong man to their knees. Except I don't want him on his knees, just looking at me the exact way he is now.

"I don't think you could ever be boring" he expresses his opinion with a frown and I really want to lean over a kiss him between his eyebrows to remove his slightly baffled expression.

"Huh, well you'd think different if you knew I could sleep until three in the afternoon and wake up looking like death" I joke and he raises his eyebrows playfully.

"Like death? Not possible and I can sleep until four so I guess I win" he smirks then shoots me a wink that almost knocks me off my stool. Dear fucking god.

"So what are you doing here alone Elijah? Hard day at work?"

"Not exactly. I came here hoping to find someone to drink with. Someone exactly like you funnily enough" he smiles before finishing his pint of beer. I watch in fascination as he licks his lips.

"Someone like me?" I ask because I want him to elaborate. I wanna know where he will go with this.

"Yes. Someone like you...you're so beautiful. Do you know that?" he says so intensely that I wonder if he's slipping up with his act.

"I'm not sure that's true but thank you for saying so"

"You're welcome. Something tells me you're pretty intelligent too"

"Nope. I'm really dumb actually. I can barely count to ten without getting confused. I don't think I'm the women you're looking for" I tease and he just stares at me for a moment, his eyes slightly glazed over. Like he's imagining something.

"You're definitely the women I'm looking for" he confirms and I shake my head at how cheesy that sounds. The thing is, I would have liked it if we had just met. However I love it knowing that he really means it.

"That was smooth. Do you say that to all the girls?"

"No. Just you Darling" he croons, leaning a little closer. His arm brushes against mine and it feels like I've never been touched by a man before. My body ignites with flames. How am I going to get through tonight without begging to be with him again?

Is that even what this is about? Do I want it to be? Can I risk being hurt again?

As he orders another drink - a whiskey this time - I realise that it's possible I'll take the risk.

"What do you do Sofia? What do you love?"

He knows I don't have a job so even if I make it up for the sake of tonight, it's not actually lying.

"Web design. I build, break and design websites for a living" I tell him and he nods as if taking in what I've said.

"Tell me more" he hums and shifts in his seat so he's facing me. He moves his foot so that it's resting on the bottom of my stool and his jean clad leg heats mine. Does he know he's doing this to me? Absolutely.

"There's lots of different coding languages..." I begin and then burst into a whole description of all things web tech. I know it sounds boring to most people but I live and breath it.

Elijah listens to my every word. I've told him all of this before of course. He's always been interested in the things I'm obsessed with other than him. I don't know if it's just politeness or if he genuinely wanted to know but there have been many occasions in which he's asked me questions.

I guess it's the same as my interest in his work. I really enjoy listening to him talk about it.

At one point we both put our drinks down at the same time. Our fingers touch and we both shoot our eyes to our touching skin.

Without thinking about it I move my hand over his. He doesn't say a word but instead turns his hand and links our fingers. Even though it's extremely distracting, I continue talking as if nothing is happening.

"I really want to help more people learn about Web Tech too. Not enough people do. Especially women"

"That's amazing Sofia. I know you'll achieve that. There's simply no way that you won't" he encourages, squeezing my fingers tightly. God. Someone give me oxygen.

"Thank you. What do you do Elijah?"

I change the subject so that the lime light is on him. He does the same as I did and spends some time talking about his many business ventures.

We end up moving from the bar to a booth nearby and somehow end up signing up to a bar quiz. I'm not entirely sure how that happened.

Or maybe it was announced and I immediately wanted to participate. I haven't had this much fun since the last time I was comfortably sat next to this man. Right before...well...right before I was kidnapped. Not many people can say that. I wish I couldn't.

We have to lean together in order to read the questions on the sheet. Which may have had me leaning my head on his shoulder just a tiny bit.

It's pretty simple really. Answer all the questions and the table with the most right answers gets free cocktails.

"I feel like this first one is a you question" I laugh and he hums in agreement. It's about the stock market and he answers it will ease. "I'm impressed" I compliment and his cheeks pink in the cutest way.

"Which illegal drug is white and powdery?" Elijah reads out the second question and I immediately exclaim "Cocaine!" Which probably isn't a good look.

Elijah laughs uncontrollably while I bite my lip in embarrassment.

"I'm a drug dealer on weekdays" I inform him and he grins.

"Fantastic, can I buy something from you?" he asks, waiting expectantly. I pat down my jacket and then pout.

"Ah sorry, I don't have it on me"

"Damn it. Maybe another time then" he chuckles and nudges me with his shoulder. It's so natural that my hand ends up on his knee. When I realise, I pull it away but he grabs it and holds my hand again.

"Sorry" I whisper.

"Don't be sorry sweet Sofia" he almost purrs and I have to cross my legs for...reasons. "How many days in three years?" he continues with the next question, his fingers soothing mine.

"One thousand and ninety five" I say without much thought.

"Wow that was fast. I thought you said you can't even count to ten" he teases.

"I can't count to ten. I can count much further than that" I say proudly.

"Wow, you're a genius"

"I know. Now come on, we need to get all of these right"

For the next ten minutes we work out the rest of the answers with our combined brain power and we're the first to be done.

Only seconds before a group of people a few tables away from us.

It doesn't take long for the answers to be checked and the same bartender that served us approaches us with yet more drinks.

We won.

"Oh we are soooo clever" I laugh but Elijah shakes his head.

"You're sooo clever"

That has me blushing all over again as a row of shots and three different cocktails are placed in front of us. Each one is labelled with its name and ingredients.

For some reason I decide on the multicoloured cocktail called Ecstasy.

However the taste does not live up to the name.

"That is disgusting" I almost gag as my face screws up in horror. Elijah's laugh fills my ears as he sits next to me, his gaze firmly on me at all times. I sure do love having his full attention.

"Can I try it?" he asks and I gladly slide the glass to him.

Then I get to watch as he has the same reaction, his face contorting in disgust.

"Fuck. That's the worst thing I've ever tasted" he exclaims and pushes the cocktail away.

The next thing I ask, I wish I could blame on the alcohol but honestly I'm still pretty sober.

"What's the best thing you've ever tasted?"

This has his eyes filling with something I know well. Desire. He's been looking at me like that all night but now it's only gotten wilder with my words. I think it's my turn to make him squirm.

"I'm not sure it would be appropriate to answer that question" he answers, keeping in character well.

"Hmm why's that? Do you have a weird taste in food?" I act oblivious to his struggle and watch as his fingers tighten on his glass.

"No but what I'm thinking about isn't food. Sofia can I be honest with you?"

Well that's not what I expected him to say.

"Yes, please do" I reply, now even more eager to hear what he has to say.

He looks me dead in the eyes and repeats similar sentences to what he said to me the real first time we met.

"I want you Sofia. I'm sure that's more than obvious. I want whatever you're willing to give me. Every second you'll let me have. I want you in so many ways. We can just talk or we can do more but I need to see you again. I need to have you next to me. Just us. Together..."

It doesn't escape my notice that this confession is more affectionate than the first time he made it. For obvious reasons.

I enjoy this time just as much. More, in fact. It's more sweet, diluted by the feelings we have for each other.

It's clear that what he just said wasn't from the role play we're trying to keep up. It's obvious because of his pleading expression and my racing heart.

"Maybe you'd like to take me home with you then?"

Okay Sofia, maybe you shouldn't let your heart go so easy again or maybe it's too late.

"I'd very much like that Darling"

"Only if you promise to be there in the morning. I don't want to be left alone" I sigh, leaning closer to him without really having control of it. My words have a deeper meaning than they seem but I think he understands.

His hand slowly and shakily, moves to my cheek. The warmth blooms over my skin beneath his touch. Oh god. I'm done for.

"I'll never leave you alone..."

"Do you promise?" I ask, my voice shaking slightly with emotion. He has to promise because I can't be hurt again. What is happening right now?

"I promise you. I promise you forever" he breathes deeply, his bottom lip quivering.

I'm a horrible mess and it only took seconds.

"How can you promise me that?" I ask yet another question because I'm terrified. I'm also consumed by him and I can't hear any noise from around me anymore, all of my senses are tuned to him.

His other hand then reaches up and he holds me so gently, both hands on my cheeks. He leans forward and presses his forehead to mine. Automatically I'm grabbing his wrists for an anchor so I don't float away.

"Sofia...Darling, I can promise you forever because...because...I love you. More than anything. Nothing else matters to me. Just you. It's only you"

Shit. It's safe to say hearing him say those words like this is a lot more powerful than when he did so in court because here I can literally feel his love pouring into me.

I can't do it. I can't walk away from him. From this overwhelming feeling that I've found my home again.

"I love you too Elijah. I wanna do better than those words. I wanna show you my love everyday"

"Fuck, I love when you say that. We can show each other. We can do it together" he growls, his eyes blazing with the love he's voiced.

"Together" I breath.

Which is the last word spoken before we're smashing our lips together, the desperation pouring from both of us.

Well...I guess my Mom is really gonna kill me now.

Elijah

    Her lips are like an antidote to all my pain, shooting through my veins and taking away all the suffering I've ever felt. Her hand gripping my shirt keeps me from ascending to heaven. Wow, that's something I never thought I'd think. Jesus fucking Christ. She really boggles my mind but in the best way.

    We pull apart slowly but I peck her lips once more just to check that this is actually happening.

    "So are you going to keep pretending you don't know me or..." she asks, her lovely face slightly flushed.

    "No, no more of that Darling. You told me before that you'd like to see what it would be like if we met in a more natural way. What do you think?" I ask, hoping that I did good. It certainly seems like she's enjoyed herself.

    "I think it's clear that it wouldn't matter how we met. The outcome would be the same"

    "You're right. There's no way I could ever resist you" I sigh, feeling as though I'm on cloud nine. At the same time I'm worried she could slip through my fingers all over again. Which is why I take her hand in mine, kiss the back of it and ask: "Be mine. For now and forever. I know I said I wasn't safe but-"

"Elijah you are my safe place. You're not dangerous. You make me feel secure and yes I'll be yours and you'll be mine"

"I've been yours since the day we met Darling" I tell her because it's the most truthful thing in the world to me. I met her and that was it. I was done for.

"What changed your mind about love?" she questions and it makes me a little bit sad that she doesn't already know the answer.

"You, of course. I've be so secluded from the whole world and on my own, so I became bitter and angry at everyone. You've taught me that not everyone is evil. You've also taught me that whatever love is, it's very much real. Just different for everyone. It's not about the words, its about the actions behind them and I want to show you my love Darling. I'll never betray you. I'll never say it without meaning it! I love you Sofia and that's never going to change"

She blinks a couple times before looking away and I realise that I'm probably overwhelming her. I mean suddenly I'm admitting all of this meaningful stuff and I know how it felt when she admitted her love for me. It almost knocked me over. Of course I've told her similar things before but everything is different now that we're letting each other in. Really in. Instead of dancing around the idea that we would actually be a couple.

"Sorry, I'll give you a minute" I whisper feeling a little guilty.

"Don't say sorry. I love how honest you are" she replies with watery eyes. And then "I love you" falls from her lips once more.

I kiss her again in the same second because I can't take the overflowing emotions coursing through me.

"I love you" I mumble against her mouth. It's so freeing to finally say it.

She actually moans in response. Which reminds me that we're in a bar and we need to get out of here so that we can really make up.

I'm not just talking about sex. I'm talking about just being alone with her so that we can get everything out in the open. Anything we still need to say.

"We should go" she says as we pull apart, as if she's read my mind.

"Yes, let's get out of here" I agree, feeling so fucking fantastic. I've felt sick all night worrying that this would end on another goodbye. Our last goodbye.

Yet here we are leaving the bar hand in hand and full of so many possibilities.

"Thank you Darling" I sigh in relief, glancing down at her.

"Thank you for what?" she replies with a frown on her forehead. So I lean down to kiss it away.

"For giving me another chance"

"You don't need to thank me. We all work things out in different ways. I'm just really glad I came tonight. I wasn't sure if we'd end up better or worse. I'm glad it's the prior" she smiles softly and squeezes my hand.

"I'm not sure what I would have done if it had been the latter"

"Well, I'd probably have been miserable until my dying day so this is a fantastic outcome" she laughs but honestly I think I would have been miserable to my dying day too.

Pulling her close so that she's tucked under my arm, I lean my chin on her head. Neither of us can drive with the alcohol we've consumed so I'll need to get my car tomorrow.

"Sometimes I still think it's crazy that I decided to join the Sugar Rush website. In fact it's certainly not something that I even contemplated before. So I like to think that something told me to do it. Something told me that if I didn't I'd miss out on something amazing. I'm so glad that I didn't just delete that email" she ponders, watching the cars drive by. Her head drops onto my chest and I hold her even tighter.

That's so fucking sweet.

"You think we were always meant to be?" I ask. I certainly think we are.

"Definitely. We'd have found each other no matter what"

"You're right. Nothing would have stopped me getting to you..."

Sofia

Getting out of the bar is the only thing we did successfully because as soon as Elijah said nothing would stop him getting to me, I couldn't help but seek out his mouth again.

The intention was to get a cab but with Elijah's lips on mine and building need that never stops, I pull him around the corner to kiss him even harder.

Which is why we're now making out in the dark alleyway, his body pressed tightly against mine while I'm pressed into the brick wall.

"I've missed you so much" he growls, his arms wrapping around me tightly.

"I don't even know how to describe how much I've missed you" is my breathless reply. My hands glide up his chest then rest on his shoulders, my thighs squeeze together as desire floods. It's the way he looks at me. The way he touches me. The way it feels like I'm the only thing that matters to him.

"We should really get that cab" I suggest and he nods in agreement.

"We really should"

Only we don't move. We stay pressed together, our gazes giving away what we want.

Sex. Love making. Fucking. However you want to say it. We want it now and badly. It's been too long. We belong together. Our bodies yearn for it.

I can feel the soft breeze against my legs, reminding me that we're very much outside. The darkness keeps us mostly hidden but all it would take is for someone to stumble around this corner and find us.

"I can't be without you ever again..." Elijah whines, his hands gripping my hips with tattered self control.

"You won't have to be" I reply, grabbing his face so I can kiss him some more.

Of course then we have no control over what's happening. Before I can even think any further I'm hooking my leg around his hip and he gripping my thigh to keep me there.

The moan that escapes me as I feel his growing hardness grind between my legs is almost inhuman. There is too many articles of clothing in the way. I want his jeans gone and my skirt and panties. I want him thrusting into me hard.

"Are you okay? Nothing hurts?" he breaths against my lips and if I'm honest I'd forgotten that there was even a possibility of anything hurting.

"No nothing hurts. Everything feels great" I giggle and he grins widely.

"Just let me know if anything does hurt though. I know you said your ribs-"

"I'm okay baby. I promise you" I cut him off because I don't want him to worry or feel bad for another second. "I need you Elijah. Please" I moan and watch his eyes darken with yet more desire.

"I need you too. You have no idea" he groans, his head dipping so that he can kiss my neck. It sends shivers through me in such a delicious way before his breath is at my ear. "Are you sure Darling? You deserve better than a dirty alleyway"

I can tell how much he's holding back for my benefit and I hate it.

"Yes, we can do all the romantic stuff later. I just need to feel you. If you're okay with it too of course" I ask in case he'd rather not do this here.

"Oh I'm okay with it Darling. See..." he gasps as he grinds into me again harder.

So that's when everything goes wild. I unzip his jeans and he pulls down my panties, holding my skirt out of the way. Our hands grip at the fabric left on our bodies as he guides his cock to my entrance in the dark.

"Ready Darling?" he asks, his body trembling with need.

"Yes, please yes!" I beg and that's all it takes for him to slam into me.

My responding scream may sound as though I'm being murderer if someone walked by but I just hope they don't try and rescue me. Elijah's swearing and yelling my name could sound suspicious too.

"Sofia!" he yells and picks me up, my legs wrapping around his hips. "So good, oh so fucking good!"

"Ahhhhhh Elijah!"

Yeah we sound like wild beasts and I honestly feel like one. There's no proper words to describe how it feels to have him around and inside me. I've missed this so damn much.

Holding him to me tightly, I squeeze my legs around him and he stumbles slightly, his body weight pushing me into the wall.

"Shit" he sounds panicked for a second before I soothe him.

"It's okay! I'm okay!" I assure him because it feels even better. Having him glued to me like this is perfect but I understand that he'd probably assume he was hurting me because of the position.

He shifts again and places a hand behind my back to support me and ruts his hips forward in a way that has his cock hitting deeper.

"Ah yes, right there" I moan and see the triumphant twinkle in his eye. He gets off on getting me there, which in turn is really hot to see. His determined face with sweaty brow is such a turn on.

The cool air does nothing to stop my temperature rising. I don't think anything could stop the heat that this man makes me feel.

With every thrust he watches me. Every move is in sync with mine.

I don't want it to end but it has to.

Holding me up with one hand, he uses the other to reach between us and tease my clit. It sends shock waves through me right before my orgasm takes over, hard and earth shattering. It's no surprise really since I've needed this for weeks.

This closeness. This connection.

His orgasm is set off seconds later and I squeal in shock as he collapses to his knees with me squashed to him. He sighs my name and buries his face in my neck.

I drag my fingers through his messy locks to help him catch his breath. He brushes my hair from my face and pecks my lips.

"Stay with me forever" he begs.

"Forever" I promise him and watch as years of stress leave his features from my words. He looks so much younger simply because he's happy. I imagine I look the same. I've never felt so free than right now being here with him.

We stay there for some time, hugging each on the ground as if we're terrified to let go.

***

We end up in the nearest hotel since going back to my parents house wasn't a very desirable idea. Especially since my Mom was less than happy about my plans tonight. She made it very clear too. Wait until she knows that we're together again. She might have a heart attack.

I'll let her know as gently as possible.

Now though I'm more focused on the man sitting across from me in the large tub. We filled it with maybe a little too much bubble bath in our haste to be naked together again.

This room is just about the only one left in the hotel due to our short notice. Because of the same reason it has two single beds instead of a double, which we fixed by pushing them together with a lot of determination.

"Now we can do all that romantic stuff you mentioned" Elijah smirks and holds out a bubble covered hand for me to take.

"Hmmm I don't think I'm good at romance" I joke moving into his arms. He pulls me close so that I'm straddling him, causing the water to slosh around us.

"No? Oh I don't think that's true Darling" he smiles softly and presses his lips against my shoulder.

Should we get some candles or..." I ponder then shrug as if I haven't got a clue.

"Sounds dangerous. Wouldn't wanting anything to catch on fire. You're hot enough after all" he winks and I automatically make a disgusted face.

"Ew, that was bad Elijah. I think I'm gonna he sick" I laugh, running my fingers through his hair, making it wetter.

"Sizzling hot..." he hums and I shake my head before hiding my face in his neck. Most of my skin is red from the heat of the water but it doesn't hide the blooming blush on my cheeks I bet.

"You're the worst" I whisper which causes him to gasp loudly. Then his fingers are tickling my sides relentlessly.

"What's the matter? I'm just being romantic" he chuckles as I squirm away from him.

"I think you've got the wrong idea. You're supposed to be sweet and gentle with me" I yell, grabbing his hands to stop the attack.

"Oh I see, let's try this"

He pulls me back to him but asks me to turn around. Then I'm secured safely with my back against his chest, his legs on either side of mine. Titling my head back, I bask in the feeling of joy that fills me and sigh as his hands move over my stomach.

"Better?" he questions, his breath hot at my ear.

"Much better" I answer before a demand falls from my lips. "Touch me more"

"I thought you'd never ask" he teases before his lips suck on the skin of my neck and his hands go to my thighs, pulling them apart to rest on his.

"How's this?" he asks, knowing exactly what he's doing to me. His fingers trail up my thighs but never quite get to where I want them.

"Torture but you know that" I pant then turn my head so I can seek out his lips. He kisses me with uncontrolled passion, his tongue diving into my mouth in seconds.

I can feel his hard cock against my back and purposely shift into him to tease him right back. He growls against my lips, his chest vibrating with it.

Then as if he can't stop himself his fingers find my clit while his other hand shoots up to cup my breast. I arch against him instantly, my body giving into the sensations he creates.

When our lips disconnect, my head is thrown back and his cheek presses against mine. The feeling of his beard on my skin makes me tingle as does the sound of his heavy breathing.

"You're so fucking perfect for me Darling. Every little bit of you, all for me. Just like I'm all for you. Would you agree?" he asks, while I writhe against him. His teeth tug on my ear lobe and I find it hard to form words.

However I do push out a small reply.

"I couldn't agree more...ohh...fuck"

He pushes a couple of fingers inside of me and instinctively I throw a leg over the side of the tub to give him more access to me.

"Sofia, I love you Darling. Fuck, I love you so much" he confesses again, his words so clear and true that I'm sitting up in seconds and turning in his lap. He snatches me up and pulls me close, my forehead leaning on his.

"I love you Elijah. Let me show you"

All he can do is give me a mesmerised nod, his mouth half open as if in shock. Then I position myself over his waiting cock and sink down onto it like I'll die if I don't.

I watch as his mouth falls open fully and his head hits the cool tile wall at the back of the bath. His chest rises and falls and his hands grip my hips, keeping him deep inside of me.

Wow he's gorgeous.

"Look at me Elijah" I command, using words that's he's used on me before. I know that he needs me to be in charge right now. I can see it in his glassy eyes as he opens them and sits up, his hands going to my back to keep me close.

"I won't ever stop looking" he promises as I rise up and sink back down on him. My moans are so loud they echo around the room. I can't help it. Feeling him inside me, so deep, hitting every spot is heaven.

His head dips to suck on my nipple as I rock my hips. Then he puts his lips to my ear as I ride him so that he can whisper so many loving things to me.

I set the rhythm and drive him mad. I go slow and then fast making him whine and beg for release.

"Ah Sofia, fuck! You feel so good. I'm gonna come baby. You first...wanna feel you...wanna see you" he pants, taking my face into his hands and rocking up into me. He pushes in just the right way to hit my clit too and I'm so close to losing it.

"Elijah, yes! Harder!" I demand and he pushes up with more force. A few more perfect thrusts and I'm crying out as my orgasm takes over.

I can hear his appreciative groans as he watches me and am able to catch his face as he comes too.

"Sofia...ah, yes. Fuck. Oh Darling"

His face is a picture of pure ecstasy - eyes almost closing, slight frown, lips parted- and I think that actually makes my own orgasm last a bit longer. Fuck he's so hot.

As we come down from our high, we end up slumped together, tired and spent.

"Was that romantic enough for you?" I sigh, running my fingers down his arm lazily.

"I think we just created a whole new definition for the word romantic Darling" he chuckles and squeezes me tight.

Yup, I think he might be right.

***

We lie on top of the make sift double bed, facing each other, entwined, still naked and still slightly damp.

His hand caresses my cheek and in the low light I see the love in his eyes. I never thought anyone could possibly want me this way or I'd ever feel so much for someone else.

He then takes my left hand and presses a kiss to my wrist.

It takes me a few seconds to remember that this is the hand attached to my fractured wrist. It healed pretty quick.

"How's this?" he asks, his fingers moving over where the damage was.

"All better and fully functional" I reply and link our fingers to try and stop him from thinking about it. "You know now that none of it was your fault right?" I return with a question, hoping that with us finally being honest with each other about our feelings there will be no guilt left over.

He doesn't reply immediately, instead he glances at me with a sad smile.

"Logically, I know it wasn't my fault but I wish I'd been able to prevent it. I feel like I let you down" he confesses. Oh no.

"Can you turn the light on please?" I ask, needing to be able to look him in the eyes properly when we talk about this.

"Are you okay?" he replies slightly panicked.

"Yeah of course, I just want to talk to you"

So he does as I ask and rolls over to switch on the bedside lamp. As soon as he rolls back I grab him and pull his lips to mine.

Okay so maybe I wanted to do more than talk.

Pull it together Sofia!

He's quick to respond and slips his tongue into my mouth, teasing me. I can't help but put my hands in his hair. I've wanted to touch it again for far too long. So now that I can do it when I want, I can't stop. Plus, I know he likes it.

Wasn't I meant to be telling him something?

Shit! Yes!

Pulling back abruptly, I catch his eyes fluttering back open. His pupils are dilated and his breathing heavy. So hot.

"You didn't let me down. You came for me. You took care of me. I can't thank you enough for that" I tell him sternly, wanting to drill it into him. Unfortunately he shakes his head, his hand dropping onto my thigh as if he's still apologising.

"It should have been sooner. I spend too much time feeling sorry for myself"

"Actually I'm kind of flattered. Which sounds strange I know but the fact that you were so upset when you thought I'd left you...I mean, I never thought anyone cared that much about me. Not that I ever want you to be upset...sorry...that's fucked up-" I ramble on but thankfully he stops me.

"I know what you mean. I get it. I'd be incredibly hurt if we broke up and you didn't care. That would mean you never cared at all" he explains, his eyes soft and inviting.

"Oh thank god. You do get it" I laugh.

"I do" he smiles and kisses my nose.

Speaking of guilt, I guess we should try and talk about why I feel so friggin bad too.

"So, your company? You're getting it back now right? Since Nadia is in jail?" I question and watch him shrug nonchalantly. Huh?

"I don't know. I probably will get it back. In fact the documents may already be null and void. Although I'm not so sure I want it anymore..."

What? Huh? Excuse me?

"You don't want it?" I repeat and probably look as if he's just told me he's a serial killer. Well, we've been there I guess.

"Not to sound too mushy but it represents everything I don't want anymore. It was what kept me going when I had nothing else. I put a lot of work into it but it's never been mine. It still seems like my Dad's. Meeting you changed my whole perspective on everything. You've made me beyond happy. I think going back and leading that company would be like stomping on our relationship. In short, I want to start a new business. A new company that I really believe in. One that you believe in too. I doesn't have to big and I don't care if I end up losing my multimillionaire status. I just want it to mean something and I want your input"

Wow. I did not expect that but the overwhelming happiness it brings me, has tears in my eyes. He's doing it for himself and I love that so much. He wants to start over and he's finally going to do something that he believes in. Whatever that may be.

"I'm not sure I'll be much help in the business sector but I can nod in the right places" I joke and he grins wide, carefree and gorgeous.

"You'll be with me every step of the way. Just like I'll be with you. I can't wait to see what you do"

"Well actually, I just had an interview yesterday"

"Tell me everything" he responds immediately looking excited to hear.

And I do. I tell him that I think it went well but I really never know. I tell him about the web tech company and that it's an entry level job. Every doubt I express he soothes it and encourages me. So much so that I get teary eyed...again.

"You know you don't have to say all these nice things. We already had sex twice" I joke, which makes him frown then roll us over so that he's on top of me. He brushes his nose again mine, his hands capturing my face again. I'm completely surrounded by him and if I'm honest it's the only way I ever wanna be. I know what he's doing because I do it too. Make him focus on me so that I can get a point across. An important point.

"I don't say nice things to you because I have to or because I want to gain something for myself. I say them because I believe them to be true. I mean every word. I wouldn't ever lie to you Darling"

I truly believe that he hasn't and won't ever lie to me. My only lie was forced by Nadia so I guess I won't count that. Therefore I've never lied to him either.

"I know baby and I'm so grateful for that" I tell him and brush my lips against his. "I know your intention wasn't to seduce me but I'd very much like it if you made love to me for a third time" I continue, biting my lip as his eyes fill will passion.

"You know I can't ever say no to you Darling"

With that, he nudges my thighs open further and slips inside me once more.

Perfection. Heaven.

He's my heaven.

***

In the early hours of the morning I'm woken up by my ringing phone. Which I have to find by searching through my thrown away clothes to find my bag.

I'm about to jab the decline button but when I see it's my Mom I decide I better answer. Her greeting is not one that I thought I'd hear.

"So did you both finally stop being idiots and make up?"

What? She was totally against Elijah and I getting back together.

"Ummmm, yes and you're happy about that?" I whisper so that I don't disturb Elijah. Although it looks like he's waking up anyway.

"Of course I am Sofia. He makes you happier than I've ever seen you. He literally broke up with you to keep you safe. I've been rooting for you guys"

Did I wake up in the wrong world?

"But you said-"

"I know what I said. It's called reverse psychology. Plus I'm you're Mom and I know that if I encourage you not to do something, you'll probably go and do it anyway" she laughs while I stand butt naked in shock. Sly very sly.

"You're a smart ass, aren't you?!" I whisper.

"Where do you think you get your attitude from Sofia? Your Dad? I think not" she laughs.

"I don't know if I want to slap you or hug you"

"I'd go for the hug because I'm still your Mom and even though you are twenty six I can still ground you"

"I'm speechless"

"Don't be speechless. Be happy. You've got the man of your dreams back. I'm assuming you'll be coming home later to get your stuff. Not that I'm in a hurry for you to leave but I want you to start living your life again. Go do all the things I never did. Get that career. I know I can be a bitch Sofia but I love you and I want what's best for you"

Wow. I don't think she's ever actually confessed that. So combined with all of the emotions I've already been going through, it has me holding back tears yet again.

"I love you too Mom"

"I should hope so. I'm fabulous. Now go back to your man. I'll see you soon"

As I hang up, that man sits up in bed looking all sleepy and confused. Yum.

"What are you doing over there?" he sighs dreamily.

Time to take my Mom's advice start living again I guess.

Sofia

After my Mom's call we fall back asleep and are in no hurry to get up. It's just too good to be wrapped up in his arms all warm and safe.

A glance at the LED clock on the bedside table let's me know it's only ten thirty am. Which has me wiggling against him to try and get even closer.

He squeezes me in tightly, his legs tangling with mine and the duvet.

"This is the best way to wake up" he sighs, his voice so dreamy that I can barely take it.

"Well you better get used to it because you're kinda stuck with me now. You're gonna have see me all wrinkly and old one day" I tease and he smiles mischievously.

"Mmmm sexy. You're always gonna be hot stuff Darling. It's you that should be worried. I already have the odd grey hair"

Oh you'll be a silver fox, baby. You're like a fine wine. You'll only get better looking with age" I assure him.

"Easy, you might make me full of myself" he replies, his fingers fluttering over my cheek.

"You aren't already full of yourself?" I ask, acting shocked.

"Not quite yet but the longer I'm with you, the more I'm gonna think I'm gods gift to the world because well...a man like me got a women like you. I must be pretty awesome"

"Meh, you're alright I guess"

My stomach rumbles and interrupts our cute moment. His reaction is to push the duvet off of us and begin kissing my stomach, making me laugh.

"I can't have my girl going hungry now can I?" he says with his lips moving over my skin. It has me wriggling all over the place especially when his tongue flicks out.

"Elijah!!!" I squeal while laughing uncontrollably.

"Yes? Did you say something?" he questions glancing up at me with glee in his eyes and a blinding smile. Woah. God I love to see him happy. "I could just eat you but then that wouldn't fix your problem" he ponders tapping his chin.

Then what are you gonna do hm?" I ask playing with his hair.

"Let me think some more" he replies and smothers me in kisses all over again.

I try to pin him with my legs and roll him but he captures my leg and kisses that too.

"What kind of monster are you?" I gasp as he moves his lips up my thigh.

"A love sick monster with no antidote" he replies giving me puppy dog eyes. He's so good at saying the cheesiest thing but making them sound so endearing.

"Oh no. I'm sorry. There's just no cure for this" I pout, gesturing between the two of us.

"That's okay, I don't want one Darling" he winks and moves back up my body so he can kiss me full on the lips.

When my stomach grumbles again he stops and hovers over me.

"We really do need to get you some food. I take my position as your lover and partner very seriously"

He's still being playful but he's not lying. One of the things that he'd do frequently that showed me he cared was ask if I'd eaten. I don't think he liked how little I'd been eating when we first met. A few times while I had long shifts at the coffee shop he'd gotten lunch sent in for me.

I returned the favour a few times too when I knew he had draining meetings. He'd seemed really touched by my gesture.

"I know you do. I'm very grateful. Yet I also don't want to leave this bed"

"That's okay. I'll go see what's in the mini bar" he announces before rolling out of bed.

I have the pleasure of watching his naked form striding across the room. I think I may have an unhealthy obsession with his ass. I could just bite it.

"Damn that ass" I call and he glances over his shoulder, his hands moving behind him to cover the goods.

"Don't, you'll make me blush" he calls back before removing his hands and shaking that ass for me. Which has me in fits of laughter again. It feels so good to laugh after weeks of crying.

"You've got rhythm too" I laugh and watch in fascinating as he circles his hips.

"Oh you bet I do!"

He blows me a kiss and I simply can't take it. I actually can't breath with laughter. Luckily he takes pity on me and begins to search the mini fridge on the table next to some tea and coffee supplies.

"We have many many tiny bottles of alcohol, chocolate, fizzy pop, potato chips and some things that I can't quite work out" he informs me, pulling out a red bottle to inspect. "Devils sauce?"

That sounds hideous. Which gives me an idea. A punishment for all his tickling torture.

"I dare you to drink it" I challenge and wait to see if he will accept.

"Is that so..." he teases before cracking open the lid and gulping it down in seconds. Holy mother of god. My mouth falls open as the substance disappears.

He puts the bottle down and shrugs as if it's no big deal but the fact that his face is turning red suggests otherwise. Oops!

"Are you okay?" I ask a little concerned. "Is it hot sauce?" I continue with wide eyes as his start to water. He nods frantically before grabbing a bottle of water from the fridge and downing that too.

"I'll get you back!" he gasps holding a different bottle of water against his forehead.

"Oh I'm really sorry" I tell him but I can't hide my smirk.

"You're in trouble!"

"It was a dare, you didn't have to do it" I giggle as he crosses his arms. He's trying hard to act serious but he's slipping up.

"Oh okay. Then I dare you to drink this" he exclaims, pulling out a black bottle the same size as the red one. Uh oh.

Fuck. I can't say no to a dare either.

Getting out of bed, I march towards him in my birthday suit and take the little bottle. He looks smug as I pop open the top. Immediately the smell hits me and I gag.

"What's wrong?" he taunts and I glare at him. Then hold my breath and put the horrible smelling substance to my lips. As I swallow it down I keep my eyes on his and just like me he looks a little worried.

He's wondering if he's made a mistake.

The taste in my mouth is horrible and it makes my stomach churn.

Slamming the bottle down I cough on the after taste. Inspecting the bottle more, I see that it was liquid liquorish. Uh! Nope!

"Are you okay Darling?" he asks, his hands on my arms as he frowns in concern. He's so sweet.

Yet I still want to mess with him more.

"No, I think I'm gonna be sick" I reply and gag again, only this time it's fake.

"Shit! I'm sorry!" he exclaims and takes my hand, pulling me in the direction of the bathroom.

Seeing him panic has me stopping my prank. I don't actually want him to worry.

So I tug on his hand to stop him and bite my lip to stop my grin.

"I'm kidding Elijah, I'm okay"

Once he understands he lifts me into his arms immediately and carries me back to bed.

"That's it! I'm going to punish you real good!"

It's no surprise that we end up forgetting about hunger because a different kind takes over.

Elijah's punishment is the best kind because it consists of him driving me mad over and over until I fall apart on top of him. I'm pretty sure I can live with these punishments for the rest of my life.

***

"What do you want to do now Darling? I mean do you wanna stay here or go back to Chicago?" he asks shyly as he buttons his crumpled shirt.

I thought the answer was obvious but then knowing Elijah he won't just assume.

Chicago feels more like home than my actual home. So the question isn't here or Chicago. It's, does he want me to stay with him again and do I want to stay with him again when I can't afford to pay my way?

"I definitely want to go back to Chicago but I don't want you to have to pay for my life anymore" I reply, trying to make my cami look more presentable.

"No more money. I understand" he nods. I know that he enjoyed supporting me because it was his form of affection but that one sentence seems to make him lighter inside. He hasn't been a sugar daddy for a long time but I think that statement is him letting go of the years he lived that life. No one is trying to take from him anymore.

Moving in front of him, I wrap my arms around his neck and lean in close.

"No more. Just you being you" I breath and he's kissing me in seconds. I want him to see how valuable he is. Money is nothing. He is everything.

"I've never said thank you but...thank you Darling" he whispers and I pull back to ask what he means.

"Thank you for what?"

"Setting me free"

Well, lord help me with this man.

"I should say thank you for that too. I don't think you know just how happy you make me" I tell him. His eyes become watery and he pulls me into a tight hug.

"That's all I want to do forever Darling" he breaths against my neck. My heart thuds and I cling to him so hard that I'm worried I'm hurting him. "You'll still come stay with me though right?"

How can I say no? Of course I want to stay with him. So maybe I'll just have to swallow my pride and pay him back once I can afford it.

"Of course, you can write me an IOU for rent"

"You don't owe me anything. It's your place too" he assures me, brushing my hair behind my ear.

"I appreciate that. Maybe one day when I eventually have a career we can choose a house together..." I look up at him through my lashes, hoping that he likes that idea.

"I'd love that so much Darling. That's definitely going to happen..."

***

Following my Mom's advice we decide that there's no point in wasting anytime. We want to go home. Our home. So that we can start our future now.

So we collect Elijah's car and go to my parents house to get some of my things. Everything else is still in the storage locker in Chicago anyway.

When my Mom sees us walking in she does nothing but grin like a mad women.

"Nice to see you Elijah" she says in greeting, looking way too smug for it to be normal.

"Mrs Westwood, how are you?" Elijah replies politely.

"Oh I'm just great. I'm really glad you two worked out your differences. No go on, get your stuff and get out of my sight. I wanna turn your room into a gym so that I can work on my bikini body" she sings gleefully while I cringe at the image her words give me.

"Right well, good luck with that Mom" I reply in mock disgust and head for the stairs. Elijah laughs at my horrified face and follows.

We spend most of the afternoon gathering my things together. Just the essentials really. I didn't bring much with me so there isn't much to take back. However I do end up looking through drawers and boxes under my bed that I haven't looked at in years.

This means Elijah finds an old diary of mine.

"What do we have here?" he asks, holding up the bright pink notebook with the words 'Do Not Touch' scrolled on the front in block capitals. Oh no.

"Something that's not for your eyes. Can't you read?"

"Yeah it says 'Please Read Me'" he jokes and pretends to peak inside. I launch myself at him as he sits on my bed and grab it from his fingers.

Dropping down beside him, I open the tattered pages and angle myself away from him so he can't see. Then I find something not so embarrassing to read.

"The new boy in school is really cute. I wonder if he will sit next to me...UPDATE, he didn't sit next to me. I guess I'm not pretty enough"

Wow. Poor little Sofia.

"I'd have sat next to you..." Elijah says softly and I lower the diary to see his face.

"You would have been too cool for me no doubt. I was a nerdy little kid if I recall correctly" I explain.

"So was I. I had black rimmed glasses and everything"

"Oh my god! Tell me you have photos of you as a kid. I have to see that!"

"I'm not so sure that I do but I think you could imagine what I looked like. Pretty much the same just less facial hair and better skin" he smirks.

"You know what, I think I can imagine it"

My fingers trace over the shape of his face as I picture a younger, less rough looking boy. I bet he was cute.

"Maybe I'll try and find something when we're home. I must have photos somewhere"

"I'd like that" I sigh happily and peck his lips. "I think I have everything. Shall we go?"

"Yes let's go home"

***

Saying goodbye to my Mom and Dad wasn't as hard as it was the first time I left home. Now I know I'll be able to visit them more.

In fact, I'm really excited to be going back to where I feel like I belong the most. With Elijah, in the city we met in.

The drive back to Chicago seems to take less time than normal. Which might be because we've done it a few times now.

It's crazy how pleased I am to see the 'Welcome To Chicago' sign and I'm even more pleased when I see the apartment building that holds Everything... and my pent house apartment on top. Still gotta get used to saying it's mine too.

I'm ecstatic when he pulls into the underground garage. I'm elated when we ride the elevator up hand in hand.

I'm at peace when he tugs me out and into the large front room. I technically haven't been away for that long but that doesn't mean that lots of different memories don't hit me all at once.

We've shared so many moments here. So many important pieces of our relationship.

The last time I was here there was a little bit more mess from Elijah's own hands. I'm glad that's gone now because the thought of him hurting here all alone makes my heart wrench. I wish I could have prevented that.

"Come sit. There's something I wanna give you" he tells me, pulling me to the couch. I do as he asks and sit while wondering what he's up to.

My mind whirls as he walks away and disappears down the corridor. What could he possibly want to give me. He's given me so much.

The anticipation makes it feel like forever but eventually he appears back in the room. He takes a seat beside me and holds out a closed hand before tuning it upward and opening his fingers.

"What's this?" I ask as I take in the little navy pouch in his hand.

"You didn't think I'd forget your birthday did you?" he asks. Honestly I guess I hadn't thought about it. My birthday wasn't something I thought worthy of much.

"You got me a birthday present?" I reply because I'm over touched by this. I shouldn't be surprised but I can't help it. Every time Elijah has gotten me a gift I've felt this way.

Of course! At the time it didn't feel right to send you it. I didn't want to make you uncomfortable but now I hope it's okay" he says softly.

I lean over to kiss his cheek and whisper and thank you before I even touch the pouch.

"You haven't even opened it yet" he laughs. He said this previously when I'd thanked him for the laptop before I'd seen it. I don't care what he gifts me because I'd love anything from him.

"Doesn't matter. I'm still grateful for whatever it is"

This has him blushing as I pluck the little bag from his hand. I can't stand not knowing any longer.

I can feel him watching me as I pull open the little drawstrings to see inside. Tipping out the contents into my hand. Two things fall out. A note and something else. My eyes latch onto the weighty silver object.

A coin. Like the one I gave him. Oh my god.

The coin has the same singular word on one side that is written on the one I gave him.

'Together'

Only the word is engraved in the form of Elijah's handwriting. On the other side there is a love heart that upon closer inspection matches the one on the note.

Before I even read the note, there's a lump in my throat.

Sofia,

This coin represents my heart. You've had it for a long time now and I'm sorry I didn't tell you sooner. I want you to keep this coin and I hope you will look after it for me. I'll look after yours in the same way. I'll always keep it safe and sound and never break it.

Yours, Elijah.

Well...shit. Don't cry. Don't cry. Don't cry!

Okay I'm crying!

"Oh hey, I'm sorry Darling. I didn't intend to upset you..." I hear Elijah say but I shake my head to stop him.

"I'm not upset. I'm happy" I push out through the emotion in my throat.

His face breaks into a smile and he pulls me into his lap.

"I'll look after your heart Elijah, I promise you"

He cups my cheeks and kisses away my tears ever so gently.

"Thank you Darling. You're the only person that it's ever belonged to. I'm yours..."

Mine. My man. My lover. My best friend and partner. Forever.

TWO WEEKS LATER

Elijah put his plans of giving away his business into action immediately. He's been working non stop to tie up lose ends because when a company is passed over correctly, it takes a lot longer than signing a few documents.

Which is why I'm currently riding up to the top floor of his building. Well soon to be Jack's building. Elijah knew that he was the only one right for the job and of course Jack was ecstatic. It was really cute to watch how emotional Jack got when Elijah offered him ownership of the company.

The reason I'm here is because I have news for Elijah. News that I can't wait until tonight to tell him. I'm too excited.

The ping announces my arrival and I try my best not to run across the lobby like a little kid.

Like always, I immediately go to Lewis to ask if I can go in to see Elijah but he holds up his hand before I can speak.

"You know you don't have to ask. I am under strict instructions to give you access to Mr Everett at all times. Stopping you from getting to him would be a crime. You guys are so cute" he explains with a smirk on his face.

"Access at all times...I like the sound of that" I laugh and he crosses his arms over his chest.

"Perks of fucking the boss I guess" he grins.

"Lewis! I am appalled at that language" I gasp and he rolls his eyes playfully.

"What would you prefer I say?"

"Maybe something like 'perks of having a magic vagina' I guess" I shrug nonchalantly and strut by as he gasps.

"You get it girl!" he calls as I make my way to Elijah's office doors, my face going red. I can't believe I just said that.

I knock for politeness because I still don't feel like it's okay for me to walk in without permission. It would be very unprofessional looking for him.

"Sofia, what have I told you Darling!" I hear and blush even brighter than I already am.

How did he know it was me?

Pushing open the door, I find him sitting at his desk with a pen in one hand and his phone in the other. All suited up and gorgeous with a lovely smile on his face. And those glasses...

"You are a sight for sore eyes. Do you have a special power that tells you when I really need a hug?" he says, getting up and closing the distance between us.

"How did you know it was me?" I ask as his arms circle my waist before he pecks my lips in greeting.

"Your knock is far more polite than anyone in this place" he explains looking smug.

"Why do you need a hug?" I ask, forgetting my news.

"It's been a long day. So many phone calls and video meetings. You make me feel better" he sighs in contentment and melts into me.

"Oh god get a room" I hear and glance in the direction the voice came from.

On the sofa by the right wall is a blonde women working on a laptop. She waves at us and I blush all over again. Lucky I didn't act on my urge to devour his lips.

I wave back embarrassed and hide my face against Elijah's chest.

"Sofia this is Anne. She's helping sort out all the finer details for handing over the company to Jack" he explains chuckling.

"Nice to meet you Anne" I greet her, smiling brightly.

"Nice to meet you too. It's nice to put a face to a name. He never shuts up about you. Which is incredibly weird because I've worked here for years and he's never talked much at all" she teases and Elijah glares at her jokingly.

"What was I meant to talk about? Nothing was ever that interesting. Anyway, I couldn't get word in with you" he sasses her back and I love the fact that he now seems more relaxed with his employees. I don't think he ever joked with them before which makes me really sad. I imagine a lot of people that have worked for him would want to have a good relationship with him. He just didn't let anyone in.

Now it's all different and I love seeing him so carefree.

"Oh I'm really not that interesting either, I promise" I tell Anne.

"You are very interesting! The women who made Elijah Everett crack a smile! To me that's the most amazing thing ever" she laughs.

"Okay that's enough of you. Out! I need to talk to my girl" Elijah commands but it's lighthearted.

"Sir yes sir!" she calls back and gathers her laptop to leave. She pats my shoulder when she passes me and makes a swift exit. I like her already. She doesn't take any shit.

"I think I'm going to befriend her and together we shall make fun of you forever" I inform Elijah, who looks momentarily terrified.

"Oh please no. I wouldn't survive that" he replies, leaning his forehead on mine.

"Okay I'll take pity on you"

"Thank you Darling. Will you come sit in my lap so I can snuggle you?" he asks and I practically drag him to his chair.

He chuckles at my eagerness and once I'm in his arms I remember that I'm here for a reason.

"What can I do for you Miss Westwood? I'm sure you didn't just come here to tease me" he asks as if he's read my mind.

"Well you never know, maybe I did"

"I'm glad you did then..." he whispers and presses his lips to mine longer this time.

"Or maybe I got the job" I breath against his mouth and he pulls back to look at me quickly.

"You did?!" he asks, his eyes big and excited.

"Yeah I did" I confirm before my face breaks into a huge smile. I can't quite believe it yet.

"Darling that's fantastic!" he exclaims and stands with me in his arms. He squeezes me tightly and attacks my face with kisses. "You're amazing!" he continues before spinning me around in his arms.

"I wouldn't go that far but I am ecstatic! Most of it is working remotely because they're a small company but I might have to travel back to my Ohio now and then if I need to be in the building" I explain. When I applied for the job I didn't think that Elijah and I were gonna be together again and I didn't think I'd be back in Chicago.

"That's okay Darling, don't worry about it. I'll take you when you need to go" he assures me.

"Oh you don't have to do that. I can get the train. I'm sure it won't be that often anyway"

"I know I don't have to do it but I'd like to. Why are you looking at me as if it would be a bother?" he asks and I shrug.

"I guess because I don't want it to be a bother" I laugh a little. I just don't want him to have to go out of his way for me.

"Nothing that involves you is a bother to me. Although I'll understand if you do want to get the train. I don't want to take away your independence Darling" he soothes and kisses my nose.

"Don't worry about that, my independence is just fine. If you don't mind then I don't mind. Plus it means we'll be apart for less time"

"Exactly my thoughts baby" he winks and cuddles me again. "We have to celebrate! What would you like to do? The sky is the limit" he tells me, glancing up at the ceiling.

I follow his gaze then bring his eyes back to mine.

"Not sure how I feel about the sky but to be honest would it sound totally boring if we just went home and ordered take out. That's my favourite way to celebrate anything"

"I think when you were created the angels mixed some of our thoughts and desires together because that sounds heavenly. Pizza?" he asks, his eyes lit up with the thought of it. It's no secret that Elijah prefers snuggling on the couch than going out. Which is perfect for me.

"Pepperoni pizza" I nod and he looks elated.

"Stop reading my mind Darling"

***

After eating far too much pizza and drinking champagne, Elijah and I found ourselves looking online at all different kinds of homes and places to live.

I'm not really sure how it happened except I remember him asking me what kind of house I'd always dreamed of. I hadn't thought much of it but now we're lying on the couch in sweat pants and t-shirts, scrolling through the housing market on his laptop.

I've honestly no idea where to start but I'm really happy that Elijah likes the idea of us getting a house together.

"Wait I have an idea!" I tell him and pop the laptop on the couch next to us.

Getting up and walking over to the floor the ceiling windows, I look out into the pitch black night then down below to all the lights of cars and buildings.

Glancing back at him, I hold out my hand for him to take. He gets up and stands next to me, linking our fingers tightly. This way we can picture the world in front of us, even though it's dark.

"You wanna stay in Chicago right?" I ask.

"That would be nice but is it what you want too?" he questions back, his need to make me happy shining through. All I want is for him to be happy too and luckily it seems we both want the same thing.

"Yes I do want that too. I love it here. It felt right as soon as I moved. Such a pretty place to be. It makes me feel grounded" I explain and he let's go of my hand so that he can put his arm around my shoulder and pull me close.

"Then we will stay in Chicago" he agrees, leaning his head on mine.

"But where?" I ponder and look through the darkness into nothing. I can't see a thing but I know that in the day light I can usually see the suburbs from here. Where it's less busy but still beautiful. A place I'd love to be.

"What about there?" Elijah points but obviously I can't tell what he's pointing at.

"Where is there?" I laugh and he takes my hand and has me pointing in the same direction.

"There is the same place that both you and I have stood here before and looked at. I've saw you and I'm sure you've saw me. I stand here and look to the outskirts of the city because it's quieter there. It's peaceful and pretty. It's where I've actually imagined us living quite a few times. My instinct may be wrong but I have a feeling that you've thought of it too"

Jesus. I really do think that we can read each other's minds. There's no other way to explain it. All I can do is stand there and stare at him like he's told me he's an alien. How did he do that?

"I love you Elijah" is all I can say.

"I love you Sofia. So much. I'm guessing you like that idea then?" he chuckles, kissing my forehead.

"I think it's the perfect idea. I'm also slightly worried that you can in fact read my mind"

"No I can't. We're just really in tune with each other" he sighs with contentment and I wrap my arms around his waist.

"We're definitely meant to be together" I reply and he whispers the last word that has now become so meaningful to both of us.

"Together"

We stand there and look into the darkness with our arms wrapped around each other.

We're looking out into nothing.

Yet at the same time we're looking out at our future together.
Just a girl and an ex sugar daddy looking out at a world of possibilities.
Maybe junk mail isn't so bad after all.
Maybe a little bit of sugar does create a rush.

The End

Epilogue available on kindle edition.

Playlist

1. Safe - All Time Low
2. Close To Me - Ellie Goulding
3. G.I.N.A.S.F.S - Fall Out Boy
4. Mother Tongue - Bring Me The Horizon
5. Love Is Madness - Thirty Seconds To Mars
6. Lights Down Low - MAX
7. Lucky People - Waterparks
8. Still Learning - Halsey
9. 11 Minutes - YUNGBLUD & Halsey
10. Need Me - Simple Creatures
11. Darkside - Blink 182
12. The Handwritten Letter - As It Is
13. Rescue Me – One Republic
14. South of the Border - Ed Sheeran
15. Hate Me - Ellie Goulding
16. Trouble Is... - All Time Low
17. Bloody Valentine - Machine Gun Kelly
18. Happiness - McFly
19. Candy - Aggro Santos
20. Bishops Knife Trick - Fall Out Boy
21. Take On The World - You Me At Six
22. Still Falling For You - Ellie Goulding
23. Stay Away - MOD Sun
24. Drugs and Candy - All Time Low
25. If The World Was Ending - JP Saxe, Julia Michaels
26. One Little Lie - Simple Creatures
27. Concert For Aliens - Machine Gun Kelly
29. Favourite Place - All Time Low

Authors Note

Thank you so much to anyone who even glanced at this book. I'm not that great of an author but I've always dreamed of writing a full novel. This was my attempt.
I appreciate anyone who gave it a shot.

Sarah :)

Printed in Great Britain
by Amazon